Also by Anita Clay Kornfeld
IN A BLUEBIRD'S EYE

VINTAGE

ANITA CLAY KORNFELD

SIMON AND SCHUSTER • NEW YORK

Copyright © 1980 by Anita Clay Kornfeld
All rights reserved
including the right of reproduction
in whole or in part in any form
Published by Simon and Schuster
A Division of Gulf & Western Corporation
Simon & Schuster Building
Rockefeller Center
1230 Avenue of the Americas
New York, New York 10020
SIMON AND SCHUSTER and colophon
are trademarks of Simon & Schuster
Manufactured in the United States of America

1 2 3 4 5 6 7 8 9 10

Library of Congress Cataloging in Publication Data

Kornfeld, Anita Clay.
  Vintage.

  I. Title.
PZ4.K852Vi   [PS3561.068]   813'54   80-12652
ISBN 0-671-25308-5

ACKNOWLEDGMENTS

From its inception, the novel *Vintage* was intended to be, and is, a cast of fictional characters born out of my own imagination and not referring to any real people, living or dead, unless by sheer coincidence. At the same time, they are often deliberately superimposed on a rich and colorful tapestry of carefully researched historical facts about this unique and special place known as the Napa Valley.

Though the Donati family and a host of other characters do comprise the main narrative of *Vintage*, they are often interwoven in the action of documented events that have taken place through the years, and often interact with actual certain noted vintners, viticulturists and political figures who did live and contribute enormously to Napa Valley's rich history.

A full intensive year of research was required before I attempted to write *Vintage*. Without the patience and encouragement and the direct informative help I received from so many, I could not have written this book.

Of those at the top of my list to whom I am most grateful is one of Napa Valley's true, noble stewards of the land, Andrew Pelissa, his daughter Dawne, and his grandson David, all of whom guided me through the rudiments during that difficult beginning.

I owe special thanks to the staff at the St. Helena Wine Library, the Napa County Library, and the Napa County Historical Society; to the wine historian William F. Heintz, who contributed vital information about Professor George Hussman; to Fred Aves of Yverdon of Spring Mountain; to Greg DeLucca of Sterling, who took me to the high rough terrain of Diamond Mountain to explain the Sterling experimental vineyards; to the Bissonettes of Chateau Chevalier; to George Altamura; Lou Ezettie; the Robert Keenans of Burgundy House; Howard Dickenson, for procuring needed legal documents; to Charles Carpy; Donn and Molly Chappellet; Michael and Robert Mondavi; Jack Davies of Schramsberg; Donti Flores and George Ortiz—and so many, many others who gave freely of their time and good will to help me through this period of research.

3

From my husband, John S. Kornfeld, I received the love and encouragement and friendship which have sustained me in all aspects of life.

I thank Elizabeth McKee, my literary agent, for having "been there," always encouraging her writers toward greater honesty and higher standards.

I express the deepest respect for my editor, John Dodds, whose sensitivity and sure third eye helped me polish the final draft.

And last of all, to "Mrs. Jordon," whose great dignity and incredible love of life made a deep, indelible impression on me which strongly influenced the last stages of writing this book.

For Uncle Marshall Walker
Who from his world of blindness has
with such joyous spirit helped me see . . .
and
In memory of Kyra, whose vintage was short-lived.

And where is he who more and more distils
Delicious kindness?—He is patient. Patience fills
His crisp combs, and that comes those ways we know.

GERARD MANLEY HOPKINS,
(*Poems*, 1876–1889)

Though I am different from you,
We were born involved in one another:
Nor by any means can we escape
The intimate sharing of good and ill.

—T'AO CH'IEN
(A.D. 372–427)

PART ONE

1894~1907

I

In an attempt to orient himself to the frenetic wharfside clamor, to the swell of noise coming from the welcoming crowd there to meet the passengers surging off the massive ferryboat that had just met the transcontinental train in Oakland, California, and brought them across the bay to San Francisco, the six-foot-two, handsome, twenty-five-year old Adam Donati worked his way quickly across the gangplank and stood near the outer edge of the milling throng and looked about searchingly.

The banker, a Samuel Linton, was to have been here at docking to meet him, he had been told by his own banker in Genoa, who had arranged the negotiable banknotes which Adam now carried in a small leather satchel clamped in a fistlike grip.

Suddenly, his jaw jutted defensively at the feel of a sharp elbow-jab in his back. Half-twisting, he saw it was an anxious-faced, rigidly corseted woman simply trying to nudge her way toward the center of the crowd to greet someone. From habit, he tipped his hat politely, then stepped back further and watched the woman's long skirts flap around her booted ankles as she plowed forward against the stiff early-morning February breeze. Then she was lost from sight, blocked out by another woman's hat—one with a giant royal-blue plume being whipped about in the wind, reminding Adam of some giant bird's wings pinned down but trying vainly to take flight.

He clamped the satchel under his right arm while straightening the dark-brown hair blown across his forehead in a gust of sea breeze; he jammed the bowler squarely on his head. His clear blue eyes squinted now as he tried to narrow down faces in the crowd, studying to see if any one of them possibly might be Samuel Linton. His mind reeled from the kaleidoscopic array of so many strangers' faces, people hugging, slapping backs, shaking hands. His ears rang with the sounds of every language he had ever heard spoken it seemed, varying in tones from low, fretful ones to the bellowing range of men shouting in Italian—one particular loud voice must surely belong to Luigi Pascarella, the giant bear of a man with whom he had become friendly on the long train ride across country, a coarse-mannered but warmhearted stonemason from nothern Italy, near his own home in Pontremoli—obviously now being met by his brothers, Cesare and Lorenzo, about whom Luigi had talked so much.

The leather satchel felt cold and crackly in the damp fog-coated air. He was grateful he was wearing his warmest dark-gray topcoat with its Karakul fur collar pulled high about his neck.

On the far rim of the crowd, Adam surveyed the line of horses hitched to parked surreys, phaetons and open buckboards. A sudden shrill, piercing blast from a nearby ship's whistle ripped across the wharfside, causing snorting horses to pull at their bits, and a wave of goosebumps to run up and down Adam's arms.

He saw Luigi Pascarella and his brothers now moving toward a two-seater phaeton, their massive arms locked about each other, their faces—so apparently brothers—beaming with happiness. A stab of homesickness like a sharp fierce toothache shot through him. He had never felt so alone! It was as though all that he had loved and left behind in Pontremoli—the century-old Donati estate now gone into the hands of a wily stranger who knew nothing, cared nothing about the famous Donati traditions of winemaking—all the good memories—yes, and even his grief over the sudden recent loss of his father, and his collected anger with his three brothers over selling the estate—all of it rushed at him in a gathered force which momentarily blurred the sight of everything around him.

After a moment, he focused again on the Pascarellas heaving valises into the phaeton and taking their places for the ride to the flat in North Beach Luigi had told him about. He longed to rush toward them, climb into the phaeton and become a part of that family's celebration. And hadn't Luigi *asked* him?—insisted many times on the train that because they were both northern Italians they were by nature then, *paesani?*

Adam drew himself up to his fullest six-foot-two, jutted his strong jaw out more stubbornly. He had important business at hand! Later on, he would look up Luigi—perhaps even hire him as his stonemason when the time came to start the building of his own winery and a replica of the Donati estate.

Just as the crowd had virtually thinned out and he was worrying about what exact next step he should take, a handsome landau carriage, pulled by two perfectly matched geldings and driven by a coachman wearing a black uniform with gold braid, pulled to a halt. The coachman secured the reins, stepped out in the open and thrust a sign stiffly in the air, its carefully blocked-out letters reading A. DONATI.

Adam hurried over, introduced himself. The coachman bowed formally, said in a crisp voice with a British accent: "My name is Jason, sir. Mr. Linton has asked me to tend to your baggage, drive you to the Palace Hotel, where he will join you for lunch tomorrow, precisely at noon—if, of course, it meets with your approval."

Adam nodded, handed over the baggage claim tickets, climbed into the carriage with a quick, agile hoisting of his lean body. As he settled back against the black leather upholstered seat and placed the satchel carefully beside him, a wave of relief flushed warmly through him. A smile caught at the corner of his full mouth. He was *here*— safely here in California at last, he thought incredulously! It had not been as difficult as he had expected—taking that first vital step toward reaching his dream.

The coachman turned left at the ferry terminal, quickly merged with the confusion of buggies, open buckboards and huge freight wagons weaving in and out up Market Street. Adam had hoped that the Palace Hotel would be situated on top of one of the high hills where it would command an encompassing view of the entire bay, the famous golden gateway, the hills to the north that his lifelong tutor, Dudley Farnsworth had so vividly described to him. But in spite of this flat route leading at an angle away from the water, Adam found himself agape at the strange raw sights.

He had come from a country where cobblestone streets had been worn down to a smooth patina from the centuries of footsteps; where most of the buildings were constructed from stone or other durable materials. He had never seen such narrow clapboard houses, one after the other, jammed side by side, looking as though they had been stuck on steep slopes with some kind of mud glue that would surely wash out from under them in a heavy rain. He was used to unfolding panoramas of richly planted vineyards lapping to the very edge of train tracks and roadsides, where every patch of earth was rationed out in layers of rock-enforced terraces, guarding every precious bit of land for growing things.

None of it fit the picture his imagination had fixed so glowingly in his mind's eye. It had not been that way, for instance, back in 1880 when his father had taken him that first time, as a boy, to the Paris Exposition (where he had heard the name of Napa Valley wines for the first time, when his exasperated father had concealed that his own entries had lost out to the Napa wines that had claimed some seventeen of the top awards). Everything about Paris had been as grand, as beautiful as anything Dudley Farnsworth had told him about this city of cities. And it was true at the other places he had visited—Rome, Venice, Florence.

The coach was now turning left, stopping to wait its turn in line to drive inside the enormous glass-domed courtyard of the Palace Hotel and make the turnaround. Adam leaned forward, his eye caught by a cluster of young ladies hurrying by. Quite fashionable ladies, he guessed, if brightly colored plumes on jaunty hats or full skirts cinched around tiny waists and flouncing above dainty ankles could be used in judging such matters.

A dimple-faced, round-eyed young lady with long blond hair turned, grinned unabashedly at him, then darted on with the others. Behind her hurried a much older woman—thin, withered face etched with a deep, worried scowl, hands clutching at long dark-brown skirts as she stepped off the curb, running to catch up with the girls, who were, he presumed, her charges.

A smile hovered on his full mouth. He was curious to know if he would find much difference in the girls in California compared to those in northern Italy; if they would be as strictly chaperoned.

But this was not the time to dwell on girls. He had to keep his mind on business—on finding the right land in Napa Valley; on Samuel Linton; on this eighty-one thousand dollars' worth of bank notes that he wanted to use as collatteral for a much larger loan.

The coach was now working into place, ready to pull into the slot where arriving guests were received. Adam pulled the small leather satchel up closer to his side. He would simply have to convince the man. He could not cut corners when it came to buying the right acreage for the vineyards and getting his root stock in, his varietals grafted on. He didn't want to cut corners on the buildings either—though he hadn't much idea, really, of what building costs in California were going to be. The Donati estate in Pontremoli had been built so long ago. Stonework—maybe Luigi Pascarella could give him a fairly accurate estimate.

This worry wouldn't be so heavy, he thought bitterly, if his oldest brother, Guido, had listened to him and come along to join efforts and combine their inheritance. He was a born winemaker. But Guido had headed for Venice. Alfredo was probably in Florence right now buying up rare old historical manuscripts or some ugly, cracked epic painting from the fifteenth or sixteenth century, allowing himself to be more influenced by an English tutor, than by his own proud father, Giovanni Donati.

Adam shrugged his shoulders. Forget his brothers! What if he had been stuck with Rudolfo—with the hotheaded, belligerent Rudolfo, who was probably in southern France by now, tossing his money to any winds of chance that happened to blow his way?

He climbed out of the coach, followed the doorman into the enormous, elegant lobby. He stopped, looked around this way and that, feeling curiously, surprisingly, as if he had stepped into a familiar place —a hotel somewhere in Europe.

Maybe he felt this way because there was a kind of universal aura to any grand hotel lobby, he thought, stepping up to the registration desk. It was something long collected—a sense of years of guests making their entrances and exits, trailing behind them varying odors, lavenders of women and cigar smoke of men, all mingled with those subtly different smells of clothing from all parts of the world. And there were the same sounds: the hurried, staccato footsteps of messengers and bellhops; the distant shuddering, clanking noise of lifts descending, ascending, of heavy doors opening, closing. The colors— yes, they were the same, too: bright prisms from crystal chandeliers reflected in mirrors, flickering against rich marbles. And people too, usually clustered in lobbies in identical patterns: nodding, smiling, chatting in properly subdued voices so that one could not guess by listening even what language at times was being spoken.

Adam's blue eyes glistened with excitement as he absorbed it.

The desk clerk was smiling up at him through thin lips. "I gather you like our hotel, sir."

Adam turned quickly, signed his name on the line indicated. "Yes —yes, I do. Very much indeed. It seems—well, European. Not as new as some buildings I saw on my way here from the ferry terminal."

The desk clerk tapped his pencil, lifted rimless glasses up high on his forehead and smiled proudly. "Since the day we opened that front door—October the second, 1875—I've been working this front desk on the day shift. I tell you for a fact, we've got the best service in San Francisco. We try to live up to our name. Make our guests happy so they'll come back." He handed Adam a receipt for the leather satchel, now locked in the safe behind the barred windows on the other side of the desk. He rang a bell, then handed a quick-footed bellhop a key. "I believe you'll be satisfied with your suite." He smiled. "We were told to give you the best. Mr. Linton demands that!"

As Adam stepped inside the lift he caught a glimpse of himself in a mirror opposite the heavy doors sliding shut. He had dark circles under his eyes for the first time in his life—the week-long gathered fatigue from the trip hitting him at once. As the lift swayed and bumped its way upward, it occurred to him that Mr. Linton had done him a big favor by allowing him needed time to get his bearings, to get such things done as a decent haircut and shave from the hotel barber, his laundry taken care of, a good night's sleep after that cramped compartment on the train—in a real bed where he could find room to stretch out his long legs and sprawl out luxuriously.

And as he was escorted into the quietly furnished, elegant suite, as the bellboy lit the carefully laid fire in the marble fireplace, pointed to a well-stocked sideboard of whiskeys, graciously accepted his tip and backed out of the room, Adam looked about, feeling for the first time since he had arrived in America that he was once again, at least for the time being, in that special, privileged world he had known throughout his life; for the moment, he felt the full sense of pride in having been born the youngest son of Giovanni Donati—who would have, himself, been quite at home in these surroundings.

From years of discipline, Samuel Linton was a punctual man. Even if he had not been so curious to meet this youngest son of Giovanni Donati—a splendid Old World gentleman if he had ever seen one, with whom he had spent several pleasant luncheons in Paris at the last exposition there, and a memorable weekend at his ancient, proud estate outside Pontremoli—he would have, from habit, arrived a few minutes ahead of his appointment.

That was especially true of one that included a lunch at the Palace Hotel. Not only did they serve the best salmon in San Francisco, but he enjoyed immeasurably sitting around in the huge elegant lobby, simply watching the people. The Fairmont lacked a certain vibrancy this one had. Here he could look around and tell by the faces of the men that they were, by and large, successful businessmen—at least they had the good sense to know where to get the most for their hotel dollar.

Another thing he liked about the Palace: because it was so big, the lobby more easily absorbed all those women cluttering up the place with their big silly feathered hats and all that rattling, empty chatter. He got enough of that at home with his wife, Sue Ellen!

He selected a comfortable chair out of the mainstream of lobby traffic, near a huge potted palm, where he had enough privacy but could still get a straight shot at the revolving doors and could watch for this young Adam Donati to make his entrance.

He took a cigar from a row of them in his outer breast pocket, bit off the end, licked the sides, plunked it into the corner of his mouth, his eyes steadily on the entrance.

He could add up the worth of any man with the bat of an eye, he told himself. And worth or no worth, he could take any man or leave him! That was what power meant in his book.

He sucked in his cheeks, keeping a good light going on the cigar. Hell, if he wanted to, speaking of *power*, he could pull the rug out from under more than one fancy Dan strutting around San Francisco acting as if they owned the gold-crusted top of Nob Hill. Not that he'd actually do that to any man, even when maybe he ought to, considering some of the shaky mortgages his bank was holding.

He squinted one shaggy white eyebrow against a cloud of acrid-smelling smoke encircling his head. *Men*—no, they weren't much problem for him at this stage in his life. If he had any troubles with people, it was with women! And if he ever felt like pulling a rug out from under anybody's feet, he sure as hell wouldn't mind giving a hard yank to one under Sue Ellen's stomping, dissatisfied ones! Damn a woman anyway who could get him hooked into a marriage for forty-eight years and remind him about every day of all forty-eight years why she should have married somebody else. Blaming him at every turn for her own failures, saying it for ten thousand times: "If I'd married Brodie Prince Bondurant from Vicksburg, Mississippi, the way my Daddy said I should, I'd be sitting pretty right now—not treated like I'm some Irish washerwoman, the way I'm treated in this city because of your boorishness!"

Hell, if she hadn't found her slot in San Francisco's high society, it wasn't because he hadn't spent enough money on her every whim along that line. He'd built her one of the finest mansions on Pacific Avenue. He had donated lumps of money to this charity and that. Sue Ellen's problem was that she never knew when to keep her mouth shut. She didn't realize that there were some people in this world who didn't give a hoot in hell about her Papa Justin Henderson's plantation on the Delta. She spent too much time picking all the ladies apart—the very ones she wanted the most to impress.

He leaned back, flicked an ash in a brass spittoon by the potted palm. He had no apologies to make to Sue Ellen. She hadn't been exactly the prize he had thought he was getting, either—she with this big *rich* Papa Justin, who had lost everything in the Civil War. And if she had driven him to the bordellos, she had no one but herself to blame for that too.

He rolled a flick of tocacco from the wet cigar across his tongue, shot it out in the direction of the palm tree. Speaking of apologies, his inner voice grunted to himself, if this brash young Adam Donati didn't arrive in—he took out his gold watch, saw that it was precisely three and a half minutes before twelve o'clock—another couple of minutes, he was going to see nothing of him but his coattails going out the other side of that revolving door. Surely Giovanni Donati had been the kind of man to teach his sons the good manners of promptness. His own father, the gruff, burly Boris Linton, who had never stressed manners so much, perhaps, but who had considered promptness a good character trait, had certainly drilled it into him enough to make an indelible impression.

Well, he had been brought up by a father who looked at life in cold black and white—by Boris Linton from Missouri, who had come to California in that first wave of foolhardy men back in the Gold Rush days; who had stood back on the sidelines—no doubt with a patronizing smile—selling them expensive supplies, and then taking their money and starting up the first Linton Bank of California. In one way, he supposed he could say that either his father or he himself had, at one time or another, built over half of San Francisco through money loaned from the original Linton Bank on Kearny Street.

And speaking of loans, it was his guess that Adam Donati might have more up his sleeve than simply looking for a reliable banker to handle his money, if he was reading correctly what the banker from Milan, Francesco Porta, had written in his letter of introduction: "Adam Donati strongly adheres to those Donati traditions, both as a viticulturist and as a vintner. He wants to dedicate his life to continuing these traditions in California's Napa Valley."

It was going to take a hell of a lot more than dedication! Or maybe they hadn't heard yet in Italy that the same phylloxera beetle that had wiped out the European vineyards not so long ago had just about finished its dirty work in California. In the Napa Valley alone, it had destroyed some eleven thousand acres out of seventeen thousand planted vineyards. Bankers besides himself were foreclosing right and left up there.

Well, maybe he could talk him into a wiser investment. Get him into partnership in the hotel business. He looked at his watch. If this Adam Donati didn't show up pretty damn quick, he'd be left to fall back on his own foolish luck.

He suddenly caught a glimpse of himself in a mirror—of a grumpy-faced, heavy-jowled, white-haired old man glaring back. Somehow, he had always managed to carry around a secret image of himself as being a much younger, much better-looking man.

Unconsciously, he tried to tuck in his middle, stand up straighter, taller, reduce his scowl as, at that very moment, he saw the revolving door spin around and a remarkably handsome, strikingly tall and slender young man in a gray-striped suit enter, stop briefly at the front desk, turn, look straight in his direction, and head toward him.

Deliberately, Samuel Linton stood his ground, taking a long, deep draw from the cigar, tapping a gold-tipped cane against the marbled floor, as if already tapping out his rebuke. He squinted, lifted his left eyebrow, measuring out a reading on this young son of the late Giovanni Donati.

Yes, there was a striking resemblance: the same astonishing clear blue eyes set beneath those thick black eyebrows, the same thick wavy dark hair, the same confident stride—though the father had had a prouder bearing, as if he were some offshoot of royalty.

And then a strong, sure hand was reaching out and he found himself shuffling the cane, allowing his own short, stubby hand to be taken over by that sturdy grip. He felt suddenly that the mirror was surely reflecting for the whole lobby to see that bald spot on the back of his head and some of the pudgy lumps on his age-shriveled body that had brought him down to shrimp size compared to this magnificent six-foot-two man.

"One more minute and you wouldn't have found me standing here waiting for you," he said gruffly, freeing his hand, turning, taking full command again. "We'll be damn lucky if they've held our luncheon reservation. The Palace Hotel is a popular eating spot this time of day."

Adam followed, a deliberate step behind. He had been completely taken aback by this odd, sour-looking man. He had expected to find a dignified, silvery-haired, reasonably tall man, more in the European tradition. This rude-acting, dumpy little man looked more as though he might be a shopkeeper than the president of a bank that was known, as he had been told, by nearly every important winemaker in California, and by a number of those in France and Italy. He was supposed to be a connoisseur of sorts, to have a pretty reliable nose for an amateur, according to the word Adam had got.

He tried not to stare at the strange array of people in the dining room as they worked their way toward their table. His thoughts were churning. He had not missed seeing the keen intelligence in those pale-gray eyes looking up at him, sizing him up. Maybe he shouldn't have held back the apology he had started to make for keeping him waiting. But he hadn't really been late! He had arrived at twelve o'clock on the dot. Besides, business shouldn't begin on a note of apology, he thought, now aware of the way this small, dumpy Samuel Linton waved his gold-tipped cane as they entered the crowded elegant dining room, as though drawing invisible punctuation marks in the air about him, announcing to everyone in the place that the president of the Linton Bank of California had just made his entrance.

Before Adam could totally orient himself to the aura of stiff-backed waiters in black jackets and bow ties, bending, carrying heavy-laden silver trays in such a way that one would think they weighed little; to the noises of glasses clinking, silverware making those scraping sounds against china, of an indecipherable buzz of voices—some muted, some rising in sudden shrill bursts of sound, and somewhere across the room a deep voice caught in a fit of coughing—the waiter was bringing the drinks Mr. Linton had ordered for them, and Mr. Linton was leaning across the table, his pale-gray eyes glinting in that cold, measuring way.

"So you've got eighty-one thousand dollars in the hotel safe waiting to hand over to me as your banker?" he blurted out in a voice as swift and sharp as a pruning knife. "Anything else on your mind?"

Adam took a breath, caught totally by surprise at what seemed more an attack than anything else. He was used to more formality. He had expected to have some sort of initiating conversation. Some small attempt at being made to feel welcome in a strange country.

A slow red fury fingered its way up the back of his neck. Slowly, he lifted his glass, took his time with a long sip of whiskey. He was used to drinking wine with his meals—not this burning drink. He wondered if the drink was part of Mr. Linton's uncalled-for attack.

"So?" Mr. Linton said, tapping the edges of the table with its crisply starched white linen cloth.

This time it was Adam's eyes that burned, a cold steel blue. "So, I think I expected a different greeting from you. I expected a polite gentlemanly—"

"*I* expected to be greeted by your presence when I arrived," Linton said curtly. "I expected the son of Giovanni Donati to be prompt."

"I was prompt," Adam shot back, his earlobes burning red. "I took a short walk. I was back on the dot of noon!" Rage burned through his very fingertips. Though he had been taught to respect his elders, he had also been taught a keen sense of pride.

Mr. Linton had seen his reaction. He waved his hand in a calm-down-now motion. Then he lifted his glass, drank the last of his whiskey, swiped at his mouth with his napkin. "Okay, young man, I'll say I'm *sorry*. I'm sorry I was quick with you. You see, I'm not at my best today. My wife . . ." He pushed a wine list at Adam. "Study what they offer here and pick out anything you want that will go with salmon.

"So what do you think?" he asked, studying Adam's bent-over dark head as he scanned the wine list. "Have you ever tried any of Senator Seneca Ewer's wine? Or any of Henry Crabb's To Kalon? . . . There's a fine 1888 Inglenook Cabernet on there. But if you see any French wines you prefer, say so. I'm a man who likes fine wine—I don't give a damn where it comes from."

"You probably know your California wines better than I," Adam said crisply, struggling to push down the last of his anger. "Any suggestions?"

"Yes, one or two. There's a fine Riesling—hell, let's order that Château Chevalier. Compare it with an Inglenook. You're not in a hurry, are you? We don't have to eat and run?"

"No, sir. I thought I would try to do some sight-seeing after we have finished our . . . appointment. Get a view of the bay from one of the hills."

Mr. Linton gave the order for wine and his usual salmon in champagne sauce to a tall, slim waiter who obviously recognized him and knew his position in the city. "I'll tell you *what*, son," he said then, folding his hands across the table. "When we finish here, I'll have my coachman take us around. If you haven't made plans with your friends, why don't you have dinner with me tonight at my place up on Nob Hill? I've got a pretty nice view myself . . . You know something? I believe I saw you when you were a kid—when your father entertained me in your home in Italy. That town that gets my tongue twisted every time I try to say it—Pont-something-or-other."

"Pontremoli," Adam said, smiling in spite of himself; enjoying now being with anyone who had known his father, had actually visited his home place in Italy.

Mr. Linton broke off a piece of bread, nibbled, then lifted the glass of wine the waiter had just poured. "Here's to Pon-*tray*-mo-lee. Did I get it right this time?"

"Yes, sir," Adam said, lifting his own glass.

"I'm not a purist like you Europeans," Mr. Linton said as the waiter scooped up his empty whiskey glass. "I *developed* a taste for wines, but I grew up on whiskey."

They were just finishing a fine chocolate mousse and a weak, watered-down cup of coffee which Adam detested, when Mr. Linton abruptly got down to business. "You realize your timing is wrong for starting out in the wine business? Or maybe you haven't heard that we've got a collapsed market on our hands over here? That the phylloxera has hit us too?"

Adam tried to hide his shock. No, he hadn't heard. He knew what it had done in Europe, from his studies at Alba. And though the Donati vineyards had escaped the disease, his father had loaned money to many vineyardists he respected in nearby southern France. He was appalled that it had hit the vineyards in this country.

"How bad is it?"

"Just about wiped out the industry in Napa Valley. Hit the lower valley first, then spread like wildfire. It got its foothold back in 1890 and is still digging its way through the roots—anywhere there are vineyards left. A lot of men are trying to save themselves from total ruin by ripping out vines and putting in orchards. A lot of prune trees going in lately." Mr. Linton looked at Adam gravely. "Young man, I hate to discourage you, but I have to tell you for a fact that if you invest your money in vineyards in Napa Valley right now you're putting it down a sinkhole. I've got more than one shaky mortgage up there. A couple of foreclosures I've got to make pretty soon, whether I want to or not." He made a slurping noise as he sipped his coffee, blew across the top of the cup. "But I've been thinking about what you ought to do. In my opinion, getting into the hotel business would be the smartest thing you could do. San Francisco is a one-of-a-kind city —on the bay. The Pacific ocean out there . . . People are beginning to come here—hell, I took a suite for you because there wasn't an available single room in the hotel. I've got some money *I* want to invest—I know a couple of men who'd like to go in with us. We could buy one of the best hotel sites on Nob Hill. How about it?"

"Mr. Linton, you don't understand," Adam said quietly. "I'm a viticulturist. I'm here to grow grapes. Establish a winery. I'm here to rebuild the Donati manor house—the very winery you probably saw when you visited Pontremoli. Of course I hope to make some money at it, but my sole intent *isn't* to make money." He bent forward, his blue eyes shining with intensity. "You must understand that growing noble grapes—"

"Let's understand one thing, son," Mr. Linton said, taking out a cigar, lighting it. "As I see it, there's not a damn thing noble about throwing your money away—ending up broke, which is exactly what I expect to happen to you if you go ahead with this idea of yours! How much money do you have? Wasn't it eighty thousand dollars according to that letter your banker sent me? Hell, that's a lot of money in any country. But it's not going to stretch very far for what you have in mind. Building a winery, your money will only get your feet wet."

"I realize that," Adam said quietly. "I ask you to consider my eighty-one thousand dollars as collateral for a loan of at least twice that. I can produce some white wines fairly quickly, get some return. I will be able to pay the loan back to you in—"

"Let's talk *facts*," Mr. Linton interrupted. "That's *my* business—facts and figures. One of the prevailing facts any banker in America has to deal with these days is that a big worldwide depression is going on. Not just in the wine market." He blew smoke in a straight shot across the table. "But for your purposes, we will limit the facts to the wine industry—if you can call it that. I happen to know quite a lot about Napa Valley particularly, since my bank has been loaning money up there since before Captain Neibaum came in and built Inglenook—hell, even before he stopped his fur-trading and shipping business. Right now there are over one hundred bonded wineries up there trying to hang on. There are some thirty registered brandy distilleries—not counting those that are *un*registered—" He saw the look of confusion on Adam's face. "The ones that are operating illegally to escape taxes. I predict that you'll be lucky to find twenty-five left in business in five years! Maybe before that. I know for damn sure that by 1900 there'll be more prune trees and fruit orchards, and more cattle raising coming back, than any attempt at winemaking. It's a dead business." He pointed his finger at Adam. "You must listen to me—you don't have a chance in hell up there! The market's dead. Stone dead."

"There will always be a market for fine wines," Adam said stubbornly, his strong jawline even more pronounced. "Historically, through the ages, there has been a market for wines. In the Bible—Noah planted vines. Further back than Noah—"

Mr. Linton shook his head. "Spoken like a true Italian, but you've got to realize one thing: you're in California now—America. People over here aren't weaned on the stuff. They don't know one wine from another." Again he was wagging his finger, puffing smoke out of the side of his mouth. "And even those who *do* . . . Take Charles Krug, who's been at this since 1861. He's hanging on by the skin of his teeth —faces being shut down too, and you won't find a more noble man in the business than Krug!" He was quiet a moment, staring off into space. Then the quick pale-gray eyes bore down on Adam's cloudy blue ones. "You may know your wines, and I'm sure a Donati does. But I'm a banker. I know *my* business. I'm telling you it won't work."

Adam spoke slowly, deliberately. "It takes four years for a vineyard to mature. Longer than than to get its best grapes. But vines will last longer than a man will live. Some vines hold out and produce for over eighty years." He saw the argument brewing in Samuel Linton's face. "From what you have told me, with over one hundred wineries and many of them forced to close down, there should be some excellent buys on the market. Fine cooperage—machinery I could buy at rock-bottom prices. Maybe there's some bulk wine that could be bought up along with it." His voice was showing his growing excitement. "With the loan I need—"

"Now, hold your horses, son! I haven't said I was loaning you any money. I thought I had made it clear that—"

"You have made it clear that contrary to what you have said, this *is* the time to begin in Napa Valley. People wanting to get out will sell for very low prices. Land—I want good hillside land. The phylloxera in Europe hit the lowlands mostly. Hillside vineyards were pretty well protected. Check your records in Napa Valley. My guess is you'll find it's about the same. And wouldn't you agree—" it was Adam pointing his finger now, though his father had always given stern rebukes when any of his sons pointed at anything—"wouldn't you agree that there has most certainly *been* a wine industry? Remember the very Paris Exposition where you met my father? Those were Napa Valley wines that won most of the prizes, right? And if there was an existing market to sustain the Beringers and Charles Krug, the man called Henry Crabb with his To Kalon, Inglenook . . ." He waved both hands excitedly. "You know them—you know more Napa Valley wineries than I do. But I ask you to consider this. That market isn't dead, even if the vines are. If I give them Donati wine to buy, they will buy it!" He sat back proudly. "They will stand in line to buy it because Donati is the best."

Samuel Linton shook his head, but he was smiling now. "I'll tell you this much—I like your spunk! Your fight. But I'm still—"

"Economic depressions—we have had them forever in my country," Adam said. "Politics, governments. A man cannot rely on them. But I am not talking about that. I am talking about something that doesn't change. There are few places in the world, as I have been taught, where grapes have ideal growing conditions. One of them is your Napa Valley. The climate, the soil, that volcanic ash for good drainage. Not too much moisture—just about enough rolling in from the ocean. Hot dry summers. And not such a big place. Don't you see? The right kind of investment in Napa Valley—*your* banker's money with *my* knowledge, my background . . ." His voice had dropped to a low, dead-level tone. "You are the only person in America who can

24

help me, who understands what I want to do here in this country. You are the only banker who knew Giovanni Donati. Give me a chance. Let me show you!"

Samuel Linton closed his eyes for a moment. Through his years of banking he had seen every type of man dreaming up every conceivable reason why he should loan him money. He tried always to use sound banking principles as his judge. There had been times when he hadn't, when he would let another man's enthusiasm carry him away from sound reasoning. But he could not escape Adam Donati's intense look. He cleared his throat, tapped at dead ashes on his cigar.

"Look, I'm an old man now." He shrugged his shoulders. It was the first time he had ever admitted it aloud to himself, much less to someone else. "A foolish one at that, at times. I've made my mark here in San Francisco. I'm—by God, I guess I'm the biggest fool around, but, I'm going to help you! I *like* you. I liked your father. I even like the wine you picked out to go with the salmon!"

He found himself studying Adam in a new light. It was not necessarily anything he could put into words, but he knew it had to do with his deep longing to have had his own son. It had to do with something unanswered inside him in—oh, more ways than that. With his wife, Sue Ellen—with a happiness he had once thought might exist between a man and his wife. And it had to do with a certain emptiness he felt, now that he was at the top, up there with the most successful men in San Francisco, certainly; with the loss of a challenge—the fight . . . This young man had fight—spirit oozing out of him! He could feel that vital sap, almost as if it were flowing in his own veins again. What the hell! Why *not* help him out? He had more money than he could ever spend. And Sue Ellen—she had glutted herself to such extremes that he doubted she could think up much more. So much of what she thought was only empty chatter anyway—words to fill up space around her.

"Do you mean you'll give me a loan?" Adam asked, his voice very even and surprisingly calm, as if he had never really seriously doubted it.

Again, Samuel Linton squinted his eyes nearly shut. After a moment he spoke, more in his usual businesslike tone. "As I mentioned, I do hold some mortgages up there that have to have something done about them. I've stalled long enough. There's *one* deal—sure, Cugnot. I believe he has some hillside acreage, but he lives in midvalley, in Rutherford. And I've got another mess up near Calistoga—he'll have some oak cooperage for you. At least he damn well *ought* to, since I loaned him enough in a weak moment to buy up every oak barrel in France. But this building business—I don't know anything about stonework, if you're planning to build something like that fine house of yours, that big winery I saw. They've used a lot of Chinese labor up there." He pushed up from the table after tipping the waiter. "The best thing for us to do is go up there and take a look around. Spend a few days checking things out. I could use a few days at the Soda Springs Hotel. A fine spa. Would you like that? Or do you have plans I don't know about with your friends?"

Adam stood up stiffly, his heart thumping. "When do we leave?"

Mr. Linton smiled knowingly. "Okay—hold your horses. Look, my coachman is waiting. Let's take that drive around San Francisco, stop by my place for dinner. Give me *my* turn at returning hospitality. Tomorrow—what's wrong with taking the afternoon ferry to Vallejo, checking in at Soda Springs tomorrow?"

"Nothing—I'd like that very much," Adam said, trying to restrain his excitement.

"Okay, let's get that eighty-one thousand dollars and drop it off for safekeeping at my bank. I don't trust these damn hotel safes." While they waited for the leather satchel to be handed over and for Adam to sign for its release, Mr. Linton drummed his fingers across the desk top, looked at Adam thoughtfully and said: "Why is it you don't have an *Italian*-sounding name? I thought the papers listed your name as being Emilio Adamo."

Adam did not hesitate. "They do. But I decided that if I am going to become an American, I want a name which comes straight to the point." He lifted one thick dark eyebrow and smiled knowingly at Mr. Linton. "I was warned by my English tutor that American men are known for being somewhat blunt—to the point."

Mr. Linton reached for the satchel, dubbed out the last of his cigar in a brass ashtray the clerk shoved toward him. "So you had an *English* tutor?—that's why you speak better English than I do." And as they walked toward the carriage entrance, his hand clasped Adam's arm warmly, as any father might with a son with whom he was pleased.

2

The Saturday-night dinner in the magnificent Linton mansion on Pacific Avenue impressed Adam, as Mr. Linton figured it would.

Even Sue Ellen, after seeing what a handsome young European gentleman her rough-hewn husband had brought home for a change—one who, for once, hadn't added even more cigar smoke to increase her bouts of migraines—had been agreeable. And if Samuel Linton's scowls had intensified as the evening wore on—as she finished a third champagne and lapsed into a thick Mississippi accent, being coquettish in a way that might have charmed some young man fifty years ago—she had not noticed.

Adam himself had thoroughly enjoyed the sight-seeing trip and the dinner in the elegant thirty-four-room mansion. The views had been as breathtakingly beautiful as Dudley Farnsworth had told him they would be, though nothing had quite prepared him for the steep inclines of the streets, where it seemed virtually impossible to Adam that any horse could climb without slipping backward.

He found himself excited about this raw young city of San Francisco. It reminded him of an excellent young wine that would need a long stretch of time yet to work its way through those intricate, invisible processes that would bring it—with the magic of luck on its side—to that full ripened essence.

The next day, however, he was anxious to leave it behind. He was finally going to see the famous Napa Valley. Aboard the S. S. *Monticello*, as they steamed toward the Vallejo wharf, Mr. Linton insisted they stay on the outer deck. "The open sea stimulates me. The air clears my head," he told a concerned Adam, who thought the stiff breezes—even though it was a warm day for late February—would be too much for a man he guessed to be in his late seventies. But even when they were crossing the cold, windy Carquinez Straits, when a bright flush crossed Mr. Linton's face, settling into a splotchy red at the end of his nose, when his gray eyes watered and his nose dripped, he still flatly refused to go inside. "I like it!" he said irritably. "I have to stay cooped up too much as it is," thinking to himself how truly wonderful it was to have Sue Ellen's nagging, for once, blown to the high seas.

When they debarked, he tried to keep up with Adam's long-legged, easy stride—this impatient young stallion of a man acting as if he thought the Napa Valley would run away if he didn't hurry and grab it by the coattails! When they got to their seats in the train coach, Mr. Linton plopped down wearily. He leaned back, closing his eyes to rest them from the sharp, salty sea air, he told himself.

The train was pulling into the Soscol depot in the town called Napa City when Mr. Linton awakened, stunned.

"We're here," Adam was saying to him as if he were speaking to a small child.

Flustered and a little confused, Mr. Linton fumbled to find his hat, his coat, his briefcase with the foreclosure papers his lawyer had drawn up and sent over by messenger barely in time, and the valise packed to last for a few days' trip.

Adam was on the platform waiting for him, a perplexed look on his face as he looked around at this roughshod place calling itself Napa *City*. Recent rains had filled mudholes to the brim in the unpaved road. Rowdy boys, playing a game of tag with an irate conductor, ducked under the couplings of the train. Bony, lop-eared dogs slunk around sniffing for food, dodging kicks from the regulars loitering in front of the depot—obviously for not much reason other than to watch the four-o'clock train come in. A sullen-looking cowboy rode by, spit purposely not too far from Adam's carefully polished shoes.

Mr. Linton stepped up beside him, a smile in the corner of his mouth. "What's wrong? Doesn't it look like what you thought?" He laughed drily. "Napa City isn't our destination. But if you're settling into this valley you'll need to accept this part too. It's the mouth—where you'll do some trading. Still a pretty busy port, on the Napa River a few blocks to the west. Hooks up with San Pablo Bay—what you might call the kite-tail end of the San Francisco Bay. No doubt you'll be shipping out grapes—wine from here, one of these days. That is, unless I can talk some sense into you and get you to come back to San Francisco—put your money where there's some future!"

The stagecoach had not arrived. Obviously, part of the ritual for the Sunday regulars at the depot was watching the stagecoach load up with passengers heading for what was referred to by them as "rich people's territory." Adam was aware that curious gazes, outright stares, had fallen on his and Mr. Linton's backs.

The delay was making Mr. Linton fretful. He pulled out his gold watch, stuffed it back into his pocket. Then he lit a fresh cigar, stared off in the direction of Napa City. In a moment he turned, the cigar in the corner of his mouth, the smoke puffing out, as though he were trying to stir up some action. "This used to be a miner's town," he said. "Sprung up along with the Gold Rush—making room for all those damn fools who went rushing out into the goldfields and then came back here with their pockets empty, looking for some kind of job to live on. A place where it was a little warmer than out there in the mountains."

Adam was half listening, but politely paid attention as he rambled on.

"Silverado Trail over there—see, where the stagecoach is coming from—that used to be busy with big freight wagons loaded down with cinnabar from the quicksilver mines up valley. Oat Hill, the Silverado Mines, one over in Chiles Valley. When the mines worked out, some people stayed on to work in lumber mills or as cowboys on the cattle ranches—a few working in vineyards. Napa City here, I guess it's got around four thousand people in it. Biggest town in the valley."

At that minute, heads turned and the sound of the stagecoach claimed everyone's attention. Adam watched, fascinated, as the perfectly matched four-hitch team of solid black horses swung into view, pulling a stagecoach exactly like those he had seen in pictures Dudley Farnsworth had brought back from California. A slim-hipped, strong-looking young man wearing a bright-red uniform heavy with gold braid on the shoulders brought the stagecoach to a startlingly abrupt stop, as though wanting to give the regulars their waiting's worth. And then Mr. Linton was giving Adam a nudge with the corner of his briefcase, urging him to climb aboard.

Inside the narrow leather-covered stagecoach they were joined by an enormous, short-breathed German man with a long, droopy moustache that seemed in constant motion. Any irritation Mr. Linton might have shown over the stagecoach being late was mild compared to the German's blustery, red-faced exasperation.

He introduced himself as Baron Klaus von Gothard. "This trip is the last time I'll ever come west!" he spluttered. "From the moment I left St. Louis, it has been one long chain of delays. And two days ago, that icebox of a train broke down on the side of a mountain! Took us eighteen miserable hours to get back on the track going again. I've already missed my nephew's wedding, but if this keeps up I won't even get there for the reception. What kind of place is this Soda Springs Hotel where we're going?"

Mr. Linton was twisting the chewed-down stub of his cigar in the corner of his mouth, both gray eyes narrowing in that measuring way of his. "Oh, Soda Springs is one of our finest California resorts. Excellent spring water. You probably drank some of it on the train. Fine hot baths—do you some good. Calm down your nerves." He lifted one eyebrow, smiling at Adam, as if letting him in on a game he was about to play. "St. Louis, eh? Von Gothard? I usually remember names . . ."

For a moment they were all three silent, busy holding to overhead leather straps as the stagecoach swerved around a curve, turning off the Silverado Trail and heading now toward the hills to the northeast.

"You probably know the big family my nephew is marrying into," the Baron said confidently, crossing his pudgy fingers over his bulging belly, making an effort to appear relaxed as the ride smoothed out somewhat.

Though Adam saw the narrowing look on Mr. Linton's face, he turned to look out the window at the unfolding landscape. It was the first time he had seen mustard—he knew it was planted to add nitrogen to the soil—in full bloom, working its way like bright golden streamers across the vividly green fields of spring hay and, to his right, straggling through a small vineyard with dormant vines that looked now more like brittle tangles of deadwood.

"What's this family's *name*?" Mr. Linton asked drily.

The Baron looked amused. "Since you are obviously a man of means, I'm surprised you don't know about the Gothard-Cugnot wedding. I was told it will be the biggest social event in Napa Valley in years." He reached for the strap again as the stagecoach suddenly burst downhill.

Mr. Linton held the cigar out between his yellow-stained fingers, studying it as though it held some secret essence that only he knew about. "Cugnot, eh? Jacques Cugnot—there's a name for you!"

Something in Mr. Linton's tone had taken the Baron off guard. "I hear it's a name that goes back to French nobility. Very respected name around Napa Valley." He twitched his moustache. "*Linton*—that's a name new to me. I don't know it at all."

Mr. Linton jammed the cigar between his teeth. "Linton—the Linton Bank of California. Ask Jacques Cugnot—*he* knows it."

Adam watched the two men with a curious detachment. This sparring they were doing—staking out a kind of territory, their own spaces of reign. Yet his ears were becoming keenly attuned at the mention of the name Cugnot; he was positive that was the name on the foreclosure papers in Mr. Linton's briefcase.

Mr. Linton let a wreath of smoke curl around his face. "The biggest social event in Napa—that would be Jacques Cugnot all right." He blew a chute of smoke at the Baron.

The Baron sat up straighter. "My nephew, Gunther—his bride's dowry is some premium land in Napa Valley, I've been told. The Gothard Brewery just might think about expanding into wine." Something about the raised eyebrow, the bemused look on Samuel Linton's face made the Baron draw back into himself. He had enough doubts about this whole wedding. Gunther was a damn-fool nephew! Who knew anything about this Jacques Cugnot or his pretty daughter, Monique? Gunther should have chosen a girl from St. Louis, where they might have checked the family's credentials more easily. Not that his marrying a Cugnot from Napa Valley meant that Gothard money would be invested, willy-nilly.

Mr. Linton watched the Baron closely, squinting one eye in his most studying way.

Adam left the older men to their thoughts. He was concentrating fully now on the truer feel of the landscape. As the stagecoach swung around a high curve or bounded over the crest of a sharp ridge, he saw here and there glimpses of the narrow valley dotted with farmhouses and outbuildings, its fields of spring hay, dormant orchards and vineyards, long stretches of pasture with cattle grazing making a colorful patchwork. He had quickly seen the contrast between the two opposing ridges of mountains, the western side being greener, richer-looking, so unlike the eastern slopes over which the stagecoach was traveling—ragged with rocks and scrub oak, with its dense scaly thickets of underbrush and its manzanita trees, its banks of sun-baked, wind-whipped pines. A smile crossed his face as a nearby covey of quail swooped into a startled low-flying formation, barely skimming over the trees as they fled the sound of thundering hoofs and clanking harness, the wheels crunching, creaking their way toward that last stretch of road. Adam sat up excitedly, catching his first sight of the glass-domed rotunda, the solid stone building that was the main hotel, the separate cottages cascading down a green, well-kept hillside.

And then they were stopping, the door being opened by a freckle-faced, wide-grinning footman wearing the same Soda Springs red uniform with gold braid. From politeness, Adam waited for the Baron and Mr. Linton to climb out. He swung down easily, stood a moment, out a few feet away from the others, gathering in the sights around him.

The sky had just begun to take on those oranges and lavenders of sunset. In every direction Adam saw long stretches of formal gardens —exotic bright-blooming spring flowers, palm trees, round raised garden beds, fountains, flower-lined pathways. Down to his right were a bathhouse and a huge pool. And off across the valley, to the west, the mountain ridges seemed to march in a ragged undisciplined flank toward the north, where he could see the famous Mount St. Helena he had read about, that flat-domed top where some eons ago the volcano had erupted and spewed its lava down across the valley, leaving that deep ash so valuable for a viticulturist.

He tried to guess which ridge would hold the land he would buy. The western slopes would be where he'd prefer—the cooler, heavily wooded slopes with their natural springs and the larger share of volcanic ash. He wouldn't mind the hard work of clearing, not if the soil was the kind he wanted!

Mr. Linton had gone over to talk with the driver of the stagecoach about hiring a buggy and horse for the trip up valley the next day. Adam looked around, pulling himself out of his own reflections, just in time to see the main doors of the hotel open, and darting through it one of the loveliest young ladies he had ever seen. He stood watching, fascinated, as she brushed past the Baron von Gothard and headed straight down the pathway on which he was standing. She was obviously a member of the wedding party—her blue silk dress flowed out behind her, along with the pink and white satin ribbons on the bouquet she was carrying in one long slender hand. She was directly in front of him now, her beautiful oval-shaped face tilted toward his, her startling amber-colored eyes filled with a mischievous sparkle, as if she had some joke of her own she was playing. Her thick dark-brown hair, the color of chestnuts, was piled loosely on top of her head, and looked as though strands would start tumbling down at any moment.

"Hello," she said, in a wonderfully laughing, husky voice. But before he could respond, she had dashed on, the pink and white satin streamers from the bouquet flying behind her.

"The Reynolds girl," Mr. Linton's voice cracked at his elbow.

A stocky square-faced boy in his midteens, wearing the Soda Springs Hotel uniform, his straight blond hair falling down over one eye, picked up Adam's valises and grinned, showing uneven yellow teeth. "I know Sarah Hubbard Reynolds. I went to grade school through fourth and fifth grades with her. That is, 'fore her mother Miss

Grace yanked her out of public school and put her in private." He grinned at Adam. "They don't know I heard them in there giggling and double-dog-daring Sarah to run down thisaway and say something to you. Christine Miller and Winifred Cobb—two of the bridesmaids from St. Helena—probably in there 'bout to have a fainting fit wondering if Miss Grace caught wind of what they was up to. Lord, if she don't watch that Sarah Hubbard Reynolds like a hawk! Some say it'll be snow in July around here before Miss Grace'll let anybody close enough to her only daughter to get a good word in edgewise, much less propose to her. Being maid of honor for Monique Cugnot might be the closest she ever gets to a wedding, if you ask me. Monique—I went through fourth and fifth grades with her too."

Mr. Linton gave a curt nod to Freddie. "Here's a silver dollar. What cottage do we have?"

"You'll have to ask at the desk. It's my guess you'll be in the upstairs suite right here. Jacques Cugnot rented out every single cottage for the wedding party. Lord, if he ain't gonna be out of his pockets when he pays all these big bills! Hired a big dance orchestra out of San Francisco. Got enough food down there at the rotunda right now to feed Cox's Army. . . . But any room here at Soda Springs is mighty nice. Best beds in Napa Valley—best spring water too. Everybody says that. We stay busy when Pope Valley over there at Aetna Springs starts getting hungry for people about this time of year. But not us, nosirreebob!"

Mr. Linton registered for them at the front desk. "What's on tonight's social agenda for young people—for my friend Mr. Donati here?" he asked the clerk.

"There's the billiard room . . . the library."

Mr. Linton signed the form, shoved it back impatiently. "That's for old fogeys like me. Didn't I hear music—a band tuning up down at the rotunda? I saw a few young people, nice-looking young ladies, heading down that way. Wouldn't they like to have a handsome bachelor introduced? Join the party?"

The clerk turned his head. "That's a private party, sir!"

"It's made up of Napa Valley people, isn't it? Mr. Donati here, he's going to buy some land. Build a big mansion, big winery. Seems to me it would be a fine time to introduce him."

"I couldn't help you with that, I'm afraid. Freddie, take them to Room Ten—the suite at the end of the hall with the balcony. We gave you our best," he said apologetically. "The cottage you requested down near the bathhouse is taken. All the —"

33

"I heard," Mr. Linton said grumpily. "I'd like to be here when Jacques Cugnot pays his bill!" He nodded to Adam. "Come on, let's wash up for dinner. I'm hungry. At least they'll serve us in the dining room, I believe. Or is *that* private, too?"

They were being served the main course and Adam was watching with amusement as Mr. Linton hacked at a tough piece of steak. "It's not the Palace Hotel," he said, disgruntled, chewing vigorously. "Look, I'll try to figure a way to get you introduced around, get you to that dance. That Reynolds girl—you perked up when you saw her, I noticed."

Adam tried to concentrate on a bite of lumpy mashed potatoes streaked with thick brown gravy. "She was attractive—"

"Hell, she's beautiful! Admit it. Though where she got her looks is beyond me. Miss Grace, her hatchet-faced mother—*she'd* certainly not win any beauty contests. Tough as nails, though." Mr. Linton waved his fork in the air. "Son, let me tell you something right now about women who come from the South! I'm married to a Mississippi girl. Miss Grace Hubbard Reynolds came from someplace down there—talks like she's got a wad of cotton wrapped around every letter *r* in the alphabet. Here's what they do. They can pour on the honey and molasses and act like their very life depends on your next word. Then, next thing you know, they're holding the reins. The Reynolds girl—watch out for her. She probably got some of her mother's crust."

"I wasn't . . . I only saw her on the pathway. I—"

"Your eyes about bugged out of your head," Mr. Linton snorted, pushing his plate aside and pulling a piece of chocolate cake closer. "I've lived a lot of years, young man. Had my share of women. I know that look when I see it. Nothing to be ashamed of."

Adam pushed his own food aside, though he had been taught to let servants take charge of all dishes. There was an informality here, however. As he looked around the huge, empty dining room, seeing the dark beamed ceilings, the oak sideboard, the gas lamps sending out a soft glow, he felt oddly misplaced. It was the emptiness, the lack of noise he expected in hotels. It Italy, wherever people were, there was commotion. Talk—everyone talking, gesticulating. He missed Luigi Pascarella, oddly. That week on the train a bond had formed between them. He wondered if this happened to men when they shared any new experience; crossing into some new, alien territory, safer by knowing they shared something in common from the place they had left behind. With himself and Luigi, there were wide spaces between them in their backgrounds; yet, how very much he would like to hear his own language right now—join in and laugh with Luigi as they relived some memory from the train ride. His ear was getting more in tune with the English language, with all those derivations and inflections that kept jumping out at him. He never realized how a native language itself made a bond, a communion of sorts.

Mr. Linton had ordered brandies for them. He swirled his slowly, his aged hand with its brown spots and rubbery-looking veins reaching in a toast toward Adam's long-fingered strong right hand now holding the glass up—while he studied, Mr. Linton presumed, the amber color, the fine clear quality of an excellent Château Mont Helena brandy, which was, in Mr. Linton's opinion, one of Napa Valley's best. In reality, Adam was not thinking about the brandy at all: he was seeing those amber-colored eyes that had sent another kind of warm, trickling sensation through him when the girl in the blue silk dress had run past.

Mr. Linton was proposing his toast. Adam forced himself to listen, refocus his attention. "Here's to my selling you on another bill of goods besides this wild-goose chase up here!"

Adam felt the click of their brandy tumblers, but he did not lift his glass to honor the toast. After a moment, he sipped quietly, noting the smooth quality of the brandy; also noting to himself that he could make a finer one.

After waiting long enough, he lifted the glass again. "Here's to bringing Donati winemaking to Napa Valley—salute!" His voice had its own quiet ring of determination.

Samuel Linton shook his head ruefully. "You're hell-bent, aren't you? You don't see it at all when I tell you I could make a rich man out of you, put the city of San Francisco in the palm of your hand?" He wagged a finger at Adam. "I've seen a lot of men come and go in my day. I've seen about every kind of failure. Sure, some big overnight successes. In every case of success, though, by God, it's a matter of timing. A man comes along with the right guts to take the right chances. He's willing to judge the odds. See a golden opportunity under his nose."

Adam smiled patiently, tolerantly. "My father taught me differently. He handed down to me what was handed down to him. From as far back as I can remember, I was taught about vineyards—noble grapes, noble wines. About pruning . . . the harvest . . . next vintage . . ." He had a far-off look in his pale-blue eyes now, as if seeing something beyond Samuel Linton's vision. "I was taught the meaning of the word 'patience.'"

Mr. Linton's voice came out in a sound like a snort. "Your father must have thought he was the Pope's right-hand man!" He reached for a new cigar. "I never met a *patient* Italian in my life."

Adam sipped his brandy. "You've met one now," he said matter-of-factly. "I know—I know it, right here—" he thumped his breast, put the brandy tumbler down and waved his hands as any Pascarella might have—"I know I will find the perfect hillside land, I know I will rebuild the Donati Winery—the vineyards, the manor house! I know it might take a lifetime to do it right. To satisfy myself. But I know I will do it. I know *waiting* is part of the game. Half of it is waiting."

Mr. Linton chewed off the end of the cigar, wadded up the band, dropped it by his brandy tumbler. "You sound exactly like old Jacob Brunner, a stubborn old Swiss vineyardist up here in Napa Valley—somebody maybe you ought to meet." He struck a match, puffed hard, then sat back, more at ease. "I loaned him some money once. On his word. No collateral, nothing but his word." He blew smoke, drummed his fingers against the tablecloth. "Not like this blowhard, Cugnot! No, Jacob Brunner's a man of his word, one hundred percent. He came into my bank one day looking like he had seen a ghost. I thought the phylloxera had got to his vines and wiped him out." He tapped ashes, caught up in his story. "Well, it turned out Jacob had this daughter—Johanna, something like that—married this big strapping Swede from Minnesota who wouldn't listen to Jacob and settle down in Napa Valley. Had to get back to his dairy farm. To his milk cows and his cheeses up there in that iceberg of a state. They had a few children. Three or four, I believe it was. Then they started falling on hard times. It was dead of winter. They were stuck out in that Godforsaken farm country, buried in snow. One night right before Christmas, the whole house caught on fire. *Phhhht*—went up like kindling. Everybody burned to death but one grandchild of Jacob's—a young girl named Erika, I believe he said." Samuel Linton was still a moment, let the smoke drift through his fingers. "Jacob is a man who thinks going into debt is the closest thing to sinning. But he needed a couple thousand dollars to go back to Minnesota and pay his daughter's debts and bring back his only surviving relative." He shook his head vigorously, as if trying to shake off the thought of a family perishing in fire. "It's a hell of a note—being buried in the first place in a goddam snowbank and then burning to death! Jacob said this girl Erika jumped out a window —woke up, and I guess saw the fire, took a blind jump out of a two-story window and landed in a snowbank. Broke her leg. Couldn't move. Damn near froze to death before neighbors a few miles off saw the flames and came to rescue her. She must've stood there and watched her family burn up alive. How would you like to live with something like *that* for the rest of your life? What kind of patience you think that young girl has to have?"

Adam shook his head, drained his brandy. "Life—I guess it hands out some strange blows all over the world. I've heard of things bad like that, back in Italy."

Mr. Linton pushed back from the table, stood, stretched. He rubbed his stomach. "That gravy was too greasy to suit me. It's sitting like lard. Probably keep me awake half the night. And if *it* doesn't, all those chirping crickets and goddam noisy bullfrogs probably will." He gave Adam's arm a friendly grasp. "I'm a city man. A dyed-in-the-wool city man. Otherwise, I'd most likely have bought myself some vineyards a long time ago. Jumped off the deep end like you're about to do and wasted all the money my father made in the bank business." They were leaving the dining room, standing now out in the main lobby. "Sometimes I wonder how men get this winemaking bug—why they can't shake it off. But why does a man get his head stuck on any foolish dream? Go charging through life like a stubborn mule wearing blinders —on one main track?" He placed a hand on the thick wooden railing of the wide stairway. "I guess I'm getting old, son—losing my sap. I'm sure as hell running out of patience with people like Jacques Cugnot— over there right now at the rotunda, probably strutting around acting like he's king of Napa Valley! Trying to pull the wool over everybody's eyes. Get somebody else's hard-earned money back in his pockets." He shook hands with Adam. "Good night. You'll find something to do until you get sleepy. Me, I have to go to bed early. Otherwise I won't be fit for much tomorrow when we go up valley. If my memory is right, Jacques Cugnot has some pretty nice land cleared off and planted in vines up on Spring Mountain. That ought to be hillside enough for you."

After Adam found himself alone, he wandered into the empty library and looked around absently at the rows of leatherbound books on the dusty shelves. Idly, he picked out a volume of Robert Louis Stevenson's *Silverado Squatters*, thumbed through it, noticing a passage here and there written back in 1880, when Stevenson had come to St. Helena on his honeymoon.

"This pleasant Napa Valley is, at its north end, blockaded by our mountain. There, at Calistoga, the railroad ceases, and the traveler who intends faring further, to the Geysers or to the springs of Lake County, must cross the spurs of mountains by stage. Thus, Mount Saint

Helena is not only a summit, but a frontier," Adam read, then shoved the book back into its slot.

He had come to the end of *his* stagecoach ride. He wasn't here as a traveler, an observer. He had come to the Napa Valley to settle in. Plant the name of Donati along with his vines.

From the bay window facing the glass-domed pavilion, he could hear faint strains of music from a lively waltz. He tried to imagine the girl, this Sarah Hubbard Reynolds, whirling about in the blue silk dress, that laughing face turned up toward someone else.

Absurdly, a shot of jealousy went through him. He didn't even know her. He hadn't even been introduced. For all he knew, maybe she was engaged to someone else.

Though he had no desire to meet the others, his arms ached with desire to be dancing with her. There were a hundred questions he would ask.

The bellboy, Freddie, came into the library. "Anything I could get for you, Mr. Donati? George told me to come ask. A newspaper? Nice bedtime stogie?"

Adam turned away from the window, glanced at the grandfather clock and saw that it was nine o'clock. "The dance—when is it due to end?"

Freddie shrugged his shoulders, checked to see if all the ashtrays had been emptied. "The orchestra is due to stop about now. The girls' chaperones will shoo them off to bed—if by any chance you had in mind they might be coming over thisaway again tonight. Everybody folds up early in the country. Even when it's a big wedding celebration. Tomorrow they'll come trouping into the dining room clacking like old setting hens."

He went over to pull the curtains at the bay window to ward off early-morning sun that would beam through otherwise and fade the red velvet cushions the next day. He peered out, his face close to the glass. "Looks like they're filing out now. There's that Sarah Hubbard Reynolds—out there dancing around under the gas lamps showing off for everybody." He yanked the curtains closed. "But I reckon anybody that pretty's got a right, wouldn't you say?"

Adam felt as if his neck, his ears, his whole face were turning red. He didn't want Freddie to guess how badly he wanted to rush to the window, get a look for himself. He tried to appear nonchalant as he strolled out of the library. "I'll call it a day," he said to Freddie, and went quickly upstairs.

But long into the night he stared at the ceiling through the darkness. Even the shadows in the room seemed to play some taunting dance of their own, with every turn and flicker reminding him of that indelible image he had fixed in his mind now of the girl in the blue silk dress with the mischievous eyes.

Adam was not alone with his restlessness. Sarah herself was having her own troubles falling asleep in the cottage where she had been assigned, along with two bridesmaids and the old-maid chaperone, Alice Greer.

The wedding had been more like a nightmare to her. First, they had had to survive her own mother's last-minute hysterics as she had tried to make each detail meet the snobbish demands of Lydia Cugnot, Monique's mother. "You should have taken charge of your own daughter's wedding!" Miss Grace had screamed out at her. "I offered to let you use my *home*—but I didn't expect to have to run the whole affair."

After that outburst had ebbed, Lydia Cugnot had begun her fussy inspection of the bridesmaids' hats, the satin streamers on the bouquets, the way Monique's hair looked under the veil.

Then had come that awful moment when suddenly Monique had lifted her arms straight up in the air, as though caught in some painful seizure, and, just when the organ music started with the wedding march, screamed in a bloodcurdling shriek, "Sarah, don't let them make me! He's not right—he's somebody I barely know, and so *ugly*—so . . . He's . . . *Please*, Sarah!"

But the matter had been taken out of her hands. Lydia Cugnot, along with Sarah's mother, had swooped in with smelling salts and with fans fluttering. Lydia Cugnot's voice had snapped out like sharp scissors cutting a ribbon, "Pull yourself together! The wedding march is *playing*." And then in what she intended to be a whisper for Monique's ears alone she added, "Monique, dear you're saving the family! Just remember that. Do it for *me*—for all of us."

Sarah had followed along numbly. At one point, just before that part of the ceremony where the ring was to be slipped on, she had had the overwhelming urge to snatch Monique's arm and pull her down the aisle in their living room, where the wedding was taking place. She wanted to run with her out to their hideout going back to their childhood—out to the stone bridge, where a bounding creek spilled down from Spring Mountain, and where beneath the bridge they used to spend hours spinning out fantasies about the Prince Charmings they would meet; where they had shared girlhood secrets, consoled each other over little sorrows. But she had stood there, immobile. She had stared straight ahead, trying not to see Monique's trembling bouquet or the tears that were sliding down her cheeks and dropping into the tiny rosebuds.

Nor had there been a chance to talk with Monique after the ceremony. The entire wedding party had left right away for Soda Springs. And once there, as maid of honor, she had felt certain obligations. She had gone about checking place cards for the banquet. Trying to tell the musicians what tunes Monique might want played at the dance. Then Jacques Cugnot had started passing out champagne as though there were bottomless barrels of it. "This is a day for a real celebration!" From time to time, Monique seemed to swim, float past on the dance floor, her eyes glazed, as though she had been drinking champagne for days without stopping. Once she had smiled wanly at Sarah, her face ashen. As she danced with her groom, the waddling, silly-grinned Gunther, she seemed to hang limp, dead on his arm.

Maybe, Sarah thought, she had been back East too long. The years at Wellesley College—of going to the Boston Symphony, to parties, to the theater—all had made Napa Valley seem closed in on itself, as though the very ridges of mountains on both sides were slowly strangling the life out of it, moving in closer and closer, imperceptibly.

She missed the sophistication of her school chums, Helene and Ernestine. She even missed their funny old house mother and chaperone, Miss Beatrice—their "away-from-home nanny," she used to call herself when girls first arrived.

Surprisingly, she even missed Christopher Elliot-Weare, even though before she said goodbye to him in Boston she had been literally counting the days to get back home to her beloved Napa Valley, away from his incessant urging to get her to say she would marry him. "Promise, Sarah—just say you will agree to marry me after we graduate. After I finish law school at Harvard and you're graduated from Wellesley. Even if you insist on waiting a year after that, honestly, I won't object. I'll be patient. Just give me your word you will marry me."

And why had she refused? She puffed her pillow, tried to settle in more comfortably on the too-hard bed with its heavy quilts. Certainly Chris had the right credentials. Even her mother would approve of him, with his lineage going back to the blueblood Pilgrims and the Weares of Virginia. She was so tired of *lineage*, of being called Sarah *Hubbard* this, Sarah *Hubbard* that! At school, she had refused to give her middle name to anyone. In Napa Valley, she couldn't escape it.

The bridesmaids, Betty and Margaret, and Alice Greer were sound asleep. Sarah listened for a moment to their varying breathing patterns. She thought back on this day, on how silly some of the conversations had seemed to her. At school, at least the conversations with her school chums—yes, with Chris too—had been interesting. Here, all they were able to talk about was the imported silk dresses from *Paris* or "Isn't this the biggest social wedding you *ever* saw!"

Her eyes were wide open now, staring at the ceiling. She shouldn't deny anyone his excitement in life. But it was just that back East she had opened her eyes to so much more—to music, art; she had developed an absolute passion about Greek history. Her vision encompassed so much more of the world than Napa Valley. One of these days she was going to travel and see that world—not only Greece but Rome, Paris . . .

At the foot of her bed, she let exhausted eyes focus on age-worn cracks that lined a dark-green window shade. Light shining through from an outside gas latern formed a kind of world map that she began to trace with her mind's traveling eye, drawing imaginary boundaries of places she wanted to visit the most.

Christopher Elliot-Weare had told her, "When I graduate from Harvard Law School and you finish at Wellesley, we'll get married and sail immediately on our honeymoon to Europe. I'll have a trust fund coming due by then. We can go anywhere."

Why couldn't she fall in love with him? With a man who was rich, from the right background, and handsome too, in a certain slight, blondish way. He was gentle, kind—yes, but *weak*. The man she had always dreamed of would be very strong—and, though at Wellesley they would tell her she was even dreaming in clichés, he would be tall and dark and handsome!

Where did the shapes of dreams begin? From what fragments of a fairy tale, a story, a glimpse of some adult shaded into the size and shape and substance of an ideal?

She rolled to one side, kicked a long, slender foot at the heavy quilt. It made no difference where the dream began, she told herself; she had seen him in the flesh and blood today. At first when the girls had dared her to run down the pathway, she had done it on a crazy impulse. But when she had actually got even with him, had looked up at those startlingly clear blue eyes, into the face of the most handsome man she had ever seen, something had happened inside the very quick of her being.

But who was he? What was he doing at Soda Springs in off season with a crotchety-acting old man?—a big banker, someone had said.

41

She let her thoughts go back over it, excitement running through her. She tried to recapture that first sight of him stepping off the stage-coach, standing there looking out across the valley as if he were search-ing for something. She fought to keep his image exact, but she was get-ting sleepy. Another face was bearing down, wiping out that of the man she had met. She was seeing the stricken, ashen-white look on Monique's face just as the wedding ring had been slipped on her finger by Gunther.

"I will never marry a man I don't love!" Sarah told herself furiously. "I will never allow myself, for whatever family reasons, to be pushed down an aisle into a marriage not of my own choosing."

The last thing she remembered before falling off to sleep was seeing a wobbly line on the dark-green window shade that she decided would be about where the Nile River should run on her world map.

Samuel Linton was out by the porte cochere making last-minute arrangements with the driver assigned to them for the day when Adam, who was sidetracked by the talkative bellboy, Freddie, caught a sudden, unexpected sight of Sarah Hubbard Reynolds.

She was taller than he had remembered. Today, instead of blue silk, she was wearing a rust-colored velvet suit, with pale beige ruffles from her blouse falling gracefully over her long slender hands which seemed to move in a dance of their own as she spoke. Her hair—which he remembered as being piled up on her head—was brushed back off her face, tied with a velvet ribbon to match the suit, and as she half whirled around, as though sensing his stare, he saw how it spilled in long, luxurious waves down her back. To his astonishment, she headed straight toward him, her entire face radiantly alive, her smile aimed unmistakably at him.

"I know I shouldn't *do* this," she said in a quick, lilting voice. "It isn't at all proper. But who could possibly introduce us?" She looked about, laughed facetiously. Her eyes were like fine amber beads caught in sunlight when she looked back at him. "I had hoped you were a guest at Monique's wedding when I saw you get off the stagecoach . . ."

He heard the question in her voice, but he had never felt so tongue-tied. He found himself stumbling for words in English, his mind racing in Italian. "I . . . no. I am here on business." His voice had sounded as curt, as precise, he thought, as Dudley Farnsworth's. "I wish I had been a guest." He tried to let his eyes tell her more than his jum-bled thoughts could get out.

Suddenly she stepped back some distance from him, as though

aware that she was being watched by others in the lobby. She kept her eyes fixed on his face, however. "I'm being forward—but I don't know your name, I'm afraid. And I would like to know it."

"Adam—Adam Donati," he said, his throat tightening. Out of the corner of one eye he saw the woman he guessed to be her mother, Miss Grace, bearing down on them. "Thank you for being . . . for asking. You've made me very happy," he said in a soft voice. "Last night—I couldn't sleep, afraid I wouldn't see you again."

He saw the color rise in her cheeks. But there was no more time. She turned as quickly and deftly as she had when she crossed the room to greet him. Her voice was now aimed at Freddie, in a tone obviously for her mother's sake. "Freddie! I haven't seen you since grade-school days. You're looking marvelous. Oh, hello, Mother—you remember Freddie, don't you? Freddie Collins?"

Adam caught the open-faced, curiously suspicious look Sarah's mother shot his way. He pretended not to see, to be studying the heavy wooden beams in the ceiling, the line of the brass chandelier. Then, trying to look as much at ease as possible, he headed toward the side entrance, toward where Samuel Linton was already climbing into the surrey, and where a driver named Kyle Plimpton was holding back the reins on an impatient chestnut mare. Adam felt the pounding in his chest, the surge of excitement almost like pain. He had had girls— buxom, soft peasant girls. But this was different. Sarah Hubbard Reynolds—she was very, very different.

As they pulled away from the hotel and started down the long, curving gravel driveway toward Silverado Trail, where they would turn right and head up valley, Adam did not allow himself to look back —for that matter, to look right or left. He had seen her! She had sought him out—had felt, surely, the same as he did! . . .

Kyle Plimpton let the mare find its own steady even trot down Silverado Trail; then at the Yountville crossroad he reined her sharply left, headed toward midvalley.

Kyle was a rakishly thin six-foot-or-so man who slouched over the reins, a battered cowboy hat shoved back on his head. Adam had guessed him to be in his thirties. There was something about him that made Adam think he had not always been a driver for Soda Springs Hotel. And then he noticed for the first time the badly crippled, scarred right hand curled in protectively, as if he were trying to keep it hidden from scrutiny under his left hand controlling the reins.

As they approached Yountville, Kyle nodded his head toward a

43

huge brick winery and depot ahead. "That building belongs to old Gottlieb Groezinger. He's been hit pretty hard by the phylloxera. Used to have some good Cabernets. You can see where he's yanking 'em out in places. Sticking in those puny orchards. Look over thataway at that big wagon loaded down with puncheons. Most likely somebody trying to sell off some stored-up brandy to try and keep the sheriff's lock off a little longer. The tax collectors stalled off as long as they can hold out. This valley's been hit awful hard lately."

Adam was studying what looked to him to be some healthy vines. "What about that vineyard?" he asked, leaning forward.

Kyle glanced over his shoulder. "Groezinger figures, I guess, when they come out of dormancy they still might be okay. Telling himself the beetle's skipped over him and headed on north. People always think it's going to work on somebody else's vines—not theirs."

"You seem to know something about vineyards," Adam ventured, leaning forward so he could talk more easily. He rested his hands on his knees to keep in motion with the swaying, rhythmic roll of the surrey as it made steady progress now past the Magnolia Hotel, onto the main county road heading straight up the middle of the narrow valley toward Rutherford.

Kyle pulled out his crippled hand, thrust it up in the air. "See this? Before the accident, I was Gilbert Reynolds' foreman. I guess I know a few things about grapes. But then I oughtta—I was taught by Professor Hussman with the U.S. Agriculture Department. One of the best anywhere. Hussman and his partner, Professor Hilgard."

"What happened to your hand?" Adam asked, shocked by the ugly sight.

Kyle dropped the mangled hand back in his lap, tucked it securely under the other one holding the reins. "Aw, hell—funny thing, life. A man gets to thinking he knows it all about one particular something or other. Then one day he comes up with a whopper—a big case of the ignorants. I was over one day helping out Mr. Reynolds' neighbor— that Frenchman, Cugnot, who treats anybody works for him like dirt under his feet. He was spouting off 'bout how I didn't know a hill of beans, more or less. I guess I was trying to prove myself." He pushed the cowboy hat back even farther, gave a flick of the whip to the mare's flanks. "What it amounted to was he had just got in this fancy new equipment from France. A new crusher. Well, we didn't have enough Chinamen around that year to do everything. Everybody and his youngins had pitched in to help get the crush done and over with. It was one of them vintages where every grape in the valley seemed to be running a contest to see which one could get ripe first. Damndest sight—Rieslings coming in about the same time as the Cabernets. Something you couldn't count on." He made a noise out of the side of his mouth, urging the mare into a little faster clip. "What it boils down to is I looked right when I should've looked left. Got my hand caught in that damn contraption . . ."

Adam saw that Kyle's neck muscles looked taut now, as if the memory itself brought back some of the pain. "I'm sorry to hear that," he said, consolingly.

"Aw, don't matter all that much, I reckon. What's done is done. I guess I was lucky somebody around had the gumption to get me pulled loose before it chopped off my whole hand. At least saved me a stump of a hand—something I can work partway with. I can handle feisty Betsy here. If it's a tame enough four-hitch, I can get along."

Adam turned to Mr. Linton, who was rubbing his stomach and pulling his city bowler down to shade his face from the bright morning sun. "It was that overspiced sausage for breakfast," Mr. Linton said grumpily. "One too many biscuits, maybe. I keep forgetting my stomach's not what it used to be." He sat up, leaned toward Kyle's back. "Any chance we could stop by Jacob Brunner's place? Thought I'd introduce him to my friend here—maybe borrow a pinch of soda bicarbonate."

"Sure—it's your time. Your money paying for the day," Kyle said amiably. "I'm willing to take you anywhere in Napa Valley you want to go. Guess I know every goat path, every wagon road."

"Were you born here?" Adam asked, looking about at the way the valley seemed to be getting narrower as they made their way north.

"Naw, I was born in Hickman, Kentucky—town on the Mississippi. My daddy worked on a big barge. One day, he just loaded up the whole family, put us on a boat and went up the river as far as he wanted to go. Then we joined up with a party heading out west. Took us three years before we ever found where he wanted to settle down. He started working on the wharf down in Napa City. Ended up owning his own barge, shipping out wine, lumber. Dropped dead back aways. Ten years ago, about. But you could say I grew up here in Napa Valley. I consider my roots here, even if my daddy always called us Southerners. Claimed Hickman, Kentucky, was the greatest place on earth, it and that Tennessee town a few miles across the border—Union City, it was. To the day he died, he was complaining he'd left his home place. Where *you* from? That accent . . . I was trying to put my finger on it. Not like any I ever heard before."

45

"Italy—northern Italy," Adam said, smiling at a huge hawk soaring by.

Kyle shoved his hat to a new angle on one side of his head, gave the mare another light snap across its flanks. "I'd never guessed that in a hunert years! You sure don't sound like the rest of the Italians—we call 'em Dagos around these parts. You not only don't sound like 'em, you look different. You *sure* about that?"

Mr. Linton didn't give Adam a chance to answer. "He's coming here to build a big winery, Kyle. He'll be as much a Napa Valley native as you in a few years. Brunner's place—are we pretty close by now?" he asked irritably, thinking to himself that old age ought to be satisfied: hitting him below the belt in one way was bad enough; it didn't have to spell it out in his stomach too.

"We'll be there in a few minutes. Just past the Reynolds place up yonder a way." Kyle spoke to Adam now. "If you want to get a good look at some of the finest vineyards ever planted in Napa Valley, then you ought to see Jacob Brunner's mountain vines. Up on Spring Mountain. He's got some Rieslings, French Colombards and Cabernets that walk off with the State Fair prizes about every year. He knows what it means—keeping 'em pruned back. You really figuring on settling in, building a winery?"

"Yes. We're scouting for land today. Maybe you have some good suggestions. Where the best hillside acreage might be—since you know vines and know so much about Napa Valley." Adam had seen the scowl cross Samuel Linton's face. But Kyle Plimpton was already answering him.

"See straight ahead—Mount St. Helena? The flat-topped beauty you see? The one looks like she got her Easter bonnet blown to hell and back? Well, that's what gives you your clues. You got to find where all that volcanic ash spewed out, like fingers. Like Professor Hussman told me, some places in Napa Valley will grow the greatest vineyards in the world, bar none. Then there's spots where you might as well turn a bunch of billy goats loose. What you want is just enough butte loam, rock, ash. Grapevine roots dig down sometimes up to fifteen feet deep. They've got to have dry feet, as they say. Good drainage. You don't want too rich a soil. Have to keep that vine struggling. Give your grapes more character. But, hell, maybe you know all that. Since you *ask* me, though—"

"These Brunner vineyards you mentioned—where are they?"

"Up on Spring Mountain—see, to the left there of St. Helena. Past Diamond Mountain—next one. Can't tell much from down here. But there's a good county road goes over the mountain into Santa Rosa. Sonoma County, that's where you'll find Señor Parrott's Miravalle, Château Chevalier, a whole bunch of smart people who know their stuff about winemaking."

Samuel Linton reached across and slapped Adam's left knee. "Don't get so many bees in your pants. Wait till you see what I've got available. It just so happens, Cugnot's hillside vines are somewhere up there, though—some damn place on Spring Mountain."

Kyle Plimpton's face was full of curiosity. But at that moment they were driving past the Reynolds' mansion. Adam felt his heart leap when Mr. Linton blurted out, "That girl—Sarah Hubbard Reynolds? That's where she lives."

Set far back off the road, at the end of a long driveway lined with oak trees, Adam saw the giant pillars of the enormous house, the upstairs gallery wrapping around all sides, it appeared.

Adam wanted to ask a dozen questions, but Samuel Linton was having no more conversation until he got his soda bicarbonate. He was leaning back against the seat, his eyes closed, his hands folded across his burning, aching belly. He was out of sorts with the whole morning. He never did like gabby drivers. And he had grown too used to San Francisco's cool days. This sun was hotter than he liked, even if it was only the last day of February. It might have seemed a good idea when he was having a fine salmon lunch at the Palace and *talking* about Napa Valley, over good food he could digest, but *being* here—surely he must be getting balmy in his old age!

Kyle was pointing his crippled hand toward the Reynolds' place. "That's where I used to work. Back then, though, old Gilbert was still more or less in control. Least, we *called* him the boss. First one thing, then another, and Miss Grace was cracking the whip. I took off for good then—even if I might've figured out a way to work with one arm. One thing I can't stand is a woman trying to act tough as leather. My daddy told me Miss Grace just *talked* like she was mushy-mouthed —she's got a brain sharp as a tack. If there's anybody in this valley's gonna figure out how to get back on their feet after the beetle wiped out their vines, *she*'ll come up with something." He bent over the reins closer, tugged his straw hat toward his forehead. "Everybody around here's hard hit these days. Future don't look so hot for grape growers, the wine business. Guess I'm lucky myself to have a job at Soda Springs. Don't pay so hot, but it's a roof over my head. Food sits with me, I guess, better'n it does Mr. Linton back there."

They were even now with two driveways running parallel. Samuel

Linton sat up, adjusted his hat, his necktie. "Let's hope Brunner's home," he said, frowning. He gave Adam's arm a nudge as Kyle reined the mare and started down the gravel driveway lined with olive trees, a carefully dug drainage ditch running alongside it. "That fancy paved drive to your right—that's Cugnot's. His valley-floor property runs alongside Jacob's place—the same up on Spring Mountain. Back to back. I tried to catch hold of him at the hotel this morning, but he must've seen me and ducked out. Running for cover. It's *one* thing—a man gets his ass in a sling and comes out in the open, tries to work out of the mess he's in. I hate a coward, a man who won't face his debts, won't come right out and ask for help if he needs it."

Kyle stopped the surrey in front of the plain two-story farmhouse. Around near the barn, a dog barked loudly. "If old Jacob ain't around, his granddaughter's apt to be," Kyle said, lowering his voice. "She's shy as a church mouse. Mostly stays home. But, Lord, can that girl cook!"

The front door opened, and a small, bent man with a shock of white hair and a neatly trimmed goatee stepped out, stopped with his feet planted apart on the edge of the stoop.

Mr. Linton made a grunting sound, allowed Kyle to assist him out of the surrey. "Good morning, Jacob," he said, yanking at his coattails, taking a few steps toward the entrance. "Remember me—Samuel Linton?"

"I paid you," Jacob said, staring hard at them. "I don't owe you nothing and I don't need nothing."

Mr. Linton stretched out his right hand. "Relax, Jacob. I'm not here about money. I dropped by to have you meet a nice young man here from northern Italy—Adam Donati. He's got some of the same crazy ideas about grape growing that you do. And since you'll be neighbors . . ."

Jacob extended his hand and nodded a silent greeting to Adam. His voice was crisp, bore still the strains of a European accent as he called out to Kyle, "Take your horse back to the barn. Wang Chi's out there. He'll take charge. Erika saw you coming—she's fixing up something in the kitchen for you." He nodded his head up and down, clasped the railing. "My granddaughter likes Kyle Plimpton. Finds him easy to talk to." He grinned, showing yellowed teeth worn down like stubby pieces of corn. "She likes to see him eat her cooking."

He motioned for them to come inside. "How do you figure we're going to be neighbors?" he asked Samuel Linton as he waved them into a sparsely furnished parlor. "Being's I got Jacques Cugnot on one side and the Reynoldses on the other. Nobody said anything to me about either one of them pulling up stakes."

They took seats in the rugless room with its heavy-armed oak chairs covered with horsehair, its spindly table in the middle of the room on which were an ornate lamp with fringe dangling from an eggshell-colored shade, two small portraits, and a vase of freshly cut jonquils mixed with almond-tree blossoms.

Adam waited for Mr. Linton to answer the question for him. "He's after mountain acreage. Up on Spring Mountain—maybe Cugnot's vineyards."

Jacob Brunner pulled at his goatee, narrowed his eyes. Adam guessed him to be in his eighties, older than Mr. Linton. Yet there was an alertness, a strength and a sense of vitality that old men of the land often keep until the very last. "I told Jacques more'n fifteen years ago if he ever decided to sell off any mountain land I wanted to be the first to hear about it."

"It's not a matter of his *deciding* to sell," Mr. Linton said, rubbing his stomach. "I gave him every chance to pay off his mortgage, even make some stab at paying *on* it. He throws big fancy wedding receptions at Soda Springs, sends his girl off to expensive schools on the East Coast—hell, he can't pay me! So I'm foreclosing."

"That land ought to go to the right people."

"That's why I'm arranging it so my young friend here can take over. This is strictly a business arrangement, Jacob. It isn't a matter of going around making a choice as to the right man or the wrong man. But if anybody ought to treat the land right, it would be a Donati from northern Italy, don't you think?"

Jacob's eyes opened, narrowed again. "I guess I didn't make the association when I first heard it," he said, his voice brightening. "Donati —the wine family?"

"Yes," Adam said eagerly. "Yes, sir. Do you know it?"

"I came from Yverdon—Switzerland. Close to that area. Anybody in the business in those parts knows the name." He gave Adam an approving eye, his face wide with pleasure now. "Cugnot let the leaf hoppers get to his Rieslings," he said to Adam. "Every vineyard he's got needs some work. He never was one for that, so much. Paid others to do it. 'Least, it's land that's cleared off. Up on Spring Mountain, you'll find that's a blessing." He stood up, reached out to shake hands properly this time. "Welcome to Napa Valley. We can use a young Donati up here right now. The whole valley's gone crazy—everybody yanking out their vines and putting in those *prune* trees." He shook his head. "Not me. Diversifying—you hear that being passed around a lot these days. I don't mind diversifying. I always have had my land broken down to where it's not lopsided. Anybody with any sense at all about grape growing—or winemaking, which I don't fool with myself —knows there's going to be good vintages and bad. You can't count on any year being one you'll break even on. So I've got some orchards. A few olive groves. My cattle. I sell produce to the local stores. My vegetable gardens can stand up to anybody's, thanks to my Erika. But I won't disgrace myself planting *prune* trees, I don't care what money they bring in!"

"Jacob, I ate some sausage at Soda Springs that's raising the dickens with my stomach. Could you ask your granddaughter if she can spare some soda bicarbonate for me? A tablespoon in a glass of water ought to do."

"Sure. She's fixing up a tray of some cookies, I believe. We don't have much company around here." Jacob shuffled out of the room.

When he came back, Adam looked up to see the frail, wide-eyed Erika in the door, carrying a tray, her eyes reminding him somehow of a trapped, frightened animal who any moment might try to bolt for freedom. He found himself smiling at her, trying to reassure her and make her more at ease. She wasn't beautiful, but there was a fragile, pretty look about her, like a fine delicate piece of china one must handle gently. She was wearing a white linen blouse embroidered with brightly colored Swiss designs. Her floor-length skirt was full, made out of a calico print that moved softly as her tiny feet hurried to the center of the room, where she placed the tray on an empty space on the table.

When she came across the room to him and handed him a plate filled with delicate pastries that could have come from any European bakery, a jump of nostalgia hit him. He saw how her straight blond hair was braided back into a knot at the nape of her neck—a neck long and slender.

"I have a pot of tea ready—or would you prefer coffee?" she asked in a thin, tentative voice. She looked flushed now, though he had noticed how fair her skin was when she had entered.

He looked at her, smiled. "Tea. I haven't had a good cup of tea since I arrived in Amerca. In Pontremoli, where I came from, I had an English tutor who insisted that we have tea every afternoon. I miss it."

She smiled back at him shyly, finished serving the others, and sat down, a teacup balanced lightly on the folds of her skirt where she held her knees tightly together.

"Where's Kyle?" her grandfather asked her, dropping a lump of sugar into his tea. "He's usually eating everything in sight."

She smiled faintly. "He ate two pieces of chocolate cake. In the kitchen. He said his mare had a loose shoe he wanted to check. He wanted to talk with Wang Chi, I believe."

Jacob turned to Adam. "If you do take over the Cugnot mountain vineyards one of these days, will you do your own work?"

"A considerable amount of it. I'll have some building to oversee. A house, winery. I plan to rebuild in duplicate the Donati estate in Pontremoli. Did you ever see it?"

"No—afraid not. We didn't have money for travel back then. I stayed pretty close to home. It got so bad we finally migrated to America. I've been here since 1856. My wife—her name was Erika too. We came here to the Napa Valley right after we first married. Had one daughter. Erika's mother—Johanna. A son too, but he died when he was seven years old. Maybe Mr. Linton told you what happened to my Johanna." His eyes moistened. "Erika here—she's my last relative. I'm trying to teach her what she ought to know about running the place. Just in case—a man never knows, I figure. I like to keep my affairs in order."

Samuel Linton was looking at Jacob Brunner curiously. He had never known him to talk this much. Maybe it was his advancing years. He was getting scared. Afraid all his hard work wouldn't mean anything to anybody. Well, he could share a little of those feelings—but he hadn't reached the stage of being afraid of dying, and doubted that he ever would. He didn't have any regrets. That was part of his belief about life—that, by God, if he made up his mind to do something, even if it turned out to be a bad mistake, he wasn't going to waste time crying about it, stewing in his own juice. He'd go on to the next thing. He'd die fighting out some new problem, most likely. But these men of the *land*, as they seemed to call themselves, they had something else they believed in. Something they seemed to think had to be handed on down to the next generation. It gave them too much a one-track mind to suit him. All that lifelong dedication to the roll of the seasons. Struggling to get from one vintage to the next.

"Is the soda helping?" Jacob Brunner asked, watching him with his own look of curiosity. "Try some of Erika's tea. It's good for upset stomachs."

They got up to leave after a few minutes. Jacob seemed reluctant to have them go. Erika smiled, looked uncertain, then began gathering up dishes, piling the tray full again.

Adam went over to her. "Thank you. You're an excellent cook."

When they were back in the surrey and Kyle was lifting the reins to start the mare up again, Jacob came up alongside them, looked up and smiled at Adam. "I hope you do settle in up there." He lifted his hand to Mr. Linton, to Kyle. "Too bad you can't find yourself a vine-yardist like Kyle here. I say too bad 'cause you won't find anybody knows what he knows. Young people today, most of them have their minds on other things. Finding work in big cities. Even the Chinamen are beginning to drift out of Napa Valley. I've got a good crew. Same crew I've had for twenty-odd years, about. I don't usually loan 'em out. Too many people don't treat them right. Think they're next to slaves. But if you find next harvest you need some pickers, let me know."

"We'll surely see each other again before next harvest," Adam called down politely. He liked this old man exceedingly. He reached down and grasped his age-cracked, leathery-looking hands and shook both of them.

The pale-blue eyes of the old man looked watery again, as if some longtime friend had surprised him with a visit. "Young man, you're going to find Napa Valley's a lot like the country where we came from. Some of the same problems too, mostly likely. But it's good—I'm happy to welcome a Donati."

The ride up Spring Mountain was a long tedious one. The narrow county dirt road wound its way around the sharp curves as if its route had been made for it by some giant snake in a hurry to get across the mountain into Sonoma Valley to the west.

Adam listened attentively on the way up when Kyle Plimpton would point out landmarks and make some comment about them. At the beginning of the upgrade, there had been the enormous estate on the left belonging to a Señor Tiburcio Parrott. "He's a dandy," Kyle told him, a sneer in his voice. "You'll know him if you run into him down on Main Street in St. Helena—wearing his city clothes and tipping his hat at all the ladies. But, hell, any man could do that if all he had to do was sit back and hold his palm out for a thousand dollars a month doled out by a rich family! Funny thing to me how Lady Luck seems to shine pearly teeth in a big grin at some and kick her heels smack in the face of others. Me, I'd be lucky to catch sight of her coat-tails."

Farther up the mountainside, he pointed out a stone bridge. "That paved driveway will take you back into Château Chevalier. That winery was built like a stone castle—but beats me why they stuck it down in a big gulley when all they'd had to do was move it up the knoll a ways and they'ud had a top-of-the-world view." He gave the mare a flick with the tip end of the whip. "Maybe 'cause I don't have much loose change to spare, but seems to me rich people sure can squander away money sometimes."

"Won't be the last good money thrown away up here on Spring Mountain, the way things look now," Mr. Linton said in a dry voice, then folded his hands over his stomach that was easing up now, closed his eyes, and pretended to nap.

At that point, though, Kyle reined the mare a sharp left, onto a rain-rutted dirt road, through an open gate falling half off its hinges. "Good thing you didn't want to try this a month ago. We had a lot of rain this winter. Seemed like the sky dumped out all its reservoirs on us in one big caper." He leaned forward, yelled out to the mare, "Come on, Betts—pull hard!" Then he called grumpily over one shoulder to Adam, "Cugnot don't take care of this land up here. Lets it go to the dogs. Not like Jacob Brunner, who keeps everything up to snuff."

Adam saw they were nearly to the top of the crest. "How long does your rainy season last, generally?"

"A rule of thumb, oh, November through February. But you can't keep Mother Nature pinned down on a calendar. You stake out a general rule of thumb, after that you stand back and hope Lady Luck is on your side." Kyle stopped the surrey. "This ought to be as good a spot as any for you to take a look at what's out there."

Adam jumped down, took long strides to the edge of the clearing. There he stopped, took a sudden sharp breath. In every direction the views were to him awesomely beautiful. To the south, he could see a fifty-mile distance—fingers of the San Francisco Bay, the mountain he had been told was Mount Tamalpais. To the east, he gazed across the narrowed-down stretch of valley at the ragged outline of Howell Mountain and a ridge Kyle told him was called Glass Mountain. Below, stretched out like a rumpled patchwork quilt, were brilliant greens pocked with glowing yellows from the mustard covering the valley floor.

Kyle was smiling at him. "Glad you like it." He pointed southeast. "Over thataway, those outcroppings of jagged rocks—we call that Chimney Rock. Behind that is Soda Springs, but you can't see it from here. When you get to know the landmarks better, you'll pick out the Stags' Leap turnoff."

Mr. Linton was busy taking out his briefcase and searching for a plot map. Adam strolled back across the clearing, jumped up and balanced himself on wobbly rocks atop a stone fence that Kyle told him was the boundary line between Jacob Brunner's land and Jacques Cugnot's. "Won't be hard for you to know which is which. Where the vineyards are tended, those are old Jacob's."

Samuel Linton's voice seemed to crack, split the air. "Well, does it suit your taste? Will this do?"

Adam wanted to sail off the rock wall—throw his arms out with happiness. Hug the old man. Slap Kyle Plimpton on the back. "How soon will it be mine? My own?" He had kept his voice relatively calm. "How much will be mine? How much is cleared?"

"Hold your horses," Mr. Linton snorted, peering at the plot map. "From what I can figure from this damn thing, I'd say some sixty acres already cleared off. Kyle, would you say those cleared acres are planted with vines?"

Kyle raked his left hand through his hair, pulled the cowboy hat back on. "A good chunk of it, I'd say. Some vines ought to be taken out. Some new root stock put in and grafted onto—like Hussman's got everybody doing around here these days."

Mr. Linton rolled the map up, tucked it back in the briefcase, headed toward the surrey. "It's roughly one hundred twenty acres. Some you won't get cleared in a hundred years from now. Some you might. A lot of timber up here."

"There's a hell of a fine spring over there," Kyle said, pointing beyond the clearing. "Wouldn't take much to cut a road back toward it. If it was me, I'd want to build my house close to water. That's about as good spring water as you'll find anyplace." He let the mare get one last nibble at the clump of bright-green grass, then took the reins, got back into the surrey. Adam was reluctant to leave.

"Come on," Mr. Linton said irritably. "There's a lot of legal work to get finished before this land will be yours by law. I've got to tackle a tiger by the tail tomorrow when I call on Jacques Cugnot and give him the word." He placed the briefcase in a secure place on the floor of the surrey.

Adam took his seat beside him, still looking all about. A deep sigh escaped him.

"It's going to be yours—don't worry," Mr. Linton said, holding on as the mare spurted forward, going back down the steep wagon road.

Kyle seemed gloomy.

"I've got a lot of work to do, haven't I?" Adam asked, leaning toward him.

"Looks to me like Lady Luck is on your side. I wouldn't worry about the work ahead—not with that kind of roll of the dice in your favor. No reason why the Cugnot vineyards couldn't match or maybe even top Brunner's. The right attention."

A thought had hit Adam. "Kyle, why don't you come work for me—be my foreman? Take charge of the replantings."

For a moment, Adam thought Kyle had not heard him. He tried again. "I've got to hire someone who knows Napa Valley. Knows vineyards. The soil. Someone on whom I can depend." The wagon bumped over a deep rut. "How about it?"

Adam was leaning forward, trying to see Kyle's face. He saw a muscle on the side of his neck twitch. Saw Kyle's good hand clench the reins.

"What would anybody want to hire a cripple like me for? You can't be that much a greenhorn. You ain't even looked around yet to see who's around for hiring."

Samuel Linton was looking out of one eye at Adam, studying him closely. His mouth rolled the cigar he was ready to light to one side, as if ready to add something to the conversation, but thought better of it. He struck a match on the sole of his shoe, puffed vigorously.

Adam was smiling. "It's the way you said, Kyle—Lady Luck is on my side today. Brought me the best there is without my having to waste time looking. If Jacob Brunner says you're the best, then I'm willing to take his word."

Kyle jerked his right arm out and held up his mangled hand. "Take a look! A man working with vines needs both hands. A man works with both." He yanked the reins, guided the mare out onto the county road and headed back down the sharp curve.

"I plan to hire other workers. You could be the boss—teach them what they need to know. If you can handle a horse as well as you do, you can do plenty of other things. I mean it. I want to hire you, Kyle. I can't pay a big salary at first, but I should be able to do better perhaps than what you may be earning now at Soda Springs."

Kyle shook his head. His voice sounded strained. "Wouldn't have to stretch your purse strings much for that."

They were silent for a moment. Kyle seemed to be concentrating hard on his driving, on braking the surrey as they took on speed going down the sharp incline. Samuel Linton thumped one finger against his cigar, as if biding some time of his own. He looked up through smoke at the trees draped over the narrow road, raking limbs together. Birds overheard chirped noisily, fluttered from treetop to treetop. In a ravine to the right, the sound of rushing water tumbling over rocks made its own song. Off to the left, crows were sending out their commanding *caw caw*.

"You *mean* that?" Kyle blurted out. "You mean to tell me you'd hire a cripple like me? Trust me to take charge? Be your foreman?"

"Why not?" Adam responded, his voice filled with a new excitement. Kyle would be a perfect worker. And he had found him the very morning he found his land!

Kyle cleared his throat. "Well, you might as well know what some people around this valley think of me. It ain't all like what Jacob Brunner told you."

Samuel Linton spit out a speck of tabacco from his tongue, gave Adam a knowing look. But Adam was listening only to Kyle.

"Since it happened—the accident . . ." Kyle pulled back on the reins as the mare bolted at the sight of two deer standing near the edge of the road. In a split second the deer leaped across in front of them and scrambled up a steep bank for safety. "I guess I've been known to go off on a bender or two. Big whopping drunks, is what they are. It's —I get this sinkhole of a feeling inside me sometimes. So I get drunk— dog drunk." He looked back over his shoulder at Adam, then turned back to his driving. "I wanted you to hear it from me first."

Adam thought a moment. His voice rang out confidently. "I'll keep you too busy for that," he said, matter-of-factly. "If you get those vineyards in the shape we'll both want to see them in, you'll have work enough to keep your mind out of any trouble."

Kyle was shaking his head back and forth. "I'll be damned if I ever thought anything like this was going to happen to me today—happen *any* time!"

Mr. Linton licked his teeth with his tongue, flicked out ashes from the cigar, sat slightly forward. "Come on, Kyle, tell him yes. What do you have to lose? I want you to get it said so you can get your mind back on your driving. I'd like to get this buggy back to Soda Springs before dark!"

Kyle let out a startling whoop, lifted his hat, slammed it back on. "Lord, Lord! Me a foreman again. If it don't beat all. When do you want me to start? I've got to give notice at Soda Springs. It might not be the best job in the world, but they've been good to me. Let me come back after I've left 'em high and dry a few days in a row. But I give you my word. If I take this job—and I'm saying yes right now—I won't go on no more benders! It's a promise. I give you my word on my daddy's grave. On his honor."

They were nearing the foot of the mountain. Adam took another glance at the Parrott mansion, at the manicured gardens, the groves of orange trees, the greenhouse, the iron gates he could see from the road. "I need a few days to find a boardinghouse somewhere in St. Helena, I suppose. Look around for some good buys on cooperage. Some equipment I'll need. As soon as you're ready, I'll be ready."

"Then it's settled," Mr. Linton said for both of them. "I'm your witness. Adam, I suggest, as your banker, that you start Kyle off at three dollars a day. After you get some return on your investment, then you can raise him. Maybe put him on percentage of whatever you sell your grapes for. You can work out the details. But you need a base for a start. Does that suit you, Kyle?"

"It sure beats what I'm making now. 'Course, I do get free room and board at Soda Springs. But I guess I can stay with my cousin Henry Plimpton and Coleen. They'll put me up for not much money. A few extra dollars ought to help them out right now, too."

"As soon as we get some buildings put up, I'll give you a nice place to stay up on Spring Mountain," Adam said.

"Well, you'd better take things in their proper order," Mr. Linton cautioned. "First, let me get this title squared away. Get the foreclosing done. Get Jacques Cugnot informed as to what's what." His voice sounded more like a bark now. "Kyle, I'd appreciate it if you'd take the shortest route back to the hotel. My stomach's acting up again. I'm not a young man like you two. I don't have this big bag of patience you men-of-the-*land* keep slung over your backs. I'm too old for these damned wild-goose chases to hell and back."

Adam looked at him, concerned. "The soda? Maybe you need to stop for something to eat?"

"I need to get back to Soda Springs."

"I'm sorry you aren't feeling well—but you won't regret this, Mr. Linton. I promise you that," Adam said intently. "The Cugnot land is exactly what I want. I'll show you! I'm going to build the Donati Winery, the house, everything, up there. One of these days you'll—maybe you'll be glad you helped me get a start."

"I'll be glad to get back to San Francisco where I belong," Mr. Linton said sourly. "You young people—you think what you're seeing is unalterable truth. Well, I'll tell you this—I wouldn't trade places with you for all the prize bottles of wine in the world! For a ninety-nine percent return on every dollar I loan you! If the powers that be gave me the chance to trade shoes with you this minute, I'd say no. I'd turn youth, everything, down flat. *Why?*" He snorted, flipped the cigar down beneath the crunching, whirling wheels of the surrey. "Because I wouldn't have the nerve to face what you're going to be facing in the wine business. Okay—so you end up proving you can grow all these goddam noble grapes and make wine that will win you prizes at the State Fair, maybe some medals in Europe. When you reach the end of the line—and let's face it, I'm getting closer every day to the end of mine—are you going to march up to Saint Peter with one of your prize vintage bottles and propose a goddam toast? Is that the end of your dream?"

Adam deliberately let a silence ride in motion with the swaying surrey. "I can only say I have to do what I have to do. I'm . . . I was born to the land. My father called it stewardship." He let his voice drop off, looked up through the shapes of leaves as the mare pulled out from under the last thicket of mountain trees and broke into a steady trot on the hard-packed surface of the valley-floor road. It was as though he felt his father's silent approval—as though Giovanni Donati had seen the land he had chosen and was happy about it.

What was it his father had said once about owning land? "No man every really *owns* the land. He can at best be a good steward and try to treat it with the respect it deserves."

A part of Adam wanted to speak up and say more to the disgruntled Samuel Linton. He wanted him to be happier. More content with his place in the world at this time of his life. But Samuel Linton had made a statement of his own: that he wanted quiet and peace right now. He had pulled his hat squarely down over his eyes, was leaning back against the cushioned leather seat of the Soda Springs surrey, his hands clasped in a kind of finality across his stomach.

Even Kyle Plimpton looked lost in his own thoughts as he sat hunched forward, his elbows propped on his long bony knees, the reins dangling loosely between his fingers while Betsy, the mare, sensing that the Silverado Trail she was now on meant that last home stretch back to the stable, made a steady, even trot of her own choosing.

At breakfast the next morning, just when Adam was accepting a second biscuit and a third cup of coffee, the waiter informed Mr. Linton that a visitor, a Mr. Jacques Cugnot, was waiting to see him in the library.

Old age had got to both of them, Mr. Linton was thinking as he walked in and got a close look at the portly man, slickly bald, his eyes large like frog eyes, who had the look on his face of a man who might have eaten more than one greasy sausage for breakfast and found them sitting heavily.

He got straight to the point. "I sent for you, Jacques, because—as much as I hate to tell you, I'm foreclosing."

Jacques Cugnot let out a spluttering sound, more like a gasp. The infuriated protest came out like an explosion: "You can't do that to me! Not now—not when I'll finally have some outside assistance coming in. My new son-in-law . . . he's—" He waved his arms out wildly. "What kind of rotten game are you playing with me?"

"Business is business. I've given you a lot of dragged-out months to come up with the money. With some kind of *promise* even of the money. I come up here and find you throwing a wedding that must have cost—what, Jacques? All those imported dresses from Paris I kept hearing about, the French champagne, the orchestra, renting all those cottages." Mr. Linton took out his watch, checked the time, jammed it back inside his pocket. "I've been in this rat race of loaning money too long. There comes a point where any banker has to consider a sound dollar as his main principle."

"Principle! What kind of principle would let you run a man into bankruptcy? Outright disgrace?" Jacques Cugnot's bloated face was beet red now.

Mr. Linton sat down at the long oak table, took out a sheaf of papers from his inside coat pocket. "Let's say I have *some* heart left, Jacques." He paused long enough to light his after-breakfast cigar. When he had his light going to suit himself he shuffled through the papers, waited for Jacques Cugnot to sit down opposite him. "I've got a more than fair compromise worked out here. A deal that will get you off the hook, let you save some face in Napa Valley—keep your house and valley-floor land—and still help me by getting my board of directors off my back."

Jacques Cugnot looked at the papers suspiciously. "I . . . my lawyer ought to be here. I don't sign papers without my lawyer."

"You don't really need him. It's pretty clear and simple. Too good a deal for you to refuse." Mr. Linton put the cigar on the edge of an ashtray, pulled out a deed of transfer. "You see, Jacques, I'm willing to settle this whole loan, at a loss to me, the whole kit and caboodle for the title to that piece of land you own up on Spring Mountain—I believe one hundred twenty acres."

"Why that? Why my Spring Mountain vineyards?" Jacques stormed. "You know damn well those are prize vineyards!"

"My adviser tells me they're in bad shape. Badly neglected. Most of the vines will have to be replanted. New root stock." Mr. Linton took a long puff of the cigar, let the smoke drift between them. "You and *I* know that means a lot of work. Big expense. But I happen to have a foolheaded client who thinks he can bring them around. Willing to spend his money trying, at least. You're lucky, this wine industry being at rock bottom the way it is, to have anybody crazy enough to buy them."

Jacques let his hands hit the table helplessly. "You don't understand. My new son-in-law, Gunther von Gothard, is from a *very* rich brewery family—"

59

Samuel Linton waved one hand, as though casting the remark into the ashtray. "I know that. I know all about that. Dowry and all, Jacques." He let that sit a moment. "It's no use. *This* is my offer."

"All I need is time to talk it over, but they're on a ship heading to Europe right now. On their honeymoon. It would depend on those mountain vineyards—the deal I wanted to work out with the Gothards."

Mr. Linton shook his head slowly. "As I said, that's my offer. Either you come up with the money in full in three days or you sign your name right here—*or* I foreclose. Take your pick."

"This is blackmail!" Jacques bellowed, getting up from the oak table, his whole enormous body shaking with rage.

"No, it is simply an offer. One I was instructed to talk over with you—instructions that came from one of the best lawyers in San Francisco." Mr. Linton got up himself, folded the papers, stuffed them back inside his pocket—all except the deed of transfer, which he slapped against the tabletop. "Take it or leave it. But me, I'm getting on the twelve-o'clock stagecoach out of this place. If you haven't signed it, I'm going through with the necessary legal steps for foreclosure on every foot of land you own!" He started toward the door.

"Is it that Wop in there who thinks he's taking over my mountain vineyards?" Jacques Cugnot shouted after him. "That's the dirty Italian that Miss Grace said made advances toward her daughter Sarah right out there in this very hotel lobby at *my* daughter's wedding reception! Are times getting so hard for you that you're doing your banking these days with Dagoes?"

Mr. Linton turned around slowly, held the cigar out almost daintily and flicked the ashes as though flicking away a fly bothering him. His voice sounded as though it came off a grating board. "Understand this. Adam Donati is a fine young *gentleman*. His father, Giovanni Donati of northern Italy, was a marvelous man—a good friend of mine. A highly respected vintner in Europe. It might pay you, Jacques Cugnot, to watch your foul mouth!" He reached for the deed of transfer. "Forget my deal," he snapped.

Jacques Cugnot's hands slid the deed out from under Samuel Linton's stretched-out fingers. "I was just passing on to you exactly what Miss Grace told everybody in the dining room yesterday morning after you rode off in the surrey."

The cigar was being rolled from one side of Samuel Linton's mouth to the other. "Are you signing or not?"

Jacques Cugnot's hands trembled as he picked up a pen from its inkwell. He held it fixed a moment, looked at Samuel Linton with sheer hatred. "What does a banker like you know about what those mountain vineyards mean? About the work clearing that land? Planting vines, cultivating, lasting out one bad vintage after another waiting for the right one to come along?"

"We'll need witnesses to your signature," Mr. Linton said calmly. He went to the door, motioned to Freddie, asked a guest standing at the front desk to come inside the library.

"He's got me over a barrel," Jacques Cugnot said to no one in particular, then signed his name with a wide-sweeping flourish. He handed the deed of transfer back to Samuel Linton, drew himself up, a cold glint settling in the eyes like frog eyes. "You may still hear from my lawyer about this little paper of yours—in the courtroom!"

When he stalked out of the room, he looked like a man who had already begun planning his counterattack for the next battle.

It was five minutes before twelve o'clock that same morning when Freddie came into the lobby of the Soda Springs Hotel yelling out the announcement "The stagecoach is loading up. Any guests wanting to catch it better board now."

Adam went out the porte cochere entrance with Mr. Linton, stood back a few feet waiting while the footman assisted Mr. Linton up into the coach. Then he stepped closer to the window, spoke quietly, his voice, however, full of feeling. "I don't know how to thank you for all you've done. I know you made a compromise deal. Probably cost you money. I—I promise—"

Mr. Linton poked a finger at him. "Look, young man, I never regret deals I make! Bad ones included." He looked grumpy, out of sorts again. "It's been a policy I've lived by. Something you might remember in the years ahead. Don't blame yourself. Don't come crying to me, either, if you lose your ass up here!" He sat farther back in his seat, adjusting his coat behind him, trying to settle back comfortably before the trip began.

"I don't intend to lose," Adam said, smiling, trying to show him that he felt confident. "I intend to show you—"

"All you have to show *me* is the payment in full on April the fifteenth, 1899. That'll give you plenty of time, as I see it, to either make it or sell out. Either way, I'll expect my eighty thousand dollars paid back in full plus—okay, I'll give you a break and charge you only five percent instead of my usual eight percent interest. I'll send papers to that effect. Which reminds me, as soon as you settle into a place to live until

61

you get your buildings built, I'll send any documents to general delivery at the St. Helena post office. Is that okay with you?"

Adam nodded. "Maybe I'll come to San Francisco. We can have another lunch at the Palace Hotel. I—"

The driver had taken his place, cracked the whip, let out an accompanying commanding yell, and the impatient four-hitch team lurched into motion. Adam stepped back out of the way. "I'll be in touch!" he called out, waving in a saluting way.

But if Samuel Linton had heard and given back some answer, his words were lost in the rumbling clatter of the harness, the pounding hoofbeats as the stage rounded the wide curve of the driveway and lunged toward the great stone gates marking the exit of Soda Springs Hotel.

During the next few weeks, while Adam waited for the title to his Spring Mountain acreage to be cleared, he went about searching for bargains of cooperage and equipment he thought he could use in time.

Kyle Plimpton did, it seemed to Adam, know every goat path and wagon road, just as he had claimed. As soon as he was free from his job as driver and general stablehand at Soda Springs, Adam had presented him a fine gelding mare and a nearly new buckboard he had bought from the William Spires stables in Calistoga. Each week, they found some new forced sale, some auction in progress.

At one point Kyle Plimpton ventured, "Why are you bothering to build a big stone winery for yourself way up there on the mountain when you could buy the big Greystone, I hear, for a few peanuts compared to what it cost that rich miner Bourn to build it? Biggest stone winery in the world, he claims. But he don't like being hitched to something that don't make money. He's heading back to the mining fields, and somebody told me Charles Carpy and some of them from down at the California Winemakers Association were looking into buying it."

Adam shrugged his shoulders. "I didn't come to Napa Valley to buy some other man's secondhand dream. I came to rebuild the Donati Winery of Pontremoli. I've already got my plans on an architect's drawing board, my stonemasons lined up. My father used to tell me, 'Build your own mistakes.'"

"My daddy used to say a mouthful of advice to me, too," Kyle said. "Nothing much took, I guess. Maybe he'd like seeing me now, though." He grinned, took his cowboy hat off, set it back on his head. "Except my daddy thinks every man ought to get married, settle down.

How about you, Adam, building a great big house and all? It'll be a lot of room for a single man."

"I'll keep my eye out for a nice girl to marry," Adam said, smiling.

"Wouldn't be you already got a big eye on that Reynolds girl, would it?" Kyle hesitated, seeing the red color creep up Adam's neck. "Freddie over at Soda Springs was saying something about Miss Grace raving and ranting—how you were flirting with Sarah Reynolds right out there in front of God and everybody." His voice seemed to carry a gentle warning. "My guess is a man would sure about have to hang the moon to meet Miss Grace's approval when it comes to marrying *her* daughter."

Adam didn't answer, but Kyle knew he had definitely hit a tender spot. He decided against telling him the rest of what Freddie had said Miss Grace had blurted out in front of the whole dining room: that if her daughter, Sarah Hubbard Reynolds, ever dared marry a Dago it would be over her dead body. There was a point where a man had to hold his tongue.

If Adam had any secret hopes of seeing Sarah again during the busy weeks ahead, it was something he kept to himself as he got caught up in the engulfing plans of designing the buildings on Spring Mountain. He had found an architect, finally, who seemed to understand what he wanted and was reasonably excited to help Adam follow his own ideas of how the buildings should look rather than superimposing his own—as one man put it—"architectral integrity."

After exchanging several letters, including a set of the architect's plans and returned estimates for labor costs calculated by Luigi Pascarella's oldest brother—the *padrone*—Cesare, it was agreed that Luigi would start the job, and at a certain point, Cesare would join the crew. Adam was looking forward to seeing Luigi again. Though he had, by now, adjusted to the inflections Americans gave the English language, and could speak fluently with anyone, he missed talking in his native tongue. He missed *home*, even though Napa Valley was living up to most of his expectations.

Luigi Pascarella arrived and in one afternoon's time found a place to stay, a boarding house on Madrona Street, run by a plain, practical-minded widow named Fanny Martin. Adam was given the largest room, with his own bath. For an extra five dollars a month, she let them use an empty barn for storing the cooperage, the freight wagons, the innumerable odds and ends that Adam kept buying because he could not resist such low bargain prices. "We'll surely need this later on, won't we, Kyle?" he would say as they made trip after trip where farms were being forced into bankruptcy sales.

"Cesare said you ought to try maybe to find a good job for Vittorio Alfieri," Luigi told Adam one Saturday afternoon when they had just finished a huge midday meal Fanny Martin prepared special on weekends. "Vittorio came over the same time Cesare did. Had a nice winery going—big house. Lost everything. Lost his pants, Cesare said, and needs work bad. A big family—lotsa' mouths to feed."

"I know where he's hiding out," Kyle said, tossing out a stick of cedar on which he had been idly whittling for Fanny's bulldog to fetch. "He's got his whole family crammed inside a chicken coop of a place up on old Petrone's place on Howell Mountain. Ashamed, they tell me. Won't show his face since the sheriff put the lock on his place and they auctioned it off out from under him."

Adam got up, stretched. "Let's ride up." He was getting restless, waiting for the final word from Samuel Linton that he could take over Spring Mountain. He had completed all the necessary banking transactions. His money was set, ready to go. He had been told it was only a matter of a few days now; that Jacques Cugnot had given up his efforts to fight back through the courts.

The three men piled into a two-seater phaeton Adam had bought for his personal use. Though he felt like handling the reins himself, until he found the stallion he was looking for he'd let Kyle work his own gelding mare. It was the third week of March. All around were signs of spring bursting into the growing season of summer ahead. Those vineyards still intact from the ravages of the phylloxera disease had been carefully cultivated. It was a time when a late killing frost could bear down, but the old-timers were predicting it wouldn't happen this year.

It was also a time when the sky was alive with puffy cumulus clouds; when birds had migrated back and were in virtually every tree-top, it seemed to Adam as the phaeton made its way out of St. Helena, then started the climb up Howell Mountain, on the road that would lead past the St. Helena Sanitarium.

All the way up, Luigi told him this story and that: about Cesare's children; about Lorenzo's determination to open a restaurant and the widening gulf between his two older brothers because of it. He was worried, he said, because work was off in San Francisco. "This big depression everybody keeps talking about—I thought we left that behind in Italy."

Kyle, who had been whistling out of the side of his mouth, looked at Luigi through his "black-Irish" eyes, as he called them—eyes that were truly more black than brown at times, that did not seem to go with his fair skin, which turned red in the sun. "Well, you've hit the right spot now. Adam Donati is going to bring us all good luck in Napa Valley! We're going to whip that old dog trying to drag us all down in the mudholes. We'll all get a fresh start up there on Spring Mountain, is how I see it."

He had gone a mile or more past the sanitarium when he stopped the gelding in front of a massive stone barn. Down below, the valley worked its way in slivers between sharply rising mountains. But before Adam could take in the beauty of the scenery, a huge black dog in a crouching position slunk around the corner of the barn, its teeth bared, a menacing growl in its throat. "Damned if he don't look mean as a snake," Kyle said, holding the gelding back.

A small olive-skinned man with eyes deeply set, glistening in the sunlight like polished buckeyes, stepped around the barn, called out to the dog, who then began an open barking. "*Basta!*" he cried out, then waited for it to quiet down and move over to where chickens were pecking at the ground. He was looking at the three men in the phaeton, a puzzled but resigned look on his face, as though he expected bad news. Adam was shocked by the haunted look in those eyes—a man who must be no more than fifty years old, he'd guess, but who could pass for seventy, the way his shoulders had sagged in.

With the dog at a safe distance, Adam was the first to jump down, reached out to shake hands with him. "My name is Adam Donati. I come from Pontremoli—northern Italy. My friend here, Luigi Pasca-rella, has a brother who—"

A wide grin spread across Vittorio's face. "Cesare! Sure. *Buono!* You gotta be the young one, huh? The baby brother I hear so much about?" He grabbed Luigi's hands, pumping them hard. "Your brother was a smart man." His head was bobbing up and down. "He told me, 'Vittorio, stay in San Francisco. Forget winemaking and growing grapes.'" To Adam's dismay, tears had filled the little man's eyes and were sliding down his weathered cheeks. "I lost—everything is gone! They took it away from me."

At that moment, a small, pear-shaped woman eased her way like a shadow in behind Vittorio. Behind her came a string of children, two of them clinging to her skirts, peering out wide-eyed, like startled baby does who thought they would be safe if they stayed close to their mother. Her voice was as soft, as coaxing as her gentle eyes. "Vittorio—these are nice men. They have no papers." She moved forward slightly, as if about to step in front of him to shield him from embarrassment. She spoke to Adam next. "Pontremoli—did I hear you say that? I came from La Spezia. On the sea, not so far away. Vittorio—he is from Padua." She was squinting, studying Luigi. "You look so much like your brother, Cesare! Sure, you got to be a Pascarella! Good—you got here, too. You come see us, but . . ." She looked about, flung her hands out.

Vittorio seemed to have something snap inside him. He squared his shoulders, gave a slight push with his arm, as though reminding his wife, Delfina, of her place. It was a gentle push, in its way, Adam saw. He sensed the love running like an intertwining rope between them. He saw, too, the hurt, the defeat they were trying to conceal, mask with a deeper pride. He stepped up, quite formally now.

"Vittorio, we rode up here today to see if there was a possibility of talking you into coming to work for me. I'm buying some nice acreage up on Spring Mountain. I'll be starting very soon now building a big winery, a barn, a house."

Luigi broke in. "Vittorio, you know the wine people Donati? Him, he's one! A big shot. Here to show Napa Valley how people in our country make wine, huh?"

Delfina was gathering her children about her, her hands fluttering this way and that with excitement. Vittorio was standing now with his hands on his hips, looking at Adam with a blank stare, as if he could not quite comprehend what had just been said. Too much had happened to him in recent months. But before he could gather words together to speak, Adam was going on. "When I'm through with the building, I'll need a winemaster. But right now—" he looked at Luigi —"Luigi will need a crew. Do you think you could work helping—"

"Me—I work any job! These—" Vittorio held out his hands— "with these I built my family a fine big house. A winery—not so big a winery maybe. But we had a nice place. A good brandy still. Taxes, forms—I don't fill out something. Don't pay some fees—lotsa things I don't do right, the government men tell me." Again his eyes were moist. "I tell them to give me time—more time. Show me what is wrong . . ."

Delfina stepped up beside him, touched his arm, pressed down as if kneading bread. "These are such nice men, Vittorio. From Italy! A Donati—think of that, Vittorio!"

Again his head bobbed up and down. His eyes were wide open, like a child's. "Sure—I will be proud to come work for you. Any job you say. When do you want me to start?"

Adam had seen the desperate look on the faces of the children. He guessed they had been hungry. "Monday—how about Monday morning? Come by Madrona Street—ask for Fanny Martin's boardinghouse. People all seem to know where she lives."

"Madrona—sure. Fanny Martin. Sure, I will be there."

Adam checked his watch, as if in a hurry on his own. "We have to get back, I'm afraid. But you come Monday and we'll discuss salary. A few other things."

"See, Vittorio—didn't I tell you today would be a good day?" Delfina was beaming, her own eyes brimming.

They were on their way back down Howell Mountain when Kyle blurted out: "It's a damn shame what they did to that poor fellow! Nailed his place shut. Dumped him and all them kids out on the county road." He shook his head. "One of the hired hands over at Soda Springs saw it all, said they were auctioning everything off—holding up the wife's drawers and laughing, asking who wanted to buy a pair of Dago drawers. Said Vittorio tried to knock him down. Everybody hollering and yelling. The sheriff finally made the family drive off. Told the auctioneer to hold his tongue. That Dagos were human beings like everybody else. Said when the wagon was pulling out, that big black dog barking its head off and all the kids crying like stuck pigs, Vittorio shook his fist at everybody and said he'd get 'em all back. He'd show them. Sure hurts to see a man's pride drug out like somebody's dirty wash for the whole world to point at and laugh about to his face. All these people calling themselves big *Christians*, then doing something like that! Every bit as bad as the crazy nuts hiding behind sheets and burning crosses. They do that up here in Napa Valley too. Big bunch of Ku Klux Klanners. Slipping around holding meetings and trying to scare the daylights out anybody don't agree with them on something. They don't like Catholics, they don't like Jews. They *hate* niggers—which is why you don't see none up here. Hate—everybody sure holds on to their grudges, don't they, usually calling 'em by some other name that sounds better to the public, though. Sometimes it's enough to make a man go on a bender! People laugh at me sometimes, too—call me 'cripple,' mock me behind my back holding their hand up funny. Yep, sometimes I think it ain't a fit world—even in Napa Valley, which ought to be the most peaceful place on the face of this earth."

Adam, who had listened, holding back his fury over what he had heard, bit his lower lip. "If they did that to Vittorio, then I figure it's up to us to see if we can help get him back on his feet." It was more a statement than a question.

They rode the rest of the way home in silence.

3

Adam had made up his mind, on seeing the plight of the Alfieri family, to find a decent place for them to live.

He asked Kyle to look around, find out what modest homes were selling for and what might be on the market in the immediate area. If Vittorio was to work on Spring Mountain, he would have to live closer anyway.

On Sunday afternoon, the very next day, Kyle took Adam to a place across from the Bale Mill owned by a native Missourian named James Lester Jenkins, who had got tired of one bad year after another in Napa Valley—even grapevines he had leased for management had fallen victim to phylloxera—and was selling out, lock, stock and barrel. " 'Least back home a man can make a living raising corn, a few hogs and some dairy cows," he grumbled.

He pointed out to Adam what went with the sale: five acres of pasture, a grove of almond trees, some scattered fruit trees of various kinds, the simple seven-room farmhouse he had just freshly white-washed, the shutters painted a bright green, a tin-roofed barn and wagon shed, a dilapidated buggy, a large flatbed wagon, a few tools, and two workhorses still capable of some light work but not up to making the long trek back to Missouri. After a few moments of consultation with Kyle, who knew more about the prices, Adam offered him nine hundred dollars cash for everything.

James Lester Jenkins put his thumbs behind his overall straps, looked around at what he was leaving behind. "I reckon a bird in the hand is work two in the bush. Ain't nobody else offered me nothing and I want to make the trip back before cold weather sets in." He shook hands. "I got the papers. It's yours, looks like. Don't seem like much—trading paper for money. But what you're getting for nine hundred dollars stands for a whole lot more than what this paper makes it out to be."

On Monday morning, a full thirty minutes before he was expected, Vittorio arrived at Fanny Martin's boardinghouse. At everyone's insistence, he joined them for breakfast, then was taken by Kyle, Luigi and Adam to see the Jenkins place.

"I thought it could be included as part of your wages—free rent," Adam said matter-of-factly.

Vittorio went around as if suspended in some weightless space where at any moment he would regain his foothold. He went from room to room in the house; then through the barn; stopped to pat the workhorses, whose names were Buster and Maggie. He looked up at Adam, his eyes shining with a blur of tears. "Someday . . . someday I will do a big thing to thank you. You will see!"

"Forget it," Adam said gruffly. "Kyle, why don't you and Luigi see about hitching those workhorses to one of the freight wagons over in the barn at the boardinghouse. Go up and help Vittorio move his family down."

"Tomorrow—could they come tomorrow?" Vittorio asked quickly. "I want to get everything packed up. It is not very much. I can have it out in front of the barn ready to load up. Save time."

Adam guessed that Vittorio did not want anyone to see how his family had been forced to live. His guess was that they were living in the barn itself. "Sure—you work it out with Kyle and Luigi."

So on Tuesday afternoon the big freight wagon lumbered to a stop in front of the farmhouse, its sides draped with excited children. One by one, Luigi swung each out into the air, whirled him about, set anxious feet on the solid ground of their new home.

Adam had made sure the pantry shelves were stocked with basic supplies: that a spare twenty-dollar gold piece was left in the sugar bowl for Delfina to buy whatever she might need before Vittorio's first pay. He had offered him an advance in salary, but Vittorio had flatly refused. "I don't take a handout. I work—then you pay me."

Now he and Delfina stood with their arms locked about each other. Her voice came out in a rush: "Vittorio says next Sunday we will fix a big dinner. After Mass is over, we invite you to come share our celebration."

Vittorio beamed. "This time I will have some wine."

The Alfieri celebration, with Delfina having loaded the table with freshly made pasta, a roasted hen, an enormous birthday cake to celebrate all the past birthdays that had gone without a cake, marked more than one transitional time. Though the toasts were given to salute their climb back, their health, the fresh beginning, they marked as well the beginning of a long period of feverish activity taking place on Spring Mountain.

From sunup to sundown, six days a week, the mountain rang out with noises of sledge hammers, buzz saws, trees being felled, lumber cut, stumps pulled out, stones squared off, men shouting in Italian. Chinese workers darted about in that scuffling, straw-sandaled way of theirs, long braided queues flapping down their backs as they followed the barked-out orders of Cesare Pascarella, who was appointed boss by Luigi.

As the summer heat bore down, Adam suggested they take a longer break at lunchtime.

"We've got to get the roofs on before winter," Cesare told him. "Me, I will go back to San Francisco then. Now we work!"

Adam found himself going from the building sites to the vineyards, where he wanted to keep a close eye on Kyle's reconstruction work and the plantings of new root stock. He knew that Kyle was capable, but to Adam his vineyards were the most personal of all. He wanted his own hands to know the feel of vines—of the earth itself. He had to know it was *his*!

There were trips down Spring Mountain. He visited with Professor Hussman. He bought root stock and special varietals to be grafted onto some existing roots he was advised to keep. He was invited to a countywide grape growers' meeting, and then, later on, was introduced to members of the California Winemakers Association, where he met the noted taster Henry Lachman, their chief chemist, Charles Ash, and the venerable Charles Carpy, who told him, "In this valley we must join forces and work together to swing this industry around. It can be done. More progressive marketing, higher standards in winemaking."

If the days were long and exhausting, Adam was nonetheless exuberant. Though his first vintage would come from vines Cugnot's stamp were on, it would be a harvest with some salable grapes. In time, he would have the large bulk of Golden Chasselas—a grape he did not like—removed and replaced with more Rieslings, Zinfandels, Gamays, Pinots, Merlots, Cabernet Sauvignons, and some cuttings from Pontremoli of Nebbiolos and Barberas. Though he was willing to experiment with some of the newer varietals Hussman suggested he might want to try on Spring Mountain, he wanted to stick, by and large, with grapes he knew—grapes with a characteristic composition and flavor he thor-

71

oughly understood when it came to making wine. To him, his vineyard management would make the mark of the quality of his wines. After the grapes could come the right fermentation techniques, the processing and aging. Each step was essential, but none more vital than the vineyards.

If only he understood as much about building! He had never dreamed it would cost so much money to erect a simple stone stable, a —granted, not as simple—winery. But the stained-glass quatrefoil windows were a Donati trademark; just as were the original designs of the wrought-iron circular staircases he was having forged with their patterns of grape leaves and clusters of grapes. Too, he must have a fine tasting room, hand-carved doors. It was part of the dream. He was letting too much of it get chipped away as it was. Even his keen anticipation of his first vintage on Spring Mountain was being deadened by the blow that there weren't workers enough to go around. Jacob Brunner —hadn't he suggested that Adam contact him if he needed pickers when the crush began? He might have to take him up on that after all. When he found the spare time to take a trip to Napa City—and it was going to be essential soon that he do so, Luigi had told him, handing him a new list of supplies that were not available in St. Helena—he would stop by Jacob's place.

It was Cesare who came to him one day and warned, "If you don't get your stained-glass windows ordered, it might be this time next year before we get them put in. I'm just here for the summer. Wintertime comes, I've got to get back to San Francisco. Line up more work. Get the kids in school. I can come up for special jobs. Me, I'd better be the one to install the windows when they're ready. Help hang the big doors when your woodcarver finishes them."

Before Cesare had finished giving him dimensions, Luigi came up with his latest order for special brass fittings and French doors that would have to be milled in Napa City. Adam stuffed the lists into his pockets. Lately, everyone was getting on his nerves. *Money*—all he seemed to do was dole out money, more money! And the latest thing was an unbearable heat wave that kept tempers hot among the workmen.

He could use a break. A change of pace, he told himself, hitching his fine Arabian black stallion, Hajib, to his phaeton, heading out for his trip south to Napa City.

As he pulled out onto the main county road, Kyle Plimpton stopped him. "I was just down at China Camp in St. Helena trying to line up a crew of pickers. This heat wave is bringing up the sugar too damn fast to suite me. At this rate, if we hold out two more weeks before picking we'll be lucky."

"Jacob Brunner told me that day we stopped by that if we need extra help, we could use his regular crew of Chinese."

Kyle reached down, his lame hand on the saddle horn, and patted the gelding's sweat-drenched neck. "I envy you taking a breather. This kind of heat wave is enough to send a man off on a bender if anything ever would." He lifted his cowboy hat, swiped his forehead. "Don't look so worried," he laughed dryly. "If I give you my word from here —" he hit his belly—"there ain't no way in hell I'm going back on it without a mighty good reason—which I ain't got." He started to ride off, then reined the gelding around in its tracks. "Yeah, maybe you ought to line up Brunner's Chinamen. When I used to be Gilbert Reynolds' foreman, we had Chinese lined up begging for work. A dollar a day got the best. It ain't like that now. There ain't no use trying to hire any of those Indians from Lake County either—not for picking grapes. They'll hire out if it's a job where they can reach up, pick fruit off trees. It's against their religion to hire out for any stooping-down labor."

Adam waved goodbye, then gave the high-spirited Hajib a loose rein until they reached the first sharp curve going down Spring Mountain. On Madrona Street, he stopped briefly at the boardinghouse to change into a fresh shirt and a nice suit. As he was straightening his tie, checking his shave in the mirror, he saw how bronzed his skin had become in the hot, dry Napa sun. He liked the color—what it did to his blue eyes. Kyle was right, he needed a breather. If he was lucky, maybe he'd catch a second look at Sarah Hubbard Reynolds. He would be riding past her place. There was always a chance . . .

All the way down the straight main county road toward Rutherford, Adam allowed the stallion to find its legs in a fast, steady trot. He hadn't had much opportunity to work this splendid animal. A sense of exhilaration worked through his fingertips. He sat upright, proudly, feeling the luxuriousness of the padded seats of the fine phaeton, the luxuriousness of the entire Napa Valley stretching toward that last full ripeness before the crush.

He had just come up even with that length of road where the Cugnot and Brunner driveways diverged on the right. He had noticed vaguely a carriage coming down the Cugnot driveway a distance back from the road, where the huge mansion was set against the foot of the mountains. Though Samuel Linton had told him to keep an eye out for Jacques Cugnot, to avoid him if possible, he had almost forgotten him by now. He figured that any fury Jacques had had in the beginning had died out by its own specific gravity.

But suddenly, without warning, Adam's hands tensed on the reins and he was fighting Hajib for control.

It had happened so quickly. At first he had not been sure what was taking place. He was aware of the loud, swift cracking of a whip, of the pounding, sudden rush of the horse coming straight at the side of his phaeton. And then had come that crucial moment of having to fight the bucking, screaming Hajib rearing up on his hind legs and trying to bolt off the road. He had heard that whanging, zinging sound as the flying whip barely missed his own ear and landed instead on Hajib's flanks. Between his shouts at his stallion, over Jacques Cugnot's loud menacing laughter, he saw the second whiplash come down with dead accuracy in the same place, this time ripping open a huge gaping wound on Hajib's right flank.

Before Adam could let the blinding swift action register—find his bearings as he still fought to calm down the frenzied, injured Hajib—the sound of Jacques Cugnot's voice from out on the main county road cut at him: "Let this be a lesson to you, you bloody Dago! Stay out of my way from now on. Just because you stole my land doesn't mean you can take up the whole road with your fancy carriage—blocking *my* driveway! I'm not through with you yet by a long shot!" And then he was driving his own horse with the whip's end, sending it at a dead run north toward St. Helena.

Adam jumped down from the phaeton. His hands shook visibly as he patted the stallion's neck. In English he was saying softly, "It's all right now . . . it's all right," and then he broke into Italian, murmuring over and over, "*Mi dispiace . . . mi dispiace.*"

When the horse was quieter, he eased alongside him to check the gaping wound. At the sight of the ugly gash, the numbness of shock was replaced with a fury that shot through him. What kind of coward would take out his vengeance on an animal? On this splendid thoroughbred? What kind of crazy man was this Jacques Cugnot? He had bought the Spring Mountain vineyards fair and square! If Cugnot had an argument, he should take it out in the open with Samuel Linton. And what was this "bloody Dago" business? He was from an entirely different class of Italians. Or didn't Jacques Cugnot know the Donati name in Europe?

His head was thumping, pounding with off-rhythm beats, as if his skull were suddenly full of flying hoofs.

He took out a handkerchief and gently touched the bloody

wound, felt Hajib's flanks quiver, heard his hoofs paw, stomp the ground, the high-pitched squeal come from him.

There would be doctors in Napa City . . . His head was spinning. English words he thought had been indelibly stamped by repetition slid from his mental grasp. Animal doctor . . . animal doctor—there was a word for it, he kept saying to himself.

He began working his way gently back into the phaeton, trying not to further startle the still-frightened animal. He sat quietly in the seat a moment, his hands still trembling from the delayed reaction to the violent assault. He glanced toward the mountain's base on the west side of the valley and saw this time the modestly imposing outlines of Jacob Brunner's simple farmhouse. He would like to turn down the Brunner driveway, find what solace he could with the wise old Jacob who had spent his life tending the land, being a noble steward if ever there lived one. But there were the lists in his pockets. Luigi and Cesare needed the supplies. He had started the house, the stable, the winery, the vineyards—he couldn't stop now. If he felt better on his way back, maybe he could stop in then. He had promised Kyle he would ask about hiring the Chinese who worked for Jacob on a regular basis.

"*Lento . . . lento*," he called out in a soft, coaxing voice to Hajib, finally getting the stallion back on the even pace that came so naturally to him.

He did not look right or left as he made a steady pace toward Napa City. Even when he was passing the Reynolds mansion with its huge pillars, its driveway of giant oak trees, he did not seem to notice or catch a glimpse of the fantasies that had been lurking so vividly in his thoughts these past months: fantasies all wrapped around a beautiful girl with laughing amber-colored eyes and an oval-shaped face. His mind was churning with sobering realities, with uncertainties he had not included in the glowing package of his initial dream.

In Napa City, he went immediately to a livery stable and asked for help with Hajib's wound. A slow-talking middle-aged man wearing dirty overalls, his thumbs tucked under the bib, introduced himself as Buster Hembry from Missouri, then looked at Adam suspiciously, another kind of anger in his voice. "Any man whips his horse like this ought to have a rawhide taken to his bare back."

"I didn't whip this horse!" Adam said, furious, his back stiff. "A man in Rutherford who thinks I took . . . deprived him of something took aim at me and hit my horse instead."

Buster Hembry rubbed his grizzly chin, looked carefully at the wound. "Any man done a thing like that to *my* horse—even if it was a plain ole mule and not a fine purebred like this stallion—I'll tell you what *I'd* do!" He wagged a finger in Adam's face. "I'd fill his ass full of buckshot. I'd tie him to a tree and turn a rawhide on him. He'd deserve it, too."

"Is there a doctor . . ."

"Yep. Me. I'm a better horse doctor than Doc Baer, who calls himself one but sits down in a saloon on Main Street all day. Give me a couple hours, I'll fix him up for you."

By three o'clock, Adam had finished his errands. The special order for the French doors, the stained-glass windows, the brass fittings had been given, deposits left. He had bought special nails that Luigi wanted; some rolls of tar paper for roofing. He had hoped to get to a couple of lumber mills to compare prices, see if they were being charged too much for lumber in upper valley. Surely there were cheaper prices—for everything!

Hajib was nervous, stomping at the hay. "That liniment I put on his gash stung him. Got him stirred up," Buster Hembry said matter-of-factly. "He's sure a fine animal. I fixed him up. Pay me a dollar—that ought to do."

Adam was not sure he had done the right thing. The wound still looked raw. He paid the money, drove Hajib out into the hot sun, let him take his time on the way back.

There was no question in Adam's mind when he arrived at Jacob Brunner's driveway. He had to let Hajib rest. He was himself oddly exhausted. Maybe it was still a shock reaction. Maybe it was worry creeping up. He found his thoughts riddled with doubts about everything—even the upcoming harvest. He was sure that a late rain would come and that he'd find every vine with cracked berries, bunch rot or something to wipe out his first vintage. Or when he got back to Spring Mountain there would be some disaster up there—Luigi or Cesare would have built those high scaffoldings wrong. Someone would get hit with a falling tree. Bitten by a rattlesnake . . .

This "Lady Luck" Kyle Plimpton was so convinced was always grinning down on Adam Donati—where had she gone? What had he done wrong to chase her away?

The sun was just beginning to take its orange-glowing slide over the tops of the mountain ridges, dropping westward into the ocean, when Adam stopped Hajib in front of Jacob Brunner's.

At the sound of the dog barking, Jacob came out, his shaggy eyebrows lifted, his goatee twitching. He saw Adam, then broke into a welcoming smile. "You should've given us some notice. I'd had Erika fix something special for supper. She'd like that." He extended his leathery, age-wizened hand. Then he saw Hajib's wound, drew back. "What's *that?*"

Adam hesitated. He was holding Hajib's reins up near his neck. He patted the horse reassuringly. "Your neighbor seemed to think we were in his way when he was coming out of his driveway this morning."

Jacob seemed to jump, bounce on his toes. "That lowdown sonofa-bitch!" he sputtered. He examined the wound more closely. "I've seen Cugnot take his whip out before—back when he used to think he had the right to use it on Chinamen. Ask Wang Chi what *he* thinks about Cugnot." He half trotted to the corner of the house, peering in the direction of the barn. "I hope Wang's back from the vineyards—he's been out checking the sugar acids on my French Colombards and Ries-lings. I'd like to have Wang take a look at this horse."

He gave a shrill whistle through his ragged yellow teeth. In a moment, Wang Chi bobbed around the corner of the barn, his aging shoulders stooped, his cone-shaped straw work hat pulled down low on his head, the long braided queue swinging as his sandaled feet scuffled toward them in a half-run. He smiled, bowed to Adam, then quickly went around to examine the wound, his hands making gentle strokes around it. He sniffed the smell of the liniment, made a disapproving face. "Burn it worse. I got good herb. I make paste. Keep flies off. Heal up fast. Take out sting." He led Hajib around to the barn.

"Unhitch him," Jacob called out. "I'm going to talk this young man into staying for supper, fancy or not." He grinned at Adam. "She's a good cook any day of the week, my granddaughter. Today's her bread-baking day. Maybe you won't get a stuffed hen, but you'll get some fine bread fresh out of the oven."

Adam smelled the rich aroma of bread baking as soon as he set foot inside the door. A wave of nostalgia hit him. In Pontremoli, as young boys, he and all his brothers would troop into the kitchen when the giant ovens were stoked specially for baking days. They played games with spare scraps of kneaded dough. They spread giant chunks of oozing butter over broken-off slabs of hot, steaming bread. They got in the cook's way, pestered her, but it was always like a party. And as they got older, they drank wine instead of milk, ate cheese with the fresh bread, and sat around the kitchen swapping growing teenage boys' stories that sometimes made the cook slap her hands over her ears and shoo them out with a broom.

Erika came out, a startled look on her face as Jacob summoned her from the kitchen. She swiped her hands on the sides of her apron. A smudge of flour was streaked across the tip of her tiny bobbed nose. Recognizing Adam, her cheeks flushed red with color. She pushed with the sides of her hands at a strand of straight blond hair that had worked out of the pile of it on the back of her head. "I—I didn't know you were coming," she said shyly. "I'm . . . a mess." Her floured hands fluttered like startled white dove wings.

"You look fine," Adam said cheerfully. "Reminds me of home—of Pontremoli. The smell . . ."

Jacob gave him a nudge toward the parlor. "He's spending the evening—having dinner with us," he called back to Erika. "Set an extra plate. Meanwhile, I've got a good Beringer Riesling I want him to sample." He made sure Adam was in agreement. "You stay in there where it's cooler. Take off your coat and necktie. I'm going down to my cellar. Maybe we'll do a little tasting." His eyes were alive with excitement now. His goatee seemed to be saying *yes, yes, yes* as his head bobbed up and down. "You remember I told you I don't make wine on my own? But I grow the best grapes in Napa Valley. Every vintner worth his salt wants to buy my grapes. They bring me their best vintages. Erika and me, we don't drink much. A little sherry. Some brandy. Now and then a dessert wine." He beamed proudly. "I would match my wine cellar with anybody's in Napa Valley. They keep bringing it to me, I keep putting it away. I've got Krug bottles going back to 1868. Probably turned to vinegar by now. I've got To Kalon —wines you can't buy if you looked for them. I've got samples of every Napa Valley wine that won a prize at the 1889 Paris Exposition. I've got samples of every wine that ever won a State Fair prize. You name the prize—I've got the wine." He chuckled at his own secret now shared for the first time. It was known around Napa Valley that old Jacob Brunner must have a substantial wine cellar, but he was also known to be tight-fisted, to hoard every dime he ever made, and most likely every wine bottle ever given to him. But with Jacob Brunner, no one asked; no one really knew his business.

By six o'clock, when Erika appeared in the parlor doorway, her face freshly scrubbed, her hair braided neatly, a richly embroidered Swiss pinafore over a pale-blue cotton dress, Adam and Jacob Brunner had tasted their way through an astounding array of bottles. Jacob was having a wonderful time. He waved a wobbly hand at Adam. "To hell with ritual! Progressive tasting, right? Sample this 1887 Cabernet that Senator Seneca Ewer turned out. See if you don't like it better than Inglenook's same vintage. But then, go back to Inglenook's 1884—no comparison." He was visibly tottering for balance, but his faded eyes

were aglow. It had been years since he had found someone who understood where he was coming from when it came to growing grapes.
This young Donati knew viticulture. He knew what he wanted. He
was a fine, *fine* young man . . .

Erika sat down primly on the edge of the horsehair-covered sofa.
"Dinner is ready," she said quietly.

Jacob smiled a lopsided smile in her direction. "If *she* had been a
boy, I would've taught her everything you know! She's inheriting my
property when I pass on. I get some things across to her. Erika, one of
these days you will break out of that shyness. Maybe you won't ever
turn into a Miss Grace Reynolds—" He laughed, his shoulders shaking.
He pointed at the row of empty bottles. "You must learn to appreciate
fine wine, my little dear. When I die, you ought to know what's down
there in my cellar. Adam, you promise me you will show her the difference. What's what about wine. What she ought to know to manage
my vineyards."

"Grandfather . . . you should eat. Supper is getting cold. The table
is set." She looked helplessly at Adam. He gave her a knowing wink,
then took Jacob firmly by the arm. His own feet felt wavering, as if
searching around on their own for the right direction. It had been a
long time since he had drunk that much wine. Certainly, he had never
had such an unexpected tasting. All excellent—surprisingly excellent
wine.

The table was impeccably set, the linen cloth starched and ironed
so that not a wrinkle could be seen. Erika had folded the three napkins
in a quaint old-fashioned way so that they stood up like flag bearers. A
small bouquet of mixed flowers stood in the middle of the table. She
had prepared, to Adam's surprise, fresh fish, boiled new potatoes, peas
in young pods, a plate filled with crisp radishes, green onions, freshly
sliced tomatoes from the garden. "Wang Chi caught the fish for me,'
she said, pleased at Adam's enthusiasm. "In the Napa River."

The food began to bring Jacob around. He was anxious to go on
with his conversation. "So I taught you a lesson, didn't I? That you can
tell a wine by its grapes? The Châtaeu Chevalier you tasted—sure, the
terra rosa—it comes out so you can't miss it. I could show you a wine
made from Rieslings grown in the Carneros region put up by Carpy at
Uncle Sam's Cellars. You taste the difference between it and one from
Inglenook. Not because of fermentation—the kinds of oak they use.
The *grapes*—I taste the grapes!"

From time to time during the meal, Erika would excuse herself
from the table, her starched ankle-length pinafore making a crisp, rus-

tling sound as she hurried back to the kitchen; she would return with fresh hot bread, with a bowl of strawberry jam, a special jar of loganberries that one of the Swedish relatives from back in Minnesota had sent to her at Christmastime. When she was out of the room at one point, Jacob Brunner leaned across the table and said in a lowered voice, "Its good to see her so happy—color in her face again. She is like a scared doe. Her mother, Johanna, was not like that. She laughed, sang songs, all the time. When she was in the kitchen she would yodel—get all the birds singing around in the big lilac bush out there. My wife—*my* Erika—she was jolly. Laughed! All that fancy embroidery work on that apron, these napkins, my Erika used to sit sewing. Her work won prizes at the State Fair in *her* department, *my* grapes won in mine. I could show you a trunk full of blue ribbons. But this one, my granddaughter Erika—the fire burned something out inside her. Seared her mind with scars. She doesn't talk about it. She keeps her ghosts to herself. But I keep trying to draw her out of herself. Tonight—tonight is the best! She drank some wine. Did you see? Sure, she is coming out of her shell." He sat back, beaming. "Tonight I am a very happy old man."

"Don't say *old*," Adam said lightly.

"I am eighty-eight years *old*. Swiss people, we live to be old men." He kept nodding, tugged at his goatee. "I've got to stay on awhile—can't die yet. Erika still needs me. The shell is just beginning to crack open a little." Adam was not sure if it was the wine or some loneliness of Jacob Brunner's own that brought the tears brimming suddenly in his faded-out blue eyes with those white rings around them. But the sound of Erika's skirts coming down the hallway made the old man sit up, collect himself. "Look at dessert—now, there's a Swiss chocolate cake for you!"

"A *Swedish* recipe this time, Grandfather," she said.

"All right, all right. Swiss, Swedish—your cakes are the best."

The moon was up by the time Adam bid them good night and a smiling Wang Chi led a much quieter Hajib around to the front door. "Your horse he fine now."

Adam waved goodbye, drove down the driveway feeling inordinately better than when he had arrived. As he turned out onto the main country road and passed Jacques Cugnot's turnoff, he looked back at the Cugnot mansion, where only one single light glowed in the gathered darkness. For a moment, a shadow seemed to fall over Adam's shoulders. He shrugged it off, felt the welcome cooler breezes of a valley night brushing across his face. The sounds of early night filled the flat valley floor with songs different from those he heard up on Spring Mountain. The moonlight brushed across the fields, made dancing shapes across the smooth road packed hard from the hot, rainless summer. His spirits picked up. Napa Valley was big enough for all of them! He would last—his dream would long outlive the likes of Jacques Cugnot, he told himself, letting the reins loose so that Hajib could find his happiest pace back to Madrona Street.

4

The next day, word had reached the workmen on Spring Mountain about Jacques Cugnot's whip hitting Hajib. It seemed that he had stood outside the St. Helena bank bragging about the incident to a group of men. Vittorio Alfieri, coming out of the bank, had overheard and, in turn, told Luigi and Cesare Pascarella about it immediately.

"He is saying how he is gonna break Adam's back up here. Tear up his place before he is finished," Vittorio said, his eyes wide, glazed with his own hurting memory.

When Adam rode up—having left Hajib to rest and saddled up a white mare Fanny Martin loaned him—he was met by Luigi.

"That crazy damn Frenchman—he's no good!" Luigi bellowed. "I don't like this business—him bragging how he's gonna come up here and do his dirty work. Maybe he'll get his head cracked open with something more'n a whip if he comes to Spring Mountain."

It was a nerve-wracking day for Luigi anyway, with his new scaffolding going up and with two inexperienced workmen to show how the ropes worked, to teach the dos and don'ts of working on a scaffold. He turned, his voice sounding as if it had been cracked down the middle with a chisel. "Double-check those ropes!" he yelled at his crew, just beginning to pull themselves up. He turned back to Adam. "My men—I watch out for my men. I don't need Jacques Cugnot up here."

"Jacques Cugnot is not after your crew, Luigi," Adam said, giving him a reassuring slap on his shoulder. "This problem with Cugnot—it's my worry, not yours." He squinted through the bright morning sun at the buildings. "You're making progress. Will you get any one weather-tight before winter sets in?"

"The stable. The living quarters for workers in the back. Roofs on —temporary walls. Some of the stonework will have to come next spring. But we can get a lot done on inside finishing. We're on schedule."

Kyle sauntered over, took a bandana from his back pocket, swiped at his forehead. "Another scorcher, looks like." He had taken to smoking a pipe; he loaded it now, lit up. "Adam, I've been checking out the acid sugars. There's four to five acres planted in Gray Rieslings that look to me like they got caught sometime last spring in a bad windstorm. Not enough leaves on half of 'em to keep the grapes from getting sunburned. Some as hard as acorns. Not worth a tinker's damn." He puffed his long, lean cheeks around the pipe stem, his black-Irish eyes lost in his own thoughts a moment. "That Cugnot fellow—he sure as hell was uneven when it came to tending these vineyards up here. Some he's got in pretty good shape. The Cabernets—pruned 'em about the same as I would've done. Left about the right number of buds. Then on some Zinfandels, he's overcropped them and they ain't bearing much now. Must've worked 'em hard, bilked those vines to death." He shook his head. "Men get greedy. Hussman used to drill into us like he was teaching us the arithmetic tables, 'Maximum yield but optimum quality.' When it comes to pruning, it's a man's nature to leave too many buds on. But if you keep vines healthy—if you're after the best grapes for the best wines—somebody's got to take a firm grip on the pruning shears." Kyle had not heard yet about Jacques Cugnot, Adam guessed. He was grinning now. "Cugnot knew a *few* things. These vines could run plenty a close second. But wait till we get our own stamp on Spring Mountain—right?"

It was during the lunch break that Kyle's face reflected that he had heard the news from Luigi. He stalked over to Adam, who was rechecking the architect's plans on the scaled-down main house. "If Jacques Cugnot sets foot up here he won't crack a whip again," Kyle said, his mouth grim.

Adam stood up, let out a long, hot sigh. "I don't want any of you men building up a case of hate up here. Seems to me there's enough of that around."

Vittorio was pulling a thick crust off an end of bread, adding slabs of salami from his lunch pail. "Plenty people in this valley hate Italians. I know that for a fact."

Kyle started fishing in the lunch pail that Fanny Martin packed daily for her working boarders. "Damn, I thought she put in two drumsticks." He looked at Vittorio, tore a strip of thin meat from a chicken wing. "Hell, it ain't just *Italians* people hate. Some hate Jews, some hate the foulmouth boys from Missouri. You got a chip on your shoulder, Vittorio—not that anybody blames you. Jacques Cugnot is plain lowdown. He'd cheat you blind but is the first to accuse every-body else of what's on *his* mind. I wouldn't be surprised if he didn't cheat somebody out of this land up here on Spring Mountain in the first place."

Adam stood up. "We've got enough on our minds up here without worrying over things we don't really know about." He cast a slow, deliberate look at Kyle. "I'd appreciate an estimate of what you think we can get from the vineyards when we do start harvesting. I want records kept of the yield per acre according to variety—what we sell them for. I'm running a business up here, as of now."

He saw the men exchange glances. They were not used to seeing Adam Donati show his temper. When he stalked off toward the vine-yards, Vittorio nudged Luigi. "He's worried. Italians—we gotta stick together. What does Cesare say?"

"Cesare's gone back to San Francisco. He's decided to pack up his family and move everybody to Napa City. He sees a future up here for us—which maybe says he's not worried much, being *northern* Italian." Luigi stood up, bellowed out at everyone, "Okay—eating time is over! I want every Wop, every Chinaman, every black Irish back on the job!"

As Adam plunged through the vineyards, making his way toward the outer edge where he could get an overall view of the valley below and the eastern ridge of mountains to the east, he was arguing with himself. It wasn't fair to take it out on the men, this anxiety he had about money, this gnawing concern over Jacques Cugnot's last shout-ing threat that he wasn't finished with him yet. He needed every dollar he could get off these grapes that had come with his purchase of the 120 acres on Spring Mountain. He had, at best, thirty acres of bearing vines right now—counting the diseased ones, the deadwood, the new plantings that had gone into the additional thirty cleared acres. In time, surely he would have another thirty. But right now, on the brink of his first Napa Valley vintage, he didn't need Kyle Plimpton's bad news that he was losing close to five acres he had counted on. Every dollar, he could see now, was going to count.

He was taking longer strides than usual. Even Luigi was getting on his nerves lately. The building—why was everything creeping along so? Why did Luigi have to be a perfectionist with every last detail? All that measuring—squaring off, getting things level! He knew it could go faster. And why had Cesare just walked off, giving him one day's notice that he was heading back to San Francisco? That he'd be back. What did that mean? *When?* And for how long the next go-round?

At the edge of the vineyards, he stopped and stood looking out at the vast stretch of valley below, at the vividly clear outlines on this sparkling, sun-scorched day of the San Pablo Bay, and then on south to the tracings of Mount Tamalpais. A giant horsefly swooshed annoyingly around his head, finally flew off. A tree with its branches filled with birds—a flock of blackbirds Kyle had told him had recently located the vineyards—seemed alive with pests. More losses from his profit, no doubt, by the time they got through feeding on ripe grapes!

It was damnably hot. He unbuttoned the top buttons of a blue workshirt he was wearing. The woods nearby, just down the slope from the vineyards, looked invitingly cool. Back in Pontremoli, he used to take long walks into the heart of the forest behind the old estate buildings. He could use a shadowy, quiet haven right now, he thought. A place to gather his thoughts. Find himself, his enthusiasm again.

And then he was bounding down the narrow dirt trail made by the Chinese who came from Jacob Brunner's to tend his mountain vineyards.

It felt marvelous to stretch his long legs. The very sounds of his own footsteps were hypnotizing. Down and down he kept going. Now and then he stopped to push aside an overhanging limb, remove a sticking briar snagging his trousers.

The trail wound along a tumbling creek which had its origin in a natural spring on his own property. The gurgling was a refreshing sound. He was forgetting now the workmen up there with their common jug of grappa and their snaillike methods of putting up his buildings.

Abruptly he had come to a place where the hillside made a steep slope down toward a small stone bridge. He realized that he was standing almost parallel with the roof of a barn built into the hillside. Because of the steep incline, he had to watch his footing carefully. He would go as far as the bridge, he told himself, rest a few minutes there, then head back.

He stopped, his breath caught in his throat. She was standing just beyond the bridge, wearing a pale-beige riding habit, holding the reins of a chestnut mare as its long neck bent down to drink. She was gazing down at the rushing water tumbling under the bridge, lost in her own thoughts. But something had made her sense his presence. She looked up, startled.

"Why—oh, hello! I didn't hear you. I—what are you doing *here*, of all places?"

Her hair was pulled back with a ribbon, the same way it had been that morning at Soda Springs Hotel when she was wearing the rust-colored velvet suit. Her amber eyes sparkled, as beautiful, as alive, as he had remembered them. Yes, she *was* beautiful! So very beautiful.

His voice seemed to have been wrapped in cotton. "I'm here—why? I don't know. I was taking a walk down a path."

He walked to the middle of the bridge, waited for her while she led her horse up away from the water and tied its reins to a tree. When she joined him, she extended her hand in greeting, but he reached for both of them. "Do you—do you believe in fate?"

She lifted one eyebrow, a smile slowly lighting up her face. Then she pulled away from him, sat down on the edge of the bridge and dangled her riding boots over. "Join me," she said laughingly, indicating the space beside her. As he lowered his long legs, easing into a sitting position, she said, "Fate? Yes, I suppose I do believe there's a larger force at work than our puny lot. Fate, God—I seem to lump them into one category."

The side of his leg brushed against hers. He felt his heart racing. His body taking charge of his senses. He tried to concentrate on the swirling patterns of the water beneath, calming himself down.

"You have been avoiding me," she said, lifting her face, forcing him to look straight at her. "I thought you would make some attempt to call on me after that day at Soda Springs—or did you promptly forget me? Was I just another girl to you?" Her face was serious, her eyes filled with tiny yellow flecks.

"I—no, I didn't forget for a moment! I remember every word you said. How you looked. What you wore. How you had your hair tied back with a ribbon, just like today." He reached over and touched her hair, his fingers trembling in spite of his efforts to control himself. "I have been very busy up on Spring Mountain. Vineyards to bring around into some kind of decent shape, the buildings—so many reasons why you haven't heard from me. Your mother being one big one. I understand she doesn't like Italians. I was told that."

"I wondered if you had heard. She made a dreadful scene in the dining room at Soda Springs. I was horrified. Mother's standards are so Old World—'Old South.' Being an only child, I take the brunt of her idealism. I wish she had had six, seven children. She'd have less time to dote over me." She kicked her boots out at the air. At that moment his fingers touched hers on the edge of the bridge, worked their way in between hers.

They sat silently a long moment, letting the flow of electricity run through them. Her voice was lower, with that hint of huskiness. "You are right. Mother has made up her mind that you are *not* to be in my life. And yesterday Jacques Cugnot came over to add fuel to the fire—

telling her how he had to give your horse a lash with his whip to make you stop blocking his driveway."

"That's a lie!" Adam said, his voice fierce with the rush of conflicting emotions. "I was driving my phaeton, going down the main county road. My stallion, Hajib—I—" He wanted to quit talking. The smell of her hair, the pressure of her fingers against his telling him her responses.

"I know Jacques Cugnot well," she said, her voice tight. "Monique and I were best friends since we were five, maybe six years old. She is an only child, too. But he was never doting with her. He actually hated her because she wasn't a boy. He rarely paid any attention to her at all. My father—poor Daddy Gilbert is washed up now, but he used to be such a dear! Monique would spend almost as much time at our house as her own. This—this very bridge was our special hideout." She looked up at the treetops, smiled, shook her head sadly. "I couldn't count the times we hid under here making up stories, dreaming silly dreams about the man who would come along. Poor Monique—she was forced into that marriage. Jacques Cugnot pulled strings, lied, whatever it took to get that marriage arranged. I worry so about her. She was so miserably unhappy at the wedding. I—I doubt that I'll ever see her again. Something I just know. . . ."

He was unable to take his eyes from her. A shaft of sunlight glinting through the overhead thicket of limbs brought out red highlights in her dark-brown hair. He saw the pert nose, the smooth skin, those long slender hands now free of his grip moving in dancing motion as she spoke.

"Has the right man come along—for you?" he asked abruptly.

She jumped up, her motions swift, agile, and stood on the narrow bridge, one hand lightly on his shoulder. "Perhaps . . ." she said, and moved away, went over to a mossy bank, placed one hand on the tree trunk, smiled across at him, her eyes mischievous, as he had remembered them. "What about you, Mr. Donati? Don't you have someone special?"

He got up slowly, feeling awkward. He did not take his eyes off her face as he went toward her, took her roughly by the shoulders. "That day at Soda Springs—you have been the special one for me. I haven't missed a day when I haven't thought about you. But I haven't dared. I am just beginning. So much work. I cannot offer anything to you—*yet*. When I am ready . . . does it matter to you if I am not the man your mother would choose?"

"I am so glad—so glad you said what you have just said," she whispered. "I think I would have died if you had told me there was a girl in

Italy. I was afraid you might even say you had a wife you were planning to send for!"

They were in each other's arms then, and together easing down on the mossy bank, their bodies wrapped in a desperate embrace. It was Adam who was the first to pull away.

"Your mother doesn't like Italians," he said in a whisper against her hair. "How do we convince Miss Grace that I am—What do we tell your mother?"

Sarah sat up, sighed, picked at a single blade of grass. "We simply can't tell her anything yet. There's no need to get her upset. I'm leaving for school very soon. My last year at Wellesley. After I graduate —next June—then it will be different. A year—she won't know we've met. We can write letters. At Christmas I'll try to come home. Or perhaps you can come east."

"I can't," he said matter-of-factly. "My work here—I have to see that our house is finished. That I'll have a place ready for my bride. When—when do you think we can—"

"When do you think we will be formally introduced?" she teased. "I believe one should wait at least a year after that."

"I am serious," he said, pulling her against him.

After he had kissed her until he no longer dared, she drew back, traced her finger down the bridge of his nose. "Let's meet here next June!" she said, pulling herself free, standing up. "Right here. I'll be here at sunset. I'm due to return on June the fifteenth. Meet me here then. Will you promise? Will you wait for me?"

"But can't we see each other before?"

The horse let out a loud shrill whinny, as if hearing another one nearby. She hurried across the bridge. "If I can. At least there'll be next June," she whispered and ran to untie the reins; quickly mounted.

He sensed that he must not be seen. He hurried back up around, above the barn; stood up at the top of the steep slope, waited until she had disappeared, his whole being alive, his heart racing.

The climb back up the trail took much longer than the easy, rapid plunge downward. But he was glad for the added exertion, the sweat it brought out on his neck, that ran down the middle of his back, dampened his shirt under his arms.

He had gone about halfway up when he heard the unmistakable sharp crack of a broken twig, the sound of a horse. He stopped, stood with every sense alert, looking across through a clump of trees where he had heard the noise. There, astride a gray-dappled horse, sat Jacques Cugnot, a rifle in his hand.

"If you step one foot on this side of that path I am going to put a bullet through your head," he said in a voice that had its own ring of lead. "Get this, Dago—you may have *temporary* legal claim to my Spring Mountain land, but you are this minute standing on the edge of property that still belongs to me in the eyes of any law. Property posted with 'No Trespassing'!" He had the rifle aimed. "Come on, Wop! Step over this way. Let's see what the law says when I shoot you for trespassing."

Adam dared not move. His whole body quivered now with animal instinct to survive. He knew he was looking at a man half crazed. A man who wanted an excuse to pull the trigger.

The defense tactic he used was not one Jacques expected. Adam began speaking in French, softly, as expertly as possible. "Pull the trigger," he was saying, "and you will have to answer to my stonemason, Luigi Pascarella. He is never very far from my side. You do not know what an expert he is with a chisel. A sledgehammer. He is like a bull charging when it comes to cracking things open—so don't *you* step on *my* land!"

Adam saw the unsure look cross Jacques Cugnot's face and his hand quaver slightly on the gun. He spoke now in English, his voice crisp, precise, in much the same way that Dudley Farnsworth used to speak. "May I suggest that you put that gun down? May I further suggest that in the future you watch around whom you use those words 'Dago' and 'Wop'? Luigi Pascarella and I both have split heads open for less cause."

At that exact moment, Jacques Cugnot's horse felt the change in the nervous hands on the reins. It backed up at a fast, frantic pace, then tried to rear, to fight off in any way it could the harsh, cruel bit.

Adam took advantage. Now it was his voice lifting, carrying weight across the clearing. "I see your horse doesn't obey you too well! Maybe you have hit it too many times with a whip. Horses, you know, never forget!"

And with that, Adam turned and headed up the trail, taking long, even strides, his heart thumping like a war drum inside his chest.

Adam did not tell Kyle Plimpton or Luigi about the incident with Jacques Cugnot. They were upset enough as it was. Maybe Luigi had been right. Maybe he should have his men take extra caution. But, on the other hand, he wanted to keep down as much anger and fear as possible. *Patience, the cardinal rule for a viticulturist,* his father had always said. Maybe he should apply it to other things as well.

He went up to Luigi. "I'm sorry I was short-tempered today. I guess I'm just anxious to get this place up here livable. I'm not cut out for Fanny Martin's boardinghouse."

Luigi looked at him with a narrowed, measuring eye. "I see lotsa things," he said quietly. "I see this costs too much money. So we push ahead faster, okay? Luigi is a man of his word. If you got money worries, me, I can hold back. Don't pay me for a while. I don't need much to live on. The boardinghouse don't cost so much. I am paying Cesare and Lorenzo back." He looked around at the buildings. "When we get through, you gonna have the finest stone buildings in all of Napa Valley. I give you my word."

Adam went over and looked at the recently shaped outer stonework on the quatrefoil-shaped windows. "Maybe we could hold back on some of the stained glass. It cost more to have them made over here than in Italy, I'm finding out. How does that sit with you for right now?"

"Sure, hold back on some of the fancy stuff. Cesare said you ought to do that anyway—the carved doors for the tasting rooms, that fancy paneling you said you wanted to have shipped over from Europe. Save the trimmings."

Adam clasped Luigi's arm lightly. "One of these days we'll get it all built exactly as the plans say. As close to the way I *see* it as can be done." He glanced over at the mare nibbling grass. "I'm taking off early today," he said to Luigi apologetically. "But I'll stay with the job all day tomorrow."

Luigi was studying him closely as Adam tightened the saddle, mounted for the ride back down Spring Mountain to Fanny Martin's boardinghouse. "Good, you take a little time off," Luigi said softly. "I'll take care of this place up here."

"I would hate it if your workmen—if anything should go wrong because of—"

"Look, I see plenty things! I see this Cugnot fella has got a bolt loose in his head. Don't you worry about Luigi Pascarella's men! We keep our eyes open."

But even with Luigi's reassurance, that night Adam could not sleep. His thoughts were tumbling. One moment he would be seeing Sarah's face, reliving every word she had said; the next, he would be seeing Jacques Cugnot's gun aimed at him and hearing his voice shouting out.

The next morning he stumbled out into the day, his feet like dead weights, his eyes dry and red with exhaustion. None of which put him in the right mood for what took place on Spring Mountain that day at noontime.

He had just walked out into the vineyards to look for Kyle and check the picking that had started—or should have started now that the crew of Chinese had made their way up the back trail from Jacob Brunner's. Adam found them sitting under the shade of an enormous live-oak tree. They were squatted back on their heels, their gourds of tea and their bowls of rice being emptied.

Kyle was standing on the wagon road that skirted the vineyards, squinting into the sun. "Look yonder who's coming," he mumbled as Adam greeted him.

Adam, jumpy, turned around, glared into the blinding noonday sun.

"It's Jacob Brunner and his granddaughter, looks like." He put his lunch pail down without opening it. "Reckon he's come to check and see if the Chinamen got here. If we're picking."

Adam saw immediately that Erika looked different—more at ease, a smile on her face. In fact, she looked quite pretty, wearing some kind of ruffled bonnet to match the pale-blue dress that brought out what color she had. Golden highlights shone in the blond hair that was now braided in one long loose braid falling down her back beneath the bonnet. She was so tiny, he thought, offering to help her down from the wagon. How light she felt as he swung her down; how soft the small round breast that so briefly brushed across his hand.

Jacob Brunner refused assistance from anyone, making his own scrambling way down. He turned to help Erika take out the picnic baskets, the bottles of wine. "We came to celebrate your harvest," he said, crinkling his eyes nearly shut against the sun. "We do that every year up here."

"I knew there was good reason I didn't tackle Fanny Martin's lunch bucket today," Kyle said cheerfully. "Mr. Brunner, do you remember the first time I ever laid eyes on your granddaughter? That time when everybody down valley was being neighborly and pitching in trying to help Miss Grace save what was left of her grapes? That year it rained so hard and we had bunch rot so bad? Don't you remember that? Erika came in toting a big picnic basket, just like she is now."

Jacob Brunner shook his head. "Neighbors in Napa Valley pitch in most anytime there's trouble. Yeah, I guess I recall." He was busy now passing around tin cups for the wine.

At the mention of the name "Miss Grace," Adam had been sure his neck and ears were beet red. He tried to focus his full attention on Erika as she began spreading out a huge picnic cloth on the ground and taking food from the basket. But her small busy hands seemed to swim into the larger, slender dancing ones belonging to Sarah Reynolds . . . .

Jacob shoved a tin cup into his hand. "Some people have the priest give blessings when it's time for the first crush. Me, I drink toasts." He made a wide, impatient motion with one arm, beckoning the Chinese to come join the circle. "It's not so much *how*, but it's bad luck not to celebrate your harvest every year. Don't forget that." He lifted his wine. "*Salute*—here's wishing Bacchus always smiles on your vines!"

The picnic was indeed a feast in its way. Adam saw that preparing food was Erika's speciality. He smiled, admiring the huge round loaf of bread with the insides scooped out, the top fashioned in the shape of a lid. Before putting the fried chicken inside the scooped-out breadbasket, she had poured in melted herb butter, and she told everyone to tear off pieces to eat with the chicken. Clusters of grapes spilled across the picnic cloth. There were chunks of cheese and small apple tarts. "Enough for Kyle to have seconds," she said shyly.

Jacob had chosen a Beringer Zinfandel for the toasting. Adam sipped it appreciatively. He needed something to relax him. But he had to force the food down. It was good, but his stomach had drawn into a tight fist of its own and stayed that way since the day before when he had had the encounter with Jacques Cugnot on the trail—then, and when Sarah Hubbard Reynolds had let him know so inescapably how she felt about him. . . .

Jacob Brunner's voice brought him out of his drifting. "Let's step over here a minute where we can talk," he said, touching Adam's elbow with his knobby, age-worn right hand that even in so light a touch had a firmness and a sure sense of purpose that men who have tended the land a lifetime get.

They moved to the edge of a clearing, one where, recently, stumps had been removed in preparation for a new vineyard. At first, Jacob looked carefully at the holes from the stumps. He squinted at Adam. "Every time you pull a madrone out they say it's a tree that cries."

He was carrying his tin cup. He lifted it, waited a moment, as if finding what he wanted to say in the red liquid. "I got word this morning that Jacques Cugnot caused you trouble yesterday. Not just the whipping of your horse—the *other*."

Adam's whole face flushed. "What was that?" he asked, trying to keep his voice even.

Jacob was watching him closely. "I think I told you the other night that I've known Cugnot's nasty ways a long time. Which is what bothers me. He can stoop pretty low." He tugged at his goatee. "I don't know what makes some men need to spout off. Try to convince the world they're important by how loud they talk. By how much they show off what they have—what they want people to *think* they have." He looked off across the vineyards. "Anyway, he's saying you stole this land. He seems to think any money come from these grapes this year is his money, by right."

"It's *my* land! I bought it fairly and squarely. The lawyer, Norman Jaspers—ask him! Or ask Samuel Linton. He arranged the deal. It is legal. I paid a lot of money for it."

Jacob waved his hand, quieting Adam down. "Look—I know Jacques Cugnot is a lot of hot air. I told Miss Grace that, when Jacques was saying things to her about you and—well, the Reynolds girl. Saying how he saw you—" Jacob's voice broke off. "What I wanted to say was, I guess I thought you ought to know."

"Why doesn't someone come ask *me*?" Adam cried out. "Why don't they hear my side of the story!"

Jacob turned the empty tin cup around. "Some people in this valley are funny. For no good reason, they have something against anybody who's Italian." He shrugged his shoulders. "People usually listen to me around here, *when* I decide I've got something to say, I've told the ones who count just who the Donatis are." He grinned, chuckled. "People who count to me are people who buy grapes. Now I want you to listen to me. Sell to Inglenook. And Uncle Sam's Cellars—Carpy will buy some from you. Beringers usually buys what Spring Mountain Cabernets they can get." They were strolling back toward the others now. "Here's how *I* see it. Jacques Cugnot is about washed up—about flat broke, is my guess. He's had some rough spots before, but with the phylloxera wiping his vines out down valley it's just a matter of time. Most people quit paying much attention to him a few years ago. But there's always a bunch of roughnecks who keep their ears open hoping to hear a good excuse to fight. Cause trouble." He put his hand on Adam's arm, stopped him. "Be careful. What I'm saying is—until Cugnot's steam blows over a little, keep a watchful eye out in all directions. He's mean."

"But I really don't see how this could be happening to me! In Pontremoli no one would ever talk to a Donati the way he talked to me! Or say things behind my back."

"Look, Adam—this country is still raw, like some of that grappa Luigi drinks. Napa Valley, particularly, has got a lot of varietals besides grapes. Some don't mix, that's all." Jacob made a grunting, angry sound. "I can't tell you why men the world over seem to want power and more power. Why they can't look around and see nobody really needs to be king of the mountain—the big boss at the top of the ladder. Maybe I'm *too* old. Seen too many harvests come and go. Maybe I think the land, what comes from it, is what's important. Not men, who all die sooner or later. Take Cugnot. Comes from France by way of New Orleans. Says he goes back to nobility, but my guess is he just *wishes* he did and what really happened was his own father came over to get out of prison for cheating somebody in France." He shook his head, biding time to let Adam calm down. "So let's forget about Jacques Cugnot. I'm sorry I brought it up. The real what's what is that this is a harvest celebration. We don't want Lady Luck to hear us talking about Jacques Cugnot."

But Adam was still furious. "This ladder business—I have my own ladder! I'm not stepping on anyone else's rungs and I don't expect anyone to try to step on mine. I came here to do honor to my father's name. To plant the Donati traditions in these hillsides. And I am *proud* to be a Donati. Proud to be the son of Giovanni Donati of Italy.!"

Jacob tried to wave him down to a calmer state. "Look, let's go help Erika pack up her picnic leftovers. I don't want her hearing any of this. She's had enough bad news. Enough trouble for a lifetime. I like to see her happy. See how happy she looks laughing at Kyle Plimpton. Come on—smile for Erika's sake! Let's forget Cugnot. Forget I said what I said. I think Napa Valley needs all the young men like you it can get. We need real men of the *land*—not another bunch of rich hobbyists." He forced a grin. Gave Adam's elbow a nudge. "Okay? *Salute?*"

"*Salute,*" Adam said, trying to return the old man's smile, but his voice was grim, stripped down, as though many of the fruitful buds of his dream had just been severely pruned.

The next day—a Wednesday, the first week of September—Kyle had been at work with his crew of pickers since sunup. When Adam rode up on Hajib to the building site, a huge freight wagon loaded to the top with Rieslings was just pulling out.

"Where are those going?" Adam asked, surprised to find he was late on the job when he had thought, at seven o'clock, he would have been early, ready to begin with the others.

"Krug is usually first in line for these. This year, things being bad for him the way they are, I figured you'd want Inglenook. Next year how about getting contracts signed ahead of time? Make it easier finding the best price." Kyle looked nervous, on edge. "We'll be lucky to bring down twenty-two dollars a ton this year. It don't help—this heat spell bringing the sugar up fast. This is one year you ain't going to get that 'noble rot' on your Rieslings. You sure got yourself some fruit flies, though!" He swiped at his forehead. "I like picking early to beat the fruit flies. And those damn bees! I believe we got Napa Valley's bee population swarming up here on Spring Mountain this year."

A short, stocky Italian, a friend of Vittorio's from Howell Mountain, named Alberto, was driving the big freight wagon pulled by a six-hitch team. He was waiting for Kyle's command to drive on.

Adam frowned. "What's the delay—what's holding this up?"

"We're waiting for Virgil Martin—Fanny's nephew we hired to ride double. Waiting for him to get out here with his loaded shotgun."

Adam, who had been busy staking his stallion to a long rope for grazing, walked over to Kyle, a deep frown burrowing in between his clouded-over blue eyes. "Shotgun? What's that all about?"

Kyle's expression twisted into a fierceness Adam had never seen there before. He lifted his cowboy hat, set it back down squarely on his head. "The word's out that Cugnot's out to get you, one way or another. It won't be the first time he's been known to hit below the belt. So last night Luigi and all us got together and took a vote. We're riding double from now on, all the time. One does the watching the road, one watches the bushes. One of us will be ready if a shotgun is needed!"

Adam took a deep breath, his eyes a steel-cold gray.

"Since when are votes taken behind my back? What else have you been talking about?" His voice fell in a cold, deadly fury. Alberto, who was new on the job, pretended to be absorbed with holding the reins back on a six-hitch that seemed more preoccupied with swishing flies off with busy tails than with lurching into any forward motion.

Kyle looked embarrassed; his face flushed. He took the hat off a second time. This time, however, he held on to it tightly. "Well, we wasn't gonna say anything, but seems he's got Miss Grace all riled up, too. She's running around like a chicken with its head cut off squawking about how you've ruined her daughter's reputation. Cugnot's fault —telling everybody he comes across how he saw you and her in the bushes."

For a moment, a blind white anger made Adam stand as if the shotgun Virgil Martin was carefully aiming toward the ground as he climbed up on the freight wagon was aimed squarely between his eyes. His hand clenched, unclenched.

Kyle spoke in a softer voice. "When you hire *me*—and I can speak for Luigi too—you're hiring more'n common workers. We stick by our boss in every way. We have a lot of respect for you—me and Luigi. Just in case you want to hear that."

96

Adam turned, his back half toward the building site, half toward Kyle. Then he turned again, full face. "Thank you. Well, let's get those grapes down the mountain. They aren't making any money sitting over there."

From that point on, the day went feverishly, with the crew picking until late in the afternoon, and with the second load (this one driven by a Giuseppe Pascoli, who had worked for years in the magnesium mines over in Chiles Valley and was glad to have a new job, even a temporary one, doing what he knew best) being taken to Groesinger's winnery in Yountville.

When Adam got back to Fanny Martin's boardinghouse, he was low-spirited, totally exhausted. Fanny herself met him at the door, holding an envelope. She was a plain, rawboned woman who, like Jacob, didn't waste words. "It was brought here by a Chinaman—one works for the Reynoldses." She whirled on one foot, marched back toward the kitchen. At the doorway, she turned and stared hard at Adam. "I've got me a couple new boarders coming in Sunday, a week from this one coming up. I figure you and that friend of yours from Italy—you'll be moving pretty soon anyway on up to Spring Mountain. Boarders don't come a dime a dozen these days. I've got to look out for number one—like everybody else around here seems to be doing these days."

"I see," Adam said, his hands shaking as he clasped the letter and stared for a moment at the now empty doorway.

Adam took the steps two at a time. He shut the door, fell across the bed and ripped open the letter.

My dearest Adam,

This is being written in extraordinary haste. My mother insists that I leave Napa Valley on Friday. As you might have heard by now, Jacques Cugnot spied on us and is having quite a heyday telling his version of what he saw.

Regardless, I am determined to see you again to say goodbye. My only possible chance would be tomorrow night around six or six-thirty at the bridge. Jacques Cugnot has planned a meeting at that time. If you cannot be there, or if something goes wrong here on my side, please let this letter be our temporary goodbye.

Love,
Sarah H. Reynolds

That night, Adam's restless sleep brought dreams juxtaposed by fitful waking periods, both bringing about kaleidoscopic distortions ranging from the nightmarish to the sublime.

The next morning when he went back up to Spring Mountain he felt ridiculously attired: wearing a necktie, a white shirt, a suit, up to the building site. He carried something else new: a revolver in his saddlebags—though he did not intend to let Kyle or Luigi or any of the varied assortment of newly hired workers know he was doing so.

If anyone noticed his different attire, nothing was said, and any curious looks exchanged took place behind his back. He spent most of the day in the makeshift office inside the finished rooms in the back of the stable—rooms designed for future workmen's steady living quarters.

At sunset, when Luigi and he and Kyle usually joined to ride down the mountain together, he looked up from his crude desk at a puzzled Luigi. "I've got more paperwork. By the way, Fanny Martin has given us notice. Did she tell you?"

Luigi nodded a silent yes. "But I figure we could make do up here. I've got another ten days to add some finishing work. Or is this not right for you?"

Adam looked about. "An excellent idea. Sure—when you have our quarters ready, say so. I'll see about buying some mattresses for the bunk beds. Make out another list." He smiled ironically. "We can't quit making up lists now, Luigi."

"I've been trying to cut back expenses every place I can," the massive, sweat-drenched Luigi said, taking his hat off a nail. "Cesare's got himself a good job lined up for the winter down in Napa City. Found a nice house to rent. Cost less than what he paid for his flat in North Beach, he says. Lots of room. A nice yard, fruit trees. Close to school. He's settling down in Napa Valley. Figures he can start up his own business in due time. He sees the future in lumber—*wood* houses. Being a stonemason over here—it's not the same as back home."

Adam was anxious for Luigi to leave, but he had seen something haunted in his face. "I'm glad your brother sees a good future for himself up here. He's a nice man. I like him." In truth, he found it hard to be around Cesare, who he suspected disliked him for spending his money too fast, for God knows what else. He had enough worries. But he wanted Luigi to stay happy, and part of that would depend on Cesare's state of mind. "I guess you're pleased to have him up here. Does that mean you'll be staying after you finish my place?"

Luigi shrugged his shoulders. "I used to think it would be different. Stonemasonry—that's what I know. I'm one of the best. Even Cesare will tell you that. You'd think it couldn't be—what did Cesare call it?—'a dying art,' not in a brand-new country like this one." He put on his hat, started out to get on his horse. At the door, he called out more cheerfully, "In Europe, though, we don't have trees like they've got over here. Like Cesare says, use what's at hand. Take advantage. Don't put on mule blinders to new opportunities."

"A talented stonemason such as you—you'll always be needed in this valley, Luigi," Adam called after him, not liking the dispirited look on his friend's face.

Luigi looked at him for a long moment. "I guess time and Lady Luck will tell us what this Napa Valley needs out of us. You want me to tell Fanny Martin you're coming late? To save you some supper?"

Adam thumped his pencil on the stack of papers. "I expect to be there around nine o'clock. I'll skip tonight's mashed potatoes and gravy, thank you."

"Nine o'clock, huh? Then I won't worry about you till after nine," Luigi said, as if knowing what was really up.

As soon as Luigi's and Kyle's horses had clomped out of hearing distance, Adam quickly mounted Hajib and headed toward the back trail. He rode with the easy style of a man who had been taught the finesse of fine riding.

The shadows cast in front of him seemed to glow with the orange-pink from the muted sunset. Across the valley, in those spots where the trail opened up and gave him a view, the vineyards seemed bathed in a soft blue hue. Birds were sending out their last-minute trills of the day, making the woods echo with their songs. A soft breeze blew across his face. The leather saddle squeaked, swayed beneath him as he adjusted himself, pulling at the vest, the rather tight suit jacket, from where the hard summer's work had expanded his muscles.

After he had passed the clearing where Jacques Cugnot had stopped him with the gun that day—where instead he now saw a herd of deer grazing, who paused to stare at him with startled, on-guard eyes the size of black walnuts—he began to relax, to anticipate meeting Sarah.

Then he had reached the top of the slope above the bridge, where he dismounted, secured his stallion, eased his way down alongside the barn built back into the hillside.

She was leaning back against the tree trunk, wearing her riding habit, blending in with the background so well that at first he had not seen her. Then she looked up, called out softly, her voice lilting, "Here —oh, I'm so glad to see you!" She hurried to meet him. "Let's go down here by the creek bed—a special hiding place of mine since I was a little girl."

As he followed her down the moss-covered bank to the place

beneath the bridge, he felt his own heart hammering like Luigi's chisel against a piece of granite.

They sat down, their knees drawn up in a cramped position. He had not needed to wear a necktie and suit, he was thinking ironically. And then he was leaning back against the stone bulwark, staring at her beautiful profile in the flattering, muted light of an early dusk. He could not stop looking at her.

She spoke first. "I thought you wouldn't come. I have been here since five-forty-five. It seems like hours." She reached out, traced one finger along the strong line of his chin.

He wanted to pull her down against the damp mossy place beside him, never let her up, away from his need of her. Neither of them touched after that one brief moment of her finger on his chin. It was as if they did not dare.

"I won't see you again until next year—until 1895! That sounds like an eternity away, doesn't it?"

"It's not quite an entire year," he said huskily. "We will write a lot of letters." But just then the dusk played magic with her face. He could not resist. They melted into each other, and then she was pulling back.

"No—we won't do this," she said matter-of-factly, buttoning her blouse where his fingers had been working. "We will wait until we can be married."

"Until we are introduced?" he had attempted to say with his former lightheartedness. He stared gloomily at the water in the stream near his feet.

"I love you, Adam," she said softly.

" 'Love' is a strange word," he said, more to himself. "It is more like that phylloxera beetle—eating away at the roots. Maybe it is not such a good word." He wanted so desperately to reach for her again. He felt his entire being pounding with frustration, with its own volcanic force of desire.

Suddenly quiet tears were rolling down her lovely face. "There's so much against us, Adam," she said forlornly. "They—tonight, that meeting . . . Jacques Cugnot is telling them how you have . . . He made up things about us here—when he saw us under the tree. He made it sound as if more happened than actually did. And my mother—she accused me. She . . ." the tears kept coming. "For the first time in my life she slapped me. Called me names. Made me feel as if I'm a common . . . a . . . ." She buried her face against him. "I'm glad I'm going! Maybe by the time I get back things will have quieted down. Maybe

Monique's husband will make Jacques feel important again and he'll forget us. Maybe I will forgive my mother. She will be less bullheaded. Though she won't ever forget that I told her I love you. I did, you know."

In spite of his agony, Adam felt his heart jump. "We won't worry about your mother. About what Cugnot says! I will go on and finish the house. My bride's house—for you. When you get back next summer we will get married. If she will not give her permission—if you still love me—"

"I know that I can't help that, Adam."

"Then what will stop us?"

"I don't know. But I—I get so afraid sometimes. I feel so helpless. That she—that my mother is so set in her ways she won't let me do anything except what she has mapped out for me."

They were both silent. He placed his hand lightly on hers, and they stared down into the dim shadows beneath the small bridge.

"Adam, if it works out, if we ever have children of our own, let's be so very good to them! Let's not put them inside our own ropes, keep them from having the freedom they deserve. Mothers—do they always hold their children down in some way? Or *am* I terrible? *Am* I those names she called me?"

"You are the woman I love," he said simply. "You are going to be my wife. That is the important thing for us to remember. Now maybe you should go. I don't want you to have any more trouble because of me."

They got out, stood for a moment getting rid of the cramps in their stiff legs. He kissed her one last time, found it unbearable to let her go.

"Please be careful, Adam," she called out to him as he started slowly climbing the steep incline toward his horse. "I don't trust Jacques Cugnot. He has never been a very nice man. Monique was my best friend. She used to tell me that he was mean. Mean to her mother. Mean behind people's backs. That he was one thing in public, another behind closed doors. You cannot turn your back on him."

"You mustn't worry. You will write? Send your letters in care of Vittorio Alfieri, general delivery, at St. Helena. That way, no one will ever know. Okay?" he called down to her.

"Yes—oh, yes," she said. "Goodbye, Adam." And then she was hurrying to mount the chestnut mare, was galloping away.

"*Arrivederla . . . arrivederci,*" he called after her in a husky whisper.

．　．

That first week after Sarah was gone from Napa Valley was the most difficult one for Adam. But the harvest was still not completed. A late hot spell—Indian Summer, the natives called it—had brought even the normally late-ripening Cabernets up to excellent sugar levels, so there was no lull in the picking.

From time to time, Adam would walk to the edge of the vineyards, stare out in the general direction of the Reynolds place down midvalley. He had never experienced such turbulence. He felt alternately ill, alternately the most alive he had ever been in his life.

He tried to keep a rational outlook on what was taking place on Spring Mountain. On the gloomy side, the harvest was not bringing in the kind of money he had hoped to get. Somewhat more positively, the tension seemed to be easing up about any impending threat from Jacques Cugnot. Kyle had remarked that he had heard a rumor that Jacques's lawyer had told him he didn't have a legal leg to stand on, but that Jacques still spouted off now and then about how he wasn't through with Adam Donati, he had his ways.

As the harvest tapered off, the crew began to change. More and more Adam discovered that his workmen were Italian. Word had spread among them about Adam Donati being rich; that he was hiring men. Word had also spread through their own special grapevine that Jacques Cugnot had declared himself Adam Donati's enemy. It was unspoken on Spring Mountain, but it was apparent to Adam that the Italians had decided, as Luigi put it, to stick together.

And in its way he found it comforting. More and more he was falling back into his native language. He enjoyed hearing Italians' laughter, their voices breaking out in bursts of songs, their sharing of a common jug of grappa. Though it was not the same as the Donati estate in Pontremoli, there was a certain ring of familiarity. And when he went into the vineyards, saw the lugboxes of grapes being tossed into the freight wagons, heard the rumble of wheels and the crack of the driver's whip, when he smelled that thick, half-sweet, half-sour smell of ripened grapes, he realized that harvests were essentially the same the world over.

But he missed the actual crush. He longed to have his own winery in operation. Have his first true Donati vintage! He mustn't rush that aspect of it, though. Winemaking was, in one way, one of the simplest processes; in another, it had the nuances of needing a master's hand, of needing every process to *work*—including the magic, as Kyle said, of Lady Luck's hand on your head.

Luigi announced that their living quarters would be ready before the final deadline Fanny Martin—who made no pretense now of liking them—had given them. On Friday and Saturday the workmen were brought down to help move out all the stored equipment and cooperage Adam had bought at the distress sales and kept in Fanny Martin's barn.

Though Vittorio Alfieri normally didn't work on Saturdays, saving that day to tend his own vegetable gardens and do chores around his house, he pitched in that morning. "It doesn't take much time to collect a lot of stuff. Buy maybe too much things." Then he smiled apologetically; reached in his back pocket.

"I almost forgot—you got a letter." He handed the envelope with a Boston postmark to Adam.

They had been standing at the front steps to the boardinghouse, where Adam had one last trip to make, going inside to pick up his packed valises and a few boxes of loose belongings. An unsmiling, stiff-backed Fanny Martin stood at the front door, watching every move.

"I see you got a letter. Handwriting looks familiar." When he didn't volunteer anything, but started up the stairs, she shot out after him, "Be sure you don't leave anything behind! Pick up after yourself. My new boarders are coming in early on Sunday."

Adam took a deep breath. "Miss Martin, I trust I've thanked you sufficiently for your many kindnesses?" His voice cut like a knife. "But I'm somewhat concerned, and since in my country it is customary to leave a gratuity for servants and the like, I have this twenty-dollar gold piece. Shall I give it to you now or leave it in my room?"

Fanny Martin's finger shot out like a pointed gun. "No Dago talks to *me* in that tone of voice, even if you think you can go around this valley defiling our nice girls! You get your things and get out of my house in five minutes' time or I'll get my nephew Virgil to go get the sheriff and throw you out! And don't think Miss Grace wouldn't like to know about that letter you crammed in your pocket. Ha!—you didn't think I saw that little squirrely friend of yours slip it over to you!"

Adam stormed up the stairs, got his things, charged back down, his arms loaded. Fanny Martin was waiting, her arms crossed over her flat chest.

"I'll have you know, furthermore, that I ain't *nobody's* servant! But you can just put that twenty-dollar gold piece right there on that side table. I figure it'll cost me that much hiring a scrubwoman to get rid of the traces of you and that greasy bear of a man you drug in here with you!"

Adam's knuckles were white. But he managed to march out, dropped the gold piece down, pleased that it fell to the floor and that she would have to stoop to pick it up. He slung things into the phaeton; tried to keep his hands loose on Hajib's reins.

Though Adam longed to read Sarah's letter, he did not open it until he had unpacked and settled into the bunk room of his choice in the back of the new stone stable. While Kyle and Luigi and three other workers who decided to live permanently on the premises—Paulo, Giuseppe and Antonio, all former workers in the magnesium mines in Chiles Valley—were deciding on bunks and getting settled, he closed his door, slid the new bolt lock into place, and went over to his bunk.

A brandy, poured into a tin cup, which Kyle had offered him as a toast to their new living quarters, was in his hand. He sipped, let the liquid warm him. As he tore open Sarah's letter, his fingers felt as if they had lost their strength.

DEAREST ADAM,

I am trying to imagine you in your sunny Napa Valley. Here in Boston, we are already shivering and snow is a possibility.

But I am not writing to discuss the weather. I am writing hoping to bring back those sharp clear edges of memory—of certainty about us. These past lonely weeks have been dreadful ones for me. I have tried to keep cast aside that gray shadow of disgrace—my mother assures me that I am a *walking disgrace* forever and ever in Napa Valley! I try to find those little framed mirrors in my mind that bring into perfect focus the reflection of your blue eyes, your strong, straight nose, your stubborn jaw. I try, at other times, to make myself forget how it was, your holding me, the way we knew—oh, we knew so much about each other that day! I try to think about the sound of the water under the bridge. How I searched to find my old friend Moses the crawdad backed into his little castle there. I try to remember only the lovely things and forget about Jacques Cugnot and the ugly lies he has told. I try to forget my mother's having slapped me. I try to think of her good intent; tell myself that she did what she felt was right.

It is not always easy. Before I met you, there was a man in my life. Though I never felt for him those same feelings that have torn my life apart over you, I did see a lot of him. He has, in the past, asked me on several occasions to marry him. His name is Christopher Elliot-Weare.

I am telling you about Chris because, even now that he knows

I have fallen desperately in love with you, he insists that I postpone saying a positive no to him until the year is over. Because his mother and my mother are friends from their childhood days down South, the matter is further complicated. Mother is writing urgent letters to his mother to get me to visit New York as a guest of the Elliot-Weares this coming Thanksgiving. I have little choice in the matter. I tell you this because I suspect that my mother will see that this item appears in the *St. Helena Star*, which will be *her* way of reminding Napa Valley of her contacts in the world and just who her daughter really is. I would not want you to read about it in the newspaper and not understand what is behind it.

I have no intentions of marrying Chris. He is a charming man. Bright, wealthy. He has credentials my mother adores. But I love you, Adam. I pray to your god Bacchus—I pray to all the gods of all people and to some nebulous force out there *I* believe is God, that this year will pass swiftly and that by this time next year, I will be your wife.

> Love,
> SARAH H. REYNOLDS

Adam sat on the edge of the bunk, the letter fixed in his hands. He was torn with jealousy. With a frustration he had never dreamed possible. He grabbed the cup of brandy, drained it down.

Patience—hadn't his father always stressed that word as being the most cardinal, necessary word in any language for a viticulturist? He had no patience these days, Adam thought, looking about at the partially completed bunkhouse. He saw the space where the stovepipe dangled loosely against the flue. "I'll get that taken care of tomorrow," Luigi had said. Everyplace he looked he saw something that would "get taken care of as soon as we can get to it"—which was the problem! Nails half driven in by Vittorio Alfieri, a reminder to Vittorio to return for the less needed finishing details. Caulking splashed across windows hastily put in—"We'll get that cleaned off as soon as we get the roof on the main house."

Not any one job was totally finished. Everything was "in progress." It was all such a sharp contrast—this cracked mirror of reality, to that orderly, finished dream he had painted so brightly and framed so neatly in his mind's eye.

Kyle Plimpton knocked at his door. "Hey, Adam, we've got some supper together out here in the mess hall. Want to come try out the famous Plimpton Saturday-night hash? 'Mule stew' is what Luigi called it." He laughed, waited for Adam's response. "The new boys living with us now from over in Chiles Valley brought two gallons of Nichelini wine and some of that good bread Nichelini's wife Marie bakes."

Though that first supper in the Spring Mountain bunkhouse was a jovial occasion, Adam decided then and there that the next essential line of duty was to hire a permanent chef.

"We can't let you waste your talents in the mess hall," he told Kyle when the last of the second gallon of wine had been depleted. "Where do I go to find a good chef—someone who will keep this bunkhouse clean, too?" He was still secretly chafing from Fanny Martin's implication that he and Luigi had been dirty. "We've got to keep a new shine to the place."

Kyle scratched his head, whirled the rich red burgundy around and around in the bottom of his tin cup. "Well, my advice is to try first off at St. Helena's China Camp. Go to Old Lee's store. He's the only one down there who reads and writes English. Runs a kind of Chinese bank of his own, they tell me. Gives out credit and writes up contracts for some of those ragtags left. Not so many Chinese around as there used to be." He squinted his eyes. "If that don't work, you could go on down to Rutherford, look up Man Sing at his store. But don't let China Mary grab hold of you! She might win Spring Mountain off you in a gambling game."

Adam twisted an end piece from a long loaf of crusty Italian bread very similar to that he had eaten most of his life. "You suggest this Mr. Lee, then?"

" 'Old Lee' is what everybody calls him. He'll most likely make you sign a contract and put up some front money if he does have anybody to hire out. He's set hisself up to look after his people, I reckon —ever since back around 1886 when some hotheads started a St. Helena chapter of the Anti-Chinese League. Didn't take Old Lee long to wise up." He shook his head, leaned back in the simple cane-bottomed chair. "Some people around here still think they can ride herd over 'em. But it ain't easy like it used to be. Not with Justice Bell cracking a whip of his own lately. 'Bout time we had somebody not afraid to send some of these culprits to jail, give 'em a stiff fine. I read in the newspaper the other week where Justice Bell said he was't gonna let a nice place like St. Helena turn lawless, where a man, even a heathen, couldn't walk down a sidewalk and feel safe."

The next Monday, around noon, Adam drove down Spring Mountain and looked up the man Kyle insisted was "Old Lee." He found him hunched over a long wooden counter in a narrow, low-ceilinged hut of a building. The counter was loaded down with jars of spices, ginger candy, rice, sugar and an array of Chinese goods unfamiliar to Adam.

"Mr. Lee?" Adam ventured, his hat in his hand.

The man looked up curiously. He was wearing a small black satin skullcap with a knob the size of a walnut perched on top. He quickly reached up and removed the cap, held it in both parchment-looking hands, and bowed. The light was poor inside the cramped, scarcely ventilated room, but Adam saw the intensity in the eyes that seemed to bear like black holes into his own.

As explicitly as possible, he explained the type of help he was seeking. "The accommodations I can offer now aren't the best by any means," he apologized. "I myself, along with some of my workmen, are living in the bunk rooms that are still undergoing some finishing details. But by this time next year, I should be moving into my large home, where I believe I will offer comparably the best there is in Napa Valley. I want someone interested in long-term employment. Someone honest. Who will be loyal. Who will work hard. I would prefer a good cook—someone who will also do cleaning and some laundry. Do you have anyone?"

The old man had not wavered his steady gaze at Adam. He bowed again, backed a few steps, pulled aside a thick dull curtain, spoke in rapid Chinese. In a moment a very young-looking boy—Adam guessed he could not be more than eleven or twelve years old—wearing clothing identical to the old man's, his black eyes showing the same intensity and alertness, came forward, bowed.

"This is my nephew, Li Po. I teach him many things. He is soon fourteen. He can work for you. But first we try two weeks. You pay only two dollars first two weeks. But if it works out—you like him, he like you—one dollar a day. We sign paper."

He brought forth a written-out contract form. "I make everybody sign," he said matter-of-factly. "Have room for special terms. For my nephew, he must be free to come here to stay with me. You bring him here every other Saturday morning. Li Po came back to your place on Sunday by one o'clock. I see to it he gets back."

Adam nodded in agreement, all the time curiously studying the young face staring so intently at him, the expression coming from those black eyes seeming to belong to a much older man. The thin arms, the small graceful hands holding the black satin skullcap seemed lost dangling from the huge loose sleeves of his black Chinese jacket. His thinly braided queue was not as long as his uncle's, Adam noticed. But the most striking peculiarity was the way his small ears seemed stuck on the sides of his head, as though designed to jut out a little farther to pick up added nuances of sounds.

The uncle was now looking puzzled. He was afraid Adam had not understood his terms. He was, in turn, looking Adam up and down, taking careful note of the gray-striped suit, the pearl stickpin, the leather spats, the handsome face so cleanly shaved. He had heard about the young rich Italian on Spring Mountain. He had not expected him to look like this. On two occasions, Italian miners, back in the early days when he had worked in Chiles Valley, had befriended him, kept a whip off his legs. "I must continue training my nephew how to mix special herbs. He is not a full herb doctor yet. He must study other things."

"The terms are suitable," Adam said quite formally. "When shall we begin the two-week trial period? I need help now, badly."

"You nice man. I like your people. They laugh. Have good faces." The man's head bobbed up and down fiercely. "I see you have honest face. I need two, three hours to instruct my nephew. Fix supplies. Do you have some jobs to do in town? Excuse us two, three hours?"

Adam spent the time drifting in and out of stores on Main Street. He went to the bank and withdrew more funds to meet the coming week's payroll. Then drifted into the hotel dining room for a drawn-out cup of tea.

When he got back to China Camp, the old man and his young nephew hobbled out carrying a huge wooden trunk, a leather-covered smaller one, and a lugbox filled with various pots and pans, carefully packed bottles of special herbs with labels in Chinese, and something wrapped in a richly embroidered silk cloth. When Adam offered to help, he was waved aside, as though he had done something wrong. Then, the loading up finished, the old man was waving up at him, as if bidding him goodbye. Adam looked around for Li Po; did not see him.

"He rides on back of carriage."

"Why can't he ride up here with me? I'd enjoy his company going up Spring Mountain."

The black eyes beamed with pleasure. The old man muttered something in Chinese to Li Po, who scrambled from his perch on top of the luggage rack and into the leather-covered front seat of the phaeton. "You will be good to my nephew," Old Lee said matter-of-factly, stuffing his hands inside his flapping sleeves and bowing low.

5

Li Po's adjustment to Spring Mountain's bunkhouse seemed, from all appearances, to go well. Kyle, Luigi and the three good-natured Italians from Chiles Valley treated him with warm good humor and from time to time gave him helpful advice. Kyle urged him to use more salt in the food; Luigi asked for less grease. But his cooking was a decided improvement over Kyle's efforts, everyone concluded.

In the one small room Adam assigned to Li Po, he had quickly arranged his wares, spread out his mat he used for a bed, and in one corner set up a small altar, where each day the smell of incense would sift through the bunkhouse. Adam did not question Li Po about anything pertaining to his private life. He had observed that the silk-embriodered cloth was part of the altar. But after taking that one look to see if Li Po was settled in or needed anything more for warmth—there being no potbelly stove in that particular room—he had fully respected his privacy.

The two-week trial period passed swiftly. Hammers pounded, saws ripped through lumber, more windows were put into place. At night the men ate, drank the Nichelini wine, exchanged jokes and stories. Bedtime came early.

Then came the Saturday morning when Li Po was due back. Adam drove him down on promised schedule, tended some errands, and returned to Spring Mountain. But on Sunday, by three o'clock, Li Po had not returned.

It was a brisk, chilly November Sunday afternoon. An early-morning misty rain had blanketed the mountain with a gray dampness. The valley floor below was heavy with fog in the morning and had only begun to clear just about the time Li Po had been expected back at the bunkhouse.

Kyle and Luigi had built a good crackling fire in the one open fireplace in the main mess hall that had become their overall gathering place. Kyle had been sitting in a cane-bottom chair, propped back, a thin piece of cedar in his crippled hand, whittling with his left, good one—a habit he had purposely developed to increase more precise use of it. Luigi had been hunched over one of the eating tables, his arms spread out over the blueprints turned over to him by the architect, trying as best he could to sort out first things first and schedule the coming week's work. Adam, getting restless, had taken Hajib out for a long racing ride, practicing jumps, now that Hajib was well again and had only recently demonstrated to Adam that he was a natural jumper. The other three men were not expected back until close to dark, since they had gone, on Saturday, to Chiles Valley to visit relatives still living in the area, and—on order from Adam—to bring back a good stock of Marie Nichelini's Italian bread and enough jug wine to last the week.

Kyle suddenly flipped the shaved-down stick of cedar into the fire, closed his pocketknife, stretched his long, thin raillike body, and said to Luigi, "Wonder where that young Chinaman Li Po is? Ain't he overdue? I thought *one* o'clock was the time Adam said to expect him back." He let out a long, sleepy yawn.

Luigi looked up curiously, tapped his pencil against the tabletop. "You're right about that. He is late. Did Adam say there was any question? He was here on a tryout. Maybe he didn't want to put up with our rough talk. You'd never know—he stays so quiet. Back there burning those sticks."

"But it ain't like Old Lee to go back on his word. He'd have said something to let Adam know." Kyle worked his crippled arm slowly into his field jacket, rammed his left arm through solidly. "You don't reckon we ought to ride down the mountain aways and see if we see him coming? Some fresh air—wouldn't a little do us both some good? Wake us up a little?"

Luigi got up, went to the hooks where his red-plaid wool jacket was hanging. "We can hitch up my buggy. It's got a good solid top—case it starts raining again," he said in his deep voice, as if there was no question about going.

"Might as well take along the shotgun," Kyle said, trying to sound casual. "Maybe we'll run across a good tender rabbit for some stew. Find us a fine fat wild turkey."

Both men had a serious, determined look as they went out into the main stable. They decided on taking Luigi's own more dependable dappled mare rather than the newer stallion Adam had asked them to work out any chance they got. "A day like this, I want to know my horse," Luigi said quietly, hitching up quickly—much more quickly than usual.

Kyle sat on the edge of the seat, the shotgun perched across his knees, the barrel safely aimed out toward the side. "Sure is foggy out," he said, as they drove down the mountain at a steady clip. "Fact is, it's right hard to see down here in some of those real low spots, down there in the ravines," he said, keeping a steady watchful eye as Luigi took the mare around a sharp hairpin curve.

Suddenly Kyle flung out his crippled arm. "Hold it a minute," he said, his voice dropping in a hushed way. "What's that noise?"

Luigi drew the mare to a stop, sat still, listening through the sounds of the gurgling creek rushing down the mountainside and the scraping of branches being tossed this way and that by the wind.

"*Hear* it?" Kyle said, his good hand tightening on the shotgun.

And then came the unmistakable moaning. A high-pitched wail. "Damned if I didn't!" Kyle said, jumping down to the roadbed. "It's down here in the hollow! Tie 'er up—come on," he yelled back to Luigi, already on his way, scrambling, sliding, gaining a foothold, working his way through dense undergrowth to get to the sounds. "It's me—Kyle Plimpton! Who's down here?" Kyle yelled out, cupping his hand to his mouth. He listened. Then came the crashing sounds of Luigi half falling, half tumbling his way down.

The moment Kyle had identified himself, the moaning turned into a shrieking, hysterical cry. Both Kyle and Luigi saw at the same instant the terror-stricken face of young Li Po—his arms bound behind him, the blood running down his face on one side from a cut under one eye and from under his nose that had been hit with somebody's driving fist.

"Okay—hold on there, fellow," Kyle was saying in a soothing voice, working his way as easily as possible toward him. "Here—nobody's gonna hurt you. I'm gonna cut you loose. We'll take care of you."

Li Po was too frightened to speak. As soon as his hands were free, he began pointing wildly toward the pile of rocks on down by the creek. Finally he blurted out, "Wang Chi—Wang Chi!"

"Jacob Brunner's old Chinaman?" Kyle cried out, passing Li Po over into the big comforting arms of Luigi, who had already taken out a handkerchief and was wiping away some of the blood, trying to check the extent of Li Po's injuries. His hands, as big and as thick as they were, moved gently. Sensing this, Li Po seemed to regain his voice.

"I tried to make them stop," he squealed, tears running down his face. "It was Wang Chi—they would not stop whipping, kicking him. They hit me when I got in his place. I tried to make them stop! They laugh and laugh . . ." And then his frail shoulders seemed to cave in and the hysteria ebbed into deep, body-racking sobs.

Luigi patted him awkwardly, straining all the while to see what was happening with Kyle, who now yelled at the top of his voice.

"Luigi—come 'ere! Help me carry him out. He's half-dead-looking. Maybe we ought to— Those sonsabitches! Goddam bastards who did this to this poor old Chinaman!"

"Sit here—stay right here by this rock," Luigi told the still-sobbing Li Po. "I gotta help Kyle out a minute." He stumbled, crashed through the thick bushes toward the pile of rocks and Kyle's voice.

"They just dumped him here for dead," Kyle said, his face white with shock setting in. "Wonder he didn't land face down in the creek bed and drown. Look—his arm's sure broke. His jawbone—ain't that broke, too?"

For a moment Luigi did not speak. His whole massive body seemed to go through a vibration of disbelief. Then he seemed to come to, snap into action in the manner he had been taught by his father in Genoa in case a man fell from a scaffolding or was hurt in any way on a masonry job, as did happen all too many times. He was taking the same blood-soaked handkerchief, wrapping it, pulling it up under the sagging chin, trying to bring the jaw back into line. He asked Kyle to find two smooth sticks for a splint. Took Kyle's red bandana handkerchief and one of his own shoelaces and tried to bring the arm into a straighter line. Wang Chi groaned, one arm flailed weakly, then dropped back into limpness.

"He's unconscious—but 'least he's alive," Kyle mumbled. "Luigi, how we gonna get him back up that bank?"

Luigi was arleady bending over, lifting the crumpled, mangled form as though it were a child. "Find the easiest place to climb. Get that young fellow. Help him," Luigi said, the way he might give orders to a workman during a delicate part of a masonry job. "Take it easy— okay? Lead the way."

They made it up the bank, got into the buggy and propped Wang Chi between them, with Li Po on Kyle's lap. Luigi took the reins.

"Do we head back up Spring Mountain? What is best?"

Kyle's eyes widened. "Damned if we risk riding down like this— they might think we did it. Let's head back and find Adam. He ought to be back from his ride by now. He'll know."

Adam had just given Hajib that last freeing pat on his flanks and was carrying the bridle in his hands and heading back to the bunkhouse when he heard the buggy coming and Luigi's bellow, "Adam—wait! We need help."

The tone of Luigi's voice told him there was trouble. Adam's whole body tensed as he broke into a run and met them at the doors to the stable.

For a moment, the sight of the bloodied Wang Chi and the look of horror etched inside those black eyes of Li Po's, the blood still trickling from the wound under his eye, made Adam gasp, draw back with a wave of dizziness. A hard sick knot jumped inside his stomach. But he fought through the shock and sprang into action. "Get them inside—my bunk. *Easy*—who *did* this?" he asked in a whisper as he lifted the sagging limp form of Wang Chi and helped Luigi get him inside the bunkhouse.

Kyle brought in Li Po, set him down on the opposite bunk across from where Luigi was easing out Wang Chi's legs, trying to get him in a straight line.

"Might have a broken bone someplace we can't see," Luigi said, rechecking the splint he had put on the obviously broken arm. "We need a doctor fast. But we thought—"

"We thought somebody might think we did it—that we might get jumped going on down the mountain," Kyle put in, his face still white.

Adam was fighting his rush of emotions: anger, confusion, a deep hurting worry that Wang Chi might die, a sense of shame—a shame he didn't quite understand—and a guilt that lashed at him like a cat-o'-nine-tails. "Yes, and we must let Jacob Brunner know. The sheriff—we must get him up here. Kyle, are you up to it?"

Luigi got up. "We'll both go. We'll saddle up your better horses."

Adam went across and poured out two quick brandies, handed the tin cups to Luigi and Kyle in turn. "Drink it. You need it." He went back to Wang Chi, stared down at the moaning, crumpled man and saw suddenly that the long queue had been chopped off. The rage nearly blinded him. "Look—his hair!" he said, barely able to speak now.

"If we find out who did it they'll get that cut-off piece of plaited hair stuffed down their throat, tied like a noose around their goddam necks!" Kyle stormed.

Adam saw tears on Li Po's cheeks again. With relief, he saw that the boy's hair had not been touched. He went to him, put his arms around the trembling shoulders. "I am so sorry. You are safe now. We will see that the men who did this are punished. Did you hear any names? Do you know them? Do you feel like telling me before the sheriff comes?"

"J.T. I hear that. I don't know what J.T. means. I hear Frenchman's name. I can't say. 'Dago'—they say that over and over. 'Dago' . . ." He was sobbing again.

Kyle, Luigi and Adam exchanged white-faced, grim looks. "I know who J.T. is!" Kyle said, his voice more like a thin rasping sound. "I know that lowdown snake in the grass from way back when." He had the shotgun under his arm, the barrel pointed toward the floor. "Come on, Luigi."

By dark, the bunkhouse was alive with men's voices, with the moaning outcries from Wang Chi when the doctor resplinted the broken arm correctly and rearranged the misplaced jaw. While the worst part was taking place, Kyle, Luigi, the sheriff and the three wide-eyed Italians who had just returned from their trip to Chiles Valley sat uncomfortably around the fireplace in the mess hall.

Jacob Brunner came in, stalked out a small circle of his own. He had just insisted that the doctor give Wang Chi a shot to relieve the pain, but had run into resistance: "Jacob, it might kill him—the shock. He's an old man. He can't handle it."

At that moment, Li Po's uncle slid in behind Jacob, whispered to him, "I give Wang Chi some special powder when the doctor goes to wash up." Then, quickly, he was gone back to the bunkroom to look after his nephew and Wang Chi, who was sleeping now.

Jacob doubled up a gnarled fist, shook it in the air. "They won't get by with this!" He glared at the sheriff. "If I have to go to the highest courts in this country—and I *will*—the culprits will be punished. Where is law and order around here, Sheriff?" His voice quavered with rage.

The sheriff, a loose-jointed, open-faced man who had lived his lifetime in Napa Valley, flipped a hand-rolled cigarette into the ashes of the fireplace. "Now, come on, calm down, Jacob. We don't want you working yourself into a stroke here. Let *me* tend to law and order. That's what I was elected for. That's my job."

At that moment, Adam and the doctor entered the room.

Jacob then turned toward Adam, narrowed his eyes. "Why would they take out their spite on you, on *my* old Chinaman?"

Adam threw his hands out helplessly. "How could they take it out on any one of them? What is this about?" His eyes were wide with the shock now working its delayed reactions. His body felt limp, torn apart in another way.

Jacob glared at him. "I've lived next door to Jacques Cugnot too many years. I know he told half the people in Napa Valley he was out to get you. When he saw he couldn't get to you through his lawyer, he figured out the best way he knew where you couldn't hit back." His face was shaking with rage, his faded blue eyes ringed with white fury. "Cugnot always hits below the belt. He knows the word is out now that he barely missed getting the sheriff's lock on all his property. That so-called new son-in-law's money s'posed to get in his open pockets hasn't come to his rescue. He's flat broke—and the long and short of it is that everybody knows it now. He can't fool anybody any longer. He struck a blow in the only weak spot left open to him."

The men were awkwardly silent a moment. The sizzling damp log Kyle had tossed onto the fire made a loud hissing and popping noise. Jacob Brunner was not quite finished. He pointed a finger straight at Adam. "What did you expect here in Napa Valley—a garden of Eden?"

The sheriff made a move to take over the center of attention. "Now, everybody listen here." His huge bony Adam's apple worked up and down vigorously. "Just everybody get off the high horse! I want every one of you to know that I didn't come all the way up here to settle another brawl. I wantcha to know that my family came across this country in a covered wagon to find law and order. I'm living up to helping keep it. I swore on a Bible on my mama's deathbed I'd uphold the *law*. Now I want it said here and now, I am plain sick and tired of seeing it happen over and over where a man gets shoved around and kicked and whipped on just because he's this color or that. I helped run the Ku Klux Klanners out of here. I helped break the backs of that anti-Chinese chapter. I kept more'n one arson fire from setting off China Camp in St. Helena. I don't condone this kind of stuff!" He hit the palm of one hand with the doubled-up fist of the other. "You got to realize *one* thing—ain't everybody in St. Helena and Napa Valley stands for this violence. Good people around these parts outnumber the bad—the same the world over, in my opinion."

Old Lee, who had just come into the room again, having taken a quick inspection of Li Po—sleeping now from an herb medicine of Lee's own secret concoction administered to him earlier—dug his hands deeply inside his flapping sleeves, bowed, then looked at the sheriff through narrowed eyes. "*My* people don't know this. They get plain sick and tired, too. Many go back to China. Give up all the way. Some go to San Francisco. Find plenty of our own people there." He nodded toward the three Italians who were now sitting in a row in cane-bottomed chairs on one side of the main eating table. "My people stick side by side, too." He looked around slowly. "I try to teach my nephew good and bad. You are good men. I leave Li Po here. He stay with you." He looked staight at Adam. "From now on you look after my nephew. Keep him safe. I am old man. I got money saved up. A little nest egg. I go to San Francisco. Sell my store now."

Jacob Brunner took a deep breath. The doctor, who had slipped back into the bunk room to check on Wang Chi, came back in, snapped his leather bag closed.

"When can I take Wang Chi back to my place?" Jacob asked stiffly. "Is it okay to move him now?"

The doctor thought a moment. "Might be a good idea—before the opium wears off. He gave Lee a knowing, disapproving look. "That is, if you've got a flatbed—something where he's stretched out and rides as comfortably as possible." He folded his stethoscope, put it into his coat pocket. "He'll be sore a few days. Bring him in to my office in about ten days. Sooner, if anything worries you about him."

"I'll escort you down the mountain," the sheriff said, putting on his coat, reaching for his hat, adjusting the guns strapped to his waist.

Jacob looked around. "Maybe your men can hitch up, then," he said to Adam. "Get something soft in the back of your buckboard." As Paulo, Giuseppe and Alberto hurried out to get the buckboard ready, Jacob turned to the sheriff again. "When Wang Chi has recovered—as soon as he is strong enough—I'll expect you to come by my place and take a statement. I want formal statements from every man here. I'm warning you *now*—I'm going to the highest courts, if I have to, to see that justice is done. That whoever did this to my Chinaman is punished. And that goes for Jacques Cugnot! I've had enough from that sonofabitch through the years. This is the last straw. This time, *I'm* going after Cugnot. This time he's stepped his big flat foot on the wrong territory."

"Didn't I tell everybody to calm down—take it easy?" The sheriff buttoned his jacket. "I can't promise you action in one day. I can't even say we can get all the goods on Cugnot—*if* Cugnot proves guilty, as you claim, Jacob. But I can promise you this, I'll gather every scrap of evidence and we will take it through the due process of law."

Kyle shoved a chair back with the toe of his boot. "Better start off then with J. T. Price and that lice-headed Vern Woods! And if *you* don't, somebody else sure will."

"Listen to me, Kyle, how many times have I seen you one foot out of the clinker? You and that hot temper of yours, back in your bender days?" The sheriff's face was grim. "You've got a good thing going for you now, up here working for Mr. Donati. I know you've had your bad breaks in life. But you've carried that chip around on your shoulder long enough. Keep it knocked off. You'll get along fine without it.

People think a lot of you—pulling yourself around, stopping drinking and all, holding down a nice steady job as foreman. You remember that before you start going around with a nervous trigger finger or some other dumb idea!"

"And I'm just telling *you*, Sheriff, that it seems to me like nobody does much around here enforcing law and order."

The sheriff's neck muscles tightened. He put his hands into his outside jacket pockets, stared hard at Kyle. "I'll tell you what I've done, so far. I've given Cugnot a warning myself—back a while ago when he was spouting off about Mr. Donati here and the Reynolds girls. I told him to watch out for slander. I told him he ought to carry around some *proof* of what he was claiming he saw over there by that stone bridge near Cugnot's place. I furthermore told him that if he messed with any single one of the freight wagons hauling grapes during the crush—your very own freight wagons coming off Spring Mountain here—he'd have *me* to answer to. You don't know all that goes on in St. Helena, Kyle Plimpton. I've got deputies. I've had my deputies on the lookout more times than one just making sure Jacques Cugnot minded his own business. Some signs of law and order ain't always out posted up on somebody's bulletin boards!" He waved his hand, as if motioning to anyone who was heading down Spring Mountain and wanted the sheriff's protection that they should come along.

Adam's face had flushed a bright red. He stepped forward. "I must defend myself—and Miss Reynolds. I must assure you that anything whatsoever that transpired between myself and Sarah Reynolds was of —the highest decorum." He saw Jacob Brunner's stare boring through him. "I have utmost respect, admiration for her. I would not do anything to harm her—her reputation."

The sheriff shrugged his shoulders. "I guess for whatever reasons, the cat's already out of the bag. Right or wrong. Besides, how you regard what took place between you and her is strictly your business, as far as I'm concerned. As long as no complaints are filed across my desk and as long as I don't have evidence of wrongdoing on anybody's behalf, I keep my opinions to myself."

"But you do believe me?" Adam protested.

"Look—this ain't a time for me to discuss what I believe and don't believe. I'm here on a duty. I'm trying as best I can to carry it out. Now, if you've got some spare lanterns, they'll come in handy on a night as dark as this. Beats the hell outa me why when things do happen it's hardly ever on a full-moon night. We'll be lucky to keep the buggies and flatbed on the road."

Adam instructed the men from Chiles Valley to ride down, taking over the driving. "Luigi and Kyle have had their workout for the day," he said quietly. "I'm not feeling quite up to it myself —and I want to keep a close eye out for Li Po. I'm keeping him in the spare bunk in my room," he added, more for Li Po's uncle, who was standing over in one corner of the big mess hall, politely keeping a distance. Adam walked over to him. "Do you have instructions for me?" he asked.

The old man handed a bottle to him. "Take this powder," he said softly, being sure he was not overheard by anyone. "Give him two pinches—mix with some wine. Little bit of wine. Maybe two days he needs. Young people—it does not take so long. It will be hard for Wang Chi." He shook his head sadly, bowed, hiding his eyes.

Adam placed his hand on the hunched-over shoulders. "I will be proud to look after your nephew. I will see that he is treated with the fullest respect. That he is well taken care of. I want you to know that."

"I know that," Lee said simply. "If I did not think so he would go with me to my sister's place in San Francisco. No—he stay with you." And, like a shadow, the small black-clothed form seemed to slip out into the night.

Adam went out, watched, helped where he could to get Wang Chi comfortable in the back of the buckboard. Paulo was driving. Jacob Brunner sat huddled beside him. Adam walked around to him, reached up and touched the old man's hands. "I am so truly sorry," Adam said, finding it difficult to speak. "I didn't know Wang Chi would be bringing Li Po back. I thought somebody else . . ."

Jacob's voice sounded as though it had dropped down into some space of tired resignation. "It was not your fault. I told Wang Chi to ride up and check with Kyle, see if we could work out a schedule on pruning. Set a time for working both up here and down on my place. Double up—save some money between us." He was looking at Adam, but in the darkness Adam could not totally determine the old man's full expression, which usually rode in his pale faded eyes. "This will pass. Everything does. Life goes on. People always pick up, figure out some kind of way to keep going." His voice sounded nearly spent.

"I'm worried about you," Adam said quickly. "Will you be able to rest? Would you send for me if you need help? I will come immediately."

But at that moment the sheriff rode up, his saddle making a squeaking noise as he adjusted his boots in the stirrups. Adam smelled the warm hot air snorting from the horse's nostrils so close to him. "We're set to go up front. I'll ride behind the buckboard. Okay, men —pull out!"

Adam stood watching the bobbing lanterns fade, blur into the dismal night. The combined sounds of the men's muted voices, of horses' hoofs, of wagon wheels crunching joined in with the closer eerie call of a lone hoot owl. A damp mist was falling now. Adam felt it on his face, the backs of his hands. He had not put on his coat. The mountain wind whipped against his shoulder blades, sent shivers up and down his back.

"Better come in by the fire," Kyle called out to him. "Luigi's poured us all a stiff whiskey. You need it same as we do."

Inside, the fire in the fireplace was sending up a flurry of sparks from a damp new madrone log Luigi had dumped on. A sluggish draw in the new chimney on the damp, close night belched back smoke across the mess hall. As Adam stepped closer to the warmth, the smoke burned his nostrils, made his eyes smart.

He pulled a chair up alongside Kyle's and Luigi's, accepted the tin cup Luigi thrust in his hands. The first swallow of the whiskey burned as if Adam had swallowed a live coal from the ashes in the fireplace. Tears streamed from his eyes; he fought through a fit of coughing.

"It'd take the hide off a mule, wouldn't it?" 'Kyle said, making a face of his own as he drank. "Luigi, where'd you run across this stuff?"

Luigi looked a little embarrassed. "A friend of Vittorio's, up on Howell Mountain. Used to operate a registered brandy still. Got shut down because he didn't pay his taxes. Lost his license. Now and then, they run off a batch of whiskey on the side, just to keep their own tastes supplied. Nothing they put out on the market."

"Well, won't be the only still running on Howell Mountain that the revenue men don't know about. Hell, a man has to cut corners where he can these days. Taxes on liquor, brandy. It's sky high. Enough to make a man duck certain parts of the law." Kyle drank again, screwed his face into a fierce knot. He looked across at Adam. "I'd like to say *this* to you—this is the first drink of real bona-fide whiskey I've touched since I came to work for you. A little wine or a swig of brandy once in a while ain't the same thing. Don't get to me like hard whiskey does. But just because we're tasting a little tonight don't mean I'm taking the habit back up. I reckon tonight makes taking a hard drink fall into its rightful place."

Luigi lifted his cup. "*Salute*—here's to better times."

"I'll sure drink to that," Kyle said, waiting for Adam to join them. "This has sure been one hell of a windup for your first harvest, ain't it, Adam? We started out with old Jacob toasting to good luck. Seems the devil rode in on a broomstick." He stared at the fire when he finished his drink. "But look at it thisaway. Next harvest will be different. It'll show the results of our hands on the vines. It'll be one hundert percent our pruning and picking. I figure I'll have most of the vineyards coming around again—that is, *if* Pierce disease or a whole new crop of leaf hoppers don't hit below the belt, *if* it don't hail baseballs, *if* it don't rain cats and dogs at the wrong time, and if it don't do a dozen other things Lady Luck might decide to toss out of her Easter basket on us."

Adam got up, placed his empty tin cup on the edge of the rough-plank table Luigi had nailed together for temporary use. His stomach felt as red hot as the smoldering fire. "I'll go look in on Li Po, see if he's still sleeping," he said quietly. "Guess I'll call it a day. As you said, Kyle, it's been a hell of a windup."

"Aw, tomorrow's a Monday—starts a whole new week," Kyle said with attempted cheerfulness. "Look at it thisaway—can't get no worse. Things are bound to get better."

Just as Jacob Brunner had vowed he would do, he pressed charges against the men accused of assaulting Wang Chi and Li Po. When the sheriff arrested J. T. Price and the man known as Vern Woods, holding them in jail until the trial date could be set, Jacob had his own personal statement printed up and went about, this man of few words, posting it anywhere he could find a place and handing it out personally to people he hoped would listen.

> *Assaulting Chinamen will no longer be tolerated by upright, honest citizens of this fair town. To those ruffianly men now in jail for their brutal assault on my long-devoted and loyal servant, Wang Chi, we must see that prompt punishment be dealt out so that those men of another color we have called heathens may walk the streets and sidewalks without fear of abuse from men calling themselves Christian. I ask for your support by attending court when the date of the trial is set.*
>
> Sincerely, your neighbor,
> JACOB GUSTAF BRUNNER

Though the formal statements from Wang Chi, Li Po, those men involved at Adam's, and from the doctor and the sheriff himself had been entered as circumstantial evidence, the sheriff surprised the courtroom and the defendants' lawyer by bringing in an actual eye-witness to the beating, to testify.

It turned out that an unemployed cellarmaster named Alvin Upton had been out that Sunday afternoon hunting for game to help feed his large family. He had been down in the ravine by the creek when he heard the commotion up on the road. "I heard this squealing and hollering—sounding like stuck pigs. Them two over there came right down the bank after they knocked both that old man and little boy down. I seen 'em tie one to a tree, laughing and saying ever' cuss word you ever heard. Throwed that old Chinaman nearly at my feet. I was hid behind a rock, 'cause I figured I had this one shot left in my gun and I couldn't kill them two with one blast." He had sensed the wave of ridicule coming from the jeering crowd. "Plus all that, I'd been laid up in bed three weeks with a bad case of bleeding ulcers. As it was, I was fighting for strength to keep on hunting till I took home something for my family to eat. If them two had caught sight of me, they'd turned the whip on me too, I figured." He heard the derisive laughter and snickers. His eyes widened desperately. "A man gets down on his luck —he pushes hard as he can trying to keep his kids from going plain hungry. But that don't mean he's got to risk his neck and what support he's got left for his family saving some heathen's necks! That don't mean I think its *right* what them two did. It was worse than seeing a dog beat to death. Stomped on, like I seen a man sitting right out there laughing at me right now do one time! Then when it came out in the newspapers, I decided to tell the sheriff what I saw up there on Spring Mountain."

Voices buzzed, curiously now.

The defendants' lawyer jumped up. "Mr. Upton, didn't you testify earlier that you cannot read or write? Yet now you are telling us that you read this in the newspaper?"

The bewildered man rose half out of his chair. "I didn't say no such a thing!" Tears welled in his eyes. "I ain't ashamed to say I can't read or write. Never had a chance to go to school. But I got four of my kids in school and I got one boy reads ever' word of the newspapers before he goes out delivering. I might be poor. I might have a hard time finding a job these days and keeping shoes on my kids. I ain't no liar!" He swiped at his weathered, gaunt face. "If the sheriff had told me testifying 'ud be like this, wouldn't been no team of mules strong enough to drag me in here and be made fun of!"

"Your being here makes it possible for us to carry out justice," the judge said, pounding his gavel, and then giving the courtroom his own stern lecture.

His verdict was equally emphatic: "Six months in jail or leave Napa County for good."

J. T. Price opted for the six months in jail, while Vern Woods decided that leaving Napa County would be to his best advantage.

Another result of the trial: local missionary societies joined forces and saw to it that the Upton family had food and clothes delivered, and when the true plight of their needs was made known, there was a community outpouring of furniture, blankets, even clothing that could not be used, and finally a volunteer crew of men to patch the roof and repair broken windows went into dedicated action.

Part of the fervor had come from the fact that Christmas was near at hand. The natural benevolence and spirit of giving had been heaped on the Upton family as a symbol, a reminder to anyone reading the newspapers that the community was, indeed, a fair community with more than its share of *true* Christians.

Kyle Plimpton had just finished reading the account of one of the wineries giving Alvin Upton a job as a janitor. He was peeling thin shavings from a cedar stick, his cane-bottomed chair tilted back near the mess-hall fireplace. "The Donati name sure got spread around in the papers over this. Least you got up on the map, Adam," he said, smiling ironically. "We'd better be thankful it's the rainy season right now, else every long-necked gawker in Napa County would be riding up here trying to find the bloodstains where the beating took place." He saw Luigi looking at advertisements in the newspaper. "Thinking about going Christmas shopping, Luigi?"

Adam looked up. He had been thinking about the upcoming holiday. "Why don't you men take a week or two off?" he said matter-of-factly. "Spend a vacation with your families."

Luigi looked up, a huge grin on his face. "I was hoping you might want us to close up shop. Cesare's been after me to come to Napa City and see his new place. He's talked Lorenzo into patching up their differences—getting everybody together for Christmas up here." He shook his head. "He can't talk Lorenzo out of his restaurant, though. Can't get him up here to go in business the way he wants him to."

Kyle stood up, stretched. "I'll try and last out a week with my cousin Coleen and that brood of hers. Lord, you ought to see them fighting over who gets what toy on Christmas Day! But she's a good cook. Adam, if you don't have a place to go for Christmas dinner, Coleen's always got room for one more plate."

Luigi looked embarrassed. "Cesare—he'd want you to be with us if you don't have family."

Adam smiled. "Vittorio Alfieri has already invited me for Christmas Day dinner, and I'll be stopping by the Brunners' on Christmas Eve for supper."

It was settled then that everyone would depart, except Adam, the following day. Apologetically, Luigi explained that he and Kyle had not managed time yet for Christmas shopping and did not have a gift for Adam. Kyle broke in: "We'd made up our minds if you don't have a place to go and worse came to worse, we'd stay up here with you and take you down to the St. Helena Hotel for a big turkey dinner on Christmas Day—let that be our present."

Paulo, who had been listening, slipped into the bunk room he shared with Giuseppe and Alberto—who were playing a game of checkers, but who got up and came into the mess hall to present to Adam a huge keg of Nichelini wine. Adam, in turn, gave everyone a twenty-dollar gold piece and assured Luigi and Kyle he had not expected gifts from them.

It was then that a now-fully recovered Li Po scurried out, returned shyly with small packages of ginger candy and passed them around; bowed and accepted his shiny gold piece; backed out of the room, smiling.

The next day, Adam drove Li Po to Napa City and dropped him off with Li Po's cousin, who ran a store near the wharf. Then he went to the best hotel on Main Street and checked in. He needed a change. He had shopping to do for Erika, Jacob, the Alfieris, and he wanted to check and see if the package to Sarah had been sent out on schedule, as promised, from a purchase he had made weeks before. Though he had not heard from her in over seven weeks, he would not allow himself to think that she might, by now, be engaged to this Christopher Elliot-Weare from New York. When the doubts tried to creep into his thoughts, he pushed them out, closed his mind to it.

Adam longed to go to San Francisco and spend Christmas at the elegant Palace Hotel, perhaps manage an invitation from Samuel Linton to spend a sumptuous day in his splendid mansion on Nob Hill. But he must hold on to as much of his cash reserves as possible. Even a few days' stay in this simple Main Street hotel was an extravagance.

But he found himself enjoying the small town called Napa City, with the shop windows filled with tinsel and brightly wrapped packages. He had gone from shop to shop, buying gifts he would need for Jacob and Erika, for the entire Alfieri family, and once more checking in the jewelry store to see if they had mailed the garnet necklace weeks ago to Sarah as they had promised.

He took long walks, aware of the pretty girls smiling at him as he wandered down Main Street, across to the residential section of the finer homes, on down to the wharf to look at the loaded barges, the sailboats rocking, their masts listing back and forth as strong winds whipped in from the ocean to the west.

As he returned to the hotel, a pretty redhead smiled invitingly at him, sending his whole being into a sudden, surprising quickening of desire. When he entered the hotel, the bellhop whispered to him that she was a girl for hire and he could arrange to have her come up to his room, if he so wished. For a moment Adam almost said yes. He sternly rebuked himself, hurried to the elevator. If he loved Sarah he must not cloud that pure memory of her with a dirty woman for hire! But that night, in his dreams, he had them both.

On Christmas Eve he checked out, loaded the phaeton with wrapped packages, and headed up the main county road toward the Brunners'. Passing the Reynolds' driveway, he glanced across at the massive pillars of the mansion, at the graceful row of oak trees lining the driveway. One day, he thought, his place on Spring Mountain would be completed and it would be as grand—yes, even more impressive in a different way than the much-talked-about Reynolds place; for on Spring Mountain he had the most commanding view in the valley. He and his wife would live as if they were king and queen on the top of the world itself!

He gave Hajib a lighthearted flick with the whip. He must not doubt fate—Lady Luck, as Kyle Plimpton called it. He must remember that Lady Luck smiled on him. So why wouldn't it turn out that Sarah Hubbard Reynolds would be his wife? She loved him. He most certainly loved her. He must keep strong faith in every aspect of his fullest dreams. . . .

He realized he had arrived much too early for the Brunners. He headed on to St. Helena, stopped at the post office to check the private box he had rented following the episode over the letter at Fanny Martin's boardinghouse. As his hands worked the combination, his fingers began trembling slightly at the sight of a letter. But after he had jiggled the tiny door open, his heart sank as he saw there was no word from her. The letter was from his brother Guido in Florence.

Adam decided against ripping open the letter then and there. He had time left for a pot of tea and some pastry at the St. Helena Hotel dining room. He put the letter into his pocket, walked briskly down the street, nodding now and then to strangers passing by who made friendliness a part of the Christmas season. Over a cup of tea he read:

Via Ricasoli, Florence
October 5, 1894

MY BELOVED BROTHER, EMILIO

I have been here for a month now visiting Alfredo, who is writing a book on the famous people buried in the Basilica of Santa

124

Croce, and a history of its paintings and sculpture. We spend what free time he has going from campanile to cloisters to the chapel of this cardinal or that. He asks me to send his love. He writes so many words each day on this monumental manuscript that he does not have words left for letters, he tells me. But he is well and happy with his life; his only complaint, he says, is that he knows he will not live enough years to write the history he sees and wants the world to see through his eyes.

For me, I am not as happy. My wife has decided she must spend most of her time with her mother. She was very glad to see me come to Florence. I have been asked to go to Pontremoli and take charge of the winery by the man who bought it. He has not found it the peaceful pastime he thought it would be. He is a nice man, I believe. But he misses Milan, and it is my guess he misses his factory he sold. I am considering accepting his offer. It is a shame to see our father's life's work fall into ruin. It will also make my wife happy. She will not have to worry about having to listen to me complain so much about how I hate working in a glass-blowing factory. My dear wife simply cannot understand that a son of Giovanni Donati was not born to be an artist blowing glass!

I have no word from Rudolfo. Nor does Alfredo hear from him. He is probably spending all of his money gambling. But even so, maybe one day we can reach him, and one day you will be very rich, and we will all come back to Pontremoli for a big family celebration.

Until then, we send our love to our baby brother. We send our prayers, our best wishes for your happiness. May Bacchus's smile rest upon your hillsides.

Your loving brother,
GUIDO

When Adam started toward the door, he turned, made a sudden decision that he would not go back to Spring Mountain tonight, but would sleep in the St. Helena Hotel after he had had dinner with the Brunners. The letter had made him feel the loss of his family, the vast distance of the ocean separating them. He did not anticipate sleeping alone in the crudely furnished bunkhouse in the back of the stone stable. It was not that he was afraid of Jacques Cugnot any longer—the trial having brought Jacques into bad public light, and with his having left the valley, supposedly for a long visit to St. Louis to see his daughter. But there was still something awesome about being alone up there, alone anywhere, when night's shadows took on grotesque shapes and caused very ordinary sounds to reverberate in threatening waves. Since early childhood he had been afraid of being alone, abandoned. He could remember still, terrible nightmares back then where demons took diabolical shapes born out of his fears and swept in on their own tidal waves, their faces hidden, their arms waving like bat wings under ghostly-white sheets. He could remember trying in his dreams to run, but his feet would be like vines rooted in rock, and when he would try to scream out his voice would fade in some paralyzed place in his throat.

He went to the front desk and registered, paid for his room in advance.

He had spent much more money this Christmas than he had intended to spend. But it *was* Christmas—it was his way of celebrating. What had Samuel Linton told him: *Don't regret decisions you make.*

Even if it was somewhat deliberate, his step was jaunty as he walked down the sidewalk, went to the hitching post where he had left Hajib, and started his drive back to the Brunners'.

He presented Erika a lovely small cameo brooch, the carved-out face on it reminding him of Erika herself. He gave Jacob a new gray wool muffler and a pair of dark-gray leather gloves that, though they were a size too large, Jacob proudly claimed fit perfectly.

Erika presented him a box of Christmas cookies she had made and a linen handkerchief she had embroidered with the letter *D*. Jacob then, in a rare burst of generosity, took Adam to the barn and pointed up to an elaborate saddle. "Used to belong to a Spanish general who rode through here in the old days. Solid silver. All the trimmings. It is yours —for Hajib."

Adam thought Erika looked charmingly pretty in a dress over which she wore a brightly embroidered black velvet jacket. Jacob pointed to the jacket with pride. "My wife made that fine jacket, when she was about the same age as Erika here—twenty years old. She was pretty like Erika too." He smiled at both of them, his faded age-old eyes alive with excitement.

The next morning, Adam did not accept the Alfieris' invitation to go along and attend Mass with the family. But he did arrive promptly at twelve noon at the small house he had bought and turned over to them, across from the old Bale mill.

From the moment Adam stepped inside, he was greeted with a burst of excited happy children, all radiant from the happy discovery of so many presents under an enormous Christmas tree on their return from church. Delicious odors permeated the entire house. Adam hugged and kissed each child, presented to each in turn a package containing a small toy and an additional silver dollar. To Delfina he handed a small package with a brooch in it, almost identical to the one he had given Erika. To Vittorio he gave a larger package holding a handsome navy-blue sweater with brass buttons down the front. Vittorio put it on immediately, held out both arms, called out to his children, "Look at your papa now! A prince. I look like a prince."

He presented to Adam an exceptionally fine bottle of claret from Château Chevalier. Adam insisted they open it. While Delfina scurried about putting finishing touches to the dinner, Vittorio took out two crystal glasses, beamed while Adam poured the wine. "*Salute*," Vittorio said, his eyes suddenly moist. "Because you come to Napa Valley and help me and my family. Who knows?—maybe we would still be up on Howell Mountain. Crazy-scared. Like rabbits hiding in dark holes. *Salute*—God bless you, Adam!"

At that moment, Delfina hurried in carrying a tray loaded with olives, pickles, salamis and cheeses, and a long thin load of freshly baked bread. "The turkey is so big it needs more time." She leaned over, kissed Vittorio lightly on the cheek, turned to Adam and proudly showed off the new cameo brooch pinned to her high collar.

Vittorio watched her until she had disappeared into the kitchen. He helped one of the children untangle a lead string to a pull-toy Adam had brought. Then he raised his glass a second time.

"*Salute*. This time we drink to the good woman you find someday to marry! The wife who will make you happy like my Delfina makes me."

But when Adam looked into the rich, ruby-red claret, his fingers felt ice cold, uncertain, as he lifted the glass to his lips.

6

On New Year's Day, the men were back on the job. Kyle had gone to Napa City to pick up Li Po. It had rained on them most of the trip back, and when they came inside the bunkhouse Adam insisted both of them get dry, come in to warm up by the roaring fire Luigi had built.

Everyone's spirits seemed revived. "Lord, sure is good to get back up here away from those squalling kids," Kyle said.

Luigi presented to Adam a huge box of Italian sausages and salamis that Cesare had sent as their Christmas gifts. Only Paulo and Giuseppe returned from Chiles Valley. They offered no explanation why Alberto had remained behind, but Adam was relieved. It would be one less salary. He paid regular workmen two dollars a day. It mounted up. He paid Luigi and Kyle three times that, plus bonuses. He paid Vittorio. He was hiring a steady stablehand to keep the stables cleaner. There was too much work to get done.

But by the middle of February noticeable changes were now taking place. The inside finish work was nearly done in the main house, where Vittorio had spent most of his time. By May or June, Luigi predicted, it would be finished, at least enough for Adam to move in and for the building crew to be cut back, including those who rode up the mountain each day and went back at sundown.

The third week of February, on a Wednesday, Adam received a letter from Sarah. He pulled the phaeton off the side of the road, heard the pelting rain against the top, saw the water trickling in rivulets off Hajib's flanks. His hands trembled as he ripped open the envelope.

Wellesley College
January 17, 1895

My dear Adam,

Forgive me for not having written. I have tried to sort out my life and make some rational conclusions. For me, time, where you are concerned, has had little interruption since I said goodbye to you that day. I feel as if we just stepped apart.

The lovely garnet necklace arrived the first week of January, in time for my birthday. I adore it! How beautiful and delicate it is. The color of the stones is the color of wine. I think of you in that way. I imagine us drinking a toast—a garnet toast.

Since my last letter, I have made two visits to New York. One —the first, at Thanksgiving—was spent in New York City itself, where I was entertained at a breathakingly rapid pace, and on such a grand scale, as the Elliot-Weares do things, that I felt as though I had taken on the nervous tic of that big city itself. During that mad whirl of events, I confess, dear Adam, that for a while I lost sight of your face, of your words, of what we had vowed.

At Christmas, his family—and my mother, of course—insisted that I spend the holidays with them. This time, we were entertained in their large Larchmont home, where the Elliot-Weares spend summers and Christmas holidays.

Oh, we ice-skated, had sledding parties, and on the last night, a large formal dance was held in the ballroom.

Adam, I do not know exactly when—or even where—but suddenly it happened: I could not bear to have Chris look at me or touch me with even the slightest romantic suggestion. I asked myself how I could have ever imagined marrying him. Then I admitted honestly that I had been overwhelmed, seduced by a kind of brilliant ambience the entire Elliot-Weare family collectively share—a brilliance, not of the mind, but of things dazzling; of that ever so enticing surface luster of life. To be enormously rich—one might often dream about that; but to be caught up even in the peripheral glow of it with these oh-so-witty, oh-so-charming people who seem to more or less glide through life as if skating on solid gold blades across surfaces strewn with diamond dust—yes, I *was* impressed. And for a few weeks, I was convinced, along with them, that the figure-eights being cut with the golden blades on that limited glittering surface were indeed the all-encompassing dimensions—man's ultimate dream route in the world!

Then suddenly I was seeing *your* face—hearing *your* voice. I was experiencing, vicariously, the dream you were trying to build on Spring Mountain, and I knew that my life would never be real unless I was able to share that dream, that struggle with you.

I am writing now to say, with my whole heart, soul and body, that if you still want me I would be your wife. I will be home, if the schedule goes as planned, on June the fifteenth. Let us try to meet at sundown at our special place. Please ask me again!—we will coax the crawdad, Moses, out of his castle under the bridge to be our witness!

My love on wings to you,
SARAH

After Sarah's letter, it was as if new energy and meaning came back into his life. The weeks fairly flew by, and, in what seemed like days only, the growing season was upon them, the valley floor had strung its streamers of golden mustard across the vivid green fields of new pasture grass. Kyle was in the vineyards from sunup until sundown. Adam went about as a man obsessed with finishing every job still waiting completion. *June the fifteenth*, he kept saying to himself.

The last week of May, it became necessary for Adam to make a trip to San Francisco to untangle a mixup on a bill of lading on furniture he had ordered from Italy.

On the second day, he stopped in the Linton bank and asked to see the president, Samuel Linton. A tight-lipped teller was just ready to brush him aside with a flat refusal, since he did not have an appointment, when Mr. Linton himself came through the main lobby, the usual cigar poked in the corner of his mouth.

Adam was delighted to see him, and the feeling seemed mutual. Mr. Linton insisted that he come along and join him for lunch at his regular table at Jack's. When they entered, they were escorted promptly to "the Linton table." Automatically, without anyone ordering, fresh cracked crab and sourdough bread were placed on the table, along with a bottle of wine—French wine, Adam noticed, checking the label instinctively.

It did not take long for Adam to fill Mr. Linton in on all that had been taking place on Spring Mountain, including the Jacques Cugnot episodes, the trial, the newspaper stories, and Cugnot's departure to St. Louis.

Mr. Linton squinted his eyes against the smoke. "Don't count on Cugnot being gone for good. I'd keep my eyes open. Just because a snake sheds its skin doesn't mean it quits being a snake." He looked at Adam thoughtfully. "My board of directors raised hell with me about that whole deal I made with you. These aren't the best times. They're —we're all clamping down these days. Money's tight," he said, as if reading Adam's mind.

Adam dabbed butter on a piece of bread, sampled the crabmeat. "It has certainly cost me a lot more than I had planned," he said cautiously. "Building supplies—stained-glass windows alone have cost—"

"Don't give me a rundown on your expenses," Samuel Linton said bluntly. "I told you then to limit yourself, *if* you were so hellbent on throwing your money to the winds. My advice to you now is to stop everything that isn't absolutely essential, to get through the next couple of harvests." He narrowed his eyes. "The market reports are dismal. I expect you haven't begun to see the bottom of this thing yet. Krug—he's folded tent, I hear. I don't see how this wine market will get on solid ground again—and even if it should, it won't happen until after the turn of the century. Maybe in 1900 you'll see a shift." He pointed his finger. "If you are going to make this thing work, you had better tighten every loophole!"

Adam cupped his hand around the wineglass a moment. "I have total faith in an upswing happening sooner than that. I have talked with growers—with Charles Carpy. With many of the important vintners in the valley. The mood is optimistic." He got to the point. "So much so that I would like to ask you to increase my loan so that I will be fully prepared to meet the demands of the expanding market."

Mr. Linton slammed his wineglass down as hard as he could without breaking it. "Listen to me, young man! Count Agostin Haraszthy —the first man to bring in European varietals—when I knew him in the early 1860s was the biggest optimist ever to hit the wine industry. The one who trotted all over the world spreading the good word about California wines. And what happened to *him*? Have you found that out yet—that he left America with the jaws of a big scandal trying to clamp down on his flying coattails? And where did he end up? I'll tell you! Fell in a river in Nicaragua and was eaten by crocodiles. Which is just about what I think of your optimism."

Adam took a deep breath. He had heard the story before. He was trying to think of a retort, a new side to his argument. Mr. Linton got up abruptly, checked his watch. "I take just so much time for lunch. I loan out just so much money, too, young man. When you pay up the loan you've got outstanding, then we'll talk more business. Don't forget —1899, your note will be due."

They walked out into the narrow alleylike street. Adam hesitated, ready to go off in another direction, then decided to give his appeal one more try. He walked alongside Mr. Linton, dodging in and out as people hurried by. "I still think you're wrong," he said stubbornly. "With men such as Hilgard and Hussman there is new knowledge—an entirely new attitude among growers and vintners alike. A determination to stick it out, recover from the phylloxera damages. It can be done." He waited as Mr. Linton tipped his hat to a cluster of older women getting out of a carriage. "I assure you that any money you invest with me will be paid in full."

"I told you back in the beginning, Adam, that if it was *money* you were after I could make you a rich man right here in San Francisco. Didn't I offer you a share in a new hotel? Do you know what that would be worth in one year's time of appreciation?"

Adam felt his neck flush red with frustration. "I believe I told you then that it is not *money*—that I was not born to live in a house stuck on the side of a hill like a cardboard box!" He clasped Mr. Linton's elbow while they stopped, waited for the traffic to clear before crossing Kearny Street. "Wait until you see the magnificent buildings that are nearing finishing now. The stonework! And wait until you see what we've done with the vineyards. Won't you come up and see for yourself? I know you would be happy to advance more money to me, with the buildings alone being enough collateral to more than double the original loan."

Mr. Linton turned, looked him steadily in the eye. "This is where we part company," he said gruffly. "I have a meeting in that building over there with a young man who's got another dream—a dream about mighty buildings, shooting these cardboard-box houses you mentioned up to the damn moon. I think *he's* crazy! But I'd be willing to give *him* money before I would risk another dime on anything to do with the wine industry, the way it stands right now." He patted Adam's stiff arm consolingly. "Look, I like you. I liked you back then and I still like your gumption. But I deal with cold facts. I deal with what adds up and what slides right off the ledger into a sinkhole. I have helped you as much as I can—as much as I am willing to. If it's the way you think, then you won't need my help. You will find a way on your own."

Adam waited politely while Mr. Linton crossed the street. Then he turned, charged blindly in the direction of the ferry building. If he hurried, he would still have time to get on the last boat to Vallejo, a day ahead of his original plans. Why waste time? He would show Samuel Linton. He would show all of them what he could do!

It was on a Tuesday afternoon in early June, the week before Adam was expecting Sarah home, when the unexpected happened.

He had just spent a marvelous morning being escorted by a proud Luigi through the now finished main house on Spring Mountain. He had been shown how smoothly the new doors swung open on their hinges, how well the locks worked, how nice the plain glass windows were where they had thought stained glass was essential. It was not the exact duplicate of Pontremoli, as he had first envisioned, but it was close enough. He clapped Luigi on the back, congratulated him. "You have done what you promised, Luigi. You have built the best stone building in all of Napa Valley. At least to me it is the best."

He paid Luigi his wages, added a generous final bonus. Luigi would be working from then on, he had told Adam, with his brother Cesare's new construction business, Pascarella Enterprises. "I'll come up to see you now and then. When you're down in Napa City, stop by on Brown Street at Cesare's place and look me up. *Paesano*—it will stay that way, huh?"

After Luigi rode off on his dappled mare, Adam had saddled Hajib for a ride down to Jacob Brunner's place. He was in one of the most lighthearted moods he had known for weeks. His house was ready! He could bring his bride to live in it with full pleasure and a deep sense of pride. He would not have to apologize. To ask her to wait for something nicer.

Adam decided to take the back trail down instead of the main Spring Mountain road. He rode out through the middle of the vineyards themselves, looking happily this way and that at the lush growth on the full-blooming, mature vines; at the progress of the young, newly planted ones that would take a few more years yet to reach that stage.

Stages—life, like the vineyards, took its stages, he thought, feeling the wind against his face as a breeze rustled the tops of the vines. From that first push from dormancy in early April, on to the blooming in May, the growth of berries in June, the ripening in July, the final stretch toward full maturity through hot August and into September. Each step vital. So many variables along the way to change the predictable pattern.

He let Hajib run through the last flat stretch before reaching that sudden plunge downward toward the back trail. Yes, life and love had their variables! But one stepped, sidestepped, as the need came up, he thought, his heart singing.

What a beautiful early-summer day! What beautiful vineyards! What a magnificent stallion! And with a burst of enthusiasm he took Hajib over a stone fence, pulled him back into a pace for finding his way down the fast descent. The trees were alive with birds. A mountain wind whipped his thick dark-brown hair off his forehead. His proud head was up, his back straight, even on the difficult trail, for he had been taught impeccable *haute école* by Mr. Kologz, the famous Hungarian horseman.

He was making the special trip to receive a gift from Jacob—a new varietal Jacob himself had brought into being, saying only that it came in part from the French Colombard. He would share it only with Adam, he had told a young student from the University of California in Davis—"an upstart," Kyle Plimpton had called him when bringing this story home to Adam—who had blatantly asked for a sample of the new varietal, as if it were his rightfully.

"Why would you give it to this Adam Donati but you won't give a sample cutting to me?" Kyle had told Adam the conversation went. Jacob Brunner had snorted in his face, "Because Adam Donati comes from Europe where *appellation d'origine* means something. He's from a famous family of grape growers and winemakers, is also why. Go back to school, young man, and maybe in a few years you will really know something about grape growing."

Adam was smiling, trying to envision Jacob's face in rage. It would be pleasant seeing him, having lunch with Erika. In a way, they were like relatives.

At the foot of the steep trail, Adam let the restless Hajib stretch his legs in a long hard run, deciding to give him a full workout on a dirt wagon road leading through Jacob's fields, then bring him out onto the county road and back down Jacob's main driveway. He missed the long flat runs himself. Though he had been enjoying the jumps up on Spring Mountain, he loved this open full gallop, the wind in his face, the sound of Hajib's hoofs pounding the smooth rich valley-floor dirt. He felt it was the closest thing to flying. What had Sarah written?—"I send my love on wings." He felt as if he were racing toward it. "June the fifteenth—it is almost here, Hajib!" he said under his breath.

On the main driveway, he let the stallion find a smooth even trot. They were just approaching the Brunner house when Adam caught sight of the unmistakable Reynolds carriage, the gold letter *R* on the back, and Miss Grace herself sitting in the front seat of the carriage, perched there as haughtily as he had remembered her, holding the reins of a spirited, obviously well-bred chestnut mare. Erika was standing alongside the carriage, holding her skirts down from the wind, looking intently up at Miss Grace.

Instinctively Adam had adjusted himself in the saddle, and, having automatically slowed Hajib down at the sight of Miss Grace, he was now checking himself, as if ready to pass by the strictest ring of judges in a dressage event. Just as he came up even, where he knew she would see, bearing in with his left leg, tightening the reins, he led Hajib into his smartest off-fore canter; nodded politely to Miss Grace, smiled openly at the shy, timid Erika, who seemed puzzled and perplexed by her visitor.

Adam had not missed Miss Grace's disdainful look. His heart was pounding as he entered the quiet shadows of the barn, dismounted, put Hajib in a stall, then stood a moment, trying to collect his thoughts. He supposed it wasn't that extraordinary to have her drive by. They *were* neighbors. But he had seen something else in her face, a smug look, that riddled him now with anxiety.

Jacob entered the opposite end of the barn, his shoulders hunched over as he carried a basket of vegetables he had just gathered. Oddly, Adam thought, even Jacob seemed ill at ease. He dropped the basket, looked closely at Adam. "I guess you saw we've got a visitor?" he said matter-of-factly.

Adam found himself buttoning the top button of his shirt, wishing he had worn a tie, his full riding habit. He scolded himself. He had come here to get special cuttings. A gift from Jacob Brunner. He had been invited to lunch. And the Brunners were simple people.

Jacob shook hands with him, bent over to pick up the basket of vegetables.

"Let me—here," Adam said quickly, scooping the heavy basket up easily and starting with Jacob out of the barn toward the side entrance to the main house.

"Let's skip *her*," Jacob muttered in a gruff voice. "She's on her high horse! Anytime you see Miss Grace coming, you know either she wants to wheedle a favor out of you or she's got something she wants spread all over Napa Valley. This time she's got the last one on her mind." He opened the door for Adam, waited for him to put the basket down on a table on the screened-in porch where Erika sorted and cleaned the fresh produce, deciding which should go to the market to be sold and which were culls that she could use in cooking.

Adam's eyes had clouded. His fingers felt stiff, as if he had been out in the cold without gloves; yet Jacob had found the day warm and was wiping perspiration from his wrinkled forehead, from under the flaps and folds of skin beneath his silvery goatee.

In the kitchen, Jacob waved him toward a chair at the table where he and Erika usually ate their meals unless Adam or an occasional rare guest had come to see them. As Adam sat down, to his dismay he saw that his right boot had dung on it from a misstep in the barn. He felt a wave of embarrassment, as if Miss Grace herself were seeing it, were ready to point to his dirty boots. He excused himself, hurried out on the stoop, scraped them clean, took a leaf from one of the squash in the basket, dabbed, looked around anxiously.

Miss Grace was turning her carriage around, making a wide sweep, so that he caught only the sight of her profile, her rigid posture, and her own quite correct position of hands on the reins. She had not seen him, he thought, relieved, hurrying back inside and going to the sink to wash his hands.

Erika came in, flushed, upset. At first Adam thought it was because she had been interrupted in her preparations for lunch. She was such a tentative, shy creature—her movements through life were fragile steps in a very circumscribed area. If Miss Grace intimidated him, she must surely shatter Erika.

Jacob sat down opposite Adam, pushed a cup of hot tea in front of him. "Americans don't understand a good cup of tea," he said, relaxing a little. "The same with wine—most *talk* wine but don't know much. They talk grape growing, don't understand vines. *Talk*—I heard Miss Grace out there spouting off something a mile a minute," he said grumpily to Erika. "What was on her mind today?"

Erika looked at her grandfather, seemed to snap her head around and hurried over to the stove, where she lifted a lid, stirred vigorously at something in a large stewing pot. "Something about a big party she is giving for her daughter, Sarah. Something about a letter she had just had from her best friend in New York who is coming out with her son for a visit." The lid clattered back in place. Her face looked flushed, damp with the steam that had risen and enveloped her. She wiped her small, fluttering hands on her checked apron, looked suddenly trapped, as if she wanted to run from even two people around with whom she was usually comfortable. "She . . . Miss Grace said . . . I think she said they were arriving in Napa Valley ahead of her daughter. A surprise—the party. This man . . . he is in love with Sarah, she said, and Miss Grace thinks there will be an engagement announcement. The party—she is more or less calling it an engagement party. At Soda Springs—a very big fancy party." Her hands flew out. "Papa Jacob—don't make me go! I would die if I had to go. I can't dance. I can't see so many people. I . . ."

Adam saw the tears in her eyes. He wanted to help her, but his own body seemed frozen, the blood drained.

Jacob rapped sharply on the table. "Erika—get hold of yourself. We have company." He got up. "Adam, she is very fussy with her cooking. She doesn't like anybody watching, getting under her feet. Let's take our tea into the parlor."

Adam's voice felt stuck in his throat. "I—I'm sorry, but I don't think I could possibly stay for lunch. My—I have some men who can start work grafting. The cuttings . . . I . . ."

Jacob was watching him closely. He looked angry, tired. "So the Reynolds girl is getting married?" he asked; though his question, Adam thought, could have been directed at him as well as at Erika. "If any young man has won Miss Grace's approval, you can bet your boots he's a rich pureblood," Jacob said, as gently as possible, his eyes resting totally on Adam's face now. His look was one that might have told Adam, under less trying circumstances, that he had seen a lot in life, and that he could pretty well guess right now what was troubling not only Adam but his own miserably shy, upset granddaughter Erika. But Jacob Brunner was known to be a man of few words. He worked with his hands. He understood life in a way where words usually, if anything, got in the way. At the same time, he had to try now to do something for both of them.

"If you can't stay to eat with us, Adam, let's skip a second cup of tea. Come on out to the barn with me. I've got the cuttings out there. Plus, I want you to take home some of our fresh vegetables. One of these days, you'll have to put in your own garden up there on Spring Mountain. One of the first things I taught Erika when she came here to live with me was how to raise vegetables. Next thing, I'm going to have her entering her tomatoes and maybe some pole beans in the state fair. Maybe I'll even get you started entering competition, Adam. My wife —she used to breathe and talk blue ribbons. Sewed all year for the next State Fair. 'Course, if I talk you into entering your grapes 'gainst mine, Adam, I'll be talking myself into a *red* ribbon instead of a blue one."

Adam's teacup and saucer clattered against the tabletop. Somehow he got outside. He realized numbly he had forgotten to say goodbye or to apologize to Erika for his change of plans. He felt as if a sudden dizzying heat wave had hit midvalley. He followed Jacob into the cool, shadowy silent barn.

Jacob dumped vegetables into a burlap bag, waited for Adam to climb on his horse. He handed him the vegetables, then went over and got the carefully wrapped cuttings he had in an oak bucket. "See if you can hold these in front of your saddle there. You're going straight home, aren't you?" He was studying Adam closely. "You might look a little like a peddler—a handsome one at that," he said, trying to sound cheerful, put Adam more at ease. He had seen the hurt and confusion in those pale-blue eyes, the sudden set jaw, the red flush riding up Adam's neck. And, what Adam didn't know, he had also seen that part of Erika's going to pieces was because she knew that Adam was in love with Sarah Hubbard Reynolds instead of with her. He had known from that first time when Adam Donati set foot inside their house that

Erika had felt something snap inside her; only then had she started working her way out of the turtle's shell where she had been hiding ever since he had brought her to Napa Valley from the tragedy back in Minnesota. He had delighted in the change. Encouraged every step of it. His granddaughter was smart. She wasn't, perhaps, as beautiful as the Reynolds girl; but she was pretty in her way. She was certainly one of the best cooks around. She'd make a man a fine wife—with careful handling. With a lot of patience. He didn't like to see any man suffer, and he saw the pain in Adam Donati's face. But maybe it was best it was happening now. Get it over and done with. Time healed a man's wounds. And with Sarah Reynolds out of the way, there might be room for Erika to find a path into his heart. *If* that happened, he could die at peace. He could quit pushing himself out of bed every morning. Forcing himself to get through one day after the next. He was tired. He was old—very old. He had served his stewardship. And if there was a young man in the state of California who could better take over the reins than this Adam Donati, he would like to meet him! Most of the young men who came around asking about his vineyards thought they knew it all. They studied viticulture at the university, listened to a few lectures from Professor Hilgard or Hussman and thought they had all the answers. Thought all they had to do was barge in and hold a hand out. What was it that smart aleck had said who had asked for the same cuttings he had just handed to Adam? "I was told you growers and vintners in Napa Valley worked closely together and shared your common knowledge." That was true, he had told him. "But there are so few real viticulturists and vintners around. Dabblers, talkers, hobbyists. Rich people needing to fill up some space in their lives. I don't give them my special varietals!"

Suddenly, Jacob Brunner did a very uncharacteristic thing: he reached up, clutched Adam's wrist, clung to his hand with both of his. "Young man, I want to tell you—I want to say to you that I have become very fond of you these past few months. I never had a son. I guess I always wanted one. To teach him what I know. You would be the very son I'd want, if I could just wish on the stars and get my wish. I—I just wanted to say that. I'm old. I have never talked much. Words don't come easy for me. But there are some things I want to say before I die." And before Adam could fully grasp what had just taken place, Jacob Brunner had turned and headed out toward the far end of the barn, an empty vegetable basket under his arm. He did not once look back, and after a moment Adam made his way out the front of the barn, headed Hajib back toward the trail.

When he reached the base of the mountain, he did not start up immediately. He veered left, headed for the very stone bridge where he had made plans to meet Sarah on June the fifteenth. He tied the stallion to a low-hanging branch, worked his way down to the tumbling creek's edge, crawled under the bridge, drew his knees into a cramped position, where his chin fairly rested on them. With one finger, he traced a line in the smooth, damp earth. He gazed at the pile of rocks, his eyes looking as if a pale film had been pulled across them. After a moment, he got out, went down to a special rock, looked closely to see if he could find the crawdad, Moses.

He stood up, kicked a large stone hard into the water. "Damn you, Sarah Hubbard Reynolds!" he said, his voice cutting the still, warm summer air. "Damn you to hell—you and your mother! Damn Miss Grace! Damn all of you in Napa Valley!"

He went back to his horse, untied him, remounted. He looked about wildly. Shadows played hide-and-seek games across the tumbling water. A bluejay above squawked mockingly. His hands tightened on the reins. For a moment he had a wild impulse—he would ride down the main county road, right up to the Reynolds' front door! He'd insist that Miss Grace hear him out.

He rubbed one hand across his eyes. *What good would it do?* He was nothing more than a dirty Dago to her. He was not *good* enough for her fine daughter, Sarah Hubbard Reynolds! His back stiffened. He gave Hajib a strong sure command with the insides of his legs. Hajib spurted forward, his hoofs sending small stones and dirt flying as he started up the steep trail.

Adam's thoughts were racing blindly. He would go back to Spring Mountain. To his newly finished manor house. Yes, it was a manor house! Donatis lived in manor houses, didn't they?

Sarah Hubbard Reynolds wasn't the only woman in Napa Valley. He had seen many pretty girls turn an interested eye in his direction. And there was Jacob's granddaughter. Sure—there was Erika. At least he could *trust* her! She would be *his*. She would belong to him, a girl like that.

Hajib was struggling to follow the conflicting commands unconsciously being given to him by the irate, disturbed Adam. At the top of a knoll he suddenly bolted, stopped dead, pawed the ground, his ears back.

Adam snapped back to his senses. He leaned over, patted the fighting stallion on the neck. "*Va bene . . . va bene . . .*" he soothed. "Okay . . . *mi dispiace . . .*"

After a moment, the horse quieted down. Adam rode at a steady trot, guiding Hajib this time around the edge of the vineyards, the easiest route back to the stone stable.

It was on Friday of that same week that Kyle Plimpton came into the mess hall at the bunkhouse, plopped down at his regular seat at the table, accepted a plate from Li Po and, with a long, steady look at a dispirited Adam, said,

"I was down to the bank. Sure heard a big whopper being grafted on the tongue-waggers' grapevine."

Two deep ridges elided between Adam's stormy eyes. "*So?* What's the big news now?"

Kyle made a tunnel through the steaming rice. "Seems Miss Grace is going around town with some rich dude from New York City riding her arm. Says it's the man gonna marry her girl, Sarah, one of these days." He saw the white line around Adam's mouth. But he felt that Adam should hear it from him. "Seems there's going to be a big party at Soda Springs. Word is that if the wedding comes off like Miss Grace seems to *think* it will, it'll be a wedding to outshine anything Monique Cugnot pulled off. Make that look like dollhouse play compared to what she's rigging up."

Adam's fork clattered across the table. He stood up, gripped the edge of the rough, plain table. "Is that all you have to tell me—*gossip* from busy women! Is that what you were doing on your afternoon you just *had* to take off for business?"

Li Po had just started into the mess hall from the area of the huge kitchen stove. He heard the tone of Adam's voice, saw the angry look on his red face. He backed silently out of the doorway, disappeared from sight.

Kyle's crippled hand had dropped back under the table in his lap. He looked squarely at Adam. "I thought you ought to hear it from me —in case you didn't know about it. I know her letters have meant a lot to you and all . . ."

Adam did not answer. He stalked out of the mess hall and headed up toward his new house that stood empty, waiting for the furniture to arrive and be moved in. It was a night when the moon was pushing toward being full. In the valley below, a soft golden glow made a patchwork quilt of oddly shaped patterns as Adam stood out on the stone veranda facing east.

He stayed there until nearly midnight. Kyle had tried a game of checkers with Paulo. He stood up, stretched, went over and looked out the window. "I reckon he's still up there gazing at the moon. Ain't nothing worse than being *love*sick! I had it bad one time. Over this little flibberty-jib Mulligan girl. She ran off with some cowboy from Nevada or someplace. A man thinks he'll die, throw up, roll over and start frothing at the mouth." He started toward his bunk. "It don't kill, and thank God it ain't catching! Once is enough for any man."

Paulo placed the checkers carefully in the box. His huge black eyes were soft. "A girl—my papa has sent to Italy for a nice girl for me. I have her picture." He took out a small round locket, opened it, smiled broadly. "She is very pretty, huh? I have not met her. But I feel this boom-boom sick stuff. I would turn the table upside down if, say, maybe she wanted Rocco or my brother Antonio instead of me. Adam Donati—he is a fine man. That girl must be very stupid!"

In spite of the gossip, Adam made up his mind to live up to his end of the bargain and be at the bridge on June the fifteenth, at sundown.

The sun was still high when he arrived at that spot above the barn, where he dismounted, tied Hajib to a tree. It was shortly past four o'clock. Matter-of-factly, he worked his way down the steep slope, stood on the bridge itself a moment; then, on impulse, decided to go beneath it to wait.

The winter rains had washed out some of the old rock formations that had been there when he and Sarah had held each other, he thought, working himself into as comfortable a position as possible and leaning back against the stone buttress, glad the moss that had been awash with mud had thoroughly dried now.

There is something that happens when one waits. Sounds become intensified. Time takes on its own humming, buzzing noises in the back of one's head. A thousand fragments of thoughts splinter like fuzzy stars across the Milky Way. Tracks from a colony of trailing ants become monster tracks. A pestering fly becomes an enemy one must kill.

At the sound of the heavy, crunching footsteps, Adam knew immediately it was not Sarah. He sat up, tucking his long legs in as closely as possible, his whole body alert now.

The sound of the two men's voices—he had heard them both, he thought frantically, trying to identify them. Then, unmistakably, he detected that certain splintery sound in Jacques Cugnot's tone. He had not heard that Jacques was back in Napa Valley—in fact, he had heard his place was going up for sale and the Cugnots were planning to stay in St. Louis.

The other voice—gruff, crude. *Yes, he had heard it.* But it was Jacques doing the talking now, almost directly above him.

"I sent for you as soon as Miss Grace stopped by last night and asked me to take charge," Jacques was saying. "She brought me this big love letter from that Dago up there on Spring Mountain—saying how he was going to be here at this bridge at sundown on June the fifteenth."

"Well, he'll sure run into a different kind of mush, won't he?" came the deep burly voice Adam thought he knew now. "I'd sure like to get hold of that sonofabitch! You think he's gonna chicken out—think he's heard about that other feller?"

"I'll say *this*—if he does show up, I want you taking the rawhide to him. Tie him to a tree—any damn thing you want to, short of killing him. I can't let my name get attached to any of this. Remember that, J. T. *Whip* him, but don't kill him. You got that?"

"Yeah. But what if he don't show? What then?"

"We'll get him. Sooner or later. Nobody robs me of my land! It might take me till the day I die, but I'll get even with that dirty bastard."

"Dagos are slippery. Hard to catch hold of."

Jacques Cugnot's voice sounded edgy, nervous. "I've got to pick up my wife and drive her to Soda Springs for that party. Can I trust you to take care of everything?"

"I told you I'd fix him! I don't spend no six months in jail without wanting to get back, too. If it hadn't been for him, that Chinaman and all . . . Sure, it's *his* fault."

Jacques Cugnot was walking off. "If anybody ever asks, you didn't see me. Don't get any big ideas, J. T. Remember this is a job you're getting paid to do."

It seemed that time had stopped. Adam knew that J. T. Price was standing directly above his head. He dared not move a muscle, take a breath. A fly had found his neck, his nose. At any moment, he was afraid a round stone on which one foot was resting would give way and send a cascade of rocks tumbling into the creek bed. Then, on the very edge, he could see the actual toes of J. T. Price's boots. In a moment, a noisy yellow stream of urine splashed into the clear rushing creek water.

His body was cramped. Surely, even if he had to, he could not move quickly. He had no idea now what time it was. The sun had set. The gathering dusk would shortly become darkness. At least then, he thought, J. T. would give up and go home.

But then, to Adam's horror, came the loud, shrill whinny from Hajib, followed up by another snorting, pawing sound. Then there was dead silence, where J. T. was obviously listening. At the tromping tread of the boots overhead, heading across, up in Hajib's direction, Adam's every muscle tensed. He quickly untangled himself, slid out from under the bridge, realized he had left his loaded revolver in the saddlebag. He cursed himself for his stupidity; searched frantically for any kind of weapon; picked up a rock in one hand, a stick he hoped would prove solid in the other.

He took long, stiff strides up the creek bank, on up the slope behind the muttering J. T. Price. At the sudden piercing cry from Hajib, adrenalin shot through Adam in a blinding fury. "If you hit that horse with that whip I'll kill you with my bare hands!" he cried out, all fear replaced by seething rage.

J. T.'s hands were up in the air, the whip back ready for its first hard lashing out just as Adam reached the top of the incline and came into full view. Adam stopped, his feet apart, ready to hurl the stone, flail out with the stick—anything to keep that whip off Hajib's back.

"I told you—come down with that whip and I'll kill you!"

Like Adam, J. T. Price was over six feet tall. The six months he had spent in jail had just ended, and he still had the paunch from the jail's starchy foods around his middle. In that moment of measuring his opponent and his chances, Adam saw how this man's face seemed to droop with some evil force of its own.

But J. T. was whirling around, the whip making a zinging noise, a sharp crack at the end as he tried to aim it on Adam. When the whip missed, Adam lunged forward with the stick, making J. T. himself change attack and charge down with his full bodily force.

Later, Adam tried to figure out exactly how it had happened. The sheer momentum of the hulk coming at him must have made him take one sure agile side step—surely a blind instinctive move, for he did not remember deciding to do that at all; or, for that matter, even having done it. At any rate, J. T. had lost his balance and plunged down the twenty-foot, heavily overgrown slope. And during that crashing, twig-breaking jumble of confusion, Adam had grabbed Hajib's reins, mounted, and galloped off at top speed up the trail.

When Adam arrived back at the bunkhouse, the place was dark. It was Li Po's weekend to spend with his relatives down in Napa City, now that his Uncle Lee had departed for San Francisco. Kyle had left, still chafing from Adam's cold shoulder to him all week, having told Paulo and Giuseppe (who had gone to Chiles Valley, where plans were in the making for Paulo's approaching wedding to the bride his father had arranged for him) that it was about time he loosened up with a bender. "Not a rip-snorter," he had said. "Just one to shake the bugs out of my head."

Adam lit an oil lamp, went into the kitchen, fumbled around for a glass, knocked over something, bumped his elbow. He stood rigidly still, as if expecting someone lurking, ready to jump at him from the shadows.

His heart hammered as his thoughts jumped out instead: he could have nearly lost his life tonight! He could have been whipped as badly as old Wang Chi. The brutality of what might have happened left him numb with shock.

He went into the bunkhouse mess hall, found a small amount of brandy, drank it down. Every nerve was on edge.

Every shadow in the large, sparsely furnished room loomed like an incomplete ghost shape. He went over to a partially opened window, closed and locked it. The winery that had been left unfinished until he could recover some cash reserves—until he would truly want to have his own first crush—jutted against the mountainside like some lost abandoned fortress. From the depths of the stable, through the thick closed doors of the bunkhouse, he heard the snorting of a horse, a loud whinny. His entire body tensed. That had been Hajib's noise. *Someone was out there!* He had been followed.

Adam put the lamp out. Reached across the table for his loaded revolver. The night was bright enough to cast light through the windows—enough so that he would not bump into anything. He eased his way around the table, over to the wall, made his way on tiptoe to the door, listened, his whole body straining, every nerve on edge.

There was a definite scraping sound. He could see the flickering of a light approaching the door. It would give him a decided advantage if the other person was holding the light, he thought, and in a rush of motion he flung the door open, yelled out, "A gun is aimed between your eyes! One move—"

It was then that he saw the pale-blue silk skirts, heard their rustle —saw the wide-stricken, startled eyes of Sarah Hubbard Reynolds. He had frightened her so that she almost dropped the lantern.

"Oh . . . oh, thank *God* it is you, Adam," she said weakly, tears of relief, as well as of her gathered fright, surging over her. "I—it never occurred to me there wouldn't be anyone here. From the way they were talking, it sounded as if you had an army of armed Italians up here in wait for trespassers. I was determined I'd convince them I wasn't an enemy."

His arm had reached out to guide her inside. He found his own hand trembling so that it was difficult to assist her. He took the lantern, relocated the lamp, lit it after fumbling with a match.

He did not have to ask her to sit. She fairly collapsed in the nearest chair, propped one elbow for support against the edge of the mess-hall table. "I have never been as frightened in my life," she said, letting out a long sigh, then suddenly a laugh. "Oh, Adam, you looked so funny with that gun! You really meant it, though—you *were* going to shoot me, weren't you, if I had been the wrong person?" She was looking at him intently. Before he could answer, she hurried on to say the rest. She reached across with one hand, touched his arm. "They didn't get to you, then? Jacques Cugnot and that man he was hiring to beat you up? I heard them. I slipped over and hid and listened. I knew my mother had found your letter."

Adam did not want her to stop, yet he knew she could use a brandy, wine, something. He got up. "Just a moment, please. A cup . . . glass . . . somewhere around here I have something. You need a brandy." He found a cup, but he had finished the brandy. "Come on—I have some more in my room," he said quietly, trying to keep down the rush of his own need to hear everything, to ask his own questions. The anger he thought he had against her—where had it gone? All he could see were those eyes, the blue silk dress, those long slender hands in frenzied motion. It was beginning to hit him: she had come here to *him* —*run away*! Risked—in her mind's eye—an army of guns . . .

"Come—I have some brandy. It will be more comfortable. Here— this mess hall is too large. I keep seeing—hearing noises." He took her hand, handed the two cups for their brandy to her, carried the lamp, and made his way down the narrow hallway to his bunk room.

She stood near the window, looking out in the direction of the new house. He found the brandy, placed the lamp on a table across the room and came up behind her. "It is a beautiful house," he said in a husky voice. "It—I had planned to move into it with you as my wife."

Still he did not touch her. He handed the brandy to her, motioned for her to sit on the closest bunk.

Her voice had that merriment that even the fear of the night, the unresolved unspoken things between them, had not taken away. "Isn't this ridiculous? My very best dress on! Adam, you should have seen me trying to find my way on back streets, driving a *buggy*—I haven't done that in years! I used to ride my own mare, but rarely a buggy. I was sneaking into the barn, trying to hitch it up—trying not to tear my dress, of all things. It's my lucky dress—I wore it the night I first met you," she said softly. "Tonight my mother had this elaborate plan

146

up her sleeve. I was not supposed to know that Christopher and his mother were in Napa Valley! She had them staying at the Cugnots'. I was to be so overwhelmed and see my error in having told all of them that I did not love him. She insisted I go to the party, telling me it was my delayed birthday party and she had invited all my friends. Friends! I have no friends here!" She sipped the brandy. "When I heard Jacques Cugnot tell that horrible man to take his whip and wait for you at the bridge, I was frantic! I wanted to warn you, to tell you not to come. I knew—I just *knew* you would. That if you had heard anything, you would give me a chance to explain. I had to pretend I was going to the party. I was supposedly upstairs dressing. I slipped down the back stairs and out to the barn and—somehow I got here." She drank another sip of brandy. "Adam . . . I have to say all this. I have to explain—you must understand . . ."

He had been looking at her as if seeing her for the first time. He was on the edge of the bunk opposite her. His hands were cupped around his brandy, his shoulders hunched forward, his eyes like bright lanterns themselves. "I am listening," he said, his voice sticking to his throat. "Go on. Tell me everything."

"I wasn't sure when I came to this road. And then, driving back in here when it was getting dark, with no sign of anyone around—wondering *where* you were . . . *if* they had found you at the bridge . . . *if* your men might shoot me on sight. And then coming inside that stable —those horses peering at me as if they were my enemies, too."

He could not bear it any longer. He was across the room, pulling her to her feet, drawing her into that space against him where he had held her so many times in his dreams, in every waking thought of her. He knew that he was holding her too tightly, kissing her too furiously. But he wanted never to let her go. Her hair, her forehead, her nose, her mouth—oh, again and again her delicious mouth! Her neck. . . . No, he could not kiss her enough.

"Adam, I thought this would never happen for us . . . I love you . . . I—"

"I will never let another man have you!"

He was pulling her with him in the direction of the lamp, holding her as if she might try to bolt away. Then he was blowing out the lamp. His fingers were working with the buttons, finding gaping places where he was trying to grasp those rising-falling, rising-falling soft mounds. All the while he was kissing her, tugging again at the dress.

"We mustn't rip it . . ."

"These buttons . . . these *things*," he muttered huskily.

147

"Please . . . No, Adam, let *me*." For a moment he stood back, allowing her space to unbutton the dress to her waist. "Adam . . . more brandy. Perhaps we should. . ." She stepped back from him. "While I take it off—we mustn't tear my lucky dress—pour brandy, please."

His boots clumped to the floor. His belt buckle made a clanking sound landing on top of one of the boots. He was ripping at his own buttons . . . trying to pour brandy with a trembling hand into cups that he couldn't find. And then they were standing in the middle of the room, hushed now, stunned by their own nakedness—or, for Sarah, her near-nakedness, for she had not been sure about removing the new silk teddies her roommate at Wellesley had given her, saying, "A man will find you more appealing with something, anything, on. These are for your wedding night."

Adam was trying to juggle the brandy, tug at the silky things, get whatever it was *off*. And then nothing but the brandy cups were between them. They drank awkwardly, and it was Adam who put them someplace—spilling, he guessed—on the opposite bunk bed. And then they were tasting each other's brandy with their tongues, and their mouths sealed in a bonding force that brought them in unison, back and back, working their way to the bunk bed where Adam slept and had dreamed so many dreams. He kept her mouth beneath his, pulled her down beside him, working all the while to keep that bonding heat—that unbearable bonding heat pulling and pulling them into position.

He raised his head from her mouth, finding other parts of her. The smell of the down mattress on the narrow bed, of bed ticking, of some kind of sachet powder she had rubbed under her arms and her breasts combined with his own strong musky odor as his body worked itself now into place. "I must not hurt you . . ."

Her own voice sounding far removed, reaching him from some swirling vortex of sound, saying, "It won't hurt . . . let me help . . ." And their mouths together again while her legs found their natural separated place, out, around him, and those rising mounds of her breasts, like pillows, like clouds beneath him. He was lost—on a sea of rising, gliding, falling, caught in whirling winds, of tuneless songs, of an all-consuming passion that was too exquisite to end. *It must not end. . . .* It must go on and on and on . . . but it was pulling . . . pulling . . . down and down into the garnet-red depths of the vortex . . . and then the winds were ebbing, the sea was still . . . *so very still and silent. . . .*

She was, he realized, crying. Soft, warm tears were sliding down his neck where her head was cradled. He propped himself up on

one elbow, looked at her with worried concern. "I *hurt* you? I know
—I could tell it was the first time. But you said it did not hurt." He
traced one finger down her cheek, swiped gently at the tears. "Please . . .
only don't cry."

"I am not crying because it hurt," she muttered in a muffled voice
against his neck.

"Why, then? Please . . . I love you. You aren't *sorry?* You still
love me? It was all right, wasn't it? Or was I rough—too big a hurry? I
waited so long . . . I couldn't help . . ."

She put one finger to his lips. "No, not that. It was—I love you so
much, Adam. I love you!" The tears were pouring down her face now.
"That is the trouble. Too much—I love you too much. And it is
wrong. Everything is wrong! We should not have done this—spoiled
our wedding night. Hiding—running away from such ugliness. It
should be beautiful! *Right*, in the eyes of—oh, whatever God is, and in
the eyes of my family! It matters—it does matter to me, Adam. I have
tried to convince myself that it doesn't. That loving you is the most
important thing. But they—she is my *mother*! She doesn't understand
what she is doing. She doesn't mean to be evil. I am so mixed up,
Adam. I had to come here to try to keep them from hurting you. But I
didn't come here for—to do what they have all accused us of doing
before now. Everyone looks at me that way, as if I'm spoiled—ruined
. . . I feel—they make me feel *dirty*."

He propped himself up again, looked at her fiercely. "Don't use
that word! Not with me. Never again say 'dirty'! I want to marry you.
My house up there—it is finished now. All but the furniture. It is waiting for you, me, to move in. It is the most beautiful house in Napa
Valley now. . . . I love you, Sarah, I would give my life, everything I
have worked so hard for, to prove it. You must stop crying—that is
spoiling what we . . . the other. To me, it was beautiful. It was so right.
Perfect. There could not be anything *wrong* about something that perfect."

He waited a minute for her to stop. He wiped her tears with the
edge of the sheets that Li Po had put on fresh that very day, taking the
soiled laundry with him to Napa City where his cousin would iron and
starch linens to that clean crispness Adam himself insisted upon. He
tried to cradle Sarah closer against him, felt the dampness beneath his
hip—knew that there must be blood there where he had penetrated her
for the first time.

"Nothing is *dirty* about this, Sarah. Nothing is wrong about it in
the eyes of God either. Not when we love each other and will get mar-

ried. Not when you are, to me, already my wife." The sounds of the night on Spring Mountain wrapped around them for a moment. Instinctively, he was listening through them, checking, evaluating their safety. Shadows flickered about them, encased them on the bunk bed, danced against the rough ceiling, made a snowman's shape out of the potbelly stove.

"You must realize, *love*—it is bigger than all of them down there! What has happened between us tonight . . . Do you love me?"

She lifted her head, looked down at him. "Yes . . . I love you."

For a dreadful moment, Adam had a feeling that he was losing her. Even as his arms closed about her, she was slipping away. "We could not help what we did, don't you see that?" he whispered. "Even now I cannot help wanting to—"

She moved his hands from her breasts, tugged her leg free from under his where it was beginning to climb over again. "No—I must go! I have to get back before they return from Soda Springs. I haven't much time. How . . . how will I manage it?" She was out of bed, suddenly stricken with her own nakedness and reaching frantically for the silk teddies, the petticoats, the blue dress.

Adam was pulling on his trousers, his shirt, carefully hiding the place on the sheets with a blanket. He bent over to relight the lamp when he realized she was having trouble with her slippers.

"No! Please don't light it," she cried out. "I—I know I look terrible. I don't want you to see me like this!"

She was feeling the sticky dampness and how the silk underwear was clinging in the wrong places. She was sure that her silk dress was torn, that the burning places on her face were red and raw where his beard had scratched her. Her fingers trembled so that she could barely manage the buttons on her dress. "Why do I feel so guilty, Adam?" she suddenly blurted out. "Why do I feel dirty—spoiled?"

"You are not either of those things," he said, his blue eyes cold now. "I will not let you think it! I tried to tell you, Sarah—you are the only woman in the world for me and I want you to be my wife. Can't you understand? Your family—it does not seem to me that they love you. What kind of trust do they have in you? Tell me that. Oh, don't you *see*? You have nothing to go home to. Here—here on Spring Mountain is where you belong. With me!"

She had started crying again. "Adam—I—she is my *mother*. I am her only child. And poor broken-down Papa Gilbert—he loves me so much. I'm all he has, in a way. I understand him—I don't make him feel inadequate the way Mother makes him feel. No, I— I have to go home!" She put her frenzied hands on his arms, her amber eyes looked smoldering black. "Look, I will bring Mother around if I have the summer to work on it. Oh, she will stay in bed with one of her migraine headaches, for days, probably, and not speak to me. The Cugnots will go back to St. Louis. Jacques will leave again and we'll be safe from him—" Her voice broke off. "Adam, I'm—I'm afraid in another way. It's as if fate doesn't want us together! Did you know it was by sheer accident that Jacques Cugnot was here at all in Napa Valley? That just two days ago that terrible man he called J. T. was let out of jail? I feel sometimes the whole world is against us. And doesn't that make our—our union *wrong*?"

He shook his head. His voice was soft, gentle. "You cannot fight this, Sarah. It is so perfect—that is why you are afraid. Love—how many people find this kind of love? No, it is not wrong. For me, our union, as you call it, was our wedding vow. Our wedding night. For me, it was perfect."

She seemed caught, as if trapped between two equally destructive forces. "I never thought it would be so—so difficult! *Why*, Adam? when it seemed so perfect to me too. The dream . . ." She seemed agitated now—even afraid of him too, Adam thought. "I have to do this my way, Adam. I—You have to help me! I have to go back. If you will not help me, then I'll go alone. I got up here, I will get back down somehow. The lantern—where is my lantern?"

He took her roughly by the shoulders. "You will not go alone. Stop this. Listen to me—please! I must tell you again, I believe it is a mistake for you to go back down there. They will try to do—I don't know what. But I believe they will try anything now to keep us apart. Jacques Cugnot is a crazy man. He blames me for his failure in Napa Valley. Right or wrong, he does. He will get *me* through you, if he can find a way. Your mother—she will never listen to me, or I would try to explain all this. Try myself to make her see. I have thought about it before! I nearly went there alone. I—"

"Adam, I must do this my way. Please help me—we are wasting valuable time."

He led her, reluctantly, out into the stable, being sure first that he had his revolver, his keys. He bolted the bunkhouse securely. Then he checked the buggy's harness for her, got Hajib out, saddled him, tied a lead rope for him to follow behind the buggy. "I will drive you down. I know the road well. This horse—I believe it must have been sent to pasture. She is very old," he said, trying to cheer her up. He helped Sarah up into the buggy, climbed up, took the reins, urged the old horse into motion.

Sarah was edgy. Her hands fussed with the folds of her silk dress.

There was enough moon to let him see that she was worried, her face strained. He patted her hands clasped in her lap. "Don't worry. We will work this out."

"If I run into someone, will they *know*? Can they tell by looking at me that we . . . that . . ."

"You look *fine*—beautiful," he said, reassuringly.

"I suppose I can slip back up the kitchen stairs—*if* we get home before they do, that is." Her hands clenched, unclenched. "I can get into bed and pretend *I* have a migraine for once. Cover my head—lock my door. Have some sort of female 'spell,' as Mother calls them."

Then they fell silent. Adam maneuvered the buggy around the steep curves, felt the soft, warm summer's night breeze against his face. At the foot of the hill, he turned and took back streets, avoiding St. Helena's Main Street. It was around ten o'clock, he guessed, but the town looked asleep. After a while he was forced to work his way back to the main county road. To his relief, it was deserted. The mare was making a reasonably steady pace. Hajib's hoofs followed restlessly behind them. Clouds drifted across the quarter moon, darkening the road, then drifted on, leaving it hanging there like a tilted golden grinning thing mocking them.

They drove past the Cugnot driveway, past Jacob Brunner's. Soon they had reached the Reynolds' driveway. Adam pulled the buggy off in the darker shadows of a large oak tree, jumped down, handed the reins to her, went behind and untied Hajib's lead rope, led him back to Sarah's side. He reached up, clasped her arm, the silk dress soft, more like satin beneath his fingers. He forced her face where he could kiss her goodbye. He felt her tenseness. "When will I hear from you?" he asked in a whisper.

She looked about anxiously. "As soon as I can. But now I must—I have to hurry. If they were back, she would have someone out here waiting, looking for me. At least we got here before they did."

"Sarah . . . remember," he said, restraining her a moment longer, "if you change your mind, we will elope. We will go to San Francisco the moment you give me the sign. I will meet you there—anywhere. I want you to be my *wife*. To live with me up on Spring Mountain. I will be there, waiting to hear from you." And then, seeing that she was no longer listening but rigid with nervousness, he gave the old mare a vigorous slap on the rump to get it in motion again. He mounted Hajib, waiting under the oak tree until he was sure that she had made her way to the house. But even as he sat there motionless, his eyes glued to the disappearing swaying, rattling buggy wheels, listening to the thudding clomp of the old mare's hoofs, he felt as if he had been caught in some giant invisible network of cobwebs closing in around him in a steellike vise.

He gave Hajib the command to head back toward St. Helena, falling into his own preferred high-stepping canter, his spirit as dynamic, as proud, as ever. Adam's own spirit was draining now. The magic of what had taken place earlier was fading, slipping from his grasp.

He could not understand it. Why couldn't it have been the perfect union? Why the accompanying violence—the ugliness imposed not of their own doing?

Again, clouds closed over the moon. Though it was a warm night, Adam hunched his shoulders forward, as though cold. Then he felt something snap inside him. He sat up, the way the Hungarian Kologz had told him always to sit in the saddle. His head went up, his chin jutted in its usual stubborn line. Tomorrow something would happen! By Monday, he'd think of something.

7

By Monday, Adam had forgotten his anxieties; he was remembering only that magic he had had with Sarah at the bunkhouse. Sometimes, simply remembering, in desperation, he would fling himself down in that very place where he had known the reality of her beneath him, he would relive it vicariously. Then, revitalized, he would take long, striding, confident walks through the vineyards, marveling at his good luck, at the glory of Napa Valley and particularly of his hillside land on Spring Mountain.

Naturally, it would require a few days for Sarah to work through her situation there, he would tell himself; after all, it was not going to be easy. He must be patient, give her time.

So he tried to occupy his days with work, with involvement in grafting on the new cuttings from Jacob Brunner, along with some experimental ones George Hussman had asked him to try out in one particular place in his vineyards where the volcanic ash lay in places like fine white powder. He took a trip with Kyle up the back of Diamond Mountain, where Adam ran that powdery chalklike soil through his fingertips, gazed down at the valley, and still opted for his Spring Mountain vineyards. "The best—I will be giving my bride the best," he would tell himself secretly.

He received word his furniture had arrived at Napa City's wharf, and he took the young Paulo, whose wedding was coming up at the end of the month, down with the big freight wagon. When they unloaded the beds, chairs, couches, tables, chests, and odds and ends he thought he would need, he tried to place them in the big empty house so that it seemed fully furnished. "I need rugs. I need to have a woman help me," he said, his blue eyes alive.

Waiting—it was so difficult to wait, he thought desperately. Yet it was simply a matter of time now before Sarah would tell him they could be married. Before he could tell the world she was his wife!

· ·

The first blow came on a Wednesday, only two weeks after Sarah's return. It was Wang Chi, Jacob Brunner's old Chinese man, who rode the gelding up the back trail; was flailing his arms about wildly, yelling in Chinese to some workmen helping Kyle graft on some new vines where the old Golden Chasselas had been. Kyle got the message straight finally; hurried over to find Adam.

"Wang Chi says old man Brunner is bad off. They want you to come down there right away! He's asking for you."

Adam ran to the barn, threw a saddle on Hajib, took the lead back down the familiar trail; soon left the frightened Wang Chi and his gelding far behind.

Dr. Williams had just given Jacob a stimulant for his heart when Adam slipped into the bedroom upstairs. A white-faced Erika, her voice sounding as if it were being sifted through a net, whispered to him, "I waited for him to get up—come down for breakfast. I—he was like this . . ."

Dr. Williams nodded to Adam, who stepped closer to the bed. "The Donati young man is here, Jacob. Can you *hear* me?" Dr. Williams called out to the shallow-breathing limp form.

Adam grasped Jacob's hand in both of his. "I'm here . . ."

Jacob's voice was barely audible. "I want your promise—you marry my Erika. Take my land. Take everything. You must marry my granddaughter. Promise me . . ."

"I will tell—" But before Adam could say anything more, Jacob seemed to lurch his head back, as if making one last attempt to suck life into his worn-out body. His mouth gaped open, revealing his ragged, age-yellowed teeth. His breath had cast a sour, stale odor that sifted up, made Adam feel as if he would gag and was trapped in an airless place. Then the frail, spent form beneath the brightly colored Swiss coverlet was still.

It was Erika who first reached down. Her fingers spread out hesitantly, fan-shaped, hovered above his face. Gently, she touched his weathered cheeks. With her fingertips whe closed his eyelids and fixed his mouth so that his teeth didn't show. "I *love* you, Papa Jacob," she said in a barely audible voice. And then she began to cry. It was as though all those unshed tears from her past horror, from that frozen-off time in her life, now rushed through a sudden weakened spot.

For Adam, it was a terrible thing to see. He had never heard such sounds or witnessed the type of agonized convulsions that ripped her small, fragile body. Both he and Dr. Williams came to help her; led her out of the room, across the hallway to her own pristine, crisply clean bedroom. While Dr. Williams removed her ankle-high small boots, helped her loosen her tighter garments, Adam turned back the covers.

"I must help her get some peace," Dr. Williams said, preparing a hypodermic. "While this sedative takes effect, could you stay here with her?" he asked. "I have a few arrangements to make—the funeral."

"Of course," Adam said, pulling a chair closer to the bedside, taking Erika's lifeless hand inside his own.

"I am alone—so very alone," she mumbled, her eyelids fluttering, heavy with the sedative. "Papa Jacob tried to help. But I can't possibly manage. I simply cannot."

"Don't—you mustn't cry. Please don't cry," Adam coaxed, patting her hand with both of his. "I will help you. Wang Chi is still here. No, you aren't alone. There's Kyle, Luigi. . . . We will be your family."

"But you do not love me," she said in a voice that seemed to be drifting. "I know that you could never really love me."

"Please . . . try to sleep," he said, pushing her damp hair off her face. "Please . . ."

When word got out that Jacob Brunner had died, it was as though something came awake in the valley. Neighbors from all directions came to call, to leave baskets of food, to take turns sitting watch over the casket, receiving guests, seeing that coffee, tea and refreshments were passed around. To Adam's bewilderment, he did not see any sign of Miss Grace Reynolds or of Sarah, though the haughty Lydia Cugnot swept in and out, leaving behind a tall wicker basket filled with gladiolus.

As often happens after a man dies, Jacob Brunner's talents and assets to the community came into sharper, more meaningful focus. Though his blue ribbons from the State Fair were an acknowledged fact, it was as though the awards were being bestowed again, and with their first true significance. All the important vintners came to pay their respects and to stand around in clusters exchanging their memories of what year produced the greatest vintage, which rare varietals were Jacob's finest, the ones he would be most remembered for. "Out of the eighteen awards from the 1889 Paris Exposition given to Napa Valley wines, it is my bet that fifteen of them were made from Jacob Brunner's grapes," one grizzle-faced cellarmaster from Inglenook commented. "Hasn't been a label of any note come out of this valley without his touch on it someplace," came the answer.

Adam tried to stay in the background but keep his ears open for responses in general. To him, Jacob Brunner had become the closest thing to a father he had known—certainly in this new country of

America, if not, even, in Pontremoli. In a few brief months, really, he had learned to love him. They had exchanged something he could not easily put into words. A burning lump of sadness rode in the pit of his stomach as he stood listening, watching faces that had known Jacob through the years.

Erika moved like a figure fashioned out of her own now noted pastries. She wore a simple, nunlike black dress. Her hair was pulled back into a tight twisted knot. The gray eyes seemed to have rounded out like marbles, and the medicine Dr. Williams had Wang Chi administer to her every four hours had given her eyes a shimmering, glassy look. She nodded, bowed, extended her hand as though responding to some automatic timer inside her. Concerned women from the Catholic church and Father O'Brien himself seemed to hover about her as though trying to seal off any further hurts.

Adam had just stepped out into the hallway, on his way into the parlor to see if Kyle or anyone from Spring Mountain was still around, when he heard one neighbor say in an excited whisper, "Look—there comes Miss Grace herself! Draped in black from head to foot. Acting like Jacob Brunner was her nearest and dearest in this wide world. Coming in with her big basket of dried-apple cake and that boiled custard she takes everyplace—you wait and see! Coming in taking charge—being the boss."

Adam felt the color drain from his face. But it was too late for him to go out the side entrance. Miss Grace was entering the front door, her face veiled in black, the enormous hat riding her proud head like buzzard wings. He saw her look at him as if he were the empty hat rack; brush on past the two neighbor ladies with a curt "Good afternoon, Charlotte. How are you, Nellie? Isn't it too bad that it takes a funeral to bring this valley together? I never see you. I understand Erika is sleeping. Which room, please?"

Adam decided to stand precisely where he was. He folded his hands quite stiffly, stood as though waiting for someone just outside the dining-room door. He pretended an aloofness, that he was not listening or watching. His blue eyes had faded to a color almost as pale gray as that of the cotton dress and sunbonnet the round-faced, heavyset woman named Nellie wore. The thinner, nervous-looking, colorless woman called Charlotte seemed to shrink back, as if trying to find an open door where she had bumped into solid wall. Obviously, he thought, they were frightened of Miss Grace Reynolds. He saw their false smiles, their patronizing nodding up and down.

"Yes, isn't it dreadful. . . . Oh, you mean your daughter isn't here? She's gone *where*?" Nellie was asking.

Adam felt the blind fading of his reasoning. He whirled about, went into the room where Erika was sleeping. He was standing at the foot of her bed, his hand gripped around the cold brass railing at the foot. Erika's small face looked white, childlike. Her blond hair had come loose from the tightly twisted bun. The covers barely moved as she breathed in and out, regularly, the afternoon's sedative having taken its effect.

He heard the movement in the doorway, sensed the gathered black skirts, the hand clutching them, moving around behind him, on to the side of the bed.

Both his hands clutched the railing now. His chin was jutted forward, his eyes like chiseled ice. Miss Grace did not look at him. She bent over, placed her hands lightly on Erika's right arm that was out from under the cover.

"You poor, poor unfortunate child. . . . But don't worry. Now that my own daughter has gone, I will adopt you as my child. Do you hear me, dear? This is your neighbor—Miss Grace. Mrs. Reynolds. You do *hear* me? I want you to know that you won't be alone. I had planned for you to meet my daughter. That you two would be friends. The party I told you about—that is, the small *girl* party we were going to have as a kind of bridal shower for Sarah?" Miss Grace was patting Erika's still arm, her fingers like wet, wrinkled crepe material, interlaced with ripply blue veins, heavy with diamond and ruby rings. A lace handkerchief clutched between two fingers waved like a small flag of victory. She looked up at the ashen-faced Adam, who felt as if his head had been filled with leaf hoppers addling his thoughts, his reason. "My daughter has gone to New York—we presume she has decided eloping is much easier." Her face with its pouches of gathered fat, of lines like boundaries on a road map, blurred, came back into focus. "But we won't talk now. I know you are exhausted." She had seen Erika's fluttering eyes, the movement of the arm, like a bird with an injured wing trying to fly. "I will call again soon, dear. I will see what needs doing around here. I understood your mother's old school chum, Gudrun, is on her way here from Vallejo. That she plans to move in and stay with you."

She had not spoken to Adam; nor he to her. When she was through, she stood for a moment, her back as stiff as if it were the very flagpole for her triumphant banner. The black hat and veil and the black suit with its rows of buttons, its tiny pleats around the flounce of the floor-length skirt went past him like one monstrous unfurled black sail that had successfully flung an enemy into the sea to drown.

Wang Chi scuffled into the room. "You go home now. Maybe *you* need some powder? I sent Li Po some medicine for you. He—Mr. Brunner loved you. You a son to him. Maybe you marry sad girl? Make her very happy." His whispering voice sounded to Adam like mountain wind whipping around the corners of the giant stone house. Corners of a bridal tomb . . . "You okay, Mr. Donati?" Wang Chi asked, his own grief-ravaged face struggling to keep that inscrutable expression.

"Yes," Adam mumbled. "Tell her—I'll be back later." He did not remember leaving Erika's room.

He half stumbled into the barn, led Hajib from his stall, tightened the saddle, mounted, the reins burning his hands like ropes. He headed out, automatically turning toward the back trail. When he caught sight of the stone bridge, he pulled Hajib to an instant stop. The arch of the bridge, the sound of the tumbling water became Sarah's face, Sarah's words, Sarah's vow to him.

And then he was yanking Hajib around, racing at full gallop back past Jacob's house, down the driveway to the main county road.

If Hajib was sensitive to the tension of the hands on the reins, he did not rebel, but it was as if his own spirited legs were racing with the wind in search of something unnamed. His hoofs pounded the hard-packed surface of the main county road. If men standing on China Mary's front door stoop looked up curiously as the handsome man in a black suit riding what was surely one of the most magnificent black horses in Napa Valley tore past, it did not matter to him. *Appearances . . . impressions . . .* He had spent too much time on such matters in the past. *Truth . . . There was only the truth*, his father used to pound into them. He was going after the truth! If Sarah Hubbard Reynolds was still in Napa, he must know. If she had really gone to New York, he must know!

He did not let Hajib slow down. He was riding down the Reynolds' driveway under the huge oak trees. The pillars loomed like the Parthenon pictures he had seen. The driveway went around the south-western corner to the back, where a frowning Chinese man came scurrying, his wizened face bobbing up and down in puzzlement.

Adam leaped off the horse, tossed the reins at him, and without speaking took long angry strides back around to the main front entrance. His boots made dull, thudding sounds across the brick terrace. At the double doors, he pounded furiously.

He did not hear any sound. He looked up at the underside of the second-floor gallery. All around him the massive pillars marched like encircling tombstones. A wind warm and gentle swept across his face.

He sucked in a deep determined breath, pounded the door knocker, banged with his fist on the doors.

When it opened suddenly, Adam took a quick step back. He had never been this close to a black man before. He had not seen any black people at all in Napa Valley. In New York and Chicago he had seen them. On the train there had been porters, but they were always in uniform and never face to face, in command of the situation.

"Yas, suh?" came the thick, languid Mississippi drawl.

"I want to see Sarah Hubbard Reynolds," Adam said, his entire six-feet-two pulled into a ramrod command of its own.

"Sorry, suh, she ain't heah."

"Who *is* here!"

"Mistah Reynolds—he's heah, suh. But he ain't receivin' company. Sorry, suh."

But at that moment a moon-faced man, whose tongue seemed swollen, more or less waddled, teetered up to the opened door. "Come on in. Since *when* am I not receiving company, Matthew? Shame on you, Matthew, telling this nice young man a big white lie like that. This fine young man in a black suit on a day hot as this asking to see Sarah Hubbard Reynolds. Why, Matthew, I'm *surprised*. Miss Grace taught you to be hospitable to strangers come knocking at the door, didn't she?" He reached out and grabbed Adam's upper arm. "Go on, Matthew! Get us something nice on a silver tray. Bring out those *Hubbard* silver goblets. Miss Grace'll kill you on the spot if you don't serve us a drink in those Hubbard goblets. Whiskey? A brandy? What suits you, young man?"

"I didn't come to drink! I came to see—your daughter."

"Well, now, I wish I could just snap my finger and, *click*—" Reynolds tried to make his thumb and forefinger come out with a snapping noise, but the effort made him lose his balance slightly. He batted his eyes, held on tightly to Adam's arm. "What we need aroun' here 'sides Matthew, who oughtta go back to Mississippi and claim his freedom from Miss Grace's slave-driving ways—right, Matthew?—what we need is a nice fairy godmother who could just *whisssh* . . . bring out Sarah." His eyes clouded, watered, and now he was clutching Adam with both hands. "They took her away! They didn't even let her come tell me goodbye. Sarah wouldn't do that to me."

"Where is your daughter?" Adam asked, tight-lipped.

"First sit down there—make yourself at home. Let's talk. Get acquainted. Sarah'ud want me to get to know you. You're that young man she was in love with—the one she was telling me about, aren't you? That one from Italy? Lives up on Spring Mountain? See, I know a thing or two! I'm not totally *blotto*—yeah, that's what Miss Grace, her highness, calls me, *blotto*." Reynolds tried to sit down somewhat grandly, but barely made his way into the chair and sat down more with a big plopping motion. "Tell me this, young man, how in the hell did I ever land up in this place, married to her royal highness? Me—from Illinois. Out here with the big drove of bug-eyed men trying to find a big strike. Here comes Miss Grace, bowls me over with all that molasses. Found out I was due for a big inheritance—and look around, see what it got me! Furniture straight out of New Orleans and Natchez. *Hubbard* silver goblets . . . and Matthew here—keeps me quiet, don'tcha, Matthew? Give the old goat enough to keep him *blotto*." He took a goblet from the silver tray, waited, saw that Adam was refusing a drink. He waved the black man out of the room. Then he bent over, pointed a wavering finger at Adam. "I guess you and me both struck out. Miss Grace fooled us both. Got her out of here—on the same train headed back to New York as that snot-nosed Christopher Something-or-other went back on. Jacques Cugnot took her out, right under my nose. Didn't even let her come tell me goodbye. *Whisssk*—that's what happened! And old Jacob Brunner dead now. Everything dead . . . Everything gone . . . everything but the Hubbard silver goblets." He did not seem to know that his drunken tears were sliding into the whiskey, trickling off the end of his nose that was as red and bulbous as an overripe strawberry. Nor did he even look up when Adam stormed out of the parlor and ran across the brick terrace to find his horse.

It was the next week when the letter from Miss Grace Reynolds arrived. Adam did not read it immediately. He opened it as he might have opened a new form to fill out from the government regarding getting his winery bonded. He was resigned to those things inevitable: "Lady Luck's hind-leg kick," as Kyle Plimpton would have referred to what had happened to him.

New York City, New York
July 20th, 1895

DEAR MR. DONATI,

I have just joined my daughter here in New York. At her request, I am writing this letter to explain why she did not personally contact you when she made the right decision to marry Christopher Elliot-Weare. The wedding date will be set this coming late fall. In the meantime, I am taking my daughter, in the company of my long-time friend, Veronica Elliot-Weare, to Europe. (The Hubbards and the Elliots had plantations next to each other in Mississippi before the dreadful War Between the States; a fact I relay to you, Mr. Donati, since you do not apparently understand that in this country, heritage means a great deal to some of us; we do not accept just anyone who steps off the boat and decides he is free to marry whom he so chooses!)

In view of our upcoming plans, it will be impossible for you to attempt to contact my daughter, should you entertain such a foolish notion. I have been informed that you are a man of temper, of emotional outrageousness: traits from your background which have already done my daughter great harm. She is most fortunate, indeed, that Christopher Elliot-Weare is still willing to marry her after what has transpired!

If our paths should ever cross in the Napa Valley again, I warn you that I shall never speak to you or acknowledge you in any manner whatsoever. The same shall be said for my daughter, Sarah.

Accept this letter as a final goodbye. My servant, Matthew, has been instructed that should you trespass on our property, or bother Mr. Reynolds in any manner, he will send for the Sheriff.

Most sincerely,
MRS. GRACE HUBBARD REYNOLDS

The first thing that Adam did on Spring Mountain after that letter arrived was to have all the furniture he had ordered for the master bedroom removed and that room permanently locked. The large fourposter bed with its canopy was moved into the room in the northwest corner, the only room in the entire house, it seemed, without a view.

One month after Jacob Brunner was buried, Adam called on Erika and proposed marriage in a solemn, matter-of-fact voice.

"He wished it, on his deathbed," Adam said. "I don't think I will be the best husband for you. For any woman. But I have become very fond of you and I promise you that I will be good to you. I will be kind and protect you from harm. I will be a lucky man if you will marry me."

He studied her face, the slight fluttering motion in her delicate hands. He saw the gray eyes soften ever so slightly. Her voice came back quite calmly, surprising him: "It does seem the right thing to do. It would be practical. There was a will—a will with certain provisions, should I—should *we* get married. He didn't name your name, but we know he was thinking of you."

163

"I suppose—yes," Adam said quietly, holding her hands.

"You have full use of all the land. You would, I believe he said, become the steward of it. As a dowry, you would receive outright the vineyards up there on Spring Mountain."

Adam's blue eyes were alive with their first true sparks of greed. He could not help it. The Brunner vineyards on Spring Mountain were the best anywhere in Napa Valley, his own included! And now they would be *his*—all his very own!

This time, Erika was studying him closely. "The other—the terms he placed on his valley-floor land are complicated . . ."

Adam released her hands, walked over and poured sherry into two glasses. "Never mind the land. Let us drink a toast to Jacob. To your grandfather—to my friend. To a man who was quite like a father to me. I loved him. And I love you too, Erika." In a sense, that was not a lie, he told himself quickly.

She lifted her glass, smiled over the rim, a peculiar gleam in her gray eyes, he thought. "You will never love me the way— the way you love the land," she said in a hurried, breathless voice. "But it doesn't matter. I love the land, too. Papa Jacob taught me that. He taught me to respect it."

"Then there is no reason why we shouldn't have a very nice life together, is there? We have much in common."

The wedding was a simple one. Since Erika was not a Catholic, they had a justice of the peace come to the Brunner home, where Erika preferred to hold the ceremony. She had placed full arrangements in the hands of her mother's friend, the big, lumpy Gudrun, who seemed to stand in doorways, Adam thought, as if she were there on guard.

"Why doesn't she ever *smile?*" he asked Erika, before the ceremony took place and an unsmiling Gudrun had gone about adjusting flowers, rearranging cookies on a tray, setting wineglasses in precise rows.

"She's German, I guess that's why," Erika said lightly. She seemed to have taken on a kind of girlish giggle—a nervousness, Adam supposed, with no one but himself and the hefty Gudrun there as family. He must remember that she had lost everyone. He must never forget.

Erika had agreed that after the ceremony their wedding dinner could be held with the friendly Alfieris. There, a smiling Delfina, surrounded by her large family and a beaming Vittorio, brought out a wedding cake with pink icing. Vittorio passed champagne. There was a kind of giddiness in the air after several bottles were consumed, but even Kyle's jokes and Luigi's booming laughter did not bring a true note of hilarity and happiness. Something was missing, and it could be seen in quick, serious looks Vittorio would now and then exchange worriedly with Delfina.

At one point, Gudrun lumbered up to Adam. "Erika wants me to come live with her up on Spring Mountain," she said flatly. Erika seemed to swim in a blur behind her. Adam felt his head whirl in a dizzy, near-black spell, as if he were sinking down and down. Somehow, the reality of actually moving into the big house on Spring Mountain with Erika Brunner as his wife was just hitting him. Now he was looking into the square face of the big Gudrun. He simply could not imagine either's presence where he had, in his dreams, walked through every room with Sarah Reynolds!

He should smile, he told himself frantically. He must look convincing. Jacob would be smiling if he were alive. But if he were alive, Adam wouldn't be married. *The land—the dowry* . . . No, he mustn't think like this! Smile . . . yes . . . yes. That was what he should be doing. . . .

Erika's voice seemed to drift up from some tunnel. "Gudrun knows about vegetable gardens. How to manage a big house."

At that point, Delfina came up, her oldest daughter, Theresa, in tow. "She is going to play the piano for us. Vittorio has bought a new upright piano. Come, see how proud we are. Someday, if she is good, maybe we will buy a big concert grand piano."

Soon Luigi, Kyle, Vittorio and the other children were clustered around the piano, everyone singing as Theresa's fumbling fingers tried to pick out melodies.

"*Salute!*" Adam called out, his voice thickening, one arm pulling Erika into an all-engulfing circling motion. "To my wife."

"Yes, to your *wife*," Erika said, her voice strangely flat, a curious smile fixing itself on her small, porcelain-like face.

The drunken, loud-singing Luigi and Kyle headed the wedding procession up Spring Mountain. Erika had placed her head on Adam's shoulder, she herself now tipsy. When they arrived at the main house, Adam insisted that everyone come inside to christen the hearth. He introduced Erika to Li Po, who bowed, grinned shyly, and said, "Welcome to your new home. Your suite is ready."

After the wineglasses had been emptied and thrown in ritual against the hearth in the parlor, Kyle and Luigi exchanged knowing looks, said goodbye, went down to the bunkhouse, still singing, fresh wineglasses in hand. An unsmiling Gudrun was taken by Li Po to the northwest bedroom with the giant fourposter bed.

As Adam and Erika climbed the new, highly polished stairway,

Adam realized through his alcoholic haze that he was a good foot taller than Erika. With Sarah, she had come to the end of his nose. Their bodies—they had fit so well. *They had been perfect.* This little girllike woman—how could he manage? Would it work at all?

Li Po was waiting at the door to their suite. He bowed. "A hot bath is ready for the lady." He hurried down the hallway, disappeared down the back stairway.

"A groom must carry the bride over the threshold," Adam said, scooping Erika up as though she were a doll, a tiny child he could swing around in the air. She snuggled up against him, wound her arms around his neck. He set her down in the middle of the enormous room, tilted her chin up. "Do you want to take a hot bath?" he asked, actually stalling for time, expecting her to be grateful for any delay he might offer her before he would, in essence, he realized, violate her body. *Hurt*—he would surely hurt so fragile and petite a child. In fact, he could not imagine anything—anything at all.

She stepped away from him, light-footed, as thought she might suddenly start dancing. Her arms went out in a slow-moving windmill. Then she stopped and began removing pins from her hair. She ran her fingers through it, let it fall in its own shimmering clouds slowly around her shoulders. A ripple of a laugh slipped from her and, to his amazement, she was shedding her clothing. The wedding blouse, a delicate oyster-colored lace, she dropped daintily onto a chair. She stepped out of the skirt, the petticoats. She was wearing some sort of white ruffled lace. Her arms, thin and white, reached toward him. "Undress me. . . . Please undress me and carry me into the bathroom and put me in the tub and wash me," she said softly.

Adam looked at her, uncertain. But she seemed relaxed with her whole being. With Erika, the shy, traumatized Erika, he had expected a tedious introductory period. He had most certainly not expected this sudden naked, taunting elfin creature, tossing her hair back, twisting it in braids, unashamedly standing there waiting!

"I am your *wife*," she said, again in a mocking, teasing way. She lifted her arms toward him, and he was carrying her in to the bathtub, placing her in the sudsy, foaming water. His hands were sliding down across her back, around slowly, finding her small firm breasts, reaching on down in front, down, the sleeves of his shirt making a bubbling, squishing sound. Steam poured up into his nostrils, his open mouth. Again, to his amazement, she was reaching toward him, her small hands undoing the buttons on his trousers. *She was a child—a woman! She was a strange devil with gray eyes gleaming like cat eyes at him.* And then he was a victim of forces new and overpowering to him. He was lifting her out of the water, carrying her, dabbing at the dripping, foaming soapsuds with a towel. He put her on the bed and was barely able to wait long enough to get the damp trousers out of his way before he was spreading her legs apart, and her own slender doll-like hands were helping him find his way inside her.

"I knew . . . I always knew if I waited I would someday be Mrs. Adam Donati," a small, matter-of-fact voice said under the groaning, animalistic cries escaping him as this tiny woman named Erika he thought he knew so well claimed him as her husband.

If the next morning Adam expected to find a childlike, snugly sleeping Erika nestled up against him (as he secretly now hoped), he was disappointed. She had slipped up at the roosters' crowing, dressed in a plain, to-the-floor, severe brown cotton dress, pulled her long blond hair back in a tight knot, and was going about the huge new stone house making notes.

"Papa Jacob would expect me to be efficient. To run things well for you," she said, giving no hint whatsoever of what had transpired the night before.

He was to learn it was a pattern, a way she had. There were definitely *two* Erikas. He began to watch the one by day, trying to detect signs of the child-woman he found at night. He began to want darkness to fall. To be there for her to claim in whatever new way she seemed to decide was her spur-of-the-moment fancy. They took baths together. He would sit watching as she played with soap bubbles floating across the surface of the hot, foamy water. He was like some toy she found, played with, used as she wished. At first, he gave in to the bodily enchantment, the excitement of the unexpected. But as the weeks passed, he began to notice the gleam in her gray eyes. He became somehow afraid of what had at first intrigued him, driven him to delirious physical joy: the hands cupping a soap bubble, closing suddenly around him; a certain laughter she would let escape when his whole being flowed away from him, became her possession.

But any fears Adam had about Erika's strangeness had to be put aside, temporarily. It was September and the crush was on.

There is an excitement, a kind of feverish pitch that takes hold during harvest time. From those very first blessings and toasts to the crush, it is as though some long-stored-up energy releases itself in a swirling vortex around the vineyards and wineries. From sunup into the night, frenzied separate activities form an overall well-tuned synchronization: one that takes the grapes from the vines into lugboxes; from there onto transporting vehicles that dump them into the stemmer-crusher; then on into fermentation vats; and finally into cooperage for the wine to sleep. A pungent odor from flowing ripe juice sweeps across the valley floor, is caught up by ocean breezes wafting in at night and sifted across the very mountaintops. Fruit flies swarm in tiny dark clouds. Bees and flocks of birds and wide-eyed deer make their own private feasts and celebrations. It is that peak, that acme, of seasons!

And even that year of 1895, when the industry was at one of its lowest ebbs, when the sad news had just spread that Krug, the Napa Valley grandfather of commercial wines, had indeed folded, and even the California State Viticultural Commission on which Krug had served had been abolished, there was still optimism riding those few thousand acres of bearing vines left after the phylloxera's devastation. It was harvest! For some, that seemed enough in itself.

Kyle Plimpton came up to Adam after the picking got under way. "I guess my rule of thumb that we'd start fifty days after the first color hit the grapes was off this year. It's been a spotty growing season. Hot, cold, rain—now this blistering heat spell."

"There are variables always, I guess," Adam said. "How bad do you think the market really is right now, Kyle?"

"E. C. Briber—was our Napa Commissioner—he was saying the other day all the vintners ought to hold back their wine. Store it away in good cooperage and wait until all those consumers he *says* are out there someplace start hollering for good wine." Kyle wiped his perspiring forehead, downed a cool drink of water. "Wonder if he's figured out how a man's s'posed to hold back—how he's gonna stretch his pocketbook in the meantime. But E. C.'s smart. He's got a good idea of how to beat the market, I guess."

Adam looked at Kyle thoughtfully. "Did I tell you to hold back our Spring Mountain Cabernets? Just to sell Jacob's valley-floor ones? I got my license. I'm even bonded now to make brandy on the pot still I bought on Howell Mountain. Vittorio says we can manage a moderate crush. Paulo's cousins have scrubbed out the oak—those small barrels, which I prefer to use on my reds. We're set with a couple of redwood fermentation vats." He saw Kyle's studying look. "Oh, I know the winery itself is still a shell, so to speak. But we have a roof, and walls without windows. It will be rustic, but we have the gravity-flow principle and aren't dependent on fancy equipment."

Kyle squinted one eye, smacked at a sweat-bee on the side of his face. "I'm mostly a *grape* man myself. But you pick up a few things hanging around wineries the way I have all my life. I was wondering if you'd noticed those two acres over there in the hollow—those Rieslings we thought had bunch rot so bad, thought they'd fall right off the vines a while back? It's my guess they might end up having that 'noble mold' everybody seems to think is like solid gold when it does happen once in a blue moon. If it is, will you be turning your hand at some late-harvest Riesling?"

Adam shot Kyle an appreciative look. "I'm glad you saw it," he said quietly. "I've been keeping my eye out on them—hoping. There are so many factors, though. They have to have more than that shriveled-up raisin look they've got right now. We've got to get that high concentrate of sugar—a metabolized acid. If it's true that we'll have *Botrytis cineria* working into a genuine noble mold, then maybe I could win my first blue ribbon at the State Fair! Who knows? Yes, if those grapes turn out right, maybe we'll get a few rare bottles this very first vintage."

"With your kind of good luck, wouldn't surprise me," Kyle said, going back to the vineyards to oversee the next freight-wagon load nearly ready now to head down Spring Mountain.

Adam watched him take his long, loping, lean-legged strides back to his crew of pickers. A rush of affection, akin to a pure brotherly love for Kyle Plimpton, spread over him. He missed Luigi Pascarella— whom he rarely saw these days, who came now and then to visit on a Sunday afternoon and admire his own buildings or show them off to some future customer; but with Kyle, he shared that bond of the land. It was something he could never put into words to him, but he hoped Kyle knew the implicit trust he had in him and the place he had taken in his life.

He was smiling. Kyle and his Lady Luck, he thought. He wished he could believe in her as Kyle so irrevocably did! Luck—yes, he granted it a space, but somehow it got diffused with Napa Valley itself, with Mother Nature, with God, with all of it grafted onto the same vine somehow. However, he did not bud onto that the scion of love. Love had its own separate forces, he thought bitterly. Even Kyle could not come up with a rule of thumb on that one!

It had come as a relief to Adam when Erika announced she wanted to go to her grandfather's place for a few weeks to tend to the work that needed doing there. She had been taught to keep his books up to date. She also wanted to do some canning. See that his house stayed cleaned. She would take Gudrun, since she did not want to be alone, she told him.

Adam had taken them down himself, and assured her he would come down, hopefully, every day to check on them and eat supper with them. He was the officially hired foreman of the six hundred valley-floor acres Jacob had willed directly to Erika. Jacob had specified that a capable foreman be hired; perhaps with sharecropping terms worked out, if necessary. Erika herself had said to Adam, "He would expect you to be the foreman. I will pay you by the terms of the will." Her delicate features twisted into a tight, hard look. "You will have to manage your own Spring Mountain books. I will tend to those of Papa Jacob's."

Adam had noticed that same look—a kind of stinginess—cross her face anytime they were discussing business. He decided it was because she had lost so much in her life; what she had left she was determined to keep in a tight-fisted grip of her own. He tried to keep himself reminded of this when he would see her gray eyes cloud over suspiciously over a new item. But if the terms of the will specifically applied, she would inevitably brighten and say, "Papa Jacob would be pleased. Yes, he wants it this way." Her voice would sound as if she had just discussed it with her grandfather. "Papa Jacob wants me to be fair—do what is best for the *land*."

Caught in the swirl of harvest taking place (now largely on Spring Mountain), Adam found it advantageous to take the daily rides down the back trail. He also found it easier to have one hot meal there in the simple, sparse kitchen. In a way, it was as it had been—except there was no Jacob; there was the sour Gudrun in his place.

He was relieved in several ways that Jacob Brunner had diversified his six hundred acres on the valley floor as he had done, rationing out so many acres for pasture, for barley, for hay, for cattle grazing, for orchards. And after the phylloxera had wiped out his original vineyards, he had replanted with the new root stock only some thirty acres of Zinfandel, twenty-five of Cabernet Sauvignon, and five acres of Merlot. Once he had said to Adam, his eyes alive with his own secrets, with the excitement of sharing, "You have the nose and palate to tell the difference! You'd know by blind-tasting which Cabernets come from Spring Mountain and which ones come from down here in Rutherford. I'd bet money."

The old man's wisdom about the land—his use of it—was making more imprint on Adam each day. If more of the six hundred acres were in vines right now, how could his exhausted crew manage? And, the market having shrunk, what good would it do? It would be the profits from the diversification that would carry them through this year. He didn't need Erika's precise figures to see that. Had Jacob known all along he might fail without Erika? Without the dowry? But why had he handed over complete control of the valley-floor acreage to her? Had he guessed that Erika herself might change her mind? Or was it Adam Donati he doubted? Or, in the long run, had Jacob Brunner known too much about Napa Valley—what it could give a man and what it could take away?

The questions haunted Adam's mind at times. Yet, it was the middle of harvest. It was all he could do to keep an eye on the loyal Chinese men down in Rutherford, work his way through spiritless visits with an increasingly agitated Erika and the sullen-looking Gudrun. If he had noticed a certain pale, drawn look on Erika's delicate face, he had little time to worry about it. Ching had told him they would be ready to pick the Zinfandels, and then the Cabernets would be ready. There was not going to be any lull whatsoever between the work on Spring Mountain and that down in Rutherford. They would be dovetailing.

He had just arrived back at Spring Mountain one sundown, following a particularly difficult supper with Erika, who had decided not to speak to anyone and had even left the table midway in the meal without explanation. Kyle Plimpton was sitting on the stone veranda. "I hope you don't mind—it was hot as Hades down in the bunkhouse tonight. I like sitting here looking out at the sunset bouncing its colors off the east slopes over there. Look west, you get bright orange. Look east, it's rosy-pink." He got up to go.

"No, stay—I need to talk with you anyway," Adam said. "We've got to start picking in Rutherford too, sooner than we expected." He sighed. "It's piling up. We're so short-handed."

Kyle chuckled. "Harvest wears you out all right. But sometimes—even when sometimes I get down on myself and start thinking how Lady Luck has hopscotched her way right around me, I get to figuring I still have to be one of the luckiest men alive to get to take part in the harvest again!" He sent a series of tiny puffs of smoke into the still, warm early evening. "I feel like a kid waiting for Santa Claus, wondering what's going to be wrapped up under the tree. Even if you get disappointed, you always figure next year it'll come out right. I guess we've had some mixups in ole Santa's bag. Damn, this year I was sick to see where those leaf hoppers did some more damage! And we must be feeding every deer on Spring Mountain. I know grapes are way off—

hardly worth the effort picking 'em this year. But damned if I still don't feel proud to be part of it! It's a feeling—kind of like I've got an extra rib grafted on about the vines, the land. It's like the harvest means to me what Thanksgiving and Christmas all wrapped up in one mean to some people. It's what makes everything else that takes place all year come to a head—mean something special to me." He looked at Adam, to see if he understood. "Yep, I start feeling that way from the first minute Erika brings out that picnic basket, to the last—when some of us sneak off for a finishing-up bender."

"I guess that's okay," Adam said, smiling, seeing the guilty look that had crossed Kyle's face. And suddenly he was quoting something his father used to say: " 'And Noah began to be a husbandman, and he planted a vineyard; and he drank of the wine and was drunken.' "

Kyle stood up, stretched, took one last look at the fading-out sunset's deeper colors reflected on the eastern mountains. He laughed down at Adam. "You mean that same old man Noah, with the Ark and all—that he went off on a big toot, a whopper of a bender himself?" He chuckled openly. "Then maybe it ain't gonna chalk up so hard against me in that little book where Saint Peter scores things, huh? Maybe I won't get as thirsty in hell as some people claim is gonna happen to me when I die."

In November, Erika came back to Spring Mountain. Gudrun, she told him, was staying behind to keep the Chinese from taking over the place and running it to the dogs behind their backs.

"You don't mean you'd expect that to happen from Wang Chi or Ching?" Adam asked, giving her a welcoming kiss on one thin, pale cheek, taking her suitcase and handing it to Li Po.

Erika looked at Li Po suspiciously, waited until he had gone upstairs. "Gudrun says they carry diseases. They're *heathens*."

At the look on Erika's face, he decided it was best not to argue. "I'm glad you're home," he said, taking her hand and leading her into the living room. He had hardly been inside the room since the harvest began. It was a chilly afternoon. He went over and lit the fire that Li Po kept ready for lighting. "Let's have a brandy—let's drink to our first true vintage," he said pleasantly. "Vittorio has just finished our own crush. We've just put our first Cabernet Sauvignon to sleep in all those oak barrels you were asking me about that time. The wine is out there right now bubbling, working its own magic."

Her eyes had narrowed, and a strange icy glint seemed to ride across them. "He looks at me funny," she said flatly. "He doesn't like me! He didn't want you to marry me because I'm not . . ."

"Not what, Erika?" he said gently, holding her hand, alarmed, trying to coax her into a better mood. He was glad that the dour Gudrun had stayed behind. She was not a good influence, he decided. He must bring Erika back to the way he remembered having seen her when he and Jacob would let her serve them, fuss over them. "Vittorio *likes* you. Of course he does."

"I'm not Italian! He likes only Italians. He doesn't like my cooking. Kyle likes it. But Vittorio doesn't. I've seen him give Kyle one of my best chocolate cookies and then wolf down that stinky sausage."

"I like your cooking very much," he said, getting up, pouring out brandy. "In fact, I've missed it. I'm glad, very glad, to have you back." He handed the glass of brandy to her, but she waved it aside.

"I hate cooking! I hate anything to do with food," she said stiffly. "I'm sick. I'm going to have a *baby* and everything makes me sick! Your lies make me sick. You are telling me *lies!* You don't like my cooking. You don't like me either. Her—that Reynolds girl. You wish *she* was your wife! Not me. I know about you, Adam Donati. Don't lie to *me!*" She got up, ran from the room and up the stairs.

For a stunned moment, Adam stood there, trying to stop his spinning thoughts; to decide if she were making it up about the baby, just as she had made up the other. He saw Li Po, like a hovering shadow out in the hallway, his eyes startled. Adam called him into the living room. "Did Mrs. Donati say anything to you?" he asked quietly, trying to pull his own thoughts in focus. But Li Po looked down at the floor, his hands stuffed into his sleeves. "Did she, Li Po? Please—I must know what she said!"

"She said—don't touch her. Stay away. I'm—she thinks I am sick. Dirty."

"Please forgive her," Adam said solemnly. "Mrs. Donati is going to have a baby. I—someone told me women sometimes behave differently when they are—well, that way."

Li Po's head bobbed up and down affirmatively. "My Uncle Lee —yes, he says that, too!" He smiled shyly, pointed to his skullcap. "Sometimes they get strange here. They get scared. But we can give herbs. I know the herb medicine for such things."

It did not take them long to realize that Erika was going to refuse anything she thought Li Po had touched. Adam promised her that he would personally bring trays to her room. He slipped the herbs into tea, which Erika did seem to enjoy and keep down. By December, the nausea was subsiding, and she was up and about. But even as color came back to her face and she began filling out, looking softer, prettier than

173

Adam had even seen her, she would narrow her eyes at Li Po and clamp her mouth shut until he was out of her sight. "*I* will do the cooking!" she said. "Send him to the bunkhouse. I don't want him in this house!"

Adam took Li Po aside and explained the circumstances. "This will pass. When the baby is born, she will change. I have sent for Gudrun. You must stay in the room that used to be mine. When conditions improve, then you may move back into your quarters in the main house. You do understand, Li Po?"

Li Po bobbed his head up and down, smiled. "You are a good man. You are my boss. Kyle Plimpton—he will take care of me," he said, solemn understanding riding his coal-black eyes.

Adam explained to Erika that Li Po had received other assignments, that Gudrun was on her way to Spring Mountain. He had been removing his trousers, ready to put on his nightshirt, when he glanced at Erika, who had climbed into bed early. He saw the hostile glare, the way her hands were clutching the cover. He pulled his robe on, neatly arranged his boots under a chair, hung up his trousers. He came over, pulled a chair up alongside the bed. "Erika—are you angry with me because you are going to have a baby? Is that it? Because your ankles are swollen and it is hard for you to get around these days? Dr. Williams tells me that because you are small-boned, you will get big more quickly. That it might be very uncomfortable for you. I want you to know I am sorry about that part of it, but I am glad, very pleased, that we will have a child. I am very, very happy about that."

He reached out and placed his hand quietly over her clenched one grasping the coverlet. He saw her eyes fill with tears. "Tell me—please try to share with me what you are thinking. What is troubling you."

"Babies—they can't walk! They can't do anything. What if there is a—a *fire!*" she screamed out in a shrill voice that sent a chill up Adam's spine. "I don't *want* to be a mother!"

He sat on the edge of the bed, placed his arm across her sobbing shoulders. "You will feel better now that you have said it. It will help if you say these things that are bothering you. I want to help, Erika. Please know that I am willing to do anything to make it easier for you."

Her eyes narrowed again. Her cheeks were still damp, but the face was not one crumbled with tears. "Then sleep in another room," she said crisply. "You keep me awake. You roll over on your back and you snore. You make noises and I can't sleep. I start seeing—the shadows start . . ."

"Yes? *Please*—what?"

Her lips were tight, as if she were holding back words she didn't want him to hear.

"Erika—please, *tell* me. I promise you—I will sleep in another room. I want you to be as comfortable as possible. You will have three more months at least before the baby is born. Dr. Williams says that they will not get easier. Let me help you, *now*. The shadows—if we know what they are, then even if you awaken for other reasons, you won't be—are you *afraid* of the shadows?"

"I am not afraid!" Her voice came out in a reedlike finality. "I will tell you! They are *her*! She comes and dances around the room and laughs at me. She mocks me!"

"*Who* mocks you, Erika?" he said, alarmed now, a fear as cold as ice creeping over him.

"That Reynolds girl! I *heard*—Gudrun told me how you ruined her reputation! How you *did* things to her! I *know*—I know you lie."

"Erika—whatever took place between myself and . . . the person you mention, it is something of the past. It is over. I am married to you. *You* are my wife, and I want to do the very best I can to make you happy. Dr. Williams tells me it is natural for women to get alarmed, exaggerate ideas. But you must listen to me! There is nothing to the shadows but what your imagination works into them. Look—see my shadow. See that from the furniture." He was standing beside her, smiling down, trying his best to reach her and reassure her. He saw the genuine torment in her eyes. "Please . . . promise you will *believe*—"

"I want to go to sleep," she said, as if speaking from some sealed-off space. "You promised you would leave me alone!"

8

At Christmas that year, Erika took to her bed and would not participate in any form of celebration. Adam did some quick shopping in St. Helena, took gifts to the Alfieris, joined the men in the bunkhouse for a celebration around a small tree Kyle had brought in. He dared not leave Erika too long at a time. Dr. Williams had warned Adam that she had developed high blood pressure; eclampsia, he told him, was not that uncommon in young mothers having their first babies. But he was also getting concerned, he told Adam, that her dark moods were not improving. "I am afraid myself. She is beginning to have suspicions of me too. She seems to trust this Gudrun woman. You—I'm sure she doesn't trust you at this time, but that will pass, perhaps. Some women are scared to death of having babies. Becoming responsible. In her case, we have to understand. Be patient."

Adam spent more and more time in the winery. Even on cold rainy days with the mountain wind whipping in through windows that were waiting for stained glass, when he knew that Vittorio had topped the barrels and all was done that needed doing he would wander through his modest first vintage, thumping barrels idly, looking about at the enormous space, seeing it in his mind's eye as it would look someday, running full capacity, the wine industry back on its feet, the Donati name an important one in America.

Though Adam could not understand the plodding Gudrun or the burning looks she cast at him from time to time, he was still grateful that she was there tending to Erika. "I owe it to her mother," she said gruffly to Adam once when he had tried to acknowledge aloud to her his feelings. "She was good to me when I was growing up. She was my best friend. This child—she is tormented." And though she never said it, she left the unmistakable impression that she blamed it largely on Adam.

In January, Dr. Williams came every week to check Erika's condition. In early February, alarmed by her high blood pressure, her swollen face and legs, her fingers that would not reduce in size to slip the simple gold wedding band on her finger, he mentioned to Adam that he wanted to give her a shot that might start labor early. "I am very worried about her. I don't like any of what I see."

When the long, tedious labor began, Erika flatly refused to let anyone except Gudrun be at her side. The labor pains started slowly, at one o'clock on a Friday afternoon, February the eleventh. The seven-pound, two-ounce baby boy was born on Saturday, just as the sun was setting. Adam looked at the strangely shaped head, molded nearly into a point from the long, difficult birth.

"The head will round out after a few days," Dr. Williams assured Adam. "He's a healthy lad—already kicking and bawling his lungs out. Came out looking mad as a hornet, which you can't blame him for. It's hard on the little tots." He hesitated, started to say something more to Adam, changed his mind. "Don't worry—she'll be fine. It will take a while for her to regain her old self. Women—sometimes they get depressed after giving birth. Particularly if there's some guilt involved. She said so many times she didn't want this child. She will probably see him and be repentant. You must be very, very patient with her. Understand as much of this as you can."

Adam went into the darkened bedroom, looked down at the white, still form asleep, the coverlets flat again where before there had been that huge mound of her swollen belly. Gudrun sat opposite him, as if daring him to touch Erika, to awaken her after what he had put her through.

"If you need me, I'll be in the library," he whispered.

"Get some sleep," Gudrun said calmly, as though talking to a child. "I'm here with her."

On the third day after the birth, Adam found a more cheerful-looking Erika propped up on brightly embroidered pillows, a bed jacket that had belonged to her grandmother buttoned up around her neck. Her hair had been carefully brushed and braided in one long plait by Gudrun, a bright ribbon tied around it. A vase of early jonquils was beside her bed. She smiled tentatively at Adam, who sat down, happy to see her improvement.

"He's a lovely baby," he said softly. "Thank you for giving us a son. What shall we name him?"

"You are the father. You should name him," she said tonelessly.

He had been thinking about the name, hoping he would have the opportunity. But he had made up his mind that he must pamper her wishes. His eyes shined. "Joseph—Joseph Jacob Donati. How does that sound?"

"Yes, I like that name." She picked at the coverlet. "I want Gudrun to be the godmother. You should choose the godfather."

"Then I will ask Luigi Pascarella," Adam said brightly. "He was my first friend in America, and our son is full-blooded American! Think of that, Erika—we have an American citizen!"

Her gray eyes had that narrowed-down look. "I'm glad you didn't choose that dreadful little Alfieri man," she said crisply.

Adam took a deep breath. Of all the men he had ever known, Vittorio was perhaps the most gentle and kind of all. How, why, he asked himself desperately, had Erika built this case against him? But hadn't Dr. Williams said that it would take time for her to regain her old self? And weren't most of the other suspicions fading? He must be patient. He must give her time about Vittorio.

After that, Adam made a habit of visiting with Erika each morning before he went about his busy days. It was springtime, which meant a hectic work period in the vineyards. There was cultivation, the clearing out of deadwood, using whatever innovations one could to protect the young shoots from frost; Kyle's latest device had been piling huge mounds of stones in strategic spots to collect warmth. And now, for Adam, he had to meet those agricultural needs on Jacob's diversified six hundred acres. Along with all this, Adam had also begun to involve himself with the local politics, seeing how the government could help or hurt any man in agriculture, at any level.

Kyle had seen Adam's plight, and on his own had gone to the growing Portuguese population—that year of 1896, their number had reached roughly seventy-five people—where he found capable, low-cost help: a man for the stables, one to bring a crew into Jacob's orchards, and a family happy to sharecrop the hay and barley and tend the cattle. It seemed that Wang Chi, ailing and disillusioned since Jacob's death, had simply taken his countrymen and disappeared one night.

"We're getting this place organized," Kyle told Adam confidently. "Just give us three, maybe four more harvests and we'll sail right over the top!"

But where Kyle seemed happy, Vittorio had come to Adam with his black eyes troubled, moist. "Your wife—she wants me to go away. She told me." He held his hat in his hands. "She thinks I know something about that—that other woman. That Reynolds girl. She won't listen. But Luigi offered me a job. I go work for Pascarella Enterprises.

I got work to do around my place. Maybe if I go, I pay you rent? One day I buy the house you gave us. Pay you cash."

Adam had tried to reassure him. "Don't worry about that. Stay there as long as you like."

"Maybe I pay rent. I send my boy—the oldest, that Kyle likes. Kyle calls my Roberto 'Bobby-Boy.' Maybe I send him to work off the rent. He would like to do that. He could stay under Kyle's supervision."

Because Vittorio seemed stubbornly fixed on that idea, Adam agreed to let the thirteen-year-old boy Bobby come live in the bunkhouse. He knew that Erika would not recognize him, and she never went around any of the men anyway. Maybe with Vittorio—an obsession to her—gone, she would soon return to normal, he thought.

Then came the day the baby was to be christened. "I want him sprinkled to be a Methodist," Erika had said flatly. "You are not a faithful Catholic. I don't like priests and nuns."

He had agreed. Anything to keep her more cheerful, as she seemed to be lately. He could talk with a priest later on—out of honor to his mother and father, to the way he had been brought up.

Luigi and Kyle donned suits and ties for the occasion, and Adam served his own bottled late-harvest Riesling that was excellent but not the rare quality for which he had hoped. Even Gudrun and Erika accepted a glass of the wine. It was the happiest Adam had been in weeks. That the baby cried and drew its legs and fists into a rage did not seem to matter. Luigi laughed: "A big strong fellow, this one! Hey, he could be a Pascarella with those lungs."

After that, he went with Adam and Kyle to inspect the unfinished winery. "When you get ready for me to come back and put on the last touches, just say so. Cesare and me, we got too much work lately. Not only the stonemasonry business is pretty good, but the lumber business, and Cesare is trying to talk this banker guy, a Mr. Goodman down in Napa City, into loaning him some money to start building houses. *Wood* houses. But the Donati Winery on Spring Mountain—that is my pride! That is my masterpiece!" Luigi beamed. "I will come here first. Just you say when."

Adam shook his head. "I'm having to hold off. Until we get on sure solid footing again. I have my loan to the Linton Bank coming due in 'ninety-nine. My brandy—I'm bottling some brandy as soon as I've let it age. I won't put a Donati name on it. When the real good Donati brandi is ready, it will be ten years from now. Only then!" He took

Luigi on a tour of the pot still. "One day I will buy a new still. Everything will be the way we used to plan, Luigi!"

Because people are comfortable with habits, a general routine soon settled in on Spring Mountain. The men in the bunkhouse and Adam had their world; Gudrun and Erika had theirs. The baby Joseph was growing, sitting up now, and would occasionally laugh and try to say what Adam was convinced was 'Papa' when he came around. Usually, on those occasions, Gudrun would thrust the child at him. "Hold your son—he won't bite! Every boy ought to be held by his father."

Gudrun had become to Adam a kind of fixture around the place. Actually, he had grown to depend on her a great deal. He was immensely pleased when he saw how she had got Erika back into the kitchen baking her fancy pastries again, putting huge loaves of bread into the oven. He would see them sitting in the glassed-in sunporch sewing, talking to each other, now and then laughing.

He was taken by surprise, then, when one day Gudrun caught him as he was going out the kitchen door toward the winery. She was pouring tea, and he turned, sat down at the kitchen table across from her.

She came straight to the point in that blunt, square-faced manner of hers. "It's none of my business what married people do behind closed doors. I never had a husband myself. But it is my advice to you to move back into Erika's bedroom. The sooner the better."

Adam felt a red flush creep up his neck. It was a very personal matter, and he did not enjoy having Gudrun be so flat-footed about it. Her face was grave. Her thick fingers with their chewed-down nails drummed across the tabletop. "I spend more time with her. I see things you don't. You see just one Erika. The one wearing clean dresses I insist she put on. The one who has brushed hair because I brush it. The one who smiles and talks because I tell her she ought to make the effort. But I see the other one! The Erika who wouldn't drag out of bed if she wasn't pushed. The one who talks to herself when she doesn't know I'm looking." She picked at a frayed piece of cloth on the napkin. "Something ought to be done. You're her *husband*. You ought to—" She shrugged her shoulders. "But what do I know?"

"Really, this . . . it is a subject that—"

"Yes, I know that. You needn't think I like bringing it up. It's the baby I'm worried about." Her face was twisting into a different shape now, one of genuine worry and, he sensed, a real love for the baby Joseph. "I can't be here full time. I've got a sister lives in Michigan. She's expecting. I told them I would come stay with them four or five months. They have sent me train fare and I want to go. I've never been outside of the state of California before. Hardly out of Napa County. I don't want to run out on her—on what I owe her mother. But I owe something to my sister too!"

"Why are you so concerned about the baby, Gudrun?" Adam asked in a thin voice, a deep fear knotting inside him. He had pretended to himself that he had not seen that look in Erika's gray eyes, a look she had got with him before when—yes, when they were in the bathtub together. He had seen it one day when Gudrun was bathing the baby, when the soapsuds were floating around the chubby, kicking legs and Erika had moved across the room, looking down at him as if about to close her hands around his genitals.

Gudrun's face was troubled now, with no attempt to hide her doubts. "She doesn't seem to see him as *real*, her own live baby! She looks at him—oh, like a toy. Maybe one she doesn't even want around sometimes. I—it worries me, is all. I thought if you moved back in with her . . . At night—sometimes she gets up at night. I'm—I'm afraid she might hurt the little fellow!"

And suddenly, to Adam's astonishment, tears were sliding down Gudrun's plain raw cheeks. "I know I won't ever have kids. Look, I know who—what I am. A big clunker like me. Men never paid much attention to me, and I—frankly, I never gave two hoots about men myself. My own papa saw to that. Used to beat the hell out of all of us, my own mother included. That's why I got to know Johanna Brunner. Came to school once black and blue. She told Jacob. He told his nice wife, who was already sick then but nobody knew it. They opened their home to me. Took me in. They lived simple like you could say. But it was the most peace . . . the happiest home I ever knew. That is why this one—I hate to see her lost off in some funny place inside her head. She—I don't think she's always right up there. I hate to say it. But I don't!" She wiped at her face, got up. "Don't know why I broke down. It ain't like me. I guess I've been worried about it. Kept it bottled up inside me. I was—well, you seem so grand-acting. I didn't know how to say it. Finally I just made up my mind to blurt it out as best I could."

He stood up. "Gudrun, thank you. I—I guess neither of us has known quite how to approach the other. What you've done for Erika has been more than payment back for what her grandparents and her mother did for you, I'm sure. Take a rest. Enjoy your trip to Michigan. When will you want to leave our employment? I would like to hire someone else, perhaps. Do you have any suggestions?"

"Maybe you shouldn't bring anyone new around her yet. But there's one thing . . ." She seemed uncertain.

"Yes? What?"

"She's got some letters you kept from that Reynolds girl. I wasn't snooping—prying in anybody's business. I was just looking for some baby clothes I thought I put away in a dresser drawer in her room. I came in, right in front of her. It wasn't behind her back or anything. I opened up the drawer and, well, there those letters were, under that stack of flannel nightgowns—I had been right about where I put them. Wasn't more'n a minute and she was flying at me, clawing like a tiger! Said that Reynolds girls would kill her if she knew. Was blubbering something about the Reynolds girl and that Alfieri man and that nice little Chinaman working down at the bunkhouse."

Adam felt a chill through his entire being. His fingers felt numb. "The letters—I should have destroyed them. In fact, Gudrun, I thought they *were* destroyed." His blue eyes were desperate, wide with concern. "That girl—believe me, she belonged to my past. I don't dwell on the past, on mistakes I may have made. She married some rich man in New York. She isn't anywhere near Napa Valley. How could she hurt Erika? How could Erika even imagine such an absurd thing!"

Gudrun shook her head, pushed her straight hair off her coarse face. "I can't figure it out. Any of it. God knows I've tried."

Adam looked at her as though seeing her for the first time. "Gudrun, I'm sorry we—that it took us so long to come to an understanding. I would appreciate it if you would come back to work for us when you return from Michigan. Maybe by then I can pay more."

"It isn't the *money*. It isn't the money at all," she said slowly. "I can't promise. But I will keep it in mind."

Before Gudrun had made her preparations to leave for Michigan, Erika announced one morning in a white-faced fury, "That baby is sleeping all day just so he can cry all night and keep me awake! I want him out of my sight! I hate him."

As soon as Adam could get Gudrun out of hearing distance from the distraught Erika, he said in a desperate, pleading voice: "I have one idea. Could you possibly consider— You said you liked the child. Would you mind, perhaps, taking him for a few months down to the Brunner place? You can keep him safe there—if there is a chance that Erika might do harm to him." His face was white with a deep, confused agony. He had been trained to expect and accept the unkind hand-outs Mother Nature could deal any man of the land, but no one had prepared him for what could go wrong with women—with love, and this institution called marriage where a man was supposed to be head of his household.

Gudrun bit her bottom lip, closed her eyes a moment. "I think sometimes it's my fault," she said miserably. "When she first came down with me at harvest last year, I thought she was unhappy because of you. She said a few things, how you took advantage of her and . . . maybe she was making up things about your . . . you know, what married people do. Anyway—" Gudrun had dropped her head in embarrassment, was scraping a big, plain foot across the floor in the kitchen— "I thought you must be as lowdown as what some people had said—Fanny Martin, for instance. We go to the same Methodist church together. I used to go every Sunday. Never missed Sunday school or a Wednesday-night prayer meeting. Since I came to work for you—well, anyway, I let Fanny Martin's wagging tongue turn my head against you. And I believed Erika's tales. I made a mistake. I want you to know that. I want you to forgive me. I—I told her what Fanny Martin told me and everybody else who'd listen. So I'll keep the baby for you. I owe that as my atonement, if nothing else. But I'd be happy to keep him anyway. He's the sweetest little thing. I know he's just a little baby, but I swear he can tell his real mother don't like him. He knows the minute she picks him up it's her. I've seen his little face start pinching up, ready for a squalling fit the minute he feels her hands touch him. When I take him, he stops that second. Maybe he's got it all mixed up—thinks I'm his mama."

"Will your sister in Michigan get along without you?"

"I reckon she'll just have to," Gudrun said matter-of-factly. "Looks like I've got my own baby to look after." The smile that crossed her face was the closest to a truly happy smile. Adam had ever seen on it. But in an instant it was gone. She was the old Gudrun again. "I guess I'd better start packing. I think I ought to take him out of here right away. I've got the house key. If somebody could drive me down in a buggy with our things . . ."

The very week that Gudrun departed with Joseph, Kyle came to Adam one evening, a deep frown on his face. "I'm worried over this turn in the weather. It's colder'n bejeesus. A bad frost right now, this late—I hate to think about it."

Adam walked with him toward the vineyards. It was a gray foggy early evening. An unusual late spurt of rain had pounded the valley. Adam buttoned his jacket, rammed his hands into his pockets, hunched his shoulders forward against a burst of wind whipping across the mountain. "We're more protected here on Spring Mountain than they are on the windy Mayacamas. We're safer than vineyards down in the valley."

Kyle shook his head. "Sure, we've got some sections that ought to be skipped over. But we've got some damp low spots too. If it frosts, we can stand to lose pretty big."

Adam's sigh seemed to trail off with a wisp of fog being lifted, turned in a spin. "I guess this isn't my luckiest year. Where is that Lady Luck you're always talking about, Kyle?"

"Hell, I don't know what she's up to! Beats me. Sometimes I tell myself she's a right friendly ghost. Sometimes I could swear she's riding on a broomstick." Kyle looked at Adam thoughtfully. "Why don't you come on down to the bunkhouse and eat supper with the men tonight? You ought to sample Li Po's cooking. He's improving every week. We've got a good bunch down there now. I'm crazy about that Alfieri kid. That Bobby-Boy is smart as a whip. I don't guess you've run into that funny old Italian I've hired off Howell Mountain to take charge of the stables, have you? Lord, he's got a last name a mile long which I ain't about to try and twist my tongue around. I call him Adolfo. He's old, but he's got a good hand with the horses and he knows all there is to know about maintenance of the gear."

Adam bit his lower lip. "I'd like to join you. . . . I have to keep an eye on my wife. She's not been well. But she's much better."

Kyle looked at him through pipe smoke. "That's good to hear. But anytime you need company, you know where the bunkhouse is."

When Adam told Erika that Gudrun and the baby were living down at her grandfather's, largely to keep an eye on the place, she had looked at him a moment, her gray eyes shining with tiny specks of bright light. "Good! She can keep those dirty Chinese—those *heathens* —out of the house!"

He did not tell her that the Chinese were gone. He said in as gentle a voice as possible, "It is time that we have this house to ourselves again." And without further word he moved back into his bedroom, the first night being careful not to touch her, except gently kissing her good night, and turning over on his side, hoping he would not snore.

After a few days, Erika seemed to reach back into some happier place in her life and revive old habits. She went about cooking, dusting, fussing with the arrangement of dishes on the shelves. It was as if she were playing house, had found a new game. And then, on a Sunday night, Adam came into the bedroom to find her wearing a softly ruffled nightgown and smiling at him in an obviously inviting manner.

At first he was tentative, concerned that the glint would come

185

back into her eyes and he would be afraid. But she was different. And soon his arms were about her, and his long abstinence caught up with him. She was placidly soft, compliant according to his simple directives. He made no attempt to talk. He must accept what was there. Handle it as delicately as possible. But even as his bodily needs took possession of him he felt a kind of numb, despairing anger inside him. Why should he feel *grateful* that his wife was being soft, yielding, behaving without those signs of madness! His last groaning thrust into her was such that he did not care if he ground some of that anger into the limp thighs, the slim pale legs spread so quietly apart. "More . . . there should be more," he mumbled into the pillow. He was startled then, when, propping himself up on one elbow, she pushed her hair off her damp neck, traced one playful finger down his nose, and said, "I haven't been a very nice wife for you. I am sorry. You may have more—yes, whenever you wish."

But there was no passion left in him. He kissed her lightly on the forehead, heard himself saying ironically, "Thank you," and then turned over, pretending to fall asleep. This time, it was for Adam that the shadows turned into Sarah's shape and form; but they were soft, loving shadows. And as the wind wound its chortling, whistling way around the corners of the huge stone house, rattled a shutter as if in added mockery, a knot of bitterness settled like a hard black growth beneath his heart.

But that night when he finally did sleep, his dreams were not of Erika or of Sarah: he was a very young boy again, snuggled deep into a down mattress, and the wind blowing, rattling the window, had brought his father into the room, and for a long time his father seemed to stand there, staring out frowning at the vineyards, his face dark with worry.

He and Kyle examined the vineyards together the next morning after the frost had indeed found its mark all across Napa Valley.

"We can't tell yet, but we're going to lose some. Jacob's valley-floor vines—it's my guess we might as well forget them," Kyle said, his voice thick with disappointment. "But, hell, you never know what the damage will really be until picking time."

Soon after that Adam attended a meeting where Professor George Hussman spoke to growers and vintners alike. He stood before them, tugging at his whiskers, shaking his kindly face, and warned, "Gentlemen, we must rally our forces. We must make a solid effort to improve marketing or all our efforts at practicing higher standards of viticulture and applying the latest knowledge to winemaking will be of no avail.

My figures show that we have thirty-nine registered brandy distilleries and one hundred and four wineries in Napa County, thirty-four of which are here in St. Helena. There's an estimated ten million gallons of cooperage. But it wouldn't surprise me this year at harvest if some of you won't be turning your hogs into your vineyards rather than picking."

After the meeting broke up, Adam found himself falling into one of the clusters of discouraged men standing in groups talking about their plight. He felt comforted, knowing that there were others trying to beat the forces against them. One grizzled farmer was saying, "I'm not a wine man. I raise cattle mostly. But I'm part of this valley. I figured you ought to see this pamphlet my wife brought home from church. That big bunch of Anti-Saloon Leaguers—they're pushing in along with the Woman's Christian Temperance Union."

Adam looked about, bewildered. "I don't understand." He studied the pamphlet. "Do you mean they think winemaking, brandy, whiskey —those are *sins*? Something to take to the courts?" His face was flushing red with anger at the thought. "Isn't this America? Doesn't freedom make room for everyone's beliefs?" His look was so genuinely incredulous, his bafflement so sincere, that the men stopped laughing.

"They call it the 'temperance movement,' " said a well-dressed gentleman Adam was later to learn was Senator Seneca Ewer himself. "Several states in America have already passed prohibition laws. It started as a movement before antislavery did. I was reading some figures the other day. Back as far as 1834, the American Society for the Promotion of Temperance had five thousand chapters with over one million signers in every state of the union. They started fighting over what other stands to take, and finally fell apart. Then we had a group of reformed drunkards who called themselves 'Washingtonians,' and they got a big following. On local and state levels, yes, I'm sorry to say, we've had prohibition legislation taking place for a long time. It's gaining momentum again. Which is why all you men should get active in politics and defeat these people before they bring us to our knees!"

"They can't bring Napa Valley to its knees," a tall man wearing a huge straw hat called out cheerfully. "*You're* a wine man, Senator. Don't you know that!"

"I know it is much more serious than you men give it credit for being. Don't always think it will happen out there to someone else but never hit home. We have more to fight than phylloxera, poor marketing, a killing frost!"

From that point on, Adam attended every political meeting he could find that dealt with any matter concerning the wine industry.

The bad blows dealt out by Mother Nature would balance out in time, for he firmly believed in point-counterpoint in all matters concerning nature itself. For that matter, with effort, he believed that to be the case with human nature as well. If he had had his disappointments in life, he had had his share of pleasant events. If his marriage had been an offshoot, an event grafted on with a surprising varietal, it had its advantages. He had received that counterbalance of a son, of land, of Jacob Brunner's wise eye looking into the future and giving him profits on the ledger. Erika herself seemed to be coming around now—behaving really quite normally in all regards and making life pleasant enough for him on Spring Mountain.

She had taken even more interest lately in her baking, as if diving her hands down into the soft, silky flour bins, kneading the dough, decorating the delicate pastries with fancy rosebuds and designs akin to embroidery work, were her main happiness and meaning in life. She had begun asking questions about Joseph, about Gudrun, though she made no effort to see either of them. "I'm so glad everything is going well," she would say lightly. And if Adam was riding down the back trail on Hajib, she would sometimes send along some of her baked goods.

He had sealed off a part of his mind that might ask for some added dimension to lovemaking. That too took on its ritual that summer. If, on occasion, he would suddenly realize Erika had been staring at the ceiling, as if waiting for it to be over, he tried to tell himself it had been only that one time; that he had looked at the wrong instant. He began keeping his own eyes clamped tightly shut when he made love.

One day, Adam suggested to her that perhaps they should take a trip. "We didn't have a honeymoon. I would like to take you someplace. San Francisco—anywhere you want to go. We can afford something."

A slightly smug, secretive look came over her face. "Papa Jacob left me a little nest egg for—oh, travel, whatever I want to do. I have funds for my son's education too. Would you like to see Papa Jacob's *will* sometime?"

He looked at her intently. "No. That is your business. If you wanted me to see it, you would have brought it out," he added gently. I didn't mean that we should use *his* money—*your* money. I have a little put aside. I save all that I can. I have a loan payment due soon."

"I don't want to go anywhere," she said abruptly. "I like it here with just you and myself. No one else!"

He smiled at her tolerantly. "But this house—it was built the way my own home in Pontremoli was built—for a big family, for parties. Don't you want that too?"

Her face tightened. "I want it exactly the way it is now. I cook for you the way I used to cook for Papa Jacob. I do the work, don't I? Nothing is dirty. I keep everything clean—very, very clean." He saw her eyes fill with tears.

"Everything is *fine*," he said, working his strong jaw, his blue eyes clouding with a veil of their own.

"No it isn't!" she cried out, getting up from the wicker chair on the veranda where they had been sitting. "You want *people*! Big parties! You want dances and—"

He got up, put his arms around her, held her against him. "Don't —please don't say those things, Erika," he said desperately. "We've—it has been nice lately. I just want you to be happy."

"Then take me to bed. Make love to me!" she cried out.

Later, when it was over, he looked down at her. "Erika, do you *love* me? Do you love me, really?" When she did not answer, he looked at her more closely, saw that she was crying. "Why are you crying?" he asked.

"Because . . ."

"Because you *don't* love me? Is that it?"

"No, I do love you. But sometimes . . ."

"Sometimes what, Erika?" His voice was gentle, coaxing.

"Sometimes I don't know who I am! I get all mixed up."

He had seen that look creeping across her gray eyes, the look he feared. He held her against him. "You are my wife. That is who you are."

"I am—but I am not," she cried in a muffled spurt against his chest. "I have a son—I don't have a son. I want to see him—I never want to see him again! I sometimes see my mother and my father and my brothers and sisters sitting around the kitchen table watching me cook, but when I get everything ready they are gone. And sometimes I see *her*—that woman you wanted to be your wife. She comes sometimes and laughs at me or she sends that Chinaman Li Po sneaking in and out of the kitchen stealing my herbs, probably putting poison in my jars!"

"Erika!" Adam said firmly. "Li Po left many of his own spices in the kitchen. He is cooking for the men down at the bunkhouse. If he *slips* in to get something, it is because he is afraid of you and he is merely getting what is his."

Her voice had taken on that eerie suspicious sound and she was pulling away from him. "See . . . you take up for *him*. For her too!"

She was sitting up, naked, her breasts firm, heavier than he had remembered. She clasped her hands across her small rounded belly. A look of triumph crossed her face. "But she can't have you. I fooled you. I got another baby here so you can't leave me!" She stretched her arms above her head, then glared down at him through strands of her long blond hair falling across her face. "Why do you think I let you do those things to me?" She ran across the room into the bathroom, slammed the door and locked it. She was calling out through it. "But you can't do it to me again. Ever again. I won't let you touch me *any*where."

Adam sank down into a huddle on the bed, a low, deep moan of the blackest despair he had ever known in his life smothering him. He thought he would not breathe again. *All this time she had been mad.* She had been playing some kind of horrible demented game with him. When she had been there beneath him so placidly, she had been there like a spider pulling in her prey! And then he was lunging out of the bed, snatching his clothes, his boots, his belt, his winter jacket, even in hot August, and going down the hall to the library. He had done what he could for her. She had tricked him. He was not mad, as she was, but there were two of them now who would not be touched again!

The next day he went to see Dr. Williams and told him the news about Erika. "Quite truthfully, I think my wife is insane," he said, his voice barely coming out. "I cannot manage. I have to do something."

"You cannot divorce her. You cannot get a judge in this state to give you a divorce simply because you *think* she is insane. But I do think you are correct in your assessment. I also fear for this second child—assuming she is pregnant. Is it possible?"

Adam buried his head in his hands. "Yes. Yes, it is." When he looked up at the gentle probing eyes of the short, round-bellied doctor, a cry, like a cry for help, came from him: "What have I done? Why is this happening to me, Doctor?"

There was a long silence. "I am a physician, I have seen many strange things in my day. Long ago I quit asking *why*. Why would an innocent child be born with its brain damaged so that it cannot speak or control its body? Why is a child born blind? Deaf? With hideous defects? Why was your wife born with a mind that cannot handle her own anguish?" He shook his head, let out a long, exhausted sigh. "I have no answer for you. I have learned to try and help where I can. To patch up. To fix up. To lend a hand. I have *some* magic that comes out of my 'little black bag,' as some people call it. But not often. And never, never, enough. No, Mr. Donati, this is not the time to ask *why*

—it is the time to ask what we must do about it. We must put your wife in a safe place. At the St. Helena Sanitarium we have facilities that might be satisfactory for a short term. We can keep her there until the baby is born. Maybe—who knows?—maybe she will suddenly snap out of it. She seemed to be doing all right there for a while. Did any one thing bring this on?"

Adam shook his head miserably. "She only covered it up so that we were fooled. She—no, it was not ever all right."

Dr. Williams stood up. "Then I will make arrangements to have her admitted to the hospital. It will be your duty to get her there tomorrow. Will you be able to manage?"

"I will manage—a man does what he has to do. Somehow. Isn't that the way it works?" he asked with dry-lipped bitterness.

The next morning, Adam tried to go about as though nothing at all were different. She was in the kitchen when he entered. The table was set. She placed a plate of eggs and thick sausage before him, turned to take biscuits from the oven. She was white-faced, with dark circles under her eyes.

"I am sorry I was upset with you," she said tonelessly. "It was the shock—about knowing I was going to have another baby. I don't *want* a second baby. It made me . . . say things I didn't mean."

He sipped coffee, pretended to concentrate on the eggs. "I understand. I'm taking you for a checkup. Dr. Williams wants to see you."

I don't want to see *him*!" she cried out. "I want to stay right here. Why should I see him?"

"Your appetite—you aren't eating well."

"How can I eat with this baby—this thing inside me!"

"You said you planned to have another baby. You told me—"

"I won't see Dr. Williams," she said, and stormed out of the kitchen, ran up the back stairs.

Adam went out the back door to the bunkhouse in search of Li Po. He quickly explained to Li Po his problem.

Li Po bowed, his dark eyes alert. "I have herbs. You put in milk— anything. She will go to sleep."

It was noontime when Adam drove the phaeton down Spring Mountain, the limp, drugged Erika propped against his right shoulder. It was impossible to avoid seeing a few people, even when he drove on as many back streets through St. Helena as possible. He had dressed her as nicely as he could, having the nervous Li Po assist, and finally going after Kyle to come from the vineyards and give him a hand in getting her into the carriage. The hat he had placed on her head had tilted askew. Her mouth was open. He saw two ladies staring at her. He felt at once embarrassed and protective of his wife.

By the time he arrived up the mountain slope to the east at the sanitarium, she was beginning to get restless. Dr. Williams had been expecting them and had left orders for additional sedatives to be given on her arrival. After the nurse and the attendants had taken the drowsy Erika and led her away, Adam was called in to talk with the doctor in charge.

Adam missed the portly, kind Dr. Williams. This Dr. Zuber was thin-faced, somewhat rigid in his appearance, in much the manner of German or Swiss physicians Adam had known during those summers at the Lake Como resort, when he was a small boy, and notable gentlemen would join his father for a game of chess or simply to discuss wines, if, as many physicians were known to do, they fancied themselves connoisseurs.

"How long will it take for my wife to get well?" he asked.

Dr. Zuber lifted small round glasses. "No promises can be made on that matter. I will be quite frank. From what your family physician has told me, the symptoms do not sound encouraging." He leaned back, folded his hands over his thin stomach. "Now and then these conditions are precipitated by pregnancy. And your wife has had those terrible shocking tragedies in her life." He paused, looked at Adam calmly. "She seems to think there is some other woman in your life, Dr. Williams tells me. She seems suspicious of *you*—"

Adam felt his heart thumping, his hands clenching. "There is no other woman. I have been a faithful husband. I have tried my best to care for her."

"I am not accusing you, Mr. Donati. I am trying to find out what I can that might be of help to me in treating your wife."

"I used to love another woman, yes. I admit that. But that was in the past. I have been a faithful husband!"

"I understand that. Suspicion is a main symptom of this disease. This illness. This malady. People search for names to make themselves feel better. Let's just see what we can do. Perhaps we can make your wife well again. That is our goal, at any rate. We will do our best."

That harvest of 1896 and the following winter months were nightmarish ones for Adam. As Kyle had predicted, they lost much of their crop; the frost had cut heavily into the productivity as well as the quality of those grapes worth picking. As this became apparent, Adam decided they would crush their own Spring Mountain grapes. He

192

would make a bulk red, a limited amount of Cabernet Sauvignon, five thousand gallons of Zinfandel. The rest of his grapes—his French Colombard, Folle Blanche and Trebbiano (he refused to call the grape by its French name, St.-Émilion)—he would distill in a larger production of brandy. He had found an improved pot still, had seen to it that some welding repair was done on the worm condenser, and had enough wood stocked to keep the preheater stoked.

But everything required an inordinate amount of time, of manpower. He asked Kyle to send the old Italian Adolfo over among his friends to find men skilled in running a still. Adam had had only limited experience running the still, but knew that it required a man with a good nose for sensory examination to determine when to make the transition at the end of the run.

Kyle had scratched his head, looked puzzled. "I thought running a still was pretty simple. Plenty people have got 'em tucked in around these parts, ducking the taxes. What's so different with brandy?"

They had been sitting in the bunkhouse—where Adam now ate his meals and spent any free time he had, the main house having begun to haunt him. "Just how much do you know about the actual winemaking process, Kyle? I know you understand grape growing."

Kyle looked up from his whittling. "Around you experts, not so much, I reckon. I know you get the grapes hauled to the stemmer-crusher as quick as you can. If it's red wine, the grapes get crushed, run through that basket press—"

"Not right *after* the crushing—not if they are reds."

"Well, mistake number one. Okay, you crush 'em, then get pulp and all into open redwood fermentation tanks. Dump that yeast in. Then when it gets to going—all that bubbling! Lord ain't that a sight? But I get mixed up as to what exactly causes it."

"When fermentation takes place, the sugar gives off roughly equal parts of alcohol and carbon dioxide. Those bubbles from the heat—what you are seeing is carbon dioxide being released."

"I heard you saying last harvest, when you did that little bit of crushing, that your fermentation was running too hot."

"I'm used to our way of doing things back in Pontremoli. We had cool caves that helped keep the heat down. One of the reasons why I'm not working with whites yet is I need better cooling devices. The right cooperage. I hated to see those excellent grapes go last year. But winemaking has to be done by certain fixed standards. There are all kinds of variables winemakers implement. But certain things simply have to be done right."

Kyle flipped the cedar stick into the kindling box. "Is this part right—you get *white* wine because it's fermented on mostly juice alone, kept off the skins and pulp? The difference is that with the reds they get color from the skins?" When Adam nodded, Kyle chuckled. "I'll tell you something else I know for damn sure: if you want a red-hot argument, just put two winemakers side by side who don't agree on those variables you mentioned. But seems to me, no matter who is right, a lot of it is hit or miss. A lot depends on old Lady Luck's mood!"

"You're right again, Kyle." Adam smiled. "You were asking me about brandy-making, and I wanted to explain the difference. The Donati way—which is the one I'll stick to—is to use the pot still. Take wine right after vintage that hasn't been clarified. It goes into a pot over direct heat. Above the pot is an enclosed air-cooled space. There some volatile materials condense. Then it goes into the worm condenser, where the remaining vapors turn into liquid. You get more volatile constituents in increased concentration in the condensate vapor—"

"Hey, that's over my head. But would you explain one thing? What is this heads and tails I hear them talking about?"

"The heads are the first volatile constituents—the first fractions coming off. You see, when liquid boils, molecules escape from the surface as vapor. In an alcohol-water mixture, the vapor leaving the surface contains a higher percentage of alcohol than the original liquid. This is the basis—fractional distillation. It is what gives us brandy from wine."

"Okay, Professor! what is grappa, then? That rotgut Luigi drinks?'"

"It *is* rotgut, as you say. Brandy made from where pressed skins and seeds have been placed in a pile for weeks or months. Then the surface is taken off and what's inside is put into the still. When it comes out—that first run—you've got grappa. It is raw, strong stuff."

"Answer me one more dumb question—what is proof?"

Adam smiled reassuringly. "I learned what 'proof' meant from my old English tutor, a man named Dudley Farnsworth. He was proud of that word because it came from his country originally. Used to be, when black powder and an alcoholic beverage were mixed, when a flame was put to test it, if it burned well, it had proof, otherwise it didn't. Absolute alcohol is two hundred percent proof spirit. Your average brandy has eighty—can be less or more. That would run between forty and fifty percent alcohol by volume. With my brandy, I prefer a lesser proof. I want a high quality, which means redistilling."

"I'll look into getting you somebody," Kyle said, casually.

"It has to be right away. I'll start right after we pick. We won't clarify the wines. The first run will give us about fifty-four proof. We'll empty the still, start again. The next run we'll have about a hundred and forty proof. This we'll cut with water and store away in those fifty-gallon oak barrels I've been saving. After about a year, we'll move the brandy into bigger cooperage and then let it sleep at least fifteen years. Up to twenty would suit me better."

"I think it's best working with the *grapes* out there in the vineyards," Kyle said. "You just have to try to make it come out right on the vines and into the lugboxes. Jacob Brunner—he used to agree with me. You didn't see Jacob messing around with it! He said he had enough trouble with government not to get mixed up with the Bureau of Alcohol, Tobacco and Firearms. Plus, they stick you for that high tax on one hundred percent proof alcohol. Somebody said it was two dollars every 100 percent proof gallon! Seems to me from how you explained it, if it's that easy to fire up a pot still—whether you're running off sour mash or brandy—it's a wonder they don't have more *unregistered* ones going around these parts than they do, with times being so hard and grapes bringing no more a ton than a bunch of potatoes, hardly."

During the frenetic weeks of harvesting, of tending to the crush, and then distilling his brandy, Adam found little time to get to the St. Helena Sanitarium to see Erika. And when he did go, a nurse was always in the private room with her and usually had to prod Erika into saying anything. If she recognized Adam, she did not give him any indication that she did. She would turn, her eyes glinting in that peculiar way, a smile on her face, as if she had some secret he wished he had.

By Christmas, she was beginning to look enormous. But the swelling was not as severe as it had been with Joseph. He had taken a warm shawl for her, a new flannel nightgown the nurse had suggested would make a lovely gift. He had tried to kiss her cold cheek, but she had pulled away, as if not wanting him to touch her.

From there he had gone back down to the Alfieri place, left off toys for the growing children, a large box of chocolates for Vittorio and Delfina. Then he had gone to Gudrun's, his arms full of toys for the baby Joseph, who was walking in a toddling off-gait, his hands busy at all times pulling on Adam's hair, his nose. He was a short, stocky baby, with legs fat and dimpled. His eyes were not round, like those of some babies Adam had seen, but were wide-set, and a pale blue that made him seem oddly very old. Adam tried to play with him, to reach for some outpouring of love for this son, but nothing deeply special seemed to happen.

Gudrun was pleased to see him, and presented him a rather crudely made sweater she had knitted. "I'm not very good with knitting needles yet, but that sweater kept me busy this fall. It'll be warm. It's solid wool at least."

In turn, he had given her a new large umbrella she had hinted she wanted, and a box of chocolates the same as he had given the Alfieris.

As he rode Hajib up the back trail, a cold misty rain was falling. It was the most dismal holiday he could imagine. And when he got to the bunkhouse, to find the men already on a drunken song, even Li Po's black eyes looking fuzzy, Adam found himself accepting eagerly the straight whiskey Kyle thrust his way. Around midnight, he went into an empty bunkroom and fell in a stupor across it. The sound of Kyle's voice trying to sing a Christmas carol went round and round in his head, spiraled down toward a tiny blinking light far off in the dark recesses of his memory. And when he dreamed, he was a child, carrying a candle, in a procession with his brothers attending Mass. His mother was smiling at him and handing a warm sweater to him. He awakened, his teeth chattering, the bunkhouse freezing cold and filled with snoring drunken men. Li Po, with a blanket around his shoulders, had gone to sleep huddled near the smoldering fireplace. Adam stalked out into the gray, fog-thick dawn, through the eerie dormant stalks of the vineyard, out to the very edge, and looked out at the swirling gray void where he knew the Napa Valley to be. For a long while he stood there, the dampness from the fog mixed with his own hot, bitter tears.

"I will never spend another Christmas like this!" he mumbled, as if the vines themselves might be listening, caring.

Though Erika's due date for delivering the baby had been estimated to be in early April, Adam received word the first week of March to come to the hospital. By the time he got there, the family doctor, Dr. Williams, had delivered a second son.

"This one has got your long legs. Long, lean, healthy boy. Your first one was short, fatter. Both nice healthy babies."

"How is my wife? How is she?" he asked, feeling as if the floor were moving beneath him.

"Adam, you are going to have to hear the truth. Your wife is hopelessly insane. Dr. Zuber says so—everyone says so. We're not set up here for permanent care. We've been investigating some places where you might want to have her committed—private institutions.

She was brought here in the first place because Jacob Brunner was a supporter of this sanitarium, ever since his wife was brought here with tuberculosis and died here. They felt they should try to cure his grand-daughter. But now, just as soon as she physically recovers from the childbirth, she has got to be taken elsewhere. I have orders." He waited a moment. Then he pushed a form at Adam. "What name do you want on the birth certificate?"

Adam looked at it blindly a moment. From the time when he had changed his own name, Emilio, to Adam, before coming to America, he had decided that any children he might ever have would be given short, to-the-point names. His head was spinning. He had had a good friend once named Antonio, he thought frantically, looking down at the forms. He supposed he could shorten Antonio.

The name seemed to blurt itself out: "Anton—I think we could name him Anton. How about Anton Brunner Donati?"

"Sounds okay to me," Dr. Williams said, writing it down. He looked up at Adam suddenly. "What about Gudrun? Is she up to taking on the care of another baby? She's got her hands full with that rip-snorter Joseph. She brought him to my office to have me look at his ears where he'd been crying with an earache—didn't want to bother you, since you have so much on your mind. He's a healthy young fellow!" He smiled, shook his head.

"Gudrun seems to enjoy her surrogate role as mother," Adam said tonelessly. "She said she would take the baby. Do her best by both of them. I try to get down often to look in on them."

Dr. Williams had seen the agony in Adam's eyes. He clasped his arm. "You've had a rough go in this marriage. I'm sorry life's treating you so harshly. But, all in all, Napa Valley's a fine place to be. At least you've got that going in your favor. You couldn't suffer in a better place." He started walking out with Adam. "One thing you're going to have to do, though, is hurry up and get a good lawyer for yourself. You're going to have to have legal control of your wife's affairs to get her committed. Do you have a lawyer?"

"Not—no, I guess I haven't had anyone special." Adam's voice was numb-sounding.

"May I suggest a young man, new to Napa County? Good friend of mine, lately. I give him free medical advice, he gives me legal advice. Norman Jaspers—young bachelor, maybe a couple years older than you. You could use a good friend as well as a lawyer. Want me to arrange a meeting?"

"Yes—yes, I suppose I'll have to."

And so it was that Norman Jaspers came into Adam's life.

· ·

Norman Jaspers was a man who, at thirty-three, after having practiced law in Napa County for over five years, still could not believe he was actually settled into a relatively isolated agricultural pocket on the West Coast. In every way—geographically, culturally, intellectually—he was removed from his Eastern background, his Boston-reared, Harvard-educated past.

When he tried to figure out exactly why he was here, he usually came up with more or less the same answer. Some sixth sense had told him to get as far away as he could from those rigid Eastern standards where one must always achieve, must keep one's emotions under the strictest control, must have been a Bostonian since the Pilgrims—must always be something more, it seemed, than one really was. Whatever he accomplished, it was never quite enough. Even at Harvard Law School, when he had graduated in the top ten of his class, he had not been in the top three, and it had been those top three who were hired by the law firm of his choice. Nor had any of the Bostonian women found him up to their standards. Granted, he was five feet tall, portly, round-faced. But he had developed a keen sense of humor, a fast-thinking business acumen. And he had also developed—among his scrambling efforts to become someone special, somehow out there ahead of the others—a love and knowledge of wines. "Ask Norman what wine to choose," his classmates would say. So, in a way, it had made sense to come to Napa Valley—after he got over the disappointment of being turned down, and when he found statistics supporting his decision, indicating that indeed he could make a reasonably profitable living for himself in the area.

Once there, he had gone about with his usual drive to *achieve*. Automatically, he had tried to get that Harvard-trained "overview" on his situation—tried to fully understand this rather strange locked-in narrow valley (in places he had discovered it was less than two miles wide, and at its widest only about five miles across) that seemed to have been deliberately sealed off from the rest of the world to keep it that unique grape-growing region it was. The opposing ridges of mountains running east and west were themselves like unrelenting sentries keeping it pinched in on itself, and when that thirty-five-mile stretch to the north ended it was because the formidable Mount St. Helena, like an angry dowager of a mountain, furious because she had lost her jeweled crown to the volcano, had put a firm foot down to stop it, demanding that as payment in return the valley give back the most noble of grapes.

Another startling discovery he had made, having found a report on population statistics of foreign-born that year of 1890 when he arrived in the Napa Valley, was that this tiny area contained some 140 Scots, 38 Australians, 323 Scandinavians, 1,098 Germans, 216 French, 454 Swiss, 51 Austrians, 320 Italians, 15 Spanish, 74 Portuguese, 183 Mexicans, and, to his delight, that the Irish outnumbered the English 887 to 448; the rest of the valley's people seemed comprised mostly of Southerners ranging from the roughneck Missourians to the articulate Professor George Hussman to the haughty Miss Grace Reynolds from Mississippi. It was a strange amalgam. Yet, in one way or another, they all seemed to have been drawn to Napa Valley by some magnet force of the valley itself—each held, fixed irretrievably to it. And if, he reasoned, this disparate mixture of people had any one thing in common, it was one main fulcrum, like an obsession, around which they rotated: the vintage.

And hadn't he too, after getting his practice launched and money in Goodman's bank—wasn't he finding himself pulled into that collective obsession? But even if that were true, was that really what was bothering him lately? he had asked himself.

Maybe he had been too busy getting established, going about in search of that constant "overview," to the point where he had lost sight of himself. What about other standards—the theater, the opera, the symphony, another entire world out there that was not necessarily and arbitrarily fixed to the pivot point of the harvest?

He should face it. From all indications, he was slated to be a lifelong bachelor. There wasn't a wife's third eye to help keep him on his toes. It was up to him to pull himself out of the valley, make regular trips to San Francisco. Force himself to keep a broader perspective.

Norman Jaspers had just reached this decision when Dr. Williams came to him and explained Adam Donati's plight.

"This young man, like yourself, Norman, is well educated, has excellent breeding." The doctor had looked perplexed. "But somehow he doesn't fit in socially around here. I suppose it has something to do with his being Italian, though it shouldn't. People pick their scapegoats. He isn't like the others—they're mostly miners, short and dark, from southern Italy. It's my guess, even when Italians stick together so closely, that he doesn't fit in with them either. He's stuck off up there on Spring Mountain, married to that pitifully deranged Brunner girl. He's father of two sons, babies that that horse-faced Gudrun Meyers is trying to bring up on her own down at the old Brunner place." He rubbed his eyes, took a long, exhausted sigh. "Look, you're a misfit around this valley, too, in your own highbrow way. Why don't you try to be this man's friend as well as his lawyer? When you take him to San Francisco to take the necessary legal steps to commit his wife, take him around a little. Try to cheer him up. You can see guilt all over him. I hear he was in love with the Reynolds girl and that Miss Grace, along with Jacques Cugnot, took care of that! He married this girl at Jacob's deathbed request. He profited from it, but now he's got this totally insane woman for a wife. He's bound to her for the rest of his life. Do me a favor—see what you can do."

So when Adam Donati walked into Norman Jasper's office on Coombs Street that April morning in 1897, he was being appraised by a measuring eye searching for more than his legal problems. Norman liked him immediately—envied him, secretly: his good looks, even that somber stance with the pain behind it. Love—it was an emotion that had eluded him, a confrontation he might not ever have.

Because he was not one for wasting time, he got down to quick business. He had asked Adam to bring in Jacob's will, all the records that might be of help. Because Adam had been troubled over his own separate problems about how he would meet the loan coming due all too quickly with the Linton Bank of California, he had brought along his agreement with Samuel Linton. And when Vittorio Alfieri cautioned him to be sure he had filled out all the proper forms for the Bureau of Alcohol, Tobacco and Firearms, he had brought along an enormous stack of forms regarding the brandy distillery, and others for his winery.

It took Norman some time to study them, during which Adam wandered along the wharf, went inside Uncle Sam's Cellars to visit with his acquaintances there. By the time he returned to Norman's office, the short, round-faced man with rosy cheeks and a bright intelligent gleam in his black eyes looked at Adam intently. "We can bring all this around into solvency," he said matter-of-factly. "I see no reason why, as legal executor of Erika's affairs, you can't invest these funds and make them highly profitable. *She* has been sitting on them; the old man, Jacob, must have hoarded money like a squirrel with his winter walnuts. According to these terms in Jacob's will, you can, as official foreman of his six hundred acres, increase your salary. You've been too modest, in my opinion." He saw the look on Adam's face. "Look at it this way: you owe it to your wife who is irreparably incompetent, to your young infant sons, to do your best for them. You owe it to yourself—to all the work you've put in so far. Now, as soon as we finish with the painful ordeal of committing your wife, a step you are going about in the most humane way possible, we will try to get your personal affairs in better order. This is ridiculous! You're a winemaker—a viticulturist. You're obviously no good with books." He tapped his pencil on the desk. "Look, you have to trust me. I specialized at Harvard Law School in estate management, wills, trusts. Napa Valley is lucky to have me," he said lightheartedly. Then he looked seriously at Adam, lifting his round face so that the double chin made one continuous curve, so unlike Adam's strong jutted jaw working back and forth in unison with his conflicting thoughts.

"I realize I need someone to help with the business end."

"From now on you have me. And from now on we will be friends as well. Count on that. You're the only single man—available man with whom I have anything intellectually in common, it seems. In San Francisco, we'll both take a break. I'm getting tickets for us at the theater. If there's an opera on, we'll go to that too. San Francisco has so much going on we'll find something to give us a needed change of pace. By the way, do you have any preferences regarding hotels? I'll see that reservations are made for us."

Norman Jaspers' matter-of-fact, good-humored manner was beginning to work on Adam. For the first time in weeks he felt a faint lifting of his spirits. A change—yes, he needed that. "When I first arrived in California, I stayed at the Palace. I had a lovely suite there," he said hesitatingly.

Norman had seen the cloud that crossed Adam's eyes, as if looking back had been a painful trek of some sort. "How long ago was that?"

Adam shook his head, seemed to be looking at a space just beyond Norman's shoulder. "It's strange. In one way, it really hasn't been long at all. Three years—February, 1894 . . . ." His voice trailed off. "It seems, right now, that it was twenty, thirty years ago."

"I understand," Norman said quietly. "You've been through a lot." He got up from his desk. "But you are going to feel much, much better! Believe me. I intend to see to it."

When he came around the desk to shake hands with Adam, it was the first time that Adam realized he was a full foot taller than Norman Jaspers, that at most Jaspers must stand five feet tall; yet, at that moment, he seemed indeed a giant of a man.

9

With Norman Jaspers by his side, virtually in charge, Adam managed to get through the numbing ordeal of committing his wife to the San Francisco Clinic on Bush Street. The sedatives given to her at the sanitarium for the trip to the city were still keeping her half asleep in a wheelchair. Two attendants had come along at the doctor's request, to keep her safe and to make it easier on Adam. At the clinic itself, the supervisor, a hefty, plain-faced woman named Grace Pruitt, who reminded Adam of nuns he had known, took Adam and Norman into her office.

"I want to assure you, Mr. Donati, that your wife has been brought to the best, most modern facilities in northern California. I realize it costs dearly, and I realize that this is very difficult for you in *other* ways." She looked at Adam closely, as if trying to determine any reaction he might be having. "We have a staff doctor on duty at all times. We're well staffed. Our food is excellent. You do understand that we don't encourage visitors? Unless the physician specifically requests a visit, we prefer that you trust her to our care. It usually works best for both concerned."

Later, when he and Norman arrived back at the Palace Hotel, Norman insisted that he down a stiff whiskey. "You don't look so well, which is understandable. But life goes on. Tonight I am taking you out to dinner. I have tickets for the theater tomorrow night. If you would like to go along with me, I plan to explore Chinatown. I collect Ming porcelains, and anything before that period as well, *if* I can find a bargain. I'm considered a bit of an expert at it."

Adam slept fitfully that first night. But, as Norman said, life went on. He found himself going about after that as if in a daze. If Norman suggested something, he followed along. They took walks in the downtown district; along Fisherman's Wharf; they took a streetcar to the end of the line and back, trying to get Norman's "overview" of the city and its everyday people. And one day they ambled through North Beach. When they came even with the sign LORENZO'S NORTH BEACH RESTAURANT, even though Adam had promised Luigi that he would go inside and introduce himself, and though he could see the man who was unmistakably a Pascarella, a sincere boyishness on that friendly face, now laughing with customers, his arms waving about in wide-sweeping gesticulations, cigar smoke encircling his round animated face, he could not bring himself around to going inside and facing such warmhearted immediacy. There was something inside him too leaden—a lump like granite made up of guilt, sadness, a frustration because he felt there should be something that could be done for Erika that would bring her back to life in a conscious sense of the word.

He did not even acknowledge that he knew anything about Lorenzo, but kept walking alongside Norman Jaspers, who was enjoying the Italian atmosphere. With every step, surrounded by people who reminded him of his homeland, Adam felt as if he were caught up in, some stitched-on pocket of Italy itself.

Norman had seen the deep melancholy like a heavy weight on Adam's strong shoulders, burrowed into the ridges of his handsome face. On the way back to Napa, aboard the steamboat, and standing on the upper, outer deck at Adam's request, Norman watched at a distance as Adam leaned over, his arms propping him up on the railing as he stared blankly out toward the open sea. He walked up to him, standing now taller than Adam, the way he was stooped over so low. As he clamped his arm reassuringly down around those burdened shoulders, Norman thought how glorious it must be to have the physical stature of so fine-looking a man as Adam Donati.

"You are going to feel better with time," he said quietly. "Some things change—*some* things can always be improved upon."

After that, Adam tried to bring some pattern into his life to make things work out as well as possible. He made purposive frequent trips down the back trail to visit his small sons. If he did not feel a deep emotional outflowing of love, he most certainly appeared to be a dutiful, loving father, the way he arrived with gifts, the way he would sit on the floor trying to teach the busy, disruptive Joseph patience to build with wooden blocks, to fit any two things together instead of throwing things in all directions or grabbing, pulling everything around him down in a tumbled mess on the floor. The small infant, Anton, was a quiet baby who seemed contented to grasp at nearby objects, study them with pale-gray eyes that seemed unusually alert for so young a child.

Adam also began stopping by regularly to visit Luigi, who had purchased a small frame house at the very end of Madrona Street, out of sight of Fanny Martin's boardinghouse, and who was at work in his spare time building a huge stone barn to house the equipment he and Cesare used when working jobs in the upper valley. Their reputation was growing, their business booming. Though Adam enjoyed his more intellectual visits with the bright, educated Norman Jaspers, with Luigi he felt as if he were visiting a relative, a kindly cousin. He looked forward to knocking on the door, seeing that big open bearlike face of Luigi's break into a grin; being welcomed inside his small house, where Luigi would bring out mounds of salamis and delicacies he kept on hand, a jug of wine, and where they would sit for hours talking, laughing, recalling how they first met.

Also, routinely, Adam made a point of joining the Alfieri family for Sunday dinner about once a month. These visits took on a familiar pattern: after the oldest girl, Theresa, played the latest tune she had picked out on the upright, the second-oldest daughter, Lilliana, would join her to sing and show what a clear lovely soprano voice she had. The entire family usually joined in a chorus or two. And after an enormous meal Adam and Vittorio would sit on the porch on hot days or around the fire on cooler ones, talking over problems with the winery, market reports, and matters in general.

One day Vittorio told Adam, "I am working double jobs. Soon I will have enough money to pay you for this house. Then, one of these days, I will save more and sell this and buy a fine big place for my family—bigger than the one they took away from me! I will buy down in the middle of the valley, around Rutherford maybe. One of these days I will show them!"

That early evening, as Adam rode Hajib back up Spring Mountain, in spite of the warm glow he always got when he spent an afternoon with the Alfieris, an overwhelming sadness came over him. He dreaded going back into the huge stone house with its rooms like caves, his steps like hollow echoes going through it. He had mentioned, not long ago, bringing his sons and Gudrun back up on Spring Mountain; but she had herself requested to stay on at the Brunner place, where she could look after the property and be closer to things. She wanted to take the boys to church just as soon as they were old enough, she told him. And there would be school to think about. Besides, didn't he have his hands full enough trying to keep up with running everything?

He had given in, seeing her practical point, ignoring some vague sense of warning inside him over this decision. For even if Gudrun was building her life around his sons, establishing her own household, so to speak, it was a dedication on which he could depend. She was, after all, tending to his sons in a better way than he could ever manage. If it weren't Gudrun, he would have to hire someone else. And wouldn't Jacob Brunner—wouldn't poor Erika herself if she were rationally aware of things—want the Brunner house lived in? Cared for?

Though Kyle Plimpton still called the bunkhouse his home and was more or less in charge of it, Adam had noticed that he was spending less time there. He would be gone for nights in a row. Yet, if he might have feared Kyle was drinking, going off on his notorious benders from the past, he soon erased that idea from his mind. Kyle kept up with his work—in fact, seemed more intent on doing things well, earning as much money for Adam as he could, since Adam had put him on a salary plus percentage, at Norman Jaspers' suggestion.

But even that had not been the real reason for the change in Kyle Plimpton, as it turned out. Kyle had met a widow, buxom, jolly-faced Emma Case, and fallen in love, just as he turned forty.

That harvest of 1897 limped past, prices for grapes still lower than anyone had imagined, hitting an average of eighteen dollars a ton. But Norman Jaspers, who kept all Adam's books now, reported they had an increased margin of profit from the Brunner holdings, and he had made some money for him in the commodities market. "If you keep your sights limited to Napa Valley, you won't ever get ahead," he told Adam confidently. "I have contacts on the East Coast. My roommate at Harvard, Addison Fisher, is tops as an investment counselor. We have been corresponding. I have several ideas to make both of us some rather substantial sums of money. Do I have your approval to act on your behalf if I have to make a quick decision?"

Adam had come from a background where wealth had been accumulated through the generations, slowly, steadily, by one long-proven means: Donati winemaking. He understood his vineyards, he understood, as much as any man could in the current plunging wine industry, about wines. He felt a wave of panic over simply turning over money—Jacob Brunner's long-hoarded, tight-fisted accumulation that had come from his own careful planning and back-breaking hard work —to a little bouncy man jumping around with excitement over ideas Adam did not comprehend.

"Look at it this way, Adam. If you are sick, you go to Dr. Williams to find out what's wrong. If you want a stone building put up, you go the the Pascarellas. If you want the best foreman, you hire Kyle Plimpton. You yourself are the finest winemaker. I've been hearing rumors about that first Cabernet Sauvignon you put up that's just now getting around the tasting circle—men who know their wines! I know you are a man on whom I would place my chips if I were gambling on wine futures. But *I* know what *I'm* doing with money on the open market. In New York, in Boston. Trust me. You have a huge payment coming due to the Linton Bank in 1899. Do you want to meet it? Or do you want to lose everything?"

They had been sitting in Norman's office, going over the harvest reports, facing the cold hard facts of figures added up and subtracted. Adam stood up, bit his lower lip, jutted his chin out. "All right. I give you my say-so. Do what you think is right. I trust you. You are my friend."

Norman waddled around the desk, his eyes beaming with pleasure. "You will not regret your faith in me! You know your wines—you know a lot, Adam Donati. I have my talents, too. We will make a fine team!"

Ten days before Christmas, Kyle drove up Spring Mountain, helped the broad-hipped, buxom Emma out of the buggy, and said, "I'd like to have you meet my wife. We slipped off and got ourselves hitched. Rode the train all the way to Reno, Nevada. Spent a nice honeymoon up there all snowed in." They brought Adam a colorful Indian rug. "Thought the bunkhouse mess hall could use some livening up," Kyle said. "Leave 'em behind a little memory of me, since I'll be staying at Emma's place on Spring Street, naturally." He had gone inside the bunkhouse, gathered a few of his leftover belongings and loaded them in the buggy. "Never thought I'd settle down, let myself get hooked," he told Adam on the side. "Emma's maybe not a raving beauty, but she's an awful good woman. She don't seem to mind atall about my crippled arm. I used to think a woman wouldn't want to crawl up next to that ugly thing." He looked embarrassed. "She's got a way about her—makes me feel like I'm the biggest fish in the Napa River! Best catch she could've ever made." He laughed, pulled his old faithful cowboy hat down in its usual lopsided position on the back of his head. "I didn't say she had such keen eyesight—that she might not be as blind about some things as a bat. I figure I'll just enjoy, pretend I'm the man she thinks I am!"

Adam was happy for Kyle, but a sense of added loss swept over him. He had always known that Kyle was there, readily at hand. He liked knowing he could wander down to the bunkhouse and find him sitting by the fireplace whittling on his cedar stick or making jokes with the crew—a crew, Adam realized, that would be one hundred percent Italian, with the exception of Li Po, now that Kyle was moving out.

Kyle had seen the clouded look cross Adam's face. "Hey, don't start thinking I'm going to backslide on my work! I'll do everything the same as before. Maybe even better. Have more reason to work hard —something different from myself to spend it on when we do strike it rich."

Kyle's early visit, delivering the Christmas present in advance (since he and his bride Emma were planning to spend the holdiays with her family in Sonoma), reminded Adam that he should make a trip to San Francisco to see Erika and to do his own Christmas shopping. Norman Jaspers was ready for a break, too, he told Adam, so on Sunday, a week before Christmas Day, they checked back into the Palace Hotel. It was agreed they would go their separate ways during the day—Norman had business meetings with other clients, and Adam wasn't that keen on standing around in Oriental antique shops. They would take in a performance of *La Bohème* that evening, meet for an early dinner at the hotel at six o'clock.

As soon as Adam arrived at the hotel, he sent word to Grace Pruitt at the San Francisco Bush Street Clinic that he would be stopping by at one o'clock on Monday afternoon and requested persmission to see his wife.

He had not stated why. It would not have made any sense, even if he could have forced himself to try to put it into words—how, lately, his dreams had been nightmarish dreams of Erika screaming out into the night, the total darkness. He would try to find her, reach out for her, but not be able to touch her; he'd hear only her voice screaming in this hideous wailing. He was secretly obsessed with the fear that some-how they weren't treating her right. Who knew what went on behind those locked doors? Hadn't Grace Pruitt jangled those keys around her waist as if they gave her some sense of power? Or was that his imagina-tion? Hadn't everyone assured him that Erika was getting the best pos-sible care?

Even so, he must, he had decided, see with his own eyes. He wanted to look Erika in the eye. *Her eyes*—he always knew when she got that look if she were really there with him or off in some place only her own mind's eye knew about.

He arrived carrying a bouquet of roses and a large box of candy, which he presented to Grace Pruitt. "You said it was advisable not to send gifts directly to my wife, but these are for you. For everyone who takes care of her," he said, his voice tense, nervous.

Grace Pruitt looked at him with piercing black eyes. "Mr. Donati, we do not advise you to go back and see your wife." Her voice was decisively professional, as if some lock and key had been clamped down on it. "Your presence is going to—will most likely upset her. Her condition has not improved at all since she was admitted here. If anything, it is much worse. It is, unfortunately, the nature of this particular mental illness. Our head physician, Dr. Berblinger, suggests that it will be a mistake—for you, mostly—if you *insist*. However, it is up to you."

Adam's jaw was like a ramrod of determination. He had allowed too many people to take matters directly involving his life completely out of his hands. Gudrun had charge of his children; Norman Jaspers had charge of his finances; and now these people, about whom he knew very little, had his wife locked up and he had only their word for it that they were treating her right! He had to see with his own eyes. If they had nothing to hide from him, why should they be so reluctant?

"I insist on seeing my wife," he said flatly.

Grace Pruitt sighed, shrugged her shoulders. "I had hoped, for your own sake, perhaps even for your wife's, that you would change your mind." She began sorting keys on the huge key ring. "We've had others before. They come in here looking at us as if they think we use whips, torture racks. Then they see for themselves. They usually wish they had listened to us. But come along—you won't be satisfied until you do see with your own eyes." As she unlocked the main door to the ward, she turned and said over her shoulder: "Just as I instruct my attendants and nurses, I must remind you—do not turn your back on your wife when we enter her room. Stay beside me or the two attendants who will enter with us."

Adam nodded, followed behind her, his heart pounding. His first impression was the overwhelming odor—an unclean odor covered up with strong disinfectants. Then, through small open windows in each door, only large enough for faces to peer through, he saw eyes and noses and mouths—human faces, yet somehow inhuman. Up and down the long corridor he heard eerie sounds—a laugh here, a shriek, some voice croaking out the vilest language he had ever heard, and, as they passed one door, fingers reached through the tiny bars and a voice screamed, "Damn you, Pruitt! You said you would bring me some butter and yellow roses for my hair. You promised! You slut! *You* are the whore, not me!"

They had reached the far end of the ward. Grace Pruitt took out one of the keys, placed it in the lock, but before opening the door said in a whisper to Adam: "The mattress is her only furniture because it is all that is safe for her in her present condition. She has been very violently upset lately."

Erika had her back to them when they slowly entered. She was standing over in a corner, her hands picking, endlessly picking, at a hole she had torn in the side of her dress—a dress that hung like a limp short sack off her. Then Adam saw her hair.

"What happened to her hair! Why is it cut off like that?"

"We had to do that as a safety measure," Grace Pruitt said in a low, coarse whisper. "Otherwise, she might have strangled herself with the long braid. She *tried* to." She moved up closer to Erika, the attendants close behind. "Erika—your husband is here to see you. Would you turn around, please?"

Adam felt as if his feet had turned into stones that would never move. "Erika?" His voice did not sound like his own. "Erika . . . hello. . . . I wanted to come see if—" At that moment, he saw the floor where obviously she had relieved herself. The color drained from his face, his arms now felt limp.

Then Erika turned with the swiftness of a cat pouncing. Her eyes were like glass. Her arms raked toward him, trying to scratch his eyes, his face, grab him by the neck. Her shrieks were more like what he would imagine would come from a jungle. Her bare feet were kicking at his shins. She was trying to bite him. The two attendants were there at once, taking her arms and pulling them away.

"Quickly," Grace Pruitt was saying. "Hurry! When she gets disturbed, it is not easy."

She was pushing Adam toward the door, her hand firmly on his right arm. The two men, as strong as they were, were having difficulty restraining the screeching, biting, flailing Erika. Adam felt as if he were stumbling, that any moment he would fall. He would never get out of the locked ward. He would hear for the rest of his life those sounds— he would never forget that smell!

"Why can't she be taken to the *bathroom?*" he asked, unaware that tears were sliding uncontrollably down his cheeks.

Grace Pruitt did not answer. She took him rapidly down the corridor, opened the door, led him across the waiting room into her private office. For a moment, she let him pull himself back together. "I am sorry. I would have spared you that. But at least now you *know.* You must realize that we are trying. We are doing our best for her. She gets a bath every morning. There are times when it requires four—once six —of us to get her fully bathed. When she is disturbed, she has the strength of ten women. We do attempt to get her to the bathroom. It does not always work out that she will go on schedule. I am—believe me, Mr. Donati, I am so dreadfully sorry to see you this upset! Is there anything, anything at all, I can do for you?"

Adam half stumbled out of the clinic, walked blindly down the street. He continued walking and walking, turning this way and that around corners, going he knew not where. And then he was on Columbus, recognizing the location. Slowly, miserably, he made his way to Lorenzo Pascarella's place on Stockton.

Lorenzo was out on the sidewalk, sweeping, a cigar in the corner of his mouth, a large white apron wrapped around him to keep the dust of the broom from getting on the dark-blue suit he wore as owner-manager of the restaurant. Lunch was over; it was that time of day when he got the place ready for his dinner customers. He looked up, frowned, as Adam hesitantly introduced himself. A grin spread over his face. He tossed the broom against the wall, untied the apron, flung it at a waiter standing in the doorway taking a break.

"Come on!—make room for my friend here," he said, pushing the waiter aside, clamping one arm around Adam's shoulder. "Hey, Luciano! Come outa the back there, Luciano—look who's here! The friend of my brother's. The Donati fellow—you know the one I was telling you about?" He was directing Adam to his own private table with a reserved sign on it. He puffed vigorously on the cigar, as if stirring up the movement with his smoke that he expected from Luciano's footsteps he did not hear or see. "Hey—maybe I see you got something the matter. Maybe you just get off the ferryboat, huh? A little sick here in the stomach—butterflies maybe?" He waved his hands in a fluttering motion like flapping wings.

Adam stared at him blankly, as if a wordless grief had been interminably harnessed around his spirit, his very capacity to make utterances. "My wife—she is . . . sick. The clinic . . ."

Lorenzo's thick black eyebrows rose in exclamation points of their own. "Clinics—that is serious business." He shook his head. "*Very* serious?" Lorenzo's waiting silence was more commanding than his question.

"She is—it is her mind. . . . I am sorry. . . . I cannot talk. It is—I was just there to see her and . . ." To his shame, he felt white-hot, hopeless tears blinding his eyes.

Lorenzo and Luciano looked at each other, both trying to speak at once, then Lorenzo was taking over. "Look, we don't talk, then. But, hey—my brother Luigi tells me you need more markets for Donati wine. What do you say if I got a big order for you? I take seven hundred fifty gallons Donati wine the first shipment! My people drink lotsa wine. The better it is, the more they drink." Lorenzo was frowning, as though adding up figures in the back of his head. "Hospitals—

any kind of hospital costs money. A lot of money, huh? Hey, Mario! Come here. You need a barrel of wine? The best there is? Sure, you can buy a barrel—thirty cents a gallon. Tell Flavio. And what about the guys down on Columbus at the Cigar Store? Sure! Maybe they can use five, six barrels. Look, Adam, we got lots of customers around here. So from now on we buy your wine. Is that a deal?"

Adam nodded numbly.

Lorenzo said, more softly now, "Look, everything will be okay. She will get better. Next time you will feel better, too, and stay for dinner. We have our own fishing boats—nothing but fresh fish every day. Pasta—we make it here every morning. The bread is the best you can buy."

Adam tried to thank him.

"Hey, what is this thanking business!" Lorenzo laughed. "You were good to my brother Luigi. Now Luigi and Cesare are getting rich up there in Napa Valley. Because of you. Sure, why not we do something for you too? Pascarellas, they never forget nothing! I make plenty money here in my restaurant. Now we make you plenty extra money too, selling your wine."

That evening, when Norman Jaspers insisted they attend the opera, Adam found himself latching onto every sound, every movement of the plot, to keep his mind off what he had seen at the hospital. He had not told Norman what he had done during the day except to say he had visited friends in North Beach.

During intermissions, Norman talked animatedly about the singers, the orchestra, the acoustics of the hall. "I have seen better productions in Boston," he said lightly, "but it is a treat to see any performance!" During the last act, when Mimi was dying, Norman looked across to see Adam openly weeping, as if he himself were up there on stage holding the dying woman. He smiled, reached into his pocket and handed him a handkerchief. As the audience roared their bravos and applauded thunderously, he waited while Adam hurriedly wiped away the tears. "Don't look embarrassed—everyone knows you Italians are emotional about your operas! Sometimes I wish the rest of us could be." If he had guessed that Adam was crying because of Erika, because of all the sadness and accumulated loneliness inside him, he did not let on.

Norman Jaspers made the arrangements to repay the money to Samuel Linton, quite matter-of-factly telling Adam it was done. Curiously, Adam felt himself glaring at Norman, furious with him that he had simply just done it—made it seem as if it had been nothing, when getting the loan had been so difficult, a milestone in his life, actually. He felt vaguely stripped down, impotent.

Norman was sitting back, his hands folded across his round belly, his desk chair squeaking as he turned rhythmically back and forth. "What's wrong? You've got that mulish look, Adam. You *did* want it paid back? There was no real alternative. *I* thought it was a considerable feat! It is all legal, every penny that went into that payment! Come out with it—what's wrong?"

Adam shrugged his shoulders, his face a mixture of rage and acceptance of the sense of what Norman Jaspers had just said. "Donatis, we mind our own business. A Donati is always head of his house!" He turned, stalked out, feeling tattered. He had not gone far down the hall when he turned around, charged back in, his face furious. "From now on, you talk to me first! Maybe I would want to be the one to go there and pay off my debt. Maybe I wanted to see my friend again!"

Norman Jaspers sat at his desk, his face twisted with puzzlement. "Italians!" he muttered to himself. What kind of emotionalism was that, when he had worked a near-miracle to bring Adam's finances into the clear? Was that the kind of thanks he was going to get for his efforts? The kind of appreciation? People—east or west, he would never understand the capriciousness of the human spirit, much less the range of Adam Donati's moods! He'd let him cool his heels. Stew in whatever his own juice was. Maybe he himself had taken too much for granted. But he had needed that opportunity to meet Samuel Linton. He had plans of his own. One of these days he was going after a big loan. He would open his own winery, perhaps. Besides, he hadn't done anything to take away from Adam Donati's fortunes. He had made Adam money, and himself some money in the process. A deal was a deal.

Adam did not have time to dwell on his fury with the short little man who, he had decided, was trying to grow a foot taller in *his* boots. The harvest was upon them. And though, as usual, everyone went about following the rituals of blessings and making toasts, it was as if a shadow had crossed the valley. The harvest that year made an all-time record: grapes bottomed out at an average of eight dollars a ton! Only 407,612 gallons of wine were produced. Over fifty wineries were foreclosed on. Even the phylloxera louse took one last swipe, with the El Molina vineyards reportedly succumbing to it.

With the help of Bobby Alfieri and the old Italian, Adolfo, Adam made arrangements to get casks of his bulk red wine loaded and shipped to North Beach to Lorenzo. He would, from now on, he told himself, keep in his own books any sales he made from his winery. Let Norman Jaspers handle the business end of the Brunner estate. He would show him he could manage Spring Mountain from here on out. He had just received money from Vittorio—a cash payment of $1,575 for the house across from the old Bale Mill.

"It is not enough," Vittorio apologized. "But I thought it might come in handy, the harvest being so bad on everybody this year. Pascarella Enterprises pay me good money. I saved this up. I figure if my boy Roberto works one more year for you, then maybe I have paid back." He looked at Adam intently. "I could never pay enough."

Adam had accepted the money, grateful for it, touched by his friend's loyalty. This year he would enlarge his brandy distillery; the bank had agreed to loan him extra for buying the big copper Sanders column still he needed. He could use this money from Vittorio to buy some new oak cooperage from France. It would help him keep hanging on, paying his own way; though, granted, he could not manage without the salary he earned as foreman for the Brunner property in Rutherford. But even so, he kept a sharp division in his mind between that money earned down there—those books Norman Jaspers kept—and what he, Adam Dontai, made on his own.

Kyle Plimpton continued managing the Spring Mountain vineyards. That spring of 1900, when he had just finished the cultivating, he stopped by to see Adam. "I was talking to some fellows down in St. Helena the other day about that bummer of a vintage last year. Everybody figures we hit bottom. From here on out, it's going *up*. It weeded out the weak from the strong. What we've got left are vintners—growers who know the ropes. 'Course, some blame Hussman for pushing so hard on that Missouri root stock, that *Vitis riparia*, when the *Rupestus* was better. Ain't it the damndest thing how men turn against each other when times get hard? Looking for somebody else to blame. Used to, Hussman was everybody's man to swear by. Now he's not worth a tinker's damn."

Adam flared. "He knows more about viticulture than all the growers in Napa Valley put together!"

Kyle laughed. "Well, don't get on your high horse at *me*. I like Hussman—always did, always will. I don't turn against a man so easy. I figure you don't, either."

A wave of guilt spread up Adam's neck. Hadn't he turned on Norman Jaspers for no real reason? He missed his visits with Jaspers.

The long talks. The trips to San Francisco. Sure, maybe he stepped out of line by paying off that note on his own. But didn't every man have to have room for shortcomings? Maybe there were some things about *him* that Norman Jaspers didn't like, too. He'd have to try to do something about it—patch up a fence he had torn down without thinking ahead.

It was mid-June. The work was essentially caught up now, the growing season on them. He sent word to Norman Jaspers that he wanted an appointment the third Monday in June at eleven o'clock.

He would have gone before that, but Gudrun had told him she wanted him around Saturday, since she was having a belated birthday party for Joseph, who had been in bed with a bad case of croup when his real birthday came along. "I'm giving him his first real party," she told Adam. "The Alfieri younger kids are coming, and a couple of Mulligans. Try to surprise him—be here with Luigi about one o'clock."

The idea began to intrigue Adam. He alerted Luigi, the godfather. He asked Kyle where he might find a pony. It was time a five-year-old had a pony! Kyle, with the help of old Adolfo, located a Shetland, a brown-and-white spotted one, from over in Lovall Valley. It had been brought to Spring Mountain earlier in the week. So on Saturday, when it came time to start out for Joseph's party, Adam himself put the lead rope on it, mounted Hajib, and headed down the back trail.

It took some doing to get the pony to follow along. Finally, a laughing Kyle and Bobby Alfieri gave it a shove. "You got yourself a baby mule there," Kyle had called out after Adam. "Ought to tickle that kid pink, *if* you get it down the mountain."

Adam found that it required prodding and a degree of patience to coax the young pony down the steeper areas on the trail that by now he knew so well. Even the normally impatient Hajib, who liked to take his jumps, seemed to sense he had to slow down. Flickering shadows on the pathway were enough to make the pony balk. When Adam reached the top of the steep slope above the barn, the place where he had once fought J. T. Price to keep the whip off Hajib's back, he dismounted, tied Hajib to a low bush so that he could graze, then began trying to bring the pony down the steep grade. He was himself backing down, tugging at the rope, trying to keep his own balance in the process, along with his temper.

It was the sound of her voice, that lilting, unmistakable laugh he would never forget his life long, that caught him from behind, from down there at the very bridge itself! He turned, color rushing to his face, to his earlobes. Then the pony was sliding stiff-legged and he was having to turn back and keep himself from tumbling head over heels.

"Oh, *Adam*!" She was laughing hard now. "How funny you look. . . . I'm sorry, I didn't mean to laugh."

He was standing there staring at her, his feet as though fixed, the silence between them stifling. His gaze was trying to absorb the full sight of her—the shocking impact of Sarah Reynolds as a full beautiful woman now. He saw the gentle movement of the pale-yellow dress blowing back with the wind, her brown hair shining with red highlights as the sun found outlets through the thick overhead trees and seemed to fasten its playful rays on top of her head.

She was the first to move. She stepped forward, reached out and touched the pony, ran her fingers down its coarse long mane. "How adorable he is. Does he bite?" She looked straight into his eyes then, her own amber gaze unflinching as she saw the wavering smoke-blue of his.

Her hand was so close to his holding the lead rope on the restless pony. "No, he doesn't bite," he said, huskily. "It's—he's a birthday present, for my oldest son, Joseph." He felt his neck burning red. He thought he could not breathe.

"I heard about them—your sons—and about Erika. I'm *sorry*," she said, her voice dropping. She reached over, touched his hand ever so lightly, her eyes clouded now and her lower lip showing a slight trembling. "I'm so sorry about everything, Adam. Life—it seems so unjust at times, doesn't it?"

He could not restrain himself. He blurted it out, his voice thick, mixed with anger and the certainty that he still loved her—that he could never stop loving her. "*Why*? How could you have just gone away like that—after making me think you loved me!"

She shook her head back and forth, pain crossing her face. "Adam, I could ask you, why didn't you have enough faith in *me*? Why didn't you trust me—know that I would never, never marry Christopher Elliot-Weare?"

He stared at her incredulously. "You mean you *didn't* marry him? No one told me! Why—why didn't you let me know? Write and tell me? All this time I thought—I was sure you married him."

Their fingers had interlaced, strands of the pony's mane caught in their tense grip. "I didn't get a chance, at first. Jacques Cugnot saw to that! My mother paid him to see to it." Her laugh was dry, bitter. "Oh, he did a good job."

"How? What happened?" Adam asked, barely able to speak.

"They arranged a party—a kind of farewell to the Elliot-Weares."

She looked at Adam desperately. "I should have suspected something. But I had made my own careful plans to run away that night, just as soon as the party was over. I was going to come to Spring Mountain to you. After we drank the farewell toasts, I felt drowsy. But I thought I was just tired from the mental strain and that a little nap would revive me. Besides, I figured I should rest—to be awake late into the night, if it called for it." She bit her bottom lip. "The next thing I knew, I was being carried out of the house, wrapped in a blanket. It was dark. At first I thought I was having a nightmare, that I would wake up. I wanted to cry out, but my tongue—it was as though my throat was numb. I tried—I couldn't speak. I tried to lift my arms, grip my fingers. I kept sliding in and out of sleep. When I started coming around, this horrible sensation of being a prisoner—not only with them and that grim-faced woman watching me like an army of guards, but a prisoner inside my own head . . . The sensation of being aware but unable to *do* anything. I could cry—and I think I cried all the way to New York."

The pony was trying to nudge its head around to bite Sarah's skirt. She tugged it free, blinked back tears that were eddying as though ready to join the force of the water gurgling under the bridge.

"But you didn't write to me when you got to New York," Adam said in a strained, clipped voice.

A quick flush of anger crept across Sarah's face. "I could say to you that you didn't *wait!* But what good does it do for either of us to fall into accusations! Blame—it doesn't make things any different now. It doesn't repair anything."

"I'm—does it help if you know how sorry, how heartbroken, I am to learn this! To know that it could have been different?"

She stood helplessly staring at him. Then she seemed to snatch the pony's lead rope and tug at it, get it in motion heading toward the Brunner barn. "I came here today never dreaming I'd see you. Out of old habit, I guess. Looking for something else in life besides the bitterness and the outright mess of the life my mother has created. But maybe it's not her fault either. It won't help Papa—the poor gibbering old drunken soul. Or make old Matthew hold out any longer." She broke off. "I'm sending him back to Mississippi. I can't stand seeing him with that dogged loyalty, trying to do what is expected. It's like keeping an old dog alive in spite of its pain—forcing it out of our own selfish sentiment to keep it going, following patterns that give us a false sense that life hasn't changed any. Nothing in life has turned out for me, for us, the way I once dreamed it would, Adam!" she cried out miserably.

Adam could no longer bear it. He pushed around the pony's nudging long nose, drew her to him, his voice agonized. "*Why?* I still don't understand why. One letter—any word . . ."

She pulled back, swiped at her damp cheeks, looked up through the dappled leaves overhead. After a moment, she spoke, her voice slow, deliberate. "When we arrived in New York, my mother insisted I wasn't well. I was kept in bed three days, always drowsy, always watched. I had made up my mind to escape. Then Mother waved tickets to Europe under my nose. She kept saying, 'When we get home, if you insist that you love this Donati upstart, then *I* won't insist. I'll let you have your way, in spite of my disapproval.' I took her word. I knew she might change, soften with time. And I was so sure down deep that you would understand. Would *wait*, Adam. It never occurred to me—ever—that you might marry someone else so quickly." Pain joined the tears, and her face drew up in contorted grief. He dared not go to her. Out of combined guilt and desire, he felt as if he himself had been drugged, would never move again. She went on: "In Europe—oh, Mother was like a child. *Her* dream did come true. And in that way, I'm glad for her that she had it. Paris—oh, how divine, that city! And we went to southern France, to Italy—Adam, to Lake Como, where the strangest thing happened." A tattered laugh split mirthlessly the space between them. "It had to do with wine, with a label. She saw the label—this bottle of wine with the Donati label on it. She started hearing about the *great* Donati family, and found out that your home place wasn't all that far away. Adam, I *saw* your home," she said softly. "We went to Pontremoli and I even met your wonderful brother, Guido. He sent his love. But I didn't—after what happened, it was too late to tell you about it."

"But *why*—why didn't you write!"

Her eyes widened, then seemed to close in. "Because I had just discovered I was pregnant. I didn't want to write because I didn't want to tell you in a letter. I was so sure you would be waiting when we returned. And Mother was so impressed by then with the Donatis—telling me she had, she realized, made a mistake. That we must make a point to invite you to dinner on our return." Suddenly Sarah was running. She turned her back to him and was fleeing down the path.

"Wait! You can't leave me like this. You mustn't!"

He dropped the lead rope to the pony, plunged down the path after her, grabbed her by the shoulders and pulled her roughly around. He was shaking her. "*Tell* me. You were pregnant. Did you—what happened?"

"I had our son, Adam—David Hubbard Whitmore. Don't ask me

why I named him Whitmore! It was a *name*—one that seemed as good as any. He was born two months before your Joseph," she said in a choked whisper. "In a way, he is your firstborn, you might say." The bitterness had drawn her face into a tight intertwisted knot.

"Where is he?" Adam's fingers were gripping her shoulders.

"In Napa City, staying at the house of one of my old school chums. He's a beautiful child, Adam. You will meet him in time. He is so much like you—so very much like you."

She broke away from him, pointed to the pony wandering down toward the creek bed. "You'd better tie him to something or you won't have a birthday present for your son—"

Adam looked into her face again, still reeling from the shock of all she had told him. He went over, tugged at the rope, dragged the pony back up the bank and tied the rope to a limb of a nearby tree. He stood a few feet away from her, his heart now thumping as if it had run away from itself. "Where have you *been* all this time? How did you get along? I've—"

She licked her lips, had got control of her tears now and was struggling to gain back her usual composure. "My mother found out about it on the way back. When the doctor alerted her that my seasickness was a little more than that." An ironical smile tilted one end of her mouth. She kicked at a pebble beneath her foot, slapped the sides of her skirt. "When we got back, Mother left me in New York and headed here to call on you. She was met with the news that you had already married Jacob Brunner's girl. After the hysterics, somehow I found, on my own, a place for . . . 'unwed mothers,' they call it." They were several feet apart. Her voice floated over a gulf that could have been two hundred feet deep between them. "David was born. I worked for the house itself—'secretarial,' they called my functions. Then, because I did have my degree from Wellesley, I finally found a position in a girls' school—Montague Hall, basically set up for slow learners from wealthy South Carolina families. Oh, they had students from all over the South. I was *quite* the bereaved widow there. The reclusive widow, Mrs. Whitmore, whose husband was lost at sea!" She laughed drily. "People need those empathic answers, and their curiosity quickly diminishes. One must simply state a truth. At least, it must appear to be truth." She shrugged her shoulders. "I must get back. Poor Mama, huddled there helpless. And those big impressive columns on our house—they were supposed to answer everything for her, weren't they?"

He looked at her, perplexed. "I'm sorry."

"Down South where she came from, the house with big pillars—

the black servant answering the door—it used to mean so much. Heritage . . . *Hubbard* traditions."

"What does she say about . . . the baby? You haven't married anyone since he was born?"

Sarah's look was like something on fire. "I don't love that easily. Mother? Something has caved in on her on the inside. She doesn't seem to care much about anything any longer. They're on the edge of bankruptcy. I took what little I had saved and paid off the taxes. I've kept the roof over their heads. The house—haven't you seen it? It's in shocking need of everything! It's—oh, I don't want to talk about it, Adam! I do, I really do, have to get back, and you have your party." She was walking away now, obviously intent on no further delay. "Let's talk some other time. I will be staying here. I have to try to care for both my parents. There simply isn't anyone else. I have a job in St. Helena. *Mrs.* Whitmore will be teaching high-school English and history." And then the path was empty.

Adam stood a moment, as though caught in some invisible net. Then, very slowly, he went over, untied the pony. But as he pulled it along, he felt that the pony was like some giant boulder on the end of the rope. He was in full view of the barn. Luigi was standing there with the two Portuguese hired men.

"*Paesano!* We thought you got lost. Here-come look what I got for my godson's birthday!" Luigi bellowed. "Come on, saddle up. Let's go see Joseph's eyes light up like saucers!"

Adam tried to appear as if nothing at all had happened as he helped with numb fingers to strap the new leather saddle that was Luigi's proud gift onto the Shetland pony.

10

On Monday, Norman Jaspers received Adam as though everything
between them was quite the same as it had been before.

Actually, Norman decided, he was relieved he had had this time
and distance away from Adam. He had been letting himself lose
perspective on what this friendship and client relationship really were.
All of his life he had had a little too much tendency to live vicariously,
and with Adam, this ideal physical specimen of a man, he had been
unconsciously trying to turn him into the full man he *wanted* him to
be.

He had no time for nonsense. Besides, his life was taking on a new
pattern lately. He had had his first taste of success as a trial lawyer,
having won a big fee for himself along with a favorable decision for
his client, and one of the keenest senses of exhilaration he had ever
known. He enjoyed success—winning. He was admitting to himself
that he *was* ambitious, and though it might reflect those very tenets he
had come west to escape, that was a realization he'd shrug aside. In the
long run, a man was judged by what he *did*—the marks he made in a
given space and a given time. He might as well face it: he was going to
always be five feet tall and basically unattractive, in the physical sense
of the word. But he could have his compensations. In a few months he
would be thirty-six years old. He had made up his mind that before he
turned thirty-seven he would have made enough money to make his
move up valley—to buy the house he had decided would become
known as "the Norman Jaspers place." For it was apparent—since he
had heard the inside story from a fellow lawyer—that the Gilbert Reynolds mansion soon would be up for sale. When it did become available, he would be ready to buy. And once it was his, he would restore
those magnificent columns, the grounds, the entire place inside and out.
It would be *the* showplace of Napa Valley. And then he would invite
his Harvard friends who sent such glowing reports of their own suc-

cesses back east. He would show them something none expected to find in the wild and wooly West!

All this was on his mind that Monday morning when Adam Donati entered his office. If, by paying closer scrutiny, he had seen the strange new glint in Adam's pale-blue eyes, a certain new lift to his shoulders, he would most likely have shrugged the observation aside. Emotions—maybe they were second nature to Italians, but they were not a part of his program for the future. He needed Adam Donati as a client—yes, and as a good friend—but he was going to keep this relationship at careful arm's length from now on.

He missed, then, seeing that Adam was like a tightly wound clock suspended, not allowed to strike or in any way ring out its measurements of time segmented, marked off. Nor did he see a new intent in Adam's determined face—an observation that might have left him less surprised when Adam made his announcement that the will he had only recently drawn up for him had to have a codicil.

Adam blurted it out, more or less. "Before we talk about anything else, I want you to add something to my will—this morning!" His jaw worked back and forth. "But before I say what, I want you to make it clear to me once more exactly what my two sons stand to inherit from Jacob Brunner's will."

Norman had barely had time to extend his hand in greeting. He was annoyed. He had planned this meeting out in his mind's eye quite differently. He found himself fumbling through the Donati file. He came up with his copies of the two wills in question. Deliberately, taking command again, he studied Jacob's will in a long silence, now and then, reading snatches out loud, more to clarify points to himself. Adam was jiggling one leg impatiently, working one hand against the palm of the other.

" 'If second party to said first party' . . . 'deems proper to act as ancillary Executor' . . . 'representation of the interests of unborn or unascertained persons shall be . . .'

"What this boils down to," he said after a moment, leaning back in his swivel chair, placing his reading glasses high on his forehead, "is that, obviously, Jacob hoped you—or someone like you—would marry his granddaughter, Erika. However, he wasn't sure, so he left a will that protected her, one way or the other, and one that would pass on his valley-floor property in Rutherford to any blood heirs Erika might, in time, produce. He made generous stipulations for such 'unascertained' persons, we'll call them, regarding education or costs that might arise in various areas. Also, he must have suspected that Erika was not well, since he left openings for covering any medical costs. What is it you want to know, specifically?"

Adam bit his lower lip. "I want to know: if our sons, Erika's and mine, inherit the Rutherford property, do I have to leave them what I own on Spring Mountain too? Could I leave it to a—a third party? One that . . ." His voice broke off, uncertain.

Norman looked at Adam curiously. "I would advise you to leave something—a small token. Of course, assuming that you have this third party definitely in mind?" He had made the statement as though it were a question, but Adam ignored it.

"Then I want you to write my will over. I want it where Joseph and Anton don't get Spring Mountain but somebody else does."

"And to whom will it go?" Norman tried to keep his voice professional, without any sign of curiosity.

"I will say just this much: to my son, David." Adam stood up, pointed a finger at Norman Jaspers. "Remember *this*—what I tell you is business. Strictly business. You don't tell anyone. Just write that in my will—to my son David. That is all you need to know. And nobody else needs to know!"

"A lawyer is obliged to keep confidences of his clients. Consider that done." Norman was smiling now, pushing up from his chair, feeling the weight of his stomach. He was going to have to cut back eating so much. "Now let's forget the business and go have some lunch." His thoughts were spinning. So there was a *third* son out there? And he had been so sure he had figured out Adam Donati, knew all there was to know about him. Secrets—did every man have his potholes of tucked-away secrets? And in spite of his resolutions, Norman Jaspers found himself, as he followed down the hallway behind the long-legged Adam, watching him enviously: seeing the tall, slim, easy swagger, the strong shoulders, the proud tilt of his handsome head. He *was* jealous —in spite of everything, he was jealous! He wondered how many women Adam Donati had made love to. What it would be like to be he. Regardless of his own secret longings, he had never known a real woman—only his own vicarious ways, his own secret fantasies of how it was.

It was Adam himself who cut the lunch short. "I have to get back to St. Helena before the bank closes," he said.

Adam looked a little too secretive, Norman thought, squinting one eye. "By the way, I'm having a new accountant I hired to reduce my work load bringing my books up to date. If, by chance, you have any bank accounts I don't know about, you should get the figures in for—"

"You have what you need," Adam said stiffly. "I keep some of my business my own!" He pretended not to see the startled look in Norman's black eyes.

When Adam arrived at the bank, he went up to the teller he liked, asked to withdraw fifteen hundred dollars in cash. It was the money he had put aside for buying new cooperage; but that would have to wait. He had to help Sarah. He had seen that lost look of desperation in her face. If she had spent her savings on taxes, she must be broke. Even if she would be teaching school, what was she living on in the meantime? There would be doctor's bills for her mother. *And there was his son.*

As soon as Adam got back to Spring Mountain, he wrote a brief letter to Sarah, put the money into a large envelope, sent for Li Po. "If you take the white mare and the buggy, you can get there before sundown. I want you to request—*wait* for a reply from a Mrs. Whitmore. Sarah Whitmore. Get back before dark. I don't want you taking any chances. And, Li Po—it must go only to her! See with your own eyes that she receives this envelope."

His letter had been a simple one, considering the complexity and wide range of thoughts he had churning in his head that he wanted to get across to her.

MY DEAR SARAH,
    Since our brief visit, I have not had you off my mind. The enclosed is money I send as a small gesture, hoping it will help you out during this bad time. I wish I could send more. Right now, it is the best I can do. If I can be of help in any other manner whatsoever, please don't hesitate to send word to me.
    I long to meet David, to see you again, and to know how you are. I have instructed Li Po to wait for some reply from you.

Love,
ADAM

Adam had been pacing the veranda when Li Po came hurrying up the pathway from the stable. "You *saw* her?" Adam asked, his voice slightly trembling. "How was she? Was she alone? Did anyone see you —recognize the buggy and the mare?"

Li Po was looking at him with quiet, shining eyes. "I did see her. First, I saw big man—very dark. Big eyes! He speak funny so I don't understand everything. I stay, I tell him I won't go away without letter from Mrs. Whitmore. He did not like. He go away long time. She come to door—but he hand me letter." Li Po ducked his head, then looked up, his eyes burning with some hurt Adam wasn't sure about.

After a moment, Li Po said in a soft voice, "Black man say, 'Yellow boy, go back where you come from. We don't want you here.' " Li Po handed Adam Sarah's letter.

Adam got up, went over to Li Po's hunched-in shoulders, clasped him securely. "Li Po, you belong right here with me! This is your home for as long as you wish. I hope you are happy here. It's not the best place, I suppose. You do see your relatives in Napa City enough?"

Li Po's head was bobbing up and down. "Yes. Yes, sir. I like it. This is my home. My cousins—they happy for me."

Adam took the letter up to the room in the main house he had claimed as his own. Originally, on the plans, it had been intended as a second-floor library. A large fireplace was buried in rich walnut paneling. A window seat was built in the tower that gave a view all the way to San Pablo Bay. Below, the entire Napa Valley lay spread with the muted gray-lavender tones of dusk. Adam's fingers trembled as he opened the letter and began reading.

My own dear Bacchus

(I do not call you "Adam" now because only a god would have known how desperately I needed the money), I cannot refuse it. I can only be grateful and try my best to apply it where it is most urgently needed. I can only say a deep, humble "Thank you!" I know your Chinese lad is waiting, and my words stumble as I try hurriedly to send my heart's message back to you.

Yes, my mother is gravely ill in the hospital. Dr. Zuber tells me it is only a matter of days before she will *expire*—he seems to prefer that word to *death*, and I believe it is because he thinks it makes it sound less final. I have, however, reached the point where I will welcome her death. She does not recognize anyone. She has lost total control of all basic bodily functions. I stand by her bedside and look down at this unseeing, unhearing, unconscious woman, this shrunken form under the blankets who used to be the powerful woman who was my mother, who directed my life, who was known to everyone as the formidable "Miss Grace."

How truly your letter revived me. I have been so utterly distraught. Fortunately, I was able to keep David staying on a few weeks in the truly sun-filled home of Martha Cantrell, a grade-school chum of mine. She has four children of her own. David adores being part of her big family.

At this time, I cannot place even a guess as to when we can arrange it for you to meet David. It will happen. But right now I must do all that I can for my parents. Whatever their mistakes in life have been, they were responsible for my being here. I owe them all that I can give at this time.

Please forgive me for unburdening myself in this way. It is almost the way I used to feel when I was at Wellesley and about to sit down and write a long letter to you.

Again, thank you for your generous help.

I love you,
SARAH

Adam read the letter twice, three times. Long into the night he sat there on the window seat, staring out at the distorted shadows in the dark, moonless night.

Before he could manage to see Sarah again, the harvest was upon them. The stepped-up tempo left little time to think. He was short-staffed this year. He had missed three Saturdays in a row visiting with Anton and Joseph, even had missed going to school with Joseph on his first day, something Gudrun had specifically asked him to do. There was just so much time, so many hands, and much too much to get accomplished, he told himself.

It was Kyle Plimpton who brought Adam the clipping from the paper telling about the death of Mrs. Gilbert Reynolds; or, as the obit itself stated, "better known to residents of Napa County as 'Miss Grace Hubbard Reynolds.' " It stated that she had died from natural causes; that the funeral had been private.

> Mrs. Reynolds is survived by her husband, Gilbert, a noted agriculturist of our fair valley, and by an only child, Mrs. William Whitmore, known in these parts as Sarah Hubbard Reynolds. Mrs. Whitmore attended school in St. Helena and graduated from Wellesley College. She is now widowed, and plans to live in our area, with her young son, David Hubbard Whitmore. She has been employed to teach in our local high school.

Kyle, who was staying in the bunkhouse for the duration of the picking and the main height of the crush, told Adam to keep the clipping if he wanted it. As he ambled back down to have the evening meal with the crew, he was thinking how good it was to be back. Marriage to Emma was okay, he guessed, but it wore down some after a while. It got on his nerves, just sitting around listening to one woman talk on and on, raving and ranting about how everybody knew Sarah Hubbard Reynolds was little better than a common you-know-what, and that baby boy she had brought back sure reminded a lot of people who had seen it of you-can-guess-who, and, for that matter, if she had ever been married to any man named William Whitmore, it was sure mighty odd why Miss Grace didn't have anything put in the papers about it when, Lord knows, everybody and his uncle who ever even stood up before a justice of the peace around Napa County got his name stuck in the papers.

Kyle took a long sigh, then went inside the bunkhouse. He went over to the fireplace, straightened out the Indian rug he and Emma had left as a reminder of him. "Hey, Li Po—where's the chow? Where's everybody around this place, anyway? Come on there, Bobby-Boy— how about a game of checkers for old time's sake?" As he sat down, he realized he had not been this happy in weeks.

As soon as the fever pitch of the crush began to ebb, Adam called Li Po into the main house one evening. "Li Po, most of the crew will be leaving the bunkhouse this week. Old Adolfo, a cellarman I'm keeping on—maybe four at the most will be left. Do you think you could manage down there but spend more time up here? Move into your old room off the kitchen?" He saw the open delight rush to Li Po's face. "I want to get this place cleaned up—put a little shine on it by Christmas-time. Maybe we'll have a party. Give this place some of the lift it deserves."

Li Po's black eyes beamed his approval. His long queue flew out behind him as he darted out the back door in that kind of scuffling trot he had developed through the years.

Adam planned to send word to Sarah that he was getting caught up with his work now and would appreciate setting a definite date for him to meet David and see her again, when Kyle brought him word in an offhand remark: "I hear old Gilbert Reynolds kicked off the other night. Finally had that one last bender too many. They buried him day before yesterday. I saw the hearse go by and her—Sarah Hubbard— riding along with the Cantrell family. 'Case you might be interested." He jammed on his cowboy hat, sauntered off toward the new vineyard being extended with cuttings from Jacob Brunner's secret varietal— which Kyle had dubbed the Brunner white until Adam gave it a name for the records.

Adam went immediately to his desk and wrote a letter for Li Po to hand-deliver.

MY DEAR SARAH,

I just learned today that your father recently died. Surely, you must be busy settling the estate, and with all that goes with the tragic loss of your parents in such close succession. Should you need any legal assistance, I would strongly recommend my own lawyer, Norman Jaspers, whose offices are located on Coombs Street in Napa City. Most likely, you have already procured someone. I mention his name, too, because he has expressed an interest in someday buying a nice home up valley, and perhaps would be interested in your property, should you be planning to sell. I was concerned that you would be going back and forth every school day for teaching, and in bad weather the ride could be very long and tiresome.

I long to see you as soon as possible. If there is anything I can do right now, please let me know. I am sending Li Po and two of his cousins down to help with any odd chores needing doing, including housework, laundry, or general outside cleanup. I was afraid you might not have enough help. If you do not need them, however, just let Li Po know. They have been instructed by me to work a full day for you, and I have taken care of their wages. Please send some reply back with Li Po.

Love always,
ADAM

When Li Po returned, Adam met him anxiously, bombarded him with questions about Sarah, the boy, the house.

"A nice little boy—so high," Li Po said, grinning. "Dark hair. Curls on top. Big blue eyes . . . Nice boy."

"And her?—is she?—"

"Nice lady. Very pretty lady. Here letter for you."

DEAR ADAM,

Hurriedly, because I am in the throes of moving to a small house I found in St. Helena, across from the park on Main Street, on the northwest corner of Madrona and Main. Thank you for your letter. I had already been contacted by Norman Jaspers, and he is indeed a marvelous help to me right now. He had dreamed of buying our home, he told me; so it works splendidly for both of us. I had no choice but to sell. He has wonderful plans for restoration. It is hard to give it up, but I cannot look back.

After a few days, I should be settled in. Please stop by any Saturday or Sunday afternoon. I long to see you and to have you meet David.

Love,
SARAH

It had become a custom for Adam to eat Thanksgiving dinner with the Alfieri family. On his way that Thursday, he stopped by the house he thought was the one Sarah had described to him, but there was no answer. He did not know that she had taken David and gone to visit the Cantrells in Napa City. He found an excuse to spend the night at the Magnolia Hotel in Calistoga, wanting to check on some cooperage he heard was in good condition and up for sale on Tubbs Lane. It also gave him a day or so to delay, then try again to see if he could find Sarah at home.

It was about noontime when he drove the phaeton around to the side of the house at Madrona and Main Streets, took out a large wooden rocking horse he had found for sale, and came to the back door, lugging the ungainly toy.

She had been grading test papers. A pencil was rammed through her hair on the right side of her head. She was wearing a dark-brown skirt and a plain beige blouse with a high collar. "Adam! What have you *done?*" she cried out pleasantly, her face full of surprise. "I didn't expect you—I haven't—the house isn't very tidy, I'm afraid. But come in."

Awkwardly, he bumped through the narrow back door, wedging one rocker of the enormous toy against the jamb, freeing it, finally placing it in the middle of the kitchen floor. He looked about expectantly. She saw the look, threw her hands out. "He'll be here very soon. He is playing at a neighbor's house. I'll call him—"

Adam took her hands. "No, please. Not yet. Let me look at you. I—" They were in each other's arms then, each kissing the other as though it would be their last kiss on earth. He drew back, barely able to speak. "I—maybe it is best that I came in the back door."

She was flushed. She stood back, smoothed down her hair. Both were on edge, as though afraid someone had seen. "Some coffee? Could I fix something for you?"

But before he could answer, Adam heard the sound of tiny footsteps running through the house.

"Mother—I saw a buggy in back! A beautiful big black horse that's—"

At the sight of the boy, Adam's breath caught in his throat. He was wearing a tweed overcoat, a tiny cap to match. His short pants and new shiny boots jutted out like doll legs below the coat. He was removing his cap, extending a chubby hand toward Adam as his mother had taught him to do with strangers. "My name is David," he said in a clear voice, his enormous blue eyes peering at this man he had never seen.

In Adam's own childhood, at about that same age, he guessed, a daguerreotype portrait had been taken of him and placed in a silver frame on his mother's dressing table, along with portraits of his brothers. Looking into the child David's face, for Adam it was as if the portrait had come alive. It was his own child-face, the same eyes, nose, chin—yes, so much his chin. But he could not remember ever in his lifetime being as happy and clear-eyed as this child looked now.

Unconsciously, he had bent down on one knee, lowering himself to a even eye level with the boy. A surge of love, like a seizure of its own, seemed to rush to his fingertips as they closed around those tiny fingers curled inside his strong grasp. "My name is Mr. Donati," he said in a voice that surprisingly held together. "I am so pleased, so very pleased, to meet you. I brought a present for you." He turned with his arm crooked around the tiny tweed-coated shoulders. "There—a fine horse, about your size."

The sound of delight, the sudden clamping of those tiny arms around his neck was one of the most painfully exquisite moments of his life, Adam was to think later on when he had time to sort out his feelings and go over the events of that Saturday.

Sarah stood there smiling through her own hazed-over vision as Adam lifted the boy and placed him astride the rocking horse. She poured coffee then, and they sat across the kitchen table watching him take his first imaginary ride. The huge stack of examination papers she had been grading were in a rumpled heap on the table. Adam flipped through them, curious as to what she had been teaching. He wanted to know everything about her! To try to envision her in a classroom.

"It's frustrating to teach these young high-school students," she said, shaking her head. "I'm astonished at how little they know about current events outside Napa Valley. I've been trying to bring them up to date on what is taking place in the world at large." She lifted her eyebrows. "Some of them had never heard of last year's Boer War even! When I asked if the war is still going on, if anyone knew who was fighting whom, not one could answer. So this examination covers a crash course I instituted, trying to bring them up to date on events of the past five years."

Adam took a cursory look at some of the questions: "Name the husband-wife team who discovered radium and polonium . . . . Explain briefly what is radium . . . . Where was this discovery made? Who won the Spanish-American War? Why was it fought? . . . Describe Admiral Dewey's assault on Manila Bay. How much money did the United States pay for the Philippine Islands? What other countries were acquired by our country as a result of the treaty signed between our country and Spain? . . ."

He laughed, pushed the test questions aside. "I do not believe I would pass your test. I could tell you how many gallons of wine we produced. How many wineries have gone broke. I could tell you the price of a two-hundred-gallon oak vat from Nevers. How much I paid for a Sanders copper still."

Since David's head was bent low that moment as he hugged the wooden horse by the neck, Adam's fingers quickly grasped Sarah's. They stared deeply into each other's eyes.

"Some lessons are very hard to learn," she said softly. "Sometimes there are those who always fail." She stood up then. "I think you should go now. The neighbors—this is such a small town. People talk. They do enjoy that."

Adam gave a farewell pat to David's shoulders. Sarah stopped the rocking, asking David to thank Mr. Donati for the nice gift.

"Thank you. Would you let me ride the big black horse someday?"

"Yes. Someday I will take you on a long ride. Maybe all the way up Spring Mountain and show you where I live."

"Mother, may I? *Now*—may we go now?"

"No, David. But someday, perhaps. We must wait and see."

Shortly after Adam's first visit to the house on Main Street, Gudrun asked him during his regular Saturday-afternoon visit with Joseph and Anton if he would mind keeping the boys during Christmas. She had decided to take a trip to Detroit and would need at least a full month to make it worthwhile.

Adam was delighted. He encouraged Gudrun to leave even earlier— having sent her off on the train, with a large bonus to make her trip more enjoyable—and brought the boys up.

He had made up his mind definitely to have a big Christmas party. He sent out handwritten invitations to the Alfieri family, to Kyle and Emma Plimpton, to Luigi Pascarella, and one to Sarah and David, along with another to Norman Jaspers—to whom he also sent his own tally sheets of profits and losses, expenses, estimates for next year's production of various crops on the Brunner property. Too, he needed some advice on the new forms from the Bureau of Alcohol, Tobacco and Firearms regarding his larger-capacity Sanders still and new tax rulings. "Be sure your lawyer checks everything," Vittorio had warned. "The forms—they closed me down because I don't fill out the forms right, don't pay right taxes. Don't fool around with the forms. You could lose everything!"

From then on, until Christmas, the giant stone house became a beehive of activity. For the first time ever, an enormous Christmas tree was cut and brought into the main parlor and decorated. Adam took a trip to San Francisco, stopped by the clinic briefly, left off gifts for the staff, new warm slippers and a robe for Erika. He had a marvelous dinner at Lorenzo's restaurant; made a stop by the Linton Bank on Kearny Street, to be told Mr. Linton himself was in New York on a vacation and would go from there to France.

Every tiny thought about Sarah would send him into diabolical moods. Alternately, his heart would soar; then guilt about Erika, about all that had happened to make any relationship with Sarah wrong in the eyes of the world, would plunge him into dark despair. But this was Christmas—he was going to have her in his home! For the first time, his three sons would be under the same roof.

While he was in the city, he not only finished his Christmas shopping but bought special things for the house. He wanted it to be exactly as he had once dreamed of it being.

Li Po had been instructed to bring extra help from China Camp to stay during the holidays. "It must be perfect. Everything must be the best we can do, Li Po," Adam said, going about checking that rooms had been aired, that the crystal was sparkling, the linens were starched.

It had been arranged that the Alfieri family would arrive on the twenty-third, spend two nights, and be back in their own home for their traditional Christmas Day dinner. When Delfina arrived on the morning of the twenty-third, she looked about the kitchen, threw her arms out. "Adam, as nice as that little Chinese boy is, you need a woman to get those pots clean! Come on, Theresa and Lilliana, let's give this house a woman's touch." And all that day she was in charge, arranging the baked goods she had brought along, preparing the enormous menu for the Christmas Eve dinner that would be Adam's first in the huge stone house.

Adam himself went about gathering holly, pine and cedar boughs for adorning the staircase, the mantels, and in general trying to recreate the atmosphere he remembered from his childhood in the big house in Pontremoli.

Outside, he could hear the sounds of Joseph and Anton playing with the younger Alfieri children, and wondered how David would fit in when he arrived. David seemed so much quieter—"Eastern," he supposed Sarah might call his polite behavior compared to an admitted rowdiness on Joseph and Anton's part. But he couldn't blame Gunrun. She had done what she could by them, and, should there ever be a good chance to bring them under his roof, with the right circumstances . . .

He tried not to think about that. Today was today! He wanted to enjoy every moment of it. That night, bedding all the children down, sitting around the kitchen table with Vittorio and Delfina, while she waited for extra Christmas bread to come out from a late yeast rising, he was filled with happiness. He had family—the house was alive! All the delicious odors, the presents under the tree, the anticipation of more things to come—yes, it was the closest he had come to his dream.

The next morning, Luigi Pascarella arrived at ten o'clock, his buggy filled with presents. All the children raced to greet "Uncle Luigi" and help carry the packages to dump under the tree. At eleven, Kyle and Emma Plimpton drove up, Emma having draped herself with shawls that would accommodate either her hot spells or the cold ones she was lately prone to. Since reaching her fifties, she had become quite fretful and attentive to the discomforts accompanying her "change," as she referred to it. Yet, in spite of her apprehensions, she seemed genuinely fond of Kyle, of being included in the festivities, and now and then would break out in sudden spurts of laughter, her jellylike hips and big bosom shaking.

Though Adam was the only one to know about it, he had asked Norman Jaspers to stop by and pick up Sarah and young David, and to try to arrive around one o'clock. Delfina had decided four o'clock would be a good dinner hour, considering the different ages of the children and all their excitement. It was now close to one, and to curb his nervousness Adam had asked the men into the library to sample some of the fine wines he had allowed himself to bring up from Jacob Brunner's cellar, assuaging his sense of guilt by telling himself it was in honor of Jacob, in memory of Erika, and to toast the future of Joseph and Anton, Jacob's blood heirs. Vittorio had brought along his favorite jug of grappa, a special Christmas gift from one of his friends on Howell Mountain. Though Adam had not wanted to wipe out his taste buds with the raw grappa, he could not resist Vittorio's eager offering of his own favorite drink.

Kyle tasted the grappa, twisted his face up and grinned. Then he heard his wife talking to Delfina down the hall. He nudged Adam, said sheepishly, "Wonder why she don't compliment me to my face?"

The men stopped to listen. "There I was, thinking I'd have to spend the rest of my life, a plain-looking widow-woman like me. Let's face it, Delfina, I'm the closest thing to *ugly* you'll see around this house today! Anyhow, there I was figuring I'd just have to spend the rest of my life settin' on the front porch watching the rest of the world go by, and here comes Kyle Plimpton making me feel I'm the one won the blue ribbon at the County Fair. Lord, I could just wring his neck sometimes—he does have his ways of getting on my nerves with all that mess he makes whittling on that cedar stick day in and day out, or leaving those smelly pipes around. But I consider myself the luckiest woman around, having so good a man care for me. Somebody to laugh with and cook for." There was a pause, and Adam was just ready to lift his glass in a toast to Kyle's happiness, when Emma's voice hit him between the shoulder blades. "I feel so sorry I could die for that poor Adam Donati. His wife in the crazy house and him stuck up here in this big house and—Wonder where the men *are*—I wouldn't want him hearing me say that . . . ."

Kyle began swirling his grappa around. Luigi was studying the wine bottles Adam had brought up, trying to read everything on the labels. Vittorio suddenly thought the fire in the library grate needed chunking vigorously.

Adam walked over to the side table where he kept special glasses for tastings. "Vittorio, how about sampling a Krug Zinfandel from 1886? And there's a fine Cabernet that Senator Seneca Ewer bottled— that vintage 1890." His voice was full, robust. This was his holiday. He didn't care what anybody said! He had made up his mind to get the most from it. *And any minute now, Sarah and David would be arriving.*

It was Li Po who hurried up to Adam, his black eyes gleaming, his hands hidden in the folds of his best silk jacket, his skullcap perched on his head, and said in a soft voice to Adam, "I see nice lady coming with the boy. The short fat man—he come, too."

"Excuse me," Adam said quite formally to all the others, who had by then assembled in the parlor and were admiring trays of food Emma was helping Delfina and the girls bring out. "The last of my guests are arriving."

Emma looked up, having just placed a huge silver tray piled high with the salami, olives, pickles—all the things which Adam enjoyed so much when he was a guest at the Alfieris' and which Delfina had made especially for him. "You mean we've still got people coming?" She was having one of her hot flashes at the moment, and stood up, swiped her damp forehead. "We've been in there trying to juggle seats at the table, finding room for everybody."

"My lawyer, Norman Jaspers, is arriving—with *his* guests, the widow Mrs. Whitmore and her small son, I believe." Adam saw Kyle stop his wineglass in midair, then drink too fast. He was standing his fullest six feet two, his chin high. "Do you know them, Emma?" he asked testingly.

"Well, everybody in Napa County is talking about her! Lord, I never dreamed she'd be *here*. Your lawyer must be scraping bottom, coming up with the culls or something worse."

"Emma! You got no right. You ought not say just anything pops to your mind," Kyle said, his voice as thin as one of the shavings off his cedar sticks.

"Well, excuse *me* for living!" She shrugged her shoulders, lifted her eyebrows at Delfina, as though women understood these things. Adam had already gone out of the parlor, was waiting with Li Po at the huge front door for them to come across the veranda. He longed to fling the door open, rush out to greet them. He stood quite stiffly formal, waiting. Li Po's bright eyes were beaming up at him, telling him that he understood.

Kyle had walked back over to Emma, lowered his voice. "You've got no right talking like that, Emma. Adam Donati is my boss—my friend. If he brings in Andy Mulligan and sets him down at the head of his table, it's not up to *you* to criticize *who* walks in that front door!" He looked around, being sure no one could hear.

Emma, not being used to Kyle speaking out his anger at her, drew up huffily. "I have to speak the truth, don't I? And if you want *my* opinion, I'd just as soon sit down with Andy Mulligan, the biggest sot to ever hit Napa Valley, as to sit at a table with that you-know-what!"

Kyle's crippled hand tried to balance the wineglass while his good arm gripped her elbow firmly. "I'm warning you, Emma. Christmas spirit or not, if you say anything out of turn I swear I'll move out—back up to the bunkhouse. I mean it!" At that moment, the full glass of wine tipped, splashed down his new Sunday suit. "See there, dammit to hell!"

"Talk about Christmas *spirit*," she fumed, and walked over across the large room so she'd have one of the first glimpses of the notorious Sarah Hubbard Reynolds who called herself *Mrs.* Whitmore.

At the sound of their footsteps on the veranda, Adam motioned to Li Po to go ahead and open the door. She stood there, holding David's hand, only her eyes telling him in that brief exchange her own mixed, throttled joy over being there.

He had never seen her this beautiful, he thought, trying not to stare at the mink-trimmed flowing velvet cape and bonnet to match, both of them the color of her eyes. David had on the same tweed overcoat and cap he had seen before. The small hand was reaching out to him.

"Good afternoon," the tiny voice said in that same bright, clear way. And then he was looking around Adam's long legs at the eyes of other children now crowded in the main hallway staring at him curiously.

Adam found himself awkwardly trying to greet Norman, who had stood politely behind—himself having guessed by now that David was the David whom Adam had wanted put into his will; that this exquisitely beautiful Sarah was the woman he truly loved. He had also guessed that the others might think he was her companion. He found himself suddenly caught up with that role, and he helped Sarah through the door, proudly holding her elbow, and assisted David with the removal of his tweed coat and hat so he could dash off with the other children already inviting him to join their games out on the sunporch, where Luigi had got all of them organized with puzzles and building blocks he had made with his own hands. It was Norman himself who, with a rather elaborate flourish, guided Sarah into the parlor and introduced her, as if he were the sole force responsible for her astounding presence, as well as being—for all they might know—the recipient of her affection. If, when they came to Emma Plimpton, either was aware of her frozen, disapproving fixed stare, Norman deftly moved Sarah on to the gentle pear-shaped Delfina, who took her extended hand in both of hers, shook it warmly. "We are so happy you come today. Your little son is such a beautiful boy—like you! Vittorio, look! She is the most beautiful woman." Her head bobbed up and down. She looked straight into Sarah's amber eyes. "I tell only the truth. I tell you you are the most beautiful woman I ever see in my life."

Adam began passing wine. Then Theresa and Lilliana were pushing trays under even Emma's uplifted nose. Kyle came over, insisted that she take a glass of wine.

"You know I hardly touch it. Makes my spells worse," she rasped.

"Go *on*—it's Christmas," Kyle said firmly. He forced her to click her glass in a toast. "Here's to loving kindness—that Christianly brotherly love you were telling me about yesterday. Come on, Emma—give me a smile. Just for me. Let's make this a *fun* Christmas."

Reluctantly, she lifted her glass, let Kyle's commanding gaze win her over.

By the time everyone was seated at the table, Emma Plimpton was on her fifth glass of sherry and was overflowing with love for the whole wide world, and as Kyle directed her to her place she took Sarah's arm, weaving toward her. "I had made up my mind you would be the spitting image of Miss Grace—that you'd walk in here like you hung the moon. I want to say right now I am *sorry*." Kyle gave her a firm push toward her chair, where she more or less plopped down.

Delfina had tried to rehearse Li Po and his three helpers. Adam saw him peering out from behind the screen over near the pantry door, the silk skullcap bobbing this way and that as his cousins from China Camp, wearing black cotton jackets and caps, hurried in and out serving course after course. Luigi had taken charge of seeing that the children were served and had their turkey meat cut. Vittorio made the toasts. Adam tried to keep from staring at Sarah, at the beautiful oyster-colored taffeta dress with the lace cuffs, the beautiful necklace of topazes set in gold filigree and the long dangling earrings that matched.

He was glad when Norman asked about the jewelry. "Sarah, I can't help admiring your unusual necklace. Is it old?"

Her long slender hand went to the largest stone dropping like a pendant from the rest of the necklace. "It was my Grandmother Hubbard's from Mississippi. I never knew her. But my mother told me she had a—a large collection of semiprecious stones such as this particular necklace, as well as some very valuable emeralds and diamonds. Most of it was lost, of course, during the Civil War. Only a few pieces remain. I put them on in honor, I suppose, of my mother, who believed so much in tradition." She looked for one quick moment straight at Adam. "I think she would have loved this Christmas dinner. Your china—my mother adored beautiful china. This is lovely. Your silverware and crystal—everything is beautiful!"

After dessert, Luigi took control of the children. It was planned that the children would open gifts, be put to bed early, which would give the Alfieri family plenty of time to get back down Spring Mountain in time for Mass and then on to their home, and allow Luigi time to get to Napa City to celebrate with the Pascarellas' combined families.

Norman looked about, undecided. He had, regrettably, invited clients from San Francisco with property in Napa Valley to come to his place and be his first guests in the remodeled Reynolds mansion. His secret plan was to take Sarah back, insist that she join them. He would be delighted to have her officiate as his hostess. So as soon as he thought it polite, he said quite confidently, standing near the center of the parlor, "I do hate to be the first to leave, but, Sarah, if you don't mind, I do need to get back early. I have out-of-town guests arriving tomorrow morning, who will be with me for two or three days. Shall I get your cape? Is David ready with his toys?"

There was a stunned look that crossed Adam's face, a strange startled look on Sarah's, since she had thought everyone was to spend the night. Delfina had taken her to the guest room; David had already moved into the children's "bunk room," as they called it. It was Delfina who hurried over, her busy hands aflutter. "Oh, Sarah can't possibly leave! But don't worry. We will give her a ride home tomorrow. We have plenty of room."

Luigi stepped up, his voice mellow from so much wine and the rich food. "I have room in my buggy. No—the kid is too excited. The little ones are already upstairs in their nightclothes."

Norman looked flustered. "But I thought . . . " He looked at Sarah searchingly.

She placed her hand on his arm. "If you don't mind, Norman. Thank you for coming by for me. Being so helpful. I promise—very soon I will accept your invitation to visit you and see how you've restored the old home place." Her voice was soft, the words were spoken directly to him. "It is the only home I ever really had. I'm so grateful someone as nice as you bought it. Someone with whom I can be friends."

Kyle stepped up to Norman, winked at Adam. "Don't worry—I'm taking Emma home. She's been upstairs sick to her stomach. Had too much excitement for one day. Too much sherry, I reckon. We'll ride along behind you."

It was decided that those left would get to bed early. If Adam had secretly hoped there would be a chance of talking with Sarah, he had to forget it. Delfina had more or less taken charge, and Sarah had said good night, gone up to help get all the children into their various beds for the night.

He slept very little, his thoughts filled with one bright image after the next. But even the creaks normal to the house were friendly, happy sounds. The house, to him, had finally come alive.

Luigi was in charge of rounding up all the children, of helping this one and that gather toys, belongings, find his place in the giant freight wagon ready to head back down Spring Mountain.

David had slipped up to his mother. "I want to go, too! I want to go home with the Alfieris!"

Joseph and Anton, each holding Luigi's big hands, each quite at home with him from his regular visits at Gudrun's, turned to Adam. "We want to go with Uncle Leege. We want Alfieris!" Joseph's broad forehead, his pale-gray eyes, his straight blond hair whipped around angrily at Adam. "I don't want to stay up *here*!"

Adam went over, swooped the younger up in his right arm. "You, Anton, do you want to stay with your papa?"

Anton's four-year-old face had lost its baby look. It was lean, slim, expressive. "I want to play," he said, looking toward the Alfieris.

Vittorio came up then. "Look—let all the kids go with us. My family wants it that way. We've got plenty of room. They are like one big family, huh? Delfina and me, we would be very happy to take all three boys." His eyes were soft, full of sudden understanding and a reasoning of his own. "Maybe they spend the night. We can bring them back. Roberto, he will bring everybody home the day after Christmas— the day after that?" He shrugged his shoulders, leaving it up to Adam.

Delfina came up, put her hand quietly on Sarah's arm. "Adam can drive you down Spring Mountain. He needs a nice visit. Quiet—not so many people." Then, very briskly, she was walking down the pathway, holding Vittorio's hand, hurrying toward the huge freight wagon down near the stable where they could hear Luigi's voice bellowing out, "We got everybody loaded up! Anybody riding with me in my buggy?"

Vittorio called back over his shoulder, "Don't worry. Luigi goes first. Leads the way. I will bring your boy by your place—when you say?" He had directed his question to Sarah.

"Tomorrow," Adam said quickly. "In time for supper. Four, five o'clock."

They stood out on the veranda, waving as the enormous decorated freight wagon with its musical bells bounced out of sight. Then Adam led her back inside, asked her to wait in the parlor while he saw that the Chinese received their pay and Li Po his Christmas bonus. In the kitchen, he gave Li Po his gift, then added in a businesslike voice, "You've more than earned a vacation. Take a few days to spend with your family. Be back next Monday, if that suits you."

Li Po bowed, grinned shyly. And then he was scurrying, speaking orders in Chinese to his cousins. In moments, they were gone down to the bunkhouse to gather their belongings and head back down Spring Mountain to China Camp in St. Helena.

She was sitting in front of the fireplace, her oval face cupped in her hands, leaning toward the crackling flames, her gaze fixed there on some vanishing point only she had seen. He poured sherry, walked over with the two glasses, waited for her to take hers, stand up and lift the glass in a toast.

"*Sa—salute,*" he said, huskily.

Their eyes locked. "*Salute,*" she said in a whisper.

He sipped the sherry—tasted nothing. He felt as if he had been caught in some capsule of space and time that would break open, hurtle him against ragged, uncut rocks. It could not possibly be a reality that they were *alone*, here, locked safely inside the two-foot-thick stone walls, with the rest of them gone!

He reached out, traced with his forefinger the cool, glassy surface of the largest stone in the topaz necklace; looked slowly up from it, back into the depths of her shimmering amber eyes so near the same color of the topaz. He smelled the oak log burning, a rich fragrance of cedar boughs, the luxurious sweetness of the perfume on the inside of her wrist which he had drawn to his lips. He inhaled the odor there; drank it, along with a lingering taste of the sherry clinging to his tongue. There was no rush. It was, in one way, a snatch at time; in another, he had the day ahead, the night!—the full long night and on through tomorrow until four o'clock. He would not sleep. He would savor every full, ripe moment. His hand slid across the huge topaz pendant. He took her glass, his own, and placed them on a nearby table. And then, in one easy, effortless movement, he was lifting her, carrying her slowly toward the main staircase. Her arms had slipped gently around his neck. It occurred to her that she might be heavy, but he did not feel her weight.

At the door to the room that had been originally designed to be the master bedroom—the room where Sarah had slept alone the night before in the enormous fourposter bed with its canopy—Adam placed her briefly on the floor, tilted her chin. "A man always carries his bride across the threshold," he said in a thick voice. "You *are* my bride—my only bride."

He placed her gently on the edge of the bed. This time, as his fingers found the buttons down the front of the oyster-colored taffeta dress, there was not the frantic fumbling there had been that time in the bunkhouse. He took deliberate time, as if each tiny covered button was itself symbolic of each step he would be taking before he would find that ripest, fullest moment, and then on and on, to all the possible moments awaiting them through the rest of this day, through the black silken night ahead, through the reach through tomorrow.

One by one the buttons opened. And then, one by one, the different textures of her layers of garments eased through his hands: the crinkly taffeta, the lace, the silk, the thinner silk—until there was that remembered satin feel of those mounds of her breasts in the cup of his hands, and again their mouths fixed in that tortured seal, repeating again and again their permanent bonded vows of love; their joined bodies readily forming their own liquid wedding ring. . . .

II

After that Christmas, if local gossipmongers looked for scandalous goings-on in the little white frame house across from the park where the widow Sarah Reynolds Whitmore lived with her small son, David, they found little to talk about. Adam made a point of openly parking his phaeton in front of her house, usually on a Saturday or Sunday afternoon, and quickly dashing inside and calling for the little boy, who would then sit perched in the two-seater carriage along with Joseph and Anton as if in fact he were merely a playmate. What they did not know, however, was that he had found his ways of now and then riding Hajib down and leaving him at the livery stable, taking long meandering walks until he was certain his entrances through the back door were unobserved. Both hated the sneaking in and out; but neither wanted to ruin her chances of keeping the job as teacher at the local high school. To Adam, he must not risk losing her again. Any small, sporadic visiting was better than not having her in Napa Valley.

The year of 1901 passed without any overall significant world events, according to Sarah's astute eye at determining such matters. Adam found the year one in which he struggled, along with the other surviving viticulturists and vintners, to hold what small recovery he had made. He had heard from his brother Guido in Pontremoli that matters weren't much different in Italy: the assassination of King Umberto by the anarchist in 1900 hadn't made that much impact that Guido could tell; Itlay would always have its ups and downs, would repeat chaos after chaos, politically.

China Camp was burned to the ground in January, 1902. Li Po brought his three now homeless cousins to Adam, who, in turn, seeing the aging Adolfo's painful arthritis, hired all three to be his helpers and allowed them to live in the bunkhouse's back rooms.

Soon after that, the Magnolia Hotel in Calistoga burned to the ground, but even Emma Plimpton's hysterics about a mad arsonist out there on the loose died out: the spring rains had come. "Worst flooding on record, I bet," Kyle told Adam. "The railroad tracks are under three feet of water in Napa City. But up here on Spring Mountain, hell, nothing can't get us, right?"

In his way, Adam was beginning to believe that. He had escaped phylloxera. His grapes were now considered to be the finest grown in the entire area, with many past prize vineyards having been destroyed and the new replantings not yet producing. Even when the overall average per ton that year was nine dollars, Adam's sought-after grapes brought down fifteen dollars a ton. Too, he had some very promising wines in the making, out there in their oak vats sleeping. For instance, that secret varietal Jacob had given him (Kyle thought it was more like a Folle Blanche, with a trace of a spicy taste on top of the fruity, tart flavor; Adam thought it leaned more toward a Riesling); he had bottled the past vintage under the label Donati Chablis, and was entering it in the upcoming State Fair, along with his 1897 Cabernet Sauvignon, private reserve. His brandies were gaining a fine reputation, his Donati bulk red sold through Lorenzo was having remarkable success in North Beach.

So, if, as his brother Alfredo said, there was some insidious force at work out there among the silent masses that might turn and destroy him (how could anyone take seriously these factions calling themselves Prohibitionists—these scattered hotheads trying to make winemaking or any alcoholic spirits against the *law*!), he could not perceive it or become alarmed.

Even on the domestic side of Adam's life, he felt better. Though Gudrun had the boys back, he had routine weekly visits with them, usually trying to combine that with a visit that included David's company. He wanted them to know David—if not by recognition as their half brother, then by association.

As the boys grew, Adam found himself fighting hard not to show partiality. He would concentrate on the finer points of each. For instance, with the youngest, Anton, he saw how always he seemed to hesitate, *think*, before he made a move. He was surely as bright in his way as David. Yet he did not have the open-faced direct look and the easy personality that David had. In contrast, Joseph was the "all-boy," as Kyle would say. "Look at him, Luigi! There's a born fighter for you. Nobody's gonna mess with that one. Got the Donati temper and old Jacob Brunner's stubbornness."

For that matter, Adam had noticed how much Joseph resembled Jacob. But he had so little patience, he worried. And he rarely seemed really happy as most young boys did. He was undoubtedly his best when he was riding his pony. By the time he was seven, he was attempting daring stunts. "Look at that cowboy go!" Kyle would say proudly when Joseph would stand up on the saddle or hang over the side, one leg flying out in the air.

Adam saw these things; but it was David with whom he felt identity. The blue eyes would look into his as if he anticipated what Adam was going to ask, to say next. And on those nights when Adam would feel safe to stop by Sarah's and would sit at the kitchen table helping David with homework while Sarah graded papers or prepared a study course for her students, he was delighted to find that David's interests seemed to go toward things having to do with the land—with nature. "When I grow up, I will be like you," David would say emphatically. "I will grow blue-ribbon grapes, make wine, and ride a big black stallion!"

If there was rivalry, Adam passed it off. Even Gudrun, with just the two of them, would shrug her hefty shoulders and say, "Boys will be boys. Of course they fight."

With Napa Valley on the upswing, its recovery apparent, Adam found that one harvest seemed to elide into the next; then, without warning, winter's dormancy period would suddenly burst into spring's bright promise. He would sometimes sit over the kitchen table at Sarah's and shake his head about how time was getting away from him. "There's so much to finish. By this time, I thought I would be so much further ahead. A wall full of prizes."

"You have a few State Fair ribbons, any one of which should make you proud," she would tell him.

"But not a *real* vintage yet!" he would say, smiling at her.

He had grown to depend on Sarah's keeping him up with world events. It was through her that he learned about Colonel Goethals of the U.S. Army Corps of Engineers getting down to the difficult business of building the Panama Canal, of conquering, along with that, the battle with the yellow-fever-carrying mosquito. She tried to keep him informed about the Russian–Japanese War and how Japan was appealing to our own President Theodore Roosevelt to mediate a settlement—a settlement which brought Japan into the world powers that September of 1905. But though Adam always listened attentively—it had become their way of passing time until David would most assuredly be sound asleep, when they could safely find that sense of freedom and space to make love—his real obsession was inevitably cen-

243

tered on Napa Valley, on world events that might be of interest to his struggles on Spring Mountain. Yes, he would try to assure Sarah, he found it interesting that the Wright Brothers had flown an airplane at Kitty Hawk, North Carolina; that Albert Einstein, a twenty-six-year-old dabbler in physics, had published a special theory of relativity; that Russian workers had marched peacefully on the Winter Palace in St. Petersburg and seventy of them had been killed and 240 wounded by a hail of bullets from Russian troops; that the world's largest diamond, the Cullinan diamond, had been discovered and would be given as a birthday present to the King of England when it was cut. But even while he watched her lovely lips forming the words, delighted in a certain tilt of her head, was grateful for the warmth of her presence, her company, her love, he would usually have his own secret thoughts running in the back of his mind: he would be figuring new oak barrels he had ordered from France; the new press he wanted to buy; the slight change he would like to make on the Donati label; the varietals he had heard were being used on the graftings taking place in Oakville at the U.S. Agricultural Department's experimental vineyards, now being managed by the son of the old scholar Hussman. He had been distressed when the old man had died, and had mentioned this to Sarah; had been amazed that with all her worldly knowledge and facts, she had not realized Hussman's significance here in Napa Valley, the great work he had done in helping the viticultural world everywhere find the right root stock to conquer the phylloxera.

One night, when she told him that a group of radical and socialist labor leaders had met in Chicago to form the Industrial Workers of the World; that it was a movement she thought would bring about broad-sweeping changes in time, he looked at her thoughtfully a moment and said, "I guess it's what matters to a person in the place where he happens to be. Here we won't ever have any problems like that. With labor, grape picking is different. Here men work because they choose to be here in Napa Valley around grapes—winemaking."

"Adam, I think you believe the whole world rotates around wine-making and your oak vats up there!"

He left her place earlier than usual that night. Women, even Sarah, didn't understand the land, what it meant to some men, he thought, riding Hajib hard up the mountain.

It was soon after that, in the year 1906—when Napa Valley was richly green with that wonderful fullness of spring, and when the main excitement around St. Helena was about the extension of the electric railroad all the way up to there—that the history-making fateful morning of April 18 made its entry in the books by ripping open San Francisco—an earthquake that broke through the earth like some giant monster bursting loose after a long, enforced sleep and, angry with the world, hurled its fury about in roaring, rumbling thrusts. Screams of the injured and the dying were diffused with the crashing sounds of glass and bricks flying, of walls crumbling, and then of the crackling flames licking like dragon tongues until one giant seething wave of fire turned its force to destroy a large portion of the city.

And as though that disturbed demoniacal force had summoned other gods from the bowels of the underworld to make a show of support in outlying areas, in Napa Valley its wine god Bacchus took a giant supportive swipe around and about—breaking open huge vats of wine that were knocked off their foundation, and pouring over 100,000 gallons out the front door of a winery in Oakville; bringing down brick walls on top of choice cooperage at the Matthews and Migliavacca wineries in Napa City; toppling the chimney on the Beringers' Rhine House and caving in their tunnels; and, on Spring Mountain, cracking one of Adam's favorite stained-glass quatrefoil-shaped windows, breaking glass in his laboratory, tumbling new empty cooperage about, and caving in one of his tunnels and sealing off at least ten thousand gallons of brandy. In San Francisco, over twenty million gallons of stored premium wines were destroyed, adding that fatal financial blow to vintners trying to hold on and counting on that wine to bring in the money they needed.

It was Kyle Plimpton who rode up Spring Mountain earlier than usual to see if Adam had heard the news, and to tell him what he knew about San Francisco. He found Adam wandering about, still stunned from the eerie disorientation he felt from the swaying movements that had hit Spring Mountain during the aftershock waves in the fault—what Kyle called "mule kicks." Kyle went with him to inspect the damage in the tunnels. "I'd write off that ten thousand gallons of brandy, if I was you," he said, shaking his head. "Might lose your life trying to get it out, and no brandy's worth that."

Adam brought him into the kitchen for coffee, and it was there that Kyle voiced his fears. "Emma was saying—once we got her calmed down and put to bed—that she wondered if your wife might be all right. I hate to bring you worries when maybe there ain't a thing to worry about. Everybody's ganged around the depot trying to get the latest word off the telegraph. You never saw so much jumping up and down and hollering from people worried over their families. Even

Luigi was white as a ghost—headed out to Napa City to Cesare's place. They say it's pandemonium. Like the gates of hell opened up."

"Lorenzo—*Erika*!" Adam was not aware he had uttered a sound. He grabbed his hat and coat. "I'll go to Luigi—see what we ought to do."

At the stable, Adolfo helped him saddle Hajib. "Every horse here is jumpy, and the Chinamen are sure every rattlesnake in Napa County is coming after them and won't help!" His old hands trembled, and even his Italian was broken. Adam himself didn't attempt to speak English. He saw that Adolfo was in greater pain than usual. "Knocked me out of bed," Adolfo grumbled. "Scared hell outa me. Hurts bad enough every day when I get up easy. Crazy place, this Napa Valley!"

Li Po had been standing by the bunkhouse stove, his eyes wide, startled. Tin cups had rolled across the floor, pots and pans had been knocked off their nails.

"It's over now," Adam said softly. "Try to convince your cousins we're all right now. Adolfo will kill any snakes that come around."

Kyle asked if he could ride along with him to Napa City. "Don't want to get Emma going again with her raving and ranting. Dr. Williams had to give her a hypo to calm her down."

All the way to Napa City, everyone they passed seemed to want to stop and talk about the earthquake. Each had a story he wanted to tell —where he was, what he had seen, how he felt when the earth was shaking, how one man's dog went crazy and barked a full hour before the earthquake hit, even kept barking after its owner had whipped it hard for disturbing people sleeping.

They went straight to Cesare's new, impressive fourteen-room house on Brown Street, near the Napa River. Adam had never felt that much at ease around Cesare, who he felt disliked him and only tolerated his presence because he and Luigi were such close friends. A grim-faced Cesare opened the door, looked suspiciously at Kyle Plimpton, as though at such a trying time only family should be coming around; but he opened the door and silently motioned them inside.

"Luigi, he's gone to the bank. We've got to find out about Lorenzo and his family. They say no, but we get in there and see if Lorenzo is okay, if we can help anybody. Nobody tells us anything!" he suddenly cried out. "Luigi is getting money out of the bank 'cause maybe Lorenzo lose everything. I *tell* him, 'Lorenzo, come to Napa and join up with us. If you got to run a restaurant, open up in Napa City. Families ought to stick close, stay together.'"

Luigi came in, his face drawn, his hands filled with envelopes.

"Here's the money, the tickets. Maybe the ferryboat won't be running, they say. Maybe we find trouble." He shrugged his shoulders. "One of the guys owns a fishing boat says we ought to hire him. Go in on his boat. One hundred dollars, he says!"

"Then we pay. We pay two, three, five hundred dollars if we have to," Cesare yelled. "*Quando sarà pronto*—how long will it take? We go now if he is ready."

"Could I go along, too? I'll pay part of the trip," Adam asked, gripped with the need to see, to know about Erika.

Cesare looked at him, not sure. "Maybe—if they got room."

At the wharf, when Cesare took a look at the creaky vessel, he changed his mind. "We try the other way. Maybe we find a better boat in Vallejo. We will get there some kind of way." He looked at Adam and the hanging-back Kyle, who was staring wide-eyed at the massive Pascarellas moving like a big team of workhorses. "You stay here," he said to Adam. "Maybe word comes here soon. We will find out what happens to your wife. You stay at my place and look after my family?"

"Yes. Of course," Adam said hurriedly. "Luigi, don't forget—it's the San Francisco Clinic on Bush Street. Down close to Kearny, that area, and it's a Miss Grace Pruitt in charge. I—"

"Don't worry, *paesano*. We will find out what's what."

Adam decided he would rest better staying in the room he usually took at the hotel on Main Street. Angelina, Cesare's wife, was busy trying to keep up with her six children, getting them off to school, doing the day's chores as she had always done. "Cesare, he is strong. He will get there and find out," she would say, hurrying about from this to that, as if by her staying busy it would work better for everyone.

Kyle finally went back to Emma in St. Helena and, at Adam's request, left word with Sarah and with Gudrun where Adam was. Though neither Adam nor Kyle had ever mentioned it, Kyle knew that David belonged to Adam, and Adam accepted that fact. It was not a subject needing words. But he needed Kyle's sympathetic looks, his encouragement in little ways: "That kid of hers—that David! He's the smartest boy I ever saw. 'Course, you've got two smart boys in Anton and Joseph. It's just you don't usually see a little boy like that David come up with names of grape varietals—hardly ever gets his tongue twisted on a big word. Talks like he's born on a damn vine!"

Adam found himself hanging around clumps of men talking in the hotel lobby, hearing exaggerated stories, some stories that weren't exaggerated. He read the Napa *Register*, seeing to his horror pictures of the fire, the collapsed buildings. He was tempted to get on the train, head for there himself, but the papers stated there was martial law, that pandemonium existed, so that all but those with emergency reasons were being kept out. He would have to wait for word to come from Luigi and Cesare.

He was having trouble sleeping. He had planned on visiting the clinic in May, as soon as they had finished the cultivating, he told himself. "I *tried*—I tried to do what was right!"

But guilt had made its own earthquake inside him. An accusing voice counterpointed: "Why didn't you go visit her more often? How could you simply forget her? And face it, Adam Donati, you haven't thought of your wife in weeks. You think only of Sarah—a woman who is not your wife. A woman with whom you must slip into bed, hide under the blankets and hope the world will not know—hope that your own son who does not have a legal name will not hear."

Cesare and Luigi were gone three tortuous days and nights. On the morning of April 22nd, Adam stopped by Cesare's house at ten o'clock. He had just finished his third cup of coffee with a nervous Angelina when suddenly she jumped up, ran to the door. When the bleary-eyed Cesare and Luigi came inside, Cesare hugged her briefly, pushed her gently aside, seeing the question on her face.

"The family is *okay*. Lorenzo's place, the old one, burned down. The new fancy one—it is a miracle, it is fine. His house—it's busted up. We sleep—everybody stayed at the restaurant." He looked at Adam then. "Lorenzo passed out free all the Donati wine. Fed everybody without charge. So many good people walking around—lost everything. No money, no house, no nothing! Looking like they still don't believe it, like any minute another big shake comes and puts everything back the way it used to be—bring dead people back to life, build back their places."

Adam could not bear it. "My wife—what did you . . . was there . . .?"

Cesare reached out, clasped Adam's shoulder. "The clinic burned to the ground. Look, they don't know yet. The whole place is crazy. Everywhere in San Francisco people are looking for somebody lost. I asked. Somebody says maybe if she was *off*—crazy up here—who knows, maybe she is out running around someplace lost and . . ."

He went over to where he kept his wine locked in a bureau, took a key from behind a clock, came out with a bottle of brandy. His wife hurried out for glasses; came back in. Cesare's huge hands, always steady on a chisel, on anything concerning a building, felt the glass shaking in his fingers. He handed brandy to Luigi, to Adam, placed both hands around his own glass. "A lot of people are dead. That is for sure. But they won't have a list of everybody for—who knows? You cannot imagine what it is like!" He shook his head. "Ask Luigi! Me and Luigi rode in on a fisherman's boat. We could not believe what we saw around us. But we found Lorenzo's place. We helped out a little. We gave all the money away. It wasn't much—people lost everything! They just take money and cry and cry. We told Lorenzo to come to Napa. To close up and come here. He says he can't leave his people. He belongs to North Beach, he says. When he can, he will come for a vacation." Cesare drank the brandy down in one long burning gulp. "Maybe you will get word about your wife in a few days."

"I guess . . . yes, maybe," Adam managed to get said. Blindly, he lurched outside, heading back to Spring Mountain.

It was not until three weeks after the earthquake hit that Adam received positive word as to what had happened at the San Francisco Clinic. Grace Pruitt had written the letter.

DEAR MR. DONATI,

Perhaps by now the officials have contacted you. But I felt it was my duty to write to you personally. You were always so kind to the staff at the Clinic, and attentive to your wife's needs, as so many weren't.

When the earthquake hit, I was not on duty. I always got to the Clinic at seven o'clock sharp. My night nurse, Maude Finley, was in charge. As soon as the earthquake hit, I started fighting my way to get there. But by the time I made my way within five blocks of it, the street was blocked off. The fire had already started burning. Maude, with the help of anyone she could find, managed to save nine of the patients. They tell me that is a miracle in itself. But we are not comforted by that. We lost twenty-seven patients in that fire. Your wife was one who perished. Maude Finley herself tried to save those on the back ward, and was seriously injured in her attempts. The police had to help me drag her away, even when it was all over.

I now pray to the good Lord that your wife and those others who died will rest in peace at last. I used to think that every day each one lived, each lived in his own private flames of hell. I pray that their families will find peace. I pray that all of us will one day recover from the horrors we have lived through. For myself, I will go to my grave heartbroken.

Sincerely,
GRACE PRUITT, SUPERVISOR

249

Erika's death was reported briefly in the county papers.

Mrs. Adam Donati, the former Erika Swanson Brunner, daughter of the late Johanna Brunner and granddaughter of the late respected viticulturist Jacob Brunner of Rutherford, was a victim of the San Francisco earthquake. Mrs. Donati, who had suffered a long illness, was a patient at the San Francisco Clinic on Bush Street. She was one of several patients who perished when fire ravaged the hospital. Survivors include her husband, Adam Donati of Spring Mountain, and their two sons, Joseph and Anton.

He waited until his usual Saturday afternoon to call on his sons and Gudrun. She had read the obituary notice in the newspaper. When Adam entered the house, she flung her thick, strong arms out as she might do to a child.

"God gives and God takes," she said in that flat, matter-of-fact voice of hers. "It is God's blessing. She is better off this way." She sat down then, shaking her head. "It just does not seem right, though, that God would have her die like the others in her family—everybody but Jacob going by way of fire!"

Adam put both arms around his sons. "Your mother is dead, boys," he said, for the first time feeling the tears streaming down his face. "You didn't know her. She was a good woman. A very beautiful lady."

After that, Adam threw himself into his work. There were always things to be done. That summer, he announced to Gudrun that he thought the time had come for the boys to move back to Spring Mountain on a permanent basis. "They are old enough now to ride their ponies to school. I have things I want to teach them about the land, the winery. I was about their age when my father in Pontremoli started teaching me."

She had looked stonily out into space, then shrugged her massive shoulders. "I have always known this day would come," she said, her voice stricken. "I've tried to gear myself. I've prayed to God to give me strength and understanding. I know they are *your* boys, not mine." Her face was twisted with grief, combined with a rush of anger at Adam, which she held back.

He had seen the look. "Gudrun, there is always a place, a need, for you with the boys. I didn't mean I wanted to take them away from you. I want you to come with us. I took that for granted, I suppose. I thought you knew that."

She looked about wistfully. "I guess this place—it's home to me now. It's been the only happy place of my life and I thought . . . Of course, I know it *isn't* mine."

Adam was trying to decide what was best to do. "About coming up to live at my place—how would you like to work out an arrangement that, say, you are there for the weekdays, getting the boys off to school, helping them with homework, the same things you've done with them? Then you can spend your weekends here in this house. Have some privacy you've certainly earned. Gudrun, you have been— well, how would I have managed without you?"

"I have tried. I treated the boys like they were my own. I have raised them since they were babies. I—yes, I think your idea is a good one. It should work out fine."

With Gudrun in the house, Adam found it easier to make trips down Spring Mountain. Too, now that he was truly a widower, he did not feel the compulsion to more or less sneak in and out of Sarah's life. By Christmas, that same year of the earthquake, they were beginning to talk openly about getting married.

"I think people regard a year as being proper—one should wait a year at least," Sarah said to him one night after they had made love and he had dressed, was sitting in the kitchen of her small frame house drinking a brandy before taking the long ride back up Spring Mountain.

"It will be a year in April since Erika died."

"What do you think about next June?" she asked quietly. "Isn't June the month for brides?"

He noticed the irony on her face. "I'm sorry it has been like this —so much to keep us apart. So much that didn't work out the way we had planned—dreamed it could be."

She looked up, ran her fingers through her hair that was hanging down loosely over one shoulder. She pulled her flannel dressing gown closer around her shoulders, as though she were suddenly cold. "It could have been worse. What if I had married Chris?" she said lightly.

"Don't say that—ever again," Adam said, a wave of jealousy sweeping over him. "I don't like to think of anyone else with you."

"There never was anyone else except you," she said softly. "It's odd, but somehow I was never really jealous of Erika. Oh, maybe when I first heard about your marriage I was. But that was mostly self-pity on my part. Of her—no, I never was jealous. I felt sorry for her." She looked up at Adam. "I used to sit there in that dreadful place for all of us 'unwed' mothers and feel sorry for Erika. Imagine!" She laughed drily. "Most of the girls there were terribly disadvantaged. I thought of myself as being lucky not to be they." She drummed her fingers idly against the tabletop. "I guess I'm the eternal optimist. Or handy at justifying my place in life."

Adam had never asked her about the birth. He had wanted to, but it had never seemed quite the right time to bring it up. His voice was low, gentle. He reached out to find her fingertips. "When David was born—was it . . . did it hurt much? Were you afraid?"

She thought a moment, smiled down into the glass of brandy that was quite the same color as her own eyes. "Yes and no, to both questions. I wanted it to be over more than anything else. All those months of sitting there—virtually in jail *waiting*. You feel the heaviness, the discomfort. This kicking, busy thing inside you." She was staring across the room now, as though looking into some space he would never be able to see. A dry sound escaped her lips. "Funny, all the girls used to refer to their unborn babies as 'it.' If I heard them say once I heard it fifty times: 'When *it* is born, I will tell you *this*—I will never get myself in this kind of fix again!' " She swirled the brandy, stared back into its depths. "There is a paralysis that takes place. Even time seems to stop. You wait and wait. And then suddenly the pains start. *Hurt*? Yes, it did hurt. But I was glad that it did! I guess I wanted it to hurt. One is conditioned to expect it to hurt. But one wants that because—well, because it is that big dramatic moment that all that waiting was about. Then there is the feeling of guilt. Not only because the baby doesn't have a legal father. No, more than that! I think I would have felt guilty anyway, that I wasn't worthy of this—this thing that is bigger than we are, Adam! The labor—the process of giving birth takes over. It has total command. And then . . . then they hand over this little *it* to you, and the *it* is a *he* with perfect little toenails and fingernails—I was so amazed by that! And hair, eyelashes. You cannot believe that all of that took place inside *you*! That this perfect formation came from such a strange beginning, really."

Adam felt she had pulled away from him, into this private world of remembering, a world he had not shared. He found himself oddly jealous. Yet he had never loved her as much as he did at that very moment.

Her voice seemed caught in some haze of its own. "When you think back to that night up there in the bunkhouse . . ." She seemed a little surprised to find him there so close, so very immediate. "I guess we were caught by forces bigger than we were then, too. By letting our bodies grab hold, were we trying to define ourselves? Define the forces? Or were we vehicles?" She seemed to draw herself up; then slowly, as though now very tired, she got up from the table. "I've asked myself a hundred thousand questions these past years. I have gone through the guilt—the guilt is the worst. It always is, isn't it? But then I see this miracle that, to me—yes, David *is* a miracle! Do all mothers think their children are miracles? As special as I think David is? It scares me sometimes, Adam. . . . I love him so very much. And I feel so—so *terribly* responsible. You see them when they are so newly born —that fresh, untouched entity that has come out of you. Come from that night up there under the blanket." She shook her head. "Somehow I forgot that you had anything to do with it. Motherhood becomes such a private event. So excruciatingly personal. The pain—even the pain is so personal. Yet I know you *are* his father. One only has to look at him for a moment to see that!" She was leading him toward the back door. "He is so much you that now it is hard to remember he was ever mine."

His arms were around her, he was holding her as though he would crush her. "I—I am so sorry that I ever caused you pain," he said, his voice coming over a lump in his throat. "When we are married, maybe I can make it up to you a little. And to my son. Sarah, I have another question to ask you. A very private kind of question."

"Yes," she said, standing back, searching his face.

"My sons . . . I have *three* sons."

"Go on."

"Should I feel guilty that I love one more than the others?" He looked at her intently. "I try—I honestly try to be the very same with each one. But there is something about David that— He is like me. I understand him even before he says what he has to say. I look at him and I can see *me*. Really see myself again through him." He was reaching for the doorknob. "It frightens me a little. I love Joseph and, sure, Anton too. But—"

"You don't have to explain," she said quietly. "I think I understand."

He kissed her lightly. "So June will be the month we get married, then?" He had opened the door, and a cold November wind was whipping through, causing him to pull his jacket in closer. He felt, for the first time in his life, old, and strangely sad.

"June—sure! Why not?" She reached up, lifted his collar closer around his neck. "Just think—once we are married, at least you won't have to take these late-night secret rides up Spring Mountain." Her voice was serious. "I will be happy to be married. To give David his real name. You *will* legally adopt him, won't you, Adam? Give him what is rightfully his?"

"Of course. He is, after all, my firstborn."

253

"The other two—do you think once it happens they will resent him? Will it hurt them, make a difference?" She seemed genuinely worried. "I wouldn't want to take away from—"

"Don't talk nonsense," he said, trying to make his voice sound lighter than his mood. But beneath, he felt a cold knot—oddly, a knot akin to fear—drawing into a tight fist in the pit of his stomach.

There was good reason why so many brides chose the month of June for a wedding, Sarah told herself as she stood gazing out the window of the second-floor master-bedroom suite there on Spring Mountain that first Sunday of June, the year of 1907.

Though she had been in this house, this very room, on other occasions, this was her first time to truly absorb this particular view with its brilliant colors of an early northern-California summer spread out like gala streamers, strips of color undulating, twisting their way across the pockmarked valley floor with its strange textures of vineyards mixed in with its orchards of prune and walnut trees—colors working their way like flagging kite tails across and up the mountain slopes to the east. When she turned to face directly south, she saw the misty blue haze that had drifted across the San Pablo Bay. How breathtakingly beautiful it now seemed to her.

If only everything else in her life—in this marriage about to take place any moment now between herself and Adam Donati—could unfold as perfectly.

A long, heavyhearted sigh seeemed to pull itself out of the very core of her being as she tried to shrug off the peculiar feeling that it was too late, something was missing, ruined, when this was the day she had dreamed of, waited so long to have happen.

The Chinese houseboy, Li Po, had carefully steam-pressed and spread out across the fourposter bed the pale-blue silk dress she had selected from her existing wardrobe to be her wedding dress. She was still wearing just her petticoats and was putting off until the last minute lacing herself into the tight waist-cincher she would have to wear in order to fit into the dress, which was well over ten years old now. Gathering the dress up carefully, she began examining it to be sure that all the tiny buttons, the intricate maze of hooks and eyes, the rows of snaps and tiny ribbons were in place and that no spots might be on it from that time she had worn it at the Soda Springs Hotel—yes, it had been years ago, though at the feel of the familiar silk, seeing again the still like-new blue dress, she felt as if only a few months had gone by.

For a moment she stood in front of the full-length mirror in the dressing room, holding the dress against her. A look of irony twisted into place at the corners of her mouth. It had been the most expensive dress she had ever owned or would probably ever in her life own. Her mother's last extravagance, she used to call it; a dress that had been ordered exclusively from Paris for her to have for those special occasions, particularly those her mother felt were bound to happen back East. "You will meet very important people at Wellesley College. I want my only daughter as well dressed as the next!"

Sarah pulled the dress over her dark hair, restraightened her hair piled high on her head, then began snapping snaps, hooking inner stays, buttoning the seemingly endless row of tiny silk-covered buttons that marched up the front.

At the dressing table, she rubbed dabs of rouge across her cheeks, which seemed paler than usual to her. But at her age—she would soon be past thirty—she needn't expect to look the part of a young blushing bride. She peered at herself, at the tiny laugh wrinkles beginning to show around her eyes.

Eyes, she thought, fixing her gaze on herself. Wasn't it always the eyes which spoke and told a person's age, his suffering, his basic awareness of life?

Then what was that look coming back at her now—that kind of layered look, as though a pair of back-up eyes were peering out from a deeply hidden, piled-up wasteland of things that didn't happen while she and Adam waited, hoped, dreamed for this day to come?

Regrets—no, this was not the day for regrets over what never happened. It was her wedding day!

She was standing in the middle of the room, rubbing her long, slender fingers across her forehead, as though trying to rub away all that had been unpleasant these past years since she had first fallen in love with Adam. All the whispers; all that had happened wrong for her mother, for Papa Gilbert. And for Erika—tragic, deranged Erika. Why was she so sad for Erika? It was her wedding day! *Hers*. She must not let that joy slip between her fingers.

There was a knock on the door. She welcomed the sound, almost ran to open it. And when she saw the smiling, pear-shaped Delfina standing there with her two daughters, ten- and twelve-year-old Lilliana and Theresa, who were wearing their best Sunday dresses and grinning shyly, Sarah impulsively threw her arms around the startled woman, who patted her awkwardly.

"Ah, the happy bride! Sure, girls, all brides are so happy they cry. One day you both will see for yourselves." She turned to the oldest,

Theresa. "So, has the cat got your tongue? What do you say to the bride?"

Theresa stepped forward, handed Sarah a bouquet of freshly picked lilacs, sweet alyssum and a few small roses, all tied with a white satin ribbon. "We wish you a long life of love and happiness," she said with the stiffness of words memorized and practiced.

"And you, Lilliana!" Delfina prompted.

"And good health—lots of babies."

Sarah smiled through her tears, seeing their dark-brown eyes swim away, blur, come back again. She buried her nose in the fragrance of the lilacs, tried to stop crying.

From downstairs, the sound of Luigi Pascarella's deep-chested voice boomed out: "Is everybody ready for the song we sing when the bride comes down the stairs? Where is our piano player? Where's Theresa?"

Delfina became a flurry of instructions: "Remember, Theresa, you don't get nervous fingers. You play very good. But you play *softly*— not so hard on the loud pedal."

When the girls had hurried down the stairway, Delfina turned back to Sarah, patted her on the arm. "Everybody is so excited. The wedding—that is all Lilliana and Theresa could talk about. The flowers —they are not so good this year. My roses got hit by that funny bug —what you call it, that earwig bug? But they look nice with your dress. Lilacs—they look nice against the pale blue."

Sarah drew the bouquet to her nose, felt the trembling of her hands. She tried to quiet herself, to pull the rush of feelings into one long white satin ribbon of happiness—of being fully with this moment for which she had waited so long. "They smell divine," she said softly.

"Adam is a lucky man!" Delfina said, peering down the stairs to see if everything was ready. She came back to Sarah, fussed with her hair a little where a strand had come over one ear and was slightly damp from her crying. "And such a *happy* man. Vittorio and me, we know Adam for a long time and we see him too many times so *sad*. He is such a good man." Her face brightened. "So good and so handsome, huh? And you—so beautiful. Ah, yes. Everybody will see what a fine couple you will be!" She fluttered her hands nervously. "Now look who gets nervous. My girls, they will get everybody started right in a minute." She looked back at Sarah. "From now on, everything works good for you and Adam. This big fine house! Gudrun to help you with the boys, be here so you can go away a few days—how do you say, the bride and groom and the honeymoon?" She laughed softly, looked suddenly shy. And then she began to cry. "I cry—but I cry *happy* crying. Like you—the happy bride. I say one more thing. Me and Vittorio and our family, we are your friends. Anytime in your life you need a friend, you come to us."

A methodical knock came at the door Delfina had gently closed while they waited. Gudrun pushed inside, tugging at the sides of the navy-blue skirt of her best suit, which had become snug across the hips. "I've got the three boys lined up—'least I *had* 'em lined up before I came up here." She gave Sarah and Delfina a tentative smile, took a quick, disapproving look at her own plain face in the mirror. "I don't know much about weddings. They sure can wear you out, though."

Delfina fluttered her hands across her lavender- and pink-flowered silk dress riding over two layers of petticoats and straightened the cameo brooch Adam had given her long ago. She peered out the door. "Here comes that lawyer, Mr. Jaspers. Adam said he will escort you downstairs. I see Judge Bell, and there's Father O'Brien who said he'd be happy to give a blessing on his own, even though he can't marry you in the church."

Gudrun looked undecided. "Is there any special place you want me to stay put? I feel like an extra cog in the wheel."

Sarah reached out, touched Gudrun's thick arm. "If anything, you're more the hub of the wheel. I couldn't manage without you today."

And then Norman Jaspers seemed to waddle into the room. He had gained even more weight since Sarah had last seen him. But his round face was aglow, his puffy cheeks were well flushed from the champagne they had been drinking—sampling, as he called it when he opened a bottle ahead of the cake-cutting. His breath caught a moment as he crooked his arm and as Sarah's hand slid through. It was not exactly what he had dreamed of—guiding a woman he longed to have for his own wife down the steps to hand over to someone else. But maybe any participation was better than nothing, he told himself, amused by the irony, telling himself that at least through the years he had developed a sense of humor about his shortcomings.

"I'm foolishly nervous," she whispered. "Don't *fall*."

"You're *supposed* to be nervous," he whispered back.

As they slowly descended the stairs, Theresa's playing jumped ahead of the wobbly voices. But to Sarah it seemed suddenly as if a distant magnificent swell of music had enveloped her; for across the huge entryway, standing by the parlor door, was Adam, his proud head high, his blue eyes fixed on hers, drawing her to him. And then she was giving herself in to that magnet force—just as in the past, letting them take command. She saw in a blur the finely tailored dark suit Adam had so carefully chosen to wear for his wedding, the buttoned vest, the rose Luigi had jutted into his buttonhole at the last minute. All the rest began to drop away: the very faces of those dearest in her life; the children lined up trying to keep from giggling and whispering or throwing ahead of the signal the tiny bags of rice Lilliana had handed to them; Luigi Pascarella's bearlike face with a grin ear to ear; Kyle Plimpton by the door, looking uncomfortably plastered into his new striped suit that Emma had insisted he buy for the wedding, and Emma herself dabbing at her eyes with a lace handkerchief that didn't match the off-green dress she had thought was a pale yellow inside the store; over by the fireplace, the black robes of Father O'Brien, across from the kindly face of Justice Bell; to one side of them, her own dear friend Martha Cantrell with her shy husband, Frank; over in the corner, the Chinese standing like shadows; and, next to Adam, Vittorio Alfieri and Delfina holding hands, as though recapturing some faraway moment in their past.

Then Norman Jaspers seemed to be pushing, nudging her forward, as though handing her over reluctantly to stronger forces than his own, as he might push a client in front of the judge.

Adam's hand was reaching for hers, closing around her ice-cold fingers. She kept her gaze fixed to his steady, clear blue eyes that now encircled her, claimed her openly in the eyes of the world as his.

Yes, it was right. It was that moment that belonged to them—the moment Sarah knew with a full, ringing clarity was the acme of her life. Even the one jutted-out rose in the middle of the bouquet had stopped trembling now. She knew that her own voice would be clear, sure, and that not once would she falter when Justice Bell asked for her vow.

Her face had taken on a translucent glow as together she and Adam lifted their heads proudly to face Justice Bell as he began: "We are gathered here . . ."

PART TWO

1907-1922

12

Adam had waited until only a few days before their actual wedding date to discuss where they might go on their honeymoon. Being proud, he could not bring himself to tell Sarah that he couldn't afford the luxury trip he longed to give her.

"I always thought that when the time came, should we ever get to marry, I'd take you to Europe. Take our time. No worries." A half-smile of apology had been on his face. "First we'd go to my home place, to Pontremoli. Then to Florence, Venice, a week in Rome. And I like the town of La Spezia, on the sea. Maybe a little time around Lake Como, end up in Paris." He shrugged his shoulders. "But this harvest coming up means a lot to me. It's—"

She stopped him. "Adam, we couldn't possibly be gone that long. We have the boys to think of right now." She thought a moment. "What's wrong with going to San Francisco for a few days? I hardly know the city. All those years of growing up in the Napa Valley, the only times I went were when my mother was feeling extravagant and took me on shopping sprees. We never went to the theater, to concerts." Her voice shifted in intensity. "I guess the only thing I ever miss from back East is that cultural side of life that I knew there. Here, well, life does rotate pretty much around the harvest, and though I know it is important I—please? Shall we settle on a few days in San Francisco?"

Adam looked at her curiously for a moment, as if trying to register fully what she had just said. Cultural excitement—he guessed his life did pretty much rotate around the fulcrum of the harvest, at that. Theaters and concerts had never been a big part of his life, though his father had seen to it that at least once a year he took his family to either Genoa or Florence to attend the opera. Once they had made a special trip to Rome for that purpose. And in Paris, in 1889, he had attended the Paris Opera, had seen his first classical ballet. But obviously these things meant a lot to Sarah; he had never before seen that particular intense, hungry look in her eyes.

He thought about it a moment. He had such mixed feelings about spending his honeymoon in San Francisco. The truth was, he had carefully avoided the city ever since the earthquake, being secretly afraid that it would start up the nightmares again: those sweat-drenching nights when he would awaken grabbing at thin air, trying vainly to reach the trapped and screaming Erika in her barren, locked-up room engulfed in flames. For the past year, he had transacted his business by mail or telegraph, going only as far as the Napa City wharfside to see that his shipments were loaded on barges and shipped out across the San Pablo Bay. But at the same time, it would be pleasant to see San Francisco with Sarah—for once, not being yanked along by a frenetic Norman Jaspers, who went like a leaf hopper from one event to the next.

"If you want to go to San Francisco, then we'll go," he said after a while. "I'll make arrangements."

But that had not been easy. Since the earthquake, hotel rooms were at a premium. Through Norman Jaspers he was able to make reservations at the prestigious Ruckers Inn, a place that before the earthquake had been one of San Francisco's most elegant mansions, there on Broadway near Fillmore.

Norman had once legally defended Lamar Ruckers (had, in fact, been the one to suggest they convert the mansion into a temporary paying establishment to bring in essential income for holding on to it) when, following the earthquake, Napa Valley vintners had filed suit to reclaim some of their bitter losses from the more than three million gallons of stored premium wine that had been destroyed in the Ruckers warehouses near Mission and Market Streets. According to Norman's version, the mansion had been built by Matthew Conover, a silver baron, who had left it to his only child, the patrician spinster Elizabeth. Soon after his death, Lamar Ruckers had come along (as Norman put it, "from an undetermined background, claiming a little too adamantly to be from high New York City gentility"), married Elizabeth, and, with Conover money, established the Ruckers warehouses and managed to wedge his foot into high society. "You'll find he doesn't accept very graciously being in this current position, and will probably greet you as though he's smelling through his beak nose for some new foul odor wafting in," Norman had cautioned them. "But Elizabeth, being more truly born to the manor, will make up for what Lamar lacks."

So, with the Ruckers Inn reservations secured, Adam decided they would leave for San Francisco immediately following their wedding ceremony on Spring Mountain.

That Sunday had been an unusually warm day in Napa. Adam had insisted that Sarah bring along her rust-colored velvet cape trimmed in mink and the hat to match, though Sarah had thought them terribly out of season. As they stepped off the ferryboat that gusty, fog-threaded early Sunday evening, she clutched the cape gratefully in closer about her shoulders, and was happy to sit snugly closer to Adam when they got inside the elegant gold-fitted landau that the Ruckers Inn had sent for them.

The driver took the spirited team of black horses at a fast, steady clip up Market Street. Adam found himself looking out the carriage windows in stunned awe at the badly scarred city, at places still thick with rubble, adjacent to empty lots where damaged buildings had been razed and debris hauled off; at places where new buildings had been erected and looked more like hastily applied bandages trying to hide some hideous gaping wound. Adam gripped Sarah's gloved hand tightly as they passed an empty corner, the very place where the Linton Bank of California had once stood. He felt as if the breath had been suddenly knocked out of him. None of the pictures of the fire or of the wreckage crews at work had prepared him for what he was now seeing. He simply couldn't believe that swept-clean void space, the only traceable remnants of what he had known being two still-intact marble columns lying side by side on the ground, like monuments waiting to be hoisted into place. His mind was reeling with images of Samuel Linton. Where were all those fixed assets he used to talk about? The Linton Bank of California had seemed a marble mountain in itself, like the Pyramids, like the very Statue of Liberty that would ride the times, last out all human frailties.

Sarah had felt the tension in his grip on her hand. "What is it, Adam? What are you thinking?" she asked softly.

He did not seem to focus his look on her, though his blue eyes were staring straight at her for a moment. "When I first came to California, the president of the bank which stood right there on that empty corner sent a carriage for me and made reservations for me at the Palace Hotel. He was the one who got my loan—got the Spring Mountain land for me."

"I remember him. He was with you at Soda Springs, wasn't he?"

Adam seemed to shake his head in some wordless despair. "Yes . . . that was Samuel Linton. I was thinking, he's better off to have died of a stroke before the earthquake hit. At least he died thinking he had left behind something that would last, that would remind San Francisco of what he and his father had done for it." His voice dropped. He was looking right, left. He was trying to decide how close they were to the place where Erika had perished. But the fires had destroyed those few landmarks he remembered. He felt disoriented completely. He did not even recognize the street when they passed where the Palace Hotel had stood. He had read that the decision had been made to raze it completely and build a new Palace Hotel on the spot; that the razing had begun that past October and reportedly had been finished just this recent May. If he saw signs of new construction taking place on that two-acre span to their left on New Montgomery Street as the landau wheeled rapidly by, he did not in any way connect it with the permanently etched picture he carried in his mind of the Palace Hotel—of that first unforgettable sight of it when he had rolled under the arched entrance in Mr. Linton's carriage into the Grand Court, had looked up to see the seven pillared stories with their balconies adorned with rich potted palms, hundreds of gas jets flickering, casting golden hues across even the glass-topped dome so high overhead. It was unfathomable to him that a palatial hotel some one quarter of a mile in circumference, with its eight hundred rooms, its banquet halls, its French tapestries and rugs, its entryway that had seen the entrances and exits of the likes of General Ulysses Grant, Dom Pedro II, Emperor of Brazil, Presidents Harrison, McKinley, Theodore Roosevelt and William Howard Taft, along with innumerable other famous names that had impressed him when he had been informed of its prestige—that it was no more. *Razed.*

It was as though Sarah had read his thoughts. Her voice was gentle, consoling. "I hear they are rebuilding the Palace Hotel, more splendidly than before. When they do, maybe we can stay there sometime. Have a second honeymoon."

He looked at her numbly, held tightly to her hand. They rode then in silence, giving in to the movement of the landau as it made its way toward outer Broadway. The fog was thicker now; it trailed swirling wisps across rooftops, encircled gas lanterns with muted golden halos as they passed stone gates of houses that now loomed larger, grander. And then the driver was turning into the carriage entrance and directing them to the giant front doors of the mansion that seemed to Sarah to have been built on top of the world's highest, steepest hill.

Elizabeth and Lamar Ruckers officiated as host and hostess, greeting arriving guests at the front door as if they were indeed someone invited to drop by, spend a few days. Though Lamar stood somewhat in front of the tall, proud Elizabeth, she seemed in total command of the moment. Sarah herself detected it immediately; the quickly appraising and measuring eye; the long-schooled gracious air—actually, so much like what Miss Grace had tried to project—that pleasant but carefully polite detachment which let her assert and maintain her separateness, her position as head of the house. In contrast, Lamar's peevish, pasty-gray face, with its beak nose and thinning hair riding back on a high, wide forehead, had a perpetual look of contempt, a pompous impatience with any circumstances that could reduce him to such a demeaning position.

Elizabeth Ruckers had, however, sensed something quite exceptional in this handsome couple. It was more than their quiet, gracious manners, the proud look on Adam Donati's face; there was something hauntingly lovely about his wife, as if those amber eyes were looking out from deeper places than most. There was a look of a survivor there —a woman who, like herself, could make compromises, meet the unexpected, irrational demands life threw at her. And there was a sadness there, too, as though she knew all too well that happiness was a fragile, short-lived moment . . .

Elizabeth found herself extending her hands in a strangely welcoming way, as though she were greeting some distant relative, a cousin perhaps, of whom she could grow quite fond, circumstances allowing. With Adam Donati, she did not feel that immediacy. There was that distance the proud male maintained—that certain lurking fear she sensed in him behind all the surface bravado. But how marvelous it would be, Elizabeth Ruckers was thinking, to have her own fretful, insipidly tiring husband possess some of that same quality! How boring he had become with his raving and ranting about their "paying peasants."

Before Lamar could go into his tight-lipped listing of dos and don'ts, she stepped up briskly. "Lamar, for the Donatis we are changing the rules." She ignored his eyes narrowing like slits. "In fact, I am assigning my own personal maid, Nevada, to answer your bell, should you need anything. Should you decide to join the other guests at our regular dinner hour, I would appreciate knowing. Otherwise, consider yourselves ensconced in total privacy. Please feel as if you are at home, *alone*," she said, giving Lamar a decisive look. And then she herself took them upstairs to show them their suite.

The suite itself spanned the entire width of the bay-view side of the upstairs. French doors opened onto a balcony that would, on clear days, provide them with encompassing views of most of the bay and the distant hills north and east. Elizabeth Ruckers had refurbished the suite only months before the earthquake, having the French fourposter bed canopy covered to match the pale-blue satin brocade drapes and chaise longue. An exquisite pale-blue Oriental rug covered most of the floor. The furniture and the oil paintings were French, eighteenth-century.

"It is beautiful!" Sarah exclaimed, trying to absorb it in one quick admiring glance. "Thank you for letting us be here."

Elizabeth Ruckers smiled, drew herself up quite formally, afraid suddenly of a wave of emotion sweeping over her, as if her own collective sadness might at any moment spill over in the presence of Sarah Donati's immediate threshold of happiness. "Nevada will bring champagne, then your dinner in front of the fire."

As soon as the smiling round-faced woman named Nevada—whom Sarah guessed to be part Spanish and part black—brought in their champagne and trays of stuffed capon, delicate vegetables, crusty French pastries, a small wedding cake for dessert, Adam filled their glasses, then led Sarah to the balcony.

For a moment they stood in the fog-crisp air, staring down at the diffused shapes of rooftops cascading down the steep hillside toward the edge of the bay. Quick bright color from the cold came to Sarah's cheeks, the tip of her nose. Adam drew her back into the warmth of the room, and their glasses clicked.

"*Salute*," he said huskily. "*Salute*, to my wife."

"*Salute*," she replied, barely able to speak—as if the moment itself was as delicate, as exquisite as the effervescent liquid working its way down her throat tight with happiness. When she sat down across from their elegant silver dinner trays, she arranged the folds of her blue silk dress quite primly, feeling oddly shy, afraid that some imperfection of her own might spoil this most perfect moment in her life.

From then on, the week spun them into a giddy vortex of discovery. The license that had made their union right in the eyes of the law and the world had given them unspoken license for exploration with each other that they had not dared before. At night, they flung themselves joyously into lovemaking. During the days, they climbed into the Ruckers' carriage, accepted Elizabeth's advice about places she thought they would enjoy seeing, restaurants where they should eat, and even contributed her own Tivoli Theatre tickets to them for a concert where Luisa Tetrazzini was singing with a visiting opera company.

Adam and Sarah went about as if caught in a gloriously rapturous bubble. They were like children on a treasure hunt. Sarah squealed with fearsome delight as the carriage would suddenly seem to plunge down a steep hill. She pointed out the varying colors of the bay, of the sky, of the changing patterns brought on by a sparkling sun with its shifting darks and lights as fog rolled in across the Marin hills like a silvery river. Adam insisted on taking her into dress shops and buying her two new dresses, slippers, a gold-mesh bag for the theater.

When they would return to the Ruckers mansion, hot baths awaited them. They would sit in front of the fireplace, sipping champagne. Adam would find himself remembering incidents from his childhood and would relay long memories to her, wanting her to be a complete part of his life. "The first time I tasted champagne was when my brother Guido and I slipped away from Alfredo and we . . ."; or "I want us to celebrate Christmas in our new home together on Spring Mountain the way we used to do in Pontremoli. We must gather boughs of greenery—just like last year. We must . . ."

And Sarah, in turn, would tell amusing incidents about Papa Gilbert or Miss Grace. About some school chum at Wellesley. But Adam did not like to hear the stories about Boston. "Forget Boston—forget back East! You are my wife. *Here*, in California."

Then came their last day, on Saturday morning. Adam hurried through breakfast. "Today we celebrate Italian style!"

They said a warm goodbye to Elizabeth Ruckers, who insisted that they must come back as her private guests, while Adam was equally insistent that she come to Napa Valley and stay with them on Spring Mountain. "I am sending you some of my private reserve wine," he told her proudly. "My prize wines!"

Sarah clasped her hands, gripping them almost too tightly. "We could never thank you enough. It has been wonderful!"

The Ruckers' landau dropped them off at Lorenzo's restaurant in North Beach, where Adam had secretly made plans for their arrival. When they entered, Lorenzo, as if conducting an orchestra, waved his arms and the entire restaurant was filled with guests standing, lifting glasses filled with complimentary Donati wine in a toast to the bride and groom. And then Lorenzo was taking charge, hugging Sarah and Adam, leading them around from table to table introducing them. And then he was waving his arms calling for Luciano and Mario. "Come on! Where are the oysters? Today you get the best that North Beach has to offer. From my own fishing boat, fresh crab, fresh everything! Pasta —we make it here. Bread—we serve the best bread in North Beach. You will see. Today, the works!"

True to his word, tray after tray was brought forth to Lorenzo's private table. And then he produced his own surprise: a rare prize-winning bottle of Donati 1886 burgundy wine. Adam felt the warm rush of tears, a wave of longing for any one member of his family to be here with him sharing this celebration.

Lorenzo was beaming. "First we gotta let it breathe! Old wine—come on, Luciano, you know how to decant this. Glasses—fresh glasses over here, Mario, for the real Donati toast!"

Before the dessert—big boards of cheeses, dripping with fruit, another tray heaped with pastries—Adam realized they had to leave in order to get aboard the ferryboat. Lorenzo dropped his napkin in a disappointed heap, but cheerfully led them to the door, summoned his own carriage. "Treat your beautiful wife good—you picked a wonderful girl," he said, nodding his head up and down. He slapped Adam's arm. "Anytime you come to San Francisco, you come to my place. Yeah, Adam, we gonna need more wine quicker than usual. I got more and more customers." He shrugged his shoulders, motioned one arm toward his crowded restaurant. "Every day it is like this. Every day it gets busier and busier." He laughed. "And every day they drink more Donati wine. Double the usual order—okay?"

Once they were on board, Adam directed Sarah to his favorite place to ride, on the upper, outer deck by the railing. They needed the fresh ocean breeze to clear their heads. Sarah was woozy from having consumed too much food and wine. She leaned wearily against Adam's shoulder, pulled the rust-colored velvet cape closer about her shoulders. "I wish it didn't have to end. I wish this honeymoon could last forever."

"Why should it end?" he muttered against the top of the velvet hat, the mink trim tickling his nose.

"They say it does. It always ends. Life takes over and gives love a—" she giggled, the wine making her more giddy-headed than she had thought it could—"Life gives love a swift kick with its boot."

Adam frowned down at her. "That is not nice. I don't like it, you saying things like that. No. Besides, we waited too long for our honeymoon. We will hold on to it better than some because it was so hard to get. Everything will be good—you will see. Everything will be the way it is supposed to be when two people love each other and get married, raise a family."

She tilted her head, looked at him, serious now. "But what happens when the family is already *half* raised? Won't there be problems?" She shut her eyes against the stiff wind pushing her hair back, turning the tip of her nose pink.

"Look at the sea gull," Adam said quietly. "Look at the white wings of the sea gull. Look—see how it dips and then dives for the fish and comes up with its dinner. *See*—what did I tell you!"

Sarah bent over the railing, pretending to look at what Adam was seeing, but a sudden swell of water, a strand of hair blowing across her face, momentarily blinded her.

Adam's arm was close about her shoulders. "You see what I mean?" he asked her softly in her ear.

"Yes, Adam," she said, firmly shutting out the doubts that were beginning to cross her mind about the future. "Beautiful—yes, it is all very beautiful."

"So, from now on everything stays that way—okay?"

During the time Adam and Sarah were away on their honeymoon, Gudrun had made up her mind to try to do the best she could to help everything work smoothly.

And for several weeks it worked. If from time to time Sarah might have noted a certain wooden-faced look from Gudrun, as though she had nailed down shut her true thoughts—about how, for instance, Sarah had tried to get something across to Joseph and Anton, or how she had gone about trying to establish some specific routine for the household in general—Gudrun did not give any further sign of the furies beginning to swarm inside her. If Sarah sensed the resentments brooding, gaining a force inside that massive bulk, there was nothing precise taking place that she could express, talk out with either Gudrun or Adam.

The first incident—an incident which began, irrefutably, the deep chasm between them that could never be bridged—came about one Sunday evening after their dinner guests had departed.

From the start of their actual marriage, Sarah had made up her mind it would be beneficial, for both family and business reasons, to establish a weekly Donati ritual of giving an elegant, rather formal Sunday-afternoon dinner, conducted at an early enough hour for guests to drive back down Spring Mountain before dark. It would be a time to bring out the fine linen, the heirloom silver, crystal goblets and bone china she had inherited, along with nice things Adam had acquired, introducing the children to a style, a decorum they would need to know as sons of Adam Donati. Too, it put a certain stamp, a label of its own, on the way she wanted guests from Napa Valley and the wine world at large, who frequently made their way to visit the major wineries of the area, to remember the Donati name. She would leave the wine tastings and the choice of wines to be served entirely up to Adam, just as she would leave the main selection of guests up to him. But she wanted to combine with them a little added refinement, incorporate some of the teachings she had drilled into her since birth by her mother, Miss Grace—who had preached that if one mastered the art of good manners and diplomacy in general at the formal dinner table, one could get by in any given social encounter on the highest levels of society anyplace in the world.

On that particular Sunday when the incident with Gudrun came about, Adam's lawyer, Norman Jaspers, had brought along a former Harvard classmate, a young, enthusiastic lawyer from New York City named Martin Mueller who had a natural tendency to gesticulate rather wildly, in tempo with his excitement while talking, sometimes waving a knife or a fork about as though drawing invisible punctuation marks to underscore some point he was about to make. Martin was exceptionally bright, unreservedly vocal. His interest in winemaking—one he had originally taken up through Norman's influence at Harvard—had been rekindled after a two-week visit with Norman in his Napa Valley home. In fact, he was so enthusiastic, he told them, that he was strongly considering giving up his lucrative practice in New York City and going into partnership with Norman in Napa City, both as a lawyer and as a future winemaker.

Also at the dinner table that Sunday was a distinguished agriculturist from southern California, a Dr. Warner Yuill-Thornton, who had launched his own individual fight against those forces trying to bring about total Prohibition. He was a tall silver-haired articulate man in his mid-sixties who enjoyed lively repartee. The conversation had been just that—vibrantly so, Sarah had thought; their very best dinner yet.

Part of the ritual with the children at these Sunday dinners was to seat one of the boys next to Adam, each taking his turn. Today it was David's turn at Adam's right; Dr. Yuill-Thornton was seated to Adam's left. He had asked David several questions and had apparently been impressed that a lad so young, as he put it, could be that knowledgeable about vines.

At the same time, at Sarah's end of the table, Joseph and Anton had become increasingly fidgety and had invented their own game of making tiny dough balls from the center of their bread and had begun flicking them across the table at each other, seeing who could score direct hits. Even Gudrun had noticed; but it was Sarah who realized she must do something to stop it when, at one point, Joseph's kick aimed under the table at Anton's foot had caught her own ankle.

Sarah got up quietly, excusing herself as unobstrusively as possible, and told each in a low whisper to leave the table, taking their dessert to the kitchen.

Unexpectedly, Joseph stood up, threw his napkin to the floor, and blurted out, "What about *David?*"

Gudrun's gaunt face clouded. She got up, pushed back her chair more roughly than necessary, went around to Anton, snatched his hand and followed Joseph into the kitchen.

Li Po looked at Sarah, unsure of what to do next. He followed her format exactly, and this incident had thrown his serving pattern askew. She motioned for him, asked him to clear the boys' and Gudrun's places and go on as usual serving the dessert, the coffee, and the after-dinner sweet wines Adam had placed on the sideboard.

Dr. Yuill-Thornton cleared his throat, lifted his glass of wine, tilted it in a half-toast, as it were, toward Sarah. "Boys will be boys, my dear. Hard for them to sit still—with the exception of this young man, David."

When the guests had gone, Sarah sent for Joseph and Anton to meet her in the kitchen; but when she entered the huge room (already put in order by Li Po and his three cousins) she caught them all off guard.

Gudrun was standing in the middle of the room, holding a table knife high in the air with one hand, picking up a fork with the other. Her entire expression was mocking. "Now, boys, we use *this* for fish, *this* for soup, *this* for meat, *this* for dessert!" Her exaggerated mockery had brought out delighted laughter from both Joseph and Anton. Gudrun went on—still not having seen Sarah standing in the doorway behind her, her face rigid with shock and fury.

Gudrun waved the fork around in a circle above her head. "My name, ladies and gentlemen, is *Herr* Mueller!" She slid the knife and fork across the table, placed both hands on her broad hips, spoke in a commanding voice. "Oh, it is perfectly all right if the *guests* wave around their knives and forks or put their elbows on the table, acting like *they're* the ones raised in a barn! But when it comes to you two boys, nosireee, you're supposed to sit there like little wooden soldiers. Taste a little of this, be like a mouse nibbling on cheese!"

"Gudrun! How dare you!" Sarah's voice shot out. She had never been so angry in her life. She came around on the opposite side of the table, glared at the bulwark of hatred across from her. "How *could* you undermine my efforts to teach Joseph and Anton basic table manners—manners which they should have been taught some time ago."

Gudrun turned, twisted her lip, placed her hands more squarely on her hips. "You're the first to complain about their manners. Their father never said anything before *you* came around. We used to get along fine, just fine, around here." Her face was like a block of stone.

"We will not discuss this in front of Joseph and Anton," Sarah said, rage bringing a tremor to her hands. "If you are bothered about what I am trying to do for my stepsons, then I suggest that you come to me privately to discuss it."

Gudrun placed her flat heels down like a bass drum beat. "You are hardly anyone to tell *me* about what is proper!" She stalked toward the back stairs, her footsteps thumping against the linoleum that Sarah had had put down across the bare planks. Before she started up the steps, however, she flung one last retort at Sarah. "That is a *joke*—that is really something to wave all the knives and forks in the air about!"

"Gudrun—you *cannot*—"

But Gudrun's thudding, heavy footsteps rushing up the back stairs were her only response. Joseph and a white-faced Anton were heading after her.

"Please, boys—just a moment," Sarah said, putting out a restraining arm.

Joseph clenched his fists, screamed at her, "I won't listen to *you*! Gudrun is my boss." He flung himself out of the room, raced up the back stairs.

Sarah caught the slighter shoulders of Anton, guided him firmly back to the table, as she might guide a recalcitrant student in the classroom. "Thank you, Anton. Thank you for sitting down and hearing me out." She waited a moment, catching her breath, trying to quiet down the trembling in her hands, the anger, the frustration inside her. "I know none of this is easy. It is hard on everyone, getting used to a new family, new ways. All of us are learning to live together as a unit. I have tried to teach you certain things—manners . . ." She searched the white face, tried to force him to look at her. He kept his head down, his eyes lowered. "It's because I want you—you and Joseph and David too—to realize you are sons of a very honorable, noble man. A proud man. A famous winemaker."

Anton looked at her frantically, pushed back from the table. "May I—I need to throw up!"

She hurried to his side. "I'm sorry! Here, hurry. This way—use the downstairs bathroom."

Sarah found Adam in his study upstairs. He was bent over his desk, intently poring over some of the printed material Dr. Yuill-Thornton had left behind in the hope that Adam would join him in his struggle to defeat some of the new measures the Prohibitionists had got on the upcoming ballot. Adam had just finished reading it, was pulling at his hair trying to grasp how any such nonsense could be taken seriously; trying to believe Dr. Yuill-Thornton's plea, "You *must* take it seriously. They are out to destroy once and for all the wine industry!"

He was just beginning to digest the full implications of the propaganda when Sarah burst into his study, her eyes wide, startled, her face tight with anger, her voice shrill in a way he had never heard before:

"I'm sorry to barge in on you in this manner, but, Adam, the most dreadful incident just took place between Gudrun and myself!" In spite of her determination to stay calm, tears were breaking the walled dam against them and spilling across her eyes, out the corners.

Adam put the pamphlets down, came around the desk, put his hands on her shoulders. "What's this all about—what incident are you talking about?"

"It's so difficult to explain, put in words how important . . . how terrible it was. But you must listen to me!" she cried out. "Gudrun was absolutely terrible—horrible—to me. She was mocking me behind my back to the boys."

There was a noise at the door. Gudrun pushed her way into the room, her feet wide apart, her broad face set with fury. "I knew it! I knew you'd come running to him trying to turn him against me."

Adam looked from one to the other, totally confused.

Sarah jumped up from the window seat, stood in her own fixed place, her entire body quivering with a sense of injustice, of helpless anger. "Gudrun, that is simply untrue. I—"

Gudrun pushed her aside. "I am sick and tired of the way she pushes Joseph and Anton around. Makes them look dumb next to *her* David. It was a disgrace, her sending them out to eat with the common Chinese houseboys. Treating them like they're no better than *heathens*!"

"*Stop it!*" Adam barked, furious now with both of them. It was the first time he had ever been caught between two women fighting. He looked from one to the other. "Okay, there have to be two sides to this," he said, matter-of-factly. He reached out, put one arm around Sarah's shoulders. "Come on, stop crying," he said gently. "It can't be *that* bad."

He was ready to turn to Gudrun, to offer some comparable condolence. But at that moment she seemed to rock back on her heels, turn her full scorn on both of them. Then she wheeled around and stormed out, her heavy-soled shoes making hollow, clomping sounds as she marched down the hall to her room at the far end.

Adam's arms had stiffened around Sarah's shoulders. She felt it, pulled away, furious on her own that he did not take her side. "Adam, you do not realize—this is a very serious matter."

He was standing behind his desk now. He glared at her a moment, then scooped up the handful of pamphlets, waved them in the air. "*These* are serious!" He crumpled them in a tight wad. "What is a serious matter is that this whole wine industry is being threatened. You are telling me all this women's fuss over table manners, over who says what when. You women with your bloody tears!" He waved both arms about wildly. "Maybe it is all you bloody Americans. That is what! Saying making wine, drinking wine, is a *sin*. What kind of crazy talk is that? Maybe everybody here in this country is crazy. That is what I think is maybe serious!"

Sarah sat down, taken aback by his explosion. She folded her hands quietly in her lap. After a moment she said in a restrained voice, "You seem to forget that I was born here in Napa Valley. I grew up hearing about first one pox and then another, all out to bring the wine industry to its knees. Phylloxera, Pierce disease, wind damage, frosts, rain." She got up, went to the door. Her back was stiff. "I understand how vitally concerned you are," she said crisply. "But what concerns me right now is *this* house—what takes place inside it."

Adam made quick strides across the room, grabbed her by one shoulder. "Okay. We will talk."

"There really isn't anything to talk about. That woman is turning the children, your sons Joseph and Anton, against me—and, if you want to really hear the truth, against David! She has her subtle ways. She hates David and me, and our presence in this house because it takes away her power over them."

"It is not so much a question of power," Adam said, his voice curiously soft. "Gudrun has nobody but the boys. She is not a happy woman. She had never had very much and—"

"I understand that. I am sorry for her because of that. Even so, Adam, she must not get by with certain things." Sarah's amber eyes were more a green-yellow with her anger. "I am positive I overheard Joseph telling Anton the other day that David was a *bastard*. In my opinion, that came from Gudrun."

"Sarah, you're being terribly unfair to Gudrun."

"I am simply telling you what she said. What she implies." She wheeled around, walked briskly out of the room, the new ecru-colored taffeta dress Adam had bought for her in San Francisco rustling, the topaz necklace bouncing against her long proud neck.

When she entered the bedroom, she removed the dress with her usual care, hung it up, worked into her nightgown, flung herself under the covers. She felt dreadful. Her head ached from holding back tears. Marriage—wasn't it supposed to be more workable than any other way of life? And yet, right now, she wished she had never left her tiny rented house on St. Helena's Main Street.

How empty the bed felt as she lay there alone, the pillow her only softness. She tried to picture the hard-faced Gudrun down the hallway, hovering in the darkness.

Poor Gudrun, she thought suddenly. No wonder she was hard-faced, flat-footed, so protective of all she knew as family—never having known the comfort of a man's love, his arms about her.

Just then, Adam slipped into the darkened room, found his way to the edge of her side of the bed and sat down. He placed his hand lightly on her shoulder.

"We shouldn't argue like that," he said, his voice still tightly strained. "We waited a long time to become man and wife. We mustn't let anything spoil it."

She had been hunched over on one side, her knees tucked nearly to her chin. Gradually, she rolled back on her back, adjusted the pillows under her head. She tried to find his features in the darkness; reached up, found his chin with her fingertips. "Thank you. Thank you for saying that."

"A marriage—I guess it takes time. Bringing everything together in the right way—it is like the harvest. But we must be patient. We have to try to help Mother Nature along. People, marriages, maybe we have our cycles, too."

They did not make love. But for a long time he held her in his arms, rocking her gently as he might rock a child. If she was aware of a stubborn knot of concern, she pushed it aside and gave in to the enveloping comfort of his strength, his encircling arms about her.

After that, Sarah made a resolution that she would be patient and try her intelligent best to work things out amicably with Gudrun. But it did not take long for her to realize that Gudrun had planted herself staunchly on the opposite bank of an irreparable breach. And standing beside her, equally defiant, was the stocky, strong-jawed Joseph.

In spite of her plans to avoid any more confrontations, there was the problem of homework. It was that time in school when both Joseph and David were in the sixth grade, Anton in the fifth. The semester would soon be over; grade cards were coming in. She knew that David had straight A's. With Joseph, it was not that he couldn't learn if he tried; he had simply set his mind against it.

One evening, after a particularly exasperating homework session around the kitchen table—a session that both she and Adam had agreed must take place every school night—Sarah went to Adam to discuss what might be done about Joseph.

"He just sits there and draws doodles instead of trying to work the most basic arithmetic problem. I feel he is basically fighting me." She shrugged her shoulders. "Maybe you should try. I give up! He is like one of Luigi's stone walls that will never crumble."

"Maybe it's not so serious," Adam said lightly. "A stage he is going through. He'll improve, with time. We get wines like that sometimes —they take longer than others."

But Adam had been at the table with the three boys for only a few minutes when, from the parlor where Sarah had gone to catch up on some mending, she heard him explode: "Joseph—you are being bull-headed! You are not even trying to listen!" There was a moment of silence. "So who do you think you are? You think you're so smart you don't need to learn what everybody else knows, huh? One day you will be sorry. One day you will be trying to add and subtract figures. Right here on Spring Mountain, you will be working out percentages—"

"I won't be in the winery business!" came Joseph's sullen, angry voice. "Let *David* figure everything out for you."

Sarah hurried back into the kitchen to see if she might be of some help. Just as she walked in, Adam was grabbing Joseph by the shoulders, shaking him hard.

"Don't you talk to your father like that! *Sass*—you don't sass your father. You don't talk that way to me or your mother!"

"She is *not* my mother," Joseph said between clenched teeth.

Adam was shoving him back toward the stairs, his face beet red. "In this house she is your mother! Your real mother is dead. But that does not mean you won't show respect to Sarah, to your father. Do you understand?"

Joseph had reached the safety of the stairs. He ran two thirds the way up, then turned, yelled back down, "I will do what Gudrun tells me to do. *Gudrun* is my boss!"

Adam was going after him. Sarah's calm voice stopped him. "Let him cool off," she said matter-of-factly. "Try it yourself." She smiled at him, shook her head with understanding.

Adam stormed across the kitchen, slammed the tea kettle down on the hot stove. "He only cares about himself."

Anton, who had been sitting white-faced at the table, said in a sudden thin voice, "He cares for somebody. He's a good brother. To me and David too."

When Adam whirled around, ready to challenge him, Anton's large gray eyes glistened like glass marbles, both with fear and with determination. "At school, when the big tough bullies try to throw David and me in the mudholes—knock us down—Joseph bloodies their noses. Everybody is scared of Joseph. He gets in lots of trouble, just for us. He won't let them call us names—he's a good brother." Tears welled in his eyes.

"What names?" Sarah asked, feeling weak.

Anton looked from her to his father.

"Go on, son—answer her. What kinds of names?"

"Sometimes . . . well, just 'Dago.' " He bit his lower lip.

"What else? . . ." Adam's face was pale, grim-looking.

" 'Dirty Italians.' 'Wops.' And they call David a . . ."

"*Bastard?*" Sarah said for him.

"Yes, ma'am," he said, getting up, as though in school itself.

Sarah stopped him at the doorway to the back stairs. "Anton, I want you to understand right now that your father and I are going to put a stop to this sort of thing! It is inexcusable. We will have a talk with—"

Anton's eyes widened. "Then they will catch us on the way home from school, where the teachers can't make them stop!"

Adam came over, patted his thin shoulders reassuringly. "Son, I promise you that nobody anywhere in that school is going to get by calling my boys names! You are a Donati from Napa Valley. An American by birth. In my country, nobody calls a Donati a Dago, a Wop. Everybody respects the name there. Everybody!"

While Adam paced the floor, Anton slipped quietly up the back stairs, just as David entered. David sat down, his voice steady, firm, jutting his chin out in much the same way as his father might do. "Exactly what does that word 'bastard' mean? Why do they call me that name?"

Sarah looked at him sharply. She knew that look on his face too well. He knew perfectly well what the word meant, but he was testing both of them. She looked frantically at Adam.

"Some damn fools say anything!" Adam blurted out. "They call people names just to hear their own voices."

Sarah knew that David was waiting for a real answer. She sat down opposite him, motioned for Adam to join them when he finished pouring his tea. But he stood by the stove, his hands trembling where only he could know.

"David, forget that word," Sarah said softly. "There is another word I would like for you to consider in its place right now. The word 'dignity.' That is a very important word for all three of you Donati boys to remember at all times. It is yours by right—by having such a fine, proud father, having such fine breeding, not like those ruffians who call you names!"

There was a silence in the cavernous kitchen. The cat that Li Po kept in the kitchen to keep mice out came from behind the stove, stretched, arched its back and rubbed against the side of Adam's rigid leg, let out a low meow.

David's voice was still as clear, as persistent, as before. "But what does 'bastard' mean?"

"It means that some dumb people say I am not your father, but I am!" Adam's chin was like a ramrod. "Because I was not married to your mother at the time in the eyes of the law—well, some people call that being a bastard. What they say doesn't matter. You are my son. Some things happened so that we couldn't get married. But you are *my* boy. You have my blood. You are a Donati, the same as Joseph and Anton. You are half brothers."

Sarah put her head against the palm of one hand. But she could not hide from David's probing eyes. Finally she looked up, saw his angry tears.

"*Why* didn't you tell me before?" he rasped. "Why did you lie to me all this time? Tell me my name was Whitmore?" He was standing, his face ashen.

"David, I wanted to," she cried out. "People . . . there were problems. Your father . . . By the time we . . . he was married and it was impossible. Oh, I can't explain it this way!"

But David had already raced back up the steps. They heard the distant slamming of his door.

"I—I thought I was doing the right thing, telling him about an imaginary father. I didn't know, how could I know, that we'd work things out. That we'd ever really get married?"

Adam reached down, picked up the cat, rubbed it behind its ragged ears, listening to it purr. "Truth. I guess it's like old Tom here —he's going to catch the mouse sooner or later."

Sarah was sitting in stunned silence. Adam came over, patted her shoulders, then went on upstairs.

He found Joseph in his room, sitting glumly on the edge of his bed, staring at the floor. Adam went in, shut the door behind him.

"I hear you're a pretty good fighter. I know you are good at riding horses—I didn't know you were such a hotshot fighter."

"Good enough, I guess," Joseph said sullenly.

"I hear you fight off bullies sometimes. Stand up for your brothers."

"I only have one brother."

"No, you have *two*." Adam sat down, felt stiff and awkward. "Son, I want to tell you. David, he is my boy, too. Sarah is his real mother, I am his real father. Just as I was your father and Erika was your mother. Do you understand?"

The alarm clock beside the bed ticked, the only sound between them. Joseph's eyes narrowed, turned ice cold. "He's not your son. He's a *bastard*! Everybody at school says so. She—she said his name is *Whitmore*." He looked at Adam triumphantly. "That makes somebody a liar, then."

Adam took a deep breath. "She had to tell people something. She was trying her best to protect me . . . him . . . all of us. It happened before your mother . . . I . . . ." He stopped, realizing he had no way of telling his son. He had said more than he should, he thought miserably.

Joseph jumped up off the bed as if he didn't want to even sit beside him. "Then you tricked my mother! It's what they said—you married her to get your hands on her property." He was standing back in the corner of the room, as though preparing himself, if he had to, to fight his own father off. "They say that at school. They say you shipped my mother off to the bughouse so you could be with *her*. And you treat Anton and me like—like Gudrun says—like heathens!"

Adam's open-handed blow caught Joseph open-faced. Then, still blinded by rage, he grabbed him, slammed him into a chair. "Now you just sit there and listen to *me*." He ignored the tears streaming down Joseph's face, the red marks from his blow. "I want you to look me straight in the eye and see the *truth*. The truth is, I never tricked anybody in my life! *I'm* the one who got tricked. A man named Jacques Cugnot stopped me from marrying . . . ."

It was as though screaming out the words now was his way of telling the whole world—telling it once and for all to stop the whispers, the talk. He wanted the truth said out loud. His head pounded. The screaming out of him swept aside his senses. But gradually the frightened, shocked face of his son Joseph came into focus.

Adam drew back, horrified that he was using the boy, a boy caught at that time between being a child and a man—was using his own son as a scapegoat. His voice dropped. He turned, trying to undo some of what he had said; to soften the blows he had delivered with more than his hand.

"I did not mean to hit you like that. I—you must know something though, something about me and your mother. When it did not work out for me to marry your stepmother, I had already been very good friends with your mother, Erika. She was like my family a little—old country. European. I loved your grandfather. He had taken your mother in—"

"I know that. Gudrun told me all about Minnesota." Joseph cracked his knuckles, bit his lip, licked at the tears.

"Your mother was a very nice lady. She had pretty blond hair. Pale eyes—the color of yours. She was little, short. She was a wonderful cook. She got mixed up, is all."

"It doesn't matter anymore," Joseph said, tears still sliding slowly down his face.

"Yes, it matters. I want you to know that she was not shipped off to a—a bughouse, as you called it. Your mother was very sick. Here, in the brain. That is what the doctors said. The same way that we get sick in the stomach—something goes wrong. She did not know what she was saying or doing. The doctors—they told me there was no other place where they could take good care of her. I paid a lot of money. She had the best medical care anybody could get for her kind of trouble—her kind of being sick. I did not want it to turn out like that. I wanted to have her be my wife. Just the way she was when we got married. When you were born."

He had been walking in a small tight circle, one that seemed to be closing in on itself in the middle of the room. He looked down at the suffering boy. He reached out, touched his shoulder, tried to pat him comfortingly. Joseph's arms were stiff as iron. "I want you to know I did the best I could. I cannot tell you anything more than that." And suddenly his own agony caught up with him and he sank down on the edge of the bed, buried his head in his hands. After a while he said in a husky, cracked voice, "You could ask Gudrun about some of this. You seem to trust everything *she* says. Ask Gudrun if I didn't try everything! The earthquake—do you think I wanted her to die like that? Don't you know she would have been my wife right now if things had been different?"

Joseph wiped his face with the sleeve of his schooljacket. "But she —you loved *her* first. Before my mother." His voice sounded dry, as if it had come from the bottom of a huge, hollow oak vat being scraped clean of tartrates.

Adam got up, let out a long, defeated sigh. At the door, he stood for a moment, his hand on the brass doorknob. He shook his head sadly. "When this house was built, when Luigi put these doors up, installed the locks, did everything, I never dreamed we were building a house that wouldn't be the happiest house anywhere. I thought he was building a—a castle on top of Spring Mountain. Son, I hope someday you will understand that life sometimes turns things around for us. But you have to live with what is what. You have *two* brothers. I am proud of you for fighting for both your brothers. But remember this, Donatis stick together! From now on, now that you know about David, you three fight together."

As Adam closed the door softly behind him, he did not hear Joseph mumble, "*One*—I have only one brother!"

Later that night—after Adam had made a quieter visit with young Anton, who had mostly sat tight-lipped, his face white, listening, nodding, presumably understanding what Adam hoped he would—he found Sarah sitting in the kitchen, drinking a glass of warm milk.

"How did it go?" he asked, sitting down, letting out a long, exhausted sigh.

She picked at a frayed place in the blue-and-white printed oilcloth. Her eyes looked red, as though she had just had a hard cry. "I think he understands a little better." She did not look at Adam; she seemed to be searching for something white, pure, inside the glass of milk. "When does a mother—I guess a father too—when do parents *know* what is right and what has been devastatingly wrong? Or is it always too late?"

He didn't answer. He got up, went to the cabinet, took out a decanter of brandy, poured a generous amount in a regular glass. He needed a stiff drink.

When he sat down she asked, "What are you thinking, Adam?"

"I was thinking why can't people be more like grapevines? A vine has this deep root; a vine can live longer than we can. You can prune it. Graft onto it. Turn a common root stock into a prizewinning varietal. But with children, hell, life prunes *us*. Grafts us willy-nilly." He got up, holding the brandy. "What do you say?"

"Nothing, I guess. Except that I love you. Love—is that enough, Adam? Does it make all this . . . It's not like the way we once thought, is it?"

"It's what we've got. We work with what we've got." He pulled her up from the table. They went about quietly putting things away; banking the fire; turning out the lamp.

As they started up the back stairs, her voice came back to him. "At least we have *one* dependable cycle."

"So?" They walked together down the hallway toward their bedroom.

"The *night*—knowing we will wake up and it will be a new morning. Everything will look better in the morning."

He looked at Joseph's door, hesitated. He longed to go in, gather him in his arms and say—what? How could he say anything that was right?

"I guess they're asleep by now," he mumbled, holding the door open for Sarah.

It was the last week of May in that year of 1910, when Gudrun caught them off guard one Saturday morning, just before noon, to make her announcement that she was leaving.

Adam had been standing in front of the hallway mirror adjusting his tie and coat lapels, giving one last checking up on himself before he attended an important Grapegrowers' Association meeting being held near the Beringer Winery. Sarah was leaning against the dining-room archway, holding a second cup of coffee.

"It's time for me to pack up and go," Gudrun said, looking uncomfortable in a hat, a stiff-collared navy-blue suit and a corseted skirt still in the floor-length style of several years before.

Adam looked around, tugged at his bow tie. "I hate to hear that, Gudrun. Any special reason? Isn't it *sudden*?"

"It's past due. The boys don't need me any longer. Thirteen- and fourteen-year-old boys don't need a woman's hand. They need a strong *man* around to tell them what's what."

Adam cleared his throat. "What are your plans?"

"Detroit—help out my sister with her brood. She's got a new baby. A baby girl. I'll be there through the summer."

Adam saw the desperate look in her square face. "And after the summer is over, then what?"

"I was hoping you might need somebody down at the Brunner place—just to keep an eye out. Keep those Chinamen from turning it into a filthy pigsty."

Adam slid his arms into his freshly pressed, dusted-off blue serge suit coat. "Why, I think we could work out something. Sounds like a good idea. The place does look a little run down. But I can only give you a contract until Joseph and Anton both reach twenty-one, you realize? Then the place falls under their control. It will be up to them. I mention this so you'll know what's on paper."

Gudrun's lips were stiff. "I've never cared what's on paper so much. It's what's right in the eyes of God, of the world. People I have to live with." She shot a hard look at Sarah, who let her cup make a clanking noise against the saucer's edge.

Sarah moved purposefully to straighten Adam's collar. Then slowly she turned to Gudrun, her head more rigidly high than usual. "I do hope you enjoy your summer in Detroit. You will let us hear from you?"

Gudrun had one hand on the stairway railing. She glared at Sarah, making no attempt to hold back her contempt. "I'll always try to keep in touch with the boys. With Joseph and Anton." Then she stalked upstairs, as though heading toward her own battle retreat.

"She'll always hate me—blame me for everything," Sarah said, sighing.

Adam took one last look at himself in the mirror, placed his hat just so. "It should work out better for everyone. But I've got more important things to think about right now! I'm trying to keep my mind on the speech I'm going to make today against the Anti-Saloon League and the California Campaign Federation. I've got to convince them Dr. Yuill-Thornton is right. They are out to ruin us. This time, they mean business."

That year of 1910 was when there were over eleven thousand acres of bearing grapevines in Napa Valley, with another five thousand acres nearing production. By rough estimate, it was expected that over three million gallons of wine would be made and some 10,000 gallons of brandy distilled. In general, growers and vintners alike were more readily sharing their combined knowledge, pulling together to try to fully restore the Napa Valley name in the international wine world to the status it had achieved during the 1889 Paris Exposition, when they had won a large portion of the top prizes with a display organized by Professor Hussman. (Hussman's son was now in charge of the new U.S. experimental vineyards in Oakville, where by 1910 over three hundred varietals had been grafted on.)

But Adam saw that in spite of the progress that had nearly brought them back to where they had been before the phylloxera hit, if they did not fight the political forces working against them they were all doomed.

The speech he was going to make before the Grapegrowers Association was, he knew, important. So as he rode Hajib down Spring Mountain he was going over points he must stress to get across to them how solid force changed things. He was going to quote something that had appeared in the *St. Helena Star* the year before, after the newly formed organization had very quickly brought about indefinite suspension of the Internal Revenue Commissioner's ruling prohibiting the use of native sweet wines in the manufacture of patent medicine: "We have done much to show the fallacy of the arguments of the prohibitionists that the viticultural industry of California is in any way responsible for or productive of intemperance." He also had a plan for raising an urgently needed $25,000 to combat the Anti-Saloon League—a plan whereby every grower and vintner would contribute ten cents from every ton of grapes from the upcoming harvest. It was not his own original idea, but it was a plan he heartily endorsed and wanted brought up for a vote.

When Adam arrived, Bismarck Bruck, their state assemblyman, was also just arriving. He greeted Adam warmly, then took the first place at the podium as honored guest. In his speech Bruck warned them, "We have new prohibition measures coming up on the next ballot that have very confusing wording—to the point where even those of us who are actively fighting against these measures might be fooled and mark our votes in the wrong place. Our big job now is to educate. To keep ourselves fully informed. We are also going to have to look toward the next presidential election and find a candidate who is most favorable to our needs. Though this is traditionally a Republican county, we may have to move in another direction. Since Teddy Roosevelt has stated he won't run, he has, in my opinion, locked himself into a stalemate. It is my guess the next election will show a split Republican ticket that will insure a Democrat's election. Therefore, it behooves us to look and plan ahead intelligently. The answer, gentlemen, will be in government. Your votes *will* count. Never forget that!"

Bismarck Bruck had taken the very themes of Adam's speech, so that when Adam stepped to the podium he did not receive the attention for which he had hoped. Nonetheless, they voted his proposal in, and he returned home to Spring Mountain inspired. But deep down he carried a hard knot of disappointment.

He found Sarah in the parlor, working as usual on needlepoint. He poured brandy for them, then turned, perhaps hoping to get a reaction from her he had missed at the meeting. "I made a good speech today!"

She jabbed the needle through, snipped off a thread with scissors, lifted one eyebrow. "What kind of reaction did you get?" Her mouth looked tight.

He propped one elbow on the mantel, standing to get more feeling of himself. "I expect that Napa Valley will be voting Democrat next election when we vote for President!" He swirled the brandy. "I got my proposal voted in. I got a nice compliment from E. C. Briber, who thinks my wines might walk off with some major prizes this next year or so, the way I've been going."

"It's time they recognize your ability," she said, smiling quietly, looking into her own brandy, sipping slowly. "Everything takes time, I suppose." Her voice drifted off a little.

Adam felt a shadow cross his mood. He was watching her closely now as she went back to her needlepoint, then dropped it absently to allow the cat to pounce in her lap, wind itself into a purring ball of contentment beneath her stroking fingertips.

"You weren't really listening to me, were you? You don't really care what happened?" His voice was tight, bluntly annoyed. Before she could answer he went on. "You're just like them—you listen with only one ear cocked! You get that look on your face as though whatever it is I've got to say isn't as important as it would be if somebody else said the very same words!"

"Adam, what are you saying? You know that's not true!"

He put his brandy on the mantel, wagged a finger at her. "Oh, I see what they think! Sure—I get up and say what I have to say in the way my tutor taught me. I speak clearly. I don't mish mash my words together. But they still look at me with this funny look, like it's all wrong. They want me to sound the way Vittorio does sometimes when he talks too fast—gets excited and does that kind of singa-songa. That's what they want—a Dago!"

Sarah looked at him, her eyes wide. "But, Adam, they respect you in Napa Valley. I think you're overly excited, imagining it. Not that I mean to imply you aren't being *truthful*," she added quickly, seeing the look on his face. "I'm sure they are impressed with your fine manners, your excellent usage of the English language. I—"

He glared at her. "I know what I know! I see the way they look at me when I am speaking. They don't say it out loud, but I see it in their faces. 'A smart fellow, for a Dago'—that is what they say. But no matter how smart I am, it won't be smart enough to suit them. To make them listen to me all the way. One hundred percent. It's the same with you. My own wife doesn't listen!"

"Adam, really!" she said, trying to keep her voice light. "Do sit down and finish your brandy." For a moment there was only the sound of the fire sizzling, sputtering. "I admit maybe I do get preoccupied now and then. I try to follow all you're telling me about the wine world, the problems you men are battling on the political front. I'm not totally in tune with the process, dear, but I *am* interested all the same because it is your life. I want to see you happy. That is all I want."

He whirled around. "I will be happy when they know who I am in Napa Valley! When they treat me the way Donatis are used to being treated. That is what *I* want! And one day I will show them. They will listen to me with all ears open!"

13

As with any gradual erosion, the signs of decay and inevitable deterioration creep into life imperceptibly, so that one begins to accept them as a natural sequence. That Adam and Sarah were beginning to move away from each other was not at first evident to either. Routine brings about its own automatic discourse: a kind of enforced animation; that almost too polite attentiveness. It was as if they had shut off certain parts of themselves; what came forth was like water filling a glass from the tap, with the source of the supply never being questioned.

So life there on Spring Mountain took on a cadence that matched the seasons. Sarah's days were spent calculating appetites of growing boys, keeping up with the rapidly changing lengths of trousers and shirt sleeves, working in the gardens, seeing that the household in general was kept in efficient running order. With Gudrun gone, the friction was beginning to relax, and even the boys themselves were beginning to accept each other more naturally. Perhaps because of this, Adam decided it was time to begin teaching his sons things they would need to know when the time came for them to take over the land and the winery. He went about it quite selectively.

Because he didn't trust the bullish way Joseph approached any new problem, he had assigned him to working with the horses, taking part in the harvest by driving the huge freight wagons down the steep mountainside, and later, when shipments needed to be made, hauling the puncheons of bulk wine or brandy, either to the depot for freight hauling or down to Napa City's riverside wharf for barge and boat shipping. For a while, Adam had hoped Joseph's interest in riding horses would be such that he could teach him some of the finer points of horsemanship so ingrained in his own riding. But on each occasion when he had made an effort he had been handed back a rebellious look, a retort: "I'm a cowboy rider. I could stay on a bucking bull if I wanted to. I like trick riding—not that sissy stuff. Ask Kyle, ask Luigi, what *they* think! They say I'm a born cowboy."

"Then help take care of the horses. Stay out of the winery."

Joseph had planted his feet wide apart, as if the stance helped compensate for his shortness in a family of tall men. "Good! I like horses a lot better than I like people, anyway."

Adam had looked at him a moment. "Maybe when you are a man you'll be able to tell the difference."

Then he had turned to Anton. "I want you to work under Kyle Plimpton's supervision this year. He'll give you chores in the vineyards. Listen to everything he has to say. If you learn half of what Kyle knows, you'll be a fine viticulturist one of these days. He'll teach you what books can't."

With David, he had narrowed his blue eyes and said, "Kyle says he's taught you about all he knows already. If that's the case, then I'm turning you over to a new winemaster I've got coming next week."

"*What* new winemaster?" David asked, his eyes wide with excitement. "You said not long ago we couldn't afford to hire anybody."

Adam tried not to smile at the way David's voice had suddenly split, risen to a high reedlike sound, then dropped into a deeper croaking sound. He was still not used to seeing him, at fourteen, already taller than he was. David's hands were huge, like a man's hands, but they dangled still from wrists long and bony, from the thin arms of a boy.

"We can't afford to *pay* anyone. It's a felow from Europe, a recent graduate from Alba and some studies in Paris at the Pasteur Institute. Bruno Berilla is his name. Wants to work for room and board, and a small stipend. Just for the experience, to learn what we are doing these days in Napa Valley. I hear he's a bit of a nervous ninny. But I'm anxious to see what he might have to teach us. Though we'll make wine the Donati way, I like to keep my ears open. If there are improvements that can be made, I'll listen."

Anton had a clouded look of jealousy. "Why can't I work in the winery, too?"

"You're younger than your brother. You've got some catching up to do learning what Kyle has to teach first. A winery is no place for young boys. Prove you're serious first, then we'll see what we can work out. But David's ready."

"Bruno Berilla—what nationality is that?" David asked.

"Could be anything." Adam shrugged off the question. "Spanish-French-Italian—God knows what. Maybe a gypsy, for all I know. But he has his qualifications on paper. You answer to him. If he says scrape out tartrates, do that. You learn this business from the bottom up, huh?"

With the boys having most of their free time filled with new chores and having to answer to Adam instead of to her, Sarah found time beginning to extend itself like a lazy cat stretching out, then curling up for another long nap.

To break the boredom, she became more and more fastidious about the housekeeping, as if the shine on the crystal chandelier or the silver goblets reflected her own worth. But there would be times when, inspecting a silver goblet Li Po might be holding up for her approval, she would catch a glimpse of her own distorted image: a blob of something unsmiling, with deep frowns drawing out a strange map of disenchantment on her face.

She spent longer hours, in the spring and summer, out on the stone veranda, her sewing basket usually at her feet, and either some mending or a new design of needlepoint readily available. There would be those days when she had tired of working the threads in and out, when she would catch herself staring off at the cascading, undulating rows of grapevines and imagine them as real, live enemies ready to wrap their tendrils around her and pull her out into that clearing, hurl her off that distant edge of the mountainside.

"These vines are part of my life," she would argue silently with herself. Her roots were here, deeply implanted in Napa Valley—up here, now, on Spring Mountain, where once the mandrakes and the madrones rustled their leaves in the wind. She had heard from Kyle Plimpton once that when the madrones and the mandrakes were pulled from the ground they were trees that cried, according to some. Was she like those trees—uprooted, sast aside? Or was she some strange varietal budded onto alien root stock that offered her no renewal of sap, had usurped her vital flow of life juices?

Then came one night when she was sitting alone in the parlor—making that the sixth evening in a row that she had been left alone, after the boys had finished dinner and gone off to their separate rooms and Adam had gone to his upstairs library to work at his desk. Her discontent welled into anger that found its way into the needle jabbing fiercely at the design of grape leaves on the pillow she was making. She snipped a purple thread with quick, decisive scissors, then tossed the whole thing into the sewing basket, headed on fast-clicking heels up the steps, determined to break the monotony, even at the risk of upsetting Adam, who had seemed to be walking on eggshells lately.

She stood at the doorway a moment, studying his tousled hair, his drawn, haggard face. "Adam, excuse me for disturbing you, but—I'm lonely! I thought—we so seldom just *talk* anymore. I know you have business worries. You're concerned with this Prohibition madness. But if you'd only share it with me. Let me be a part of it." She sat down uninvited on the window seat. Her fingers picked idly at the folds of her skirt. "I get where I feel so, well, cut off from the world. I used to keep my mind so active when I was teaching. I see you looking exhausted, and I long to help! To understand what is bothering you."

He leaned back in his chair, at first irritably, as though barely able to mask his impatience with her for having interrupted him. A long sigh fought its way over a sharp retort. "What's there to say? It's this damn paperwork! I can't keep up with any of it. With taxes. With all these bloody forms the Internal Revenue keeps throwing at us." He crumpled a wad of papers in his fist. "These—this bunch right here— are for brandy distillation. *This* stack for the winery." He rubbed his eyes wearily. "Pour us some sherry, please. I could use a glass of something."

She got up, went to the sideboard and poured the rich amber liquid into small wineglasses and then sat down opposite him, placed the glasses on the cluttered desk. "Adam, you must remember I was a teacher for several years. I'm used to organizing paperwork. Why don't you let me help you with this? Surely I could do something to relieve you of this detail. Frankly, I would enjoy it."

He sipped the sherry, lifted one thick eyebrow and made a derisive sound. "You've got plenty to do running a big house like this. Keeping up with three boys. Their homework."

She leaned forward eagerly. "That's so easy for me. Adam, I am *bored* with nothing more to do!"

His eyes narrowed. "You said the other day you were happy up here. I asked you and you said you were."

"I'm *happy*. But I'm still bored. I—I feel so useless! I learned so much at Wellesley, and during my teaching years. But I feel everything is wasted. Do you understand?"

"You think this paperwork isn't boring?" He slapped the scattered piles of paper. "You think *these* are interesting? Take a look, huh! These are new forms for my Sanders column distillery. Since I'm going from a thirty-thousand-gallon capacity to fifty thousand gallons, everything changes. Go on—take a good look!" He leaned back, smiled mockingly, sipped his sherry while she thumbed through the stack of forms.

"What's this affidavit of sureties? This thirty-and-a half, twenty-five-and-a-half, twenty-seven-and-a-half form? Why the one-half business?"

"Why? What sense does any of it mean except to keep all white-collared workers busy in the government? What's the A-2s and A-4s and that one you're picking up now—that new one, 003?" He pointed his finger at her. "The government ought to quit so much paperwork and start worrying about making sense with the laws. I spend half my time filling out these crazy papers. I ought to be writing letters protesting what's going on the ballots for voting next election. I ought to be out there helping get the First, Third, Fifth Supervisorial Districts organized against these stupid Drys." His face sagged in wearily. "Bruno Berilla—I thought when he wrote that he would be a godsend, come over here and help out, make things run smoothly for a change. But he's messed up the forms. Insulted one of the government men here snooping around. Now I've been slapped with a fine I didn't need, on top of everything else!"

"Let me see these. Look, I know I could figure them out after a little study. I could take that responsibility off your shoulders. Release you to do your political campaigning. Books—seriously, I'm very good keeping books. Let me try."

"Keeping the books is a man's job. A man manages the finances of his household."

"This is entirely different. *Please*."

He was looking at her as though just suddenly seeing her. "Don't pull your mouth down like that, Sarah. You look prettier with your nice smile. I guess we haven't been doing much lately. I wanted to take you to San Francisco. A little trip. We haven't been giving any dinners lately. You used to like that."

"Let's face it. Nobody wanted those dinners. I forced them on everybody." She stood up, hit the sides of her skirt with the flat palms of her hands.

"Look, I'll tell you what. After harvest, after election in November and we get these Drys chased back where they ought to be, then just you and I—we'll take a few days off and go to San Francisco. Hear some nice opera. Stay at the Ruckers' again. I'll buy you a new dress. It'll be just the way it was." He saw how she was folding her hands, looking at him blankly. "Okay—you want to keep books? It's all yours! See how long you'll find this interesting." He pushed everything on the top of his desk slightly forward in her direction. "Start with these ledgers. These order forms and receipts of sales. Enter those in and add them up, subtract."

In spite of Adam's dire prediction that she would hand it all back to him within a few days, Sarah found it exhilarating to have her mind active again. But the more she delved into the book work, into determining dates that specific forms were due, what taxes were owed, what bills were outstanding in general, she began to find it inescapably apparent that Spring Mountain was operating at a deficit; the only profits were coming from valley-floor holdings on the Brunner land.

She made graphs for comparisons, using a ten-year and a five-year ratio. She saw clearly that the steady predictable income had come from the sale of barley, hay, cattle, fruit from the orchards, and fresh produce to the markets. And that income had originated on Jacob Brunner's property. What was going to happen to them when it reverted to Joseph and Anton? When Adam would no longer be on the payroll as manager? In only a few years now, they were going to be forced to make the Donati Spring Mountain Winery and Vineyards self-sustaining. At the rate they had been going, they would be bankrupt! She was simply going to have to help figure out some means of their becoming solvent. Of cutting back expenses right and left. Of cutting corners all over, in every aspect of the operation on Spring Mountain.

Her first move was to go to Li Po. "We've been overspending, and I simply have to cut back. Could you manage without a special laundryman? If I help out more, could we, just you and I, manage the household? And the gardeners—we can pay only one of your three cousins from now on. Please decide which one should remain. I'm sorry, but I have to ask them to find employment elsewhere. Do you think they can manage?'"

"My Uncle Chang will find work for them. He has store in Napa City." His head bobbed up and down. "I work harder. This is my home."

Sarah studied Li Po intently for a moment. How much a part of the household he had become. So predictably *there*. Never complaining. Keeping his personal life to himself. "Li Po, I want you to know how much, how *very* much, Mr. Donati and I appreciate your loyalty. Your devoted service. It means so much. I—I just want you to know that."

He ducked his head, as though embarrassed. "This is my home," he repeated, scurrying to the stove, where the teapot was whistling.

After cutting back expenses in her own domestic domain as inconspicuously as possible, Sarah made up her mind that she must try to determine what might be done in other phases of Spring Mountain's outlay of money. Adam was an artist with his wines, with what he saw out there in the vineyards, but one thing she had learned at Wellesley and during her years of teaching was organization. Yes, she could be of help.

But she admitted to herself that she knew very little about the basic operations. So one day, in mid-August when she saw Bruno Berilla out with a picking crew getting early grapes for making champagne —a new venture he had convinced Adam they should try in a small quantity under his direction—she decided that she would pay closer attention to the details of the main crush coming up—see if, by being an objective outsider, she might spot some way to more efficiency.

Adam seemed unusually irritably lately, she had noticed. He wasn't sleeping well. He tossed and turned all night, got up grumpily, barely speaking to anyone during breakfast. He seemed obsessed with politics. Not only did he attend all the rallies, he was organizing them on his own. He had decided that Woodrow Wilson should become the next President of the United States, and that if he didn't, Prohibitionists would surely bring all of Napa Valley, all of the wine industry, to its knees.

Sarah decided it was best to conduct her own little campaign in private, then, and not alarm him or in any way have him think she was trying to run things. She simply had to help, which was different. Efficiency—yes, and performance—whether in studying, in teaching, in running Spring Mountain, the same basic principles should apply.

When the harvest did get into full swing, when Bruno Berilla was frantic trying to keep up with the crush at the main winery and Adam was out in the vineyards working from sunup to sundown alongside Kyle and their dwindling crew of good grape pickers, Sarah decided it was time for her to learn more.

Adam had dashed in for a quick supper, was having a second cup of coffee with his dessert. Joseph was still at the stable, unhitching the wagon after the last load had been hauled out of the vineyards to their own winery. Tomorrow he would be taking the larger freight wagon down the mountain with grapes being sold to Inglenook and a second load to Oakville to the Brun and Chaix Winery. Anton had eaten with Kyle and the regular crew of pickers down at the bunkhouse, feeling at one with the men. Only David had joined his parents at the table.

"Adam, it occurred to me that I've never been allowed in the winery during crushing. But I would enjoy watching. Learning more about it."

He looked annoyed. "Some other time. We're too shorthanded as it is. Bruno—I don't know what the hell he's doing over there! He's got these hotheaded ideas about different levels of sulphur, some kind of new yeast strain he wants to try out. He'll ruin the whole vintage if I'm not there to watch. I thought I could rely on him, but he's another problem I hadn't counted on this year. No—another time."

David had seen his mother's expression. Though he had planned to get to bed early, was himself exhausted from the frantic pace of the crush, he spoke up. "I could take her on a quick tour, Papa. Just show her around. I'll keep her out of the way."

Adam was standing, taking a last swig of coffee. He let the cup rattle against the saucer. "Okay—but see that you both stay out of the way. They're still working that last load. We've hired a couple of cellarmen who don't know one elbow from the other." He threw out his hands. "This wine business! Where are people who *know*? They're all giving up—folding their tents and moving on to something else. Letting these Prohibitionists scare them!"

The screen door slammed behind him as he hurried out the back door and headed toward the winery.

Though Sarah had been in and out of the giant stone winery many times—and had always been overawed by the very size of it, the cool, pungent odors collected from the wine sleeping in enormous oak casks or being racked into smaller barrels until it reached that final clarification where it would be bottled and binned—she had never been there at night, seeing the lanterns and lamps glowing softly against the beautiful stonework, hearing the loud banter of the men, the noise of the conveyor belt, the crusher, the pumps going full blast.

David led her in on the lower cellar floor, where the old wines were racked and where the limestone caves cut back into the sides of the mountain. The winery had been built on the gravity flow principle, with the crushing going on at the uppermost level, then the fermentation taking place on the second floor, and the eventual aging and storage being on the ground, "cellar" floor, where the temperature remained at even, ideal levels. In all directions, the giant casks loomed like castle towers. The high-vaulted ceilings and the thick walls of stone gave a hollow, thick echoing sound as they made their way to the spiral wrought-iron stairway leading up to where the fermentation took place.

Again, Sarah noted the variation of shapes of tanks and vats across the vast space. David took her by the arm, guided her over to one side. She realized that, at fourteen, he was already well over six feet tall. His hands felt strong on her arm, though the wrists were still thin, like a boy's, not ready for the intensity, the energy flowing out of this gangly, bright-eyed being who was her son. His voice in the throes of change periodically shot up in high, reedlike sounds as he tried to talk in lowered, informative tones.

"Luigi Pascarella built this winery as tight as a ship," he said proudly. "Papa said you could flood the second floor with a foot of water and it wouldn't leak. Notice the tilt for easy drainage—for gravity flow?"

He gave her a moment to absorb the sights about her. Then he led her to the open fermentation tanks. "These are empty now, but next week when we start crushing the Zinfandels and later on the Cabernets, these will be put to work. Right now they're crushing white grapes, which get closed fermentation tanks. You should see the bubbling, boiling mass when fermentation gets going. They put the yeast culture in, and Papa uses sulfur dioxide to cut back bacteria—impurities—and after a few hours it starts. Those big paddles are used to punch the cap down about every three hours or so until fermentation stops."

"How long does fermentation go on?"

"Around ten days, usually. Papa likes to leave the wine sitting on the lees, the sediment, for around eight days. Especially his Cabernets. He runs the juice into barrels and bungs them lightly until his second racking so that trapped gas has room to escape. If you bung too tightly it can explode."

"Racking? How many times does this happen?" She wondered how much this process cost.

"Papa racks his red wines very little. He lets aging do the work of clarification. He lets his wine alone."

David led her then to the upper floor, where the actual crushing was taking place. Sarah stared wide-eyed as the swarthy newly arrived Italian immigrant workers from Howell Mountain—hired for the harvest period only—went about following the frenetic orders of Bruno Berilla, who gave her an irritated glance, threw out his hands, and barked something in Italian at someone pouring in what David told her was sulfur dioxide.

"They have to add just the right amount when the grapes are crushed. It helps prevent browning and cuts back bacteria. Papa lets his white wine clarify overnight. Then the juice will be siphoned free from sediment. Then the yeast will be added. He lets his white wines ferment in those smaller oak vats. Fills them about half full to allow room for the fermentation process."

She tried to follow every word, keep an eye on the scurrying men at work. David leaned closer so that he could be heard more easily against the din of noise from the machines, the pump, the men yelling. "You've got to try and prevent oxidation. When the fermented juice goes in for racking, the barrels have to be kept filled. 'Topped,' they call it."

"Explain racking," she called out.

"That is moving the wine off the sediment until clarification."

"I thought winemaking was a simpler process," she said, letting the heavy odors of free-run juice fill her nostrils.

When he smiled suddenly she was reminded of Adam. "Papa says if you put five winemakers in the same winery you'd get five different ways of making wine. But certain things have to be done. One golden rule Papa uses is to crush *gently*. That's why he spent all that money on the new stemmer-crusher so it won't macerate the grapes. Papa is particular about the size casks he uses for aging, too. When fermentation on the whites is over, he'll run it into oval oak—a little over three hundred gallons each. He lets his Rieslings stay in about three months. Some whites get longer."

Sarah noticed some of the cellarmen looking her way with uncertainty. "My presence here bothers them, doesn't it?"

"Maybe," David said. "They're not used to women being here."

"Then we should go. I've learned enough for one time."

He led her out the loading ramp, down the wagon road alongside the winery. They crossed the main driveway, went up the pathway toward the veranda. "They're finishing the last wagonload. Papa wanted those particular grapes to sit on the skins a little. They'll be crushing at sunup. Getting ahead of the flies and bees. By the time they finish the whites, they'll start in with the Zinfandels. Then the Cabernets. We're hoping the weather holds out. No rain to ruin things at the last minute." He crossed himself, a habit he had picked up from the Alfieris.

Sarah held his arm as they went around the darkened pathway. She smiled at David's imitation, lightly thinking that none of the children on Spring Mountain had much religious training. Her own training had been in the Episcopalian vein: just enough to be in keeping with what her mother had deemed "proper" training.

"You've learned a lot about winemaking in a few years," she said quietly as they stepped up onto the cool veranda, where an early-night breeze was finding its way across the mountain. "Here—let's sit and visit a few minutes. We never get to just talk these days. Just the two of us. You're growing so fast, David. Before I know it you'll be a grown man ready to take over Spring Mountain. You'll be the main winemaker."

He did not answer at first. He waited politely while she took a seat, then sat opposite her in a straight-backed wicker chair. The three-quarter moon glanced across the edge of the veranda, sent shafts of soft, golden light through the thick wisteria vines. David cleared his throat. "Maybe I'll be a winemaster someday—but I'm not sure it will be up here."

"But why in the world *not* here?" Her voice had risen in surprise. "Where would you ever find a finer winery than this one? And it's your heritage, dear. Think about that. Spring Mountain was built as a close duplicate of the old Donati estate in Pontremoli. You'll be a third generation. You do, of course, realize Spring Mountain is going to be yours? Your father told me himself—that because Joseph and Anton are inheriting the valley-floor property, he is leaving this to you."

Again David was silent, hesitated before he spoke, as if not wanting to hurt anyone's feelings but having to be true to his own convictions. "The real future—it's down there. Maybe not even in wine. The country's going *dry!* Everybody knows it now."

"David, don't let your father hear you say that! Besides, that's ridiculous. Napa Valley is known for its wine."

"Then why are so many people pulling out their vines and putting in orchards, getting ready for what's ahead?"

She rocked back and forth, stared out across the soft night. "Your father is upset about that. That some people won't listen, won't join the fight, but are giving up ahead of time. He's convinced the election will bring about a change. Put a political stop to this nonsense."

"I'm afraid Papa isn't with the majority of the people. He hears only what he wants to hear."

Sarah took a long, deep breath, leaned farther back into the new soft cushions she had made that summer for the old wicker which she had tried to revive with bright white paint. Though she still felt that odor from the pungent crush, she found here on the veranda the heavier smell of honeysuckle. She let herself absorb the full moment. Then she took a long glance at her son's handsome profile, realized what a wonderful-looking man he would be! Handsome in a way that even Adam wasn't. He had her darker eyes, though they had strange coloring as if the amber flecks tried to give way to a blue and blended out in their own unique shading. In the muted light, she could not see his eyes, but she felt their brooding—yes, even the brooding so much like his father.

David seemed to be chewing his nails. He leaned over his knees, cupped his chin in his hands, stared out quietly.

"What are you thinking, dear?"

"Oh, Mother, it isn't that I don't love it up here! I really do. But I want to make my own place in the world!" He leaned forward excitedly. "I want to go to Europe, for instance. Travel all over the world.

See how the Europeans make wine. I have so much to learn, to *see*. I just can't let myself stay stuck here on Spring Mountain."

"You could have a worse fate."

He jumped up, went over to the edge of the veranda and leaned against the redwood post. "Mother, you're a *woman*. You just don't understand what it's like when you know that one day you're going to be a man, you're going to have to *be* somebody."

Sarah cleared her throat. "David, because I'm a woman do you think I haven't had *my* dreams? That I didn't look into the fuzzy world out there when I was about your age, wondering what I would be, where I would end up in life? I did go to Europe once . . ." Her voice trailed off. "I used to think I would have visited every Greek island, seen every museum in Europe, by now. Dreams—they're always bigger than life, I suppose. Maybe even need some pruning down—how do you vineyardists say it?—for 'quality bearing.' But life seems to cut out its own shapes for us." She pulled her arms into a tight crisscross, as if holding on to something. "But you must have your dream. I understand. I understand, truly I do, how you feel about Spring Mountain. Don't worry about the future, dear. You're wonderfully gifted in so many ways. I'm sure you will do very well in life. Wherever you settle."

He came over, kissed her forehead. As he straightened up, his eyes were alive with a sudden spurt of good humor she noticed had been reviving itself lately. For a while, when she and Adam had first married, he had become gloomy, rarely laughed. But now his voice had a decided lilt. "I guess we're lucky a vine is so strong it will last even a bad pruning job. Besides, you forget something important, Mother. What about the fermentation process? Isn't that really what counts? Its all basically a process of conversion. Isn't that what growing up is all about? Fermenting, then letting the aging process take its due course. A little topping here, the right vats, a good selling label?" He chuckled. "So why should my life be complicated when there are so many casks around here to choose from?"

She shook her head, smiled after him. "Good night, son," she said, leaning back, deciding to stay on awhile on the veranda. But as she heard the sounds of his footsteps on the stairway, she wondered why having just heard a young man's bursts of confidence—her only son's high spirits—should make her suddenly teary-eyed. Why it had given her a sinking feeling of, yes, fear, as if all of them were riding on some precipitous edge like those distant ragged outlines of the mountains across the valley that in the muted moonlight made her think of dark and dangerous cliffs. . . .

It was after midnight before Adam came to bed. Sarah found herself surprisingly awake as he was plumping up his pillow, ready to turn over wearily and fall asleep.

"Adam . . ." Her voice was bright, alert. "We've been married how long—five years now?"

His drowsy, exhausted voice replied, "Yes . . ."

"Well, before every harvest when I tried to be a part—bringing out the picnic baskets, that sort of thing?" She propped herself up on one elbow, spoke to his shoulder, the back of his neck. "Do you realize that this is the first time I've really *felt* it? Really experienced the harvest, what it means? That I realize that what you are trying to do is important? Very important!"

"What you are saying—that sounds nice," he said groggily.

"Oh, Adam—it's so much more than *sounding* nice! It's a deeply meaning thing to me, as if—yes, as if I see its mystery."

"Good night, Sarah . . ." His voice was barely audible.

But her head was filled with new colorful images that were turning in a reel of their own. "Winemaking—it's a lot like giving birth. I see it that way. When you're pregnant, with the baby inside, it is growing, developing on its own. The mother is like one of those oak vats, keeping it safe, sealed in, until the time is ready. Until it is born, though nobody really knows the full outcome. One only guesses—hopes."

Adam's deep breathing, lost in sleep, was her only answer.

By Election Day that November of 1912, the harvest was over. Bruno Berilla announced that he was tired of America and was heading back to Europe. The fact that he had let the last white wine oxidize was not anything he wanted to discuss with Adam, once he discovered the disaster. Besides, he could see there was no future for a winemaker in this country, with hotheads who called themselves Prohibitionists —Drys!

But Adam was still convinced they could win out. He had organized a team of volunteers, and he himself went on rounds, riding Hajib, going door to door alerting people to get out and vote, and explaining the Prohibition measures to them. That day, November 8, he stayed at the polls, waiting for the final count. It was dark by the time he rode Hajib up Spring Mountain and came in jubilant.

"The Wets received 306 votes to the Drys' 190!" he told Sarah, giving her a vigorous hug, swinging her off her feet. "And we voted for Woodrow Wilson, 367 to 353. How about that? Come on, we drink a toast! Our work is paying off. I told you so. I keep telling these men with their hangdog looks we can make changes if we get out there and *work*."

They went into the parlor, where he poured out brandy. When he toasted, his eyes were enveloping her in the old way.

But it had not been Sarah's best day. Little things had gone wrong. It was the time of the month when she was normally cranky, on edge. And she had made the additional mistake of spending two hours with the books. She had added up new figures—the taxes coming up, all kinds of added expenses: a new order Adam was in the process of making out for more French cooperage; some kind of enormously expensive stemmer-crusher he wanted from Aix-en-Provence. And, on top of that, he had apparently forgotten that his yearly payment on the Sanders copper still was due the bank in January. The boys had all out-grown their clothes. School was monthly coming up with more and more expenses, it seemed. It was always something here that needed money, another something over there! But she was determined to cher-ish this rare mood of Adam's. So as he flung his arms about excitedly, telling her of his expanded plans to tighten their political strength—maybe he would go join Dr. Yuill-Thornton's task force for a couple of weeks down in southern California, taking her along for that vaca-tion they had kept on the back of the stove too long now—she smiled as animatedly as possible.

Then Adam was twirling the brandy, his eyes gleaming with a sudden new idea. "Sarah, I think it is time for us to give a big party," he said, putting his glass down, hitting his hands together with a burst of enthusiasm over the idea.

"A party? For whom, Adam?" she asked cautiously. She licked her bottom lip, tasted the excellent brandy, looked at the rich, clear liquid.

"For all the big shots, that's who! It's about time they come up here on Spring Mountain, see what kind of nice place we have, huh? Show them how Donatis can do things. Yeah, how about that? Get out the best of everything. Do it right. Lorenzo says he can get a butler, send a musician, anytime I give a big party. I want it to be the way we used to do things in Pontremoli—violin players maybe, the works!"

"But, Adam, a party like that—it would cost so much money."

His eyes clouded. "So who cares what it costs? It's time they see what is what up here on Spring Mountain." He propped one elbow on the mantel, lifted his chin proudly. "Look, they are beginning to listen to me. I make my speeches and now that we won, sure, now they will listen all the way! They will know this Dago knew things some of them couldn't see before their very eyes." His eyes were alive, shining down at her. "It's time they start looking past their stuck-up noses and saying, 'Sure, ask the nice Donatis from Spring Mountain to the next big party.' You wear that nice dress I bought for you in San Francisco, that necklace. We will send out invitations, the kind printed up. We will ask everybody big in this valley!"

"Adam, I do think you should stop a moment and think what you are saying. This kind of party would cost money we honestly can't afford. We have to be realistic. We simply have to!"

"What is this 'have to' business?" he flared, turning away from the mantel, glaring at her now. "I am the head of this house! This is the Donati place on Spring Mountain—or maybe you think you are Miss Grace? Yeah, maybe that is what you are trying to be. I heard how she put on the pants—everybody says that. But I am Adam Donati! You don't see *me* letting some woman push me over in a corner!"

For a moment, Sarah stared stonily at the crackling fire, trying to hold back her anger. She hadn't intended to argue with him, particularly when he had come home feeling so victorious. But she was still right—he was not being realistic. Facts were facts. And the facts on the books said they simply couldn't afford it. They'd be lucky to stay afloat, the way things were going.

She stood up, put her empty glass down, walked toward the hallway, her trailing skirts following stiffly. She turned, looked at him evenly. "Adam, before you begin having invitations engraved, ordering your musicians and so forth, may I suggest that you take a long, hard look at the books? That you try for once perhaps to *curb* expenditures instead of increasing them?"

Adam's fury caught her like a long outstretched arm yanking her back. "From now on, you stay away from the books! That is what I suggest to *you*!" He was wagging his finger at her. "Don't think I don't see the little notes you write in in red ink. Sure, I see your columns where you add and substract, where you work out these can-dos and can't-dos. But let me tell you a few things you *don't* see when you've got your nose stuck in my business—*my* books. What you can't add up or take away from in so many numbers. What you don't know beans about!" His voice had risen like Luigi's, but his color had totally drained from his face.

She saw the gray, ashen look, was frightened in a horrible way she could not understand. "Adam, *please*—please don't. I am very, very sorry I brought it up. *Have* the party if it means so much. I didn't mean to take away from—"

He was coming toward her, his hand still pointing accusingly.

"What you can't see in the books is what we have out there in the tunnels. What is taking place inside all those oak vats!" Perspiration was standing out on his forehead. "What you don't see is a whole new vineyard out there. Sure, right now you would look and think it is a bunch of sticks waving in the breeze—that is how you women see grapevines! What you don't know is what we expect next vintage from that one vineyard alone." He was only a few feet away from her, his rage so intense that she was sure he would strike her if he came closer. "What do *you* know about what really adds up in this business, out there where we are fighting to hold on? Votes—sure, there were women there adding up votes. But not you. You won't go out there, because you can't strut around like Miss Grace used to strut around! I see things, too. I see—"

She saw him reach for his chest, clutching at it. She felt as though a part of her was witnessing it; another was reeling from his lashing fury. As the sound, more like a gasp, came from him, she cried out with a shrill voice riddled with fear and guilt, "Adam—what *is* it! What's wrong?"

She reached him just as he sank on one knee, one arm trying to support himself by holding on to the settee, the other hand tearing at his shirt, as if by ripping open the restricting buttons he would find space to breathe. "The pain—it hurts so bad. . . . Sick . . . I am so sick."

"Li Po! Somebody!" she yelled out, rushing to him, easing him down into a position that she thought desperately might help. He was taking quick, shallow breaths, his lips were colorless. "Someone—*please* come here!"

At the same moment that Li Po ran in from the kitchen, Joseph, coming in from the bunkhouse where he had been exchanging stories with a new stableman from Chiles Valley, came charging into the parlor, his square face like a fist. "*Papa*—what's wrong with him?" he cried out in a stricken voice. He seemed stuck in one spot, terrified to come closer.

Sarah was struggling with sudden waves of blackness of her own. "Li Po—herbs? Do you have herbs for his—I'm sure it's his heart!"

Li Po was bending over, his small hands working with Adam's shirt, loosening his belt. He was bending his ear to Adam's chest.

Sarah grabbed Joseph's stiff arm. "Hurry—get Anton, anyone, to go with you. Find Dr. Williams. He lives—oh, where does he live! His office is on Main Street. I think his house is on—isn't it on White Sulphur Springs Road? *Ask* somebody—find him! Get him up here as quickly as you can."

Anton had come halfway down the stairs at that moment, having heard the commotion. He and Joseph grabbed at jackets, made a helpless flurry, then were running toward the stables. David, sensing more than hearing that something was amiss, came to the head of the stairs, an open book in his hand. Seeing his mother's white face, her trembling hands closing the door left open by Joseph, he dropped the book and ran to her.

"What is it? Papa—what has happened to Papa?"

She clutched David's arm. "His heart. Oh, God, David—it is my fault. I was arguing—and he was so happy! He came home from the election so *happy*." Tears were blinding her eyes now.

David pulled her into the parlor, where at that moment Li Po was struggling to prop Adam up so that he could drink down the concoction he had prepared. David hurried to help him, kneeling down, gently holding his father's shoulders. "Drink . . . yes, drink it."

Sarah heard the back door slam and Joseph and Anton running out toward the stables to get on their horses. She got pillows together, placed them under Adam's head. Li Po himself was gently pulling Adam's legs out into a more comfortable position. He made a shushing motion to his lips with one finger, nodded at Sarah and David. Then he went to Sarah.

"My Uncle Lee says give powder for heart pain. Wait for doctor. Keep very still. Help him not be scared." He handed Sarah a small cloth reeking with ammonium. "Here—smell this." David had seen his mother reeling, had put one strong arm around her and was leading her out of the parlor. Li Po followed. "I will stay with him. You rest."

Sarah and David stayed in the library across the hall from the downstairs parlor. The enormous grandfather clock seemed to sound bonging alarms, a hundred brass bells joining force; still there was no sound of anyone coming. "It takes time to ride down Spring Mountain," David said reassuringly. "Don't worry, they'll be here. Li Po says Papa is sleeping . . . He is better. He's got a blanket over him. Li Po is right there beside him."

When Dr. Williams did arrive, he was followed by Anton and Joseph, who stood wide-eyed, their faces pink from the night air and their brisk rides, from their accomplishment in finding the doctor and insisting that he come then and there.

The doctor removed his coat swiftly, took out his stethoscope, hurried into the parlor. "Good—you've kept him still. Quiet." He leaned down, making a kind of grunting noise to get on one knee where he could listen to Adam's chest.

As Sarah watched the doctor's face, having selected it as her focal point so that she would not see the ashen gray of Adam's beloved face, she felt as if time had formed a frozen block about her, leaving nothing —no air or space to breathe; yet, at the same moment, she could see any flicker of movement in the room, hear like thunderclaps the sound of the old clock in the hallway ticking off the minutes.

Behind her, she heard Joseph take in a sharp quick breath, let it out in an angry, snorting way. To her left, Anton shifted his weight, rolling off the sides of his shoes to his tiptoes, rocking back on his heels, shifting back to a self-conscious flat-footed stance. David had resumed cracking his knuckles, as if trying to keep time with the tick of the clock.

Just as Sarah was sure she would faint or scream or jump up and fling herself across Adam's laboring chest, Dr. Williams patted Adam's shoulder lightly, reassuringly, as though he suspected that beneath that masklike face Adam was listening through his swirling terror, silently begging for this destructive rampant force that had nearly claimed his life to be placed by sure hands inside limiting boundary lines.

The doctor looked about slowly, pulling himself stiffly to his feet. "I think he's going to be fine now—with proper care." He rubbed his chin speculatively, then settled a sharp piercing gaze on Sarah. "My guess is he's been under a lot of pressure lately. Every winemaker I know looks like he's been run through the stemmer-crusher himself— this Prohibition threat. Times the way they are."

Guilt, like a stab wound of pain, shot through Sarah. "I—we have had—"

He stopped her. "The harvest puts strain on us under normal conditions. If a man is excitable by nature, if there's a history of—"

"Adam has worked so hard, politically. Plus the strain of the harvest," Sarah put it too quickly, so that her voice shot high, and shriller than normal. Her hands were twisting in and out, making knots in her lap. "We've—up here on Spring Mountain, well, we've had a few personal problems that haven't helped."

Dr. Williams stuffed his stethoscope into his pocket. "What we have to worry about right now is getting our patient on the road to recovery." He looked at Joseph. "Maybe you boys could help me fix your father a temporary bed somewhere down here on this first floor. We want to rule out stairs—keep him on bed rest for a few days until this danger zone is clear. Do you have a spare cot and a place?"

"The library—his books and papers are there. He's at home in his library."

The doctor looked at Sarah thoughtfully. "A good idea. The boys and I will get it set up, then. You sit down and pull yourself together. My eye tells me you're getting a bit of a delayed reaction to the shock of what's happened. Take a few slow deep breaths. Lean back there and close your eyes while we get the bed set up. Can't have two sick patients on our hands at once."

"I—it was *my* fault!" Sarah cried out. "I—we were arguing!"

"It's not anyone's fault. Heart attacks—there's usually some history of them in the family." He wagged a finger at her. "That's enough of that kind of talk. As soon as we get the library converted to a bedroom, it's off to bed for you, young lady. I'm sending all of you to bed. Li Po and I will take turns sitting up with our patient here. Okay, boys, come on, show me where we can borrow a bed. The whole family is going to pitch in from here on out. We're all going to do what has to be done to get your father back on his feet."

While Dr. Williams and the boys were upstairs, and then through the noise of their heaving and bumping the bedsprings and mattress down the twisting stairway, Sarah sat with her hands clasped tightly, staring blankly at her sleeping husband. Silently, she was pleading over and over, *Get well, my darling! Don't slip away from me. I'll never argue again. Not about the party—about anything. I'll stay away from the books.* That voice belonged to the young woman in her; another, older woman's voice counterpointed, *This will pass. The doctor says he will be okay. You must sort out facts. Work with facts. You must keep your family together. Be in charge, like it or not. Think! Now you must think as you have never thought before. . . .*

Though after two weeks Dr. Williams announced that Adam was, in his mind, out of danger, Sarah was torn with doubt, with a guilt that wouldn't let her sleep at night.

"It is now a matter of time, of rest, of freedom from undue stress," Dr. Williams had told all of them sternly.

But where was there rest, true freedom from stress? Ever protective of Adam, her own self-confidence teetering, she felt as though a veil had fallen across Spring Mountain. She had the boys do all the errands, bring home newspapers, the mail, the local news. And though she tried to keep in touch vicariously with the world at large, it was as though she were separated from it. Even the Napa Valley floor itself and the outlines across the way of Howell Mountain seemed remote and distant, alien places.

It was, ironically, Adam himself who brought her around, as if sensing that she now needed him. He caught her in the kitchen one morning with a question rare for him: "You taught school—tell me, what about this guy Woodrow Wilson? Did we vote wrong or not?"

Pleased, surprised, she said, "He was president of Princeton, a top university. At Wellesley, I read his doctoral thesis—*Congressional Government* I believe was the title." She flushed with a shyness she had not felt in years. "Woodrow Wilson's a progressive thinker. At Princeton he instituted a new system—the preceptorial system, stressing small classes . . ."

Adam was looking at her with an old gleam in his eye as he pulled his dressing gown close about him, as though closing shut any foolish notions that might get his heart off balance again. He ran his fingers through his rumpled hair. "Okay, so he's a smart professor. But what kind of President of the United States will he be?" He smiled as she sat down at the kitchen table opposite him. Their fingertips touched lightly, and her amber eyes softened with the pleasure of gratitude, of knowing she was forgiven, that he still loved her. That he was coming alive again.

"At Princeton, he caused strong factions among faculty and students. Some thought he was excellent, some hated him. When he was governor of New Jersey it was pretty much the same. His 'Seven Sisters' bill drew a lot of criticism and praise . . ." She clutched his fingertips tightly. "I'm—Adam, we are so lucky! You and I. And—oh, I'm sure Woodrow Wilson is a good man."

During the summer months Adam seemed to respond to the growing season itself, as if some sap inside him was reaching out toward ripeness of renewed health. But when the crush began and he had to sit on the stone veranda watching Kyle and the crew at work, being restricted from participation and knowing it was a bad year at best, his blood pressure shot up and his heartbeat became erratic again. Dr. Williams instituted a stricter, sterner program of shorter walks, shorter hours out of bed, and absolutely no visits inside the winery.

"Another thing, Adam Donati," Dr. Williams admonished, "I know you Italians drink wine the way I might drink water, but from here on out, no alcohol until I say so! And no salt in your food."

Adam's mouth tightened. "I'm a prisoner in my own house! I'm a washed-up invalid at forty-three years of age. A nobody!"

"You're a sick man on his way to getting well if you'll do what I say." And when Sarah followed him to the door, Dr. Williams said quietly, "Humor him, but keep the alcohol out of his reach. If you can get through the winter quietly, I figure that by this time next year he'll be out there in charge of the crush again."

"I guess this is our unlucky year," Sarah mumbled glumly.

"It's a hard year for a lot of people. But count your blessings. You still have your husband. He *can* get well."

Sarah made an effort to keep herself reminded of all the good things. Nineteen thirteen was the year David was graduating from high school at the undisputed head of his class. And even if that fact was marred by Joseph's having dropped out of school entirely, Joseph had at least made a positive step: "I'm going to work for the Pascarellas. As a builder, a stonemason, who needs high-school diplomas? I'm moving out of this funeral parlor where you can't talk above a whisper," he had growled, but then turned and kissed her impulsively, his pale-blue eyes watery.

With Gudrun back at the Brunner house as permanent caretaker, Anton decided, that June, to move down with her, thus taking over full responsibility for managerial duties. He slung one arm around Sarah's shoulders. "If you need me, I can be here right away. I have a couple of pretty girls down in St. Helena. Joseph told me he'll come up on weekends—stay in the bunkhouse and keep an eye on things. You've got David. It'll be easier on you and Papa both. Make life quieter."

The summer seemed to drift into harvest time. Though all news which might upset Adam was kept silent, David let slip, that October, that Woodrow Wilson had ended up signing the Underwood Tariff Act. "Kyle Plimpton said Wilson has bolts loose inside his head," David mistakenly blurted out at the dinner table. "He says this new Underwood Tariff Act will turn the banks upside down. Making people pay income tax will finish ruining this country."

"So that's the kind of President he is, huh?" Adam said, redness creeping up his neck. "We've got too many taxes already! Look at the tax we pay on brandy, on wines. What's Kyle saying about this banking news? What are you talking about?"

Sarah bit her lip, glared at David. "As *I* understand it," she said quietly, "he wants to stop the dictatorship of private banking institutions and make more funds available to the average citizen. Establish a currency that will automatically expand or contract, as needed. At least, I believe I read it correctly."

"Women—what do you know about banking! You read a paper —what does that tell you?" Adam reached for his glass, glowered at the sight of the white milk, pushed up from the table and went straight to where Sarah thought she had safely hidden the brandy and the wine. He poured a hefty tumbler of brandy.

"Adam, please! You know what Dr. Williams said."

Adam sat down, deliberately lifted the glass and drank. "Freedom! Where's *freedom* in this country any longer? The government telling when a bank can loan money, making people pay taxes on top of taxes! Maybe your hotshot Woodrow Wilson ought to go back to his *books* and leave *people* alone!" he stormed at Sarah, as if it were somehow her fault.

From then on, Sarah decided to keep her political opinions to herself. When the Sunday *San Francisco News Call Bulletin* arrived on Spring Mountain, she would read it alone, pass it on to Adam without comment. She was withdrawing more and more into her own private spaces within those two-foot-thick stone walls of the house on Spring Mountain. But in the privacy of her own bedroom there were times when she would find herself brooding over something she had just read; for instance, the cover story of the Suffragettes thrown into prison in Great Britain for demonstrating for their rights. When had she ever stood up and openly, publicly fought for anything? Her life was one long series of compromises, resignations, she thought bitterly. And at that moment, she reached idly for a *Cosmopolitan* magazine, thumbed through to see a picture story of the latest dance—"one sweeping the nation," it said. She studied the women with their new hairstyles, wearing their tight-fitting, clinging dresses with long feather boas, illustrating the steps of this "fox-trot." She got up, threw the magazine down, and marched toward the door. How long had it been since she had danced *any* kind of dance step!

But at the sight of Adam's haggard face downstairs, she stopped her bitter thoughts. How could she worry about giddyheaded young girlish dreams of attending gala balls or of lost trips to the lands of gods and goddesses? She was the wife of a fine, proud man who had suffered a serious heart attack and was struggling to get well again. She was the mother of her own son; the stepmother of two more sons. Even if they were nearly grown men, she had no time for sitting around filled with lamentation. Her world was *here*, right here on Spring Mountain! It was her duty to give it her best.

Following the 1913 harvest, Norman Jaspers drove up one Sunday afternoon in a brand-new Stutz Bearcat, the first such automobile in Napa County. He was bringing up the quarterly reports from his accountant on the Brunner holdings. And he wanted to see how Adam and particularly Sarah were faring during this long illness of Adam's.

He dropped a sporty hat on the library table, was just ready to go in to talk with Adam when Sarah hurried out, a frown on her face. Actually, Adam had seen the successful-looking Norman bouncing up the stone pathway, had caught a glimpse of the shiny automobile, how Joseph and Bobby Alfieri and all the Chinese had swarmed around the car as if Bacchus himself had just ridden in on a gold chariot. He had felt his temples pound, his pulse race. He didn't need to listen to Norman Jaspers enumerating his long list of successes now when he felt more trapped than ever. Winter was coming up, and he would have to wait nearly a year before the next harvest; only then would he feel truly alive. So he had hurriedly called Sarah in, asked her to ward off Norman Jaspers, tell him that he wasn't up to visitors today. Then he had quickly locked himself into his private world there in the book-lined room that had become his haven.

Sarah led Norman into the parlor, sat politely stiff-backed across from him. She was wearing an older woolen dress to ward off the sudden cold spell that had hit the mountainside within the past few days—itself a reminder that another long winter was ahead. A simple lace collar was her only adornment. She rarely got out her jewelry or fussed with how she arranged her hair, with adding dabs of color to her cheeks, sachet on her wrists. Norman found himself staring at a lackluster Sarah who was still hauntingly beautiful, even in her drabness. She had the most startling amber eyes he had ever seen. She was perhaps a little heavier and slightly middle-aged-looking now, but she was gracefully elegant even so. He was studying the way she was sitting there with her hands folded limply in her lap, the out-of-fashion dress a nun could have felt at home in, and thinking how *he* would dress her, the wonderful jewelry he would buy for her if she were only his wife, what a marvelous hostess she would make in his magnificently restored mansion that had been her own childhood home.

He reached into his breast pocket and took out a thick envelope. "I have the quarterly reports, a couple of nice bonus checks included," he said cheerfully. "I insisted that Adam be paid his usual managerial fee —I understand Anton has been doing a fine job down there overseeing the Portuguese workers. The larger check is from the sale of a piece of property I invested a portion of Adam's own personal money in back when he first became my client. A small investment at the time, but one which has paid handsomely. A firm called the Pascarella Enterprises has just bought the entire block and are building an office-building complex. I thought this would come in handy right now, the wine business being the poor money-maker it is."

"To the true vineyardist and vintner, it is never a matter of making *money,*" she said, surprised at her own fierce defensiveness. But she couldn't bear his smug, triumphant look. What did he know about winemaking? About the long watchful waiting required of any successful man of the land? She was proud of Adam for refusing to see this balding, round-bellied upstart in his fine English tweeds, his leather boots with their narrow heels.

Norman sensed that he had angered her. He stood up, came over and stood above her, feeling for the first time taller than she. "Sarah, I only want to help as best I can. I know you've had a tough time up here. I—let me get you off this mountain for a little while! Come down next Sunday and have dinner with me."

At the look on her face, he bounced up on his toes, rocked back on his heels again.

"I couldn't possibly leave the boys—and, of course, Adam," she replied.

The tone of her voice made his thick neck flush hot at the back of his collar. "Bring the boys if you like. I'd love having you see how I've restored your old home place. I think you—*they* would enjoy it. Won't you ever come see it, Sarah? Just for memories' sake?"

She stood, now a half head taller than Norman. "That is very lovely of you to ask," she said with stiff-lipped formality. "Please do ask me again when Adam is well. I'm sure we'd both love that."

It was shortly after June 28, 1914, that Sarah read the local newspaper's delayed account that the Archduke Franz Ferdinand, heir to the Austro-Hungarian throne, had been assassinated by a nineteen-year-old Serbian terrorist. It was buried back in the paper, the front page having been devoted to a campaign speech made by Hiram Johnson, a candidate in California's gubernatorial election, and his opinions about a Prohibition amendment included on the ballot, which he said he opposed.

She kept her concerns over the incident largely to herself. Adam had been improving, she had noticed with some relief. His fretful attitude over every step he took seemed to be relaxing. She had seen him taking long walks out into the vineyards, standing there in the middle of them, as if by being near these growing, luxurious vines he would gain some of their strength, their reaching-forth process. And instead of spending every afternoon supposedly "napping" (she strongly suspected he drank brandy or Muscatel most of the time he spent behind those locked doors) he had been taking his "rest" periods out on the veranda, as if by having this overall view of the larger portion of vineyards there on Spring Mountain he would have some major control over what was taking place, get a firm grip on all aspects of living again.

When the 1914 harvest got under way on Spring Mountain, under Kyle Plimpton's direction, it was as though some of the fever pitch worked its way into Adam's blood. One night, Sarah was startled to find him in her bed. And after a tentative, cautious attempt at lovemaking—discovering that his heart remained beating, and finding himself furious because he had missed out on more pleasures in life than he had needed to—his whole outlook began to change.

He took a ride in the phaeton with David to St. Helena, but the trip exhausted him—actually, threw him into an unexpected depression. He took to his bed again, as if hiding from the new rush of noise he had found, even in quiet St. Helena, from automobiles, from the stares of strangers who seemed to be silently measuring his slowed-down step, his gaunt look, and thinking of him as a failure. He stayed that way for one full week, until Dr. Williams came and reminded him, "Regaining your confidence is going to be almost as difficult as regaining your physical health, Adam. Now try again—okay?"

It was during that interval that Sarah—who still protected Adam from undue stress—reached a final unbreakable stalemate with Joseph, who had, during Adam's long illness, become openly hostile to her, often attacking her verbally, cruelly, to the point where he made life miserable for her. This particular episode had taken place the day Adam had gone with David. It started when the old Italian, Adolfo, came to complain to Sarah about Joseph. Adolfo had made his way to the kitchen that Saturday morning; he had tottered his way to the back door, propping himself up on two walking canes, his twisted back bent over with painful arthritis. His shock of white hair was in disarray, his face a map of open rage, when Sarah dusted flour from her hands and opened the door to see who it was—Li Po having taken the weekend off to go to Napa City and visit his cousins, whom he had not seen in weeks.

"Joseph *non è buono*—no good! Bad boy!" Adolfo said, his voice quivering with rage. "He no do'a his job good. *Vada via!*—leave stable'a dirty. He say such'a mean t'ingsa!"

She brought him inside, fed him lunch, offered him hot coffee and fresh bread, and he went back feeling in a happier mood. She promised herself to discuss his complaints, as best as she could determine them, the first chance she got. She wondered if part of it was that the old man was lonely, had wanted to be sure himself that the *padrone*, Adam, was truly better.

She stopped Joseph soon after that, one night when they were alone in the kitchen and Adam had already retired for sleep.

"Adolfo was up here the other day. He seemed upset that you weren't doing your job as he seems to think it should be done. Said something about your going away on Saturday without cleaning the stables as you were supposed to do."

"The old goat! What does he have to say about what I do or don't do? He doesn't even earn his own keep, much less have the right to boss me around!"

Joseph had just poured a glass of milk for himself and was spreading fresh butter and jam on a piece of bread she had baked that day. She sat opposite him, spoke quietly.

"Adolfo is a very old man, Joseph. He has been a wonderfully loyal worker and your father would never throw him out, when this is the only home he has. He serves some functions. He is at least there to keep an eye on the horses, keep the bunkhouse from burning down."

"He's half blind. And he falls asleep sitting up. Let *him* try shoveling out all that horseshit for a change!"

"Joseph—that language really isn't necessary."

"What's wrong? You are shocked by what it really it—*horseshit?*" He leered at her, strawberry jam clinging to the corner of his lower lip, his eyes like ice chips frozen out of murky water. "Would you like for me to say *manure?* Use a special dainty fork shoveling one pile, another silver shovel on another?"

She had drawn back, aghast at his deliberate crudity, his intent to shock her. She tried not to look at the angry, square face with its recent rash of new pimples, some looking as if he had tried squeezing them; at the thick, short neck with the veins standing out like cords in his fury; at the blond hair that had once been called towhead when he was a little boy, now looking drab, in need of a good shampoo, the cowlick standing up like a ragged splinter on the back of his head. Unconsciously, she had drawn a comparison—had seen David's quiet, remarkably good looks, and Anton's leaner, sensitive face, his rather dashing, debonair way of charming all the ladies, old and young alike. Joseph's surly, unattractive face—it was more his attitude, she thought, than anything comprising his physical stature—made him a stranger in the Donati family of handsome men.

It was as if he had been reading her thoughts. "Get this through your head!" he yelled, as if purposely raising his voice. "I don't give a good goddam *what* you think any longer about anything I do. Keep your nose out of my life from here on out!"

She jumped up, tried to stand her ground. "You absolutely *cannot* talk to me in that manner, Joseph Donati! Your father may be too ill to come to my defense, but I assure you there are other means—"

From a long-trained childhood habit, he went over to the sink with his dirty glass, rinsed it out, turned it upside down on the drainboard. A strange sense of loss hit Sarah harder than if he had struck her. She walked around to the end of the table, gripped its edge.

"Joseph, *please*—let's not fight like this. I know cleaning out the stables cannot be a pleasant job for anyone. Perhaps we can hire someone else. The sales are increasing—we'll have a little more profit on the books this coming harvest, I'm convinced of that. Choose another job, if you wish. All of us are simply trying our best to keep up with everything until your father recovers sufficiently to take over. Will you *try*?"

He whirled around, his face like granite. "I have decided on what *I* want to do. I've asked Luigi Pascarella to hire me on as an apprentice stonecutter. He's asking Cesare and is coming up here Sunday to tell me if I have a job or not. If I do, I'm moving off Spring Mountain forever. I'm moving in with Luigi in his place on Madrona, until I can inherit what is rightfully mine. Mine and Anton's."

She was searching his face. "Joseph, even so, until you *do* depart, won't you try to please me—your father—by—"

A bitter dry laugh split the air between them. "*Try*! Listen, I am through trying to please you." He shook a finger at her. "Do you know how many times in the past I used to try to please you? Sure, the times I would lock myself in my room and practice in front of the mirror how I might do something a little different?"

"What, Joseph? Whatever are you talking about?"

"Whatever the hell it was I had just done wrong for the hundred-thousand-millionth time! How I walked, talked, ate—you name it!" His voice was mocking now. "Oh, don't think I didn't see that look on your face when David—Anton too—would wave their grade cards under your nose. See you saying to yourself, 'Here comes *Joseph* again, the big bull in the china shop,' huh? 'Joseph, the clumsy one. Joseph, the short, ugly one.' I am *never*, as long as I live, going to try to please you again. I made up my mind to that a long time ago—or haven't you noticed? Now I please myself. *Me*, Joseph Jacob Donati, that's who!"

"Oh, Joseph—please, please listen to me. Please don't *hate* so much. Let's try to work out what's wrong between us. I've never meant to hurt you. I've tried, desperately tried, to understand you. Both your father and I love you. *Believe* that."

"*You* believe it!" he cried, his eyes glistening as he stormed out the back door, letting it slam hard behind him.

• •

313

When, that following Sunday afternoon, Luigi did indeed arrive and offer a job for Joseph, Sarah readily agreed. "You are his godfather. I can't imagine a happier opportunity for Joseph right now than having a chance to work with you, have you open up your home to him, your heart."

Luigi stared out at the veranda, not looking at Adam, who said in a strained voice, "Joseph can be bullheaded. Stubborn as a mule. Don't take any nonsense from him, Luigi."

"The boy's good. He likes to work with his hands. Ought to make a fine mason, work with any kind of building." Luigi held out his own thick hands. "Take me and Cesare—we've got to work with our hands. But Lorenzo—he hates anything that doesn't have to do with his restaurant business. He comes up to our family reunion every Christmas. He's like somebody got a pants leg full of bees. Can't wait to get back home to North Beach, he says. See how his place is doing. If it's still there. Then you take you and Kyle and Vittorio Alfieri. Hands in the *dirt*—that's you people. Either that or working with something to do with the land, or getting grape juice in a glass under your nose. All that fancy tasting. But Joseph . . ." He nodded somberly. "He's different. He'll find out what he wants to do, though. Sure, we'll get along. Just fine."

After Joseph left Spring Mountain—essentially for good, except to come back on holidays or on regular visits, which Luigi himself insisted upon—Sarah found that life was much easier for her. Even David was rarely about, spending his free time in the winery, waiting and hoping for acceptance at the university in Berkeley that coming spring semester—a mistake in his application forms, then their late arrival at admissions, having knocked him out of the fall enrollment. He would now and then join Sarah and Adam out on the veranda, usually trying to convince them in mild tones that the time was coming for them to buy trucks to replace the old freight wagons. "Everybody down valley is changing over, Papa. We could haul grapes much more efficiently. Get them to the crusher sooner. In the long run, it would be much to our advantage."

"Tell Norman Jaspers to come up and talk about it with me the first chance he gets," Adam said good-naturedly. "Your mother tells me there's a sudden spurt in sales. Why do you think that's taking place?"

"The paper says it's because by next year over six million immigrants from southern Europe—all consumers—will have come to America since 1901. And they want California wine! The distributor was telling me the other day they all want Donati red, in bulk, and

Donati brandy, if they can get hold of it. Especially every Italian in North Beach."

Adam smiled. "Sure, I've got lots of good friends in North Beach. Someday I will go with you. Show my son around, huh, Sarah? Wouldn't Lorenzo like that?"

He seemed happier than he had in days—so happy that Sarah did not bring up her growing fears. She had been reading every account she could find of the war chains rattling in Europe. It was apparent to her by late August that a full-scale war was irretrievably closing in on every nation. So when, on August 18, 1914, President Wilson addressed the American people on his views of what America's position should be, she felt Adam should not be protected from anything any longer.

"It seems President Wilson is offering a course of mediation," she said, handing the newspaper to Adam, and sitting down in her favorite wicker chair opposite him on the veranda. While he glanced at the reprinted speech, she gazed out at the vineyards that seemed to her to be like strangely garbed soldiers themselves marching off in combat, as if leaping off slopes into the void of space below that she could not see from her vantage point. "He says he's determined to keep America out of European quarrels. But I wonder how long he can hold out when everybody else is jumping into the middle of the fighting. It's a terrible war. So many people being killed—slaughtered, it seems to me."

Adam made a scowl. "How did so many people get tangled up in this thing? Doesn't make sense to me. Like all the crazy people out there rattling chains to turn this country into a dry country!" He looked at her, the flush of rage creeping up in spite of his efforts to obey Dr. Williams' orders and stay calm. "What is any country without good wine? Tell me that! Look in your history books. What country ever won a war without wine?"

She waited a moment. "At least Woodrow Wilson is trying to keep us on neutral ground. He's ignoring the warmongers wanting to get over there in the thick of the fighting. He's kept what he calls a 'watchful waiting' eye on our conflicts in Mexico, too. Maybe he'll be successful keeping us out." She tried to add a lighter note, to relax Adam's tense mood. "David says the 'watchful waiting' ought to make our President a pretty good viticulturist."

Adam got up, heading out on his own toward the vineyards. He called back over his shoulder, "Maybe he ought to stick with what he knows—books! Obviously he doesn't care about us men making wine!"

14

Adam had managed to take part in the harvest that year of 1914, mostly in a supervising capacity. He had allowed David to manage a small crush of his own, and had seen to it that their usual run of brandy was distilled. He talked with the revenue agents (who were required to be on hand at the legal commencing of the run), discussing Prohibition and if it would or would not make a stronger inroad into the law books of the nation as a whole.

"We knocked out that Amendment Number Two on the ballot, didn't we?" said a sour-faced man, thumbing through a stack of forms to see if everything was in order.

Adam smiled. "In Napa, we voted 5,128 nos against 2,040 yes votes. We elected Hiram Johnson. Now that I'm recovering from my heart attack I'm getting back into the fight again."

The agent shook his head, went over to the government car and climbed in. "We've got a long way to go. I might find myself out of a job if this keeps up. They'll slash our department to pieces if Prohibition ever passes. Which it might. That Webb-Kenyon Act passed last March is making a lot of states move into tough positions supporting Prohibition. You've got California and Ohio taking strong stands against it, but look, you've already got Arizona, Colorado and Oregon, Texas—hell, half of the South—already practicing strict Prohibition! I can't see us holding out much longer. There's a bunch trying to get stronger amendments put on the ballot next time around. I predict that by 1916 you're going to find us all hanging by a thread." He started backing out, then called down to a worried-looking Adam, "If Prohibition does take over this state, you'll be losing a fine copper column still. You've got one of the best I've seen. You couldn't very well hide that big daddy back in the hills for bootlegging."

Adam drew himself up stiffly. "I would not bootleg with that or anything—not even with a pot still!" He stalked back into the house, mumbling to himself about revenue agents in general and that one in particular, whom he had never really liked anyway.

But after that conversation, Adam doubled his political efforts. Winter was soon upon them, and the winery was basically locked up, the wines were sleeping. Bobby Alfieri was an excellent cellarman, and he had the help of two recently arrived immigrants from Sicily, neither of whom spoke English, but who worked well with Bobby. Adam had no immediate worries. It was a big help having Anton down on the Brunner place, looking after things. He was openly frank about admitting he was glad to have Joseph down in St. Helena working with Luigi. "He's got a head like a damn rock anyway. Maybe Luigi can crack it open and knock some sense into him for a change. I never could reach him."

Then came the spring of 1915. It was an unusually warm March, when the sun seemed to want to remind the rain clouds that it had priority and had decided to come out and stretch itself in between downpours. Adam told Sarah he needed to be in Napa City for three or four days. He was going to shop for a farm truck and perhaps buy an automobile for them. "With the threat of this war about to get us pulled in, they say I might not be able to find one on the market if I wait too much longer."

Sarah helped him pack an overnight valise, putting in an extra clean shirt in case he decided to remain an extra day or so. "I'm worried about the way things are going over there," she said, adding a rolled-up pair of clean socks. "Ever since they sunk the Cunard luxury liner—the *Lusitania*—the German submarines are going after anything they see afloat, it seems. We're losing *American* lives now, and this country won't stand for that. President Wilson is trying to keep them at bay, but enough is enough."

Adam straightened his tie. It felt good to be moving around again, able to take a trip, even a short one to Napa City. If he bought the car, took enough quick lessons in driving—maybe he'd have to ask Anton to be his chauffeur for a while, in case it made him nervous and caused his heart to start acting up—he'd see to it that Sarah started getting out more. She was getting where she seemed to *want* to stay put on Spring Mountain.

"I hear the men talk at ᵗʰe political meetings," he said, ready to go now. "They think Wilson is a bloody coward. *Afraid* to fight. Wine men don't trust that sonofabitch."

"Personally, I am thankful he hasn't plunged us into war. With three sons—we might have lost our boys by now. Think of the blessings, Adam. At least David is in school now at Berkeley. He's safely studying—learning what he will need to know to take over up here one of these days when you're ready to hand over the full responsibility. Anton is being a wonderful help, isn't he?"

She decided she would walk along with him down to the stable, where a neighbor with a new car would be coming to pick him up and give him a lift into Napa City. Though it was a sunny day, there was still a dampness in the air from the recent spring rains. She took a sweater, then offered to help carry the valise. "I know you say it isn't heavy, but we can't risk another heart attack," she said lightly, pleased from their shared grip on the same handle, the clasp of his fingers on hers as they made their way down the stone pathway. It was so good to see him like this, taking his long strides, his proud chin up in the air, his blue eyes shining again. And it would be good for her to have a few days alone at the house to get some cleaning caught up—cobwebs clinging to the high ceilings swept down, the crystal chandelier taken apart and washed, a job that had been neglected far too long now. And she would ask Li Po to take some of the smaller throw rugs out into the sunlight and beat the dust out of them with a broom handle. Yes, this would help her give the house a polish to match the new life they would begin to have now that Adam was well.

She waved goodbye until Adam and Frank Daniels had driven out of sight, the Ford bumping over the winter ruts in the road. She stood a moment, listening to the sounds of birds twittering, a distant whinny of a horse from within the stable. She was just hugging her arms about herself, pulling the sweater closer, when Bobby Alfieri hurried out of the stable.

"Mr. Donati—he hasn't gone yet, has he?"

She saw his worried look. "What's wrong, Bobby?"

"His horse. Hajib's bad off." He put his cap back on his black hair. He was so much like Vittorio, she thought, seeing the huge black eyes, the short, stocky build, the darker skin.

"What's wrong with him?" She held her skirts down against the March wind. The sun had dipped in behind fast-gathering dark clouds.

"A couple of days ago I thought he didn't look so hot and I told Mr. Donati about it. He had Kyle take a look and Kyle brought up some medicine from the livery stable in St. Helena that old Doc Meyers gives his horses. I thought he was getting better. But he won't get up. And he's foaming at the mouth—quivering like he's having convulsions. Old Adolfo says we've got to shoot him. It's too late for anything else." He dug his hands into his pockets, kicked at the ground.

319

She looked about, uncertain. Somehow, she could not imagine the proud stallion as Bobby was describing him. She saw him only with Adam riding so straight-backed and handsome, taking him over jumps that used to frighten her terribly. Though she had been a reasonably good rider, she had never jumped a horse over anything. She thought it was one of the most splendid sights, even when it took her breath, to see Adam clear one of the stone walls, Hajib's black coat glistening, his elegant, thoroughbred lines in one fluid, muscular motion.

"Your houseboy, Li Po—is he good with a gun?" Bobby asked tentatively.

"Li Po? Good heavens, I wouldn't think so! What about yourself? You know guns."

He looked embarrassed. "Yes, ma'am, but that's not a regular horse. That's Mr. Donati's stallion! I—I sure wish I had caught him before he left."

Old Adolfo came hobbling out, barely able to move. He tried to wave an angry arm, then gave in to letting his voice carry his rage. "Somebody shoot'a the horse! *Così basta*—all so much talk, talk. *Doloroso*—the horse'a hurt so bad."

Sarah went over to the old man, patted his arm consolingly. "Please go back inside, Adolfo. We'll take care of it. Bobby and I— we're trying to decide. We're getting a gun."

When he had left them, Sarah looked at Bobby with a puzzled frown. "I can shoot a gun myself. Adam showed me how once, just in case there ever should be a rattlesnake around." She shook her head. "It's really best that you didn't tell him about Hajib. It would have spoiled his trip. He's killed sick horses before, but with *Hajib* . . ." She had made up her mind. "I'll go get Li Po. Stay with the horse. I'll be right back."

She found Li Po at the springhouse lowering jars of fresh milk into the clear cold water flowing from the natural spring out of the mountainside. He was taking out fresh watercress, baby onions and radishes from his own early garden.

She explained her problem. "Please go get the shotgun and a box of shells. Bring them to the stable right away. I'll be with Bobby and the horse. Maybe—maybe we can still save it."

Li Po looked at her with a stunned, bewildered look. Then he dropped the vegetables back into the water, bowed, ran in that bobbing-up-and-down way of his toward the main house.

As Sarah entered the stable, she felt dwarfed and awed by the strange, huge size of everything—of the horses' eyes like black walnuts staring at her from their long faces hanging out over the stall doors. On every nail, hanging from rafters, were saddles, harnesses, ropes, horseshoes, pitchforks. Much used wagon beds were parked here and there; an old dilapidated buggy tilted forward, propped against a haystack out of which a pitchfork jutted. A strong pungent smell—the combined odors of hay, sawdust, the sweat and dung of the horses, the leather saddles, a mustiness accumulated during the recent dampness from long spring rains—hit her with overpowering force.

She made her way toward the back of the huge stable. An orange-striped tomcat came out from nowhere and rubbed against one leg as she stopped to keep from snagging her skirt on the open stall door, where a nail was sticking out from a loose board that Hajib had kicked off during the throes of his first seizure. "Go away, kitty!" she said, startled.

Bobby pointed to where the stallion was stretched out on its side. Sarah walked around Hajib slowly, seeing the heavy breathing, hearing the awful sounds escaping.

She looked up wide-eyed. "We can't shoot him in here, can we? The other horses . . . old Adolfo being already so upset?"

Li Po came in at that moment, carrying the gun straight out in the air.

"Li Po! Point that at the ground," she cried out. "We don't need to blow somebody's head off!" She put her hands on her hips, looked at Bobby. "How do we do this?"

"Maybe we could get him up—out into the woods." He bent over, made soft, clucking clicking sounds out of the corner of his mouth. "Come on, old boy. Hajib, *up.* . . . Okay, good old boy."

The horse seemed to shudder, make a long, faltering effort, then slowly got to his feet.

"Thataboy . . . this way . . ." Bobby was leading him. Sarah found herself walking behind, as if ready to push, to prop up the stallion's wobbly legs. Li Po trotted along behind, holding the gun down.

"Aren't there any cellarmen around?" she asked desperately as they approached the woods. "Are we the only people around today?"

He shook his head. "Yes, ma'am. Afraid so. Come on, Hajib. Thataboy . . ."

Sarah turned to check on Li Po, saw the look on his face, the way he was holding the gun out away from him as if it were a live snake ready to bite him.

They were making their way down the dirt wagon road that was used to get in and out of the vineyards during harvest. By the time they reached the first dense clump of trees, a long slithering froth was coming from Hajib's mouth. Then they were in a clearing where all around them were tall, skinny saplings reaching up for sunlight, fighting their way for space between larger age-old redwoods. A straight shaft of sunlight, like a filmy ribbon, shot down at an angle through the tall, spiral opening near the top of the tallest trees.

"He's not going to make it any further," Bobby said as Sarah stopped to pull free a briar caught on her skirts. At that moment, Hajib's legs began to buckle and he fell in a gradual, stuttering, horrible kind of way that sent twigs crackling.

Sarah whirled around to the startled Li Po. "Can you shoot that gun?"

His head looked as if it were on coiled springs. "Oh, no—no, madame!" He thrust the shotgun straight out.

Sarah saw the look on Bobby Alfieri's face. "I'll try," he said, stepping up, his color gone. "I never liked to kill things—not even rabbits. I . . ." He looked ashamed. "Men aren't supposed to—"

"Never mind!" Sarah said, pulling herself up. "Li Po, you and Bobby go on back down the road, I will do it. It is my husband's horse. It is my duty, not yours."

Bobby was looking at her doubtfully. "My papa—he would take a rawhide whip to me if he knew I let you do a man's job, a job I ought to do."

The horse was kicking at the damp mulch in the grove. His nose was turning, his neck bent backward. A hideous sound came from him, like a shriek combined with some horrible scream.

"Is this cocked—ready to fire?" she asked Bobby.

He looked at it. "Yes, ma'am. Do you know how to aim?"

"My husband taught me how to shoot several years ago," she said, taking the gun and trying to get a feel of it. The barrel felt ice cold. The handle jutted under her arm was a heavy weight. Her hands were steady, but she felt as if a shattering quake were taking place inside her. She had never liked pulling the trigger, even when it was aimed at tin cans on a stump. She dreaded that one painful waiting moment just before drawing back on the trigger, before that blasting, body-riveting noise exploded. "I'm ready. You two go on now. Out of sight, *please!*"

The woods had taken on an eerie hush. Even the nervous twittering of birds had stopped. The stallion was now trying to grind his nose into the ground, his legs flailing. His eyes were like enormous burning coals.

Sarah did not remember actually pulling the trigger back. Sud-

322

denly there was the ripping, tearing force of the gun going off; her fear that she had missed or not even come close to the center of the head where Bobby had told her she should aim. Along with that explosion of the gun, Hajib had let out a loud final cry. She fired two shots in quick succession. She could not bear to have him suffer another second.

Then there was silence. She felt as if the silence itself would smother her, would join forces with the thundering echoing rings going round and round in her head. The smell of the gun, of the close dampness from the grove of trees, made her reel.

But she forced herself to look at the animal. The sight of the mangled head, the eyes still staring, made her rush toward the outer ring of the woods and put the gun down, come back running, carrying armloads of twigs and mulch—anything to cover up the sight, keep anyone from seeing that proud magnificent animal like this! She made trip after trip. And then it was done. The huge mound had covered him, all except his hind legs. But she had given all her energy out. Her arms hung limply at her side, like rag-doll arms.

Li Po bobbed back into the clearing, followed by Bobby Alfieri, who sank down on the ground, buried his head in his hands.

"I should've done it myself," Bobby moaned. "Papa will kill me if he finds out!" He looked up, his eyes pleading. "I am so sorry. I don't know what made me lose my nerve."

Sarah walked over slowly, as if she had some of the arthritis old Adolfo had; bent over and picked up the gun; went over and handed it to Li Po. "Come on—it's done. The horse is out of his misery. That is the important thing. It was my duty, not yours, Bobby. So let's forget it."

"But I was a coward! I was just like Woodrow Wilson—"

"You're a sensitive young man. You are *not* a coward."

"I would kill a German if I had to!" he said, jutting out his chin. "A Hun—I wouldn't be afraid to shoot one!"

"Please, Bobby, please forget it. Hajib is different. He was not an enemy."

Bobby looked at her gratefully. "Yes, I guess that's it. Hajib—he was different."

With Adam's recovery nearly complete, the spring and summer of 1915 passed with relative normalcy on Spring Mountain. Adam had been advised still to get plenty of rest, not to overly exert himself, or do any physical work in the vineyards or the winery as yet; but he was getting out more and had increased his walks, had started some mild exercises to get himself back in shape.

While Sarah sometimes fretted and stewed over newspaper accounts of the war raging in Europe, Adam pored over increasingly disturbing reports about the Prohibition forces gaining added strength. In the first week of June—only days before their eighth wedding anniversary—he received an urgent form letter from Bismarck Bruck's Sacramento office:

There are two new amendments that will now definitely appear on the 1916 November ballot, which we must begin fighting against immediately. Though the California Campaign Federation is calling them *Anti-Saloon* measures, it means a death blow to California's grape industry if either wins. What it boils down to is: 100,000 persons working in this industry will be out of work; over $150,000,000.00 invested in the industry will be lost; the state and federal governments will suffer enormous loss by giving up revenues accrued through taxation. Please attend the upcoming meeting of the California Grape Protection Association in Napa County. It is urgent!

Adam did not show the letter to Sarah. Women did not vote; politics were matters for men, he thought. She, in turn, wondered if the heart attack had numbed Adam's concern for humanity as a whole.

For instance, when, that recent May 31, the Germans had dropped the first incendiary bombs ever used in warfare, some three thousand pounds on London from a Zeppelin LZ-38, she tried testing Adam's reaction. "What will those Germans do next, Adam? One would think they would be satisfied by having already introduced that horrid poison gas! What murderous lengths will this war take us? Will mankind even survive?" She had seen Adam's preoccupied look. "What do you think about Woodrow Wilson, Adam? Are we *wrong* to keep out of the war?"

Annoyed, he had put down the propaganda pamphlet he had been reading, one that the Woman's Christian Temperance Union was passing out on every street corner in St. Helena, and answered, "He's not worth a damn about anything! He says he's not for Prohibition, but he signs these bills that help it along. This Food Leverage Act—that hurts us. He ought to go back to teaching college!"

Exasperated, Sarah had added, "I was thinking more in terms of the war—of *humanity*. As for Prohibition—Adam, these blights that hit the grape and wine industry, they usually have short life cycles. You vintners and growers always survive somehow." She had taken a long sigh, then asked, "Aren't you concerned at all about the Germans? About the horrible war going on in Europe?"

Deliberately, Adam had bitten his lower lip, gazed up through wisteria blossoms dangling in grapelike clusters from the redwood trellis across the veranda. He latched his gaze onto one clear patch of bright-blue sky, as if drawing a sharp line around it. "Sure—sure, I'm concerned!" He glared at her. "I can do just so much with my life. My father taught me that. 'Be the best viticulturist and winemaker you can be,' he used to say. 'Let the rest of the world run its business.' A man has got just two arms and legs. One damn heart—right? I look out there at my vines and see, right now, ten big jobs I'd like to get my hands on. Sure, I could look out over there across Howell Mountain and worry about what's wrong on the other side. I could worry about that dumb bastard in Washington, D.C. I could worry about the Huns. About every soldier getting blown to bits. But will that help you and me? Will it save our necks when the Prohibitionists come into power and shut us down? Oh, it'll happen! Don't look so smug. You don't read any of *my* pamphlets, do you? You don't know one amendment from the next!"

In June, then, when Adam decided he was up to working on the newly formed committee—along with a slate of directors that included such important vintners and growers as C. N. Pickett, Joseph Migliavacca, Alwyn Ever, Bismarck Bruck, and D. A. Dunlap—and told Sarah he was attending a meeting at the Liberty Theatre in St. Helena, she asked, "Exactly what *are* these amendments, Adam? Why are they so important?"

He was getting dressed after a hot bath. His legs were still muscular, his body was lean, but he did not have the sinewy strength of his youth. Wrinkles had worked their way alongside his full mouth, crinkled around the corners of his still clear, vivid blue eyes. His hair was still thick and wavy, but was now gray at the temples and at the nape of his neck. He turned, buttoning the top button of his crisply starched shirt, worked into his trousers, pulled the belt in around his still-lean waist. When he sat down to pull on his socks, he looked at her, saw she was serious about the question.

"Amendment One calls for preventing wine from being made, sold or introduced within California after January first, 1920." He brought one knee up, straightened his shoelaces, yanked at the tie. "That's Number *One*—okay? It says wine could only be made for medicinal, sacramental or scientific purposes."

"But that's absurd!" she said, handing him his spats.

"Amendment Number Two says vintners who manufacture wine could sell it to buyers outside the state or to customers within the state

—but only *two* gallons, and that has to be delivered by a common carrier to their permanent home." He stood up, worked his arms through his vest, into his suit coat. He looked in the mirror one last time, rubbed his fingertips down the sides of his face, checking his shave.

"January, 1920—that's an awfully long way off."

"Not if it becomes law, it won't seem so long!"

She followed him out into the hallway, held on to the railing and went downstairs to tell him goodbye. "They can't pass it—they really don't think they can do that?"

He jammed his hat on his head, opened the door. "Unless we get our forces going stronger than they are, it *will* pass." He looked at her, pleased with her sudden interest. "Come on, walk with me down to the car. Watch me crank up the Ford."

As they were going down the stone pathway, he waved one arm out toward his vineyards. "Those are special grapes growing out there. Very special grapes. Do you think if I replaced them with *prune* trees I could make them grow and give us a living? I see all those nervous ninnies down valley yanking out beautiful vines and putting in prune trees, every kind of orchard. That's how sure some are that Prohibition is going to happen."

Sarah stopped just short of the shiny new Ford, stood back while he cranked it and climbed up into the high front seat.

He smiled down at her, gripping the wheel tightly, still not being used to driving, and still carrying some anxiety about another heart attack. "Bacchus didn't design this land for prune trees!"

Sarah stood, watching him drive off, partly wishing she had ridden along with him and gone shopping. But Anton had sent word with Li Po that he might be up either today, Thursday, or on Sunday afternoon. She always enjoyed Anton's rare visits.

As it turned out, she could have gone along. Anton did not show up, which was not a surprise. He was not always reliable about living up to his word. If a party, a good time of any sort, was at hand, he could become easily distracted. But even so, she was not impatient with him. She rather enjoyed his flamboyant attitude; looked forward to his debonair charming wit. He reminded her, in some ways, of young men she had known back East.

For that matter, in most ways she was becoming less impatient as she grew older. She was beginning to find a certain contentment living largely within the boundaries of Spring Mountain. And there were always things to keep her busy, she reasoned. Adam was right: there was just so much any person could do. Being enlightened about what was taking place in the world at large didn't mean that she should fret about it. And didn't she have plenty for which to be grateful?

So on that particular afternoon she took mending out on the veranda, found herself idly taking stock—or what her mother, Miss Grace, would have called counting her blessings. First, Adam was essentially well, active again, his gloomy moods largely having disappeared along with his illness. Secondly, she was pleased that David was so happy at the university—though he had written recently that as soon as he finished two basic years at Berkeley he might transfer to a straight agricultural program. He was staying on for summer school, making up the credits he had lost when he missed out on the fall semester.

Joseph was still a problem. When he occasionally did come for perfunctory visits, inevitably she would forget her resolution to try to accept him exactly as he was, see in him only the positive traits, but instead would usually find herself biting back tip-of-the-tongue reactions: "Joseph, couldn't you wear a shirt that at least smells—looks clean?"; or: "Joseph, please don't say *me and him, he ain't*!" During any visit, she had to struggle constantly with herself, and mostly came out with inane remarks; always sighed with relief when he left with Luigi.

But on this particular afternoon, she found reason to be grateful even in thinking about Joseph: he had Luigi giving him steady supportive encouragement. Dear "Uncle Luigi," trying in his generous way to help, always handing out compliments in the presence of others: "You ought to see Joseph's steady hand and razor-sharp eye with a chisel!" During their last visit he had said, "Joseph could be a real sculptor carving with wood, chiseling marble if he wanted to—if he'd save some of his spare time away from Amy Mulligan. Right, Joseph?"

Remembering that remark even now made Sarah wince. The Mulligan family was notoriously unkempt, a dirty rowdy group—with the father, Barney, going out on public drunks, beating his wife, sending their numerous children to school filthy, often with bruises. She would hope that Joseph—a son of Adam Donati—could seek his company from a higher level than the Mulligans!

A hummingbird had come near her shoulder, its frantic wings making that oddly static noise. She smiled. Forget Joseph, she told herself! Think about Anton, who might arrive any moment: Anton, who had such promise—along with the opportunity to go east to school, something she wished desperately could happen for David.

It was to be another three weeks before Anton finally showed up, having forgotten in the interim to send any excuse or apology.

He came on a Sunday afternoon, the third week of June, just after Adam and Sarah had finished a quiet, simple lunch and were sitting out on the veranda. Adam had brought along a scratch pad and a pencil to try to word a letter he wanted to send out to several people —his assigned duty as a member of the newly formed committee fighting the amendments. Sarah, being unconsciously driven still by her mother's dictates—"One simply doesn't sew on Sunday, religious or not," Miss Grace had always insisted—had brought out a favorite book, Emerson's essays, and had just read:

> Society is a joint-stock company in which the members agree for the better securing of his bread to each shareholder, to surrender the liberty and culture of the eater. The virtue in most request is conformity. Self-reliance is its aversion. It loves not realities and creators, but names and customs. Who so would be a man must be a nonconformist. Nothing is at last sacred but the integrity of your own mind.

Seeing the dashing Anton swing out of his racy new automobile, stride up the pathway, a white linen jacket tossed casually over one shoulder, a pale-yellow pongee shirt, tieless, open at the collar, made her put the book aside, get up and go to the edge of the veranda, hands outstretched, a broad smile on her face.

Though Anton was not as tall as David, he appeared so, the way he walked with such bounding confidence. And though basically his features were not as handsome as David's, he was a striking young man, his skin a smooth, rich bronze color from the summer sun, his light-brown hair bleached nearly blond, his blue-gray eyes a startling contrast.

David could use some of his debonair charm, she was thinking as she kissed him. David was almost too serious—too inclined, like his father, toward brooding, toward hunching his shoulders in when he dug his hands deeply into his pockets, as if lost in some contemplative world of his own.

"A new suit?" she asked, standing back admiring him. "Anton, you stay away too long. I forget how dashing you are!"

"And I forget how lovely you are!" he tossed back lightly. "Hello, Papa." He reached out, shook hands, a formality Adam preferred to the way he had been taught to kiss his own father, first one cheek, then the other.

Anton tossed the elegant jacket across the back of one of the wicker chairs. "I forget how much cooler it is up here," he said, staring out for a moment at the breeze rippling through the vineyards thick with midsummer growth. "I forgot the view. I've stayed away too long. Indeed I have! How about a glass of Donati Muscatel?" He went inside, without waiting for a reply; came out carrying glasses and one of Adam's favorite bottles, from the 1911 vintage.

Adam accepted the glass, but did not smile. "What's on your mind? You came this time because you need something—right?"

For a moment, Anton savored the Muscatel, licked his tongue across his full lips, leaned one shoulder against the redwood trellis. "Papa, you look so formidable! When I was little you used to scare the daylights out of me with a look like that." He lifted the glass, as if in some silent toast to himself. Then he sat down next to Sarah. His tone was still light, confident. "Actually, I came because I wanted to ask your advice about something. Get your opinion. I had a long visit with Norman Jaspers yesterday about exactly what funds might or might not be available for me. Regarding my education, that is," he added quickly. "According to Norman, I can use some money going east to check out the universities I might want to attend."

"Which ones are you considering?" Sarah asked eagerly.

"Princeton . . . Yale . . . Harvard." He squinted one eye, studying closely the clear amber liquid, then took a savoring sip. "Norman has contacts at Harvard. He assures me he can help get me accepted there. I have excellent marks from high school. I think I could survive, scholastically." He reached over, fished around in the linen jacket, came up with a box of thin cigars, offered one to a stony-faced Adam, struck a match and let smoke drift through his slender, long fingertips. "Mom Sarah, you have influenced me a great deal. I'm convinced, along with you, that Eastern schools are far superior."

"What is this cocky 'Mom Sarah' business?" Adam flared. "Is that the kind of talk you hear around this Stags' Leap place? Something you picked up at one of the wild parties over there?"

Anton looked secretly amused. "Papa, Stags' Leap is remarkably sophisticated—for Napa Valley, at any rate. Haven't you heard? Even visiting royalty comes there now."

Adam shook his head, shrugged his shoulders, dismissing Anton's remark. "Visiting royalty stays in San Francisco at the Palace Hotel. If they come here, they head for Soda Springs Hotel. That's where *nice* people go. I know all about the little houses in back of Stags' Leap!"

Adam's neck had turned an angry red. He didn't like this smart-aleck son of his acting as if he had all the answers—spending Jacob Brunner's hard-earned money on fancy roadsters and white suits that would get dirty on one wearing! Jacob would turn over in his grave.

Jacob would tell him he wouldn't amount to a hill of beans, wasting his time on wild parties and wild girls, and spending money going *east* to school.

"What's wrong with the university in Berkeley?" he asked, glaring openly now at Anton. "Your brother is doing very well there. Bringing down all A's. Learning something that will make him a fine oenologist one of these days. A man who will keep his head on his shoulders. Back east what do they know about making wine? Growing grapes?" This time he looked at Sarah, as if this decision was somehow all her fault. "What is all this 'back east' stuff?"

Anton quickly lifted his eyebrows in secret understanding with Sarah. "Papa, I'm afraid oenology is not a very healthy venture these days for any young man entering college. Let's face it, the Prohibitionists are winning out. I've been asking around. Norman Jaspers says so, too. We should be diversifying right now. You really should be, up here on Spring Mountain! Grandfather Brunner was always sensible in that regard, I'm finding out. I wish I could have known the old man."

Adam was livid. He jumped up, put the wineglass down so that it teetered for a moment on the wicker table beside his chair. He let out a sound like something spat out. "Jacob Brunner would give you an earful if he were alive! You wouldn't be wasting his money that he earned working with his hands—with the *earth*—on fancy cars and white suits! If you have already got all the answers from Norman Jaspers, why are you up here pretending to ask for our advice, huh?" A vein stood out on the side of Adam's neck like a knotted blue rope. "If you want to ask *me* anything, next time ask before you march into my wine cellar and open up one of the few bottles of my prize Muscatel left!" He stalked off the veranda, taking furious, long-legged strides out into the thick of his vineyards.

Anton shrugged his shoulders helplessly, looked at Sarah with startled eyes. "How do I manage—every time—to upset him?"

"Your father is a very proud, Old World European. Oh, he claims to be strictly American now. But he's used to being boss—the *padrone*. The one who makes decisions. It's hard for him, having had this heart attack. Knowing he is getting older."

"Should I go out there and apologize?" Anton asked quietly.

"Leave him with his vines for a little while. He'll come back with his own answer. He's like that. He'll probably end up apologizing to you—in his own way. He'll never say he's sorry." She waved Anton back to his chair. "Forget it. Turning forty, accepting middle age and younger generations stepping up, is hard. Let's talk about *you*. I'd like to hear your opinion on President Wilson. Do you think he is a coward or simply being strong in a passive way? The country seems so divided about him."

"I think he's a brilliant man. I think he's made a brave stand, holding out for what he believes. The pressure is on from the hawks to go to war, though. The German submarines have sunk too many ships now—have taken too many American lives. I don't see how he can keep us out much longer. What do you think?"

She sipped the sweet wine, thought a moment. "*I'm* the coward, I suppose. I don't want any of you boys going to war—though maybe military life for Joseph might do him some good."

"Forget Joseph! He's impossible. Luigi had to bail him out of jail the other night, I hear. He got into a fist fight with somebody making a crack about Amy Mulligan. A drunken brawl in a bar in Napa City. He goes wild when he drinks."

"I hate to hear that about Joseph. Though I'm not surprised, really. He fights so many little wars with himself. But about the *real* war—I lose sleep sometimes worrying over those gallant British, Frenchmen, the Belgians, all of them putting up such courage. Last year, do you recall when the Germans rolled over the poor Russians at Tannenberg?" She shook her head. "All those young men gone, killed before they had a chance to live. *Why*—why must there be wars?"

For a long moment, they were both silent. In the distance she could see the very top of Adam's head, a strange configuration—that solid shape in the midst of the winding entanglement of vines set in straight even rows, their luxurious leaves protecting the rich clusters of tender young berries reaching toward the harvest.

"Your father—look at him. His world is out there. His wars rotate around those vines—or their product in the oak vats stored away out there in the tunnels." She sighed. "Anton, sometimes I wonder about the relativity of things in life. I think when I sit out there looking down at that rich valley floor, at the place of my birth, across at those mountains over there—" she waved one arm slowly, gracefully—"it should be enough. This should be the most peaceful place on earth. But there are all these little wars here too. It is the same, I suppose, everywhere. Yet sometimes I think about what's out there, over the ridge of those mountains. I know that all the valleys and mountains march to the seas, and the seas touch, link us with all those other places. In a way, we are one. Yet, read any newspaper! Waves of little wars lapping and lapping, mounting and swelling into this gigantic devastation, this suicide! Could Woodrow Wilson, could any man, do the right job? Does man *want* the right job done? Is man's destructiveness part of the seasons?"

Anton was looking at her curiously. They had never talked in this way before—as friends, actually. He heard the despondency, saw the cloud over her face. How truly lovely she was, he thought. How fond he was of her! Yes, there were moments when he realized how much he loved her. How much she had, alone, influenced him.

Suddenly he stood, impulsively kissed her on the forehead. "Mom Sarah, wouldn't it be delightful if you could come east with me? Wouldn't you adore visiting some of your old haunts? Seeing old friends? Going back to Wellesley for old times' sake? I'm sure Norman Jaspers can find a way to release money for you too. He's so terribly fond of you. He worries about your never going anywhere, always being up here on Spring Mountain."

"How nice of Norman," she said absently, her mind busy with serious consideration of Anton's proposal; trying to imagine the actuality of a trip back east.

"Come on—what do you say? We'd have a wonderful time!"

She smiled, shook her head slowly. "No, Anton—I couldn't."

"And why not? I tell you, I can arrange it through Norman!"

"It isn't the arrangements I'm worried about. It's . . . I've been back here too long now. I'd be totally out of step. Back east, everyone is so bent toward accomplishments. Even if I found old school chums, we'd be so out of touch! And I'm sure I'd end up feeling terribly inadequate—I'd find they had all done something marvelous with their education." She forced a frown off her face, thought a moment, then smiled at Anton. "I was just thinking the other day how very much Napa Valley *is* my life. My roots are here. Oh, there have been times when I have thought I'm a strange varietal grafted onto alien root stock —one that could never produce anything worthwhile. Times when I've felt . . . isolated. Yes, *resentful*. But maybe I'm getting old. I've come to love Spring Mountain. And of course I love your father." She glanced out, saw that Adam was slowly coming back toward the house. "Just as those vines are his main fulcrum, he is mine."

Anton had seen her face soften, the lines ease, a trace of her once great beauty creep into the still-lovely amber eyes. He was thinking about what Norman Jaspers had said: "Your stepmother was the most beautiful young woman I've ever seen."

She sipped the last of her Muscatel. "I'm glad you are going east, however. You have the flair, the personality, to do very, very well. Had we had more money—yes, I always wanted David to go, actually. But when I really think about it, I wonder how happy he'd be away from Napa Valley. He's so much like your father—as though he were truly born to the land. To be—how is it your father calls it?—a *steward* of the land."

Anton picked up his white linen jacket, slung it over one shoulder. "I must be going. I have promised a lovely young lady we'd have dinner together tonight." He looked down at Sarah. "I too love the land—in a certain way. Yes, even Napa Valley." His voice became intense. "But I have to live my life! I can't stand seeing people in this valley plodding along from one harvest to the next, their noses to the ground except for that one brief fling at looking up, feeling alive, every crush—then, like the vines, going into dormancy. Dreaming about next vintage. Me, I want to live my life now! Frankly, I love dancing, drinking—*and* girls." His eyes sparkled, a lighthearted smile crossed his handsome face. "Girls are delicious—like Papa's prize Muscatel." His face was turned now toward the vines, watching Adam's steady, even approach. "I hate the thought of war. Of having to go over there and fight with guns. But I would, if President Wilson declares war. I'd fight for our country if everyone else does. I'm just not going to rush into the Army and volunteer to get my head blown off in a trench."

"Anton, if we avoid the war, do you plan to come back here to Napa Valley when you finish school? Take over down valley?"

"Who knows? I'm not nineteen years old yet. I have time—a lot of time to decide."

She smiled with her own sense of irony. "Goodbye, dear. Wait for your father."

And, as she suspected, in his own way Adam was apologizing. "Son, let me see that fancy new car. Norman said he was going to let you have it for a good price."

Anton beamed. "He all but gave it to me. But Norman has so much money. He can afford it. Come on, I'll let you drive it if you'd like. I see you have a Ford."

"Nothing special. But it gets us where we're going," Adam said quietly. "I spent my money on a good solid truck for hauling grapes. Me, I don't have so much money. I don't have much of anything, sometimes. Maybe my temper eats it up, huh?"

Anton gave Sarah a wink across one shoulder. "You have plenty, Papa. You have Spring Mountain—the best vines in Napa Valley. Don't forget that."

Harvest was late that year. The grapes had been slow ripening, and growers throughout the valley were concerned they would lose the late ripeners to rains. Adam had made up his mind to crush heavily, stocking up as much as possible on bulk red wine and distilling a double amount of brandy in preparation for a long dry spell, should Prohibition become a reality. He would cut back on white wines, which, by and large, needed to be consumed more quickly and would not always ride out time.

Sarah was worried that he might overdo. "Hire extra help," she urged. "You're showing a bigger profit margin, I see. Norman said the price of grapes is going up steadily each harvest."

But even with added help, Adam still looked exhausted as the pitch of harvest got under way. Because of that, Sarah kept any disturbing war news to herself, not even telling him when the Germans executed the British nurse Edith Cavell for helping prisoners of war escape from Belgium to Holland.

It was the first week of November, after harvest was over, when Adam suddenly came to her one night after dinner and said, "I forgot to tell you." He rubbed one hand across his forehead, as though chastising himself. "Kyle Plimpton told me a few days ago that he heard Delfina Alfieri was sick."

"What's wrong with her?" Sarah asked, getting ready for bed.

He shrugged his shoulders. "I don't remember if Kyle said she was still sick or had been sick. How long has it been since you visited her?"

"Good heavens—not since the Fourth-of-July picnic."

"I was planning to go to Napa City tomorrow to try and catch Joseph Migliavacca and Alwyn Ever to talk over some new committee plans. Why don't I drop you off at the Alfieris' and pick you up on my way back?"

"Of course. I'd enjoy that. Yes, I'd like that a lot."

Adam looked at her thoughtfully. "Sarah, we didn't celebrate our anniversary at all this year. I guess we both forgot. Why don't we get away pretty soon? Take a trip to San Francisco—maybe we could go to Los Angeles. Dr. Yuill-Thornton would like some help down south. The Wets are gaining ground much too fast down there. We could work pleasure in with business. I know you're practical—you like everything to pay for itself," he said teasingly.

Adam did not get out of the car when he drove up in front of the rambling Alfieri house on Rutherford Crossroad. He was late; he wanted to catch Migliavacca before he went home for lunch. Sarah waved goodbye, went quickly toward the front door, unaware of what she was going to find inside.

The new Vittorio Alfieri home was a large white frame house built in 1910. A sprawling front porch wrapped around two full sides of the house, ending on the west corner in an octagonal-shaped dome, off which one entered a glassed-in sunporch, which the family referred to as "the childrens' playroom" and which was filled with several years' collected toys, books, those varied leftovers from hobbies taken on or abandoned through the different growth periods of the seven children. It also contained a large rectangular work table surrounded by a dozen straight-backed chairs. Scattered across the scratched, pencil-and-ink-marked table surface were hundreds of loose pieces of a jigsaw puzzle about one-third worked, a medium-sized spinning globe of the world, a large dictionary, a crumpled map of Italy spread open, a stack of tablets and a large glass filled with every possible size of broken crayons.

Inside the main house, most of the furnishings were of the late Victorian period: heavy overstuffed chairs, a red velvet settee with brass claw feet, an elaborate rosewood grand piano over which was draped a brightly colored silk scarf with long dangling tassels. On every flat surface—tabletops, desks, the mantels, the piano—stood variously shaped framed photographs that ranged from the babyhood of each of the seven children through their different Communions; snapshots showing wide, openmouth grins proudly displaying missing front teeth.

A sober-faced Lilliana, followed by the oldest girl, Theresa, both girls in their last year of high school (the oldest having been kept back a year during that period when Vittorio had taken his family into hiding on Howell Mountain), met Sarah at the front door. Immediately, she sensed the hush of severe illness in the house, having known it so well during Adam's long recuperative period.

She hugged and kissed each girl in turn, surprised at how beautiful Lilliana, particularly, had become since she had last paid attention to her. She held them at arm's length, seeing how both girls were taller than their mother; that both had that smooth olive-colored skin which seemed to glow. Lilliana was taller than Theresa, and, as if her added height had given her a fuller dimension in personality, she did not have the hesitancy, the shyness, of Theresa.

"I hear Delfina has been sick," Sarah said softly. "I just found out about it last night and came immediately. Is it—anything very serious?"

At the look in the black eyes staring at her as if groping through some fuzzy hurting space for reassurance, Lilliana's eyes filming over with tears, Sarah knew there was something terribly wrong. "What? How long has she been ill?"

Lilliana saw her sister's face crumble. She reached out and patted her shoulder. "You were up last night. Go get a nap, Theresa. I'll visit with Auntie Sarah and take her in to see Mother."

"Theresa, may I help you, dear? Oh, I'm so *sorry*!"

335

"I—I can't talk about it," Theresa blurted out. She turned and fled, going on tiptoe up the first six steps to the landing, hesitating, looking back at the stunned Sarah. "I'm awfully sorry—I'm so tired and upset. I will go take a little nap while you're here."

Sarah followed Lilliana into the parlor, sat down on the red velvet settee, looked imploringly at her. "Tell me, dear."

"I guess she had trouble a long time before but never told anyone. She used to have to go to bed at times to keep from hemorrhaging. She would just say it was 'female trouble.' But she started getting run-down, very pale—a strange color."

"I guess I did notice at the picnic that she looked tired. I commented on the fact that she had lost some weight, but she said she needed to, and I thought she was pleased about that."

"Papa finally made her go to the doctor in Napa City and get a checkup." Tears now spilled out of the corners of Lilliana's eyes. She swiped at them with the back of her hand. "I'm tired right now, too, I guess. Theresa and myself—we've tried to take turns sitting up wih her at night so Papa can get some rest. He's so upset he can hardly see straight as it is. He works so hard. He thinks it is all his fault—that if he had made more money back when . . . when he lost everything, that this wouldn't have happened. He thinks she worked too hard. Worried too much."

"Is it—it isn't *cancer?*"

"Yes," she said miserably. "All over. The doctor said it was too late to try to do anything. They operated on her, but they sewed her right back up and Papa insisted he bring her home. She hated the hospital so much. She knew . . . She must have heard somebody talking when they thought she was asleep. She said she wanted to come home to die."

"But no one told me! I would have been here long before now to help. Couldn't someone have told me?"

Lilliana looked bewildered. "Papa said we mustn't do that, because Mr. Donati—Uncle Adam—had helped us all so much as it was, and he had been sick and all with his heart attack. He said we must not."

"I must help now, then! As soon as Adam comes back, I will tell him to bring down some of my things. I will stay and relieve you girls. May I see her now? My dear Delfina . . ." Sarah was shaking her head, stunned so much by the news that it was difficult to grasp that her friend was about to die.

She stood up, found herself catching a glimpse of the photographs on the back of the piano, as though a panorama of the Alfieris' past was spinning rapidly before her eyes. She felt snatched back in space, in time.

Lilliana was leading her toward the stairs in the hallway. A large group photograph was there on the wall—a photo that had been taken, she gathered, on a recent Easter Sunday. The four girls and Delfina were standing in front, their faces dwarfed by their huge new Easter bonnets; behind them stood the three boys and Vittorio, standing in a stiff-backed, self-conscious row, looking as though the new neckties and high, stiff collars were more like harnesses around their necks.

She paused, one foot on the bottom step, as if caught by the strange silence in this house usually so alive with children's voices, with wonderful thick odors coming from the kitchen, with men's voices crackling with laughter and robust conversation, with wineglasses clicking in repeated *salutes*. Then she was following quickly behind the soft-stepping Lilliana, picking her way as lightly as possible up the squeaky stairs.

The sallow, emaciated form lying so still on the puffed-up white feather bed reminded Sarah more of a living skeleton around which somehow the flesh had managed to stay wrapped thinly than of the plump, pear-shaped, jolly Delfina she had always known. Automatically, Sarah's hands had seemed to grab at her stomach, as though pushing back at some lurching pain of her own. For a moment, she stood there in stunned horror, staring down at the dry, cracked lips and hearing the rattle of the shallow breathing. She hardly realized she herself was crying. A hot wave of near-nausea hit her—a burning guilt that she had not been down here long before, had stayed up on Spring Mountain wrapped in the cloak of Donati needs and issues, blind to her own dear friend's impending death.

She reached down, touched the damp, clammy forehead with light fingertips. Then, at Lilliana's motioning, she followed her out of the room into the hallway.

"The doctor was here a little while ago and gave her a big shot. Something for the pain. Would you like some coffee—to come to the kitchen with me? I'm fixing a puree the doctor wants me to try and feed her as soon as she wakes up."

Adam returned at four o'clock, only moments before an exhausted Vittorio and his sons came into the driveway in a pickup truck. Sarah ran out on the porch, where she could more easily prepare Adam for the news about Delfina. "You must go to Spring Mountain and bring down some clothes for me, all that I might need to stay until—until it's over. I can't leave her. I would have been here before, had I known."

Adam went in with her; came out of the room looking as if a horse had kicked him in the stomach. When Vittorio arrived, wordless, Adam threw his arms about the defeated little man who had been his friend and loyal worker, both of them unashamedly crying hot bitter tears.

"You should have told us," Adam scolded a little later, when Vittorio accepted a brandy Adam forced on him.

Vittorio's work-riddled hands shook as he lifted the glass to his lips. "I try . . . I decide if maybe I pray a lot, don't drink wine—maybe the Drys are right, it is a sin. God punishes me for everything by taking my Delfina."

"Drink!" Adam commanded. "You need a brandy. Are you sure there are no good doctors someplace? Maybe we can take her to San Francisco? They've got doctors. Maybe they can get her well again."

Vittorio shook his head forlornly. "She never complained. Too good to say, 'Vittorio, *sono ammalata.*' I say, what can I do? *Cosa c'è?*" Tears dripped off his cheeks, slid into the thin black beard which he kept neatly trimmed.

"How long? *Per quanto tempo?*" Adam asked gently.

Vittorio shrugged. "A few days—weeks? *Morte un estraneo qui.*"

Adam saw Sarah's questioning eyes; she did not understand Italian. "Vittorio, death is a stranger in most places, not just here. Sarah—she is moving in to help. I will be back with some of her things." He got up to go. "You stay," he said, then hurried out of the house.

The next few days seemed to go by in a blur. Yet Sarah had dedicated herself to bringing a sense of order, to trying to open some light into what seemed like a house of suddenly stricken mute people.

She insisted that the younger children do positive chores the moment they came home from school each day and had a quick refreshment. There were still some late-blooming fall mums, which she insisted be brought in, along with anything else that would suggest a bouquet. She gave the boys jobs of stacking winter wood, of raking the yard free of the leaves from the few deciduous trees. They took hulls from walnuts. She insisted that Lilliana and Theresa keep the cooky jar filled, urged them to help her with baking bread. "Your mother would not be happy to think there was not plenty of good food always on hand," she would tell them reassuringly.

"Neighbors bring food in," Lilliana said lamely.

"That is lovely and what they should do," Sarah said matter-of-factly. "But we must also have something to offer them when they do these nice things. It is hospitable. Delfina would want it."

By her presence, the girls were able to study for the examinations coming up before the Christmas break. She spent hours with them, trying to help them structure their thinking in a more conceptual manner, gathering those vital facts that would at least help them pass.

With the younger children, she had them draw pictures. "Draw cheerful pictures you think your mother would enjoy seeing if she were awake and feeling better." She put her arms comfortingly around each in turn as often as possible. "All of us feel pain," she would say when sometimes Delfina's cries could be heard through the house before the medicine could take effect. "We must try to replace the pain with something that is happy. Maybe it will help her, too."

After her first night in the house, she insisted that a cot be brought directly into Delfina's room, where she would sleep. "I am a light sleeper anyway," she told a protesting Vittorio. "It will make me very happy to be able to tend to her should she wake up. I'll be right there if she needs me. That way, you can relax a little more and get some rest that you need—for the family's sake."

Delfina did not seem aware too often of anything around her. Only of the pain that would bring her up from that protective web of unconsciousness and cause her to cry out, "Help me! Won't somebody please help me?" Sometimes she would say just the one word in Italian, "*Aiuto! Aiuto!* . . ." At which Sarah would rush blindly to her bedside, soothing her as best she could: wiping her clammy forehead with a cool wet cloth, plumping up soft feather pillows where Delfina's bones were beginning to break through and cause huge raw bedsores.

Then she sent word to Adam that Li Po must send his powder—a lot of the powder. "I don't know where or how he gets it," she told Adam frantically. "Dr. Williams says he is bound by law—he can only give so much per dose. It is not enough! It is inhuman for anyone to have that much pain. If Li Po can find whatever it takes don't ask questions!"

That same evening Adam came, bringing Li Po along with him. Li Po went in, looked at Delfina, came back to Sarah, who had taken the quick break to wash her face and freshen up a little. He handed four carefully wrapped packages, told her what to do.

It was the Friday of the first week of December, about three o'clock in the afternoon. Sarah had finished changing the bed, trying to comb Delfina's hair a little, and in general doing what she could. The powder Li Po had left had worked well. Sarah carefully saved it for those intervals when Dr. Williams' shots began to wear off. She had given Delfina a dose some twenty minutes before.

Suddenly, as she was straightening some things on top of the dresser, she heard Delfina's thin voice: "Sarah? Is that *you*?"

She ran to the bedside, grasped the fingers that felt like twigs. "Yes, dear. I'm with you. I've been here for some time now. I'm tending to the children. Taking care of everyone."

339

"Good . . . *molto buono*." A smile like a hovering shadow crossed the pale, drawn lips.

At that moment Lilliana tiptoed into the room, followed by the enormous kindly Luigi Pascarella, who had just learned about Delfina's illness, having been away working a job in Lake County for the past six weeks. As soon as he returned and heard the news, he had got into his Ford and headed straight to his friends' house.

Lilliana backed quickly out of the room, having left something cooking on the stove downstairs. Sarah released Delfina's hand reluctantly, went over to Luigi, who was standing there unsure of what to do next, twisting his hat back and forth in his huge thick hands. Sarah put one hand lightly on his arm.

"Luigi—it's so good to see you, dear. The most amazing thing just happened," she whispered excitedly to him. "For weeks now she has barely spoken anything. She just now called my name—she *knew* me."

Luigi put his hat on a chair, came uneasily behind Sarah to a closer stance near the bed. He looked as though he expected to knock something over in this room with its shades pulled, the smell of sickness heavy, of death at hand. Sarah was bending over to try to tell Delfina that Luigi had come. Suddenly she straightened, stiffened her back and turned as though she were no longer seeing Luigi. "Just a minute ago she—I told you—she spoke my name. She recognized me! But—Luigi, oh, don't look now. She is *dead*. Gone!" she cried out.

Luigi's steellike arm closed quickly around Sarah's shoulders as he saw her reeling slightly. "The priest—the last rites. We should—"

"He has been here every day, and he has given those. But I'm not Catholic . . . maybe there is something else to be done. Vittorio—we must send for him. He's working in St. Helena."

"I know," Luigi said gruffly. "He is working on one of Cesare's jobs. I'll go in my car and get him. The priest too. Adam—maybe we send word to Adam."

"Yes. We must contact everyone. But first we must have just the family."

The funeral was held that Sunday. After the burial at the St. Helena cemetery, a mute, heavy-hearted cluster of closest friends joined the grieving family at Vittorio's. A few neighbors had been there cleaning the house, seeing that coffee was on the stove and dishes of every type were out on the table for anyone who might want to eat. A Mrs. Porter had taken the children to her home for the night. By five o'clock, only Luigi, Kyle Plimpton, Emma, Sarah, Adam, and Father O'Brien were left with the stunned, swollen-eyed Vittorio.

It was then that Sarah voiced an idea that had been gradually taking shape. "Vittorio, I would like to offer our home to your children—your daughters, particularly, and the youngest boys. At least until this school year is over. They will need a woman. Lilliana and Theresa are virtually grown now. They can help out. I—all my life I've really wanted to have daughters. We have such a big house and it's empty. David will be home for summer, but Anton, as you know, is in Boston. He won't be on Spring Mountain, even if he does return. It would relieve you considerably. Would you agree to that?"

"Sarah, you're talking awfully loudly," Adam said, frowning. "Isn't this a bit sudden? Maybe Vittorio needs time."

Vittorio looked at them vacantly. "I—what do I say? This—it is no home without Delfina." He started crying again.

Father O'Brien took the floor. "Vittorio, I like the idea. I would want them attending parochial school as they've been doing all along. We'll expect the family at Mass every Sunday."

Adam jutted out his chin, as if he expected to have to defend himself against the priest's stern eye settling on him. Even now, all these years later, he still felt intimidated in the presence of priests. His own memories went back to an early experience in Pontremoli, where a fierce-eyed, unsmiling Father Julius seemed happiest swinging a cane across someone's shoulders, to the point where it had helped influence Giovanni Donati to take his sons permanently out of the local school and bring in the tutor, Dudley Farnsworth, on a permanent basis.

Sarah was looking at Father O'Brien, a wave of gratefulness coming over her. She felt that somehow by doing for the children she would be holding on longer to Delfina. She had loved her as much as any woman. She had taken her so for granted! Never imagining that she wouldn't be there.

Father O'Brien had seen the look. "How much time will you need, Sarah?"

"I should be ready in a few days. A week—would that be too long? Does that suit you, Vittorio?"

He shook his head numbly. "Sure, if Father O'Brien says we should do it." It was as though Vittorrio felt he had lost all right to make decisions. He had the look of a man begging for punishment that would remove the guilt he felt.

Sarah herself felt a weariness she had been fighting off these past weeks begin to catch up with her. "I will get a little rest. Then let's say next Sunday after Mass, bring them up and we'll all have dinner."

15

That Sunday, when Vittorio arrived with five of his seven children, Sarah rushed forth to welcome them (and try to make Vittorio more comfortable with his decision to leave his children under the Donati roof for at least the rest of the school term ahead—longer, it had been decided, if it proved more beneficial, particularly for the younger children).

And as she took in the sight of the open, eager faces of the children—who ranged in age from the youngest, the plump Rudolfo, to the tall, beautiful seventeen-year-old Lilliana—Sarah was struck by a sudden realization: there was, in spite of their age differences, an unmistakable Alfieri stamp on each. Unlike the Donati sons, the Alfieris had unmistakable similarities: thick, wavy black hair, large doe-looking, velvety-brown eyes, that smooth olive skin. And Sarah noted another thing: a certain ambience, a kind of natural acceptance they had of being exactly who they were, happy Alfieri children brought up as a tightly knit unit. Sarah had never seen that collective look so undeniably there. It made her more than ever in awe of the responsibility facing her.

"Where is Theresa?" she asked, noticing her absence.

Vittorio looked at the ground, up again. "All the time Theresa was crying for her mama. Father O'Brien spent a lot of time with her. Now she has decided she wants to be a nun. It is the only way."

Sarah saw his open suffering, his confusion. "I see." She put one hand lightly on his arm. "Please tell Theresa for me that if she should ever change her mind she will be welcome to join us here. We have a place for her."

From that time on, life changed drastically for Sarah. She found herself caught dizzily in a whirlwind of new, extremely rewarding activities.

As she would sometimes try to explain it to Adam, just before both of them fell into an exhausted sleep each night, "With someone else's children I don't have that feeling of—well, *guilt*. I am more objective with them. And I think I'm good for them right now. They need *me*. And they're such receptive, loving children. So very dear."

"That is because they had a lot of old-fashioned love, Italian style," Adam mumbled. "A close family. That is it. That is all."

"But that is everything!" she exclaimed.

Though she was frequently bone-tired, though she rarely took time out for herself any longer, a new kind of radiance and beauty came over Sarah. Where there had been before an unconscious kind of perpetual frown burrowing in between her eyes, now her eyes sparkled and were surrounded by laugh wrinkles. Where she had often brushed her hair back in a careful, too rigid chignon, now, with little attention spent on it, wisps of loose hair fell about her face, softening the age lines.

All too quickly, Christmas was upon them. Adam and Sarah both had flung themselves into the holiday, trying to create a happy spirit for the displaced children. David arrived in time to help wrap huge piles of gifts and to take charge of the smaller children, with Lilliana's assistance. Then came Christmas Day. The dining-room table was lengthened to its fullest, and when Sarah and Adam took their places at opposite ends they looked down crowded sides of the table at not only the five Alfieris in residence, but Bobby Alfieri, Vittorio, Joseph, Luigi, Emma and Kyle Plimpton (Emma had become enormously fat and developed elephantiasis, so that she had to sit on one side of Adam to keep her swollen feet propped up), Father O'Brien, and David. Rounds of toasts were given, a huge turkey was cut. Li Po bobbed in and out behind the screen, bringing delicacies prepared by both Sarah and Lilliana.

Even Joseph seemed less sullen, caught up in the more relaxed atmosphere with so many young ones around taking up his parents' attention and keeping him out of close scrutiny. Even so, Sarah had noticed that his pimples had cleared up—leaving deep acne scars; his hands were rough, his nails broken off from his work with Luigi. But he seemed happier now, quite at peace with himself.

After everyone had gone (with Vittorio having clasped each child close, tears streaming down his face as he headed back down to his empty house, with only his son Bobby for company, and a tipsy Emma and a resigned Kyle had waved goodbye, followed by the bellowing, happy voice of Luigi letting Joseph drive his Ford), Sarah and Adam sauntered into the parlor, hand in hand, to have a brandy and recapitulate the happy day's events. To their astonishment, there, locked in embrace, were David and Lilliana.

Lilliana's hands flew to her face and she stepped back, sending a branch of the tree swaying, an ornament crashing to the floor. "I—oh, I—" She fled from the room, her face a mortified red, her eyes brimming with startled tears.

David drew himself up, straightened his collar, took a moment to clear his throat. His jaw was jutted out defensively. "We have fallen in love," he said simply. "The last year when I was in high school, I knew I loved her. But she was too young then. Just beginning in high school. We—at the Fourth-of-July picnics, every harvest, we used to talk about it. How one day we would become engaged when the time was right." He looked from Sarah's stunned face to Adam's belligerent, confused expression. "We can't get married for a few years yet. But I asked her tonight to marry me and she just said yes—when you walked in. I know her. She thought it looked so bad before your eyes. She'll be ashamed to face you—but we've done nothing!"

Sarah stepped forward, held out both her hands. "David, I'm happy for you," she said, then hugged him tightly. "You couldn't choose a lovelier girl! A nicer girl. As you know, I love her as though she were my own daughter. It's just that we never dreamed . . . You kept it so secret!"

Adam went over, poured out three tumblers half full of brandy. "Then we drink to that," he said, bringing himself around. He was looking at David as though he were only now just seeing him as a young man. "A fine Italian girl. She will make a good wife for you. Give you lots of nice children. Fine sons."

David concentrated on swirling the brandy. "Thank you. Thank you for understanding. I—I guess I've never been in love before. I have seen lots of girls at Berkeley, but I kept thinking about Lilliana. Not wanting to court anyone else. Just as I've always known I will probably become an oenologist—a viticulturist, I've always known I would one day marry her. I *thought* she would say yes. I was so afraid, though. I—" He lifted his head quietly, proudly. "I guess she sees something in me. She feels the same."

Sarah left David and Adam to talk and hurried up the back stairs to the room assigned to Lilliana, knocked lightly on her door, found her sitting in a chair by the window, her hands clasped tightly in her lap. Lilliana stood, looked at Sarah with wide, questioning eyes. "I hope— oh, please don't think badly of me! It must have seemed to you that—"

Sarah went to her with her arms outstretched. "I am just so very happy for you both," she said as they hugged each other, each shedding tears from different origins. "I remember how it was when I fell in love with Adam—David's father." She stood back from Lilliana a moment, searching the lovely face with the deep-set brown eyes, the complexion like smooth satin. "But you—you will have the family's full blessing. And I know that Delfina would have been so deeply happy about this. Surely yours will be a perfect union. Oh, I wish you such happiness, my dear! Delfina once said to me—Do you remember when you were in my room just before my wedding—little girls then, yes— and your adorably sweet mother brought the flowers to me and said, 'Wishing you lots of babies'? Was it Delfina, you or Theresa?"

Lilliana was silently crying. "I said it. Mother had us memorize our speeches. Yes—oh, I do remember. I think I must have decided then that I loved David. I think I knew it that far back."

"Does Vittorio—your father know?"

"David only just asked me—officially proposed tonight. We plan to tell him tomorrow. To go down home, if that will be all right with you. If you won't need me here to help with the children."

"No, of course not. When do you think you might get married, dear?"

"I want to go to school. I promised my mother I would do that. Get a college education. It was her dream—to see some of us go on through school. Papa says he will send me. I hope to go where David is. He may transfer to Davis sooner than he had originally planned now. I can study something there that will help—that will give me a back-ground to understand David's work. We want to be a team. Go through life a team."

Sarah patted Lilliana's arm lightly. "Adam and I will see if we can help. One of these days, David will inherit Spring Mountain. This will be your home. I want you to know that. It's a lovely place for raising a family!"

Lilliana smiled, but there was something restrained in her expres-sion. "Whatever David decides," she said quietly.

When Adam and Sarah finally got to bed that night, Adam folded his arms lightly around her. "How about that, huh, our own boy get-ting married! Falling in love."

"I guess I still can't believe it happened right under our noses and we didn't see what was taking place. I—I guess I expected David would one day meet *someone*, but I was thinking about sometime out there, off in the future. Are they rushing into this? Aren't they awfully young yet, Adam?"

"So who keeps love racked—stored off in a vat in some dark

tunnel waiting for it to age, huh? Since when did that happen?" And as in the old days, he began working his hands feverishly to remove her nightgown; was making love to her as with some lost, nearly forgotten passion, as though reassuring himself that his son's new threshold of manhood in life had not necessarily deprived him of his own.

The year of 1916 seemed to whirl both Sarah and Adam into accelerated, often dizzifying activities. Her days were spent trying to establish wholesome routines for the Alfieri children, teaching them a hundred and one things she thought might prove useful to them, both in character-building attributes and as tools to use in the educational process. Adam, in turn, was working full time helping solidify forces to defeat the two amendments slated for the upcoming November ballot —as well as trying to convince voters that Woodrow Wilson must go, that any President would be better for the California wine industry.

In early January he went along with Bismarck Bruck and E.W. Churchill to attend the California Grape Protective Association's meeting in the Phelan Building in San Francisco, along with over 150 of California's most prominent grape growers and winemakers.

He decided to stay at the new Palace Hotel; signed in for a three-day visit, having several business meetings to attend.

Though Adam had always planned to come back and stay at the Palace Hotel, once it had reopened following the earthquake, he had somehow not been able to reach the point where he could coordinate Sarah, events in Napa Valley, and their vacillating finances, and pull it off. It had reopened in December, 1909; here it was January 8, 1916, he was thinking, looking about with astonishment at this glittering new hotel built on the very ashes of the old—in many ways along the same lines, though Adam thought it even grander than before.

As he signed in at the desk, he looked about at the twenty-foot ceilings, the chandeliers, the thick carpets, the marble arches. Before going up to his room—one of some six hundred—he wandered about, glancing into five ballrooms off the lobby, magnificently decorated in white and gold, constructed so that all five could be opened up to serve up to three thousand people.

He went into the Palace Bar, ordered a brandy, stared at the Max-field Parrish mural of the Pied Piper.

He had saved the Garden Court until the last. When he entered the space where once the carriages had rolled in, he felt himself take a deep breath at the astounding beauty of the palm-filled court with its marble Ionic colums, its elaborate crystal chandeliers, its lofty, iridescent glass roof.

Yes, he must bring Sarah here very soon, he told himself emphatically. He had put their second honeymoon off too long. Neither of them was getting any younger. Time . . . it wound its tendrils around you, made you forget. . . .

The meeting went well. A resolution was passed charging that the California Campaign Federation's Prohibition amendments were contrary to federal and state policies which had encouraged the growth and expansion of viticulture since 1862. Committees were formed to branch out across the state and bring voters in to the polls in November to soundly defeat the Prohibitionists.

On their return to Napa County, Bismarck Bruck addressed over a hundred Napa County grape growers and winemen formulating their stepped-up local campaign. Bruck reported to them his efforts to pass a state constitutional amendment which would guarantee compensation to all involved in the related business—grape growers, hop men, brewers, and so forth—before any prohibition could become effective. He ended his speech saying, "Let's fight *for* something, instead of always fighting against something."

While Adam intently went about working with and for the committee, having himself been put in full charge of the letter-writing campaign (his precise usage of English in the written word having been highly praised by the group), Sarah was busy instituting certain programs of her own on Spring Mountain with her new charges, the Alfieri children.

It was obvious that they had not been well grounded in the basic tools of studying—which was understandable, since neither Vittorio nor Delfina had had much formal education. They were all bright, willing to learn. And unlike the old days, when she had tried so hard to work with the belligerent Joseph and sort through frictions raging among all three boys, she found the Alfieris always cooperative.

One of her teaching tools had been to have all participate in drawing and coloring a huge world map and placing it next to the homework table in the kitchen. As the World War continued, each country was assigned a specific color, and the children took turns coloring in those territories Germany seemed to continue to take. Battles were marked with tiny flags: blue for the Allied forces; red for the German, Central Powers forces. She encouraged discussion of events as they became known to them in the local papers. "At least you will know geography and current history," she would say to them, when, for instance, they would recount how long the battle of Verdun in north-

good stuff." The veins on his neck were knotting with rising fury. "People are out there drinking wine for the first time in their lives. But you can't call that raw red vinegar *wine*! This Prohibition will set real winemakers back fifty years."

Sarah put one arm lightly across his stiff one. "Back to Anton, dear. Let's give him a chance. He's so very bright. Surely as he grows older he will—"

"He'll *what*? Look, even if repeal comes around—say it did, and I turned him loose with *my* grapes and the very latest winemaking equipment, do you think he'd know beans?" He stalked across the veranda.

"What about David? You can't say that about him," she said.

Adam glared at her. "What about David? Why did he sneak off and get married? Why is he down there at Alfieri's place and not up here learning how to run this place that will be his?"

"Adam, you aren't being fair," Sarah said, irritated now. "You know neither David nor Lilliana had any money—they struggled so hard to get their degrees. David didn't have the easy handout that Anton had." She saw Adam's stern look, added quickly, "I know Delfina would be pleased that Lilliana has such a sense of family responsibility and is helping her brothers and sisters."

"Maybe you're right," Adam said gruffly. "Maybe I'm put out with David because he didn't let us in on the wedding." He frowned, worked his jaw about. "I guess I always thought when one of the boys got married we'd have a big celebration. Fill up the whole house, the way we used to do in Pontremoli." His voice dropped. "When I built this big place I thought—oh, never mind. But with David and Lilliana's wedding, we didn't even drink a toast!"

"That *was* disappointing," she said, understanding now.

"A lot in life is disappointing," Adam said, irony etched on his face. "Come on—let's take a walk and get some exercise before dark. See what's left on Spring Mountain that isn't either bolted shut by the government's men or falling apart somehow."

They headed around the side of the main house. Just as they were about to cross the driveway toward the winery, he suddenly drew back, pushed Sarah firmly against the wall. "It's them—those dirty bastards back bothering my men again!"

"What? What *is* it, Adam?" she asked hoarsely, stunned by his abruptness and the angry look on his face.

"Prasso and his carload of crooks."

"But harvest is over. Your grapes are sold. What could—"

"They don't give up. They don't take no. They think they can talk me into selling what I have hidden. I'm not selling to them or anybody else!"

Her voice made a croaking sound. "Adam, you said you didn't *have* anything that—"

"Sarah, I want you to go back inside the house. Now!"

She clung stubbornly to the wall. "I'm afraid, Adam!"

He took her by the shoulders. "Listen to me," he said in a low urgent voice. "I am *not* a bootlegger. I never will become one. Those cheap crooks think they can scare me, but they can't. They've been trying to bribe Kyle, threaten my pickers. . . . I wasn't going to tell you. But I've hired a couple of good men to stay on down at the bunkhouse. They've got shotguns and they know how to use them. So don't worry. But, *please*, go inside."

"I don't want any shooting going on up here!" she cried out in a desperate whisper. "Why don't we get the sheriff? There are ways of keeping them from trespassing. There are *laws*, Adam. What is happening to Napa Valley? It never was like this before."

He was glancing around the corner. The bunkhouse was five hundred yards away. He could see Paulo and Gus waving shotguns; old befuddled Adolfo out waving both canes in the air. "Prohibition has happened. All the worms in the woodwork are coming out in broad daylight. But they can't scare me. And we don't need the sheriff. I've had enough of him and his deputies—and the revenue agents snooping around up here!" He was quiet a moment. "They're leaving now. I'm going down to find out what they had to say *this* time. Wait inside."

He gave her a firm push toward the house, hurried off.

Sarah made her way reluctantly around the side of the house into the front hallway. She felt cold, shivery, and headed upstairs to get a sweater. As she passed Adam's study she saw a log simmering in the fireplace and went inside, stood in front of the hot glowing embers trying to pull warmth inside herself.

After a moment she wandered over to the window seat, stared out blankly at the panoramic view of the valley spread out so vibrantly alive and still rich with late-autumn colors made more glowing in the sunset. How peaceful—yes, how eternal it looked. And how unchanged. Yet everything was so different, she thought bitterly, biting her lip to hold down her anxiety.

She heard the sound of Adam's footsteps on the back stairs. Hurrying down the hallway, she was waiting for him at the bedroom door just as he stalked up the last step.

"What happened?"

"My men think I ought to go straight to my lawyer and ask his advice," Adam said, brushing past her and going to his wardrobe, where he began searching for a suit and a clean white shirt. "Get ready. I want you to go with me. If you are afraid, the way you said you were, I won't leave you up here alone."

She looked at him curiously, then went quickly to her closet, her hands moving nervously down a row of dresses.

"Are we going to Norman's *house*?" She was frowning. "Won't we catch him in the middle of his dinner hour? Is that polite of us to do?"

"He's my lawyer, isn't he? I need his advice. It's his job."

"What should I wear?" She was staring at the dresses.

"Wear? A dress!" He was working his long legs into the trousers of his dark-blue striped suit, stuffing the crisply starched ends of his shirt into them.

She pulled out a new cream-colored light wool dress trimmed in rich brown velvet—a dress that Anton had brought to her from England, and one she had never quite found the nerve to wear, since it had been styled along modern lines, the skirt cut on the bias, shorter than she was used to wearing, with the cuffs of the long tapered sleeves tighter than she was comfortable wearing. Too, Anton had insisted that she must always wear high-heeled pumps and a brown velvet cloche to complete the look.

She felt flushed, too much in a hurry. They so rarely went anywhere, and never on the spur of the moment. She fumbled with the row of tiny velvet buttons, snapped the cuffs closed. Her hair was a mess, she thought, trying to stuff the wad of it under the head-hugging cloche and pull the hat down over her ears, low on her forehead the way Anton told her it should be worn. Adam was ready, waiting impatiently for her to finish dressing. She dabbed spots of rouge on her cheeks, reached for a purse.

He was scowling at her now. "Isn't that dress awfully short? Can you walk in those shoes? When did you buy *that* outfit?"

"Anton bought it for me—a present from Europe," she said, going out into the hallway, trying to soften the clicking, hollow sounds of the high heels against bare wood floors; holding on tightly to keep from falling as she made her way downstairs. If she heard Adam's mumbled retort "Won't be the first dumb thing Anton's come up with!" she made no sign of acknowledgment.

At the front door, Adam turned quickly to Li Po, who was looking at them curiously, his alert eyes taking in Sarah's unusual new look, his mind astutely sensing that something was wrong.

"Don't let anybody come inside this house for any reason," Adam commanded. "Keep this door locked until we get back."

Li Po's head bobbed up and down. Sarah heard the bolt click into place the moment they were out on the stone veranda.

The evening winds whipping across Spring Mountain made Sarah grateful she had selected something woolen. The velvet cloche, as strange as she thought she looked in it, did keep her hair out of her eyes. Though it was hard walking in the high heels, she felt lighter, younger on her feet. She felt oddly graceful, feeling the swirling folds of the skirt follow in easy movement as she hurried along the pathway, climbed up into the high front seat of the old Ford while Adam cranked it to a start.

While she waited for him to get in, she looked around nervously; for the first time on Spring Mountain, feeling afraid of noises she had, in the past, taken for granted: the wind rustling through the pine trees; the pawing and snorting from those few horses left in the stables, and one old mare letting out a whinny. As the narrow tires ground their way down the driveway, working in and out of ruts, she was actually relieved to be leaving her own home, she thought ironically, as Adam worked the gear pedals with his feet, moved the gas feeder on the steering wheel with his right hand.

They had just gone around the last hairpin curve near the foot of the long, winding steep road when Adam slowed down to a near-stop to allow another car to pass in the opposite direction, headed up Spring Mountain. It was an older Oldsmobile, with a crumpled front fender and broken headlight. She could see the shadowed faces of several men in the car. But the light was not strong enough to distinguish actual features. Even so, she felt nearly positive that she had seen Joseph in the back seat.

She looked at Adam's set jaw, at his hands gripped tightly on the steering wheel as he headed on down toward the level stretch of Madrona, then toward St. Helena's Main Street. Apparently he had not recognized anyone. And maybe she was just being jumpy. After all, cars used Spring Mountain's county road frequently to get over to Sonoma County and Santa Rosa.

As they made their way down Main Street and passed on through the town Sarah had known all of her life, lights were already glowing inside houses along the way. She began to relax. In one way, it was invigorating to be dressed up, going out with Adam. She let the refreshing wind from Adam's open window whip across her face. Yes, when this trouble passed, they should make a point of going out together more often, she told herself.

How strange it seemed, she suddenly thought, to be going back to the house she had grown up in—seeing it with Adam for the first time together. She wasn't sure why she had waited so long. She could have gone before. She was curious enough to see how the money Norman Jaspers had reportedly spent on the place had changed it. Yet, in another way, she dreaded going back. When she had buried her mother and father in such quick succession she had deliberately buried that part of her past. Of course, inescapably, there were times when it caught up with her—for instance, when she might be opening a drawer of an antique bureau, a piece of Hubbard furniture she had promised her mother she would keep in the family as long as there was Hubbard blood left; or, say, should she be folding a stack of choice Hubbard linens and turn, half expecting to see her mother's age-shriveled hands, with their ruby and diamond rings riding loosely to one side, waving a stern rebuke, showing her how, precisely, she should have folded the stack instead. But mostly, when her mother's face caught up with her, it was not, oddly, the face most people remembered as being "Miss Grace's," but that last sallow-skinned, ravaged face of an old woman fighting to the last to keep death away. Now and then, her father's features would float in wavery, vague lines across her memory, his image varying as it used to vary in real life, according to the particular stage of the particular binge he was on.

But now, as she slid down out of the old Ford, her toes in the new high-heeled pumps searching for solid footing, as she looked about and saw the familiar Victorian guest house, the water tower with its ginger-bread trim—both incongruous in contrast to the formal Greek Revival lines of the "plantation" house Miss Grace had constructed—it was as though the full past, in full clarity, hurtled toward her, threatening to engulf her senses.

Adam was at her elbow, his firm hand guiding her toward a white-coated Japanese houseboy standing on the back stoop looking at them with a puzzled frown. Sarah saw his immaculate starched white coat, the crisp black trousers and the carefully tied black bow tie, and thought of Li Po in his floppy, baggy pants, his old straw slippers and his long-out-of-fashion queue flapping down his back.

"We're here to see Mr. Jaspers," Adam was saying briskly.

Norman came around the corner of the brick terrace that wrapped around three sides of the enormous mansion. He was dabbing at the corners of his mouth with a linen napkin.

"Adam . . . Sarah. What a surprise." He sensed they had not come for pleasure, and he changed his tone to one he might well have used with any client at his office. Yet he felt his pulse jump at the unex-

377

pected sight of Sarah dressed more stylishly than he would have expected of her, and he realized how long he had waited to show her his renovations of her home place. "It's so good to see both of you. Come inside."

He led them across the terrace toward the front entrance, past the large Corinthian columns marching in a row, beneath the glistening, many-coated enameled ceiling of the downstairs gallery. Sarah took in the sight of the ceramic urns planted with exotic palm trees, the heavy ornate wrought-iron furniture, the freshly painted floor-to-ceiling outdoor shutters, and the gleaming white of the stucco exterior of the main house.

"Have you had dinner?" Norman was saying as naturally as possible. "Won't you join me? Dessert and coffee, perhaps? A cup of tea?"

He held the huge double doors open and directed them to step inside the wide, high-ceilinged foyer with its newly installed black-and-white marble-tiled floor laid in diamond shapes. Towering palms in porcelain urns extended the feel of the outer brick terrace on into the main house. Everywhere, it seemed, there were softly glowing crystals, either in overhead chandeliers or in sconces alongside mirrors.

Adam held his head stiffly, as if trying to shut out a full view of so much opulence. Sarah found herself looking about curiously, in all directions. She did not receive the full change and its shock until they stepped into the main downstairs parlor.

Her memories of this room were ones filled with Hubbard heirlooms: English pieces mostly, from the seventeenth century on; Oriental rugs sometimes lapping one onto the other; huge somber family portraits of long-dead Hubbard ancestors dominating every wall (portraits that were now scattered throughout the stone house on Spring Mountain). Now she was staring at dark, heavy Oriental furniture, every piece intricately carved and some inlaid with mother-of-pearl. There were porcelain jugs with dragon heads leering, Chinese lamps, smaller vases, figurines standing on every surface. Shelves that she had remembered as holding leatherbound books from the Mississippi Hubbard house now held a collection of jade—pink, white, green jade figures, vases, carved scenes in miniature bottles. Running accordion-shaped along one wall was a twenty-foot-wide screen encrusted with jadeite and other semiprecious stones. Where portraits had once hung, silk scrolls now covered the walls. The floor had one large blue-and-white Oriental rug.

"Do you like it?" Norman asked tentatively from the doorway.

"It's—it's very different. It's . . . very nice."

He laughed. "One either likes it, usually, or doesn't."

Adam said nothing. He sat down as though expecting to break something. Before the houseboy could serve the tea he had requested, he leaned forward and blurted out to Norman, "Those crooks from Chicago are back. This time they were threatening my men at the bunkhouse. Last time they were trying to bribe Kyle Plimpton into telling them where I have my stuff hidden." He slapped one hand into the other. "I need your advice."

Norman sat down, juggled his own cup and saucer. "I was afraid it was something like that," he said quietly. "There's a rumor going through the courthouse. Seems the sheriff and his deputies and a big government force of revenue men are planning a wide sweep through the valley pretty soon. A major crackdown. Maybe Prasso and his gang are getting nervous. They know the heat's on and are trying to get out with a nice haul as they run." He was silent a moment, staring into his tea. "Adam, I know you say you *haven't* been operating a distillery, running off anything."

"That's right." Adam's eyes had narrowed.

"Well, I overheard some talk. Seems the word's out there's a big important hot spot on Spring Mountain. I heard the name Donati being tossed about a lot." He looked from Sarah to Adam. "Look, I'm your lawyer—your friend. You have to be honest with *me*, Adam! If you have anything going on up there I urge you to tell me now. We've got to get rid of any evidence very, very quickly. The jail sentences and fines are going to get stiffer. I'd hate to see you—a proud and cultured man—embarrassed by either. I—I know your good name is important to you and —"

Adam got up abruptly. "What you are saying to me is that you think I am really running a still on Spring Mountain—isn't that what you are saying?"

"I am saying that there are those around who think you are. I am not saying *I* believe it, but I am asking . . ."

Adam slammed his cup and saucer down on a round black teak table with thick, squatty legs. He nodded his head at Sarah. "I told you they busted up my Sanders still and locked up what parts were left. I haven't touched a still of any kind—pot still, *any* kind of still—since then!" He shrugged his shoulders, a bitter line to his mouth, "Sure, I have some stuff hidden. My prize brandies and my premium wines. Inventory I haven't reported. But it's not for sale. Nobody has even been offered a sampling taste of any of it. I'm letting it age. Keeping it as stock to have on hand if repeal ever does come about. Sure, I make my two-hundred-gallon quota every harvest. To keep my hand flexible. My skills up. I've done a little experimenting. But that is not the same as bootlegging! Only three people know where I've got it hid. Not even Sarah or my sons know. Only Kyle Plimpton and my two cellarmen. Nobody else." He turned his hat in his hands. "Come on, Sarah. Since my lawyer doesn't have any advice for me, we'll head back to Spring Mountain. I'll take care of my own problems, my *own* way. Sorry we interrupted your dinner. It wasn't very polite of us. We won't do that again."

"Wait a moment!" Norman called out, getting up and hurrying after Adam's long strides. Sarah flung a desperate, apologetic look over her shoulder as she was pulled along by Adam's firm grip on her hand. "If you don't have anything illegal going on up there on your property, then you don't have anything to worry about! This secret cache of yours—is it truly well hidden, Adam? Is there any possible chance the sheriff or the revenue men have found out about it? You mentioned Kyle and your cellarmen. Can you trust them? I ask as your lawyer. Dammit! *Stop*—listen to me a minute, Adam."

Adam had reached the end of the brick terrace. He turned, his eyes like cold steel bands. "My men, they don't talk. They are my friends. My trusted friends. We stick together."

"These cellarmen—I don't know them, do I?"

"No. They are Italians who don't speak English," Adam said, holding Sarah's elbow, giving her a nudge to head toward the old Ford parked alongside Norman's gleaming new Packard. "Sorry again that we barged in on you during your dinner. I would have waited for office hours, but those men came late this afternoon. Next time I'll get a regular appointment."

Norman's voice sounded thin, urgent. "Please—you know I always welcome you, here or at my office. Adam, don't leave angry! If I insulted you I am—"

Adam was climbing into the Ford, having cranked it, having turned on the huge headlights. "I'm not angry," he called back down. "It's just I've got to tell my men what to do—in case the crooks come back."

The whole visit had lasted little more than ten minutes. As they headed back toward St. Helena, close to the Rutherford crossroad, Sarah reached out and touched Adam on the arm. "Let's drive by Vittorio's place. We have come this far and—couldn't we?"

He slowed down, turned right and headed toward the Silverado Trail. "I guess we *are* dressed up with no place to go. It was a mistake. I should have known he wouldn't know anything worth listening to." They rode in silence a moment. The Alfieri house was about midway on the crossroad. As the lights of the rambling house came into view, Adam said in a stiff voice, "I used to tell myself that one of these years we'd have a really good year and I'd take us on a long trip." He turned left into the Alfieri driveway, headed toward the porte cochere. "Maybe this is the time for us to go someplace. Pack up, buy some tickets for a long ship ride. Take a boat to Europe. See Paris, Switzerland. My brother says Italy's not so hot right now. What do you say? Want to go on a trip? Our second honeymoon finally?" He turned the lights off, kept his hands gripped around the steering wheel.

She looked at him thoughtfully in the muted light from a half-moon. "Adam, I don't want to go just to run away from trouble. But if this blows over, how about next spring? The weather would be better then anyway. Maybe by then people in this valley will know we're on the up and up on Spring Mountain."

"Okay—next spring." He swung out of the Ford, came around to help her down.

At the Alfieris' they were surprised to find Anton—along with his date for the evening, Diane Margolis, a secretary who worked for Norman Jaspers—visiting with David and Lilliana. They were all gathered around the work table on the sunporch, where Anton was busy showing the Alfieri children a word game he had learned back east. Sarah tried to absorb this unusual sight; but though she was pleased, she felt peculiarly left out, somewhat abandoned. Certainly it wasn't jealousy, she reprimanded herself. No, it was just that she felt lonely, in a totally new and different way. She greeted them, however, with a kind of forced animation, hugging the Alfieri children, Lilliana, David, shaking hands with Diane Margolis—an attractive girl whom she liked immediately—and then letting Anton push her back at arm's length.

"Look at Mom Sarah! You look divine. The dress is perfect on you."

"Where's Vittorio?" Adam asked gruffly, looking about.

"Working a job in Vallejo with Luigi," David said, in his easy, slow and deliberate way. He led them into the parlor, leaving the Alfieri children at work on their new game. "If I'd dreamed that you and Mother would be out and about, I would have invited you to join us tonight for our—well, celebration, I guess you'd call it." He poured out brandy for everyone. "You see, we asked Anton over. Today the doctor told Lilliana she'll have a baby in early May. Six months from now. How about that?"

Adam's jaw worked vigorously; a lump had hit his throat. "That is news, son," he said huskily. "*Salute*—to your future son!"

Lilliana's eyes were as soft as the brown velvet on Sarah's dress. "What if it is a *girl*, Papa Adam?" she asked gently.

Adam looked at Sarah, as if searching through her for a quick answer. Then he laughed. "Donatis always have boys! I am one of four boys. David, didn't I have three sons? No, it will be a *boy*. We drink to that. *Salute!*"

Sarah and the girls went out on the sunporch with the children so that Adam could talk with David and Anton about what had taken place on Spring Mountain. David looked at Adam, frowned in much the same way that Adam always did. "They came around here not long ago. Trying to get Vittorio to say he knew where you had some brandy hidden. This Prohibition business is getting mean. I don't like what's happening at all. I thought we'd see some end to it by now. But it's been over two years and I don't see any signs of it letting up. And now that the big-time bootleggers see what kinds of profit can be made, they won't *want* the country to go wet again. They'll help keep it dry!"

Anton was looking at David and Adam thoughtfully, his long, thin face like something finely chiseled. "Papa, I think David and I should go up to Spring Mountain with you tonight." He lifted one eyebrow. "Is that okay with you, David?"

"I—well, I suppose. Lilliana and I—we were—"

Adam worked his chin. "Don't waste your time. We can manage. I have good men up at the bunkhouse. Those Prasso fellows are probably in Sonoma County by now anyway."

Anton narrowed his pale gray-blue eyes. "I had lunch with Norman Jaspers the other day. He was telling me about a couple of rumors he's been hearing. I say we should go stay a few days. Look, I'll take my date home early. Head out with her now. I'll be on up pretty quickly. Leave a door open for me. I seem to have misplaced my house key from up there."

"I told you, we can manage," Adam protested.

"Look, Papa, you always used to say that Donatis should stick together. When we were in school and having that trouble with the Missouri boys, you told us to stand up and fight together. So isn't it the same thing, now that we are men?"

"Suit yourself," Adam said, looking at Anton in a puzzled way, as though no longer sure about what made him tick.

David came back into the parlor. "Lilliana says she thinks I should go. Besides, I left some things up on Spring Mountain I could use down here. And I was wondering, Papa: maybe I could bring a couple of horses down for the children to ride—that is, if you aren't using them in the fields. Maybe an old buggy? Give them a little fun. We've got good pasture."

"Sure—take the mare. Hell, take them all if you want them. I use the truck and my Ford these days. I don't ride horses any longer. Getting too old. My heart attack stopped that. The doctor advised me to curb certain things."

They decided, then, that David would ride up with them and drive the horses back down on his return. They climbed into the Ford, waved through the darkness with a half-moon shedding some muted light.

"I'll probably be back tomorrow," David called out to Lilliana, who stood with her arms around her two sisters.

Anton's roadster sent gravel flying as he backed out, the red taillights bobbing out of sight. "A nice girl, that Diane Margolis," Sarah said absently. "Anton seems to be settling down a little."

David leaned forward in the back seat, propped his chin on his folded hands, looking straight ahead at the two shoots of light from the Ford's huge headlights. "I get along with him a lot better than I used to. But I wouldn't say he's all that settled down. Anton's getting restless. He wants everything to happen *yesterday*. Patience, waiting for something to develop, is not his idea of life." He drummed his fingertips against the leather near Sarah's velvet cloche. "Papa, you certainly had three sons who aren't very much alike. Have you seen Joseph lately?"

They had just gone down Main Street and turned left on Madrona and were heading toward Spring Mountain. "No. He stays away as much as he can. Luigi makes him come to see us once in a while."

"He must be making a lot of money," David said drily. "Wearing a fancy new suit, driving a new car the last time I saw him. Being quite the big shot—strutting up and down Main Street with one of the redheaded Mulligan girls hanging on his arm like a cheap floozie from a sideshow."

"He's what he is, I guess," Adam said dispiritedly, pressing down on the pedal that put the Ford in low for the climb up. He didn't feel like talking about Joseph. He was tired tonight. What energy he had left he'd save for more pleasant topics. Maybe it was all the excitement, the added energy and exertion it had taken getting dressed up and calling on Norman Jaspers—trying to juggle that mistake around so it would sit more comfortably in his mind; then going by David's and getting the news he was going to be a grandparent—trying to fit that odd-sounding category into its right place. Now he didn't feel so hot. He felt drained. Tired to the bone. The bed would feel good tonight.

Sarah and David were chatting idly, Sarah saying, "If Anton will only choose one girl and marry her. That would help him immeasurably. But Joseph—I don't think the Mulligan girl . . . well, I'd prefer that he look a little higher up."

"Anton will marry when he finds someone rich enough," David said drily. "Joseph—who knows what he'll do next?"

"At least *you* chose so wisely, dear. Lilliana is a lovely, wonderful girl. I'm so pleased about the baby."

The Ford was making it up the mountain again, Adam thought, relaxing a little and turning off the main county road into the driveway. He'd start looking around for a new car now that he had made the unexpected profit at harvest. Now that he could afford it. Not that he'd pick out anything as flashy as the car Norman Jaspers was driving.

His thoughts seemed to bounce, jog along with the movement of the narrow tires working over and around ruts and holes in the long road leading to the stable and the main house. He'd try to get some paving done, too, after the coming winter and the spring rains were over, he was thinking, squinting without his glasses as he tried to guide the old Ford as smoothly as possible. They were nearly there. One last turn and he'd be home—only minutes away from a good night's rest . . .

As with any unexpected sudden sight, it took him a moment to register it, slot it in his mind. For a moment, the sight of the lanterns circling and bobbing outside the bunkhouse doorway made Adam think it was the harvest—a late crush, with cellarmen milling about still.

The wavering narrow slits of lights from the Ford cut ribbons across the space between the car and the men outside the bunkhouse. In the back seat, David had tensed, was leaning forward trying to see what was taking place. "What is it, Papa? Should we turn around? Go back?"

Adam himself had thought about turning around, but at that spot in the driveway it was too narrow, and in order to do so he would have to go in front of the cluster of men, whose faces were now looming into focus along with a row of parked cars—including one he recognized as belonging to the regular revenue man who had been coming around asking so many questions lately. He pulled the Ford to a stop in its regular place, his hands gripped tightly around the wheel. "I see the sheriff is here with his deputies—and the revenue men."

Before he could open the door, the bobbing lanters were closing in around the car and the sheriff's own crackly voice boomed out: "Okay, Donati—out! Hands up. You're under arrest."

384

Sarah felt the door on her side being yanked open. She grabbed at her purse, her hands fluttering, as if searching for something substantial that would give her lasting security.

"Everybody out. Throw out any guns you've got in there first," came the growl of a deputy's deep voice.

"Get your hands off my mother!" David shot out, trying to get out ahead of Sarah.

"What's this all about? What the hell you mean, I'm under *arrest*?" Adam asked, barely able to speak. He tried to shrug off the sheriff's grip. "I've done nothing to get arrested for! Most certainly my wife has done nothing—nor my son, who is here tonight as my guest only. He lives on the Alfieri place. So turn loose of his arm!"

"We've located your still, Donati," came a voice from the edge of the circle of men.

"You busted up my still and put a heavy bolt lock on what's left of it! So how could you *find* my still?" Adam spluttered.

Someone let out a sneering laugh. "We don't mean *that* one. We mean the big operation you thought you had so well hidden back there on the fringe of your property."

The color had drained completely from Adam's face. The sheriff was pushing him firmly toward the bunkhouse. A deputy had nudged David with the butt of his shotgun. "You too, Buster—inside! The sheriff wants a statement."

"You dumbbells!" Adam yelled out. "My son works for Beringers'. He just graduated from Davis, and his wife is down valley. Anything that you *say* you've found on my property has nothing to do with him, one way or the other. David, go back down to Lilliana. Get a mare—take the Ford if you like."

"Nobody's going anyplace until *I* say so," the sheriff mumbled.

Sarah pushed her way into the middle of the circle of men wearing plaid jackets, hunter's caps, all of them carrying a shotgun or wearing guns in holsters. Metal badges glistened in the flickering lights; their shadows loomed like distorted tree trunks in the muted moonlight coming at their backs. "If you have a complaint to make against my husband, then make it to him as you should to a gentleman! And *don't* call him 'Donati' again! His name is *Mr.* Donati. We have just come from our lawyer's. He will be very interested in how you are pushing us around as though we are common criminals, when we are all three innocent! How dare *you*, Henry Barnes! Oh, don't try to hide from me. I taught you English and history in high school and I'd know your face anywhere." She whirled around, the soft woolen beige dress making a graceful swirl, then falling just below her knees; the high heels wobbly on the loose gravel. She had never experienced such blinding fury. "You are all standing on Donati ground. I expect you to behave accordingly! If you have something to say to us, come to our house and we will discuss it—in a civilized manner! We will not stand here in the dark, herded like animals."

"Sarah, I—"

"Don't Sarah me! I will not be bullied by rude, inconsiderate ruffians hiding behind tin badges. There are a few things I learned from my mother. You remember *her*, don't you, Sheriff?" she asked, bitter irony making her words sound as if they were slicing through the space between them. "She used to pay your mother five dollars a week to do her ironing. She paid your father's doctor bills that time when he was down with pneumonia. She gave you the first saddle you ever had for your pony. She is probably this minute turning over in her grave over your audacity—your insane accusations!"

"Ma'am, I remind you that I *am* the law."

"Then come and bear it the respect the law deserves!" she snapped, giving Henry Barnes a firm push and heading out toward the main house, her high heels pounding like hammers on the stone pathway.

"I guess you don't argue with a woman," the sheriff said gruffly. "Come on, men. We've got that search warrant anyway. Let's hear what Donati—*Mr.* Donati has to say about the evidence we've come up with." He motioned to two of the men. "Fred, you and George stay down here and keep an eye on those two men inside the bunkhouse. Everybody stays put up here until I give the word otherwise. See to it."

Li Po's eyes had narrowed like slits when he opened the door and watched the troop of men file past into the main parlor. He caught Adam's ashen-gray nod of the head, disappeared quickly back into the thick shadows of the dining room, ducked behind the screen and made his way like a shadow into his room off the kitchen.

Adam and Sarah had taken a seat beside each other on the settee. Sarah waved one hand toward the others. "Please be seated, gentlemen," she said in a voice she might have used in any classroom. "I want to hear what this is all about. And I will most certainly expect an apology when you realize your mistake!"

A Mr. Wilson, in charge of the revenue agents, stepped forward. "I'm afraid there hasn't been a mistake, ma'am. We have known for days now—suspected it for several weeks, actually—that a large operation was working off Spring Mountain. We weren't exactly sure where. So we staked out Lovall Valley, the Sonoma County line. It's what we thought. That Chicago group had its runners from San Francisco. It's a big chain hookup. We caught them tonight with a big haul headed out of Lovall Valley."

Sarah's hands had flown to the row of buttons on her dress. Her head tilted sharply to one side. Her amber eyes flashed. "That does not indicate that *we*—that my husband or anyone associated with my husband has had anything to do with it, or knew about it!"

"The distillery is located on your property," he said coldly. "We were able to ascertain that just before dark closed in. We got one statement—from the man they left as night watchman. They're all set up for another big run tomorrow. Have over forty thousand pounds of sugar stored in that shed. The wood ready to stoke the fire. We figure we'll close in as soon as the daylight hits. We want to catch them in the act."

Adam's face was like a fist. "If there's somebody operating a still on Donati property, they are trespassers! They are not here with my permission or my knowledge. You can't arrest me for that." He waved his arm out angrily. "I will get my lawyer. This country is supposed to be a democracy, and I have my rights. There are other laws!"

The man named Wilson took command in the middle of the parlor. "Mr. Donati, you do have rights. You should know that we have come with a search warrant to go through this house. I'd like to send a couple of the deputies now to look around the house. Save time —make this as easy on everybody as possible." He showed them the warrant. "If you are hiding anything on the premises, I suggest that you tell us where to find it. Make it easy on yourself."

Adam was too angry to speak. Finally he got out: "Search! Go on —help yourself. But I am warning you—I am having my lawyer take this intrusion, this injustice, to the highest courts in the land! You will pay for this—every bloody one of you!"

"Mrs. Donati, do you have any place that you suggest . . ."

"It is my understanding that any family may have two hundred gallons of wine per year. Our wine cabinet with our racks is quite visible. There, in the dining room. I do not believe you will find that it exceeds the legal limit. There is one bottle of Donati sherry there before your very eyes. There is a bottle of spirits the doctor prescribed for bad colds in the kitchen cabinet. By all means, do look."

"I would appreciate it if you would accompany us."

"My wife has no—"

"Adam, please. I prefer it," Sarah said stiffly. "I don't like your color, dear. Please stay seated. Rest." She flashed a furious look at the sheriff. "My husband has had a serious heart attack. You may blame yourself if this nonsense brings on another!" She led them into the dining room, then into the kitchen.

One of the deputies turned the doorknob to Li Po's room. "What's back here?'"

"Our servant's quarters. Li Po, please show the gentlemen in."

Sarah glanced cautiously about Li Po's room. She smiled quietly, seeing that he had moved his prayer rug and his enameled altar directly over the cellar hatch and was kneeling there, his hands folded inside his sleeves, the incense burning. There was no sign at all of his herb bottles.

"This is Li Po's worship hour," Sarah said stiffly. "Excuse us, please," she said, lifting one eyebrow knowingly at Li Po. "Continue. That is, *if* you gentlemen will grant my servant the freedom to worship as he pleases. Or is that denied, too?"

"Mrs. Donati, our search here is not for the purpose of denying you your rights. We would not be doing this if there was not the other evidence . . ."

David met them in the hallway. "Papa says you can't go upstairs with the men. He wants you to come into the parlor."

She entered quickly, saw Adam's white face, his questioning look. She did not look at the sheriff or a deputy sitting across from Adam. "Li Po is at his altar. But if you would like a cup of tea, I'd be happy to fix it. This is his worship time."

Adam's eyes flickered. He had been afraid the men in their search would find the cellar hatch in Li Po's room and uncover his secret wine cellar. It was not his main cache, but it was still one that exceeded his legal limits. Too, the wine he had been making in small experiments with the white-grape varietal Jacob Brunner had developed and given to him was aging down there in small oak casks. He didn't want it interrupted for any reason, legal or not.

Wilson called the sheriff and his men out into the hallway for a conference. In a moment, he came into the parlor. "We've decided we'll let everybody get some rest for a few hours. Since we plan to move in on the still at daylight, we'll be staying down at your bunkhouse, seeing that nobody leaves here until the raid is over. We're not saying you are guilty, Mr. Donati, but we aren't ready to say you are innocent either. We want to see what we find—what statements we get from those people we will catch in the morning. We'll expect you to go along with us."

Adam did not answer. He thought about getting up, going to the door. But he stayed on the settee, feeling as though his blood had gone thin on him. Wilson was droning on, tapping his fingertips against the door leading into the hallway.

"We expected to complete our raid earlier today," he was saying. "Things didn't work out the way we had planned. Lawbreakers aren't always cooperative." His mouth tilted in a smile of confidence. "But the guilty will end up in jail. We promise you that is going to happen!"

Sarah was standing perfectly still. She was positive she had just seen Anton dart past the window on the veranda. "We understand," she said hurriedly. "Now if you gentlemen don't mind—my husband isn't feeling well. Surely you can see that."

The sheriff was looking at him closely. "You do look a little washed-out, Mr. Donati," he said, his voice showing that he was beginning to have his own doubts. It was the first time he had ever been inside such a luxurious home. He had taken in the sight of the silver, the furniture, the oil paintings, the fancy Oriental rugs, and he was looking at Adam Donati with a new respect. He was in awe of any man who could afford this kind of luxury—bootlegger or not.

"Okay, men," he barked. "We'll start out at the crack of daybreak. You've each been told you're to stand watch tonight. Each one of you take care to keep your eyes open. Nobody leaves Spring Mountain tonight without my say-so."

He tipped his hunting cap at Sarah, then closed the door behind him with a decisive thudding noise.

It was only a matter of a few moments before Anton slipped in the back door.

"How did you get here without their seeing you?" Sarah asked in a low voice, all of them now in the kitchen, sitting in near-darkness. Li Po had come out, was standing at the stove preparing tea.

"Easy. There are ways. I saw the cars lined up—I took the wagon road, left my car well out of sight. Came up through the vineyards and looked in to see who was here. I heard what they said when they left. But, Papa, you don't—you *aren't* involved, are you?"

"I told you, I don't do bootlegging! I don't know a damn thing about any still. That lowdown Prasso scouted out my place and took over, obviously. At least they've got him!"

Li Po bobbed his head up, scuffled over to Adam. "Here—you need herbs." He pushed a steaming cup of tea at him, stood smiling as though pleased he had done his part well.

Adam tasted the hot liquid, made a face. "It's bitter enough to kill a mule!" He looked at Li Po in a long silent stare. "Thank you, Li Po. For everything."

"What happens next?" Anton asked.

"They say we go at sunup to see the damn thing. We make statements. I am innocent—so that is all there is to it."

David looked uncertain. "Should we get your lawyer? Shouldn't Norman be here?"

"If your father is innocent, we don't need a lawyer," Sarah put in for him. "What we need is rest. As much sleep as we can get. Tomorrow will settle this once and for all. So in that regard I'm glad this has come to a head. We've had revenue men snooping around here for the past two and a half years. Maybe now they will take our word."

Anton was looking at Adam. "Papa, I know that you must have hidden your brandy. I—"

"Leave that up to me. Everything's in order. I'm not breaking any laws. I want you to know that. If I'm aging some premium stuff, that is not the same thing."

Anton laughed. "You'd be a damn fool if you didn't have something put aside. Everybody I know has sidestepped the Volstead Act in one way or another. I believe over half of Napa County is involved in bootlegging in some kind of way. It's not all big-time—just plain ordinary people who won't accept the absurdity of this Prohibition."

Sarah stood up. "We aren't plain ordinary people. But right now we must go to bed as if nothing has happened—get what rest we possibly can. Daylight will be here too soon as it is." She pushed her chair under the table, let out a long sigh. "It's been a long time since we sat around the kitchen table, hasn't it? Remember all those nights of homework? Time—where has it gone? Now so many changes."

"One thing hasn't changed," Anton said lightly. "Donatis are proving they can stick together. Right, Papa?"

True to the sheriff's word, the men were there at daylight. Adam had been awake most of the night and was dressed, waiting for them. He had never felt so drained; his very arms felt limp, deadened. He went out quietly through the front door, followed the men out into the fog-dense early morning.

In the kitchen, Li Po shoved cups of black coffee at both David and Anton, who had stumbled down the back stairs. Anton took his coffee with him, hurried out the back door. David sipped his noisily, blew across it, gave up and charged out after Anton.

Sarah was the last to come downstairs. She was buttoning a navy-blue sweater high around her neck, sat down, laced the strings of shoes she usually wore while gardening. "Have they all gone? Everybody?" She sipped her coffee gingerly.

"Everybody," Li Po said, his head bobbing up and down.

She stood up, looked at Li Po, undecided. "Do you want to go with me? I'm not asking, but should you want to go along, I won't object."

He did not answer, but ran into his room, came out tugging on his skullcap and slipping into a black wool jacket his uncle had given him long ago. Silently they went out the back, Li Po pointing to the pathway the men had taken, out around behind the winery.

The damp mist of the fog seemed to cling to Sarah's face. As they entered the silent woods, only the eerie soft cooing of the early-morning doves broke the stillness. She strained to hear sounds of the men ahead; obviously they were being told to stay quiet, or else Li Po was taking her along the wrong path, she thought, her pulse racing, her hands clenched in nervous inverted fists.

She felt the dampness clawing at her, making her nose drip, her fingers turn numb with cold. She hadn't walked much these past few years. She felt her breath coming out in gasps. They were making their way up a steep slope, through thickets and a high towering clump of pines. She could now hear the tromp of the men's heavier boots, the crackle of twigs, of dry limbs being swiped out of the way.

From a lifetime of habit, Li Po lagged behind her at a respectful distance. Sarah glanced back at him, saw him suddenly stutter to a stop, look back, begin waving at someone.

It was Kyle Plimpton, crashing along trying to catch up. She waited until he approached. He had pulled a stocking cap on under his regular cowboy hat to ward off an earache that had been bothering him lately.

"What's going on around here?" he asked, his long legs taking giant strides. "I came up early to finish pruning the Gamays. Emma made me promise I'd get my work done so we could take a vacation down in Stockton where her sister lives. I rode my horse up, saw that big line of cars. The sheriff's deputies about handcuffed me there for a minute until Gus told them who I was. I hear they're holding some kind of raid. But from what I know about where Adam put his stuff, well, ain't they heading in the wrong direction? Or is Adam trying to lead them off the track?"

"It isn't that," Sarah said in a hushed tone. "They claim they've found a big distillery working and think Adam is behind it. They've arrested some men already—Prasso and his gang."

"I'll be damned! Look, I'm going on and try to catch up."

By the time Sarah and Li Po had reached the others, they had all been stopped by the sheriff and his men near the crest of a sharp rise. Near the place where they stood was a rushing stream of water. "Look at that runoff," Wilson was saying in a low voice. "Smell the air. Smells like molasses cooking, wouldn't you say?" He looked up at Sarah and Li Po. "They got an earlier start than I thought. Okay—everybody but our men stay put. Right here, where you'll be safe in case anybody gets some bright idea about using a gun. When we get them rounded up, we'll call you over to inspect the still, Mr. Donati—in case it is something new to you." He looked at Kyle Plimpton skeptically.

As soon as the sheriff and Wilson's revenue men had disappeared over the ridge, Anton came up to David. "Come on—we know these woods. We used to hunt back here," he said to Sarah, who was frowning in a worried way.

"I'm going, too," Kyle said, yanking down the stocking cap.

"David, Anton, *don't!* Stay here," Sarah cried out.

But they had already started edging their way around the side of the ridge, working their way down toward the creek. At that point, Adam came down to where Sarah and Li Po had huddled near a huge rock.

"What are you doing here?" he stormed. "This is no place for a woman to be!"

"My place is with you when there's trouble," she said stubbornly, tugging at her sweater where a briar had caught on it. She swiped at her runny nose. "If they arrest you, they arrest me too."

He stared at her a long hard moment, then said in a stern gruff voice, "Then stay down behind that rock. Some of those men calling themselves deputies don't know beans. They're like jackrabbits hopping around with those shotguns. No telling which way they might shoot."

"Adam—stay here with us!" Sarah called out.

"I'm going up here at the top of the ridge where I can see what's going on. See who's got the nerve to use Donati land running a still. Sheriff says it's the biggest still they've found operating in the whole state." He stopped a moment, as though getting his breath. "I haven't been back in this direction in—hell, years. *Somebody* knew there was a spring back here. I want to know who that somebody was!" His mouth was a tight grim line.

Sarah tried to get comfortable leaning back against the hard cold rock, burrowing her numb fingers inside her sweater sleeves. She could have worn a scarf around her head. Some gloves. A warmer jacket. She had never been this deep into the woods, and certainly never at this time of day. It was only early November, but it felt like a winter day back east.

Li Po had squatted back on his heels, his face obviously alert, but his expression saying nothing. Down below, they could hear the gurgling sound of the spring water rushing over the rocks. Early-morning birds—a jenny wren, a thrush, a squawking bluejay—had come awake. A thin shaft of sunlight was trying to break through the layer of gray fog.

Then came the startling bursting sound of a single shotgun blast, rapidly followed by another. Then men were shouting. The woods were ringing with voices.

Sarah struggled to get up, her right foot having gone to sleep and tingling in that numb, excruciating way that made her want never to move while knowing that she must. She stomped it against the damp ground; looked about wildly for Adam, who had disappeared over the crest of the ridge. She turned to Li Po. "Are they *killing* somebody? Whom are they shooting?" Her voice sounded like a hoarse croaking whisper. "Come on, Li Po—let's go nearer to the top. Stay low."

They crept up the steep crest of the ridge. She looked from around a thick tree trunk across the gulch down below, then up another steep slope, where she could see the outline of a crudely built shed around which men were teeming. Up on an opposite ridge, where a dirt road came in from the Sonoma County side, she saw two—three cars, and someone being pushed by the sheriff and his men toward them.

Her own breath seemed to be coming in thin little gasps of air. Her heart seemed to have turned into its own hollow drum. Li Po was crouching near her side, his black eyes glued across the ridge. They both saw the huddle of men, two of them backing out of the shed at the same moment, carrying a limp form.

"Did they kill somebody?" she gasped.

But Li Po had bolted from his position, was leaping forward, plunging down the slope. At the same instant, Sarah heard David's voice shouting out, "Joseph! You *bastard!* How could you do this to your own family? Your own name?"

Then the sheriff's deeper voice was bellowing out, "Grab that Donati guy!"

Sarah was trying to grasp what was happening. She saw men holding David back, keeping him away from a shape she guessed to be Joseph.

"If I get my hands on you I'll—"

The sheriff was yelling again, "Keep them apart, Goddamit! These hotheaded Italians will kill each other."

She saw Li Po's small crouching shape working its way frantically up the opposite slope toward the men surrounding the limp form. She could see only the backs of men in plaid hunting jackets or leather coats buttoned up, caps with bills pulled down low on their foreheads. Then it was Anton's shrill cry: "*Papa!* What has happened to Papa?"

At that point, Sarah herself started down the opposite side of the ridge, fighting back briars, low-hanging limbs, her feet slipping on the damp mulch, her hands grabbing at anything to help her keep her balance. She tried stepping on rocks crossing the stream of gurgling water; gave up, plunged through the icy shallow depths; scrambled now up the steep incline, feeling that she could not possibly keep one foot going ahead of the other.

Anton caught her just short of the clump of men. "Stay here—sit down." His face was stark white. "Papa . . . when he saw Joseph—saw him with his own eyes, stoking the fire—he . . . his heart gave out. He's . . . Papa's dead . . ."

Sarah felt the buzzing, hammering sensation inside her head. Yet she pushed Anton aside, half fell through the clump of men. Li Po was bending over Adam, his tiny fists pounding on the still chest. She was pushing Li Po out of the way, her numb fingers slapping Adam's cheeks and mumbling over and over, "You mustn't—Adam, *don't* die! You *can't* die!"

The next thing she knew, it was Li Po's voice saying to her, "Take deep breath. Through mouth. Slow deep breath . . ." Her head had been pushed down between her knees. Anton and David were looking down at her, both their faces reflecting their separate horror and shock.

"Did somebody *shoot* him?" she asked faintly.

"It was his heart, ma'am," the sheriff was saying.

Anton's voice was like dry ice. "*You* killed him—you and your Boy Scouts!"

"Listen—you don't talk to the law like that! Didn't nobody kill him."

"I heard gunshots," Sarah said, struggling to get to her feet, clinging now to David's arm.

"Those shots were signals for the revenue agents to close in from the Lovall Valley side. Part of our plan."

"Aren't you *proud* of your plan?" Anton asked in the same icy voice. "Or do you arrest a dead man?"

Wilson had come up to them. "We're sorry, Mrs. Donati. We're terribly sorry it came to this. We had to do what we did." He motioned for the men to bring the stretcher and the army blanket. "Inside that shed was over eighty thousand gallons of whiskey. We knew it was on your property. We figured a Donati was in on it. We didn't know it was your son, Joseph."

"My *step*son," she said blanky.

"Your stepson was not a runner—he was just one cog in a very big wheel. He got hoodwinked. Caught."

"If you let him out of jail I'll kill the sonofabitch!" David cried out, having just looked down at his father and having seen where his mouth was gaping open, just before the men covered his face with the blanket and lifted him up on the stretcher. Tears had sprung to his eyes now. He clenched his fists.

"Take it easy, David," Kyle Plimpton said in a husky voice. "That won't bring him back."

The sheriff was looking at Sarah. "Mrs. Donati, I just want you to know that we were doing what we were supposed to do. My job is to enforce the law—even laws I don't like any more'n the next fellow. We didn't come up here to do harm, to contribute in any way to your husband's death. I hate to think you'd blame me. It wasn't—"

She was shaking her head numbly. "Where . . . are they taking my husband's body?"

"The undertaker's. You'll want to make funeral arrangements." He took a deep breath. "Could you use a ride back to your place, ma'am? We have to take the long way out of here, back through the Lovall Valley turnoff. But maybe you ought to ride back. That walk is a hard one."

"No, thank you. I'll go with my sons. With Kyle. With Li Po here."

They had turned now, David's hand gripping her arm tightly. She paused, called up to the sheriff. "Please tell my stepson that— Won't he need a lawyer, Sheriff?"

He nodded. "I'd say he'll need a *good* lawyer. One of the best."

"Tell him, please, that Mr. Jaspers will be coming to visit him shortly. The Donatis' family lawyer will represent him."

"Don't include *my* name in that," David said through thin lips.

Sarah's voice came out like something coated with lead. "He is your father's son. Donatis must stick together."

As they made their way silently back through the woods, the tree-tops came awake with the sounds of birds chirping, squirrels scampering about, a crow somewhere across the knoll letting out its raucous *caw caw*. But to Sarah, it was as though she were floating through some groundless space, like a dream, where there was absolute silence.

When they stumbled into the kitchen, they discovered that Li Po had got there ahead of them and had the tea kettle already on the stove, cups and saucers ready for them at the kitchen table. But his head sagged on his chest; he did not look up.

Kyle Plimpton removed his cowboy hat, tugged the navy-blue stocking cap off his head and smoothed down his tousled hair. He looked awkward, ill at ease. His crippled hand dangled like a broken bird's wing. "I know families like to be together at a time like this."

Sarah looked up, was vaguely aware of Kyle's Adam's apple working up and down, of his gaunt, stricken face. "Stay—please sit down with us," she said numbly.

As Kyle's chair made a scraping sound, Anton went over to a row of hooks, yanked down a jacket and a long scarf he had left behind months ago. "I'm going down to get Norman Jaspers," he said, his voice bitter. "I think we can file suit against somebody over the way they handled this raid!"

David looked up anxiously. "Maybe I ought to ride down with you. I want to be the one to tell Lilliana. The word will probably spread fast through the valley." His chin was jutted out, he was grinding his teeth. "They won't think it was *just* Joseph, though. From now on, wait and see, the Donati name will be labeled 'bootlegger.'"

Sarah felt she should make some objection. But her strength had vanished. It was as though she herself had become a void space. She was empty. She was finished. She was a fleshed-out body with no skeleton —no fulcrum left.

"We'll be back soon," Anton was saying from the doorway. "Get to bed, Mother. Li Po, see that she gets a hot steam bath and some of your herb tea. Get her to rest. We'll bring Norman."

"I'll stay with her until you get back," Kyle Plimpton was saying. "Adam—he was like family to me. If it hadn't been for him I'd be a nobody. I'd probably be rounded up in some raid myself."

After a moment, Sarah became aware of the high shrill whistle of the tea kettle. Though she had not expected to form words again ever, she was speaking out of some long-formed shell of habit. "Li Po, our guest—Mr. Plimpton could use a fresh cup of tea. . . . Do you take cream and sugar, Kyle? Adam always took two teaspoons of sugar, a touch of cream." A strange lopsided smile had worked across her drawn lips. She stirred her own tea vigorously, not even aware of the slow silent stream of tears sliding down her face.

PART THREE

1922–1960

17

Following Adam's funeral (some said it was the largest, most notably attended Napa Valley funeral since the death of Charles Krug), Sarah seemed to wander through the cavernous stone mansion on Spring Mountain as though her own life's sap had been sealed off in that elaborate steel-banded, gold-crested coffin and plunged deeply into the dark layers of the earth.

Numbly, she tried to keep busy, as if activity itself would take away that dreadful sense of weightlessness; would help fill that seemingly bottomless, rimless void inside her.

Dutifully she answered each expression of condolence the family had received. At times, reading letters filled with glowing accolades from important vintners, from various leaders in the political sector, her mouth would twist into bitter irony. Why had they waited until he died to heap on the words of praise, of deserved respect?

But soon waves of her own guilt would inundate her. Why hadn't *she* told Adam all those thousands of words of love repeated, of respect renewed, which rode now like devils in the shadows, riddling her sleep with nightmares, carving out deeper holes of loneliness? *Blame*—blame didn't repair. It didn't resurrect. It gnawed at the roots.

"The family of Adam Donati gratefully acknowledges your kind expression of sympathy . . ." she would resume writing.

But then would come the times when she could not tolerate the pressure of loss, of longing, of guilt. When blindly it would drive her out on the stone veranda, where she would stand staring out at the vineyards so unchanged, as though surely at any moment she would see him come striding out of the thick of them.

At other times, she would catch herself pausing, listening intently, through those closer sounds of the whang of wind whipping around the massive corners of the stone house, of the clock ticking, of birds outside the windows trilling out their cheerful calls, as though she had just heard him speak—the faintest distant call, in that wonderful deep voice of his.

Silence—oh, how poorly the living were prepared for that unfathomable silence death could leave in its wake . . . .

But life puts its own forces to work in a fierce fight to lay claim to the living. Sarah felt it at first in sudden fits of anger—anger which almost always spun itself out of a deep well of regrets.

If only they had not put off doing so many things together! Always waiting for that next harvest—that next big vintage, she would tell herself bitterly.

She tried to counteract those thoughts with positive ones, recalling only their happy times. What they had had together. *Count your blessings*, her mother would have told her sternly. *Think of someone besides yourself!*

But another wall of bitterness clamped down when she saw the surly, square-faced Joseph lurking behind jail bars; or the lean-faced, handsome Anton, who even on the day of the funeral had dashed off to keep an important date with a pretty girl; or her own David, the very image of Adam, the born so-called steward of the land, who seemed lately to glower at anything pertaining to Spring Mountain, as if Adam's dream was a burden to bear.

Her return to any expectancy of living came about gradually, like the slow, sluggish ooze of thick cold oil struggling to flow.

There came a day when she decided she wanted to go Christmas shopping, to buy gifts for the boys and for her adopted family, the Alfieris. The next week, she made cookies; tried to think of something cheerful to take to Joseph in his grim, barren cell.

And then one Saturday, when she was expecting Norman Jaspers for his routine weekly visit (when he usually brought new sheafs of papers concerning the settling of Adam's estate or the negotiation of some security investment he thought would be good for her portfolio), she caught herself giving extra attention to the dress she was wearing, to the arranging of her hair, neglected now for weeks. And when she met him at the door she felt a warm smile, the kind one gives naturally to an old friend whose presence is very much needed.

The contents of Adam's will held no surprises for Sarah. He had carefully discussed it with her when he first decided to have Norman Jaspers draw up a codicil. She had known for some time that David was slated to inherit all the Donati holdings on Spring Mountain, in view of Anton and Joseph having already come into their separate

Brunner inheritance. She knew, too, that she was given the right to live in the stone mansion for as long as she wished; that she had been bequeathed a twenty-five percent share of all profits accrued through Spring Mountain Donati holdings; that all securities originally invested through Norman Jaspers were hers. She was pleased he had left $2,500 cash each to Joseph and Anton, and $1,000 each to Li Po, Gudrun Meyers, and Luigi Pascarella. He requested that Kyle Plimpton continue on as vineyard manager, according to the same percentage-sharing terms they had established through the years, until his health or his own desire to stop should bring about the need for a change.

When Adam had discussed the will with Sarah, he had said, "I figure this place here on Spring Mountain should just about balance out in dollars and cents what Joseph and Anton have inherited from Jacob Brunner. If Joseph is such a dumbbell as to sell his share of some of the best valley-floor acreage in Napa County, that's his own shortcoming. Only David is a born steward of the land. He is the only one who knows what we've got up here."

Norman asked Sarah if she was sure she understood his role as executor. "I don't want you to have any anxiety about the investments I control." He took out a copy of the will. "Let me go over this one part again: 'My Executor shall have the following power, to be exercised in his discretion, without notice to any beneficiary and without order, leave or license of the court, to (1) carry on with existing securities, whereas he may vote directly or give general or special proxies for voting or acting with respect to shares or securities he deems appropriate with respect to merger, consolidation . . .' "

She put her hand out, patted him reassuringly on the arm. "You don't really have to do that, Norman. Adam knew quite well what he wanted when he appointed you as executor. I am not at all familiar with legalese. Surely you know by now that I trust you implicitly in all business and legal affairs!" She had smiled at him softly. "I don't know what any of the Donatis would have done without you through the years. Thank you for what you've done for Joseph. Getting his jail sentence reduced, his fine paid. I'll be visiting him Christmas morning."

"Joseph's a confused fellow," Norman muttered. "Who knows? Maybe this time in jail will help straighten him out."

Sarah looked at him with a worried frown. "David seems to think the newspaper stories, the bad publicity, will mark the Donati name for life. That even Spring Mountain is going to bear the stigma from now on."

Norman tried to reassure her. "Time—people forget."

• •

In view of the Christmas holidays coming so soon after Adam's death, it had been decided that any celebration would be held at the Alfieri house in Rutherford. Sarah asked Anton to plan to come by for her early on Christmas morning so that she could drop off a basket of gifts and baked delicacies at the jail. When he arrived, he had Diane Margolis with him as his date for the day. She was wearing a bright-green woolen cape, a red-and-green plaid scarf around her neck.

"You look wonderfully festive," Sarah said, adjusting her own tired black coat with its high Persian lamb collar and settling into the back seat of Anton's sleek new Packard.

"It's my Christmas gift from Anton," Diane said, her brown eyes soft, then misting over. "I wish I *felt* so festive."

Sarah caught a glimpse of Anton's look of reprimand, the tension in his voice. "Christmastime is *happy* time—remember?"

A lover's quarrel, Sarah thought absently, leaning back for the ride down the mountain, her own thoughts churning. Christmas was proving to be a very difficult time for her. She was relieved to be leaving Spring Mountain—all those memories hanging like ornaments from the ceiling, from every place she looked.

At the small jail, Joseph grinned through the bars at her. "I knew you wouldn't forget me. I just knew you wouldn't! Luigi was here yesterday. Brought me some books. Some drawing paper for working out floor plans." His pale-blue eyes squinted, blinked. "Are you okay? I—I wish Papa hadn't died . . . because of me."

Sarah looked about, unsure, aching to comfort him but not knowing how. She patted his hand through the bars. "His heart was very bad. The doctor said it would have happened anyway. Norman says you'll be out soon." She touched his face with her fingertips. "You can start all over—a whole new life." Her voice caught in her throat, would not go on.

"Yeah, that's what Luigi says. I'll try—I'm going to try hard," he said, tears now openly spilling down his square jaw.

At the Alfieris', Sarah headed quickly for the kitchen to help out with the dinner. It would be good to *do* something.

"Oh, good heavans, no!" Lilliana said, her face flushed from a wave of heat from the open oven where she was checking the turkey. "It's our first chance to wait on *you*! Go enjoy yourself."

She drifted into the sunporch, found Anton sitting crosslegged surrounded by the Alfieri children as he worked a puzzle—a little too intently involved with them, she thought, seeing Diane's clouded face as she seemed to hang limply in the corner by the Christmas tree, near the pile of brightly wrapped gifts.

When dinner was over and the presents had been opened, Vittorio passed around glasses of claret wine—"The last of my good stuff, *Donati* wine—the best for our toasts, huh?"—and lifted his glass in *salute* to the coming baby, Sarah looked at David and Lilliana smiling happily, their arms locked around each other's waists.

"Since Spring Mountain is yours now," she said, "when will you plan to move in? Maybe you'll have the baby there?"

Vittorio answered for them: "She has the baby *here*! The kids are so happy about the new baby coming to this house." Tears were swimming about in his eyes now. "My Delfina, she was always beautiful like Lilliana is now. See the color in her cheeks! How happy her eyes get —that special shine, huh?" He shook his head. "Right now I am working six days a week, sometimes two jobs. I save my money so Rudolfo and his brother, the girls, too, everybody goes to college, so we make their mother up there smile that same happy smile like Lilliana looks now!" He turned directly toward Sarah. "David has got a good job now at Beringers'. He is lucky. Not many places anywhere in America for a good winemaker to keep his skills. It is easier for the young people, down here in the valley. Getting to school. Shopping, things like that. It is not so easy up on Spring Mountain. My advice to David —I give my two cents' worth because he is now my son-in-law and so good to my Lilliana—I say, *Sell* the place up on Spring Mountain! The future is down here. Here it don't matter if Prohibition comes. We raise other things. We plant good orchards, raise cattle. Barley, good pasture. Anybody with a college education, down here they could find plenty ways to make a good living. Sure, with good educations they can make it to the top."

Sarah waited, swirled her wine, looked into its rich ruby-red depths. "There is one thing wrong with your advice, Vittorio. Adam's will says that Spring Mountain cannot be sold. It must stay in the family. Adam believed David was the only one who understood what he was trying to do up there. He figured David would pass that on to *his* sons someday." She stood up, put her glass down. "We mustn't forget that Adam is up there now, too, Vittorio. We must try to make him smile as well!" She turned and asked Anton in a crisp voice, "Would you mind giving me a ride home now, dear? It's been a lovely day. But Lilliana must be tired. We mustn't wear her out."

On the way back up Spring Mountain, Anton glanced over his shoulder at her. "I think you are going to have to close up this big white elephant of a house if David and Lilliana *aren't* interested in moving up, Mom Sarah. It's much too big for you. It's not right, your being stuck off up here, dependent upon others. I think it's time for you to buy a new car, learn how to drive."

He pulled his Packard to a stop, helped her out. "I'll be right back, Diane—wait here," he called back, taking Sarah's arm and guiding her up the pathway toward the main house.

A cold stiff wind whipped around the corner of the veranda, made a shrill, high sound through the tops of pine trees; shook the brittle trailing bare tendrils of the wisteria vine overhead. Li Po met them at the door. He had lit a crackling fire; looked expectantly now at Anton, who came in briefly, keeping on his hat and coat.

"You should have asked Diane to come in," Sarah said.

"No—we have to get on. Listen, Mom Sarah. How old are you?"

She smiled. "I don't mind saying—as some women do. I will soon be fifty. Why?"

"You are too young to be up here, living like a hermit. And I have decided that I am going to do something about it!" He grasped her by the shoulders, his gray-blue eyes shining with excitement from his sudden idea. "Next week—say, Wednesday—I will call for you. Have Li Po close up everything and take a nice vacation for himself. A month off. I will have you be my very first guest in the new wing I have built onto the old Brunner house. We will go to San Francsico for a lovely week! A shopping binge. Yes, that will be my birthday present to you. Isn't it coming up soon?"

She shook her head, laughing at his enthusiasm. "Anton, a month —that is much too long a time! A week perhaps. Two, at the most. Li Po—yes, he should have some time away."

"Your birthday?"

"In early January. But let's forget *that*."

"No. I will plan it. So be packed and ready early Wednesday morning. I have something I have to tend to in the next few days." His face clouded for a moment; he shrugged his shoulders as though wishing he could shrug aside some bothersome nuisance wrapped around his neck like a scarf too tightly drawn on a too warm day.

She pushed him toward the front door. "All right," she smiled. "But hurry—you've left Diane in the car too long."

"Diane—what am I going to do about Diane?" he sighed, giving her a quick kiss on both cheeks. "That is my problem. Women!" He lifted his eyebrows, threw his hands out in mock disgust, then dashed out across the veranda, running lightly down the path.

When Anton came for her on Wednesday, he announced, "I've changed our plans somewhat. We're going straight to San Francisco. Today."

"But, Anton, I'm not dressed for the city."

"Don't worry. You will be. I'm taking you shopping. We will throw your old clothes away."

He had made reservations for them at the Fairmont Hotel, with Sarah having a suite on the eighth floor, a view toward the east. They arrived around three o'clock. Anton ordered tea for them immediately, and as they sat back, Sarah trying to get her bearings, he suddenly asked her, "There is something I've always wanted to know—did you ever love anyone else beside Papa? I mean, when you were back east at Wellesley? Surely there was someone. You were such a knockout, I hear. Norman said you were the most beautiful younger woman he had ever seen. You're still beautiful."

She stirred her tea, trying to put her answer into words. "I was acquainted with a few gentlemen. There was one in particular who thought—oh, he was convinced we were destined to spend our life together. He and his mother made a trip to Napa once, trying to convince me." She shook her head in dry irony. "No, I never really loved anyone other than your father. I just never did." She lifted her eyebrows. "What about you, Anton? Are you in love with anyone? I sensed that you and Diane are having problems."

He sighed heavily. "Love—I'm not sure I have ever been in love. I have had girls tell me they love me. Diane—she's convinced her life is over if I—we don't get married. She has different concepts of the word 'love' than I do. I never told her, not once, that I love her." He went over to the window and stared out at the city below, at the cable car clanging by, at the bay itself spread out like a green-gray slab dotted with ships and a few sailboats listing sharply in the wind. He turned abruptly. "Let's face it! I'm a very healthy male, with healthy normal desires. I simply adore women. I particularly adore lovely young ladies who are well educated, who dress well, who complement a man." He sat down again. "So far, there has been only one girl whom I've considered asking to marry me. A girl from Boston whom you don't know—Phyllis Fuller."

"Tell me about her," she said quietly, studying him, seeing his handsome face tighten in a fierce way she had not seen before. His hands worked in and out in a nervous clasp.

"Our problem is that Phyllis is *too* rich. She comes from very big money. I can't imagine her in Napa Valley—and until I am wealthier, I can't go east, ride solely on her ticket. I won't ever be owned by any woman!" He took out a long, thin brown cigarette and lit it. "Who knows? I'm making some good investments through Norman Jaspers. I may be well off enough to marry Phyllis one of these days—on *my* terms. But I am most certainly *not* going to marry some simpering little secretary from Napa, ever!"

Sarah felt the shock of a cold shiver go up her arms. She had never seen this obvious cold and calculating side of Anton before. Maybe she had suspected it existed. But she had always pushed any such realization to the back of her mind—she supposed because she had found in Anton a charming link, her only link, to Boston, to another way of life she sometimes missed. She wished he had not said what he had just said.

She concentrated on her cup of cold tea, forced down the bitter last dregs of it. Her voice was strained as she spoke. "Diane seems like a very nice, unpretentious girl to me. I'd hate to see her get hurt. Anton, maybe you should think about—"

"I don't want to think anything at all about Diane Margolis while we are here, on *our* trip!" he said with sudden bright forcefulness. "Tomorrow I have big plans for you. Tonight I think we should have a simple dinner here at the hotel. But after tomorrow we will celebrate —in style."

"You don't really have to do all this for me, Anton. I am pleased to get away. I needed that. But you mustn't be so extravagant. Save it for some young lady."

"No, this is my way of thanking you for what you've been to me through the years. I guess I have a sentimental side. I do care about many things."

The next morning he took Sarah to a small exclusive dress shop, where soft-voiced salesladies wearing black dresses with pearl necklaces brought out repeated armloads of every possible style of dress and suit, in every fabric and color, Sarah thought. There were times in the fitting room when she felt caught in a hall of mirrors; she would see her arms up in the air, the saleslady tugging at a chiffon skirt or urging her to turn this way, that, inspecting some supposedly flattering line, and want to flee.

Anton made all the final selections; had everything, except one large box which he brought along with them, sent to the hotel. Then he took her for her first permanent. She had wanted to protest, to keep her long hair. "I'll be here when Pierre is finished," Anton said, waving her lightly on.

She was asked to remove her dress, slip into a pink smock. Then came the flurry of a hot, sudsing shampoo; of scissors doing their work; of acrid-smelling solutions, and curlers, and wires being hooked to her head; of being plunked under a dryer, with a *Cosmopolitan* magazine and a *Saturday Evening Post* being her selection from a stack of magazines. Her neck and ears felt burned. She avoided looking across into the long mirrored wall at the row of faces peering out from under metal domes. When she thought she would surely scream, someone was lifting the dryer from her head, leading her to the chair, where the unwinding of curlers, the combing-out, the dabbing here, fluffing-out there, then Pierre's own tap dance around, inspecting the final look, went on.

Then she was being ushered back into the dressing room, where a huge box Anton had brought along was spread open.

When Sarah came out, wearing the new Molyneux suit with its elaborate fur collar, the jacket that came just below her hips, the skirt only two inches below her knees, her legs in sheer hose, her feet jammed inside narrow high-heeled patent-leather pumps, she did not recognize the woman looking back at her in the full-length mirrors when Anton made her turn around and around, examining her new image.

"You look twenty years younger!" he cried. "Your hair is marvelous! The color—I'm so glad he lightened it, got rid of that mousy gray and added the henna. *Look* at yourself!"

Sarah stared, felt as if the real Sarah Donati would at any moment step out and shatter that woman in the dark-green velvet suit. And then Anton was opening another box, plopping down a fur-trimmed hat to match the suit. "I hate to see you cover up the hairstyle. Pierre, please show her how to wear the hat correctly."

Sarah allowed them to fuss over her. Then she was being asked to turn around again, and Anton was exclaiming: "The hat is perfect! Wait until your escort tonight sees you."

"What do you mean, escort?" Sarah asked, alarmed, climbing into a taxicab for the ride back to the hotel. "Your father just died less than two months ago, and I have no intentions of—"

"Relax." Anton laughed, climbing in beside her. "It's just Norman Jaspers. He's in the city for a few days and I thought his presence at dinner might balance out the evening. I have a lovely date—a girl I met in Boston when I was at Harvard. Claudia Jarvis—a Radcliffe girl. You two should find something to talk about. She's tall, blond and willowy. She has at least a dozen men in love with her. By the way, I want you to wear the jade-green chiffon tonight. I want her to see that all women from the Napa Valley aren't *farm*women. Claudia detests the country. But she's interesting. Very interesting."

Claudia was nearly as tall as Anton. She wore black satin that fell barely below her knees, with long strings of crystal beads. Her hair was cut straight, fell at an angle across her cheek. Sarah disliked her intensely, thinking she was terribly distant and condescendingly aloof. "She's very *old* San Francisco money," Anton whispered at one point. "So I gathered," she said quietly, trying to concentrate on Norman, with whom she was more at ease. If she saw that his look seemed to hold more than the look of an old family friend, she ignored it.

Norman decided to stay in San Francisco with them. Anton had plans enough to keep fifty people busy. There were lunches at Jack's, afternoon visits to museums, to matinee theater, then teatime, then dinner—always at a different restaurant each night—and usually, in the evenings, either a concert or more theater. As the week wore on, she was beginning to feel less absurd. In fact, she was beginning to anticipate Norman's admiring glances, Anton's compliments. It was as though with the soft yellow, the jade green, the shimmering gray-blue, the green velvet Molyneux, she was discovering a new rainbow of color after that thick haze of gloomy gray that had enveloped her following Adam's death.

They had planned to leave Monday morning. Anton came to her room around nine o'clock, just as she was finishing breakfast in bed. She saw by the tense look on his face that something was disturbing him. But there was something she wanted to say to him first, before she tried to find out why he was bothered.

"Anton, I want you to know how much this time here has truly meant to me. Not just the lovely clothes, my new look—no, much more than that. You have brought me out of a pit of despair. I shall always be grateful to you for that. But tell me, you seem to have some despair of your own today. Want to talk about it?"

He shook his head. "I just want you to stay happy," he said. "That helps." He began pacing the floor. "Would you mind if Norman Jaspers gives you a ride back to Napa Valley today?"

"Anton, what is it? Do you need extra money—spend too much?"

He laughed. "No, I have plenty of money, thank you." He looked up at the ceiling, clasped one fist in the palm of his other hand. "I shouldn't bother you with this. I . . . it's Diane! She's—well, she simply wasn't *careful*. She made me think everything was safe." He bit his lip, and she saw the flush creep up his neck. "She's here. At a kind of . . . clinic, I guess you could call it. It's a very hush-hush place, of course. They're going to do it today. They insist the man involved *be* there." He paced the floor. "Why do *I* have to be involved? It was her fault! Her scheme that backfired."

"Oh, *no* . . ." Sarah said, her hands trembling on the coffee cup. "You mean she's *here*—has *been* here? Alone?"

408

"A couple of days. They aren't quacks. They make the patients check in for examinations before. They don't want any kind of trouble with the law—anything going wrong."

Sarah's voice died in her throat. She was trying to let everything fall into place. All this time that they had been out having such festive dinners, with Anton being his usual charming, debonair self, bending over backward to impress Claudia Jarvis—who refused to be impressed —Diane Margolis was in San Francisco, preparing to have an abortion! She stared with disbelief at Anton—who, if anything, seemed annoyed that *he* was being inconvenienced, she thought.

"Diane—why, she must be distraught. Shouldn't you have been with her? Shouldn't—"

"I shouldn't have mentioned anything to you about it," he spluttered. "Oh, I see your look—that you're blaming me."

"Anton, sit down. I'm only trying to understand. To imagine how Diane Margolis must feel right now—so alone. Couldn't I go and be with her? A woman's presence might make her feel better. Someone who understands." She did not look at Anton. She was thinking of that time in her own life when she had given birth to David—alone. "I'd be willing to go. I want to go."

"That is ridiculous. I would never allow it, so forget it!" He glanced down at her luggage. "Will you need help packing? Norman said he would come by for you around eleven."

"No, I can manage, thank you. Norman—does he know about Diane?"

"I told him just a few minutes ago."

"And what does he think about . . . all this?" She felt sick.

Anton shrugged his shoulders. "He's furious. He doesn't say so, but I've known Norman Jaspers too long. He's blaming me, not Diane." His face tightened with fury. "He doesn't believe me when I say she had planned this all along—that it was her scheme to get me to marry her."

"Maybe he's right," Sarah muttered, trying to hold down her own anger, her disgust with Anton.

"So you're blaming me, too? Sure! I see it."

"I don't like your attitude," she said stiffly. "Frankly, you're acting so—well, cold. So unloving. I had always given you credit for being a much nicer person."

"Please, I *don't* need a lecture from you right now." He snatched his coat off the foot of the bed. "Look, I'm sorry I told you. That I brought up the subject. I'm sick of the subject. For weeks now, I've been hearing Diane simpering about it. Trying to talk me into marrying her. No woman will ever *make* me marry!"

409

"Have you considered that maybe she loves you?"

"Love!" He snorted. "Look, let's get this straight. Let's make a pact right now. We forget all about this, okay? We forget that we ever knew Diane Margolis." He took a short exasperated breath. "I hate like hell to end up this trip with something ugly like this, when I've waited so long to get to do something special for you." He shook his head. "Look, I'll see you in a couple of days. My houseboy, Tashi, will let you in. You won't need a key. Make yourself at home and we'll talk when I get back. Let's not ruin everything over this."

On the trip back to Napa Valley, Sarah tried to pull her thoughts into clearer focus. Though she had not meant to talk about it with Norman, the long years of having known him, of feeling comfortable with him, and now knowing that he knew the circumstances about Diane, made her suddenly blurt out, "I'm so upset over Anton and this —this *mess* he's got Diane Margolis into. I know he doesn't look at it that way. He's blaming it on her."

Norman's hands tightened on the wheel. "Anton had no right telling you!" he said through tight lips. "It's not something to put in your lap." He blew the horn at a car he was passing. When he was on a straight stretch of road again he muttered, "I was furious with him before. I could wring his neck now. Anton's problem is he's so self-centered! So selfish."

"Diane seems like such a lovely, sweet girl."

"She is. She's worked for me for five years. Anton—I am sure he is her first real love. I know Anton is your stepson. Actually, I've always been fond of him. But he's so ambitious, he won't let anyone get in his way, ever."

They lapsed into silence.

When Norman saw the drawn look on her face he said, "Please, Sarah . . . Don't worry about Anton. From now on, *I'm* going to see that you begin a new life. This isn't the time, but I want you to know —I have to say it. I have loved you since I first saw you, Sarah. I want, one of these days when you've had more time. . . No, this isn't the time."

She could not answer. She looked at him—at the familiar face of Norman Jaspers whom she had known so many years—as though she were seeing a total stranger. "No . . . you are right. This certainly *isn't* the time." She sat up quite stiffly. "I am not going on up valley to Anton's house. I've decided to buy a car and return to Spring Mountain."

"Sarah . . . please don't be upset with me too. If I can be of any help in buying the car—I have a lot of experience with automobiles. I bought one of the very first cars in Napa County. I've bought a new one every year since. Please, won't you let me help you make a choice? I'm executor of the estate—you *will* have to go through me to get the money released."

She took a long breath. "Yes, I suppose you're right. You would know more than anyone else. As you say, you are the executor—the family lawyer. You are a friend too. Let's keep it that way. *Please*. Do you understand?"

With Norman's guidance, she selected for her first motorcar a brand-new 1923 Buick sedan, in the two-tone shades of gray and black. Every afternoon, Norman found time to give her a driving lesson. After a week, she had overcome her fear and was beginning to discover the exhilaration of owning and driving her own automobile.

When Norman dropped by for one last period of driving instructions, wanting to be sure she understood certain points about driving in the rain, about how the windshield wipers worked, Sarah asked him, "By the way, have you seen Anton since our trip to the city?"

"Yes. Just a couple of days ago. He's been keeping to himself pretty much. The . . . incident was more upsetting than he expected it would be. He asked about you."

"Diane? Is *she* . . ."

"Yes—okay, it seems. She's staying on in San Francisco. Plans to go to college. Become something besides a secretary, she wrote to me in her letter of resignation."

"I see. But you think Anton is okay?"

He twisted his mouth into a thin line. "We know Anton will always be okay, don't we? He's already mapping out how to invest profits he expects to earn this coming harvest." He gazed out across the gleaming long hood of the new black-and-gray Buick. "He used to pick *my* brain—now I learn from him. He's very astute in business matters. He learned more than I did at Harvard."

"You've done very well, I'd say."

"I used to have some of Anton's driving ambition. I thought money was the answer to everything. Success, certain possessions. Now, as I get older, I'm not so sure." He smiled. "I'll tell Anton that you asked about him. He was afraid you wouldn't talk to him again. I know he's anxious for you to see the remodeling job he's done on the old Brunner place. Shall we go by soon?"

"Yes. Yes, I'd like that very much," she said, getting behind the wheel, ready to drive off for her first solo trip.

Norman called for her to go visit Anton that next Sunday. It was a cold, drizzly January afternoon, one that made Sarah glad to have a place to go. She peered out through the windshield with open curiosity as they drove down the Brunner driveway and the outlines of the recently remodeled house came into view.

She was glad to see that the new wing had been added on in such a way as to look integrated, as though it had always been there; yet, on the inside, she saw, as Anton rushed to greet them, it was surprisingly modern and spacious.

Anton was delighted to see them. He was bored with reading through new investment brochures and going over laborious graphs recently issued by the Grape Protective Association over projected declining profits in the grape market in the coming years ahead. He was wearing gray flannel trousers, a plaid shirt open at the collar, and had tossed a cardigan around his shoulders, tied the sleeves loosely around his neck. Sarah thought he looked quite as casually elegant as did the décor of his newly done house.

After tossing a log on the fire in the living room and fixing a drink of Scotch and soda for them, he took them on an ambling tour. The living room was tastefully comfortable, with some excellent country-English antiques, eclectically mixed with down-cushioned armchairs upholstered in a green-and-white large-checked woolen material he had had woven by a Vermont family of weavers who had been specialists in the craft since early New England days, he told them. A collection of rare Gould prints of plants were hung in striking groupings against rust-colored walls. On the mantel and various tabletops stood a large collection of Staffordshire figures ranging from the 1700s on up through the nineteenth century—peasant figures in charming simple modeling and bold colors. Sarah liked the dining room best, with its rustic country-style round table, the seventeenth-century hutch cabinet from England with its open shelves holding Anton's collection of Porto Bello earthenware. "It's something I learned about in England," he explained proudly. "The famous potter Thomas Astbury who did work for Staffordshire did these to depict Admiral Vernon's capture of Porto Bello."

When he pointed out his collection of china—excellent Wedgwood, Belleek plates from Ireland, Limoges—Sarah said, "I'm surprised at your interest in fine china."

"You shouldn't be." He smiled over his Scotch. "I remember seeing that first formal dinner table you set for us on Spring Mountain, and the lessons you used to give us on how to eat. I was duly impressed. I used to think your dining table was the most splendid sight, particularly after the way Gudrun used to slam any kind of plate in front of us, anything to get eating over with. Of course, as a bachelor, I do things more simply. It's just that I enjoy knowing that I have certain things; that I could do the other."

"Your home is lovely. Very large for a bachelor."

They were sitting in the living room now. Anton crossed his leg over one knee, stared at the fire a moment. "I've been thinking I might go back east and see if Phyllis will marry me. After the experience with Diane, maybe it's time I settle down with one woman. I don't want to go through *that* again."

After another half hour or so of light conversation, when it began to rain hard and Norman suggested they head back, Sarah took Anton's hand. "Let's forget the—the other. Good luck, dear, with Phyllis. Yes, marriage—it might be the best thing."

Anton headed east when, in May, Lilliana gave birth to a girl, who was named Anne—though Vittorio let it be known he was hurt that they had not named the baby after Delfina.

"We want our children to grow up aware of being true individuals," David said quietly. "We don't want them to feel they have to live up to someone else's identity."

Vittorio looked bewildered. "Is that what they teach in the fancy colleges? It is not the way I learned in the old country!"

Sarah had noticed that Lilliana seemed tense. She made a point to visit quietly with her. "I just want to say that should you and David change your mind, you are welcome to take over the house on Spring Mountain. I have my own automobile now. I'm getting out and about —involving myself in politics a little. Trying to help bring about repeal of this Volstead Act. I won't get in your way. I'll maintain a small apartment in the upstairs library and the bedroom off of it. That is all I could possibly use. I won't be one of those meddling mothers-in-law. I promise. You need time to be alone with your baby."

Lilliana's eyes filled with tears. "It's just that Papa—he seems to be trying to bring Mother back through me. Through the baby. I have hardly got to hold her! Either one of my sisters has her or Papa takes over. David and I—we don't have much privacy here."

"Promise me you will consider coming up. I'll see that you have a nice car. Norman Jaspers tells me I've made some money on investments Adam left me."

"David has so much pride. He won't take handouts."

"He'll accept a gift, won't he? The automobile will be my gift to my first grandchild—in your name, of course. And the house—well, Spring Mountain does legally belong to David now. He can hardly regard it as a handout."

By late June, several factors gave David no alternative but to bring Lilliana and the baby back to Spring Mountain.

In the first place, Vittorio had caused almost constant conflict, insisting that by the rules of the old country he had full say-so about running the household. Too, Beringers' Winery had informed David that they were having to cut back and his job was being terminated. In addition, Kyle Plimpton's arthritis was creeping into his hip joints as well as his hands and David would have to take over the vineyards before harvest, like it or not.

Sarah was pleased to have them. In spite of getting out more, she often got lonely. As soon as they arrived, she made it clear that she intended to stay in the background and that Lilliana would be in charge of running the household, her own way. However, she insisted on paying for a full-time maid who would be hired personally by David and Lilliana and directed by them accordingly.

"Li Po isn't getting any younger," she told them. "He will continue taking care of my needs. I guess he'll be with me for the rest of his life. But he can't manage everything."

She got out the books and explained what she knew of them to David. "These are yours now," she said, turning them over to him. "It's up to you to run Spring Mountain. If I can help, I will. But only when you ask for my advice, not before. Spring Mountain is yours now. I'm a guest here. Nothing more."

After that, she directed her main energies toward active involvement in the Democratic Party. The growing scandals erupting from the Warren Harding administration—the Teapot Dome scandal being only one of many to come—had made her decide that the next President of the United States should come from the Democratic Party. Quickly, she was made chairman of a committee to get more voters enrolled in the party and to try to figure ways of raising money. She had found it easy enough to get the help of Norman Jaspers, who looked for excuses to be with her and who needed some basic topic of mutual discussion so that he would not slip and spill out his increasing desire to marry her.

Sarah enjoyed their political discussions. Where, with Adam, she had found herself giving in always to his need to be the man in charge —the *padrone* who knew the ultimate answers—with Norman they could each air differences. And he knew so much!

414

She remembered that last week of July when President Harding had checked into the Palace Hotel in San Francisco to rest up after a long exhausting tour, and Norman, who was driving Sarah home after a dull committee meeting, had said, "From what I hear, he'll *need* a long rest, and not from having crossed country."

"A rest? From what?" she had asked.

"A scandal about to break. My friend Jason Bloom, a classmate at Harvard Law School, who works on Capitol Hill, writes to me that the scandal ready to break will rock the nation. He says Albert Fall will probably be the first Cabinet officer in history to go to jail. His old pal Harry Daugherty has been destroying bank records. One of his top aides is ready to bring evidence against him. It's the sleaziest group of men to grace a Cabinet."

"But you were just saying the other day that he had put in some excellent men. You said Chief Justice Taft was the best one ever. And you certainly like Charles Evans Hughes, Andrew Mellon, Herbert Hoover, don't you? Or are you being inconsistent?"

"I like *some* things, yes. The way he's cut back on the national debt, lowered taxes—though, granted, the cuts help mostly the rich. Myself happily included."

"It's his basic lack of humanity that disturbs me," Sarah counteracted. "Imagine—calling European immigrants 'rabble'! If it had been up to Warren Harding, I would never have had the chance of meeting Adam Donati. He would have been kept out of the country."

Norman couldn't hold back a sigh. He had hoped Sarah was forgetting a little about Adam these days.

"Why are you sighing? Do you *approve* of the way he has cut off immigration?"

He searched for a quick answer. "He isn't totally inhuman. He did free the imprisoned Socialist, Eugene Debs. He saw that the steelworkers' hours were cut back from twelve hours a day to an eight-hour shift. Isn't that humane?" He had stopped the car, was helping her out, guiding her up the pathway toward the stone veranda. Would he ever convince her how much he loved her—that she should forget the past and marry him? Aloud he said, "How are things going with Lilliana in charge of the household?"

It was her turn to sigh. "I guess any two women would run a household differently. I guess I'm used—too used to being in charge. I try to hold back." She gave Norman a light friendly kiss. "Forget what I said about President Harding. I'm sure he's a nice man. I hear he calls his wife 'the Duchess.' A man who loves his wife that much can't be all bad."

Norman let her go, bit back the temptation to spill out the rest of the gossip in the letter from his friend in Washington: that Harding was such a man with the ladies he had a young mistress who came to his Presidential office, where their favorite rendezvous was the coat closet; that Warren Harding and "the Duchess" had such bitter quarrels all of Capitol Hill reverberated with them. Besides, he did not intend to discuss such crude subjects with Sarah, whom he had endowed with his own crown. As he hurried down the pathway toward his car, pulse racing, he told himself, Let her have her fantasies about Warren Harding.

But that very week, Warren Gamaliel Harding died, at the age of fifty-seven, in his room at the Palace Hotel in San Francisco. Rumors were rampant. Because "the Duchess" had refused an autopsy, there were those claiming she herself had poisoned him—in revenge, some said; others said to save him from the erupting scandals and probable impeachment. One doctor said it was ptomaine poisoning; another team declared the cause of death to be a heart attack.

Sarah herself brought up the subject. "This means Vice-President Coolidge steps in—which means that he will most likely knock out the chances of any Democrat getting elected next term."

"Yes, I tend to agree. Coolidge is a good man. One who'll work hard to right some of the wrongs he's seen, which are plenty. Jason Bloom thinks he's a very strong man, Coolidge."

"No skeletons in *his* closet?" Sarah asked.

Norman did not know whether there was some inference behind her remark. Because he preferred to think it totally innocent, he went on to another point: "What we must work for is getting Coolidge—or whomever—to work against Prohibition. Against other rots setting in. I'm worried—I don't like a lot of things I see across country. I'm convinced the grape market is going to plunge. There's no long-range plan economically to sustain us—in any area, as I read the future."

"Aren't you being gloomy just because the President just died? Isn't that a *short*-range opinion?" she asked lightly.

"I'm a man conditioned to *long*-range analysis," he said, smiling at the secret irony that held for his feelings for her.

That harvest of 1923, the large profits reaped on grapes did not support Norman's theory. Though production in the county was off some five thousand tons of grapes, netting $500,000 less than the year before, the Donati vineyards had earned their highest profits ever, with ten new producing acres of Alicantes to add to their production. Because of this, a big celebration was planned.

The dinner was the first since Adam's death. It was being planned strictly by David and Lilliana. Sarah stood back, biting back acute urges to give Lilliana suggestions. When, at one point, she stood silently watching Lilliana put regular kitchen plates and flatware out for a casual buffet, Lilliana noted her look and said quietly, "David insisted that we keep it simple. He wants us to be—well, more relaxed than people, well, used to be."

"It's *your* party," Sarah said. "Your way suits me fine." But later, because she did not live comfortably with having spoken a lie, she mentioned it to Norman. (How strange, she was to think in retrospect, that such a mundane episode as how one set a table could be the decisive factor in getting her to say yes to Norman.)

"Why don't you marry me and give parties your own way?" They were out on the stone veranda, waiting for the guests. He asked it casually, and she, equally, tossed back the casual answer "Yes. Why not? We do get along well. We do enjoy each other's company, don't we? We should have a good life together. And I think I've overstayed my welcome up here. Lilliana and I, as hard as we both try, don't see eye to eye."

He was so surprised by her quick agreement that he did not know quite what to say. Surprisingly, he came over calmly, with only a quiver in his voice telling something of the thundering going on in his chest. "Shall we set the date? Shouldn't we—so that we can announce it at dinner today?"

She looked out across the vineyards. "Adam died almost a year ago. But I need a little more time to get used to the idea. Shall we say —what about next summer? Before harvest?"

As it turned out, other important announcements were to be made that day, when a delayed dinner got under way. Lilliana was not well organized. She had difficulty directing her maid, Judy, a big sprawling farm girl with little domestic experience. As they all balanced plates on their knees and tried to cut tough ham with a fork, Anton stood up and said rather briskly, "I'm leaving for Boston tomorrow. Phyllis Fuller will be announcing our engagement next Saturday night. Our wedding will be in June."

After a round of congratulations and questions, David got up. "*Our* news is that we're having our second child in March. We're hoping for a boy this time. We want a big family to fill up this big house. We want the children to grow up friends."

Norman waited until dessert to stand up. He tugged at his suit coat. Though, at fifty-nine, he was a short, droopy-jowled man who struggled to keep his weight down, at that moment of flushed happiness his friendly face was almost handsome, Sarah thought, clasping her hands tightly in her lap under the table, feeling the pressure from the wedding ring that she still wore.

"Since we have pretty much rounded out the toasts—to the harvest, to Spring Mountain's future heirs, to Anton's bride-to-be, I would like to add one more." He looked at Sarah, then concentrated on David's face. "Next summer, Sarah and I plan to be married. We have decided that we should have a good life together based on our long-standing friendship and our mutual understanding. I have been made a very happy man today, so I invite you, her family and friends, to join me in a toast to her. To the happiness I hope to help bring her. To our continued health . . . our life together."

David barely sipped from his wineglass. "That *is* a surprise," he said stiffly. "I guess I never quite saw you two in that light. I—"

Anton stood up, lifted his glass high. "It's marvelous! I'm pleased to hear it."

Sarah felt David's silent rebuke. Tears stung her eyes. He was her only real son—he should be the first to be happy for her. It was hard enough as it was even trying to imagine a man other than Adam Donati as her husband. At that moment, she seemed to see Adam's own shape in the shadows by the screen leading to the kitchen. But it was Li Po, scurrying over, bringing a cup of tea to her, looking down at her as though he knew her confusion.

"Mr. Jaspers a nice man," he said softly. "Good man for you to marry."

When the dinner was over, Anton walked down the pathway with Norman. "Congratulations, old boy," he said, clasping him lightly on the shoulder. "I always guessed this might happen. But I wasn't sure you could convince her."

"It takes me longer, but in my own roundabout way I usually get what I want in life, too, Anton."

They reached their cars, parked side by side. Anton propped one foot on the fender of his Packard, lit a cigarette, and in the soft light of dusk, the wind blowing his hair off his high forehead, he looked more handsome than any man—except Adam Donati—whom Norman had ever seen. "By the way, Norman, I have a little legal job for you to do for me, if you would, please. You see, when I was back east I always went by the name of Anton Brunner. 'Donati'—that was a little too ethnic to suit me. Now that I plan to be married, I want it official. I'm dropping the name Donati from here on out."

"What does your family think?"

He blew smoke toward the sky. "They'll get used to it. You see, when repeal comes, I plan to open my own winery. The Anton Brunner Winery—how does that sound?"

"Optimistic! I don't see any wineries opening."

"Nonsense. Repeal will happen. When it does, I'll be waiting and ready for it. I don't want any confusion over labels either. I figure David will open the Donati Winery. I don't want my name and his getting mixed up. I have big plans—very big plans. If I know David, he'll always operate on a small scale."

"David has a lot of high standards. Don't sell him short."

"David's trouble is that he can't see past Napa Valley." Anton looked at Norman. "You don't really *like* me, do you, Norman? I see it in your face—you're holding something back you'd just love to get off your chest." He let smoke drift slowly through his nostrils, then flipped the cigarette down, ground out the light, swung in behind the wheel of his car, but didn't close the door. "Come on—out with it."

"I think sometimes you're *too* ambitious. I think you lose sight of people—of their real feelings. That you'd step on anyone who got in the way of your big plans."

Anton's hands gripped the steering wheel tightly. "You're still stewing over Diane Margolis, aren't you? When are you going to forget that?"

"I happen to know you hurt her deeply. That she's not over it yet."

Anton closed the car door, started the motor. "Aren't you going to congratulate me on my engagement? Why don't you try *that* instead of making me feel guilty about Diane Margolis?"

"It's just that I worry about you and any woman, Anton," Norman said, stepping back out of the way. "Women need love."

"*Love*—that's an all-encompassing word. You were saying something at the dinner table about friendship and companionship."

"At *our* age, yes. At yours—Anton, you're a very handsome young man, any woman who marries you will be in love with you."

"So?"

"So, I feel sorry for her. I'd try to talk her out of it."

"Save your breath! It's all set. I'll come by your office tomorrow to sign any papers needed. Around noon—okay?" The tires of the Packard sent gravel flying as Anton backed out, sped off into the early night toward the road leading down valley.

On March 24, 1924, Lilliana gave birth to a second daughter.

"We were so sure it would be a boy, we don't even have a name!"

She looked at Sarah as though fighting back tears. "David doesn't say so, but I know he's disappointed."

"Girls are so dear—so easy," Sarah said reassuringly. "David will get used to the idea. You'll have a son next time." She took the baby out of the bassinet, handed it to Lilliana. "What names have you considered?"

"Oh, Kate, Kim, Amy . . . David likes Delia. Any suggestions?"

"Anything that pleases you suits me. The baby is perfect." Sarah glanced down at the squirming legs, the tiny hands doubled up, the face red, pinched up, ready to cry.

"You're such a nice—a lovely mother-in-law," Lilliana suddenly blurted out. "Even when we get on each other's nerves, when I know I've displeased you, I always love you."

"The same with me," Sarah said quickly. "But I'll be even a better one when I move out. By the way, Norman and I have set August eighth—a Saturday, I believe—for our wedding. We want to get it over with before harvest. Take a short trip, get back."

"Please don't rush the date because of—well, us."

"No, it isn't that. It's time for me to leave Spring Mountain. This place was Adam's dream. Oh, I was part of it. But even dreams have their cycles. Yes, my cycle here is over . . . Yours and David's, the children's, is just beginning. I know Adam would be pleased—the house finally filling up with heirs." She walked over and stared out the window at Howell Mountain across the way. "Sometimes I think I *see* him out there," she said quietly. "You know the way clouds take on shapes, form faces? I see his jaw—that wonderful stubborn jaw of his —riding the sky. Sometimes I expect to see him come striding out of the vineyards. . . . No, dear, it is time for me to leave Spring Mountain."

"You love him so, don't you?" Lilliana asked, getting the baby, who was crying now, into position to nurse.

"I will always love him—to the day I die," Sarah said, hurrying out of the room.

18

From then until her wedding day, Sarah tried to pass time by getting involved with the Presidential election coming up that fall. But she could not work up genuine enthusiasm over the Democratic ticket of Davis and Bryan. She thought the Progressive candidates La Follette and Wheeler were as interesting as anyone, though she expected Coolidge and Dawes to win easily.

From habit, she followed reports on the grape industry, predictions as to what the upcoming harvest would mean. She was concerned about the future for David and Lilliana on Spring Mountain. Though there was temporary excitement over the profits from grapes being shipped east, there was also that counterpoint of those who expected the bottom to drop out. She had read one table that indicated that extensive diversification was taking place still, with fruit crops in Napa County doubling the acreage planted in wine grapes, which had only some ten thousand acres of bearing vines.

She stopped David one afternoon as he was coming out of the vineyards and crossing the veranda. "Sit—let's talk a minute," she urged.

He had been checking to see if any of the young berries had been damaged from a recent windstorm, and, having hiked through most of the extensive vineyards, he was glad to rest a few minutes. He wiped his forehead, then his chin that was so much like Adam's. He glanced at the reports in Sarah's lap. "What are the doomsayers putting out now?"

"The Napa County Horticultural Commissioner says he thinks in another ten years there won't be many vines left. That all of the remaining grain lands will be turned into the production of fruit. I was just wondering if you thought *you* should diversify at all? If you think repeal will ever come about?"

He stretched his long legs out, tilted back in the old wicker chair and smiled. "I don't see it—that the grape industry is dead. When have growers ever made such big profits with so little effort? As for diversifying, you know Papa wanted Spring Mountain for vineyards. I'd like to keep it that way."

She felt a keen stab of pleasure. She had been concerned that David was losing his basic interest in the vineyards. "If repeal should come about, would you reopen the winery?"

"If? I don't work with ifs. I work with what we have. I've got my hands full as it is."

"Have you considered working politically? Joining some of the groups trying to fight Prohibition? Your father used to be quite active—"

"I remember that Papa became very disillusioned," David said, getting up, staring out for a moment at the vineyards. "No, I'll let the other guy do the political ball game. Oh, sure, I'd like to see repeal. See all the wineries open up again and the crush go full blast this harvest coming up. But I don't see it happening. We may never see Napa Valley return to what it used to be. Spring Mountain won't ever be what Papa really wanted it to be, is how I look at it."

"But you will *try*—try to bring his dream about?"

He seemed to be angry with her. She couldn't put her finger on the near-glaring look he shot down at her. "I have a few dreams of my own. Is that allowed?"

Before she could answer he had slammed the screen door and she heard his field boots making heavy thudding sounds as he disappeared into the depths of the huge stone house.

August 8, 1924, was a hot, blistering Saturday that was good for the ripening of the grapes but difficult for people who weren't accustomed to the heat—for instance, the musicians Norman had hired out of San Francisco to provide the dance music following the wedding. As they went about setting up chairs and music stands and placing instruments on that far end of the brick terrace where he wanted them to play, he could hear their grumblings, see them wiping off perspiration and complaining that in Napa County, of all places, they couldn't find a glass of wine even.

Norman had gone over to the leader of the orchestra. "I had planned to have champagne, but the sheriff's deputy was by here just a few minutes ago warning me. Besides, they're having some kind of Ku Klux Klan gathering in Napa County today. The deputy said over ten thousand of them have swarmed in to hold a northern California convention. Seems their main drive lately is to get the bootleggers." He shrugged his shoulders. "Wouldn't you know I'd choose not only the hottest day of the summer for our wedding but the one day in a century when ten thousand Ku Klux Klanners arrive!" He mopped his own brow.

A black musician tuning the strings of his bass muttered: "Ten *thousand*—that's a lots of sheets!"

Brad Kemper, a Harvard Law School classmate whom Norman had asked to stand up with him during the wedding ceremony, had just wandered up. "Ten thousand is a lot of anything. Are you sure the sheriff's deputy didn't exaggerate?"

Norman stuffed the handkerchief back into the pocket of his new suit, brushed at imaginary dandruff on his shoulders. "He says it's at least that many. A special train brought in three carloads. He had already counted over two thousand out-of-county automobiles."

The black musician, whose name was Jackson, lifted his eyebrows, propped his bass violin against the wall, looked at his fellow musicians. "If I see any ten thousand—if I see even *one* Ku Klux Klan—you are going to be missing a bass player!" He took a flask out of his back pocket. "You said that deputy has come and gone?"

But Norman and Brad Kemper were walking around to the other end of the brick terrace and did not see the musicians accept glasses of ice water, dump the water out and pour in whatever they had brought along to keep them "stoked," as Jackson called it.

Norman was trying to reposition a large Chinese urn filled with a palm. Brad pitched in to help. He was a cynic about marriages, having gone through three disastrous ones of his own. He looked up, his once handsome craggy face now bloated, showing the telling traces of too many years of heavy drinking. "You don't have much more time to be a single man. You're sure you know what you're doing, Norm? Didn't you tell me a few months back that she's still carrying a torch for her dead husband?"

"That was a few months back," Norman said, straightening his bow tie, taking a deep breath. He checked his watch. "Judge Bell and the others invited for the ceremony ought to be getting here pretty soon. I'm all set from this end. Look, Brad—sure I'm sure I know what I'm doing! I've waited for this day for over twenty years. I ought to be sure."

"Where is the lucky bride?"

"Upstairs, getting dressed. With her daughter-in-law. She'll be down when everybody gets here. When it's time."

At Sarah's request, Lilliana had come early to help her get dressed, snapped up and buttoned up properly in the delicate oyster-colored lace dress with its matching hat and pumps that Anton had picked out for her in New York and sent across country as his special gift to

Sarah. He had hastily scribbled out a note and placed it in the huge boxes stuffed with layers of tissue paper: "Since I will be in Europe with my bride Phyllis, I want to at least be able to imagine how you look at the wedding. I hope it fits—that you like it. See you in late August or early September at the latest. Love, Anton."

The pumps were long enough, but on the narrow side. Sarah had squeezed her feet into the shimmering satin slippers with their pearl buckles, let Lilliana pin the small hat with its lace veil into place, fastened the belt with its pearl buckle to match those on the pumps, stood back in front of the full-length mirror to examine the result.

For a moment she stood quietly, having the strange sense of being somehow detached from herself, as though she had stepped just behind herself and was looking over her own shoulder.

Lilliana's voice came from across the room. "You look lovely. That cream color is very becoming."

Sarah moved away from the mirror, let her hands drift across the folds of the full skirt of her dress as she sat down on the edge of a chaise longue covered with quilted Chinese silk. Lilliana, watching her, absently twisted the ends of the tie belt of the blue-flowered crepe dress she had made especially to wear to Sarah's wedding, having added full gathers, hoping to hide some of the extra weight she had gained with the last baby and not yet taken off. Seeing Sarah's new stylish haircut, she pushed self-consciously at a loose strand of her own dark hair that lately had seemed lifeless, dry and coarse. There was something about being in Sarah's presence—though she basically loved her —that made her feel threatened, inadequate.

"I'll never forget your first wedding," she said tentatively. "Remember how Mother made us memorize those silly speeches? How Theresa played those off-tune chords during the wedding march?" Her voice trailed off. "That seems in some ways just a little while ago. In others . . . So much has happened since then."

Sarah clasped her hands together, felt the empty space where she had permanently removed Adam's wedding ring—where so very soon now the huge diamond ring Norman had bought for her would be placed. She had the odd feeling that she was sinking. That something was vanishing from inside herself. With forced brightness, she looked up at Lilliana. "Tell me—now that you'll have Spring Mountain to yourself, aren't you and David looking forward to that?" She smiled. "Lately, David has seemed so—well, grouchy. Sometimes I feel he's not only mad at me but at the whole world. With my absence—yes, it should be better now."

"It's not because of you," Lilliana said quickly. "I guess David just feels he's missed out on certain things. Lately he's been complaining that he has never been out of the state of California. He—oh, I don't know why he's so down in the dumps! Maybe he's sorry he married *me*. Maybe he doesn't like being saddled with two babies, particularly girls." She looked suddenly ready to cry. "Maybe he wishes he had gone out with other girls. Not married so soon." She looked up at Sarah, her eyes wide, desperate. "At the time, it seemed the only thing to do. We loved each other so much. We were struggling so hard to get through school and it— Oh, I shouldn't be talking about this on your wedding day! It is selfish of me. I'm sorry."

Sarah got up, went over to Lilliana and put her arm across her shoulder. "All marriages have rough spots. You'll get over this one. I think my leaving will help immeasurably. You will feel much freer. You won't feel that I'm always there approving or disapproving. David —I think he resents me." She fussed with the half-veil on the lace hat. "It's true—David hasn't had an opportunity to travel. He didn't inherit the kind of money that Anton did. Maybe he resents Anton too. The fact that Anton and I are rather close. In a different way." Her face brightened. "But when Norman and I return from our trip to Hawaii I'll see about arranging a trip for the two of you. I can afford it."

Lilliana's eyes widened. "Oh, please—you mustn't! You mustn't say anything to David. He thinks you give us too much as it is. That you don't give him the chance to prove he can do things on his own. Oh, I'm sorry to have told you that!"

Sarah took a deep breath. She sat down again on the chaise longue. "You needn't be sorry. You should tell me. I thought part of David's problem was that perhaps he didn't want me to marry Norman. Now I see that has nothing to do with it. It's as I suspected. I'm a kind of third shoe up there."

"Sarah, no—please understand. You're not that at all! It's just that David is so independent." Lilliana looked at Sarah anxiously. "He has run into several major disappointments in life. Wanting to be a wine-maker so badly, for instance, getting trained to be a very fine wine-maker, and then having Prohibition kill the whole industry. That's hard on a man. Plus he really did want sons instead of daughters. He has not once held his daughters! He simply doesn't have anything to do with them."

"Have you tried talking with him about it, Lilliana?" Sarah saw her distress, the way she looked down at her feet, was twisting the ends of the tie belt. "Can't you bring it out?"

"David has trouble expressing himself. He's not articulate the way Anton is. Obviously I'm not, either."

"I'm glad you have been honest with me. That you're here keeping me company. I was having last-minute doubts. Come—go down with me. It's time. I told Norman I'd meet him on the brick terrace at five." But even as Sarah gripped the stairway railing, as her satin slippers found their footing going down, she felt her hand, her very ankles, tremble with uncertainty.

The actual wedding ceremony was over within minutes after Sarah appeared on the terrace. Only Brad Kemper, David and Lilliana, Martha and Frank Cantrell and Kyle Plimpton (Emma was home in bed with an attack of gallstones) attended. Other guests had been invited to arrive at six o'clock. By then, a brief round of private toasts had been made, Sarah was wearing her sparkling new wedding ring, and the orchestra had struck up the first lively waltz.

From the beginning of the long driveway, lanterns glowed like pale-yellow moons. Norman's own Japanese houseboy had hired friends from San Francisco to serve the guests, and everywhere Sarah looked she saw them scurrying about in their crisp white jackets, black trousers, black bow ties, passing trays or hors d'oeuvres, glasses of punch, directing guests to the elaborate buffet tables prepared by a catering service from Nob Hill.

The invitations had read from six until nine o'clock. By nine o'clock, the weather had cooled down; people who had brought along their own secret flasks and spiked their drinks were reluctant to stop dancing; the caviar, smoked salmon, pâté de foie gras had been eaten, the buffet tables left in shambles. Sarah was standing with Norman bidding guests goodbye.

Brad Kemper (who had just downed some straight bootleg whiskey Kyle had shared with him—a first run from a Howell Mountain still) blinked his eyes, said to Norman, "The food was *grande cuisine*. All that was missing was the Château Lafon-Rochet, a little Pichon-Baron, maybe some of that Château Mouton-Rothschild we used to sample at Harvard, eh? Any good vintage will do. Speaking of vintages, Norman, ole buddy, you ought to win a medal! Being a groom the first time at sixty." He was having trouble keeping his balance.

As Norman took Brad's arm and led him out of Sarah's hearing, asking her to wait for him on the terrace, she sank down in a wrought-iron chair, eased her aching, cramped feet out of the narrow satin slippers. David came up, looking for her to tell her goodbye. The orchestra had just started the last lively fox-trot. The music, the clatter of glasses, the sound of people's voices laughing and talking, seemed to form an engulfing wave of dizziness over Sarah's head. "I can't get up," she said with an exhausted smile. "I simply have to rest my feet. Do you have to go just yet?"

He sat down by her. "Lilliana has to get back to the baby. A ten-o'clock feeding. I guess we won't see you for a while." He was staring out at the milling party.

"David . . . I—I hope you and Lilliana are going to find a wonderful life together on Spring Mountain. I—please know that I love you. I love you so very much." She saw Li Po, who had come at her request, standing over in the shadows of a palm tree, as if wondering what he should do next. "It's a new place in life for all of us, isn't it? A kind of threshold. Or maybe I should call it a point of departure." She squinted as she looked up at him. "Does a mother ever know when to let go, whether she had done what she should have done? If I've made mistakes with you—you and Lilliana—please know they were that, mistakes. Not deliberate intentions."

He leaned over, kissed her lightly on her forehead. "Don't look so serious," he said mockingly. "It's your wedding night, Mrs. Jaspers." He looked out over the crowd, searching for Lilliana, who had gone for her purse. "Any relationship has its points of departure," he said, tilting his head in the old way that he had done back when he was a little boy, when there had been only himself and Sarah. "A man ends up sitting down with what he really is, not with what somebody else tried to make him be. Not even what he himself wants to be."

He spotted Lilliana, waved, kissed Sarah a quick goodbye. "Well —take care . . . . Take it easy," he said, as if only in their goodbye did he feel awkward, unsure of the threshold she had just crossed.

"We'll be back in two, three weeks. I'll see you then."

"Sure . . . sure thing," he said, hurring off.

David was not at all sure why he felt at such crossed swords with himself, with his mother, with Lilliana. It all had something vaguely to do with Spring Mountain. He supposedly owned it now, but he had not really had free run of it; for even when his mother held back her opinions, he could sense her approval or disapproval in the very way she would stand sometimes, or look, or walk out of a room. Besides, he wasn't all that sure he had wanted to take over Spring Mountain. It had been more or less dumped on him. Not that he didn't love the place. He did. He loved the quiet of it, the sounds of the mountain wind rustling the pine trees and the leaves of the vineyards. He loved the old stone buildings, the views of the valley stretched out below, of the mountains across the way. In his way, he loved a certain challenge of the land, the vines. He was looking forward to the day when he could oversee his own first crush, make his first wine under the David Donati label.

"What did you think of the wedding?" he asked after he had turned out on the main highway and headed north.

"Norman certainly spent a lot of money. He's awfully rich, isn't he? And he seems to want to spend his money on her."

"When I get rich, I'll spend money on you, too."

"I didn't mean it that way."

"For a dry country, there certainly were a lot of drunks there—sheriff's warning or not. Norman might as well have bought out tubs of the stuff."

Lilliana seemed to have slouched into some place of her own, leaning against the door on her side instead of against David's shoulder, as she usually did. Dotted here and there in the darkness were the shapes of lighted windows. Headlights from an approaching car bore down like huge eyes; whizzed by.

"What's wrong? You mad at me or something? What did I do wrong this time?"

"Nothing. I was just thinking."

"About what?"

"How Sarah seemed lost . . . scared. Not sure of anything, really. And she always struck me as being so very sure about everything. It was the first time I wasn't intimidated around her." She bit her lip, clasped her hands. "Are you worried about her? Her being married to Norman Jaspers?"

"Why should I be? He's a good guy. Innocuous. Vapid. But he'll be okay. Mother—she's strong. She'll look out for herself. Don't worry about her."

"Should I be worried about *us*, David? I am, really. That's what's really bothering me. Not Sarah at all."

David was squinting his eyes, peering ahead at a strange configuration glowing in the distance. "Why? When we're on a new threshold, as Mother called it. Don't you have faith in me? That I can manage Spring Mountain on my own?" He was slowing down, seeing now that the configurations were unmistakably crosses burning and thousands of torches being waved about in the air.

Lilliana had seen it by now, too, and was sitting up, looking anxiously ahead. "They're really *here*," she said under her breath. "It's frightening, David! Let's turn back. Don't go up that way. Look—they're out by the road, some of them."

"It's the deputy—waving outsiders on, I guess." He was being flagged to a stop. At the road leading back to the Lewellings' farm, David could see the sheriff's car, and a group of men milling about: spillovers or curious onlookers, he decided.

The deputy poked his face close to David's. "You a Klanner? You want in to this meeting?"

"No, thank you," David said stiffly. "I just want to pass on by and head home."

"Yeah? Where's home? We've had some threats tonight. People wanting to stir up trouble. You one of *them*?"

"No. I'm David Donati. From Spring Mountain."

"Hey—look what we've got here. One of the county's biggest bootleggers!" he roared.

It was then that at least ten men surrounded the car, Lilliana was to point out later; with no objections from anyone. It happened so quickly—the rhythmic rocking back and forth of the car, that terrible sense that the car would be tilted completely over.

"Roll up your window!" David cried out, trying to keep his balance. "*Lock* your door."

She was aware of pitching, sliding, clasping at anything to hold on to. She heard their laughter, their jeering.

"Look what we've got here—big-time bootleggers! Shake 'em up good. Tell 'em what we're going to do to 'em next go round, men! Tell 'em why we've got three crosses burning out there in the mdidle of the field."

"You sonsabitches!" David screamed out.

"*Don't*, David!" she whispered, remembering another time in her life: when the men had come to auction off the Alfieri property on Howell Mountain and had laughed at her father; when she had felt screams inside her turn mute with shame and the sickness of buried speechless horror. "Just get us out of here!"

It seemed an eternity before the sheriff pushed his way past the deputies and the thrust of men rocking the car more and more precariously. "Back off!" he yelled, pointing a shotgun. Then, pounding on David's window, he yelled, "Okay, Donati, get the hell out of here! My advice is for you to stay put a few days—until this dies down."

After it was over, Lilliana began to cry, silently, trying not to alarm David even more. She could see his set jaw, his tight knuckles.

"Goddam bunch of cowards!" David muttered. "Liars!"

Then they both fell silent, staring straight ahead, passing on through the quiet, sleepy main street of St. Helena.

"It's enough to turn me into a bootlegger!" David said as he started the climb up Spring Mountain, with his hands now clenched into fists, his chin jutting out like a wall of defense of its own. "I wish I could drive right on, over the top of the mountain—on and on and on and *never* come back to Napa Valley," he said with a cold fierceness.

"We can't do that," Lilliana said in a voice still quavery with fright. "We have the babies. Little Delia will be screaming to be fed. Judy won't remember to heat the supplement feeding. She's so thick-headed sometimes. We can't run off and leave the babies."

He did not answer. When they arrived in front of the old stone stable, he slammed on the brake, got out of the car without offering to assist her, and stalked off toward the house, leaving Lilliana to trail behind him at her own pace along the darkened pathway. When they entered the main house, she heard the baby's high piercing wail, saw a bedraggled Judy standing at the kitchen door with the young Anne hoisted on one hip.

"Why isn't Anne asleep?" Lilliana barked. "You know I told you to put her to bed at seven o'clock. On schedule. Didn't you give the baby her supplement feeding? Can't you do anything right, Judy?"

"I did what you told me to do, but nothing worked! You got no right yelling at me. My head hurts and my back hurts and I'm tired of being stuck off up here. I'm quitting! I'm leaving first thing in the morning."

Anne, who at fifteen months was still a baby, began to cry and reached her round arms out toward Lilliana.

"David, take her, *please*. I've got to feed Delia."

Before David could head on up the main stairway, where he had intended going to lock himself in the library until he could collect his thoughts, the angry-faced Judy had thrust the fretful Anne in his arms. Lilliana brushed past him quickly, hurrying up the main stairs in the direction of the high-pitched wailing of the baby Delia. He didn't know what to do with fussy, crying babies—even one fifteen months old, he was thinking frantically, ready to hand Anne back to Judy. But Judy's heavy clomping step was already in the far reaches of the kitchen, headed for the back stairway.

For the first time in his life, David felt the soft, round arms of his firstborn child wrap around his neck; felt the shape of her tiny head nestle under his chin; smelled that smell of baby powder, that freshness of her innocence. His chin was against the top of her head. She was whimpering with exhaustion from a long session of crying. "There—everything's okay now," he mumbled awkwardly into the soft hair. "Daddy's home now."

And as he placed her gently in her crib upstairs, tucked the quilt over her, then sat patting her rhythmically, trying to hum a tuneless song until she had fallen off to sleep, a new iron grip of dedication flowed through him. It was the purest, most singular driving passion he had ever known. Boy or girl, this was *his* child. His first child. His wife and his baby were in there. Spring Mountain was his home. Donati was their name. He would show everyone what that meant!

He found Lilliana tiptoeing out of the nursery. He pulled her silently into his arms, held her in a way he had never done before: with a love, a protective fierceness that needed no words. "It's okay. We're home now," he muttered.

19

It was a full year after Anton's marriage to Phyllis Fuller before he brought her to the Napa Valley for the first time, the last week of June, the year of 1925.

As soon as Sarah found out they had arrived she invited them over for lunch, being anxious to meet her stepdaughter-in-law and wanting to see if the year's absence had made any marked changes in Anton, who she suspected had been duly taken with his first-class extended trip to Europe, paid for by his father-in-law, Bernard Fuller. According to the occasional notes and picture postcards she had received, they had spent most of the time touring famous wine regions of France and being entertained in some of the most elegant châteaus, and, on their return to America, being received in grand style at Newport and in higher social circles in Boston.

She asked them to come over around twelve-thirty, on Tuesday. Because it turned out to be an uncommonly hot day for June she asked Li Po to move the large glass-topped wrought-iron table to the eastern side of the brick terrace which wrapped around three full sides of the enormous mansion. There, tucked in behind the stately row of three-foot-thick columns, with the second-story balcony overhead giving shade, they would have a cooler place for lunch. When she had finished setting the table with crisp green-and-white placemats and napkins of a fern pattern, using white Wedgwood china, she stood back, poked one last deep-blue anemone into the floral arrangement of mixed flowers she had taken from the various garden beds around the estate, and surveyed the effect. She was pleased, not only with the table setting but with the many textures—the red brick against Spanish-white stucco walls, the wrought iron, the graceful palms in procelain urns, all against the background of the Mayacamas range of mountains to the immediate west, the sea of vineyards lapping in lush green waves across the flat valley floor to the ragged base of the eastern slopes, and then, to the north, the towering volcanic-topped Mount St. Helena standing like some grand duchess herself holding solemn court.

For a long moment Sarah stood leaning back against one of the columns and staring out at the long driveway, as though intently watching for the first sign of Anton's car. But behind the gleam of bright expectancy in her clear amber eyes was a look as though a kind of transparent wax sealer had been stretched across her gaze, shutting off permanently some other vital part of herself—the look one sees in the eyes of a stranger on alien ground looking back to some more treasured place.

Consciously, she was wondering how Phyllis would fit into such a quiet, mountain-encased, small valley, having spent her life in the high hub of Boston and Newport, and having been (according to Anton's version) ruled by the tight-fisted Bernard Fuller, who had decided every course of her life—until Anton himself came along. It was not going to be easy, she guessed. She was convinced anyway that most people who had grown up and stayed rooted in any one place for a long period of time became fluid extensions of their native fixed environment. For instance, Adam had never really left Pontremoli in a lot of ways. Or in her case, when she had gone away to school at Wellesley, then on to South Carolina for those years of teaching, the picture and echoes of Napa Valley hovered like a shadow around her.

Places—yes, she'd admit they were important, she thought, taking off a floppy-brimmed large sun hat and swatting at a hovering bee attracted to her cologne. But the difficulties she had had in life had always come from nebulous sources that couldn't be drawn out on maps and pinpointed according to *place*, she told herself, digging her hands deeply into the pockets of the three-year-old yellow-and-white striped seersucker dress she had picked out to wear because it did not require a slip, and because she thought it might be cooler than anything else she owned, with its full gored skirt and its short capped sleeves. For a moment she stared out, her fingers curling inward as if trying to close around some inner conflict of her own and keep it tightly contained there in her pockets.

It wasn't that after ten months of marriage to Norman Jaspers she hadn't made certain adjustments, she told herself quickly. In fact, in some ways she was probably happier than she had been in her life—in a quiet, resigned sort of way. She still marveled that she could sit with Norman and talk for hours without once having to compromise her political points of view or carefully avoid certain subjects—such as anything pertaining to "back east"—which used to intimidate Adam

434

for one reason or another. She found a vibrant stimulation from intellectual discussions: topics that could range from the scandals constantly erupting out of the Harding administration to the notorious Scopes "monkey" trial slated to begin in court in Tennessee that coming month—which Norman had only at breakfast brought up again, having read that Clarence Darrow was going to defend the beleaguered schoolteacher John Scopes.

"How could people *any*where be that narrow-minded?" she had asked him over a third cup of coffee. "If America is a free country, shouldn't a man be allowed to believe the theory of evolution? Isn't that as valid to teach in school as the Immaculate Conception?"

"Not according to Tennessee law," Norman had said, reading the editorial page of the morning paper.

"Then I'm glad we don't live in Dayton, Tennessee!"

He had looked up and smiled at her. "Do you think it is any better here in Napa Valley? Do you think we allow any more freedom of thought? Or do you think those ten thousand people who gathered here to burn their crosses on our wedding night last year would be concerned with John T. Scopes's freedom?" He laughed drily. "People always attribute prejudice and bias to some other place, to other people. They rarely see it in their own backyard—unless, of course, it's a mass gathering. One can't quite ignore ten thousand Ku Klux Klan members swarming across the Napa Valley floor. Not that the papers made much fuss over it! A little blurb buried back in the paper."

Sarah smiled now, remembering that conversation—one of so many others that she found interesting. She let out a long sigh which seemed to ride the dry heat. So if that other part of her life with Norman—those grappling, awkward sessions of attempted lovemaking —wasn't as pleasing, at least she had learned to try to understand and to give some new tenderness she had not known she possessed, to help protect that vulnerable, very fragile side of Norman. She had discovered that being held—*touched*, even awkwardly—was better than being alone. So if she didn't look forward to lovemaking at least she no longer dreaded it. And, besides, it happened infrequently and never lasted very long.

At the sight of Anton's sleek new silver-gray Cadillac touring car with the canvas top pushed back (glistening like a giant reflecting mirror in the high-noon sun) nosing down the driveway at a fast speed, she quickly jammed the sun hat back on her head and hurried off the terrace out across the lawn to greet them.

When the car ground to a halt, she thought that at least Anton's year away from the Napa Valley hadn't changed his fast driving habits. Nor did he look all that different, she saw, watching him take his usual long-legged, quick strides around the front of the car to help Phyllis out. His hair was perhaps a little darker, not having the hot Napa sun to keep it bleached to that near-blond shade. He was still lean, as handsome as ever, and his clothes were certainly as stylish, she thought, seeing the white linen trousers, the open-collared monogrammed shirt, the red-and-blue silk ascot at his neck, as he guided Phyllis with a light touch on her elbow across the long stretch of well-tended lawn.

She tried not to stare openly as he and Phyllis took their ambling time, stopping to look about admiringly at the grounds of the estate, at the imposing Corinthian columns of the stately old mansion, at the very view she had herself studied a few moments before.

Phyllis was not, she saw immediately, the type of woman who would ever be called beautiful. In fact, her long, droopy face barely missed being what anyone would call "horse face." But even so, there was a stunning handsomeness about her—the smooth, tanned skin; that tall and lanky, big-boned, athletic look; her stylishly cut short brown hair which fell in straight bangs low over her left eye and formed a dramatic, daggerlike swoop over the left cheek. And, like Anton, Phyllis was impeccably dressed, Sarah noted, feeling suddenly that she had surely snagged a run in her own hose, or had a smudge of rouge on her cheek, or that the three-year-old seersucker dress had a rip in the hem. Why had she worn such a tired old dress anyway, she was asking herself frantically, one that had never really been very stylish?

It was too late to do anything about it, she decided as she stepped forward to greet this woman in the crisp, finely tailored beige linen dress (that must surely have been designed in Paris) who was taking such measured-casual steps in those long, slender brown-and-white spectator pumps and extending her hand in that carefully distant, reserved way. But when Sarah looked directly into those deeply set, limpid gray eyes and saw the strange haunted, sad look there, she forgot about outward appearances. All she wanted to do was to try to make this, yes, lost- and lonely-looking woman feel somehow happier.

"Welcome to our family—to Napa Valley," she said, impulsively brushing aside the coolly extended hand with its long, brightly polished fingernails, and giving Phyllis a vigorous, awkward hug, a kiss on both cheeks. She felt the immediate stiffening, that startled tenseness of someone not accustomed to open demonstrativeness from anyone, especially from a woman.

Then Anton was holding Sarah back at arm's length after kissing her lightly on both cheeks. "Mom Sarah, my, you're looking comfy!" She sensed his taking in the tired look of the yellow-and-white-striped seersucker dress, her canvas sandals, her floppy sun hat with its bright yellow and orange ribbons. "You don't look a day older. Old Norm must be treating you well. Where is he, by the way?"

They were on the terrace now, taking seats in comfortably cushioned new wicker chairs, where she planned for them to have their wine tasting before lunch.

"He had hoped to join us, but a case he thought would settle out of court went on trial today. He sends his regrets. He has selected some very special wines from his cellar he wants you to taste. His welcoming-home present to you."

"Quite a splendid present, if I know Norman," Anton said, brushing at the knee of his trousers as he crossed one leg over the other and looked about, making his own obvious measuring survey, smiling appreciatively. "I haven't had any good wine since we got back to America. This damn Prohibition—so many once well-stocked cellars have already been depleted. I suppose people thought it wouldn't last long."

While they waited for Li Po to bring out the wine, the cheese board and the freshly baked French bread, Sarah turned to Phyllis—who had that way of sitting whereby she seemed to flow back into the cushions, her long, lanky body taking on a fluidity seated it did not have otherwise. "Sorry today turned out to be such a scorcher. Napa Valley isn't always this hot. Our nights are always cool. Have you found trouble adjusting to the heat? So many people seem to when they first arrive."

"Actually, I enjoy the hot dry heat. I'm sure you remember our dreadful Boston weather—at any time of the year, our unpredictable weather." Phyllis's voice had a wonderfully rich timbre to it, a kind of throaty, crackly sound, which, with the modulated upper-class Bostonian accent, was fascinating to hear, Sarah was thinking, smiling warmly at her.

At that moment, Li Po hurried out with the glasses and the first bottle of St.-Estèphe Cabernet Sauvignon from the Médoc appellation in France. Sarah saw Li Po's disappointment that he tried to mask when Anton did not acknowledge him in any direct, personal way. She knew he had been so excited about Anton's coming home with his new bride, and how important this day was to him—it was to be his first luncheon to serve solo here at Norman's, since the Japanese houseboy and his staff usually had complete charge and seemed to resent Li Po's very presence in the household, his tending to Sarah's personal laundry and her herbal baths and bringing her breakfast in bed each morning. He had even, she noticed, agreed to put on the white coat, the black bow tie, the black tailored trousers Norman had requested that he wear instead of the usual baggy pants and the Chinese jacket with its loose, floppy sleeves. She tried to smile reassuringly at him.

When he had gone back to the kitchen to prepare the champagne sauce for the poached salmon, Sarah said, "Anton, did you notice that Li Po has cut off his long braid—his queue?"

Anton was holding the wine up, studying the color. "I guess that *was* Li Po! Of course—that bowl-shaped head. I simply didn't recognize him. He looked rather dapper, In fact. I guess I thought he was one of Norman's servants."

She turned to the tasting again, feeling better now about Anton. As she saw his smiling enthusiasm, she realized she had missed him very much during his year away.

"This Saint-Estèphe—I like its aggressive aroma, the thick texture. Very robust, which is the way I prefer wine." He lifted a knowing eyebrow, sipped slowly. "When this damn Prohibition ends and I open the Anton Brunner Winery, *my* red wines are going to resemble very closely French wines. I see no reason why California wines have to be so universally bland in comparison."

Sarah felt a sudden stir of adrenalin. She half expected Adam's own voice to blurt out irately, "Listen who is talking like the big shot about winemaking! It is easy to talk, talk, but you don't know beans!"

She had noticed that Phyllis was not "sipping" her wine at all but taking deep quick gulps of it. Surprised, she asked in her own measured tone, "What do you think of the wine?"

Phyllis lifted one eyebrow, tilted her head to one side, brushed the dagger point of hair off her cheek. "Frankly, I don't like wine—*any* wine. Even in these sparse dry times when there isn't much good stuff around, I prefer whiskey—any rye, any bourbon even, to wine."

"Well, don't admit it out loud in Napa Valley!" Anton said.

Sarah sensed the tension between them. She concentrated quickly on the wine Norman had selected. "I believe Norman wanted you to try this last vintage bottled by Napa Valley's El Molina Winery before it closed. And I believe I have the sequence right: next, this rare private reserve made by Charles Carpy, then this Georges de Latour . . ."

Phyllis pointed one toe of a spectator pump as though underscoring some invisible rating of her own. "*Latour*—I recall that name from one of the thousands of châteaus we visited in France."

"We have several French people in Napa Valley," Sarah said quietly. "Madame la Marquise de Pins, Madame de Latour . . . We used to have Jacques Cugnot. My best friend growing up was French. Monique Cugnot. I've often wondered what became of her."

"Napa Valley is an amalgam of Europeans," Anton said, his slender hand curling around the long stem of the wineglass.

"I notice that you have a Japanese houseboy. In circles back home that is becoming quite the chic thing one does."

"Do you mean Li Po? He's *Chinese*," Sarah said quickly. "He's been with me since I first married Anton's father. He's not very chic, really. Oh, today he is wearing his new uniform for your and Anton's benefit. No, Li Po is more like family."

"Chinese, Japanese! I never manage to tell them apart," Phyllis said, finishing her fourth glass of wine. "Father abhors anyone Oriental."

Anton tapped the glass impatiently, his fingernails making a clicking, grating sound. He had seen Phyllis's eyes, that fuzzy look she got when she drank too much—a look he was seeing more frequently lately, he had noticed. "Back to the tasting. One sips *delicately*, dear. One doesn't gulp down fine wine. Especially in these days when it is such a rarity to find any!"

Phyllis leaned forward, politely spread cheese on a piece of bread, then flowed back against the cushions as though she had lost her skeletal support. Her gray eyes were half closed. "Do continue with your discussion of wines, dear. As I said, I'm a whiskey—"

Anton interrupted her as though he were brushing away an annoying bee whose sting he didn't necessarily fear but which he considered a nuisance anyway. "In *my* opinion," he said to Sarah, "when we do get back to winemaking in this country, we should institute a strong appellation of origin. Since we'll have to launch an enormous educational campaign to teach Americans what fine wines really taste like rather than this abortive grape juice being fermented in any manner, I say we might as well begin on a definitive basis."

Li Po came to tell them lunch was served. Sarah noticed Phyllis's weaving as they made their way to the eastern terrace. Too, she had seen that somewhat pasty-yellow look which suggested she might be ready to be sick—that clammy perspiration on her forehead. Before they sat down she asked, "Would you like to go to the powder room before lunch? I forgot to ask."

Phyllis plopped down, spread her napkin in her lap with a flourish. "No, thank you. I do not want to miss out on hearing Anton tell you

439

about our trip through the French wine country. I have heard him tell about it, oh, several, several times now. I could almost tell you myself, having listened, about—let me see, those *marvelous* clarets of Bordeaux, those *divine* white wines from the hills of Alsace—oh, don't forget the ones from along the Loire River. Right, Anton?" She pushed the poached salmon with her fork as though with a prodding iron. "All those vintages *extraordinaire*—those Clos des Ruchottes, those Château Lafon-Rochets. Ha! You didn't think I ever listened, did you?" Her head sagged, popped back up; her large limpid eyes seemed to be searching for a focal point. "I see, I hear, I *know* a lot of things, Anton. A lot you wish I didn't know!"

"I suppose, then, that you know you should eat something quickly," he said in a voice as dry as the Beringer Chablis Norman had asked Li Po to be sure to serve with the salmon. "Obviously, you don't know how to *taste* wines. Next time, please try to remember that—"

"*Next* time I will try to remember to listen to what my father told me the first time he ever saw you!" She had a lopsided grin on her face. "I am . . . very . . . sorry," she said, pushing up from the table and propping herself, wobbling, with both hands on the back of the chair. "I wonder, could your cute little Japanese—I mean *Chinese* fellow over there in that white jacket show me the way to the powder room? I think . . . I am pretty sure I am going to be very, very sick."

Sarah was getting up quickly, motioning to Li Po. "I'll go with her," she said to Anton, who was glowering at her, his eyes as gray as his shiny automobile, as though his anger was too intense to allow any softer shade of blue to stay. "Li Po, please prepare some of that special tea you bring to me on mornings when I have a hard time getting started," she said in a quick whisper. Then she was taking Phyllis firmly by the elbow, leading her toward the downstairs bathroom.

After Phyllis had stopped retching, had washed and dried her mouth, drunk the water Sarah pushed at her, she sank down on a velvet-covered wrought-iron bench near the lavatory, dabbed at her sweated forehead with the damp cloth Sarah handed her. "I am *so* sorry," her deep crackly voice said in a sound more like a low moan. "I knew—I knew this morning I shouldn't have accepted. I—you see, Anton doesn't know. I can't, I simply can't, tell him that I am pregnant. That even the smell of wine, of his cigars—oh, God, the smell of those cigars!—almost everything makes me deathly ill."

"I didn't know. When? How far along are you in this pregnancy?" Sarah asked gently. "Why can't you tell him? . . ."

Phyllis looked up, her eyes stricken. "Because I tricked him. He made me promise when we got married that I wouldn't have a baby for a *long* time. He wants to travel, to thoroughly research the wine industry in Europe. This time he says we only scratched the surface. He has this idea that he should study oenology at the Louis Pasteur Institute. He—oh, I shouldn't be telling you this." She buried her face in the wet washcloth. "I have made such a dreadful mistake marrying Anton," she muttered miserably. "You—I see in your eyes that you understand. You *care* about people! You're not like Anton at all. Even my father, who sensed this about Anton on their first meeting and tried to warn me that I mustn't see him again—now my father thinks Anton is some walking prince! Anything that is wrong is my fault. Anton can do *no* wrong. My father has been a wine buff all his life. He's convinced Anton is some genius. The walking god Bacchus himself!" She shook her head, dabbed now at tears swimming in miniature puddles in her eyes but not spilling out.

"I still don't understand why you can't tell Anton about the baby. You can't expect him to understand—you're bound to have misunderstandings—if you don't explain."

Phyllis lifted her long face, stared at the ceiling, and when she had her tears under control looked at Sarah more soberly than before. "Please forgive me. I know Anton is your stepson. I have been taught differently. But he is not, in one year's time—oh, my father tells me I am imagining this! That I am a stupid woman who doesn't know anything about how to keep a husband or make him happy!"

Sarah wet the washcloth again, wrung it out, this time wiped Phyllis's forehead herself, sensing that she might be comforted to be touched by someone. "Please, get it out of your system. Tell me. I have a feeling you and I are going to be very good friends. You most certainly can trust me. Anything you tell me will stay between us."

Phyllis's head was going back and forth as though saying no to the world. The tears now brimmed over and fell unabated down her long, droopy face. She had stuffed the dagger point of hair tightly behind her ear, pushed at the bangs across her left eyebrow. "Anton is unfaithful to me! Even on our honeymoon, that first week, I know he disappeared with one of my bridesmaids. She—Alice—has made a game of seducing every man she meets. It's her way of feeling powerful—that she exists, I suppose. But somehow I thought that with me, knowing it was my husband and that Anton was the only man I had ever loved, she would not—out of respect." She threw out her hands. "Alice was the first—that I *know* of. But there have been others. In Paris, at more than one of the châteaus, and in southern France. He thinks he is so discreet! . . . I know the signs now. The way he becomes so very patronizing. Starts talking about all these marvelous things the two of us, just the two of us, are going to do. That is *one* way." Her face was riddled with agony. "When he is in another kind of mood, he has another tactic. He starts picking me apart. There is nothing I can do right." She flung out her hands. "I am very familiar with that. I have heard that all of my life!"

"Here—dry your eyes. You're going to have a terrible headache, I'm afraid."

"The lunch—I've ruined your lunch. Anton—he'll never forgive me!"

"Forget Anton right now," Sarah said through tight lips. "I am curious. What do you mean, you heard that all of your life? Do you mean from your father? Your mother? From whom, dear?"

"Not my mother. I never knew her, really. I vaguely remember her when I was a little girl. She was always dressed up. Dashing out to a party. She loved dancing, as I recall. And she always smelled good. . . . I was away at summer camp—I was always away at camp in summers. Anyway, they came to get me and tell me that she had died. I don't even know of what. One doesn't discuss such matters in my home. Not even the word 'death.' Oh, nothing messy—dirty!"

"Then who?"

"My father did his share. He used to say to me, 'If you're going to be the size of a boy, why weren't you born one?' But mostly it was Miss Chamberlin. My nanny. Miss Chamberlin, who liked everything *very* tidy. Even when we went to the bathroom. Yes, we had a neat checklist for that. If there weren't enough checks in the number-two column, we got castor oil. Sometimes Fletcher's Castoria, when she was in a better mood."

" 'We'?"

Phyllis looked up. "My brother—Julian—who was killed during the war. In France. The battle of Verdun."

They were silent. Phyllis handed Sarah the washcloth; pushed at her bangs again. "I had no right unburdening myself. One never really has that right. Perhaps Miss Chamberlin knew best, at that. I feel so— oh, horribly guilty having told you! Having ruined your luncheon. Having ruined everything, really. Anton—I was going to keep him by having the baby. Imagine! As if *that* would matter to him. Today, this morning when he was taking such pains to get ready, I thought surely he had other plans. I thought there must be someone out there waiting for him in Napa Valley someplace. That he had made a date behind my back. Truly, I expected him to maybe—oh, drop me off and then go on. I—do you think I am losing my mind? Could I be? Lately I've been dreaming these horrible dreams. Miss Chamberlin is always in them screaming at me about something. Washing out my mouth with soap. In each one she has this list—all these lists! I never have any of them right. 'Gawky! Don't be so gawky.' 'Keep your voice down. Softly—don't yell.' Sometimes I have the baby and she is yelling at the baby and I am trying to tell her no, but she and Anton are always there together, joining forces." She was crying again.

Sarah went to her, put her hands on her shoulders. "Pull yourself together, dear. Please. For *your* sake. I am going to be your friend from now on. I have no lists, no check marks. We will work this out. There will be a way to talk with Anton—I've always been able to talk with him when others can't. This sick stage with the pregnancy—that will be over soon. When is the baby due?"

"In November."

"Then it won't be much longer—the nausea. It's worse with the first one. A baby—you will love being a mother."

"I shall hate it!" Phyllis cried out. "What would *I* know about being a mother? What—please tell me what I am going to *do*. What is going to become of me?"

"You are going to put on fresh lipstick, comb your hair, come to the table with me and drink some very special tea that will make you feel well quickly. We will take one thing at a time. It *is* going to work. It is going to be all right. Napa Valley is a healing place. It is! You will find that out."

Phyllis was standing now, looking at her reflection in the mirror over the lavatory. "I can't bear the thought of staying here in Napa Valley," she said in a voice drawn tight now. "Whatever happens, it will happen to me in Boston. Where I feel at home. I am going home. Just as soon as the nausea gets a little better."

"I'm sorry to hear that, Phyllis. If you stayed, I feel sure that if you tried, gave this time . . ."

"Let's go back. That tea sounds good."

Sarah put one hand on Phyllis's arm. "Promise me. The drinking —maybe it is best not to drink anything. The baby, since wine doesn't agree with you."

Phyllis lifted both eyebrows, smiled ironically. "I will promise you that I won't drink any more *wine*."

They made their way out across the black-and-white marble tiles of the foyer, past potted palms, out onto the brick terrace, and headed around the corner toward the glass-topped table. Li Po came to meet them.

443

"Mr. Donati—I mean Mr. Brunner—he say he will be back about four-thirty. Maybe five o'clock. You sick—he say you ought to rest. You feel better. He come then." Li Po was bowing, going over to where he had the tea ready. "Tea not so hot now. I—"

Phyllis looked at Sarah. "I knew it! I told you I had seen the signs. He didn't have the nerve to face us." She was looking about wildly, as if searching for the right direction to run.

"Maybe you're wrong about that, dear. Why don't you come up to my room and lie down? Take a nap? Li Po can fix the tea to help you sleep."

Phyllis seemed to sag against one of the columns. "Is it possible—could you give me a ride home? I—I simply can't stay. I could not bear that right now."

"If that's what you want, yes, I'll give you a ride home. I have my car. But first, won't you come inside? I insist that you drink a couple of cups of hot tea. I must know that you're feeling a little better before I let you go home."

She took Phyllis's arm, led her inside, into the front parlor where the cool shadows in the room from the dark teak furniture and the jade-encrusted screen might, she thought, give her a more quieting feeling. Phyllis sat on a straight-backed, heavily carved wooden Chinese chair. Her fingers clasped dragon heads on the arms. Sarah saw that water had stained her beige linen dress down the front—water and some red wine. One blotch of red Cabernet was on the white side of one of the spectator kid pumps.

Li Po quickly served the tea, and Phyllis drank it slowly, balancing the cup gingerly on one knee. "You have been very kind to me." She glanced about the room, her eyes lingering a moment on the silver tray, which held several crystal decanters filled with various whiskeys which Norman had not put back into his secret cabinet after a meeting he had had with a client. Though it was unlikely that revenue officers would ever raid his house, he usually did not take chances. "Would you mind terribly if I had one—oh, anything? A whiskey, please? Just to calm my nerves. A cigarette and a drink—then I will go home."

"I don't really think you should—the baby. It can't be good for the baby," Sarah urged, alarmed by the look she had seen on Phyllis's face that brought back childhood memories of seeing her father sneaking out hidden bottles.

For an instant, Phyllis looked as if she might argue. She took a gold cigarette case out of her purse, lit it, then gripped the dragon heads on the chair tightly. "You're right. I'll have a smoke and then go on

444

home." She inhaled, blew smoke across the stale air in the room where Norman preferred that no one smoke.

"I would like to have just the two of us get together again soon for lunch," Sarah said matter-of-factly, already planning out a strategy of her own. "I've been lonely for an intelligent female friend with whom I can go shopping, take with me to San Francisco. Would you like that?"

Phyllis stood up, ground out the cigarette in a small porcelain dish on the round teak table in front of her. "If I stay here at all, perhaps. But I expect to be leaving very soon."

When they came back out on the terrace, Sarah spotted Norman's usual driver, Ito. She motioned to him, asked him quietly if he would mind driving Phyllis home. As he held open the door to the large Packard, Sarah reached out, touched Phyllis's hand. "I meant what I said when you first arrived. I welcome you to our family, to the Napa Valley. I hope you *will* stay. Give us more of a chance. If you do, I am here. I want to be your friend."

"You are very kind," Phyllis said, climbing in, tugging at the linen skirt as though it was important to keep herself neatly arranged. "Thank you . . . and forgive me. Will you forgive me?"

"There is nothing to forgive," Sarah said, standing there long after Ito had eased the Packard out of sight.

"Anton, I want to talk with you!" Sarah snapped when he came dashing across the lawn at precisely four-thirty and asked lightly, "Is Phyllis feeling chipper again? Too much wine, you know. This unaccustomed heat."

He propped one foot on the edge of the brick terrace, one hand against a thick column, loosened the silk ascot that looked just-recently knotted. She saw the smudge of lipstick on his shoulder. "I think you had better go inside and wash off that streak of red," she said, her face tight.

He looked down, dusted it with his fingertips. "Oh, *that*. Ran into an old friend. One of those brief hello kisses. Nothing more. I had to interview a man about possibly becoming my new vineyard manager. Phyllis and I plan to do a lot of traveling. While I was gone last year, some dumb bastard overcropped my vines—I had him on a percentage basis and he wanted the biggest production we could get. Where have all the good pruners gone? There's no decent knowledgeable help around, and I found this one guy. I simply couldn't miss that appointment or I would not have dashed off like that."

"I don't believe you, Anton. Nor does Phyllis. She's home."

He stepped fully up on the brick terrace, put his hands on his hips. "So she has been talking to you, huh? You've been taken in by her paranoia?"

"I am not easily taken in by anyone. I have known you too long, Anton Donati!"

"*Brunner*—Anton Brunner. If you please."

"You are clever—you have always been that. But I always gave you so much more credit. I thought you would marry and settle down. That you would—"

"It is much too hot a day to add the heat of one of your lectures to it!" He went to the front door, pulled the screen open, glanced back over his shoulder. "I'll wash up, be on *my* way."

"You are acting like an—an ass! Your father would be furious. He would—"

The door closed gently behind him. She heard his brisk light step across the marble tiles. Li Po was standing at the corner, hovering near one of the columns.

"Li Po, please take the teacups out of the parlor. See if you can air the room out quickly, before my husband returns. And tell Mr. Brunner, for me, that I have gone to my room."

Neither Anton nor Phyllis told Sarah goodbye when they left Napa Valley. When she did hear, it was a brief note from Anton in Boston, months later.

DEAR SARAH,

Phyllis gave birth to a daughter, Frances Fuller Brunner, on November 21st. The baby weighed seven pounds and two ounces; seems in excellent health, as is Phyllis.

We are sailing for a year's sojourn in Europe, where Bernard has leased a villa for all of us (himself included), south of Nice. Phyllis asks me to send her best wishes and to thank you for your kindness to her during her brief visit to the Napa Valley. I shall be studying and researching winemaking throughout Europe during our year away. Norman has power of attorney while I am gone. I have left a capable manager in charge and a housekeeper at my place, so all should go well in that regard. We sail from New York in one week. Sorry that we departed so hurriedly without telling you goodbye. We are doing well now.

Love,
ANTON AND PHYLLIS
(and your granddaughter, Frances, of course!)

The night after the letter arrived, Sarah read it to Norman, who looked at the frown between her eyes.

"Don't *brood*, dear," he said. "It sounds as if they've worked out their problems."

"But his letter is so cold—distant. He's still angry with me. They waited a week to tell me about the baby's arrival!"

"People usually resent having shared their intimacies. Revealing a weaker side of themselves. They'll both forget after a year away."

"I did what I thought was right. Phyllis seemed so genuinely distressed—in need of a good shoulder to cry on."

"I'm sure she won't ever forget that you were kind. That will last. In the long run, that is the most important thing."

That summer of 1926 seemed to slip into its hot dry slot before Sarah realized it. She had received one postcard from Anton—from Cannes, where he and Phyllis had attended the century's tennis match, he wrote, and where he had lost money betting that America's Helen Wills would beat France's Suzanne Lenglen. He did not mention the baby or Bernard Fuller. "Phyllis sends her love, as do I," he had scribbled at the bottom.

To pass time, she visited now and then with David and Lilliana (though she tried to avoid going to Spring Mountain, finding herself inevitably upset over Lilliana's sloppy housekeeping and unable to stop the silent comparisons with how things used to be). She read periodicals, subscribed to three newspapers and four new magazines. She still kept up with market reports; had read that a sharp decline in grape prices was expected that coming harvest.

In August that year, she read that in New York 100,000 people had lined up for eleven blocks to view the corpse of Rudolph Valentino, who had died at the age of thirty-one. She showed Norman pictures of women weeping, flinging themselves at the bier. "How can they be that morbid? Over an *actor*?"

"It's a crazy world. People need their idols," he said in an exhausted voice that made Sarah take sharp note.

"What's wrong, dear? You don't look so well tonight."

"Just tired. And a bit worried about some things I see on the economic front nationwide." He rubbed his eyes, placed his folded glasses in their case. "Sarah, I've tried carefully to protect my assets, in case the bottom drops out. It's important to me to know that should anything ever happen to me you're protected."

"You sound so—well, *down*. As though you're telling me something," she said, trying to keep her voice light, but sensing that he was holding something back. "Norman, are you *sure* you're all right?" She was studying the dark, puffy circles under his eyes.

He stood up, placed his hands at the small of his back. "I think my kidneys are acting up again. An old problem. I hope I'm not getting another round of stones. I had *those* once." He kissed her lightly on the forehead. "Don't worry. I'm going in for a checkup next week. I've made the appointment."

This conversation had taken place on Wednesday night, that last week of August. But on Friday, during a meeting with a client at his Napa City office, Norman became worried when he could not relieve himself by urinating. He became increasingly uncomfortable, canceled his meetings, and went straight to the emergency ward of the local Napa City hospital, where he was immediately admitted and placed on the critical list.

Sarah was sent for and rushed to the hospital. "What *is* it?" she asked frantically, in her own state of shock.

The doctor stood looking at the chart, then narrowed his eyes. "Apparently your husband has had chronic nephritis. Unfortunately, someone treated him heavily with damaging mercury salts, which have done irreparable harm. We're trying—but if he has kidney failure, there won't be anything we can do. We will have to watch." He was a small wiry man with a nervous tic. Sarah found herself hypnotized, unable to concentrate on what he was telling her. "I'm *very* sorry, Mrs. Jaspers."

After he had left her alone with Norman, Sarah went around to the side of the bed where there were fewer tubes. She sat down, placed her hands lightly on his arm, gazed down at his eyes nearly swollen shut from edema. All the good memories, those nice—so very nice—qualities she had grown to love seemed to rush at her. She watched for a moment the steady drip, drip from the intravenous feeding. When she had first married him, she had been sure that she would never truly love him. That she would die being Mrs. Adam Donati. And in one way, that was still true; yet how very much she had become Mrs. Norman Jaspers too! In such a totally different context, really.

"Norman, if you *hear* me, I want you to know that you have become so dear, so very dear, to me. I love you. I don't want you to die, Norman. I would like very much to grow old with you. We still have so very much to talk about. To share. Do you hear me, darling?"

He turned his head slightly, smiled through dry, cracked lips, licked at them with a thick tongue. "Yes . . ." he managed, his fingers clutching hers.

Nurses came in to make their routine check, their starched white skirts rustling. When one of them looked into the bottle dangling from the side of the bed holding the urine and saw only a few murky, blood-tinged drops, she shook her head grimly at the other one.

"How *is* he?" Sarah asked, looking at them with desperate pleading in her eyes, as though they could tell her something encouraging.

"The doctor is coming over. He'll talk with you."

But by the time the doctor arrived, Sarah knew that the end was near. She saw it in Norman's breathing. In the way the nurses were hovering over him now, asking her to step in and out of the room. Asking her if there were other relatives she should send for. She asked Ito to drive up Spring Mountain and tell David, to ask him to please come and be with her.

David sat with her through the night. They took turns going down the quiet polished hallways, bringing coffee, trying to keep their dry, burning eyes open. Trying to talk away the time it was taking death to make its final tiptoeing rounds.

"How is Lilliana? The girls?"

"Growing. Fine. Everyone is fine."

"The harvest—when will you start picking?"

"Very soon. This late hot spell has brought the sugar up ahead of schedule. Kyle came around, just taking a look. He thinks we ought to get started. We're not expecting much more than forty dollars a ton this year. The market's way off—a shortage of railroad cars."

"I read they're putting a new measure on the ballot in November —Proposition Nine—trying to get a repeal of the Wright Act. Is that right?" She was twisting her wedding ring.

David had looked down at Norman, heard his shallow breathing. The nurse motioned that they should step outside the room. They sat in the waiting room.

"I heard a good speech by Felix Salmina, who's trying to get a bill passed where we could make light wines. There's such a glut on the market now—so much overplanting that there's no way to absorb it all. He figures a lot of growers are going to face complete ruin. He doesn't think we'll pay our freight bills shipping grapes east this year even. But I'm still pretty optimistic."

"You have to be, dear. You must never give up faith. Your father —he believed so much in the industry, in its ultimate potential." She patted David's hand. "He'd be so proud of you, knowing how hard you're working on Spring Mountain. How you're trying to keep up the standards. I wish he could have seen his granddaughters. . . . Poor Norman, I never dreamed he was *this* sick! He's been so good to me.

449

He never complained. Always worried about *me*. About everyone else." She leaned back, closed her eyes, took a deep, deep breath.

"Are you all right?"

"Yes. I have to be. . . . Death—sometimes I think it stalks the ridges of the mountains, just searching for its next victim. Sometimes I *feel* it out there, waiting, biding its time. Poor Norman. I wonder why it singled out Norman when he's such a *good* man."

When the doctor and the nurse came toward them, she got up, stood very quietly, her face calm, composed. "It's over?"

"Yes, ma'am. He's gone."

"What time is it, David?" she asked, her voice sounding dry, hollow.

"Five-fifteen."

"The sun should be coming up, then, I suppose."

"It won't be long."

"There'll be arrangements—a memorial service of some sort. The burial."

"You'll need help. I'll—"

"No, dear. You were with me when I needed you the most. I'll manage. Just please take me home. I'll call his partners at the law firm. I'll get things started."

But when David dropped her off, he thought his mother looked as though she had glass covering her eyes; she was moving, talking, as though by rote. It was frightening. He would have felt better had she cried. Had she let down some of that rigid outward composure. But he had known her too long. She had set a certain course. He might as well go on up Spring Mountain, try to get some sleep.

Though Norman Jaspers left an impressive estate, it was not as large as he had thought it would be. When it was probated, Sarah decided she would pay off the mortgage on the mansion and the land. It was not anything Norman would have advised, but she wanted a clear deed. *The land—Adam had taught her to have faith in the land.*

For months after Norman died, Sarah went about the huge house in which she had been born, trying to get some renewed sense of belonging. Though her two husbands had been entirely different, both had, in essence, had charge of the business affairs; both had given a protective shadow for her. Now she was alone. She turned then to David.

"Would you agree to letting me *hire* you to be the manager of this place? I simply can't manage it. I don't know about hay and barley,

450

about selling cattle. About orchards. I learned something about vineyards, but not about the other. I'd pay you a regular salary." She looked at David's clouded, uncertain expression.

"Only on a strictly business arrangement. I won't take any handouts!"

"I'm not offering any handouts. Norman was afraid of the instability of our economy. We may well have to work—pull together. You do have a family to think of, David. You can use the money."

"Draw up a contract, then."

They met for signing of it, Sarah driving up Spring Mountain for the occasion, on May 22, 1927, the day after Charles Lindbergh had landed *The Spirit of St. Louis* in Paris after his thirty-three-and-a-half-hour nonstop flight.

She stood for a moment on the stone veranda before ringing the doorbell and letting them know she had arrived. Inside, she could hear one of the children crying in a way suggesting a temper tantrum. Sarah leaned against the redwood post of the wisteria trellis, stared out for a moment at the vineyards budding out. It was a warm sunny day, but she felt chilly and crossed her arms, tugged her loose gray cardigan closer around her shoulders. Huge puffy clouds drifted across Howell Mountain to the east. The valley below had a soft blue hue tinged with a faint lavender mist. A crew of workmen finishing some delayed cultivating were at the far end of the Rieslings. She found herself staring at them, as if expecting Adam to come striding out of their midst, coming toward the old stone house.

When she did announce herself, she tried to overlook the dinginess of the place. Toys were strewn about. Lace curtains that had once hung crisp with starch from Li Po's hand now sagged limply. An acrid odor of something burning drifted through the downstairs. Lilliana came out of the kitchen, the young Delia tugging at her skirts, the little girl Anne standing in the doorway with chocolate smeared across her chubby face, her fat fingers thick with icing she was trying to lick off.

"We were trying to get the cookies baked before you got here," Lilliana said, looking exasperated. "Anne thinks she's chief cook and bottlewasher around here. She just burned a batch of chocolate chips. But then she got the first one out in time, didn't you, honey? Go wash your face and hands so you can kiss your grandmother. Hurry." She gave Delia a testing pat on the bottom. "Oh, *dear*. We've had another accident. Dede, baby, we were supposed to go *pottie*. " She flung her hands out. "Make yourself at home while I go change the baby. David will be down in a moment. He's listening to the new radio. I can't pry

451

him away. Now that we have electricity, he is like a child with a new toy."

Sarah wandered aimlessly into the parlor, purposely ignoring the stains on the rug, on every piece of furniture. The room looked seedy now. Yes, that was the word, she thought, a rush of memories hitting her. It was as if she had just walked across the room toward where Adam was waiting with Luigi Pascarella, and the children had just lined up holding their rice bags, and Theresa had played her thumping wedding march. She walked over to the old upright, hit one plunking note on the out-of-tune instrument with its streaks of sticky finger markings where Anne had been playing.

David found her there. "Sorry—I was listening to Lindbergh. Fascinating. One of these days *I'm* going to Paris."

"I hope you will be able to—soon," she said brightly. "Maybe you and Lilliana can take a trip, leave the children with me. In fact, maybe you'd consider bringing your family to live at my place, David. Be closer to schools. It won't be long before Anne will be ready for kindergarten. I have so much room. Everyone seems to think the future is down valley. Prunes—I hear they expect to make more money this harvest on the sale of prunes than on grapes. Is it that bad?"

David went over and poured out brandy for both of them. "Surprise—taste this."

She sipped the excellent brandy. "Where did you get this? Isn't this *Donati* brandy?"

He smiled. "Yes. I found the cache! We came across Papa's hiding place."

"But—they won't find out? The revenue?"

"No. We kept it where Papa put it. Took out a couple of barrels and put them down in the basement. If you *want* any . . ."

"Thank you, no. I don't drink much. Living alone—I have plenty. Norman left quite a well-stocked cellar." She looked at him. "Seriously, David, how about it? How about coming down? I can afford help. You and Lilliana could have more time to be together. Have more of a life."

"We're happy up here." He shrugged his shoulders. "This place grows on you. Lilliana—I don't think we could drag her off Spring Mountain now. She loves it. The children—maybe when they're older. But right now, no, we're home here. If Prohibition ever ends, I'll open up the winery one of these days." His eyes beamed. "I've been doing a little experimenting on my own. Keeping my hand at it."

"But you won't do anything that will get you in trouble with the law? Every day I read where they've arrested someone else. Made some new raid."

"They poke around up here periodically. But they've given up, pretty much." His face was drawn. "They've got us tagged as bootleggers who were caught and learned our lesson."

"That will pass."

"Do you ever see Joseph?" Hs face was grim.

"Never. Isn't it strange how he avoids us? It's as if we remind him of only painful memories. I do try to keep up with how he is, *where* he is. Luigi stops by once in a blue moon. Luigi's not so well these days. His back—he hurt his back somewhere along the line. But he says Joseph is making lots of money. Buying houses right and left. Little houses. He's been working in Vallejo. Stays there a great deal of the time."

"Good. I never want him setting foot up here again!"

"David—don't carry such hatred. Poor Joseph. None of us ever really understood him. I feel terribly sorry for Joseph."

"*I* don't! I never will."

At that point, Anne came running in wearing a clean dress, her hair combed, her face scrubbed shiny clean. Sarah lifted her, felt the tiny arms around her neck. Then she seemed to fly into her father's arms. "Take me on the aeroplane ride, Daddy!" she squealed, grabbing his neck tightly and insisting that he whirl her round and round. When he put her back down, she climbed on his knee.

"We're spoiling them—spoiling them rotten," he said. "Okay—where is the contract? Run along, Anne—your Daddy's signing up for a new job so he can buy that tricycle you want."

20

From the harvest of 1927 on, the market for grapes made a sharp plunge downward—in spite of the fact that the U.S. Attorney General had made a ruling the year before that had, for all purposes, legalized homemade wine (since what had supposedly been manufactured "grape juices" were being fermented beyond the alcoholic content allowed by the Prohibition Law all along, and since it was virtually impossible to enforce that portion of the law anyway). The prices brought in that year had been fixed on a minimum ratio by the California Grape Exchange, where Alicante and Petit Bouschets brought in $62.50 a ton and the white Bergers brought $22.50.

David, depressed by the turn of events, stopped by to talk with Sarah about the loss he was having to sustain on Spring Mountain. "The market's sheer chaos," he complained, joining her for tea out on the brick terrace that warm November afternoon, just following the final tabulations of profits and losses. "The lack of coordination is killing us. The growers aren't pitching in—it's every man for himself. Dog eat dog."

Sarah, who was now wearing glasses full time, removed them, rubbed her eyes, readjusted them across her patrician nose. "You should get actively involved, David. I read where our lobbyist in Washington has managed, at least, to get a reduction of the tax on wines. Every bit of chipping away at the Volstead Act will help get it off the books."

David was restless to get back to Spring Mountain. He stood up, shook his head. "This industry has decayed right out from under us. The quality of grapes being shipped, all the loss of talent. The equipment—I wish I had gone into some other field!"

"You're luckier than most. At least you'll have *quality* grapes if repeal does come about. You won't have to wait four years for new finer varietals to mature. Look on the bright side."

He showed a brief flicker of interest. "I guess I would have a toe-hold, at that. I'd just have to take out the Alicantes."

"I have a recent letter from Anton around here someplace," she said, looking about through a stack of magazines on a wicker table. "Thought you might like to read it."

David was impatient to go. "What did *he* have to say?"

"Oh, mostly that he's learning a lot about winemaking during this stint in his travels. Seems his father-in-law is quite a wine buff and wants to back him in a big winery should repeal come about. He mentioned something about Bernard Fuller wanting to buy some property in Napa Valley. But he didn't say *which* property. Apparently they'll be coming back home later than they had previously planned. Doesn't seem in much of a hurry to leave southern France."

"Anton won't ever settle down in Napa Valley again—not after he's got Europe in his blood."

"Seems Phyllis is pregnant again. Expecting next April."

David reached out and broke off a small twig from a lilac bush at the edge of the terrace and twisted it between his teeth. He was staring out at the vineyards Norman had left to Sarah. At thirty, beginning wrinkles were etching into his sun-weathered face: two long ridges running alongside his full mouth, tiny wrinkles around his eyes from squinting into the sun, ridges across his forehead, between his solemn gray-blue eyes. He turned, his voice slow, deliberate, that usual air of patience about him (as though he were waiting for that eventual larger roll of fate's dice to fall in his favor). "Don't get excited about Anton's big ideas!" He spit out the lilac twig, jammed on his field work hat, leaned over and kissed her goodbye lightly on the forehead. "By the way, I'm having your grapevines pruned back severely this winter. They're not in the best of shape. It will cut your *quantity* next harvest but definitely improve the quality of your grapes—for whatever that's worth any longer."

In November, Sarah forgot to go to the polls and vote. Had Coolidge run again, she would have been more interested, she told herself. She didn't like either Herbert Hoover or Al Smith. Too, she had come down with the first of a series of bad colds that were to plague her that rainy winter. Getting old wasn't easy, she complained to Li Po, who prepared his herbal teas and concoctions for her various complaints of stiff joints, hot flashes, and overall fatigue.

She was glad when the spring broke and the hot summer sun bore down to bake the Napa Valley and her own body. She loved the sunshine. She began taking long walks, and working in her flower gardens late into the dusk. She lost excess pounds she had put on during the slow winter months and was just feeling good again when harvest time arrived.

"Are grape prices improving at all this year?" she asked David when he came by to announce his crew would start picking.

"It's bad, but it's going to get worse." He lifted his hat, ran his hands through his hair the way he did when he was upset. "Let's face it, if I didn't have this job with you, we'd be in a bad way on Spring Mountain. It's not that we spend a lot. You couldn't call Lilliana extravagant. But there's always a new doctor bill—some damn thing!" He headed off the terrace, ready to get in his truck parked near the side entrance. "Maybe I should have gone out and found a rich girl to marry the way Anton did, huh?"

"I know you are being facetious."

"I have my days," he called back, then slammed the door of the battered truck, drove off, the open tailgate bumping, rattling noisily.

Harvest was almost over on Thursday, October 24, 1929, when David hurried in out of the vineyards where they had been picking the last of her Cabernet Sauvignons. "Turn on your radio! I hear there's a panic going on with the stock market."

She led him into the kitchen, where she kept a small Philco. David was jiggling the tuning knob, gave a slap to the side of it as a loud popping, buzzing sound spluttered forth.

"Try sixty-five—that's about the only strong station lately."

"You need new tubes. A better ground wire."

"David, lately you're getting awfully impatient," Sarah said, crossing her arms over her chest. "Don't lose patience. Remember, your father always said—"

"This damn thing must be on the blink! I wanted to hear the news. This is something big—very big!"

"Take your time, dear. It's just now five. You won't miss much more than the opening remarks."

At that instant the announcer's deep voice split through the static. "Stocks nosedived amid a flurry of thirteen million shares traded. Tickers were going two hours after the market closed. General Motors, Montgomery Ward, U.S. Steel are only a few of the stocks already down some fifty percent. Bank directors across the country are planning emergency meetings to try to determine swift courses of action to restore confidence and bring about a degree of stabilization. Though

457

the plea is out not to panic, the signs are that . . ." The static blurred out the voice.

Sarah, who had been in the kitchen all afternoon with Li Po, working to find uses for two bushels of excess apples by baking pies and making applesauce, wiped steam from her glasses, replaced them. "Tell me, exactly what was that man talking about?"

"This country is in for it, is what! Not just grape growers—everybody. It means a big crash, rock bottom!"

She adjusted the glasses over her ears, pushed her hair back. "That must be what Norman was trying to tell me—what he kept fretting about that he could see coming." She looked at David's worried face. "The stock market was Norman's forte—Anton's as well. But you and your father have never had any interest in stocks and bonds. Your father was one hundred percent a wine and grape man. He invested every dime in his—his dream."

"I've never seemed to have that extra dime for investing in anything." David looked at her suddenly with a new anxiety. "Did Norman leave you heavily invested in the market?"

"A few blue-chip stocks. Surely blue chips will be all right. Aren't they always stable? Chip Brosius, Norman's partner, handles my portfolio. He's conservative—I'm sure Chip knows best."

"It's not a matter of *knowing*. You'd better get *out*, fast!"

"Don't get so worked up, David! I'm okay. I've paid the mortgage. I have a clear deed to this house, my land. Just as you own Spring Mountain outright. We're lucky. As long as we have our *land*."

"We have to have money too."

Sarah got up. "Now, you absolutely mustn't worry. I will go to Napa City and talk with Chip Brosius first thing tomorrow. I have enough money. We can manage, all of us." She shook her head. "David, you have to take things less seriously. You must look toward the bright side."

"Mother, I am a realist! This is an economic calamity—"

"The stock market always has its ups and downs. I've got to get back to my cooking. I have one last batch of applesauce to put up. Tell Lilliana I'll be sending along some to add to your pantry shelves."

As lightly as Sarah had first taken the news, on Tuesday, October 29, Chip Brosius drove to Oakville. "You must get to the bank quickly to withdraw your money. Even the banks are going to go under. You barely have time—hurry!"

"*Banks*—nonsense! Don't tell me a sensible, levelheaded young man such as yourself is going to join this panic, Chip?"

"Please, I promised your husband I would look after you! We don't have time for you to waste. Don't even stop to comb your hair, to get a coat. Just get your bank book and *hurry!*"

Because of Chip, Sarah arrived at the bank in Napa City next to last in line before it was closed down. Though she did not receive all that she had deposited there, she did get some out—$22,000, in various-sized bills. All that next week she went about the mansion searching for safe hiding places, stuffing money into porcelain jugs, under lamps, in dresser drawers, behind canned goods in the pantry.

She had received a wire from Anton that they were sailing back to America; so she sat down and wrote a welcoming letter and told him how she had fared during the crash. He answered from Boston:

MY DEAR MOM SARAH,

Thank you for your warm letter. It's good to know you did not lose everything. We got back in time to salvage something: luckily, three years ago (at Norman's urging, by the way), I convinced my father-in-law, Bernard Fuller, that he should most certainly diversify. His real estate holdings will help him ride out his heavy losses on the market; so now he is convinced I'm a worthy financial adviser and has made me head of his council. (I'm not sure Phyllis is convinced I am a worthy husband!)

At any rate, this means we won't be coming back to Napa Valley as soon as I had hoped. When we do return, Bernard wants to come with us and buy property for himself, as well as (he now says) back me in a big winery operation, once repeal comes about. (You may have all of us for neighbors in the future.) By the way, Phyllis liked you enormously—though right now she is out of sorts with the world, having discovered she is expecting a second child next April. She'll feel better soon, I'm sure.

Lovingly,
ANTON

As it turned out, Anton was not to return to the Napa Valley for another three years, in late August of 1932.

Meantime, Sarah seemed to draw a cloak of self-imposed isolation about her, in much the same way that she had done on Spring Mountain. In order to save money, she had let go most of the huge domestic staff Norman had kept employed. Rarely did she get out in the big Chrysler, complaining that it took too much gas and its repairs were too expensive. She took to driving a simple Ford that Norman had bought initially for the servants to use running various errands. Routinely, she went into Napa City, where she did most of her shopping, and where she indulged herself to a weekly shampoo at Myrna's Beauty Parlor on

459

Soscol. And, usually, after she had got out from under the dryer and been combed out, she would tend to any appointments, or run small errands that would make her trip fully efficient.

Otherwise, she spent most of her time puttering around the enormous mansion in which she had been born. Now and then she would sit out on the brick terrace, look about and take note of paint peeling off the huge Corinthian pillars, or see where the once well-kept lawn was overgrown with crabgrass or had turned brown in huge splotchy areas. If Li Po was about, she would mumble to him—though she had taken to saying what was on her mind even when no one else was about, "When times eases up, I'll spend some money to spruce up the place again." The only splurges she allowed were for gifts of clothing, usually, to David's girls, Anne and Dede—gifts he couldn't easily refuse.

None of this was easy for David, Sarah realized. The grape market, as David referred to it, was "shot to hell."

In 1930, when the speakers came around to Napa Valley trying to get growers to sign up with the Federal Aid Plan, he dropped in to the kitchen at Sarah's one afternoon in early May, after he had just finished the cultivating of her vineyards. He was exhausted, his hair needed cutting, his face shaving. She shoved a cup of hot coffee and a sandwich (made from cold chicken and early garden lettuce) at him.

"You're not taking care of yourself, David. You and Lilliana have to get out more."

He propped his elbows on the table, held the coffee in the cradle of both hands. "We get to the movies with the kids, a dance at the Grange Hall now and then. We have our church activities." He looked up, a little embarrassed. "Lilliana wants the children to have a strong faith. If we don't participate, it doesn't mean much. I'm not so religious. I like hearing the music. Seeing the sun shine through the stained glass. I *enjoy* going to Mass."

"Good. I'm *glad* you do. What's on your mind?"

"This Federal Aid—they need an eighty-five percent sign-up. You keep up on these things. What do you think? I just heard that last year's market was off another thirty percent statewide. It's going lower this year. I can't make a dollar the way things stand! But some of the men seem to think this program is a lot of baloney. Looks good on the surface, but that's about all."

She sat opposite him, pushed her hair off her forehead where Myra had tried a new style of curling her bangs. David noticed, and his eyes crinkled at the corners. "Say, aren't you dipping kind of heavily into the henna? I never saw your hair that color before."

"Myrna gave me a free shampoo if I'd let her try something out. If I could, I'd go back to long hair. I hate all this frizzy permanent mess." She looked at him squarely. "There's one thing I like about the federal program—it's brought those big corporations together and is forcing them to help out the smaller growers such as ourselves. The California Fruit Exchange and Sun Maid Raisins are *big* enough, Lord knows. But I don't like the way they've put this together. I don't think they'll be able to implement it properly. And they're charging us a dollar and a half a ton to participate."

"But aren't they underwriting up to thirty dollars a ton? Buying up all the surplus?"

"They *say* that, yes."

"What you're saying is it's the same old story, then. Washington throws these packages together, too little, too late. When it comes to the farmers, the agriculturists, we're on the short end of the stick!"

"At least the corporation has put Lloyd Tenny in as president, and I think he's smart. He was able to get $750,000 out of the plan. Even if it's a comparative drop in the bucket, it is something. We need all the help we can get right now."

"Have you been reading about the latest places that have been put on the auction block? The distress sales?"

"David, don't frown that way. You're going to look as old as I am before long. And please sit up—don't slump your shoulders in. Your father always walked so proudly, his head up in the air!" She gave a deep sigh. "He was such a wonderfully handsome man. Just as you are. You're so much like him. But do sit up!"

He pushed his cup and empty plate back, stood up. "Well, do we or *don't* we? Sign up?"

"I don't see any alternative. *I* plan to."

But that November, after the profits and losses were tallied, David and Sarah compared notes. David's fist banged against the tabletop. "Goddammit! After paying my transportation costs and my pickers, I netted $88.50 a carload. That leaves me less than seven dollars a ton profit! So much for that guarantee of thirty dollars a ton. Hell, I might as well run the cattle through the vineyards."

Sarah shook her head. "Well, don't give up. I know they're urging growers to rip out vines and plant prune trees again. The prune crop made more than grapes. Again!"

"How can I rip out the *vines?* On Spring Mountain, nothing else grows." David scooped up the papers, let out a disgusted sigh.

"We could never allow the Spring Mountain vineyards to be

ripped out, David, even if something else did do well. That would be like ripping out—yanking your father's very soul up by the roots."

"I didn't *say* anything about ripping them out, did I?" David glared, his jaw working back and forth. "If this damn Prohibition keeps up, though, I might try my hand at something else. And I mean it!"

"David—you *mustn't*," she called out after him. "Don't do anything against the law! Do you hear me?"

He let the screen door slam, stood for a moment on the back stoop, squinting his eyes against the sun. "Sometimes I ask myself why not? I see the bills pile up, and bootlegging looks damn tempting!"

In January of 1931, word spread through the valley that the Greystone Winery built by William Bourn in 1888, for a half million dollars then, was going up for sale again. In 1925 it had been bought from the California Wine Association by the Bisceglia brothers, and now they were reportedly selling it to a Chicago firm, the California Vineyards Company.

On hearing about the ridiculously low price—below $50,000—it had supposedly gone for, Sarah wrote Anton a long letter, which said in part:

> If your father-in-law is serious about buying land and property in Napa Valley, he should hasten to do so. Some fine bargains are being snapped up by those lucky enough to have any spare money on hand. Some excellent places have gone for little more than the price of back taxes.
>
> David tells me that your own vineyards look in bad shape. Apparently, whoever you left in charge either is lazy or doesn't know his business. Your house could use a good painting—as could my own. When do you think you might come see us? Do you realize I have not seen my own grandchildren? Frances is going to be six years old soon, and young Bernard is already three. They look so adorable in the photograph you sent. I was disappointed that you didn't send a snapshot of you and Phyllis. I only have your wedding pictures. I'm sure you've both changed since then. How is Phyllis, by the way? Is she happier now? Oh, I do miss being a part of your life and having that close-hand knowledge I would have if you lived here in the Napa Valley. Please do consider it.

But Anton did not write again for several months, and when he did, near the end of summer, 1931, he mentioned Phyllis only briefly:

Phyllis and the nurse have taken the children to the beach house in Clifton, near Marblehead. I've been working so hard with Bernard securing new landholdings that I've hardly seen her. I'm sure she would want me to send her love.

My father-in-law is most definitely interested in buying Napa Valley property. Right now, there are astounding bargains right here in Boston. I suppose that must be true all over the United States. This Depression is deepening. Though Bernard is a Herbert Hoover fan, I am not so sure that he can bring us out of this. What is your opinion, Mom Sarah? I recall that you used to keep up with political trends ahead of most of us.

Then, in July, that hot gloomy summer of 1932, Sarah read that President Hoover had ordered the Army to drive out fifteen thousand World War veterans who had been camped for two months in Washington demanding a bonus from Congress; that cavalry troops with drawn sabers, tanks, and infantry columns equipped with fixed bayonets and tear gas bombs, led by General Douglas MacArthur and Major Dwight Eisenhower, advanced on the veterans, with Major George Patton personally leading the final charge against the marchers; that a three-month-old baby died of tear gas; that a small boy trying to save a pet rabbit was caught by a bayonet in the leg; and that the very Joe Angelino who had saved Major Patton's life during the war and received the Distinguished Service Cross for his heroic act was one whose tent and belongings were destroyed by fire from Patton's men. Sarah decided it was time to get into the middle of the political campaign and try to get Franklin D. Roosevelt elected as President of the United States.

It was as though all the long-unused energy she had kept dormant since Norman's death suddenly erupted in its own miniature volcanic force. She was hurrying about, going from one precinct meeting to the next; not only getting voters registered, but working hard to educate voters in Napa Valley about Proposition Two placed on the upcoming November ballot—which, if it won, would mean that light wines and beers could be made in California again and sold in hotels, restaurants and boardinghouses and as packaged goods, though the saloon would still be forbidden. She was quickly given an important committee post in the Napa County Association for Prohibition Reform. As a spokeswoman for the NCAPR she went all over the county in the old Ford, touting their arguments that the Prohibition Law was unenforceable, that it engendered disrespect for and disobedience to all law, and that the federal government was annually spending a billion dollars in vain

463

trying to enforce it, as well as losing nearly that much in revenue dollars it once took in as taxes on all alcoholic beverages.

"Crime and drunkenness are on the increase!" she would shout from her stages in schoolhouses, on street corners. "Let's bring dignity back to our beloved Napa Valley. Let's restore the graciousness of sharing a glass of wine with our friends. Let's bring back the true blessings of our harvests—that ringing joy of the crush as it once resounded between these mountains. Vote *yes* for Proposition Two! Vote Democrat!"

In fact, she had just finished a speech in St. Helena at the park's pergola-topped grandstand, the last week of August—just after David had told her she should stop and be around for the harvest—when a voice shot across the park, one that made her take a deep breath and realize in an instant that she hadn't gone for her weekly hair appointment, that she had torn her hose badly, and that she must look more like an old turkey gobbler at the moment than the image her stepson Anton had surely taken with him over five years ago.

"Mom Sarah! It's *you*," he said, cutting quickly across the park, his hands extended, his neatly pressed seersucker suit, his starched white shirt and silk necktie making her feel shabbier than ever.

Because she was caught on the defensive, Sarah was scowling as she tugged at her floppy-brimmed straw hat, hoping it covered the gray streak in her hair where she had decided to let the henna rinse grow out. "Who did you *think* it was?" She busied herself stuffing in the notes she had scribbled for her speech into her purse and making a crisp stack out of the flyers she had not been able to pass out as yet.

Anton's gray-blue eyes crinkled with laughter, but he kept his voice even. "I never saw you stump-speeching before. You were wonderful!" He took her by the elbow. "Come on—Bernard is over here waiting in the car. He'll want to meet you."

She yanked her arm free. "Just a minute. I am most certainly *not* ready to meet your father-in-law! *Look* at me. Besides, I have another speech to make in Calistoga before dark tonight. You could have let me know you were arriving. To expect you! Or don't I count with you any longer?"

"Calm down. Get off your high horse. We came suddenly because —well, we hoped the trip out might bring Phyllis to her senses." He looked about at the milling people dispersing across the park, some spreading out blankets for picnics, opening big-lipped jugs of lemonade, children running about playing a squealing game of tag, a dog loping along barking loudly behind them. "I took Bernard on a drive to get him acquainted with the terrain. He's already trying to decide *what* to buy, and we've only been here since early this morning. I intended to call you. Drop by this evening."

"What's wrong with Phyllis? What do you mean, bring her to her senses?"

"This isn't the place to discuss it." He smiled at a clump of buxom teenage girls sitting in a huddle nearby and looking at Anton with appreciative eyes, then nudging each other, giggling.

"Are the children with you?"

"Yes—we came with the complete entourage. The nursemaids, the cook, the laundress, Bernard's valet, George, who has worked for him for thirty-five years. It's confusing, to put it mildly. But they're trying to get settled in. Find room for everyone. Get some of the dust out. The place is a mess. Run down. I've stayed away much too long."

"Will you be here for any length of time?"

He smiled. "That depends on Bernard. He just found out he missed the auction on the Greystone Winery."

"Auction? They just sold it last year to that outfit from Chicago! I didn't know they were auctioning it so soon."

"It sold for ten thousand dollars," he said, shrugging his shoulders. "We would have bought it in a minute, paid twice that for it, had we known. Anyway, Bernard is convinced there must be something else around equally as big a bargain, though I've tried to tell him there's only one Greystone."

"I hear the Cugnot place is up for sale," Sarah said. "But you must have known that, surely, it being your next-door neighbor."

His eyes lit up. "As I told you, we just got in. No, I didn't know! That would be ideal for him. He wants to be close by, anyway. How much acreage does the Cugnot place have?"

"At least two hundred acres, I'd think. It's in probate. Go check it out. I've got to hurry, Anton. I can't stand around talking when I've got a speech to make." She yanked at the hat again. "As soon as you're settled, give me a telephone call. But please don't just drop in on me. I'd like to have you over for dinner. And I want to look my best, certainly, when my grandchildren see me for the first time."

"You look—you look fine," he said, seeing how her face had begun to sag down now with wrinkles, how she wore those terrible rimless glasses, and that, surely, she could find a more stylish dress than that limp rag she was wearing. But at the same time, Anton found himself delighted with the way she was more or less trotting across the park, in quite a bit of a huff to be on her way. Time was turning her into an eccentric, Anton thought, a smile lighting up his face and putting a lighter bounce to his own step as he hurried back to the car, where he expected to find Bernard Fuller out of sorts from the heat and from being made to wait.

From their first meeting, Sarah and Bernard Fuller disagreed on most issues. At seventy-two years of age, Bernard Fuller had about him a surprisingly agile step, a lean body, and a mind which seemed to roll on ball bearings, turning in a precise fixed orbit: things in life were either added up or subtracted; they made sense or they didn't; there was a place for everything or it should be discarded; there was a right way or a wrong way; there were the most definite *haves* and those *have-nots* out there; there were the men in world, who ran things, and the women, who propagated the human species; and, politically, there were the Republicans, who knew about economic balance and a rational, conservative approach (even Harding, he argued, had his excesses but had had the good sense to place capable men in key positions who ran things very well indeed), and there were, unfortunately, the Democrats, who would *give* the country away, give the golden key to every ragtag immigrant who stepped off the next boat!

So when he had seen Sarah Donati Jaspers on the open bandstand in St. Helena's park, flailing her arms about and screaming in a loud raucous voice to a motley crowd to get out and vote Democrat, he had made up his mind that this so-called stepmother of Anton Brunner's was not going to contaminate *his* grandchildren's thinking. In fact, he would see to it that she was eased out of their lives totally—as long as he was paying the bills, which he most certainly was doing, forking out right and left! He was not at all sure that being here in Napa Valley was the right idea. But at least it had taken Phyllis out of the circle of friends and business associates of his who were beginning to notice her drinking. It would be a good place to hide her—dry her out, which he also most certainly intended to do, if it meant putting her behind lock and key, along with all the bottles of whiskey.

Reluctantly, he had bought the old Cugnot estate. Though he had picked it up for pennies, relatively speaking, it would cost him plenty to renovate it. It had its quaintness, however, and it was large enough for his needs. Too, by being adjacent to Anton's property, he could better keep an eye on Phyllis and the children. If worse came to worst, he would move the nurse and Frances and the little Bernard in with him; assign someone to keep guard over Phyllis, if he had to, until she could come to her senses. Genes—it was all a matter of having inherited the wrong sets of genes from her mother's side of the family! He should have known before he married Lucille Conover that she came from a long line of women with weak lungs and an accompanying weak character. Spineless! He abhorred spineless, whimpering women more than anything else in the wide world. It had been the very thing about Lucille that used to drive him into such fury that he hadn't been able to resist striking her. Even now he got angry when he realized that not once did she ever try to strike back. To retaliate—that would have made a difference! He could have respected her a little more, perhaps. In time, maybe he would not have even slapped her.

If Anton had more gumption, he would knock some sense into Phyllis. In fact, if the doctors hadn't warned him about his own high blood pressure, he'd still teach her a lesson or two. There were ways, though. There were institutions for incurable drunks, for the mentally unstable. Thank God, he had at least two sound grandchildren. Young Bernard was so bright and quick-witted. He would be a wonderful businessman. Granted, part of that he had inherited from his father, Anton.

Actually, he admired Anton Brunner. He was a fighter. A good-looking man. No wonder he sought attractive women's company. In his own case, at least Lucille Conover had been a pretty wife. Not that she passed any of those genes on to her daughter! Poor Phyllis—not only had she inherited weak character genes, but she had been born *ugly*.

But how different it had been with his son, Julian. Handsome Julian, bright Julian. Killed—gunned down for no goddam good reason, simply because Woodrow Wilson hadn't had the knowhow to keep America out of a war it had no business ever becoming involved with. Even now he couldn't bear to look at Julian's photograph in his uniform.

At least Phyllis had married a man who resembled—maybe only slightly, but enough—Julian. If he groomed him well enough, if he could bring Phyllis herself around, it would be *something*.

For weeks, Bernard Fuller had been able to stall off meeting Sarah. Then Anton had come to him one day and said, "Mom Sarah wants all of the family to come to her place to celebrate my birthday. And she's anxious to show you her home—and her husband's Oriental collection, now that she knows you have one, too."

"What is this 'Mom Sarah' business? She isn't your mother. She is no blood relation whatsoever. It is highly undignified for a man of your demeanor."

"I've always thought of her as a mother figure. She's been good to me. I like her."

"Well, *I* don't! I detest aggressive women who don't know a tinker's damn about politics but think they have the right to spout off. Damn fools, all of them!"

"My stepmother is hardly a fool. She's a graduate of Wellesley. She's astute. She's quite an interesting woman. Give her a chance. Don't be so crotchety, Bernard. You're beginning to sound like an old man lately," Anton said, lighting a cigarette, giving him his own arrogant look. He had learned quickly that Bernard Fuller enjoyed discourse that had the potential for a good fight. He needed to win, to prove himself the champion.

"Because she went to an eastern school doesn't mean a damn thing to me. I'm a self-made man. I didn't have to get a Harvard degree to wave under people's noses. I made my money by using my brains. Something you should try. Phyllis is a college graduate, too, and look at that imbecile!"

"We're invited for lunch, next Sunday. At noon."

"I will make my visit short. My driver will bring me. I have no intention of riding in the same car with your wife—until she has sense enough to give up the bottle. It would pay you, young man, to see that she does."

Though Sarah had gone through a brief nervous snit, convinced that she had made an error by inviting the old buzzard Bernard Fuller over—along with that stuffy nurse, Miss Gompers, whom Phyllis herself had asked to have come along to watch after the children. On top of that, Sarah had, in a weak moment, decided she'd like to have David and Lilliana there, more or less in her corner, giving her a support she thought she might need, not having entertained in a long time, and with only Li Po around these days to help out. Both of them were rusty. At one time, she wouldn't have hesitated to invite a host of guests.

As soon as the entourage arrived on Sunday morning, a stiff-backed Miss Gompers herded Frances (in her white stockings and organdy pinafore, her long blond curls tied back with blue velvet streamers of ribbons) and four-year-old Bernard (in his short gray flannel suit, his starched white shirt with his own monogrammed initials on the cuffs, his necktie, his polished black shoes and knee-high white socks) to the far end of the brick terrace, at a careful distance from Anne and Dede Donati (who, in their checked gingham dresses, were both recovering from bad colds, and who both stood like startled brown-eyed does, staring at the "spoiled rich Brunners," as David had explicitly dubbed them).

Phyllis was wearing a gray tweed suit, a white pullover sweater, a sensible pair of loafers. In the past five years her hair had grown to

468

shoulder length. She had it cut straight, turned slightly under, pageboy style, parted on one side, and pinned back off her face with a gold beret. The heavy drinking had left its telltale signs, Sarah noted immediately, seeing the pouches forming under the limpid eyes, the sagging lines around her mouth. At thirty-four, she looked forty-five. Her voice, normally deep and crackly, now had a coarse, split sound which came out in croaks when she made an attempt to laugh.

Lilliana had come out into the kitchen to offer to help. Sarah was trying to cut the ham slices evenly, was finding the knife dull and that big slabs of the pink meat were piling up on the platter. She looked up, pushed her hair off her face with the back of one hand. "Maybe you could get out that jar of spiced peaches, and some watercress Li Po found for me—try to make this mess look a little more attractive." She nodded toward the cabinets. "Up there." When she looked around she saw, from the way Lilliana's blue-flowered crepe dress made a definite outline across her stomach as she stretched her arm, that either Lilliana had gained far too much weight or she was pregnant. When Lilliana placed the quart jar of canned peaches in front of her, Sarah looked up from placing the slices of ham in a row on the platter and said, "Am I seeing wrong or are you expecting a baby?"

Lilliana sank down on a straight-backed chair, rubbed her forehead. "In February—possibly March. We didn't plan it. Times aren't the best for a new baby. But David wants a son so badly and I'm not getting any younger."

Sarah came over, gave her a half-hug, protecting her from her greasy fingers. "I'm happy for you! Yes, a boy for David—someone to learn about Spring Mountain. Right?"

Lilliana waited until Sarah had finished washing her hands at the sink and was standing back admiring the silver platter, now arranged for serving. "David isn't that keen on Spring Mountain right now, with this depression. It's sometimes his cross to bear, he says. I don't know if he'll want to give our son the responsibility." She got up, placed her hands across her protruding belly, as if trying to hide it. "He has days when he's like that. Other days, I don't think a team of mules could drag him off Spring Mountain. He's ambivalent about it. One of those love-hate things he seems to wrestle with a lot lately."

Sarah picked up the tray of ham. "Would you mind bringing out that bowl of salad—one of Li Po's Chinese specials—over there on the sideboard? This menu—I wonder what they serve in the Fuller house. But here they will get what *I* serve—like it or not."

Lilliana held open the swinging door leading into the dining room.

469

"You and David are happy, though, aren't you? You're both pleased about the new baby?" Sarah asked over one shoulder.

Lilliana went about helping arrange the silverware for the buffet in a neater row than Li Po had left them. She poked at a bright-orange zinnia which she thought was sticking up too high in the middle of the bouquet Sarah had quickly arranged for the centerpiece from those few flowers she had found blooming. "We don't have all that kind of time to worry about it," she said, her large brown eyes soft, a little weary-looking. "We just try to keep going, one day to the next. Keep up with the bills, the work to be done. We try to devote most of our attention to the children. Give them the best we've got. Help them in every way we can. I guess we don't think so much about ourselves."

"You mustn't neglect yourself," Sarah said, giving one last touch to the watercress on the silver plate, turning a pickled peach where it looked more in place. "You're looking a little peaked. A little drawn. Be sure you eat enough for two."

Because it was a balmy November afternoon, Sarah had set tables out on the southwest brick terrace to get the benefit from what sun was there. Being outside made her feel more relaxed. And this *was* Napa Valley, after all—she wasn't entertaining in Boston. Bernard Fuller would have to learn country ways if he was going to settle in and stay around for a while.

Everything went fairly smoothly during the main course. David and Anton were discussing the possibility of repeal being voted in in 1933.

"We've got a state ballot coming up in June next year," David said. "If it doesn't pass, if we don't get repeal soon, then they can write off a $350,000,000 grape industry."

"It will happen on the national level next November. Roosevelt is going all out for getting rid of the Eighteenth Amendment." Anton held the Château Mont Helena burgundy up to the light. "How pleasant it is to find a wine these days without precipitation. To see an honest-to-God clear red wine and not that purple high red," He sipped. "A little stemmy, don't you think?"

David took his time tasting. "No, I wouldn't say so. I like it. It's a fine, well-balanced wine." He lifted an eyebrow, trying to hold back his irritation with Anton's romantic approach to most aspects of wine-making, in his opinion. It was easy enough for Anton to sit back with his legs crossed, that disdainful look of perpetual contempt on his face, when a rich father-in-law was ladling out money right and left. But if he ever had to make a go of it on his own, David wondered how he'd do. In his own case, he was at the point where he might have to ask Sarah for a loan after all—though he would wait until the last minute, and then it would be a strict loan, paid back at seven or eight percent.

Sarah stepped up at that point with Bernard Fuller, to whom she had just shown Norman's Oriental collection of Ming china. Because she had always taken Norman's word for what the collection represented, she had never questioned any one piece on a definitive basis. Bernard Fuller had picked up a dish, turned it around slowly. "This isn't Ming—it's Tai Ch'ang, 1620."

"Perhaps I misunderstood my husband when he told me about that particular vase," Sarah had answered stiffly. "At any rate, all of it is museum quality."

"If you're talking about a Napa Valley museum, I *suppose*."

His remark was still stinging. She had thought of a dozen replies but held back on them. She had intended to go up to Anton to ask if he was ready for his birthday cake, when Bernard Fuller pushed her aside as though she were a servant. "What are you *men* talking about?" he asked in his gruff, crusty voice. "Hope you're making better sense than what I've been hearing. If there's one thing I know, it's Chinese porcelains."

"We were discussing the probability of repeal next year—since Roosevelt is a strong advocate of it," Anton said, offering a glass of wine to him.

Bernard Fuller tugged at his lapels. "That demagogue will take this country so far downhill we won't ever recover. That factious bastard! We've never had a better President of the United States than Herbert Hoover. He could have swung this Depression around with a little more time."

Sarah reached down and grabbed a cigarette. Lately she had taken to puffing on one, never inhaling, but liking the activity of it—though there were times she forgot and let the cigarette dangle in the corner of her mouth, squinting fiercely against the smoke, until, disgusted, she would snuff it out and go on to some more important matter. Now she puffed vigorously, trying to release some of her fury. Then, when she could not bear it any longer, she reached for her glass of wine, lifted it. "Here's to the next President of the United States—a man who *cares* for the people!" she added with extra fervor, having just that morning seen pictures in the Sunday paper of men standing in bread lines with burlap and newspapers wrapped around their feet for shoes. "To a man who will do more than put a chicken in the pot but will restore to the common man his dignity!"

471

Bernard Fuller's fury seemed to bounce off his thick-rimmed glasses in tiny prisms. He put his glass down on the wicker table. "The thing that makes man *common* is that he had no dignity to begin with. This country has every possible opportunity for a man to make a living. I made *my* way to the top. I didn't have it handed out to me. I worked —I used my head. Those poor people have what they deserve in life. Women! You're all damn fools when it comes to politics. You ought to stick with your flower beds, your ham bones!"

A wobbly Phyllis was coming back out on the brick terrace, carrying a glass of tomato juice in which Sarah was sure she had poured a sizable amount of gin. "Father, you have always said one shouldn't *shout*." she said languidly. She plopped down onto the wicker settee, drew one leg up under her, smiled a lopsided grin at Sarah.

"I've got more important things to do with *my* time," Bernard Fuller snorted. "Anton, do you want to go with me to see some property I heard is going up on the auction block? A place that might be perfect for your winery?"

"Well, the birthday cake is coming out. Let's wait for that."

"Suit yourself. It's your idea to open a winery. It was for *you*.'" He headed out across the crisp dry lawn.

Phyllis let out a croaky laugh. "Go on, dear . . . Daddy says jump. You'd better heel fast. Daddy might not give Anton his winery otherwise!" She drank several quick gulps of tomato juice.

"We've got to head out," David said easily. "Lilliana is trying to leave off desserts lately anyway. The girls don't need anything sweet. We've got too many dentist bills as it is."

"Go on, Anton," Sarah said drily. "Don't rock the boat."

"Well . . . I hate to run out on my own birthday party."

Bernard Fuller had his driver pull the huge Packard as close to the brick terrace as possible. He leaned out the window. "Are you or *aren't* you coming?"

"You can get home okay, Phyllis?"

"Miss Gompers will see to that—or haven't you got that one figured out yet?"

Anton looked anxiously about, then headed out quickly, climbed into the back seat with Bernard Fuller.

Miss Gompers was standing holding the children's hands. "I need to get them home now. Shall we?"

Sarah had just waved goodbye to Lilliana, David and her grandchildren Anne and Dede. She overheard Miss Gompers' remark, saw the strained look on Phyllis's face. "Why don't you take the children on home? I'll bring Phyllis. We haven't had a moment to visit since she's been here. I'd like that so very much," she said softly to Phyllis. "Won't you stay a little longer? The party's over so quickly."

Miss Gompers, a rakishly thin woman with an expression Sarah thought looked as if it had been chipped off a hundred-pound ice block, drew her shoulders back, buttoned the top button of her navy-blue princess-style coat. "Mr. Fuller made me promise that I'd see to it that—"

"Of course, he wants his grandchildren tucked in for their nap," Sarah put in quickly. "I thoroughly understand that. You hurry along. I'll bring Phyllis in a little while."

"Kiss your mother goodbye," Miss Gompers instructed the children. "Then shake hands, Bernard. Curtsy, Frances, to our hostess as you've been taught."

"Stop *pinching* me, Bernard!" six-year-old Frances said, slapping at her brother.

"Mr. *Fuller's* grandchildren don't pinch—nor do they slap," Miss Gompers said, yanking at both of them and heading out toward the waiting car with the new driver, Gunther, who had been hired and given his duties by Bernard Fuller.

As they drove off, Phyllis leaned forward. "Gunther will be back. He has orders."

Sarah sat down opposite her. "What do you mean?"

"I mean, dear, that I overheard him last evening laying down the law." Phyllis leaned back, stared hard at her empty glass. "Would you mind if I get a refill? It may be my last," she said, struggling to get up, weaving about a little.

"Phyllis, don't you think you might hold back a little? Drink a little less, dear?"

Phyllis placed both hands on her hips; the glass tilted precariously. "Don't tell me you're going to join the Greek chorus! Don't you trust me, either?"

"If you want a drink, you may have it," Sarah said, getting up and going toward the door. "Just don't sneak around about it—in *my* house, anyway. You don't have to play hide-and-go-seek with me. I don't drink gin, anway—and I notice that you seem quite fond of it."

Phyllis's hand trembled as she reached for the decanter, poured a tumblerful. "I can't help it!" she blurted out. "It helps. It's the only thing that helps!"

They were in the foyer. "Don't go back out there!" Phyllis said with a suden urgency. "Let's stay in here where we can talk a few minutes before Gunther comes for me. Drags me back."

"He won't 'drag' you." Sarah led her into the parlor.

473

Phyllis sat in the settee, leaned back, then sat upright again. "Last night he was told by my father that he could drag me by the hair of the head if that was needed to keep me away from the bottle. He was told that he could lock me in my room, if *that* was needed. He was put in charge. To see that I stop drinking." Phyllis dropped her head forward. "If that doesn't work, I've been told, then I get locked up someplace else. In the crazy house, is how my father bluntly put it."

"Your father is a—a—"

"Go on, say it. Horse's ass. But he is the boss. He hates me—he wants me out of the way. He hopes Gunther can't keep me under control so he can lock me away forever." Her head sagged and she began to cry, the tears working in and around the crevices of her long, droopy face.

"Listen to me, Phyllis," Sarah said, trying to reach Phyllis's hands, which had flopped lifelessly into her lap. "If you are telling me the truth—if—"

Phyllis glared at her, then looked about like a trapped animal. "You don't have to believe me. But it *is* the truth!" She grabbed at her glass, drank until most of it was gone. Her gray eyes looked glazed now. "Maybe you're in with them. Why else would Gunther drive off, even for a little while?"

"I want you to listen to me," Sarah said quietly. "I want to help you, Phyllis. Not lock you up or put some watchdog on your trail. I want to help you to get well. To be able to stop this—this self-destruction. Do you want to *die*? Is that it, Phyllis?" She handed a napkin to her. "There—please dry your eyes."

Phyllis blinked at her. "I might as well be dead. He killed my mother. I know that he did. I found her diary. I found it out at the beach house—hidden behind a stack of old books." She laughed. "I know all about hiding places. I'm a genius at finding hiding places." Her head sagged down, stuttered back into a level position. "My mother wrote how every bone in her body ached from a beating he had given her. She said she knew she had lung congestion but she wouldn't go to a doctor because she hoped she would die. The sooner the better. *I* don't have lung congestion. I'm as healthy as a horse! Old horse-face Fuller, huh? What else for big gawky me? Sure—how long does it take? I must have a liver, huh? I must have been given a horse's liver, to boot. It takes longer for horses to die. Did you ever see a horse die?"

"*Yes.*" Sarah looked at her intently. "It was a terrible sight. I don't want to see anyone die—not another horse, not a lovely woman such as yourself. You have got to wipe out these images you seem to have of

474

yourself! You are *not* gawky. You have an athletic look. A wonderful look. I thought so the first time I ever saw you. Patrician—an eastern patrician look. Truly you do."

Again tears spilled down Phyllis's face. "My father doesn't like you much either," she suddenly blurted out. "He told Frances and Bernard that you are not their grandmother. That you aren't a blood relative at all and that you are—let me see how he said it—balmy, a dotty old lady."

"That is insignificant to me," Sarah said crisply. "I don't care much for your father, either! Right now, let's not waste a moment. If what you have told me is indeed the case, then we don't have time to spare. I'm going to help you, Phyllis. Please, allow me to do so. There are lovely places you can go—not a place where you'll be under lock and key. There are doctors. I know of one place—I read about it recently. Down in Carmel. A spa, really. Where they cater to people such as yourself who have a drinking problem. They've had remarkable results, apparently."

"Places like that would cost money. I don't have money. *He* has all the money—assuming he would allow me to go."

"If you will go, I will, pay for it. I will make all the arrangements, if that is necessary."

"Anton would like to have me gone."

"Please—let's not talk about Anton right now. Why would you say that, anyway?"

Phyllis's face took on a narrowed, leering look. "Because he has a new girl friend, that is why. He has hired a—oh, he doesn't call her his secretary. She is going to be a kind of public liaison to help promote the Brunner name when he opens his winery."

"Seriously, Phyllis, let's—"

"Oh, this is *very* serious. This one is European. He *adores* Europeans, you know. He loves French accents! I understand that Katia Rudnisky speaks five different languages. She will be setting up liaisons in five languages—imagine that!" Phyllis's laughter sounded grotesque as it split the silence. She licked at tears in the corner of her mouth with her tongue. "Katia is a little different from the others. She is smarter. She is much, much more ambitious than the others. Katia has a long-range plan."

The doorbell rang. Li Po hurried to the parlor, looked at Sarah questioningly. "The driver, he say Mrs. Brunner must come now."

Sarah got up, marched out across the marble-tiled foyer, her heels clicking. "Your name is Gunther, isn't it?"

475

The square-faced, short-necked man wearing a chauffeur's uniform nodded, his eyes like slits. "Yes, ma'am."

"You are a driver for Mr. Fuller, is that right?"

"Yes, ma'am. I was told to come get Mrs. Brunner and take her home."

"Which you *may*—just as soon as we have finished our visit. You may wait in the car, or you may wait on the terrace. Suit yourself. But you must wait. We are not through." She closed the door firmly in his face, marched back into the parlor. "This is *my* house, and Bernard Fuller will not order *me* around! You are my guest. If you wish, you may stay here with me."

Phyllis's eyes had widened. She was trying to hold a steady appraising look. "You really are my friend, aren't you?"

"Yes, I am. I am a woman of my word. I said I want to help you, and I shall, if you will let me. If you want to get well, I know that you can. There's another way—you don't have to remain your father's prisoner. One of these days he'll die. All of us do. He's not a spring chicken. Let's face it—you will be quite wealthy one of these days. You can pay your own way."

"He would cut me out of his will. He has told me so."

"Let him! You have a good brain. It would be better to earn your own way than be his prisoner, anyway. Nor do you need to accept Anton's shoddy behavior! Just because your mother accepted your father's beatings—as you say she did—it does not follow that you must repeat her habits. You can make a new life for yourself, I know it. Let me help, right now. Stay here with me tonight," Sarah said urgently, frightened by the cold, evil look she had seen in Gunther's eyes. "I'll see that you're safe. I'll make telephone calls tomorrow. We'll get you down to Carmel, where you can receive excellent care. I'll personally take you there. *Please*, let me do this for you. Tell me right now and I will send Gunther back."

"Will you let me have a drink? You won't trick me? You'll really help me?"

Sarah took her hands in hers. "You may trust me. I would stake my life on this promise."

"My father won't allow it. He'll have you arrested. He'd burn your house down before he'd let me stay here."

"He won't do any such thing. There are laws. If he sets foot on my property, I'll have *him* arrested. He may be a big shot in Boston, but he's in Napa Valley now. This is *my* territory. Just let the old buzzard try anything!"

"Will you tell Gunther?"

"I most certainly will. Then you'll stay? You'll let me help you?"

"Yes . . . I'll try. For you I'll try." Phyllis was crying softly now, staring into the empty glass.

Sarah went back out on the terrace, looked around, saw Gunther standing smoking a cigarette as though lurking by a post, as if he might have been trying to eavesdrop.

"You may go back now and tell Mr. Fuller *and* Mr. Brunner that Mrs. Brunner is spending a few days with me. She wants to get away. Get a little rest. If anyone has a question, they may telephone. I prefer —in fact, I *insist*—that we be left alone. You might inform your employer that I will take whatever measures are necessary to prevent trespassing on my property."

"He is not going to like this. He won't accept this," Gunther said, clenching his fists, unclenching them.

"Then tell him that if he does not like it he can lump it!" This time when she closed the door, she turned the dead-bolt lock.

It was Anton who called. "What are you trying to do?" he spluttered. "Ruin everything for me? Bernard is going to call in the Army if he has to. You can't do this! Are you insane?"

"Are *you*?" Sarah held the phone out from her ear. "I have invited your wife—my *friend*—to visit with me a few days. Obviously, Miss Gompers has control of the children. And obviously, you have other things to do with your spare time. And Bernard Fuller has a nerve! I intend to help his daughter get well. If he doesn't want that to happen, that is his problem to work out, not mine! Now, please, we go to bed early around this house and I don't want any nonsense tonight with this telephone ringing off the wall. When Phyllis wants to return home, she is free to do so. Until then she is here with me. Good night, Anton."

"Don't you hang up! You listen to me. You have no right butting your nose in my life. You are not my mother. You are not a blood relative."

"I am Phyllis's friend, dear." She placed the earphone in its cradle, turned on her heel, and went back to Phyllis. "I have an idea. If I can make arrangements for a place for us to stay tonight, shall we get out of here before they can get their forces together?"

Phyllis was standing, weaving, looking about as if in a daze. "Why not? Let's have a little adventure! But could I take along the gin?"

"You have finished off the gin. Take whatever you wish. If that is what you need to get you to Carmel—please, be my guest."

Sarah led Phyllis upstairs. "Let's see what I've got in my wardrobe that might work for you for a few days. We're both tall. My clothes aren't the latest fashion, but they'll keep you warm." She motioned to Li Po. "Please prepare a hot herbal bath for our guest. Quickly. We will be leaving as soon as it is fully dark."

Li Po looked at her with wide-eyed puzzlement.

"Don't just stand there, Li Po! We don't have a moment to lose. I want Mrs. Brunner to have a bath—and a pot of hot tea. I want you to take out my old suitcase, wherever it is. It's been a long time since I had need of one. It's time I took a few days off. We're going to Carmel —but you are not to tell a soul. You do not have to answer the telephone unless you want to. Do not let *anyone* inside this house. Under any circumstances! Tell anyone who might come here that Mrs. Jaspers and Mrs. Brunner have taken a trip to their favorite spa for a few days."

Phyllis wah holding onto the banister for support. "Where will you get any money? The banks aren't open."

"I don't use banks," Sarah said, giving her a nudge forward. "I have money. Plenty of money. Don't worry about that." And when Phyllis was finally in the hot bath, Sarah went about to her hiding places, taking out the cash she thought would be needed.

21

Sarah returned to Napa Valley one week later. She had stayed until she was convinced Phyllis wanted to remain and get treatment, until she herself was sure it was the right place. She drove into her driveway just at sundown, on the Wednesday before Thanksgiving.

A bewildered Li Po hurried out to the car. "Mr. Brunner, he say if you come home you must come see him. Mr. Fuller—the old man very sick. Bad, bad sick."

"Where is Anton?" she asked, alarmed.

"Right now at his new winery."

"Where is Mr. Fuller?"

"San Francisco. Hospital there."

"Then I'll go see what he wants," she said. Letting Li Po take her suitcase in, she ran quickly in to go to the bathroom, wash her face, comb her hair briefly, then dashed back to her car. She drove straight to the winery Anton was building on the Cugnot property, close to the Inglenook Winery.

Anton had intended to get a telephone installed. He had had to be at the winery to receive an order of labels and supplies for his laboratory that had been delivered C.O.D., by truck. He was getting everything in order so that the moment repeal took effect he would be ready. But now—with the old man in a coma from his stroke—Anton, not knowing where the will was, even what it said, was jittery. For that matter, he wasn't even sure that Phyllis was still in the will, or whether Bernard Fuller had left everything to his grandchildren—possibly even something to him. Anton knew a lot about Fuller's affairs, but he had been kept in the dark as to the contents of any will, or its whereabouts. Though Fuller had pumped thousands of dollars already into this new Brunner Winery, it was not nearly finished. He was going to have to get some cash flow going—*soon*. Damn Sarah anyway! Who did she think she was, whisking Phyllis off in the night? Taking her God knows where?

He wished desperately that Katia were there at the winery with him—as she usually was every chance she could get away from her husband, Roland Rudnisky. But he had asked her to stay away until all this got cleared up. Oddly enough, Katia was the first woman he thought he had ever really loved. Or was it love? He only knew that he could not keep his hands away from her. He needed to know that she was there, that he could reach out and pull that wonderfully soft feminine body against him. To hear her saying those things she could say in that charming, high-pitched voice of hers with its singsong accent— faintly French, faintly German-Swiss, depending on her mood. She made him feel so—yes, *smart*, as though he couldn't do any real wrong. "You are so cultured—such a genius," she would say, winding her arms about his neck, her smile just beneath his, her teeth so even, her tongue so moist, so ready to receive his own. "You are so lonely—it is not right. You deserve so much more. You should not be married to an *alcoholic*. We would go to concerts, so many places, if I were your wife."

But how could he marry her when he needed Phyllis's money? When everything he owned was tied up through her? So he had tried to satisfy his need for Katia; had found the strangest places: behind building materials, with the rough concrete beneath them, or on top of uneven stacks of lumber, or out in the vineyards even, leaves hiding them, the ground burrowing into them—anyplace where he could get rid of anything in his way so that he could enter her and find that other wetness that went with that in her delicious mouth. Those incredible juices which seemed to flow from her . . . Phyllis was so *dry*—so sandpapery. Phyllis smelled like alcohol or those awful strong odors she used trying to hide it—compared to Katia's delicate perfumes.

Eventually, he would find a way. But it was going to take—who knows?—maybe years. If he could just hold out long enough to make the winery pay. There was bound to be a wild clamor for wine the moment repeal hit. He would have his labels ready. He would buy bulk wine. He might even be able to talk David out of the brandy he knew was hidden up there somewhere on Spring Mountain. He would pay him well—and certainly David could use the money. Anton had been appalled at what he had seen on Spring Mountain. That wonderful old stone house in such bad repair. Lilliana such a sloppy housekeeper. Their children so ill-mannered. Maybe his own Frances and Bernard were not as affectionate, but he could take them anywhere and not be embarrassed.

But even if David would agree to sell, he was going to have to have cash on hand. He must have ready cash. He had spent most of his own. He had lost heavily during the crash. He depended on Bernard Fuller—the old man had seen to that!

Sarah walked in without his having heard her. He looked up, startled, seeing where her glasses were loose, had slipped down over her nose, the lopsided navy-blue felt hat pulled down too far on the right side, her coat buttoned wrong, her pumps in need of new heels.

"Li Po said you were looking for me."

He motioned for her to take a single cane-bottomed chair in the room that would, eventually, become his elegant wood-paneled office but now had rough concrete-block walls, a single bare light bulb, a desk made out of an unfinished wooden door placed across two carpenter's sawhorses.

He was glaring at Sarah. "Where's my wife?"

She deliberately took her time, lit a cigarette, blew smoke in a straight chute at him. "She's enrolled for a six-month therapeutic program to cure her alcoholism. Why?" She glanced about at the new supplies stacked in boxes in one corner of the paint-spattered room. "Looks as if you're ready to open shop. Aren't you jumping the gun a bit? What if repeal doesn't happen so soon?"

"I asked you a question! Where is Phyllis? What have you done with her?"

"I just told you. She's fine. Really, she is. Aren't you pleased she might get well? Or *are* you?"

"You have no right, goddammit! You are not even a blood member of this family. Her own children and her father don't know where she is! You realize, don't you, that this brought on her father's stroke? He's critically ill. He may die any moment. She has a right to know. *I* have a right."

"Phyllis is a grown woman. She will let you know—when she is ready. She is at least safe. And what good would it do if she knew? Would she help matters? Besides, her own father was going to have her committed. I know that for a fact. He was going to simply lock her away somewhere. He hated her. Anyone could see that."

"So you know it all, huh? You have the answers."

"I know this—the doctors say they can help her. She deserves a chance. She deserves better than you have given her. Better than her family! I, for one, intend to see that she *gets* a chance. If he's out of it, what good would it do to yank her out of her treatment when she's just got started? It would ruin every opportunity she has. I refuse! *I'll* go sit with Bernard Fuller, if that's what you need."

481

"He has nurses around the clock. He has his valet, George. He doesn't need *you*. Your presence would finish him off."

She flicked ashes on the rough floor spattered with paint. "Anton, why are you so alarmed? You have a look in your eye . . . You're worried that you'll be left out in the cold, aren't you? That's all you're really concerned about. I see it. I know you now. You can't fool me again, ever."

"Goddammit! She is *my* wife. Bernard Fuller is her *father!* Even her own children don't have any idea where their mother is. If you don't tell me, I'll see that an injunction is served against you for—kidnapping. Sure—I'll say that you've kidnapped my wife!"

"Say it, then. If it makes you feel any better, I'll let her know. I'll get this information to her."

Sarah called the physician in charge of Phyllis's care and told him the news. "Leave it up to her," he urged gently. "You have done what you could."

"You have her husband's telephone number? You have all the information you need?"

"Yes, Mrs. Jaspers. We will take responsibility. Mrs. Brunner is fully coherent. She is capable of making up her own mind. You mustn't feel guilty. You have done her a great service. If you wish, you may refer Mr. Brunner to me, should he cause you any undue annoyance."

It was David who told Sarah what additional news she was to learn. "Anton came up the other day asking me to sell Papa's brandy to him. Offering me quite a chunk of money for it." David smiled in his droll way, went to the stove in the big kitchen, poured out his own coffee. "I lied. I told him there wasn't any."

"Good for you. What about Mr. Fuller? Did he mention anything about his condition? Is he going to live?"

"Yes. Anton said he's out of his coma. He's paralyzed on one side. Has gone daffy. Keeps calling him Julian. Thinks Phyllis is off at Radcliffe. Anton is trying to get power of attorney."

Again Sarah notified the spa's head doctor. "I think Phyllis should know. If anyone gets power of attorney, it is my opinion Phyllis should have it."

"I quite agree with you, Mrs. Jaspers. We will discuss it immediately. I shall tell her you called."

"Please give her my love too, would you? Tell her that she is always welcome to stay with me. No strings attached."

Sarah was not to see Phyllis again for several years. Periodically, notes and letters were exchanged between them, which gave smatterings of information. At Christmas, she received a simple greeting card, with a handwritten note beneath the printed "Season's Greetings," which read:

DEAR SARAH,

The doctors and nurses are lovely to me here. If by next June all continues to go well, I plan to return permanently to Boston. Miss Gompers has already taken the children back, as perhaps you know. If Father is still with us, I shall be taking him back with me when I return.

Meanwhile, thank you for all you've done for me. My lawyers will be sending a check to reimburse you very soon. I shall remember your kindness always.

Love,
PHYLLIS FULLER BRUNNER

Sarah, in turn, sent a box with candy, perfume, and note paper, and asked Phyllis to please keep in touch.

On March 4, 1933, four months after Phyllis went to Carmel and on the very day that Franklin D. Roosevelt took his oath as President of the United States, Lilliana gave birth to a nine-pound baby girl. Sarah had gone there to be with the children, Anne and Dede. When the doctor came downstairs and said she could go up, she found David holding the infant, his eyes moist.

He took up at Sarah, smiled. "I'm so used to girls now, what would I do with a son anyway? And look at this one! All this crop of red hair. Where did she get that?"

Sarah looked down at the tiny, squirming baby with its fists doubled in flailing knots. "My grandmother Hubbard—she supposedly had carrot-red hair. Grandmother Victoria, from Mississippi. I never saw her. My mother told me about her, though. She even tried to enlist and fight the Yankees."

"This one came out squalling—acting as if she had already fought and won her first big battle," David said, stroking one finger across the top of the tiny head, showing more tenderness than Sarah had ever seen from him. "Victoria, huh? Why not name this one that? Victoria Donati. How does that sound?"

"What does Lilliana say?"

"She promised me I could name this one, boy or girl. Okay, Victoria—back to your bassinet." He put the baby down, looked over at the sleeping Lilliana, tiptoed out of the room with Sarah. "This one's different. Have you ever seen a little baby like that one?" He took Sarah's arm to be sure she had a tight grip on the stair railing before they went down to join little Anne and Dede. "We hadn't intended to have any more children. But now that we have, I'm glad—really glad we've got an oddball redhead. I don't know why, but I feel this one is—well, different. Something a little special."

"Oh, David, don't spoil her! Parents so often spoil the baby of the family."

On the last day of June, 1933, Phyllis left in a private deluxe railroad car on the fastest train from San Francisco to Boston, with an entourage which included her father—carried aboard on a stretcher—three nurses, Bernard Fuller's valet, George, and Phyllis's own favorite psychiatrist, a Dr. Damon Stitt. Anton took the next train out, buying a regular coach fare.

He was desperate. It was obvious from the vote on June 27, when repeal had carried statewide by a four-to-one margin and in Napa County by ten-to-one, that nationwide repeal was just around the corner. It was his guess that no later than the end of the year winery doors would be allowed to open again. But he needed more backing. He had come so close, but he was still far from that point of actual production. With more cash reserves, he could buy up bulk wine that was now stored, label it, put in action the public-relations campaign that Katia Rudnisky had ready to go. Then, by the harvest of 1934, he would be ready for his own first crush—the Anton Brunner first vintage!

If only he had been able to get the power of attorney. Again, he had come so close to that! Somehow, Phyllis had got there ahead of him. How had she found out? Had Sarah somehow tipped her off? Why had he not listened in the first place to Bernard Fuller, who had seen Sarah for what she was—a damn fool? A meddlesome dotty old fool.

Sarah had not had much time to worry about Phyllis, or about Anton's absence—though she had heard through David and Kyle Plimpton (Anton had come to Kyle asking him if he knew anyone whom he might hire as a capable manager while he was gone a few weeks, possibly months) that Anton had left town in a hurry.

David had told her, "Anton wanted me to say I'd contract my grapes exclusively with him for the 1934 harvest—as if I might not have my own plans for a crush by then!"

484

Kyle Plimpton had laughed, looked at Sarah. "My wife's cousin Cora has been doing some washing and ironing for Anton. Emma said that *she* said she heard him talking on the telephone—saying how his stepmother had about done him in. Ruined him financially."

Sarah dismissed what Kyle said. She had her own plans about the upcoming repeal. Besides, she wasn't getting any younger. She wanted to be sure she had her affairs in good legal order. She figured it was time to get Chip Brosius to draw up a business offer she wanted to make to David, whereby she would be a silent partner in the Spring Mountain Donati Winery. He could have the full say-so of it; she would put up the money he didn't have, to open the doors. If her estimation was right, they'd be operating on a limited capacity at first. But David, like his father, was a stickler for quality. He wouldn't be needing the big sums Anton had been spending getting ready for nationwide distribution, the way he was telling everybody he planned to do. *Big numbers*—that was Anton, in all aspects of life, she thought.

She met with Chip Brosius in late August. "You're smart, Sarah," he told her. "Get in there right away. I predict the wine market is going to boom—just like the grape industry did when Prohibition first hit. Then, after the newness wears off, it'll probably bottom out too. Have an over surplus. That seems to be the trend. But you could clean up, if you're there ready and waiting."

Sarah was ready for action then, when, following the November nationwide election, five additional states swung their votes toward repeal, making enough states required to remove the Eighteenth Amendment from the Constitution of the United States.

The official ending of Prohibition took place on December 5, 1933. In Napa Valley, the celebrations began early and lasted until dawn the next day. Exuberant men were reported standing out in the middle of the streets pouring bathtub gin over one another's head. Fireworks were exploding sporadically across the skies. At Inglenook, Carl Bundschu threw an open house, provided music to accompany the many toasts made to the way things were before Prohibition, and to the rehabilitation of fine Napa Valley wines. Many wineries that had been closed down in 1920, those with any funds left and the accompanying fighting spirit to try it again, were making feverish efforts to reopen.

About five o'clock, a staggering Joseph climbed out of the back seat of the car, stumbled up to Sarah's front door. "I was jus' on my way to Calistoga to the American Legion dance at the Silverado Bowl. Gotta cel'brate old John Barleycorn gettin' outa jail, huh?" He tried to throw his arms around her. "I was passin' by. Told the fellas 'Turn in!

I gotta see the nicest lady in the whole wide world. Only woman ever treated me right. Only one came to see me when I was a jailbird.' "

His pale ice-blue eyes were watery, bloodshot. She guided him to the edge of the brick terrace, where he propped himself up, holding on to the pillar nearby.

"I jus' wantcha to know I own *ten* little bitty houses, one grocery store in Vallejo and a leaky fishin' boat!" He tried to count on his fingers. "One of these days I'm gonna save enough to buy a big house like this. Maybe buy back what my lowdown stinkin' brother cheated me out of! Show that sonofabitch, huh? Show everybody in Napa Valley one of these days." The horn was blowing. "My buddies waitin'. Gotta go dance. Celebrate! *Yippee* doodle dandy."

A tousleheaded, red-faced man leaned out the window of the battered 1925 Buick sedan, waved a bottle in the air. "Come *on*, Donati, if you're coming with us!"

Sarah called out to the weaving Joseph starting out across the lawn toward the car. "Be *careful*. Repeal is here now. You don't have to drink it all in one night!"

He laughed, staggered to keep his balance. "Better have a drink yourself. Everybody oughtta be cel'bratin'."

His unexpected visit had unsettled her so—all these years now he had avoided seeing her, and she hated this sight of him—that Sarah stayed out on the brick terrace a long moment; though a goose-pimpling cold wind was shooting across the valley floor, having blown in from an ocean cold front. She hugged her arms close about her, leaned back against one of the Corinthian pillars, and gazed out across the dormant vineyards toward the ridge of the Mayacamas Mountains, where the last muted orange of the sunset had just dropped from sight. A clump of trees caught her eye, a shape apart from those—there far in the distance, as though riding the ridge itself. She took a sharp intake of cold air. How much the shape had reminded her of exactly the way Adam used to look breaking across an open stretch riding his stallion, Hajib! And what a fine saddle he used to sit—how regal. How very proudly he rode that stallion!

Surprisingly, her eyes filled with hot tears. How she missed him at times. It seemed the older she got, the more she went back to those earlier days—and always with Adam; though at times she felt guilty when she knew it was Norman Jaspers who had made her life so comfortable. She barely ever thought about Norman. Right now—oh, how she'd like to drink a toast to repeal with Adam!

Li Po was standing at the door. "Maybe you come inside. Too

cold out now. You catch bad cold. I got chicken ready. Dinner served."

Sarah went quickly across the brick terrace, entered the dim, quiet foyer, walked across the cold black-and-white marble-tiled floor. "Li Po, don't you think we should drink a little toast? Welcome in this new beginning for Napa Valley? Would you join me? A glass of that last bottle of sherry we opened, perhaps?"

He was back in a moment, a smile spread across his wizened face. He poured the sherry, served the glass to her, waited politely for her to make the toast.

"Here's to—to *us*, Li Po! To seeing how long we can last through this new beginning. *Salute!*"

Li Po sipped, then looked up, his black eyes twinkling. "Maybe this not a toast, but I know poem I say for you." He bobbed his head up and down, more as though asking her permission.

"Do—please do, Li Po," she said, smiling, as with an old friend.

He looked embarrassed. "The poem—it maybe about us. Getting old. My uncle used to say it to me when it got cold every year." He ducked his head, then looked more at the light above the kitchen table. " 'At beginning of winter a cold spirit comes. The North Wind blows —chill, chill. My sorrows being many, I know length of nights. Raising my head, I look at stars in their places.' " When he looked at Sarah, he seemed to feel awkward, a little confused by his own actions. He hurried to the stove. "Your dinner—is getting cold. Better eat."

Anton's prediction had been right. The clamor for wine hit immediately.

His own trip east had not brought the results for which he had hoped. But he did get some assistance. When Phyllis had finally agreed to see him, it had been in the presence of two lawyers and three business advisers. Two of the men he had known previously—Theodore Millner and R. Jerome Shelton, both highly skilled lawyers.

Theodore Millner had taken charge, speaking in that crisp, precisely-to-the-point way Anton remembered, his eyes like steel ribbons. "Since Mr. Fuller's arrangement with you on this initial investment was a sixty—forty one, with yours the controlling interest; and since your winery had been built on Mrs. Brunner's own property, formerly known as the Cugnot property; and in order that the investment earn a reasonable return, my client has come to the conclusion that it is vital to invest further. Simply to insure the initial investment." He looked around, twitched his moustache. "Therefore, we will advance the requested forty thousand dollars, to be used for distribution and production. We shall expect to conduct our own audit annually, at our own expense. Your agreement with Mr. Fuller ends in November of 1938. At that time, proper negotiations will have to be made."

When they left the wood-paneled offices there on Beacon Hill, Anton had tried to get Phyllis alone. She looked haggard, older than before, and had lost considerable weight.

She had pulled her fur coat high around her neck, extended a gloved hand. "Sorry we can't visit. I have a dental appointment. Then I'm expected at home to interview a new night nurse for Father."

"How is he?"

"The same. He will never be any better, the doctors warn me. It is something all of us must accept—which I'm sure is bad news to you." She lifted one eyebrow, smiled coldly.

"Aren't you coming back—ever?"

"To Napa Valley? Oh, I'm sure we will have business to tend to sooner or later. We are trying to decide what to do with the house— whether we should keep it as a summer home or whether we should sell. When we decide, I'll be out."

"But as my *wife*?" He tried to take her hand.

"*No*, Anton. I will never be back as your wife, in the way I think you mean. However, I am against divorce. I have filed for a legal separation, which gives you ample freedom to conduct your life as you please. With whomever you please. Mr. Millner will get those papers to you for your signature before you leave. Or, if you prefer, we could send them to any lawyer you wish to designate."

She had walked out and climbed into the limousine before he could think of an adequate response. That very night, December 24, 1933, Anton got on the train and headed back to Napa. It was a hell of a Christmas Eve, he thought, climbing into the lower berth in a regular Pullman. He had not even been allowed to see his own children. Even his gifts to them had been taken at the door by an unsmiling Miss Gompers.

At harvest of 1934, David Donati held his first crush, working on a capacity of forty thousand gallons—ten thousand gallons being Riesling and Chablis, the rest Cabernet Sauvignon blended with Merlot. Because he had plenty of grapes left to sell, he finally agreed to sell to Anton, contracting Sarah's grapes to him as well, for the 160,000-gallon capacity Anton had planned.

"I figure we'll get our quality established," David had told Sarah. "If we're providing good wines, we'll have customers."

"I don't like what the paper says," she had answered, putting her glasses down on her nose in better reading position, and reading in part from the latest editorial by Mackinder of the *St. Helena Star*:

"The viticultural industry is facing a period of rehabilitation. Just how long this period will be, no one can foretell, but several years will elapse before the industry can be considered stable and back to the enjoyment of pre-Prohibition days. In our opinion, there rises upon the horizon a dark cloud in the probability that for several years, in their efforts to cash in quickly on the new deal, some very poor wine will be placed on the market, in striking contrast to the extraordinary fine wines marketed by California wine makers before Prohibition."

David didn't answer. He was busy reading the newly drawn-up legal papers Chip Brosius had suggested they sign to make their new partnership a binding business arrangement. "Have I got this right?" he asked, frowning, removing the reading glasses he had found necessary lately. "If anything happens to me first, or to you—either way the children become legal heirs to the winery?"

"Isn't that all right?" She studied him thoughtfully. "By the look on your face one would think you don't think that would be much of an inheritance."

He sat down across the kitchen table from her, shook his head. "It's just that I don't want any one of my children bound down by some obligation that started with somebody else's dream. I want them to have their own dreams. Their own goals."

"Well, goodness me! What if one of them just might be interested in Spring Mountain? Wouldn't you want to at least try to keep your father's dream alive? Is that so terrible?"

He got up, put on his hat, his field jacket. "Let's face it—it's not likely that any woman would want to be a winemaker, is it? I want it reworded that if one wants to keep it, she can buy out the others. If they all want to sell, they can. It doesn't have to stay in the Donati family. Okay?"

She sighed, picked up the papers. "Okay. I'll have Chip Brosius redo the papers. Make an addendum. Another *whereas*."

As Chip Brosius had predicted—along with others—it was no problem selling wine those first clamorous years after repeal, but it did not take long for marketing problems to emerge. A new type of distributor, the converted bootlegger, had taken over the wholesale market. David had been able to sell at top prices all the brandy and red bulk wine he had saved from Adam's cache. But most of the wines on the market were raw, suffering from various excesses of sulfur-containing compounds, from oxidation, from poor cooperage. In those brief years, nearly eight hundred new wineries came into being in California alone, most of them operated by men with little knowledge of the art of winemaking.

With most of the wine being unpalatable, the prices soon fell. As predicted, it did not take long for the crisis to hit Napa Valley as well as other wineries across the state.

It had been Chip Brosius who alerted both Sarah and David to the new rulings of the Twenty-first Amendment, whereby much of the control reverted to the states in determining the percentage of alcohol and putting special tax stamps on the bottles—enabling some states to place excessive importation taxes on any wine or alcoholic beverages coming in from other states.

"It seems to me we'll have to limit our distribution," Sarah said to David. "Why don't we rely on a mailing list? Establish dependable customers who like the Donati wine. You'll save transportation costs and out-of-state taxes."

"Right now, I'm more interested in establishing good winemaking techniques instead of *how* we sell," David said, clamping his teeth down on his pipe stem. "I'm working now with Dr. Cruess from Davis on an experiment on a new method of making sherry. He found out about my established Palomino vines. It won't cost much money. It's a new baking method. I can use the old greenhouse. I've got plenty of room to store it, certainly. Some will go in fifty-gallon barrels, the rest this new 'flor' yeast method, for comparison. It's a film-floating yeast —an open-air thing that gives the wine under the film a low oxidation reduction. A wood-aged, yeast-autolysate complexity." He stood up, stretched. "If we don't get any *money* out of it, maybe we'll get some nice sherry."

"You winemakers," Sarah said, going to the door with him. "There has to be a profit in this business somewhere! Some good reason for all this worry."

"Oh, there's a good reason enough," David laughed. "There's always *next* vintage, if this one goes wrong."

By 1938, the surplus was so acute that the federal government and the Bank of America put together a prorate program whereby surplus wine would be bought up and distilled into brandy in an effort to save many wineries from immediate total collapse.

The Anton Brunner Winery was one of those facing financial disaster. Anton had tried everything he could. But it had been one defeat after the next. Maybe he had been too confident, too full of theory and not enough actual experience, he admitted to himself. His 1935 vintage, of which he had been so sure, ended up with excessive oxidation in both reds and whites—for different reasons, all caused by bumbling idiots he had hired. Too, he had bought some inferior corks, which hadn't helped matters. The point was, there simply wasn't a qualified man around who hadn't been snapped up by other wineries. Katia had done a superb job of publicity. She was a genius at promotion. But those who had snapped up Anton Brunner wine had heard too many disgruntled customers and weren't reordering. He had taken extra precautions with his 1936 Cabernets, but they took time for maturing. They wouldn't be ready until 1940—maybe even '41. He could be broke by then!

In desperation, he had sent an urgent request to the Bernard Fuller Corporation, asking for funds, even though he had been advised they had lost faith in the investment.

When the letter from Theodore Millner arrived, stating simply that they would look into the matter and advise him of their decision, Anton went, as a last resort, to Sarah.

He had heard from Chip Brosius, who had become an active stockbroker, that one or two of the securities Norman had left Sarah, which everyone thought were essentially worthless after the crash, were now paying handsomely. Too, in a careless moment Chip had let it out that he himself had taken Sarah to the bank during the crash and seen to it that she got out most of her savings. Anton had been under the impression before that Sarah had lost most of her money. So, though he had carefully avoided her these recent years since Phyllis left him, he decided he could at least make the attempt. She was his only chance.

He drove down her driveway on a Sunday afternoon, the second week of August, 1938. A bent-over, scruffy-looking Li Po opened the door for him, bowed stiffly, as though he had some pain in his joints, then went to get Sarah.

She had been out gathering cucumbers from her small vegetable garden. Her apron was filled with them. She had been watering, had got mud on the tennis shoes she wore in her garden and had smeared a streak of it across the side of her face when trying to adjust her glasses to keep them from falling off. A blue bandanna was tied around her head. She stood in the kitchen door, peering through the foyer.

"Anton—good Lord, why didn't you let me know you were

coming over? You'll have to come back here. I can't track mud all over the house."

He came in, waited until she had dumped the cucumbers into a pan, had kicked off the tennis shoes and stood in her stocking feet.

"What brings *you* here?" she asked skeptically, but in spite of herself she was glad to see him. "Sit down—I'll fix tea."

When she sat down across from him, she looked over the edge of her teacup at him. "You've got that look, Anton. I've known you too long. What is it? You didn't come here for tea."

"No, I didn't." He drummed his slender fingers against the red-checked tablecloth. "I came because I need ten thousand dollars to survive. I came to offer you shares in my winery. Become a limited partner." He leaned forward intensely. "All I need to do is get through this crush coming up, put some of my better wines on the market next year. By then, my contract with the Fullers will be up and I can get rolling in a big way. *My* way. I just need the money to get me over this big crisis."

"Ten thousand dollars is a lot of money, Anton."

"I know you have the money. It isn't that you'd be giving it away! Look, I could secure it. The shares—why, the property alone is worth a lot more than ten thousand. You couldn't lose." His voice dropped. "You would be helping me in a very deeply significant way, Mom Sarah. Believe me!"

She took her time sipping tea. "Tell me, how're the children? How's Phyllis? Her father?"

He bit his lip. He had not come here to talk about Phyllis—or anyone in the Fuller retinue. He saw Sarah's look. "Bernard died—last winter. The children . . ." He looked at his tea. "What do I say? They send perfunctory notes. A birthday present. A box at Christmas. All those proper little dutiful things. I thought *you* would know how Phyllis is. I'm surprised you asked."

"I did have a letter a little while back. She mailed it from Marblehead. Apparently she likes being by the sea. She said she was going into the hospital for some remedial surgery, whatever that meant. I couldn't say that I know much from that letter, however. She didn't say if she was happy. If she was coming back to Napa Valley. She did say that she had definitely stopped drinking."

Anton suddenly leaned forward. "What do *you* say, Mom Sarah? You used to believe in me. We used to be very good friends. Would you be willing to go into business with me, on a limited partnership?"

"I'm already *in* the wine business more than I ever intended to be. I own part of the Donati Winery. So far, I haven't earned a plug nickel

492

from that investment. David's wines win blue ribbons at the State Fair, but he still struggles."

"Hasn't David always struggled?"

"Honorably. Yes, *very* honorably! He has a lovely wife and family. David has no apologies to make to anyone."

"Don't get angry. I didn't come here to make you angry."

"You came to get ten thousand dollars."

"I came to make a business proposition to you."

Again they were silent.

"I should have my head examined!" she said then. "Here this world is on the brink of another major war. We've got a man calling himself Hitler over there stripping the Jews of every right, putting them in camps because they are *Jews*. We have the Japanese getting frisky. They've bombed that U.S. gunboat—"

"I'm sorry, I don't keep up with the news, I guess."

"You never did! They sank the *Panay* and three Standard Oil tankers last December, on the Yangtze River in China. I don't like what I'm reading in the papers. I don't think it bodes well for any business investment. Not if we find ourselves in another war. And most certainly it will mean a bad investment for anything pertaining to the wine industry."

"Then you won't help me out? Is that what you're saying?" He pushed back from the table, looked down at her quietly.

"I didn't say I *wouldn't*—but I won't just fork out the money like that. You'll have to have legal papers drawn up. I had Chip Brosius make them out for David and me. A business deal is a business deal."

For a moment he stood there, his eyes lighting up. "Would you like to have Chip Brosius draw those papers up, since you seem to trust *him*? I want you to be sure of the offer. For once, I want you to know I'm *not* trying to take advantage of anyone. I'm simply trying to stay afloat. To save what little I have left."

She came to the front door with him, being careful not to slip on the marble tiles in her stocking feet. She realized she was still wearing the bandana; reached up and pulled it off her head, smoothed down her now all-white hair. "I'd like that very much. Chip does fine work. He's a capable man."

"Then he'll have the papers ready tomorrow. I'll see to it."

She walked out on the brick terrace, waved halfheartedly as she climbed into his Packard that now had a huge dent in one door and made a clattery sound when he drove off. She stood there, leaning back against one of the Corinthian columns, staring out, long after he had left. It had been a sweltering-hot August day. There was a cooling breeze just now beginning to roll across the valley in soft ripples, like whispers rustling the leaves in the vineyards. A long sigh escaped her. At sixty-four years of age, she ought to have learned a little sense. But here she was, letting sentiment rule out her better judgment.

Ten thousand dollars *was* a lot of money. True, she had made some unexpected windfalls lately, money that had come to life out of papers she had almost thrown out following the crash. How strange that seemed, even now—that a slip of paper or two could become tangible money. She guessed she was too used to grapes—to that very tangible product that must have the right acid-and-sugar balance, that must be picked, pruned, crushed, racked, fermented, topped, stored, bottled, corked just so, and must have God knows what other intangibles to make it finally bring about a profit, *money*. *Dollars*, that Anton Brunner seemed so hungry to grasp in his hand and run with.

She felt torn apart with doubt now. But hadn't she, in a way, been responsible for Phyllis's having pulled out on him? And didn't she owe a certain loyalty to Adam's son? He was a Donati, even though he went by the name of Brunner. Adam had wanted so badly a strong family bond—a unit that would stand together, fight for each other, right or wrong. Didn't she owe it to Adam—if not to Anton? And hadn't she helped David even more than David actually wanted to be helped? Wasn't he complaining that she gave too much—indicating in his way that she usurped his own confidence in himself? And didn't she have ten thousand dollars to risk? And hadn't Anton said that she couldn't lose? That she could have the property as collateral?

She went to the telephone and called Chip Brosius.

"Listen, Chip—Anton Brunner is probably on his way to see you right now, if I know Anton. When you draw up this deal he's going to present to you, I want it clearly stated that my ten thousand dollars which I've told him I will agree to invest will have ample collateral. I want something positive to back it up. I don't understand what he's talking about—this limited-partnership business. But I want you to go over it in your mind before he gets there. Figure out what is best for me. I told him I wanted you to draw up the papers, just for that reason. To protect my interest all the way. I know Anton's my stepson, but I also know he's tricky. Understand?"

Chip Brosius's voice, which sounded like a robust Irish tenor's, crackled across the wire. "Sarah, I'm glad to know you aren't letting any grass grow under your feet. That you're thinking as clearly as ever."

"I don't know about that! I think I must have pomace for brains to get myself involved with this."

22

Anton had expected to hear from the Bernard Fuller Corporation. But he had not expected to look up from his desk that Thursday afternoon, the third week of September, to see Phyllis and her entourage of lawyers standing there.

At first he was not at all sure it was Phyllis, she looked so different. As he got up from his desk—where he and Katia had just been going over a new promotional idea of bringing in cultural events to the winery—the thought flashed across his mind that Sarah had said Phyllis had mentioned in a letter something about going to a hospital for remedial surgery. Obviously, she had been to a top plastic surgeon, he thought, standing near where Katia was seated in a corner chair, trying to keep his own look composed as he took in the sight of a Phyllis whose "droopy" look had totally vanished; who no longer had bags under her eyes; whose teeth had been capped and were sparkling white and even now; whose hair was styled in a very flattering shoulder-length casual manner, dyed a natural-looking brownish-blond. On top of that, she was wearing the most elegant oyster-white linen suit and matching silk blouse he had ever seen. For the first time, she was wearing diamond rings—she had always spurned wearing the family jewels before—with one diamond surely being a twenty-carat stone, he thought, trying not to stare. She was, undeniably, stunning—younger-looking now, at forty, than she had looked ten years ago.

In contrast, Katia was having a bad day. She had spent the past three days at home with an annoying bladder infection, a low backache, a headache, slight fever. As a consequence, she had missed her regular hair appointment, so that her dyed blond hair was oily and showed a dark strip down the part. Because it was such a hot autumn day, she had worn a cool peasant-type dress. Her feet were bare, in Mexican-style sandals; polish on her toenails was worn off in places. She had not refurbished her lipstick since a hurried sandwich at lunch.

She simply wasn't prepared for the presence of this elegant woman— announcing herself as Mrs. Phyllis Fuller Brunner but appearing in marked contrast to the ugly woman Anton had painted to her as his former wife!

Anton, trying to get his bearings, motioned Phyllis toward a leather chair over in one corner of the large office; but deliberately she came around and sat opposite his desk chair, where he would have to face her. He did not like the way her lawyers were taking over his desk with their briefcases. He had never liked Theodore Millner or R. Jerome Shelton anyway, when he had been their boss.

Phyllis was sitting quite straight in her chair, looking at him in a strangely commanding way, he thought, her voice carrying a new brittle hardness. "We had hoped to let you know we would be here. It took us a little longer in Sacramento with all that government red tape than we had thought it would. And this morning we had to contract painters, plumbers, carpenters and the like to begin restoration on my father's house, since we've decided to use it as a vacation home." She let that remark settle in, then turned to Theodore Millner. "Teddie, do you have Anton's copies—all the papers ready so we can get this meeting started?"

"Wait a *minute*! What kind of meeting are you talking about?" Anton said, his face like a fist. "It so happens I'm in the middle of harvesting grapes. This is a busy time. You can't just plunk yourselves down in my office and—"

"Frankly, Anton, it is our full legal prerogative," Phyllis said, draping her long legs to their best advantage, aiming the pointed toe of one pump straight at him, he thought, just as he saw Katia self-consciously drawing her sandals under her chair, as though trying to hide her splotchy toenails and her bare legs that could use a quick shaving.

But before Anton could decide his next move, some primitive need to fight for her territory brought Katia up out of her chair over in the far corner of the room. She was suddenly busily going about, smiling that wide smile of hers, hovering, bending first over R. Jerome Shelton (who looked the least formidable), drawing on her French accent, her voice lilting. "Would you like some *wine*? A nice light Chablis? Perhaps something a little sweeter?" Her eyelids made a fluttering motion as she squinted, flashing the smile Phyllis's way. "You must be very warm in that linen suit. Here in Napa Valley we're much more relaxed. This is quite an informal place, really. Everyone dresses for the heat, you see." She gave her own attempted appraising look at Phyllis, as though forgiving her for having overdressed and committed her faux pas for the day. "Perhaps, if these nice gentlemen have some business they want to discuss with Mr. Brunner, I could take you on a little tour of the winery? It's a lovely time to visit—during the harvest, with the crush taking place. It is our busiest time, but I would be happy to personally guide you. However, before we go—" she let out a shrill girlish-sounding giggle—"in Napa Valley, always we have a little wine first."

Phyllis had not moved a muscle on her newly tight face. Her eyes, gray as the fog, slowly went from Katia's hair in need of a touch-up, down her shiny nose, down the loose folds of the peasant dress, and seemed to settle on one large toe where not only the nailpolish had peeled unevenly but the nail badly needed trimming. "I don't drink any alcoholic beverage whatsoever," she said in her most measured tone. "A cardinal rule for all reformed alcoholics is that one mustn't take that simple first glass of wine, even here in the Napa Valley." Her tone indicated she was speaking to someone not very bright. She turned to Anton just as Katia's trembling hands almost knocked over the row of wineglasses. "Now, as *president* of the Brunner-Fuller Winery Corporation, I would like to call this first meeting to order. Does your secretary have a few little letters she could write—perhaps in another office?"

If she saw the parchment look on Anton's face or the explosion of red covering Katia's cheeks and spreading out in splotches across her neck, she did not openly acknowledge it. "Temporarily, as filed in Sacramento, Mr. Shelton will be acting secretary and keep notes today. Mr. Millner is accountant and acting treasurer. You are the duly elected vice-president, Anton." She looked at the bewildered Katia, tolerantly waiting for her to leave. "Please, close the door behind you." She did not acknowledge the fierce slamming of it as Katia burst out of the room. "Teddie, do you have the reports ready? Will you see that Mr. Brunner gets a copy of the bylaws and the articles? And you should explain to him the distribution of the shares."

"Just a goddam minute!" Anton said, the words coming through clenched teeth. "What the hell are you talking about? Brunner-*Fuller* Winery? This is the Anton Brunner Winery!"

"It *used* to be—before the founding of the new corporation."

"Hold it! You can't *do* that! You can't just turn this winery—*my* winery—into a corporation. *I* have controlling interest, remember?" He reached for the telephone. "I'm calling my lawyer. Maybe I'll call the sheriff while I'm at it and have you thrown out of here!"

Theodore Millner was standing now, calmly leafing through

papers. "I don't object at all if you call your lawyer. Perhaps you would feel better about it. As you know, I am an attorney. These papers are legal. Quite legal. By both Massachusetts and California law." He turned to Phyllis. "You did inform Mr. Brunner that you bought out the controlling shares from Mrs. Jaspers?"

Anton got up slowly from the desk, his hands gripping the edge. He spoke slowly, his tone like something cut with a sharp razor. "Let me get this straight. *You* bought shares from *Sarah*? The shares I put in her name only a few weeks ago?"

"I didn't know precisely when you sold them to her. I dropped by for a visit and she told me she had a new interest in the winery. I offered her twice what she paid—explaining, of course, that I couldn't possibly allow anyone to have collateral which supposedly involves land my father owns. *Leased* land is hardly collateral, Anton. I was surprised that you would try to pull that one on your own step-mother." Her fingernails drummed against the sides of the leather chair. "When Sarah realized that in essence she had nothing but those shares as collateral—and, as she explained it to me, her son David needed money for the Donati Winery—well, it was not difficult to buy them from her. Do you blame her?"

"Blame! I could *kill* her! And you too. What do you want from me? What are you really trying to do, Phyllis?" He was pointing his finger at her accusingly.

"Please, Anton—it isn't polite to point. You know it really, truly isn't."

"I am going to find my lawyer!" He headed toward the door, where Theodore Millner stopped him.

"I suggest that you take these along—your copies. Better have him go over them and carefully explain what they mean. By the way, we would like very much to have you continue on here at the winery—either as winemaker or as production manager. We understand you have quite a marketing talent. Would you consider that?"

Anton snatched the papers, crumpled them in a tight-fisted wad. "I wouldn't consider doing anything with that—that cold-blooded bitch!"

When the door slammed, Theodore Millner turned around to find, surprisingly, Phyllis with enormous tears swimming around in her large gray eyes. He fumbled with the papers in his briefcase. The tears were sliding silently down her face; but she sat there stonily. He went over, handed his handkerchief to her. "It was, wasn't it, what you wanted? What you've been planning all these months—what we came here for?"

She dabbed at her eyes gingerly, as though afraid the scars under them might still be tender. "Yes . . . . Yes, it was exactly what I had planned." She was pulling at the handkerchief, working it back and forth in her hands, as if trying to find some strength in it. She sat up quite primly, looked now at R. Jerome Shelton. "I think I'll have that glass of wine now, if you don't mind handing it to me, please."

During the following months, a frantic Anton scurried about, trying in vain to find some legal loophole that would reverse Phyllis's takeover of his winery. He had been so confident that the shares he had turned over to Sarah were on a limited-partner basis, so that she would have to give him forty-five days' notice to allow him to buy them back. Instead, he had been the one tricked. They had been general shares. She had sold them to Phyllis legally.

"Sorry, Anton, there's nothing I can do," Chip Brosius told him. "I understand that they want to pay you a considerable salary to stay on as manager. That they're giving you your pick of being the winemaker or being in charge of production. That sounds like a good deal to me. Mrs. Brunner—"

"Don't call her Mrs. Brunner—she is Phyllis *Fuller!*"

"She said she was prepared to invest whatever sums were needed to improve the quality of the wine. Seems she's been having somebody check around and found out there are some big complaints from consumers about the wine you dumped on the market that first year or so after repeal. I heard she was even over trying to hire André Tchelitscheff and had been down south to talk with Martin Ray and the Wentes. Tried to get Jack Reorita, Louis Martini—of course, got turned down. But she's looking for the top winemaker." Chip looked hard at Anton, whom he had never liked. "I guess everywhere she turned, she got one recommendation."

"What was that—to get lost?"

"No—to hire David Donati. That he was one of the top winemakers in California today."

"Then let her! I'm not working for her. In *any* capacity. I'm tired of the whole business, anyway. Nobody can make a go of it in this market. Everybody out there wants whiskey—they'd rather have bathtub gin than a bottle of wine."

"With the kind of wine they're offered, no wonder."

After his visit with Chip Brosius, Anton drove straight to Sarah's house; was met at the door by a nervous Li Po. "Mrs. Jaspers—she's not home."

499

"She's hiding. She's afraid to show her face after what she's done to me!" Anton poked his head over Li Po's shoulder, yelled into the empty foyer, his shouting voice echoing, bouncing off the high ceiling, the marble-tiled floor. "What's wrong—are you scared to show your face, traitor?"

Li Po backed several feet away, dug his hands from habit into the sleeves of his jacket. "She's gone to hospital with Mr. Donati."

Anton stepped back, looked confused. "What hospital? Who's sick?" He never could tell what Li Po was thinking. He didn't know if he was telling the truth or lying to protect Sarah.

"Mrs. Donati—being operated on. Very bad sick. Big tumor. Here." He crossed his hands over his breasts, ducked his head, embarrassed. "Cut everything off."

Anton closed his eyes, shook his head, clenched, unclenched his fists, as though trying to shake off all his ill fortune, including this news. He had never particularly liked Lilliana, but he didn't dislike her, either. She didn't deserve that. But wasn't it David's luck? Loser David. He gave one last frustrated look at Li Po, who was still standing looking at him with that same impenetrable stare; then he hurried back out to his car. His tires spun, skidded as he roared off down the driveway.

It had been Sarah who first noticed Lilliana's color and asked her, at a vulnerable moment, what was wrong. She had been up to take the children some new clothes for the winter. David had finally allowed her to buy their winter coats each year, and now that Victoria was six years old, entering the first grade, she needed everything new. When Sarah had come in, her arms piled high with packages, it was one of those moments when the older girls, Anne and Dede, had had some argument and Lilliana was trying to get them quiet; when Victoria had caught her finger in the car door and was still crying from the pain of the swelling, soaking her hand in ice water at the kitchen sink.

"Looks as if I've come at a bad time," Sarah had said, looking about in her own state of confusion over the stack of dirty dishes, the baskets of laundry not ironed, the kitchen floor in dire need of mopping. Lilliana had looked at Sarah in her new coat, her hair freshly shampooed—her arms loaded with presents that would make her daughters happy whereas today everything she had done had been wrong—and burst into tears.

When Sarah had sent her grandchildren out, all of them startled, ashamed that they had made their mother cry—this being one of the few times any of them had ever seen her shed a tear—Sarah had looked at that peculiar chalky color and, frightened, had thought about Delfina, the way she had looked before she died. "What is it, Lilliana? Something is wrong with you. I see it. I can tell. When have you been to the doctor last for a complete checkup?"

Lilliana had buried her face in the palm of one hand. "I'm just tired. There's always so much to do. The girls—they help, but I guess I'm just not a good organizer. It never all gets done at once."

"Forget the house—that's not what I meant. It's *you*. You aren't well, are you?"

Lilliana had looked up then, her eyes wide, covered with a glaze of lurking fear. "This—here, I've had this pain lately. A big lump." She motioned to her left breast. "I kept thinking it would go away. That it was like some of the sore spots I used to get when I was nursing the babies. I—I guess I dread so going to a doctor. I hate those physical examinations. Having them—well, you know how it is."

"I'm calling my doctor immediately!"

"No—*please* don't do that. David would want to be the one to make the appointment. You know how independent he is."

"Then you must have him make one immediately. I'm not trying to meddle, but this could mean—I hate to say this, Lilliana—it really could mean your life."

"I promise. I'll tell him tonight. I'll go see a doctor."

That had been on Saturday. On Monday, the first week of November, surgery was scheduled in Napa City. Sarah had found a strong farm girl from Pope Valley to come stay with the children at her place, where it would be easier finding someone to drive them back and forth to school in St. Helena. She had reminded David that he should notify Vittorio—who, during Prohibition, had met a young woman from Sicily, married her, and moved to Fresno, where his new wife's large family had enveloped him into a busy lifestyle that made him not so close to Lilliana and her children.

Sarah received Vittorio's return call: "Tell Lilliana I will find some kind of way to get to Napa Valley. Tell her me and Sophia say a prayer she gets well soon!"

Sarah went with David to the hospital, leaving at daybreak in order to be with Lilliana before they took her to surgery. After she had been rolled out of the room, they went together to the waiting room on the second floor.

At eleven o'clock, David was pacing the floor, looking at the clock. "Why is it taking so long?"

"These things take time. Sit down, be patient." After a moment she said, "Weren't we on the *third* floor that time when you sat with me, with Norman?"

"I don't remember. I remember being here. I don't know which floor we were on. They all look the same to me."

Sarah patted his hand. "Please don't worry so much, dear. She has the best doctor in Napa County. Everyone says so."

"Maybe I should have taken her to a specialist in San Francisco."

"It wouldn't make any difference. It's the same operation."

"I hope you're right. I just *wish* . . ." When he looked at Sarah, he was trying to blink back tears. "I don't know. I didn't realize anything was really wrong. We—well, people get used to each other. Every morning she was always up first—making sure she had a hot breakfast for the girls. Hot oatmeal, hot Ovaltine. Do you think this girl you hired—will she fix the kinds of food the girls are used to eating?"

"Stop worrying, dear! The girls are just fine. Don't forget, Li Po's there. You know the fuss he'll make over them."

David cracked his knuckles. "When I think what I could have done to make things easier for her. She must have got up plenty of mornings when she didn't feel like it." He looked at Sarah desperately. "Why didn't I *know*? See what was happening? I knew she was restless at night—couldn't seem to sleep on her left side the way she usually does. But I didn't think much about it. Oh, maybe I mentioned she ought to have somebody take a look at her, give her a good checkup. But I didn't put any weight behind it. Didn't see to it that she went to a doctor."

"David, it won't help anything for you to let yourself get so worked up! Stop blaming yourself, dear. You've got to make her feel that you're as steady as a rock when she comes back from surgery. That everything is the same."

It was after two o'clock when the surgeon, accompanied by the head nurse, called them into a vacant private room, one that had the crisp, sterile look of having just been made ready for the next patient to be admitted, with everything in its proper order. The doctor plopped wearily onto the edge of the high bed, motioned for both David and Sarah to take a seat. He began fidgeting with his stethoscope, pushed the dangling mask off his neck, scratched at the edge of where the white surgeon's cap had been tied around his hair.

The nurse, a slight, thin-faced, dark-haired woman in a crisply starched uniform, stood holding a chart as though waiting to be given instructions.

"It's never easy to tell the family," the doctor began. "A surgeon goes into an operating room thinking sometimes that maybe, just maybe, he can perform a near-miracle. I knew your wife had a malignant breast-tumor. I didn't know it had metastasized to the lungs and the lymph nodes." He seemed to suck in air, hold it in his mouth, let it out like air going out of a tire. "On the table, she threw a blood clot. We tried everything to save her—we did our best. Maybe, who knows, it was a blessing. I know it prevented a lot of suffering. A lot of pain and misery she would have had to endure otherwise. You can know your wife didn't suffer . . ."

David seemed to be trying to pull himself up out of some deep hollow space. His eyes looked glazed. "Are you telling me—are you trying to say my wife is *dead*, Doctor?"

The doctor slid off the bed, nodded to the nurse. "I'm afraid so. I wish I didn't have to give you this kind of news. Nurse, why don't you get a little ammonium for Mrs. Jaspers there? Bring some ice water for Mr. Donati." He had seen David's hands trembling, that first sign of the quake taking place inside him. "Bring us some phenobarb—I'll write the order for you."

Sarah stumbled blindly toward David, the two of them clutching at each other, giving open vent to their grief. After a while, when the nurse had taken charge, Sarah mumbled, "I'll go call Vittorio. He'll want to come right away. There's the rest of the family. The priest to call."

The doctor patted David consolingly. "Take it easy, now. You and your mother stay here until you feel a little better, if you like."

David was staring at him as though blinded. "I've got to get out of here! I've—Mother, we've got to get to the children."

Sarah was clinging to David's arm. "Yes . . . we'll have to tell the children."

After the funeral that Wednesday, November 9, 1938, after Vittorio had taken his family back to Fresno, after the neighbors had gone, the priest having given his last condolence and blessing, and Sarah had gone to find Li Po to see what herbs he thought he might give the children, David came to her in the kitchen. He looked as if his face had been chiseled out of a tombstone.

"Mother, would you keep the girls for me for a few weeks? I have to get off by myself. Be on Spring Mountain alone."

"Is that the best thing for you right now?"

"I can't argue right now, Mother! *Will* you?"

"Of course. You know I'll do anything."

He went quickly to the older girls, Anne and Delia, hugged them tightly; saw they had wept until they were limp and exhausted. "Do what your grandmother tells you," he said huskily.

"Just where are you going?" six-year-old Victoria said, her mouth tight with fury, her blue-gray eyes alive with tiny specks of yellow anger.

"I have to be by myself a little while—to get where I'm used to being without your mother."

Victoria, who was tall for a six-year-old, struggled free of David's arm, stood with her tiny fists clenched. "I *hate* her for dying! She had no business getting sick and dying. Why didn't she tell us she was sick? I would have made hot Ovaltine for her the way she did for us when we were sick in bed!" Her face was a hard knot of anger that exploded in one loud wail of tears as she fled toward Sarah's front door. "I hate you too! I hate everybody!"

David looked about as though unable to see anyone, discern a shape or separate voices. Sarah put her hands firmly on his arms.

"Don't worry about the little one. It's understandable the way she's reacting. I'll talk with her. Go on, dear. But take care. Hurry back."

After Anne and Delia had gone to their rooms, having agreed to take the herb drink Li Po had mixed up for them, Sarah went around trying to find Victoria, who was hiding.

"Where did she go, Li Po? Do you have any idea?"

"I saw her running—out to the barn maybe."

Sarah took down a three-quarter-length coat she wore when she was on her walks on cool days, slipped into it, tied a scarf around her head, and went out to look for her youngest granddaughter. She saw Edna, the farm girl from Pope Valley. "Please—get your sister Cora to stay on here another month or so. I'll need both of you helping me out. I'm not as young as I used to be. With three grandchildren in the house —two teenagers and this little hellion—we'll all have our hands full."

As she hurried out the back door, headed down the road toward the old stables, she saw that the cold gray sky suggested frost. Dry, brittle leaves played a crisp-rustling dance of their own as she walked past a row of vines lapping to the very edges of the road to the barn. Ducks forming a V-formation dipped, swept around, headed toward the eastern ridge of mountains. Off through the vineyards, she saw a long-legged black Labrador hunting dog frantically chasing a jackrabbit. The recently strung electric wire leading to the barn was alive with twittering blackbirds.

A few feet from the open barn door she slowed down, softened her step. She was a white-haired sixty-four-year-old woman, but at that moment, she felt as though she had been taken back to a time when she was a little girl and would run from sorrows and the fright of having seen her father fall into a drunken heap and her mother, Miss Grace, fuming, raging through the house. She had often found the darkness of the barn corners a refuge. When she was a little older, she and her friend, Monique Cugnot, had found the little stone bridge, and a refuge under it.

So this one had inherited a few of her genes, along with her grandmother's red hair from even further generations back?

A wave of tenderness engulfed Sarah; joined forces with the sadness that she had kept pushed back since Lilliana's death, trying as best she could to be staunch, dry-eyed, there with a shoulder for the others.

It had been well over a year since she had set foot inside the old barn. The horses had been gone years ago. Yet there was that smell that stayed—that thick smell of earth and hay and horses. She didn't know why she was trembling. Why all the memories should be tossed down on her at once, as though someone had taken a pitchfork in the hayloft and decided to dump it all down on her head. It was not really any one separate memory. It was splinters of everything: of Adam; of Hajib; of David and Joseph and Anton as little boys; of herself as a little girl. Of Norman. Of Delfina. Of seeing her first snow in Boston. Of being cold; of being lonely. Of being excruciatingly happy when she had first known that Adam Donati loved her. Of being sick on the ship when she and her mother were sailing home from Europe and she accepted the fact that she was pregnant with David. Of being in South Carolina, pretending she was a bereaved widow with an orphaned son. Of waiting out the years to marry Adam. Of all that had been and hadn't been. Of death, stalking and stalking, picking off first this one and then that one, never the ones whom one expected. Of empty places inside herself. Of that big teeming world on beyond Napa Valley. Of wars, and wars repeating themselves.

She bent over the rough edge of a stall door, buried her head in her arms, let the circling sadness spin itself down and down, until she heard the tiny voice behind her:

"You're too *old* to cry! Old people ought not cry!"

Sarah turned, staring down through the gathering shadows, through the space between herself and this small child with that fierce expression to match the intensity of her fiery red hair. Suddenly she was seeing past all that into a splintered opening where the child's fear and grief were consuming her, ready to claim the fight she had put up. Sarah was bending down, lowering herself to the child's level.

"I am crying because I thought you didn't want to be with me. I thought you didn't like your grandmother. I thought I had lost you."

"Why did Mommy die? Why did she have to die!" Victoria cried out, flinging her tiny arms around Sarah's weathered neck, where the crepy folds of loose skin had gathered their own well of tears.

A few days before Anne Donati's sixteenth-birthday celebration—which was to be on Sunday, May seventh, instead of on the ninth, a school day—a letter came from Phyllis. With the letter she had enclosed several picture postcards of the New York World's Fair (which had opened on April 30 in Flushing Meadow), with its slogan imprinted across them: "BUILDING THE WORLD OF TOMORROW."

> Royal Way No. 9
> Marblehead, Mass.
> May 3, 1939

MY DEAR SARAH,

Forgive me for not having come by to tell you goodbye. I had thought, initially, that I would stay on in the Napa Valley for a while. But I simply couldn't bear to do so. We allowed the workers to continue with the repairs on the house. I'm not sure if I shall eventually sell it or not, or perhaps want to return someday. We left a couple living on the premises. It should be well taken care of from now on.

We were unable to get in touch with Anton again. Though we offered him his choice of positions with the new corporation, he turned us down, apparently. I am still trying to persuade your son, David, to become our official winemaker. If you could help in that regard, I would be most grateful to you. At this point, we have so much invested in the winery that it seems absurd to throw it away without an all-out effort. (I am not basically all that interested in the wine industry; but since I have become involved this deeply, I want it to go well, strictly as a business venture.)

I took Frances and Bernard to the World's Fair. We stayed at the St. Regis for a few days. Had an interesting time, since for once Miss Gompers wasn't there directing every moment of our activity. There are days when the veil seems lifted for me; when things my psychiatrist has tried to teach me take a firm toehold, and being a mother is not all that intimidating; when I feel I have actually touched my children. Then there are the dark days when I fall into the abyss and it takes weeks to climb out again. It is a precarious threshold on which I teeter back and forth.

Sometimes I think that only the sound of the sea, the eternal breaking of wave after wave, the ebb of the tide, the pull of some greater force, give me the strength to go on. In your Napa Valley, it is the harvest that seems to do this to people, which renders cycle of birth and rebirth. You seem to stand stalwart, Sarah, in all events in life—which is why, I suppose, I felt this need to write to you while I have another brief toehold. I felt I had to say "thank you" again.

If my request to you to beseech David on our behalf to become our winemaker is an inconvenience, please don't worry about it.

Love,
PHYLLIS

David drove down from Spring Mountain that birthday Sunday in time to take the three girls to Mass, as he had managed to do each Sunday since Lilliana's death. At forty-three, he walked with a heaviness, a world-weariness, belonging to a man much older. But today—perhaps because it was Anne's sixteenth birthday, or perhaps because it was one of those beautiful spring days when trees were again in full leaf, when the flower gardens were alive with color, and when the vineyards were forming those first young, tight clusters of berries that would burst into luxurious ripeness later on—Sarah saw that David's step was lighter. For the first time in weeks, his face beamed an open smile as the busy Victoria threw her arms out like a giant cartwheel and turned upside down as though expecting to roll the way the huge puffy cumulus clouds were rolling across the blue sky.

After Anne had blown out the candles on her cake and opened her gifts, admiring particularly the topaz heirloom necklace with its large pendant Sarah gave to her, David lifted a glass of champagne he had brought along for the celebration. "Sweet sixteen. What do you think you might want to do with your life, young lady? Any ideas as yet?"

Anne, who had put the necklace on over her lace-ruffled white blouse, came around and placed her arms loosely around her father's neck. "My music teacher at school tells me I have a natural soprano voice. A lyric. She thinks I should study seriously. That if I found I couldn't make it in opera, I could always be a light-opera singer. I was hoping—when I finish high school next year in St. Helena, do you think I could possibly go to New York and study at the Juilliard? It's the top music school, my teacher thinks."

David worked his jaw back and forth. "New York. Don't we have good schools here in California? Why do you have to leave the state? Go so far from home?"

"But you always *said* you wanted us to follow our dream, Daddy! I remember hearing you say that from the time I was a little girl the size of Victoria."

He reached up over his shoulder, clasped her hands. "If you want to go to music school in New York, then we'll find a way, somehow. As long as you know, really know, it is what you want to do in life."

Delia, whose sixteenth birthday would be coming up in March of 1940, tilted her head, smiled mischievously. "If she goes to Juilliard, then maybe I can go to Pratt. If anyone expects to make a go of it as an artist, then they have to go to New York. Anne, you can learn your way around and show me when I get there."

David pushed his fork through the birthday cake. "Wait a minute —*two* of you back east! I haven't said—"

Victoria pushed to her back the long single braid that had draped over one shoulder, got up from the table. "*I'm* not going to New York! I'm staying in Napa Valley. Right here with Daddy and Grandmother."

Anne looked at her young sister, smiled tolerantly. "When you grow up, you might want to change your mind."

"When *I* grow up, I'm going to be a winemaker!"

David scooped her up, plunked her on one knee. "You've got a long time to decide what you'll be.

"If I can't be a winemaker, maybe I'll be a stunt rider in the circus! When are you buying my pony, Daddy? You promised. You said I could have a pony and a saddle and a bridle with silver on it. I want a palomino—or a solid black horse."

"Ask your grandmother. It'll have to stay in her barn. Feed on her pasture."

"It's up to you, David," Sarah said, smiling. "I got my first horse about her age. It was my friend, my best friend, for a lot of years."

"I'll look around," David said, giving Victoria a push off his lap, picking up his champagne glass. "All this costs money."

"By the way," Sarah put in, "I had a letter from Phyllis asking me to try to help talk you into becoming their winemaker. She would pay you quite a handsome salary, I'd imagine."

He toyed with his champagne glass. "It's tempting. But I hate getting my name associated with any wine Anton has put out. I've kept the name of Donati pretty clean in the wine world so far. I've earned a fair amount of respect. I don't want it tarnished."

"Where *is* Anton these days?"

"I hear he's trying to join the Air Corps. He's sure we're heading for another big world war and he said he wanted to enlist before he was too old to get accepted. Get in while he can be an officer. You know Anton. He'll want to be the big shot—even if it's in the Army."

"Maybe it's a good idea. He seems to have made things difficult for himself in Napa Valley."

"That's putting it mildly." David laughed. "At least he found out there's more to being a famous winemaker than building a big building, printing up some fancy labels and selling a bill of goods to the public. In the long run, it's the wine that counts. Only the wine."

Anne and Delia excused themselves, went upstairs to their bedrooms. As usual, Victoria was hanging back, always nearby with both ears wide open, pretending she was busy with something else but drinking in every word.

"How are things going for you on Spring Mountain?" Sarah asked, her voice taking on a little edge. She thought it was high time David moved in with her and the girls down here on the valley floor where life was much simpler. She understood, if anyone did, how he could get attached to Spring Mountain, but there was a limit to sentiment. She was finding that out in her old age.

"I've got things pretty much shut down. Some good wines aging I've cut my crush back to twenty thousand gallons. It just doesn't pay, trying to be big for bigness' sake. I'm experimenting. I'm trying to work out a couple of blendings. I'm a jump ahead of a lot of guys because of the vineyards." His eyes lit up. "One thing Papa used to know—it was all in the grapes. Wine doesn't need a lot of help. Just enough—the right touch. Then the good winemaker lets the wine alone. I'm coming around to that opinion more and more. I'm not sorry I learned what I learned at school, technically speaking. But I'm getting back to a simpler approach. Every wine I've won a ribbon on at the State Fair has been wine made that way."

"If you go to work for the Fullers, that won't be such a small operation, will it? Aren't they thinking in large numbers?"

"Very large numbers. I hear they're thinking about selling some shares to a big brewery company. Which is one reason I don't want to get caught in their big takeover. Those big conglomerates—once they step in, the emphasis is going to be on profit. On the big sell."

"But you could use the money. And wouldn't it be a marvelous opportunity in another way? Good experience?"

"I've written her that I'll be an adviser. A consultant. That I'll have to have time to do my own Donati winemaking. My own crush. I had Chip write out an offer. If she likes it, fine. If she doesn't, well, I've held on this long, I guess I'll hang on through this last pitfall."

23

In September of 1939, World War II broke out, with the invasion of Poland by the Germans. When Sarah heard the news broadcasts she felt as if she had had the breath knocked out of her by a kick from Victoria's new rambunctious palomino mare, now out in her barn. It had been only a little while ago, it seemed to her, that they had been celebrating the armistice of the last World War—the war to end all wars. Now, at a glance, it looked as if the same countries would be lining up against each other, only this time with bigger, more modern weapons. This man, Adolf Hitler, was not the same kind of enemy as the old lion Kaiser Wilhelm had been.

When she heard the broadcast on September 28 about the surrender of the Warsaw garrison, she went out on the brick terrace to look for David. He was just coming out of the vineyards, driving a truck that was pulling a gondola filled with the last load of Rieslings picked for the day, headed out for the Brunner-Fuller Winery, where the grapes would be sold and put into the stemmer-crusher.

When David saw her frantically waving, at first he only slowed down the truck; then he thought something might have happened to Victoria, who was always into something, falling out of trees or getting thrown by her new horse, which she insisted on tring to ride bareback. "What's wrong?" he asked, leaning out the window, wiping perspiration off his head with a bandana handkerchief.

"Warsaw has surrendered! I'm scared to death we're all on the brink of another major world war. Russia is rattling its sabers at that poor little country, Finland. I'm worried sick!"

David stuffed the handkerchief into his back pocket. "Sorry to hear that. Look, I can't stop to talk now. I've had the laziest crew of pickers that's ever set foot in a damn vineyard. They've broken half the skins on these Rieslings. And the fruit flies are eating all of us up."

"Don't act so irritated with me, David. I thought you'd be interested."

"Look, Mother, this is the middle of harvest! I've not only got to get *your* grapes picked, but I do have Spring Mountain to think about. I've got the Brunner-Fuller crush on my hands and I'd like to pay more attention to my own. I can't stop and start worrying over what's happening in *Poland,* for God's sake!"

"You are working too hard, David," Sarah said, turning around and heading back into the house as the truck gears ground into low. "Sometimes I wish I'd never heard of a harvest," she mumbled to herself as she entered the cool shadowy interior of the foyer with its black-and-white marble-tiled floor.

With three granddaughters in the house, the calender seemed to flapjack for Sarah into the year of 1940. Something about that rounded-out number, that numerical progression of the decades made her take sharp, sudden note. In April, when she heard that Norway and Denmark had fallen to the Nazis, she called Chip Brosius.

"Sarah, I'm with a client at the moment. Could I call you back?" She heard his sigh, as if he might be irritated with her, too. "Is it urgent?"

"To me it is! I want to add a codicil to my will. If you are suddenly too busy to tend to your first, your steadiest client, then I'll find another young lawyer who isn't so busy."

"Calm down, Sarah. Why are you so upset? You know I'll take care of you. Haven't I always done a good job for you?"

"I'm upset because I see the Germans are winning this war. It's just a matter of time before Great Britain is going to fall, the way things are going right now. That little Royal Air Force of theirs can't hold out against those Luftwaffe bombers. It's just got me thinking. We're all so ephemeral. I'm sixty-six years old and there are certain things important to me that I want at least to be inherited by the right people. If I died tonight in my sleep, I'd like to know that certain assets of mine fell into hands that might make them a little more lasting."

"Don't sound so gloomy. You've got a long time ahead, Sarah. You're still going very strong. And don't sell the English short. They're tough. The world wasn't made in a day and it won't end overnight. We've got plenty of time to draw up this codicil."

"Just because you're a young man still green behind the ears doesn't mean that I've got a lifetime ahead of me. Either you get this codicil written for me before I go to bed tonight or I will take all my business elsewhere!"

"I'll call you back in one hour, Sarah. If you think you can last that long. Okay?"

She slammed the receiver down and went into the kitchen, where she had been helping seven-year-old Victoria with her arithmetic. Victoria looked up from the multiplication tables Sarah thought she was bright enough to learn without having to wait for a sluggish second-grade teacher trapped in a sterile routine to get around to.

"Why are you so mad, Grandmother?"

Sarah poured out a cup of tea, sat down. "Impertinence! My lawyer getting fresh with me." She looked at the round gray-blue eyes staring at her, that alertness in this odd little girl who seemed always to be listening, trying to figure out more than arithmetic problems. Sarah reached out, patted her hand. "Maybe I'm getting old and a little irascible. I'm losing patience—something one can't ever afford to do."

"That's what Daddy says."

"Your Daddy ought to know. The first thing any grape grower or winemaker learns is patience."

"Then can't I be like you when I grow up?"

"You will be like yourself, young lady. There's only one Victoria Donati. Don't forget that. This world—I'm getting to the age where I realize we're in it such a short time. You must make your name stand for something." She pointed to the arithmetic lesson. "You're going to have to learn a lot of things, some that won't be all that interesting to you. But you learn everything you can. And one of these days, you're going to find yourself with a big goal in mind. A big dream. Everything you learn will help you achieve it. And I want you to remember one other very important thing. Go *after* your dream! Don't let anything get you sidetracked." She drained the teacup. "Now, what does two times two equal?"

Chip Brosius called back before they had finished the arithmetic homework session, when Victoria was just tackling the sixes in the multiplication tables. "Write them down for me while I talk some business with my lawyer," Sarah told her, heading out of the kitchen into her own small library.

"Sarah, I think we can tend to most of this on the phone. Have you got your notes handy?"

While she was cradling the receiver under her chin, scrambling through papers, she thought she heard a click on the wire; but Chip's telephone always had clicking on it, she thought. "Okay, I have everything. Are you ready?"

"Shoot," Chip said.

"In the original will that you drew up for me, I left certain things to my stepgrandchildren, Frances and Bernard—Anton's children. I believe I designated a certain sum for Anton as well. I want that changed. Delete all of them. Phyllis is too wealthy for her own good. They don't need *my* money. Now, I want to be fair with David's three girls. Essentially, I still want a share-and-share-alike basis for division of my assets. However, I have grown very fond of the youngest, Victoria. I don't want an imbalance, monetarily; but I want to leave to her those things I cherish the most. The Hubbard antiques. My most personal, sentimental jewelry. I am making a point of giving each girl a lovely piece of jewelry on her sixteenth birthday, so each will have something from the Hubbard and Reynolds families. But I want Victoria to have my diamonds. The ruby ring. And since I own a considerable share now on Spring Mountain, I want my part of that to go to her."

"What about these remaining shares you own in the Brunner-Fuller Winery? You've not stipulated to whom—and since you only have ten left, it might not be a good idea to try to divide them on a share-and-share-alike basis."

"I thought I sold those to Phyllis?"

Chip laughed. "You sold the ones we had that were *general* shares. Sarah, didn't you read that agreement? You were also a limited partner and there were those limited shares. Anton hasn't asked to buy them back. I discussed them with Phyllis, and she's honoring them. Your ten shares are still good with that corporation. They've issued new stock accordingly. It was sent here to my office. I'm sorry—I thought we had discussed it. I've been so terribly busy lately. I'm understaffed."

"Chip, I advise you to take stock of yourself one of these days pretty soon," Sarah said curtly. "One of these days you'll find yourself being sixty-six years old and want to know how you missed out on living some of your life."

He laughed. "Okay, I'll do that. And I'll bring by this codicil for you to sign tomorrow."

"Tonight. Sorry. That was our agreement."

When she went back into the kitchen she caught Victoria hurrying to slide under the table, pulling furiously at her chair, trying to appear that she had been there all along.

"Victoria, you were listening on the kitchen telephone, weren't you? Spying on my conversation with my lawyer?"

Victoria toyed with her pencil, tapping the paper rhythmically.

"So you *were*! Sarah sat down. "There is a way that is honorable to learn all you can about life. There is a way that is dishonorable. Spying on another's personal life, being furtive or dishonest in any way —that is dishonorable. The name Donati—your grandfather came to this country to bring that name into the American wine world. To continue the honor it had earned in Italy. Your father has tried to live up to those same high standards. It isn't always easy. But if you are going to be the Donati to carry on the name, to carry on the Spring Mountain Winery, then you must learn that very important lesson right now. Do you understand?"

"Don't get mad at me, Grandmother. *Please.*"

"You do promise to remember what I've said?"

"I cross my heart and hope to die."

"Then I'm not mad. Now, what does eight times eight equal?"

When harvest arrived in September of 1940, Anne Donati was boarding the train for New York, where she had been accepted by the Juilliard School of Music. Sarah had talked David into letting her pay the tuition and buy Anne a suitable wardrobe. He was too busy to object. The Brunner-Fuller Winery was expanding. Enormous stainless-steel tanks with built-in temperature controls were being set up. Though he preferred oak, the fermentation processes he had been taught, he was curious to see how this was going to work. A young team of oenologists were being brought in at the suggestion of the board of directors of the Minnesota Brewery Company, who had, he understood, bought into the business. He didn't ask questions. He was paid twelve thousand dollars a year to be head consultant. As yet, no mention had been made that his job would be terminated. He had his laboratory. He was being left alone with making the Cabernet Sauvignon and the Pinot Noir. The new stress was going to be put on making white wine, he understood. That suited him. He had his own Spring Mountain Donati white wines. He had a surprise or two he was going to pull out and enter in the next competition. He tried to keep his name off any Brunner-Fuller labels anyway.

It helped to stay busy. It kept him from thinking about Lilliana—though at nights he still often would awaken, having automatically reached out for her. He had mixed feelings about the girls staying with their grandmother. But he couldn't run a household. Girls needed a woman's hand. It had been one thing when Anne and Delia were little, when routines were predictable. What did he know about soprano voices, all those endless scales Anne was always practicing, driving him crazy! Sarah didn't seem to mind. And how could he say no to letting her help with their education when she seemed to get so much kick out of it—seemed to get a whole new hold on life from taking care of the girls? Selfishly, he supposed, he would like to take the money he was putting aside and invest in some new equipment of his own on Spring Mountain. Everything cost so much these days. Winemaking was never inexpensive, if it was done right.

He had just finished harvesting the last of the Cabernets, which had ripened on Spring Mountain later than usual that year, and had come down with a check for Sarah.

"Did you vote?" she asked, looking up from a book she was reading to Victoria.

"I let it slip my mind. Who won?"

"Roosevelt. Wendell Wilkie was no match for him." She turned a page. "I don't envy any President trying to keep us out of war."

"Where's Delia?"

"Upstairs working on a painting. She's trying to finish a series on Napa Valley, through the different seasons. She's been going around sketching every winery she can find. Old barns. She says the lines of the mountains are very graphic. If you want to see Delia anytime, look back in the old breakfast room, which she's taken over as her studio."

"Do you think she has talent? Is she really any good?" David had his arm around Victoria's waist, was tugging playfully at her long red hair.

"Yes, I think she's gifted. She's certainly made up her mind to go to New York the minute she graduates from high school. She and Anne do seem to get along well. If they're roommates, that might be nice for both of them."

"Did Delia ask you to butter me up, Mother?"

"I want them to go!" Victoria said. "Then it will be just Grandmother and me—and you, when you come to see us."

David looked as though his feelings were hurt. Sarah spoke up quickly. "Why don't you think about moving down with us, David? Aren't you tired of trying to keep up with that big barn of a place? Aren't you tired of hot dogs and hamburgers?"

"There's a lot of furniture up there. You can't just walk off and leave everything."

"Grandmother is leaving everything to me anyway," Victoria said, excusing herself to go get a glass of milk.

"Aren't you spoiling her terribly?" David asked, when he was sure she was out of earshot.

"Yes, I am. I can't help it. Which is why you really should move in down here, David. She needs a firm hand from her father. I know she winds me around her little finger." She accepted the glass of sherry he had brought along for her to sample. "Very nice," she said. She put it down, closed the book, looked at David intently. "Seriously, I think you should pack up and move down. Just bring the antique pieces—the things of value. Leave the rest up there."

"Where would you put everything? This place is jammed!"

"Most of what you see here was Norman's. Some I might donate to a museum. I have plenty of room in the attic. I've never personally cared much for Oriental decor. I would enjoy seeing some of the pieces that belonged to my mother, to her mother, and her mother's mother back in England a long time ago—here in their old places."

He finished the sherry. "This 'flor' method—I think the sherry has a little salty taste. Maybe I added the wrong amount of mineral gypsum. I'm still working to perfect it. Getting the pH lowered isn't always easy."

David, what about it? Moving down?" She saw him fighting.

"Okay! But give me a couple of weeks. I'll have to round up some strong men to help me move all the heavy junk."

"David, it isn't junk! It's time we got it here so I can teach Victoria how to take care of it, respect antiques, which—she is right—I'm leaving to her."

On the Sunday when Pearl Harbor was bombed, that December 7, 1941, Sarah and Victoria and David sat around the radio listening to the reports.

"The dirty bastards!" David said, hearing that eighteen ships had been sunk, 188 planes destroyed, another 159 damaged; that 2,008 sailors had been killed, 710 wounded, 218 soldiers and 109 marines were known dead, and that there were no figures yet on how many others had been wounded.

"What if they attack San Francisco? The West Coast?" Sarah asked, her face white. "How could this have happened? How could we have been so ill-prepared?"

"Not everybody thinks your F.D.R. is so hot. You just heard what Clare Booth Luce said—'He lied the American people into war because he could not lead them into it.'"

"Let's not start a little war right here over who did what, David. We are in the war now. I never thought I'd live through another one. Thank God, you've got daughters. It's selfish of me, but I'm getting old. I'm glad I don't have to worry about my heirs fighting a war."

"I wonder what this is going to do to the wine industry," David sighed, clicking off the radio. "It's one guess that that surplus brandy they bought up ought to go like hotcakes."

David's prediction proved right. World War II created an active market for any kind of alcoholic beverage. During this time, David's main emphasis was still on producing château-quality wine at the Spring Mountain Donati Winery—and having won several prizes at the

State Fair, he had firmly established the name Donati with the word "quality." Since the furniture had been moved out of the old stone house on Spring Mountain, he had converted the house for part use in running the winery. He had found it easier to work in his own experimental laboratory by using the kitchen and Li Po's old room. The downstairs library, with its wood paneling and lovely old fireplace, its books on wines and the medals his father had won, made an excellent tasting room. He used bedrooms upstairs for storing bottled wine, packaged, awaiting shipment. The dining room was large and an excellent place for labeling. In the main parlor he had made an office space for files and mailing lists, where the wife of his new Spring Mountain vineyard manager, Janet Cutler, kept up with orders and sending out announcements to the growing mailing list. Janet had worked for him for only three months. Her husband, Dick, a graduate from Davis School of Agriculture, was a hard worker, a fine vineyardist. As a young couple, they were anxious to save money to buy some land of their own in Napa Valley. David was fond of both of them.

One Friday afternoon, when David was ready to leave to go back to Sarah's, Janet called out cheerfully, "We have more orders than we can fill for last year's Rieslings and your 1936 Cabernet. I don't understand it. You never take out advertisements, yet everybody seems to want Donati wine. How did that happen?"

"Good wine speaks for itself." He took down his jacket, looked in at the pile of orders she had in response to her last mailing. "Fill them first come, first served. Try to keep tab on our oldest customers. Give them some priority." He laughed with his own private bemusement. "I guess I'll always be a stickler for quality. If it's no good, I won't fill orders, regardless. I just ran across one of my brother Anton's old slogans down at the Fuller Winery the other day—'Premium Wine at an Affordable Price.'" He rubbed his eyes. "Funny thing, now I think that might start happening down there! That new brewery from Minnesota who're buying in, I hear, are dumping over a million dollars into it to make that happen."

Janet looked up. "I guess I don't know your brother. Dick and I are new to Napa Valley, just finding our way around."

"Anton—Anton Brunner. My half brother. He's in the Army Air Force now. Over in Europe training fighter pilots. He was the originator of the Brunner-Fuller Winery, near Inglenook. He's going to get a big shock when he gets back from the war."

"Did they buy him out?"

"He lost control. To his former wife. A millionairess from Boston. She calls the shots now."

"I guess I don't know her either."

"She stays mostly back east. Owns the old Cugnot house; but I don't think she ever comes here anymore. Drinks a lot, they tell me. Her corporation runs the show. A big business now."

He opened the front door of the old stone house. Janet came to hand him a stack of letters to mail, acknowledging orders received. He took them, turned, looked out across the stone veranda at the vineyards, on across at the distant outline of Howell Mountain. "If you stay around Napa Valley, you'll hear lots of stories. There are plenty of them bouncing back and forth between these two ridges of mountains. A lot of people have wandered in. Some stay, some go out like whipped dogs with their tails between their legs. As beautiful a place as the valley is, it isn't all that good to everybody. My father used to tell me—he built this place—that Bacchus smiled on the hillsides best. Maybe. Maybe not. Good men have been wiped out. A hell of a lot of heartache has rolled with the seasons in this valley. All kinds of heartache," he said softly, thinking of Lilliana as he closed the door behind him.

In September of 1945 a seventy-one-year-old Sarah went into the kitchen in the old Reynolds place in Oakville and ripped off the wall the makeshift map she had kept throughout the war (hoping to teach Victoria at least a vague concept of what was taking place out there in the world beyond the oddly still-serene Napa Valley). She wadded the map up, tossed it into the wastebasket. Then she looked at the recently filled-out, blossoming figure of thirteen-year-old Victoria and said, "If this world hasn't learned its lesson now, after this war, after Hiroshima, it never will!"

But Victoria had her mind on other things these days. For the past two years, every Saturday her best friend, Judy Rudnisky, had been coming to spend the night with her. And, usually, they would go to her bedroom, lock the door and discuss boys and how long it would take to fall in love with a handsome man in uniform. Judy preferred marines; Victoria wanted an officer who looked as dashing as her Uncle Anton, who had just returned with a chestful of decorations.

"*You'll* be asked out on a date first," Judy often complained, jealously looking at Victoria's rounded-out breasts, her twenty-four-inch waistline, her contoured hips measuring thirty-two inches. "Look at *me* —flat-chested, skinny as a beanpole. I'd give anything in the world to have hair like yours, naturally curly, copper-colored. Mine is like an old stringy mop. No wonder my mother dyes hers blond."

One Saturday night, the last week of October, just after the 1945 harvest had been completed, Judy noticed that Victoria wasn't as talkative as usual.

Suddenly Victoria asked, "Judy, how long are you going to stay a virgin?"

Judy pushed her straight hair off her face, tried to appear nonchalant. "I don't know. Until Prince Charming comes along, I guess! Why?" She sat up on the edge of the bed, looked down at Victoria. "How long are *you*?"

"I'm not sure. Maybe I would, maybe I wouldn't. I don't mean playing around. I mean I want to know what the physical part is all about so that if my real true love comes along I'll know. Really know."

"I have a secret," Judy said, biting her lower lip.

Victoria stopped brushing her hair. "You don't mean you've—you haven't already—"

"No—it's not about me."

"Who? Tell me!"

"Promise you won't tell a living, breathing soul. You'll cross your heart and hope to die? You're my best friend and we have special secrets—things we never, never tell anyone else?"

Victoria looked at her somberly. "Cross my heart, hope to die. On a stack of Bibles."

"My mother is playing around again."

"Your *mother*!" Victoria's eyes were wide, filled with yellow dancing lights. "But she's *old*! She's what—thirty-five, forty years old?"

"Forty-one. But she's still playing around."

Victoria felt a taste in her mouth she didn't like, as if the doctor had swabbed her throat with iodine for a sore throat. "Who with?"

"You promise you won't tell? You swear you won't?"

"I swear."

"With your Uncle Anton." Judy bit her upper lip, looked up at the ceiling, back down at Victoria. "When I was little I used to hear my daddy yelling and screaming at her about running around—*whoring* around, he used to say—when she used to work for your uncle. When Daddy was just starting up his new drugstore and they needed more money. One time Daddy caught them—"

"You mean—*doing* it?"

"Out behind the winery—when your uncle was first building it. Caught them out in the vineyards. He didn't let her know. He waited until she got home and when she lied to him he—he knocked her around. He really was mad! He was grabbing her around the neck, saying he ought to kill her."

Victoria was trying to think what to say. She sat there, knowing one foot had gone asleep, but not daring to move.

"I don't know everything that went on—I was pretty little. But I remember that. And then something happened, I guess. She quit working. The war started. She was home a lot. Sewing, designing dresses. Learning how to cook gourmet dishes. Teaching French lessons. Things like that. But the other night I saw them riding in a car. Mother had her head all tucked down on his shoulder. And later I heard Daddy yelling at her again." Judy started crying. "I shouldn't have *told* you. You'll tell somebody! Everybody will find out and laugh behind my back."

"I won't tell anybody. I crossed my heart."

"Then you tell *me* a secret."

Victoria thought a moment. "I can't. I could get someone in very bad trouble if I told you."

"How, if I don't tell anybody! You could get *me* in trouble. It's not fair—you owe it to me to tell."

"I'm hiding a wetback," Victoria said, her face tightly drawn up. "I found him hiding under a stone bridge, shivering and wet and scared. He's fifteen, maybe sixteen. I let him ride double on my horse, took him up Spring Mountain on the back trail. I hid him in the old bunkhouse up there."

"You mean a—a dirty *Mexican!*"

"He's *not* a dirty Mexican. He's the best-looking boy I ever saw in my life. He's half Mexican, half American. His mother worked in this big house in San Antonio. This rich oil man—he came into her room all the time. But he wouldn't marry her."

Judy tossed her head back. "You're just making that up. That's no secret! Mine was *true*. My mother is really in trouble. She's really playing around behind Daddy's back."

"Believe it if you want to. It's true though. And I'll tell you another secret. I'm going to see if I can make him—well, do it to me. How about that for a secret?"

"You wouldn't! Even if what you said was true, you really wouldn't. With a *Mexican?*"

"He's—I think he's beautiful."

"Boys aren't beautiful, stupid."

"*He* is. He has—blue eyes. The same color as mine. He looks a little like my father. He's tall. He's got dark suntanned skin."

Long into the night, Victoria was wide awake, wondering if she had taken the wetback (who had told her his name was Jerrod James) enough warm blankets. Wondering how she was going to keep slipping out her father's clothes and enough food from the kitchen before she was caught. She was going to have to do something about him. She couldn't keep slipping off up there every day. And she knew he would never really do it to her. He wouldn't even let her near enough to touch him.

Sometime in the middle of the night, Judy's voice came across softly: "Victoria, are you asleep?"

"No. Not really."

"I'm glad we're still best friends. Aren't you?"

"Sure . . ." Victoria said drowsily, finally giving in to sleep.

After that Saturday night, Victoria decided she didn't really want to be Judy's best friend any longer. She wished she hadn't, in a weak moment, ever told her about Jerrod James being hidden on Spring Mountain, or said anything at all about trying to get him to show her what sex was all about. She didn't want to find out yet, anyway! She was just seeing how it sounded, saying it out loud. She might stay a virgin all her life, for that matter—or wait until she was about, oh, maybe thirty. Plus, she was tired of reading *True Stories* and *Modern Romances*, since she could usually guess what was going to happen next and how each one would end anyway. She gathered up all she had hidden, went out to the back-yard incinerator when she knew her grandmother wouldn't be looking, and waited until she was sure the last one had burned into black, flaky ashes.

But even so, a lump of anxiety rode like a cold, thick ball of grease in the pit of her stomach. What was she going to do with Jerrod James? She couldn't just let him sit up there alone in that bunkhouse all winter waiting for spring and field work—or maybe even having to wait around until next harvest to look for wetbacks he might know with whom he could go home again.

She had sneaked out about all the clothes and food she could. She was just going to have to tell him he was on his own. That he could take the schoolbooks she had loaned him, and her good pencil set; for if he could learn to read and write English as well as he could speak it, he could get by a lot better. Maybe he could hide out on his own in a lot of places in America. He didn't have to stay on Donati property, in Napa Valley, and get caught!

Along with Victoria's secret worries over him, she had a new set of problems at school. Judy Rudnisky had every girl in the freshman class whispering behind her back, avoiding walking down the hallways with her or sitting next to her at the school cafeteria. She knew what they were saying—that she had hidden a wetback and was going to get him to do it to her! But even when she heard their snickering, mocking laughter, she walked as her grandmother had taught her—with her head high, her back straight, her chin up. And because she knew that she was the best student in class, she bore down even harder on her homework; took opportunity to volunteer and answer oratorically every question, insisting that her voice be heard among her peers, in one way or the other. But deep down, she was miserable, lonelier than she had ever guessed anyone could be. And she was afraid.

If Sarah noticed that Victoria was behaving peculiarly, hanging around her with a kind of sick-dog look, sighing a lot, and staring off into space, she passed it off as being a part of some new stage she was going through. Adolescence was never easy, during any era. And this new group of 1940s teenagers—with their "jitterbug" music, their dirty saddle shoes, their baggy sweaters, being allowed to ride around in cars with boys without a chaperone—were beyond her comprehension, anyway. Where were the *standards*, the dignified way of life?

When, on one occasion, Sarah took verbal note of how Victoria was spending a lot of time on her palomino mare lately, staying out some afternoons until nearly dark, it was to admonish her about her bad riding habits: "I wish you wouldn't ride that horse as if you're tearing down a racetrack! You could get thrown off and killed. If your grandfather were still alive, he'd show you the proper way to sit a saddle. You'd ride like a lady—not like a roughneck cowgirl tearing off into the mountains."

It was David who, inadvertently, stumbled across Jerrod James hiding out in the bunkhouse, and who was to put a stop in his own way to Victoria's problems.

It had been one of those days when nothing had gone right for David at the Fuller-Brunner (as it was now called) Winery. He had found bottles mislabeled. The new corking machine had broken down. The new team of upstart winemakers sent in by the Minnesota Brewery Company were treating him as if he didn't even exist. They simply helped themselves to anything they wanted from his private laboratory. They never asked for his opinion on anything. Plus, he had just been given the word that he would probably be let go as consultant at the end of 1945 or not later than March of 1946.

So on that Tuesday when he had finished at the Fuller-Brunner Winery, instead of heading toward Sarah's, as he usually did, he felt a pull toward Spring Mountain, a need to get off to himself and sort out his thoughts. He needed to decide if he should write a general letter of resignation or if he should list his own complaints about the new team of oenologists and send them straight to Phyllis Fuller Brunner, who was still listed as president on the letterhead, even with the new Minnesota investors.

At the junction where the Donati driveway met the Spring Mountain county road, David stopped the old Chrysler, unlocked the chain-link gate, drove through, went back and relocked it behind him. He hated the thought of trespassers at any time, and wanted no one to drive in, particularly tonight, when he realized he was wound up like a coiled clock spring waiting to strike.

Shadows thick with dusk were falling across the narrow forest-lined driveway leading back to the Donati estate. A huge buck with magnificent antlers and a startled doe stood like statues a foot away from his left fender. He stopped abruptly, waited for them to leap to safety. Though they were enemies for any vineyardist, the harvest was picked. He wouldn't ever harm them intentionally, particularly now when the doe's eyes had reminded him suddenly of Lilliana—that startled look she used to get at times. How he missed her! How he ached inside trying to accept his loss.

As he drove on through the dense trees, he pulled to a stop on the very edge of a clearing, the one spot where he could see not only the stone stable but on ahead, against the mountainside, the outlines of the huge winery, and to his left, its tower silhouetted like a finger pointing at the sky, the old mansion where he had lived so much of his life. He stopped and, though it was not the place where he usually left the car, slid out and stood looking about. It was good to be home. To feel the silence. To practically hear Lilliana's voice, see her hurrying toward him to kiss him hello and tell him what she had ready for his dinner. But something was causing his nostrils to close, open—the smell of oak logs burning! He looked about, saw the thin trickle of smoke coming out of the bunkhouse—the boarded-up bunkhouse!

Who the hell dared trespass on Donati property! He fished in his pocket for his key ring, working the keys around. He'd slip through the stable doors, sneak up that way. He looked for the right key, all the while steadily approaching the locked double front doors of the stable where huge wagons used to roll through. He eased one side of the door open, careful of creaky noises.

Inside, a pitch darkness seemed to reach for him like a gaping mouth. He stood a moment, adjusting his eyes. Gradually, muted shapes beneath the boarded-up windows began to form around the old freight wagon he had ridden as a boy, the one Joseph used to drive so proudly, his long whip cracking; around rotted lumps of hay; around stall doors hanging on loose hinges; around cracked leather saddles and harnesses draped like ghosts from spikes.

Slowly, David worked his way through the cavernous dank stable; found sure footing on the bottom step leading to the narrow corridor into the bunkhouse. His arms bristled with anger, with alertness. He eased up to the door, where a shaft of light made its way beneath it; then flung it open in a burst, his pulse racing.

It took David a moment to realize that those fear-glazed eyes, like fixed blue glass marbles, staring out from rich olive-colored skin belonged to a young teenage boy. He drew back, taking in the sight of the tall, skinny, hollow-cheeked kid who looked as if his legs and arms had grown too fast, were out of kilter with the rest of him.

"Don't you know I could have you thrown in jail for trespassing? Didn't you see the signs posted everyplace? Who told you you could just move in here and make yourself at home?"

The boy's legs looked suddenly wobbly.

"Sit down," David barked, catching sight of a fifth-grade reader and a tablet that had fallen to the floor when the boy had jumped up from the bed. David himself reached down and picked up the reader, handed the tablet to him, at the same moment noticing that the boy was wearing his very own favorite old sweater, the navy-blue one that Lilliana had mended at the elbows only a week before she died—the sweater he had been looking for everywhere these past few days.

"Just where did you get this book, that sweater?" He looked about, suddenly knowing the answer when he saw the stack of his old work pants, a pair of field boots, a baseball cap, the faded sweatshirt he had worn at college. He saw the boy's blue eyes glaze over, his hands tremble as he raked them through thick wavy black hair. A new fear was gripping David. He had always known Victoria was a kind of hellion —was as strong-willed as they came. But what had she been up to with this ragtag boy? She was old enough to start getting big ideas, he guessed—she *was* filling out like a woman.

"Goddammit, answer me! Where did you get those clothes, that book? Just who the hell are you, anyway?"

After a moment, the blue eyes fixed straight on David's. "My name is Jerrod James. Your daughter found me hiding under a stone bridge at the foot of the mountain. She brought me up here on her horse . . . told me to hide here so they wouldn't catch me—send me back to Mexico."

"Wait a minute! You're not telling me you're a *wetback*? With those blue eyes? Somebody tall like you? You don't look Mexican."

Proud yellow lights lit up the blue eyes. "My mother is full Mexican. My father was a Texas oil and cattle man. His name is Jamison Wiley James. From San Antonio."

"If your father's a Texan, how are you a wetback?" David was glaring at him.

Jerrod James ducked his head a moment, then looked back at David. "My father claimed he wasn't my father. So my mother took me to Mexico," he said in a voice so low David barely heard.

David was trying to let it all settle in. He sat down on the bunk bed opposite Jerrod James. "You realize that if I get caught harboring an alien *I'll* get in trouble with the law?"

"Yes, sir."

"What would you do? If I let you go free, told you to head out?"

"I guess I'd hitchhike, hobo my way back toward the border, unless somebody took me in, let me work for them. I'm a good worker. I speak English. People don't usually guess me to be a Mexican, unless they see me with all-Mexicans." His blue eyes were openly asking. "My mother always told me, 'Try to stay in America long enough to become a citizen.' "

David shook his head. "This has been the damnedest day! The last thing on my mind was inheriting a wetback!" He twisted his mouth thoughtfully. There was something about this boy that took him back to a time in his life when he had been tagged a bastard. He hadn't been stuck with "wetback" on top of it, but he knew a little how it felt. "How hard a worker are you?"

"I'm good at pruning grapes, picking, anything. I'm a fast learner too. I'm good at figuring things." The boy dug in his pockets, dumped loose bills and change on the bed. "Your daughter brought me this—fifteen dollars—to help me get away."

"That crazy damn kid of mine!" David said, more to himself. "I knew better than to leave her that long with her grandmother." He turned back to Jerrod, rubbed his forehead wearily. "I don't know what the hell to do with you. You say you know how to prune, eh? We're short of skilled labor in Napa Valley since the war. How old are you—fifteen, sixteen?"

"I'll be sixteen in January."

"You're sure you're not a runaway from a reform school someplace? I could swear you're Italian. You don't look Mexican."

"I know. It's why I wasn't caught before." The boy looked at the fifth-grade reader. "I learn fast. Your daughter was trying to teach me to read and write so I could get by easier. I never went to school—but I'm learning. I'm quick with figures and with reading, I guess."

David was quiet, trying to get his thoughts straight. "Okay—I'll take you home with me. But we're going to figure out a different name for you. And you'll have to get one thing straight right off—you stay away from my daughter! Understand? You're coming to *work* for me and you'll be expected to stay in your place. If you step out of line one time, I'll turn you in to the sheriff so fast your head will spin. Got that?"

"Yes, sir," Jerrod said, his eyes glistening. "My mother—she said every night she prayed for somebody, some kind man, to take me in. Teach me. Let me prove myself. She knew it would happen."

David looked away from the eager boy. He bit his lower lip, said in a preoccupied voice, "We've got to get another name for you, though. Something that sounds Italian."

"But I like my name."

"Look, I'm taking a chance harboring an alien. I don't want to get in trouble. This is a two-way street. Either we see eye to eye right now or maybe you'd better take that fifteen dollars and head out."

"Okay. Give me a new name, then."

When they got into the old Chrysler to go back down Spring Mountain, Jerrod James sat back in awe of the splendor of the elegant old car. He reached out, touched the wood paneling, ran one finger down the smooth leather seats. "It smells so nice. I always thought riding in a nice big car would be like this."

As David guided the car, braked, working his way down the hairpin curves, he saw the boy watching every move. "One of these days I'll teach you to drive," he said lightly. "You like cars, don't you?"

He nodded, his eyes shining. "Someday I'll save up money and buy one."

"Car . . ." David mused half aloud. "Carlo . . . how's Carlo Carducci for a name, huh? It's Italian enough. If anybody asked you, you say you're from North Beach in San Francisco. How do you like it—Carlo Carducci? You won't forget it—it's got two cars in it."

The boy shrugged his thin shoulders. "I'm used to Jerrod. But Carlo—sure. It's okay. Carlo Carducci. Sure, why not?"

After a while, as they neared Sarah's, David said, "I think we'll get along fine. I think there's a lot I can teach you. That is, if you're really going to show an interest. You see, I never had a son. Three girls. There's a lot I could teach a hard-working, sincere young man wanting to get ahead in life." He looked sideways at the newly dubbed Carlo. "Girls—they don't seem to understand the land. To ever have a true feel of it."

If Victoria was shocked when her father walked into the kitchen, Jerrod James in tow, and introduced him as though he had just discovered him and as though Jerrod really was Carlo Carducci from North Beach, she didn't have much chance to worry about it. David was in complete control. He selected a room adjacent to Li Po's in the servants' wing, saw that Carlo was settled in. He instructed Victoria to stay out of the kitchen after dinner each night—her grandmother would be giving private tutoring lessons to Carlo at that time and he didn't want any interruptions. On Saturdays and Sundays, David saw to it that Carlo was with him, usually out of the house, up on Spring Mountain or out in the vineyards; gone on errands to Napa City; or out getting a driving lesson, practicing for his driver's-license test.

She decided David didn't know she had ever had anything to do with Carlo Carducci's presence there—until the family dinner on Christmas, when David stood up and made a startling announcement to the family: "It's good to have you girls home, Anne and Delia. When you go back to New York next week, this place won't be the same without *any* girls in the house. You'll be taking Victoria with you, you know. I've got her enrolled in Miss Finch's Finishing School." He looked at Victoria. "Your grandmother is taking you shopping for warm clothes—so you won't be tempted to take my favorite sweater out again."

It was the quick-eyed Delia, used to observing with an artist's oblique eye, who had seen the sudden blanched look on young fourteen-year-old Victoria's face. Something was loaded in her father's remark about the sweater, whatever it meant. Certainly, Victoria was going to be the Donati girl with the good looks, she thought, looking at the incredibly fine bone structure, the flaming carrot-red hair, that satiny complexion, the tall, regal posture. She hated her own dumpy look, her doe eyes, her, yes, *Italian* look; though, thank God, Greg Little seemed to like it. But how long was that going to last?

Delia lifted her glass in toast, ran one finger under the neck of her tight-fitting, black turtleneck sweater. She was in her "all black" Village period—black boots, ankle-length black skirt, a simple piece of handcrafted jewelry made by Greg himself—made between sessions of practicing flute with a modern jazz group. He had come over as a blind date once when her sister Anne was still going to Juilliard. A lot had happened to all of them since then, she thought, squinting at the sherry.

Anne had dropped out—though she pretended to be going in order to keep the tuition money rolling in from their grandmother. She was crash-dieting, getting thin, she had just confessed to Delia, so that when she returned to New York she was going all out to become a top fashion model—to the point where she was going *blond*. Neither one of them was in a position to take on the responsibility for Victoria—Miss Finch's or not! But they both had to keep the money coming in, and their grandmother was watching them like a hawk, testing their reaction to this news about her favorite grandchild.

"How marvelous," Delia lied. "We'll do divine things, won't we, Anne? Show Victoria all the sights?"

"You'll adore it, sugarlump," Anne said languidly.

With Victoria gone, Sarah settled in seriously tutoring Carlo Carducci with intensive two-hour sessions at the kitchen table, six nights each week. How fast he learned! She used teaching skills she had learned some fifty years ago, but they seemed to work: he was reading, spelling, vastly improving with his math. However, he had little interest in history—until she mentioned some leader who, over great odds, had become victorious in some notable venture. Then his eyes sparked with alertness. She saw to it, too, that he ate well. So before the year passed, he had filled out, was becoming quite handsome.

If Sarah noticed that David seemed to make careful plans to have Carlo leave for the summers, with his departures scheduled shortly before Victoria was due to arrive home from New York for her vacations, she did not see any motive behind it other than David's interest in the boy and wanting to help him learn more about viticulture; since David had clearly made it known that he had searched hard to locate the right teacher for him, a noted vineyardist on a ranch near Modesto.

She did not worry about Carlo's whereabouts, for that matter; she was too happy each summer to have Victoria home again, to see her rapidly developing poise and elegance and to test how well her mind was expanding. She tried to make every moment count. And Victoria herself seemed happy those next two years to spend her summers close to home; to read aloud to her grandmother, whose eyesight was failing, but who kept complaining it was only that the doctor did not prescribe strong enough glasses for her.

Though Sarah cried when it came time for Victoria to go back to New York (she had come alone this time, her sisters being too caught up in their own worlds to come to Napa Valley), she had said, "Victoria, I'm so *proud* of you, dear! You're all any grandmother could ever want in a granddaughter."

At seventy-three, a noticeable change was coming over Sarah.

Where once she had kept huge maps of the world pinned to the kitchen wall, dotted with markers of battles won and lost, now she had made elaborate charts of the digestive tract, the muscular and nervous systems, a crude diagram of the heart, another of the kidneys. "If there's any glory to man," she fumed to David one day when he was late getting out of the house at breakfast time, "It's certainly not in anything he *does*, historically or philosophically speaking!" She took a ruler, pointed to the intricate mechanical function of the kidney. "There's more glory right there—in what makes him tick, biologically."

David hurried through a cup of coffee. "Mother, maybe you should get out more. Why don't I take you to a movie? How about a drive up to Lake County—over the Oakville grade for a new vista, a new panorama?"

"I don't have to *go* someplace for a new panorama!" she said. "If you want to do something to make me happy, why don't you buy me a *Gray's Anatomy*?" She sat down, poured out three vitamin pills from a bottle, swallowed them. "If I had known when I was young what I know now about the body . . . . David, listen to me. The greatest mysteries in life aren't just around the corner, out there next vintage or the one after that. Not in wines sleeping in oak vats in your tunnels, either. They are right here under your very nose." She went over to measure out an exact serving of bran cereal. "David, you ought to worry more about the magic going on inside your own body instead of what's happening to grapevine roots and wine aging in barrels."

When the legal summons was served on him in the second week of November, 1947, David, in a state of shock over trying to decipher the meaning of thirty pages of legalese, headed out to Napa City to turn it over to Chip Brosius. On his way down from Spring Mountain, he stopped by to discuss it first with Sarah, who maybe understood Anton's madness better than he could. He found her wrapped in a sweater, sitting in a wicker chair on the brick terrace, an ecstatic look on her wrinkled face.

"Don't sit in *that* chair!" she said, motioning frantically as he started to pull up one closer to her. "Don't you see that spider spinning its web? He's been working two straight hours. It's a veritable work of art." She eased out of her own chair. "We'll visit over here." On the way to the glass-topped table, she cupped her hands around a failing butterfly, guided it toward a gentler place to die. "What's on your mind, David? You look upset," she said, sitting down, looking up at him.

He felt the buldge of the summons inside his coat, but he had seen a certain frailty about Sarah. He'd handle it himself. "Not much, I guess. Just stopped by to say hello. Glad to see you're getting some fresh air. Oh, I won't be home for supper. I've got some business with Chip Brosius. I'll get a bite in Napa."

After Chip examined the summons, he shook his head. "I knew this was coming. Did you know Anton's been making a quick fortune? He saw what the rest of you winemakers missed, a way to get around the price freeze on bulk wine—found the loophole that there are no price controls on *bottled* wine. Sure, he slipped back into Napa Valley and went very quietly about buying up bulk wine at the lowest possible prices, often below the actual price-freeze rate. Then he and his girl friend set up this bottling operation in an old leased winery up near Calistoga. Printed up labels. Went east and secured contracts of sale. Which tells you why you haven't seen much of your brother since he got back. Because of that—and *this*, of course."

"I still don't see what this damn lawsuit has to do with me!" David stormed. "I have nothing to do with him or the winery!"

Chip rubbed his stubby square chin. "You're aware, I'm sure, of Sarah's new simplistic approach to life? Well, part of the way she's been eliminating certain complexities has been to get new trusts set up, to sign over her interests in securities, stocks and the like. These shares now in your name in the Fuller-Brunner Winery were to have been your surprise birthday present." Chip smiled, ran his fingers through his thinning hair.

"Some birthday present! Getting my first summons."

"Your involvement is this is more a technicality. You're not the real defendant—that's Phyllis, her corporation, and, in part, this new outfit from Minnesota. I see he's claiming that your shares which Sarah sold to Phyllis—which gave Phyllis her original controlling interest—weren't general shares to sell. I can handle that aspect. But I'm worried for Phyllis! I hear he's had detectives taking hideous photographs of her, drunk, waving brooms and empty whiskey bottles at children in Marblehead. He's going to try to prove she's been mentally incompetent all along and that her lawyers were in collusion, et cetera, et cetera. Look, you go back to Spring Mountain and make some more good wine. Leave this to me. Say, I heard you won more blue ribbons this year."

"Oh, a couple, I guess. On my white wines." David was still uneasy about the lawsuit. "Will I have to go to court?"

Chip shook his head. "Maybe a perfunctory presence, in case they need you for anything. I doubt it. This is going to take months. Phyllis's lawyers are filing cross-complaints. The big brewery firm's lawyers from Minnesota aren't sitting on their hands, either. Originally, as I understand it, when they bought in with Phyllis's corporation, their agreement was that they'd buy her out in 1955. They've got a big stake in this, too. You're just a little tiny grape in a big gondola on this one."

David got up, took his hat. "I think sometimes that's the story of my life."

"Isn't it the story of all our lives? How about putting me on your mailing list for a couple cases of that Chenin Blanc? I'm about out of Cabernet. Could use some sherry too."

"I'll ask Janet Cutler what we've got left. We sell out these days. If she hasn't got any regular stock left, I'll let you have some out of my own private reserve."

"If you do, consider that my fee." They walked out together. "The rumor's around that Anton's made a lot of money, but he's still apt to fall flat on his ass. If he doesn't win this case, he's finished. Really washed up."

"How's that?"

"I heard the prices on bulk wine aren't all that stable. Anton's got some big contracts with growers to meet. By the way, David, I'm glad, basically, that Sarah's not involved in this. This trial is going to be drawn out. Lately, have you noticed a certain kind of—well, *wobble* to Sarah's chin and head? I've been a little concerned about her, frankly. I wouldn't want her under any undue stress in a courtroom."

David bit his lip. He had been concerned about his mother lately. But she was so wrapped up in her charts and her vitamin pills and those herbs Li Po dished out to her that he couldn't get her to a doctor anyway. "Yes, it's a good thing *I'm* caught."

"David, you don't really have to worry about this now," Chip said. "At worst, you might have to make one appearance in court. And you might—though it's not likely—lose your birthday present."

The trial kept being postponed, due to cross-complaints being filed continuously and Phyllis's battery of lawyers knowing all the tactics for delays. During this time, the wine industry had another crisis: bulk-wine prices nosedived to fifty cents a gallon. Anton, who had contracted his at a fixed $1.20 a gallon, as well as having made extensive contracts with local growers, faced a debt of some $500,000. He was truly desperate now and had to win this case. "Pull out all the stops," he told his lawyers. "Let the mud hit the fence where it will."

By the time the case came to court in the spring of 1950, many citizens of Napa County were feeling the built-up tension. Though few actually knew Phyllis Fuller or Anton Brunner or anything about the Minnesota Brewery Company, they had taken sides. After all, even if Anton Brunner was from that bootlegging Donati family, he *was* "old Napa"; and if anything was going to spoil Napa Valley it would be big beer companies moving in. For that matter, the feeling was that *any* corporation or conglomerate ought to stay put in Boston or Minnesota or wherever they came from.

In regard to the complexities of complaints and cross-complaints as filed by defendants and plaintiff, the causes of action were heard before a judge sitting without a jury in the Superior Court of the State of California, County of Napa, beginning in April of 1950. The trial lasted for weeks. After documentary and oral evidence had been presented and the arguments were over, the judge issued his findings of fact and conclusions of law. Even before these findings were being pored over by reporters, news stories about the trial had spread across the country. Papers leaning toward sensationalism screamed headlines about Boston's rich alcoholic heiress, publishing pictures of her in drunken rages chasing children with a whiskey bottle. One paper told "all about" Anton Brunner's long-standing affair with his business associate, Katia Rudnisky, and published a photograph of a tearful Judy Rudnisky being comforted in the arms of her irate father, Roland Rudnisky—who, in his interview, stated he was filing suit for divorce, custody of his daughter, and damages against Anton Brunner.

As Chip Brosius explained the decision to David, over lunch at a quick-order café near the courthouse, the judge had obviously found discrepancies on both sides of the argument and had split his decision pretty much down the middle. Phyllis's side had won in that Anton was left with only thirty percent shareholdings; the Minnehaha Brewery Company of Minnesota had won in that they were being allowed to continue their five-year expansion program and would be able to buy up all shares in 1955, as previously agreed, at current market value —now, as approved by the court. However, the judge had decreed that a new board of directors be appointed by the court to manage the Fuller-Brunner Winery of Napa Valley during this five-year period, with all profits being duly audited by the court, and profits distributed according to the shareholders' various interests: thirty percent to Anton Brunner, thirty-eight percent to the Phyllis Fuller Corporation, twenty percent to the Minnehaha Brewery Company of Minnesota, and twelve percent to David Donati.

David took a bite of a corned-beef sandwich, frowned as he sipped a raw house wine. "What is this expansion program? Exactly what does all that mean?"

"It means that if everything keeps going on the upward trend, you might well be a millionaire in 1955! The expansion calls for increased storage capacity from 1,500,000 gallons to 7,500,000 gallons, and fermenting from 75,000 gallons to a range of 400,000 gallons." Chip added salt to his tossed salad; removed a sliced canned beet. "They're stepping up their bottling from five hundred cases a day to a possible five thousand—which would bring them up within the top ten of California wineries, productionwise." He chewed noisily a bit of lettuce. "Their stress, they *say*, will still be on 'quality premium wines at an affordable price, with nationwide distribution.'" He dabbed at his mouth with a paper napkin. "With the marketing trend on the upswing in this business, how can you lose? I've heard that scouts are out looking for land —big corporations have got the idea Napa Valley is hot."

David felt his gums smart from the astringent wine. "What about Anton? What does he get?"

"He got a ruling on his Cause of Action Number Three: he's been awarded $296,000 for back profits fraudulently, negligently and wrongfully diverted since the takeover. He won't have any say-so—but he'll sell his thirty percent of shares in 1955. That's big money! Very big." Chip wadded up his paper napkin. "Let's face it—it's just a matter of time, as I see it, before the wine boom is on again."

David was squinting his eyes, trying to comprehend the meaning of what Chip had just said, trying to convince himself that this kind of good fortune might indeed be his—around the corner, in five years. He'd been around the wine business too damn long, he thought, venturing another taste of the wine only because it was wet and got down the dry bread in his throat. One thing about getting used to drinking good wines, it made raw junk like this he had just been served undrinkable. He had been looking around, curious at how easily some of the customers in the restaurant were drinking it down as though it were water. "There's a big job of educating the public to what good wine is," he said drily. "If Fuller-Brunner is going to call that stuff they're turning out *premium* wine . . . Sure, it's a hell of a lot better than most —that is, for the price—but it's not premium in my book! Then you'd have to say Donati wine is *château*—right?"

Chip fished in his pocket for a package of cigarettes, pulled out a crumpled one, lit it, blew smoke across the wadded-up paper napkin and the dishes he had pushed out of his way. "Everybody knows you make the finest damn wines in Napa Valley. Call them anything you like." He leaned forward excitedly. "Don't you see what this might mean to you—to all of us who love fine wines? With the money you make when you sell your twelve hundred shares, you can expand on Spring Mountain. With *your* expertise, hell, you could put the Donati name on the international map!"

David put his money on the table on top of the bill, counted out some change for a tip. "A lot can happen between now and 1955. There's one thing you learn fast in this business, Chip. You take one year at a time." When they got out on the sidewalk, David squinted against a bright sunlight. "By the way, how much is this trial going to cost me?"

"Do you want to pay me a flat fee by the hour or do you want me to get on the top of your mailing list and get a case of your favorite top reserve wine each year for the next five years?"

"Which one suits you best?"

"I'm no damn fool. The wine—any day."

Though Sarah had, from time to time, taken note of the various newspaper accounts of the trial, she didn't have much interest these days in injunctions, exemplary damages, fiduciary duties, methods of liquidation, diversions of assets, allocations of damages, losses of profits due to volatile acidity and sloppy winemaking techniques. Where, at one time, she might have tuned in with a keen ear on conversations between David and Chip Brosius, might have even had a comment to make about "high price–earnings ratio" of stocks in a glamorous industry such as the wine industry, now she tried to keep her mind free of any subject with a barbed edge to it. She was striving to find a new kind of mind power, to decipher a different relativity and ratio of what in life was a true earning. And her only interest in wines these days was in being sure she drank two glasses daily of any reasonably good *red* wine. She had read that red wine dilated the blood vessels, helped circulation. It was no more and no less important to her than any other ingredient in her new formula for a sense of well-being.

24

In 1950, when Victoria returned to Napa Valley, having finished her schooling at Miss Finch's, she emphatically announced that she was not going back east to college but planned to enroll in the fall at the University of California at Davis. David drove her up to Spring Mountain to discuss the matter.

It was a balmy day in early June, a time of the year when a vineyardist could relax somewhat and wait for the stretch of the growing season until the busy crush in the fall. The stone veranda was still bathed in morning sunshine, so David suggested that they sit there in the wrought-iron chairs he had borrowed from Sarah's brick terrace, the old wicker chairs having fallen apart years ago. But before Victoria took a chair, she leaned against the thick redwood post where the ancient wisteria vine as thick as a tree trunk had gnarled and twisted itself around it. Her auburn hair was cut shoulder length now and fell in loose natural waves around her classically lovely face with its clear porcelain skin. David found himself staring at her, wondering where she had inherited that particular combination of looks, and how genes came down through generations—making some ugly, some average-looking, and some, like Victoria, strikingly beautiful.

They did not speak at first. The gentle breeze blew her hair across one cheek, her hands rested lightly against the redwood post. After a moment, she turned from staring out at the vineyards, at the view of Howell Mountain across the way, her eyes alive with excitement and looking more lavender now than their actual blue. "I didn't know how much I loved this place," she said in a soft, husky voice. "How much I've missed Spring Mountain."

"It gets to you. It grows on you," David said, sitting down, watching her move gracefully to take a chair opposite him, spreading the folds of her khaki cotton dress smoothly about her. She was taller than he had remembered—had long legs, like the Donati side of the family.

"How're your sisters? I don't hear from them much."

"Doesn't Grandmother share their letters with you? I know they write to her periodically."

"Sure they do—every time they want money. I get a birthday card, usually. Oh, now and then a note. Not much."

"Anne's picture was on the cover of *Vogue* last month. You mean she didn't send a copy?" Victoria closed her eyes a moment. "Anne is pretty caught up in her modeling. They're sending her on more exclusive assignments all the time. She's hoping to get to go to Europe next, all expenses paid."

"Modeling—what kind of profession is that? After all that money spent on her education to be a musician." David took out his pipe, lit it.

"It pays a lot of money. She seems to like posing in front of cameras, pampering herself. And Delia—she's gone back to calling herself Dede again, likes that signature on her paintings. She's got an exhibit coming up in a small gallery on Madison Avenue. She works hard. I'm closer to Dede than to Anne."

"She's doing okay, then? You think she's any good? This painting business—I don't know much about art."

"I like what she's doing now, since she quit trying to be Cézanne reincarnated. Since she's painting *people*, Dede style, she's good." Victoria looked at her father. There wasn't any way she could tell him the rest about Dede—that she had just gone through a serious depression, having broken up with her fourth lover since she had been back in New York; that the money Dede received from her grandmother she used to pay a psychiatrist, who had helped bring her around to where she could function again and was trying to help her gain self-esteem, break her habit of selecting men who were losers, who ended up making Dede feel that *she* was the failure. She loved her sister Dede very much. In contrast, she could barely tolerate Anne, who looked as if she was always just ready to kiss herself in the mirror—and, if Victoria's suspicions were right, looked as if she took something pretty heavy to keep that droopy-lid look the photographers were so anxious to photograph for magazine covers.

David was puffing quick, staccato puffs on his pipe, gazing out at the vineyards. "The only art I know about, I guess, is winemaking." He was squinting, as if trying to get a perspective, form an invisible frame around some unique vision of his own, out in that new vineyard of recently grafted-on Chardonnays. "So you've made up your mind to go to Davis this fall, eh? Any special reason?"

Victoria didn't hesitate. She sat up, her eyes shining. "I plan to study oenology. Become a winemaker—hopefully, one as good as you. I'd like to become your partner, here on Spring Mountain. If you ever get tired, maybe I'd take it over."

David clamped his teeth down on the pipe stem. He let smoke drift across his face, working across the weathered lines. At fifty-four, he was still handsome in a rugged, angular way. "Women aren't winemakers! What gave you that idea?"

"Why couldn't I be one? What does being a woman have to do with it?"

"It's hard work, for one thing. It's not something esoteric, some nice little glamorous theory." He pulled his legs up, leaned over, let his hands dangle loosely between his knees. The pipe, smoked down now, was still cupped in his hands. "I've been hearing a lot lately about wine being a 'glamour' industry. I guess I've never seen much of that in it."

"I know that, Dad. I've grown up around it." Her voice reflected her growing excitement. "But that's just it—I'm not a novice as some might be. Some girl just looking for something different to attract attention to herself. I've met girls like that. Spring Mountain, grapes, the crush—they're all part of my life. In my blood. And I'm strong! I'm not one of these weakling feminine characters I've seen so much of at Miss Finch's—a woman expecting some handsome man to come along and take care of her for the rest of her life. I'm smart. I'm—I'm different. I really am different!"

He tapped the ashes out of his pipe. "You're crazy if you want to be a winemaker. Look, I don't really think I like the idea, Victoria. I mean it. I've been caught up in this up-and-down profession all my life. I don't think I ever had a choice. But you—hell, you could do anything in life. We've got money now. We're not rich, but we're comfortable. I might, just might, be coming into some money in a few years. Your grandmother thinks you hung the moon, and anythings she's got, most likely, is going to be yours—so Chip Brosius tells me, and he knows. What I'm trying to tell you is, you can study any profession, travel, be anything you want to be. So don't throw that opportunity away." He stuffed his pipe into his pocket, stood up. "I wonder what I would have done if I had been in your shoes when I was eighteen years old."

She got up, hugged one of his arms. "You would have done the same thing. Winemaking, those vineyards out there, are in your blood, the same as mine!"

"Okay—come on and take a look at what we've got set up around here in the old house these days. I run the Donati Spring Mountain winery out of here now. It's not exactly the way you might remember it. There's a whole new shipment ready to go out—watch your step getting around those cases in the hallway. The truck to pick them up ought to be around pretty soon now."

When they entered the main office—the room that had once been the parlor—Janet Cutler said, "Carlo was here a few minutes ago. Asked me to give you these reports he'd finished."

David looked up sharply. "I thought he had left already. I thought he was leaving town yesterday."

"His car broke down, he told me. Had to get some new hoses, some repair work on the radiator."

Victoria was examining new labels designed with a drawing of the stone house with its tower and marvelous graphic letters "DONATI WINERY," with "Spring Mountain—Napa Valley" and "Since 1895" printed below. "These labels are the best I've seen. Who did them?" she asked, as though she weren't at all interested in the name of Carlo Carducci.

"Just a minute," David said, going over the profit-and-loss sheets Carlo had figured out. He handed them back to Janet. "Put these in my personal file over there. I want to go over them with Carlo when he gets back."

Victoria put the labels down, propped her elbows on the makeshift counter, tried to look nonchalant. "Where is Carlo going *this* summer?"

David slammed the file cabinet shut. "Summer school—in Stockton. He has a cousin down there. I guess they're good friends. He's taking some courses. Doesn't seem to want a degree, or I'd pay his way through college. He says he just wants to know certain things. He's been going every summer. Cramming in all the hours he can work off. A hard worker."

"Must be a lot of help to you," she said evenly as David guided her back to the kitchen, where he had set up a surprisingly elaborate and efficient laboratory.

"Yes, he is. I'm turning over my vineyard management to him this fall. He doesn't know it yet. The Fuller-Brunner Winery—those new guys from Minnesota lured my man Henry Ried away. You can't argue with the money they paid him. Henry's not much for loyalty. I figure Carlo will stick by me for a long time."

He poured out samplings for Victoria. "Okay—if you're going to be a winemaker, let's see what kind of natural nose you've got. Here are five blendings. One is a good one. There's something wrong with the other four. Let me see what your nose tells you . . ."

He was going over the formula he used for adding yeasts to fermentations, had just explained to Victoria that he preferred a low ratio, using only fifty to sixty parts per million, when a huge van pulled up.

Janet Cutler hurried in. "That centrifuge you ordered—it's here. Earlier than you expected."

"Look, why don't you take my car and go on back home," David said to Victoria, handing the keys to her. "It's going to take most of the day to get this thing installed. Don't wait dinner for me, either. I've got a hunch it will be eight or nine o'clock tonight before I'm finished. I'll give you a ring if I need a ride down the mountain."

When Victoria pulled into the parking area at the back of Sarah's house, Carlo Carducci came strolling out of the garage, wiping his hands free of grease. When he saw her sliding out from behind the wheel, he stopped, stood there looking at her, his blue eyes behind thick black eyelashes looking as if they were starting with her feet and working slowly up to her face. It had been four years since she had seen him. Her father had done his job well. Victoria was not prepared for the sight of the twenty-year-old Carlo—tall, sinewy, his skin a golden bronze, the thin face she had remembered as being gaunt, hollow-eyed, now one of the most handsome she had ever seen. She worked her fingers around the key ring, fussed with getting them inside her purse, taking them out again.

He was standing next to her, one foot propped up on the rear bumper of the car, his right arm resting across the sloping top of the 1940 Lincoln Zephyr sedan that Sarah had given to David when David had turned over his old Chrysler to Carlo. His voice was rich, husky-sounding. "I knew there was a reason my car decided to break down on me," he said, his eyes boring into hers. He shoved the oil-soaked rag into the back pocket of his jeans. "You've grown up. A woman now." He seemed to be laughing at her.

"You've matured a little yourself." A rush of heat spread through her entire body as she felt him move imperceptibly closer, could practically feel his breath. At Miss Finch's she had met her share of young proper escorts. Through Dede she had met an assortment of Greenwich Village types—including one Frenchman who insisted she had stepped out of a Renoir and he must paint her. She had learned, by now, the limits of back-seat petting. She had indulged quite heavily in it, in fact, until a lacrosse player from Harvard had become infuriated with her when she led him on and then stopped him just short. He had slammed her roughly back in the corner of the car, forced her hands to form a cup, and when he was through, when she was appalled at the dripping mess between her fingers, rearranged himself, then laughed a cruel, mocking laugh. "Keep it, bitch! I'll do you the courtesy of driving you home." She had cried all the way back to the Village, where she had been spending the weekend with Dede. Though he had not forced himself inside her, she felt abused, humiliated as she had never imagined a woman could be. When she had got inside, had rushed into the bathroom to wash her hands, she had nearly scrubbed them raw; but even so, she could feel that driving pressure in the palms of her hands, his wrists gripping hers together with such binding grips that she had cried out in pain as he himself emitted his own animalistic groans.

"Why do you want to get away from me?" Carlo was asking softly. "Why won't you look at me?"

She stepped away from the car door, looked at him defiantly. "I'm not trying to get away from you. I'm looking at you!" She felt the color rise up her neck, into her cheeks.

"Your father doesn't trust me with you. Or you with me. I've kept track of you through your grandmother. She's read all your letters to me. She showed me the pictures you sent home and the ones they took here every summer. But pictures don't do you justice. They don't catch the color of your eyes. They don't show you blushing."

"You're laughing at me. I don't appreciate being laughed at." She started toward the back door.

"Don't get mad, when it's been four years—when I've waited four years to see you face to face." He was behind her, coming up the back steps.

She stopped at the top one, looked back down at him, only to have him step one step closer to her.

"I live here, too," he said softly, as though guessing what she was about to say. "My room is next to Li Po's. I'm on my way to get my suitcase."

"Where's Grandmother?" she asked stepping into the huge kitchen, looking over at the wall plastered with charts.

"A neighbor took her into Napa City—dropped Li Po off at his cousin's. No one's here but us."

She put her purse on the table, was just turning, when he was sliding his hands around her waist, pulling her toward him. She heard the kitchen clock sounding out its rhythmic ticks, slow motion, behind her own racing heart. A ketchup bottle, a mustard jar, a tea kettle on the back of the old enormous kitchen range caught her eye, seemed to tilt, as his face was bearing down on hers. "It's not right—we shouldn't—Daddy . . ."

His lips shushed her. When he lifted his head again he looked into her eyes, his own glazed with desire, "We've both waited too long. It's

542

our only chance. He knows—he senses that we love each other. It's why he's kept us apart. But he can't prevent what was meant to happen."

She tried to pull free, felt him guiding her with his knees, edging her across the kitchen toward his own room just off it. "It's not—loyal to him," she managed. "After what he's done for you . . ."

"It hasn't anything to do with that," Carlo was mumbling against her ear. Then he was kissing her again. "When two people love each other . . ." He opened the door, pulled her inside, closed it, hands deftly working the buttons on her cotton dress.

"I didn't say I love you! That's audacious—you're—"

"You cannot lie to me. Don't talk. We have so little time. I have to be gone before he gets back. I won't see you again all summer. Unless you get away—come to Stockton, meet me someplace . . . . I love you, Victoria. . . . Don't—don't push my hands away. Let this happen."

When it was over, when she was lying there reluctant to let him go, her head curled in under his chin, one of his bare legs wrapped around her, she traced her finger across the line of his chin, his lips, down his nose. "Did you know that this bed has a hollow place in the middle? Did you know it's lumpy?"

"It is the most wonderful bed in the world." He pulled away from her, draped a towel about his waist, went into the bathroom. When he came out he stood looking down at her. "Come on—you'd better get up and dressed. They might come back. Your grandmother left early." He sat down on the edge of the bed, reached over, kissed her. "I love you. You know that now. You can never escape that fact." He put his hand under her chin, made her look at him. "You are going to be my wife one of these days."

"I didn't say I would *marry* you." She threw her legs over the side of the bed, got up, gathered her scattered clothes, went into the bathroom and closed the door behind her. When she came out, her hair was combed, she was fully dressed. "Your bathroom's dirty. Don't you ever clean it?"

He was hitching his pants, buckling his belt, stuffing in his shirttail. "Li Po's supposed to tend to that. I'm the vineyard manager around here. Not a latrine lackey."

"Neither is Li Po," she said stiffly.

Carlo took her a little roughly by the upper arms. "Say, what is this? What's all this about dirty bathrooms—what are you trying to say, huh?"

Victoria was looking about, saw a photograph of a dark-haired Spanish-looking girl in a small gold frame on his dresser. "Who's that? Do you bring her here, too?" She pulled away from him, lurched toward the door.

His hand closed around hers on the doorknob; he pulled her back and made her face him. "I don't understand you. I told you I love you! I've been waiting for this since the first time you, well, you let me know when you hid me in the bunkhouse—the way you used to sit next to me with the fifth-grade reader, accidentally brushing against me." He was smiling at her with a taunting look. "I knew better then than to touch you. I didn't know *much* then, but I knew I had to wait. That the time would come. I knew then that you were the girl I would love—the girl I wanted to marry someday."

"You didn't answer me—who is *she?*"

Carlo sighed. "Okay—that's Blanca. A girl I know. Lives in Yountville. Don't tell me that all this time you haven't been with anybody?"

"Not all the way. Not like now."

"I know—I could tell. I didn't mean all the way—I meant, with other men. Haven't you been tempted even?"

She pushed her hair off her face, drew away from him. "Yes . . . not anyone really, though. Not anyone whose picture I put in a frame on my dresser!"

"Good—you're jealous. I'm glad."

"You're arrogant!" This time she got out of his room, went into the kitchen, opened the refrigerator door and took out a pitcher of orange juice. "You really have a lot of nerve, Carlo Carducci—*Jerrod James.*"

He crossed his arms over his chest, leaned back against the door facing. "Ah . . . now I'm beginning to understand. 'Jerrod'— 'Stay in your place, Mr. Wetback'—is that what you're telling me?"

She slammed the refrigerator door, took a long sip of the orange juice. "I didn't say that." Before she had finished the juice, she felt tears flooding her eyes. She didn't know why she should be crying. She loved him—she hated him. She was glad she had gone in there with him —that now she knew what it was like after all these years—yet she wished she had never gone! She had waited for him; why hadn't he waited for her? What did that dark, sloe-eyed-looking girl with the full mouth give him? Mean to him? Had *she* been the first? She put the glass down. "How often do you see Blanca? What does *she* mean to you?" She was standing near the back stairs now. "She's a Mexican, isn't she?"

544

"Yes, she is. She slipped across the border, was lucky not to get sent back. Does that answer your question?"

"I think so."

He stormed across the room, grabbed her arm just as she had started up the back steps. "Don't do this, Victoria Donati! Don't ruin something very special between us. I'm not ashamed of being me, and I don't give you any extra points because you were born with a silver spoon in your mouth. That's not why I love you. I love you in spite of that. I saw in you a fight, a spirit. You would be a survivor, silver spoon or not. Just as I've been. We would love each other no matter what the circumstances were. It has nothing to do with Blanca."

"You are hurting my arm," Victoria said through stiff lips. "Let go of me! Go on to your Blanca—aren't you supposed to be in Stockton?"

He stood back then, his lips tight with anger. "Yes—I'm supposed to be in Stockton. I might stay in Stockton!"

Victoria hurried up the steps, ran down the hallway to her bedroom. She heard the back door slam, the old Chrysler back out of the garage, the wheels spin on the loose gravel. She ran to the window, tried to shout down through the screen, "Why don't you get a muffler put on that rattletrap?"

But he had gone from sight. She fell across her bed, hot tears easing down her face. She wasn't sure why she had been so angry, why she had treated him that way. She really wasn't sure of anything right now. . . .

During the next four years, Victoria threw herself into her studies at Davis. When she was home, she avoided Carlo; or, if she found herself in his presence, she treated him as though he were some casual acquaintance, if not, indeed, the hired foreman for the vineyards owned by her father—owned, too, by herself, she had recently discovered from Chip Brosius, who had outlined what her grandmother, wanting to avoid any excess inheritance taxes when she died, was signing over to her. If she was not working side by side with her father in the Spring Mountain Winery laboratory she was directly pitching in during the crush—adding yeast, learning first hand to pump over, to punch the cap down, to do the topping, to help with racking, fining, and the limited centrifuging David allowed with his wines.

And when she was at home, she spent as much time as possible with her grandmother. In January of 1954 Sarah turned eighty. At her birthday dinner—to which Victoria made a special trip to Napa Valley to attend—Sarah stood up, her snow-white hair showing a little too much blue from a rinse Myrna's Beauty Shop had put on. She lifted her glass of champagne, her hand trembling, the cords of blue veins working back and forth on the back of her hand. "*I* would like to propose a toast—now that you have all had your say," she said, her voice still steady, only now and then reedlike. "All my life I've been hearing toasts for one reason or another. We toast each other. We toast health and happiness. We toast new babies. We toast anniversaries. We toast *next* vintage, *this* vintage. We toast blue ribbons, and this or that medal. I toast *life!* Pure unadulterated life—in all its glory." She sipped the champagne, then put her glass down. "Would someone please bring a glass of red wine to me? I have one other toast." When she was handed a glass of Cabernet, she lifted it, this time staying in her chair. She looked down the table at Victoria. "This one is to my granddaughter. This one is to hoping the man who will be her true love will hurry and come along. Here's to *love*—the love of Victoria's life."

The back door slammed at that moment, with even David looking up, lifting an eyebrow and saying, "I guess the door slipped out of Carlo's hand. Or else he's got another hot date tonight in Yountville."

"Grandmother, if you aren't going to finish your champagne, I think I'll take that glass," Victoria said quickly, and with that she began her own round of toasts, ending up being very drunk indeed.

Carlo drove faster than the speed limit on his way down the main county road toward Candido's place in Yountville, where Blanca worked: the place he had gone that first time, on his sixteenth birthday, to pay Candido the ten-dollar going rate to be taught how. He had slapped the bill down on the counter, looking into Candido's broad, laughing face, and heard Candido's voice boom out across the room: "Hey, look what we got here. Come here, Socorro—this young man wants to be taught how to be top toreador! Take him back to a room and give him his first lesson." Men hunched over bottles of beer, some dancing in the middle of the darkened cramped room, joined Rod Sánchez's cheer, "*Venga el toreador! Olé! El toreador!*"

He had pretended a confidence he hadn't felt. It had been on his third trip to Candido's (he made it a practice, every Saturday night, after he received his pay check from David) that he had asked for Blanca, the new shy girl, instead of the older, bored Socorro. Actually, Carlo liked going to Candido's for more than his midnight hour out back. He missed his mother, the family in Colima. From the moment he stepped inside Candido's he spoke only Spanish. He played poker with the men, drank beer, danced—he liked the dancing, letting his body move to the liquid rhythm, his legs limber, his whole body tuning up for the ritual which he would begin at midnight. There was a reason for that hour. Candido closed his place at twelve o'clock sharp on Saturday nights. It was up to the girls to kick out the men who went in last. He made sure the ten dollars had crossed the counter. If Blanca wanted Carlo to spend the night with her, that was her business, he would tell Carlo, giving him a wink. "Sundays my girls get a holiday. Me, I take my family to Mass."

Carlo was not sure that he understood his own feelings for Blanca. In some ways, he often thought, he probably had some of the same confusions about her that Victoria had about him. A part of him could not accept the fact that Blanca was what she was. Yet, another knew the other Blanca, who had been abandoned when she was eleven years old and had managed to survive. There were times when she wound her thin arms around his neck, clung to him and wept as though she were a small, frightened child. He would hold her, spend the night with her, letting her sleep curled up against him as though he were protecting her from the world. Sometimes, on Sundays, he would stay there with her in the room where so many had made their paid-for entrances and exists in routine order. She would pretend that she was his wife. "Let me serve breakfast to you in bed," she would say, hurrying about, slipping into Candido's restaurant and bringing out orange juice, toast, coffee. Sometimes she would place the palms of her hands flat against his chest. "Carlo, if you knew me another way, if I wasn't one of Candido's girls, would you *like* me? Really like me? Am I the kind of girl you would marry?"

He never told her she was or she wasn't. He would try to make her smile, laugh again. He could never tell her that he was in love with Victoria Donati. That he wanted to marry *her*—maybe, yes, for all she stood for, but more than that. Yes, he knew that he was hopelessly in love with her. She was like the disease of anemia that Sarah would tell him about, pointing to one of her charts—his red blood cells of feeling were eaten up by the white cells of a stronger force.

"If you don't get plenty of iron, do the right things, you may end up with anemia, as I have," the old woman was always preaching to him, forcing molasses and vitamin pills on him.

Maybe he should find some kind of medicine to get Victoria Donati cleaned out of his system once and for all. Maybe he should face the glaring light of reality: he *was* an interloper. He was half Mexican. A part of him could dream about being like Jamison Wiley James himself, lord of the manor, the big landowner living in a house with pillars or a big stone mansion with a tower; another side pulled him back to Blanca: "You belong there, Jerrod—don't forget where you really belong."

On this particular January night, when he had been so sure he would be invited to join the family at the birthday celebration (they knew how much he loved "Miss Sarah," as she had asked him to call her), he had bought a present for her and had made up his mind he would do everything right at the big fancy dining-room table; would not make one mistake. And he had also been practicing what he would say to Victoria—how he would let her know that he had changed, had learned, was smart in his own way. Could be as fine a gentleman as any in Napa Valley. When he had not been asked, and when he had heard their laughter, the rounds of toasts, he had come into the kitchen, sat with Li Po, seething with hurt and rejection. He'd find Blanca all right. Maybe tonight he'd ask Blanca to move in with him! They'd rent a place somewhere. Not that he'd *marry* her, but he'd pay the rent. Maybe he'd get her to stop going to Candido's. She loved him enough to do anything for him—he knew that. Sure, he didn't have to hang around in the servants' quarters next door to a Chinaman hoping for a few crumbs of attention. Someday Victoria would come running with her arms open, saying she loved him. . . . Who was he trying to fool? He had had it with her. And hadn't Blanca said, the last Saturday night, "If you love me, Carlo, I would show you how good I am inside. I am not bad like people think because I work for Candido. A part of me never gets touched by anybody. Maybe you. . . .You can touch me. You can hold me, my whole heart, body and soul, like a robin's egg in your hand. You can help me hatch out like a nice, pretty little bird or you can squish me, break me all to pieces."

That night at Candido's, Carlo drank much more beer than he ever had before. And when he saw a burly, mean-looking Mexican (one of the new wetbacks coming in ahead of the season to try to find steady work, the word being out that there was still a shortage of good labor about in Napa Valley) putting his hands all over Blanca when he had paid for his dance with her (Candido's policy was a man paid a dollar to dance; if he liked the dance and wanted the other, he could put the rest of the money on the counter), Carlo started a barroom brawl. Beer bottles were thrown, chairs hurled across the room, tables turned upside down, and finally the sheriff was called. Were it not for Blanca, Carlo would have been in the group rounded up and thrown into jail for the night. She took him down dark back streets in the tiny town, into the crowded house where she rented a room. She washed off his bruises, his bloodied nose.

On Sunday, when Carlo washed down aspirin with black coffee, he looked at Blanca and said in a thick voice like lead, "Get your things. I'm taking you out of here. I'm renting us a place."

She stood as though the blood had drained from her body. "Where is that, Carlo? What place?"

"We'll find a place. Get your things. I've got my new car. We'll go look until we find something."

"In Yountville?"

"No. Maybe St. Helena—Calistoga, if we have to. Don't worry. I'll find something."

That afternoon, at three o'clock, Carlo drove up behind Sarah's huge house, told Blanca to wait for him in the car. Then he went into his room, threw his things into a suitcase, went into the kitchen looking for extra paper sacks to hold a few things that wouldn't fit in—his books, papers, some winter clothes.

Victoria was standing at the foot of the back stairs. "Where are *you* going?"

"I've rented a house. On Dowdell Lane in St. Helena."

"Why? Why are you leaving?"

"Because a certain person loves me very much and and needs somebody to look after her. Any objections, *Miss* Donati?"

"I wish—please, I wish you wouldn't," she said, her voice strained. "Last night I was awake most of the night. I—Carlo, I've tried to convince myself I don't love you. But—I do love you! Please, don't move in with *her*."

He found two shopping bags in the pantry, brought them out, went into his room. She followed, leaned against the door. She was wearing a tweed skirt, a pale-beige sweater. This was her last semester at Davis. She would be twenty-two years old in a few weeks. A softer womanly look graced her face.

"What happened to you, Carlo? You're getting a black eye. Have you been in a fight?"

He pushed one knee on top of his bulging suitcase, managed to get the strap pulled around it. Then he started poking shirts, neckties, socks down into one of the shopping bags. "Yeah—a barroom brawl. With a lot of *Mexicans*! Any more questions?"

"You didn't answer the other ones. Does it matter to you what I just told you—that I love you, Carlo?"

He folded the sleeves of an old topcoat in, piled it on top of the suitcase. Then he stood, put his hands on his hips, narrowed his eyes. "It would have mattered. I've loved you more than you'll ever be loved by any man. As long as you live." He went in, looked into the bathroom to see if he had left anything, came out with a hairbrush. "The bathroom's still dirty," he said, a smile hanging on the corner of his mouth. "Sorry about that."

Victoria went to him, tried to force him to put his arms around her waist. "Don't do this, Carlo. Believe me, last night I *knew*. I had made up my mind to tell you today."

He pulled her arms off his waist. "Today's too late."

"Why? *why*, Carlo?"

"Because it's not my day to kill baby robins—something you don't know anything about." He had his arms loaded now and pushed past her, hurrying before he could lose his nerve. Every muscle ached to throw down everything and crush her to him.

She stepped back out of his way. Red splotches of hurt, of anger, were gathering force inside Victoria now. She had never dreamed that he would say no to her, that *he* would be the one to walk out.

"Go on, then! Go to your own kind!"

He did not look back. He had, only three weeks before, bought his first brand-new car, a 1954 Studebaker coupe, the only maroon-colored one on the lot. He went to the back, opened the trunk, tossed in the shopping bags, worked the suitcase into place, slammed down the lid. Blanca was sitting with one leg drawn up under her, her eyes wide, in awe that Carlo knew someone who lived in such a magnificent house, much less had lived in it himself. Her own clothes were in an open cardboard box on the back seat. A royal-blue satin dress Candido had furnished was on top. A worn-down high heel jutted up out of one corner. Carlo didn't look at her when he slid his long legs in behind the wheel, turned the key in the ignition.

"Please don't get your feet on the upholstery of my new car—do you mind?" he said through tight, angry lips.

Blanca quickly placed both feet on the black rubber mat. "It's such a beautiful new car. I'm sorry. Oh, Carlo, we're going to have such a beautiful new life together. Just you wait. You won't be sorry. I promise you, you won't be sorry."

He did not answer. Though a part of him wanted to jam his foot to the floorboard, he shifted gears slowly, being as careful with his new car as always, driving out past the Corinthian pillars, past the brick terrace where he could see "Miss Sarah" wrapped in a blanket, getting her afternoon sunshine. He hadn't told her goodbye. But he would be working around in the vineyards. He'd explain to her after Victoria had gone back to Davis.

"Who's that?" Blanca asked, pointing toward Sarah.

"Don't point," he said stiffly. In a moment, when they were out of sight, he said quietly, "That woman you saw, she's a lady. A very fine old lady who taught me how to study." A bitter line crossed his face. "I used to think I was a pretty good student."

"I never got to go to school."

"Look, Blanca, do you mind if we don't talk right now? Would you, huh? I'm trying to get used to this."

"It was your idea."

"I *said*, no talking right now. Okay?"

She sucked in her bottom lip, bit back tears. "Sure—sure, Carlo. Anything you say."

Sarah had asked Victoria to come down and help her in off the brick terrace at precisely four o'clock. By that time, Victoria had dried her tears. If Carlo was like that, let him go! Let water seek its own level, she told herself, trying to push down a sick feeling, near active nausea, in her stomach.

When she came up to Sarah's chair, she found her grandmother sitting with a magnifying glass in her hand, trying to decipher the fine print on a label of a new brand of vitamins she had bought. A breeze whipping down off the Mayacamas range that blew Victoria's thick red hair off her face had turned Sarah's thin wisps of silvery-white hair with its blue tint in curls around her wizened face. A giant wave of tenderness swept over Victoria. She wanted to envelop this shrunken form and hold her grandmother as she might a small child. How truly she loved her! How well she knew her—yet how little she knew her.

She sat down by her, reached out and gently touched Sarah's hand. "Could I read anything for you? Is that magnifying glass any stronger than the last one?"

For a moment, Sarah's fingers clasped hers tightly, as though drawing strength from them. "My eyesight seems to be getting better lately. The vitamins, I'm sure. Or some say people my age get a second vision. Can thread needles." She pulled the blanket closer about her thin shoulders. "Aren't we lucky to be in Napa Valley, to have this lovely warm sunshine in January? The radio says it might rain tonight." She let Victoria help her up out of the chair, stood, then purposely stamped her feet, stirring up circulation. "I was looking out there at the vineyards in dormancy. How naked and sticklike they look." She held tightly to Victoria's arm as they made their way across the uneven brick terrace toward the front door. "Funny, though, it depresses me more right after the crush is over, when the leaves are still hanging there waiting for the first frost. I find myself *waiting* for it—waiting to practically hear those leaves start falling."

Victoria held the door opened wide, continued holding onto her grandmother firmly as they crossed the black-and-white marble-tiled floor.

"I don't like waiting for anything these days!" Sarah fussed, heading back to the kitchen for her four-o'clock vitamins and her regular herbal tea. "All my life I think I've hated waiting. Your grandfather used to tell me that patience was a must in life. A cardinal must. Maybe he was right. But I've lost mine lately."

In the kitchen, she insisted that Victoria join her for tea. Li Po shuffled out, his back bent over in a constant stooped way now, his face like ancient yellowed parchment.

"Li Po, are you burning that incense again? Is that what I smell? It's hard to tell. My nose has been stopped up lately."

"Yes, madam. Every day. Always the same time. Did you forget?" He shuffled into his room, gently closed the door.

Sarah was peering at Victoria more closely. "I won't hold up my magnifying glass, but I could swear you've been crying, young lady. Anything wrong? Tell your grandmother."

Victoria quickly sipped her tea. Finally she looked at Sarah. "I guess—oh, I was feeling a little lost maybe. Wondering what life is going to hold for me. I—I know I'll be a winemaker. I'm trained. Trained well. And everyone says that though the market is not taking any giant leaps and bounds yet, there's a steady increase. The future looks good."

"Your father and I were talking about that last week," Sarah said, more in the tone of voice she had had some ten or fifteen years ago when she was more interested in things in the world at large. "He was trying to explain to me this financing the Bank of America will give him on his wine inventory—he's thinking about expansion. And when David Donati starts getting bigger ideas, it must be safe territory. David was never adventuresome like Anton—like his father, for that matter. He's too conservative sometimes for his own good. *Too* patient."

"Maybe that's why he's such an excellent winemaker," Victoria said.

"Back to you, young lady!" Sarah snapped. "You're too young to be worried over what's out there waiting for you—a beautiful girl such as yourself. Maybe you should take a nice trip, maybe a boat cruise to meet some nice young gentlemen. Napa Valley doesn't seem to have that many around or they'd be here courting you."

"I haven't exactly encouraged anyone." Victoria took a deep breath, achingly sick over having lost Carlo, having let false pride, false reasons, keep her from him. She was afraid, by Sarah's look, that she had upset her. She turned purposely. "But at least I have the goal of becoming a fine winemaker. The first *woman* winemaker in Napa Valley, perhaps."

Sarah smiled, pushed herself up from the table. "Then you'll never be without a goal." She laughed drily. "Every winemaker I've ever known has always been looking ahead for that next perfect vintage. You'll always have that."

25

That harvest of 1954, David and Victoria signed legal papers drawn up by Chip Brosius (who was wearing a neck brace because he had fallen on the golf course and slipped a vertebra) giving Victoria half interest in the Spring Mountain Winery. They had just finished picking the Rieslings, and there was a lull before the Cabernets and the Pinot Noirs would be ready. David had poured a choice bottle of late-harvest Riesling, one with a true *Botrytis cinerea*; that one year with late rains and a period of rare low humidity, he had made a very small amount of rich sweet wine from the "noble mold."

"A special wine for a special occasion," he said, asking her to join him out on the stone veranda to escape the noise from labeling going on in the old dining room. They sat down in the wrought-iron chairs, stared out in silence a moment.

"Next year I guess I'm supposed to come into some extra money when they sell the Fuller-Brunner Winery to that brewery company from Minnesota," David said. "I've been thinking that maybe we should expand—maybe with a long-range program of around seventy-five thousand cases a year. That would make us a middle-sized winery compared with the big-time operations going down in the valley these days. I wanted to know your thinking about it—what methods you do or don't approve of. I've been watching you. You seem to have learned some new ideas at Davis that Amerine hadn't come up with when I was there. You see, I want you to understand that though I'm a bit stuffy at times about how I want things done, I'm not closed-minded about listening to new techniques, as long as they make good practical sense."

Victoria was wearing a lab coat, had pulled her red hair back with a rubber band to keep it out of her way. She turned her glass around, studied the rich golden-colored wine. "How much can we spend? This money—will it be a lot? I asked because I was hoping we could invest in a new kind of dejuicing equipment and some stainless steel." She waved her hand. "I know what you think about oak, and I agree. But I would like to discuss a method of using stainless steel *and* oak with the Chardonnays. I think Spring Mountain is an appellation of its own. Our whites particularly could be our trademark. Of course, you've built a name for your Cabernets. I wouldn't want to take anything away that you've built up. But I think the wine tastes of consumers are going to change and I'd like to see us ready for it."

"Makes sense. As to how much money I'll have, I own twelve hundred shares. Chip was saying they're already talking around a thousand a share—it might go as high as fourteen hundred a share."

Victoria looked at him with disbelief. "You'd be rich! That's a huge amount of money."

"I don't think anyone ever thought those shares would be worth much. When Anton sold them to Mother, I'm sure *he* didn't. But Anton stands to make just about three times what I'll make. He owns thirty percent."

"Where is Uncle Anton these days? What will he do with all that money? Start up another winery, do you suppose?"

David shook his head. "I've quit trying to guess what Anton will do in life. But I hear from Chip that he's planning to leave Napa Valley. Chip has worked with him for years. He knows his business a lot more than I do. It seems Anton thinks Napa Valley has given him a kick in the teeth. He thought he should have received controlling interest. The whole ball of wax."

"But three million dollars—that's so much money!"

"I guess that to Anton, who had set his aim on bigger numbers, it seemed like a drop in the bucket. Anton's always thought bigger than the rest of us. Thought he'd be king of the mountain around here, big cheese maybe in the valley. Anyway, Chip says he expects Anton will try to start up again around the Santa Cruz area. There's some interesting wine being made down there these days. Or he might head back to Europe with that woman he's been mixed up with all these years." David turned the stem of his wineglass slowly with his fingertips. "When you think about it, Napa Valley's a pretty small place, especially if you've left so many footprints of bitterness up and down these thirty-odd miles. When you think this valley's only around a mile wide in places—with those two mountain ranges riding herd on it— hiding from something in this place would be like being caught inside a hollow bass drum with sticks being pounded on it from both sides. Take us—they're still trying to keep that bootlegging beat going. Saying we all have come from that."

"Isn't truth supposed to rise according to its own specific gravity?" Victoria asked, smiling ironically. After a moment she asked,

"What happened to Aunt Phyllis? I was horrified when I saw those photographs of her splashed across one of those cheap-thrill magazines in the supermarket in New York. With all *her* money, wouldn't you think she could do better with her life?"

"I don't think money has much to do with it in the long run. Take me—those shares could be worth twelve cents or twelve hundred dollars apiece and it wouldn't matter much to me because I didn't do anything with my own hands to earn them. That's where pride and happiness are. I guess winemaking has been a good profession for me at that. I've been able to use my hands a lot, connecting with my head at times. But happiness? Money couldn't bring back your mother. I don't guess I've been happy since she died, not really happy. Right now, knowing you're my daughter and that you're interested in carrying on what we've got going up here, what my father started—that brings me contentment."

"You and Mother—were you always in love? Did you *always* know?"

David smiled. "*Love*—it's a funny word. Your mother was about eleven or twelve years old, I guess, when I saw her as a woman. Oh, I'd seen her as a little kid. I mean when I looked at her and could see that one day she'd be—well, a *woman*. I knew I had to wait for her to grow up. But I also knew I'd never love anyone else. Luckily, it worked for us. She felt the same. We had some happy years. Not always easy years, but together. We always knew we should be together. What about you? You're what—twenty-three years old, just about? You're old enough to be in love. Anybody touched your heart strings yet, young lady?"

Victoria bit her lip. "Yes. But it didn't—I don't think it could ever work. For either of us. We're not lucky that way."

David looked at her closely. "Why? Why not?"

She stood up. "You wouldn't understand if I told you."

"Give it a try. Why not?"

"I just know." She dug her hands in her lab coat pockets. "Now, we were going to talk about winemaking methods we can agree on. About Chardonnay. If it's fermented in stainless at first, it's a tidier process. Then finish off in small oak for that taste it needs—for better temperature control."

David held the door open for her and they stepped inside the high-ceilinged hallway, where a new stack of labeled wine had been cased, ready for Janet Cutler to slap on the mailing addresses and send it out to waiting customers.

Victoria went on. "I think we should also examine efficient pro-

557

duction—go over the old winery, perhaps even look into turning the stable into areas for management. It seems to me that bottling, a lot of this activity, could be more practically arranged. We have enough space up here, certainly. There's no need to feel cramped."

"I guess I've needed a woman for housekeeping all along."

The crush was over, the frenetic activity had ebbed. But even in late November Victoria was working late in her laboratory on Spring Mountain. She had poured all her energies into the winery. Her father had agreed to hiring more personnel, all, hopefully, quality-conscious. "We don't want to get so big we can't watch our wines," David cautioned. "They're like children. Each one has its own needs."

On this particular Thursday night, around eight-thirty, the week before Thanksgiving, Victoria turned out the light in her laboratory, hung up her lab coat, took her trench coat off the rack in the hallway, locked the winery behind her and started down the pathway toward the new blue Buick she had bought with her first paycheck. A stiff mountain breeze whipped the coat and her tweed skirt between her legs, blew her hair straight out. Pine trees made whistling, lonely noises. A hoot owl let out its hollow, haunting call off in the thick woods. A single light bulb from a telephone pole lit the area where her car was parked. As she hurried toward it, she saw the other car—the maroon Studebaker that belonged to Carlo. A shot of adrenalin—akin to pain, to fear, to joy—went through her. But before she could gather her senses, he was stepping out of his car, waiting for her. He had pulled his jacket up around his neck, had draped a scarf around it.

"I thought you'd work all night." His voice was low, even, commanding in an odd-sounding way.

"I work late lots of nights."

"You're working too hard."

He stepped closer, reached out, placed one hand firmly on her shoulder. She smelled alcohol on his breath, but he didn't seem intoxicated. "I had to see you. I couldn't take it any longer," he said gruffly. "I want to talk. Where can we go?"

"We can sit in the car—it's cold out in the wind."

"We can always go to the bunkhouse," he said mockingly. "You hid me out there once—remember? It was cozy enough—better than hiding under a stone bridge freezing my ass off."

"You don't have to be crude, Carlo."

"Forgive me, *Miss* Donati. I forget."

"I'm *not* going to the bunkhouse," she said, taking out her keys, unlocking her car door.

"Okay, we'll sit in the car. Is *that* okay with you?"

Her heart was pounding. "Sure—for a little while. I'm tired. It's been a long day. I haven't had dinner yet."

"I'll be glad to buy a hamburger for you," Carlo said lightly. "Or if you aren't ashamed to be seen in a public place with me I could take you inside a real, bona-fide restaurant and buy you a steak."

"Don't be sarcastic, Carlo," she snapped, getting in behind the wheel, leaning over and opening the door for him.

He slid in, unbuttoned his coat, loosened his woolen scarf. "Have you missed me?"

"Should I?"

"You love me, don't you? You said you love me. If you do, you've missed me." He slid his arm across the back of the seat, nudged her over toward him. "I've been miserable, Victoria. I had to know—see for myself." Both hands were pulling her roughly toward him. Her left shoulder bumped the steering wheel. "Come on—get in the back seat with me."

"What's wrong with up here?"

"There's no room. Are you afraid of me? I just want to be able to at least hold you. Tell you what's on my mind." He had already reached behind him, opened the door, was pulling her toward it. When she was out, on his side, he pulled her hard against him, the wind blowing their hair, his mouth grinding into hers, his hands under her coat, pressing at the small of her back. "*Say* it—tell me you love me," he said against her mouth, his hips pressing her back against the car. "*Say* it!"

"I love you, Carlo . . ."

"Again!"

"I love you . . . oh, I love you too much, Carlo Carducci! I've been miserable ever since you left with *her*. I've—"

"Leave her out of this." He was pushing her into the back seat, climbing in, taking off her coat, tugging at his jacket. "Take that off."

"You can't just *boss* me around. You can't—"

He was again pushing her farther into the back seat, determinedly pulling at anything in his way. "Quit talking. Can't you for once just *love* me—be honest with your feelings? Give of yourself without asking . . ." His mouth was bearing down, his hands busy, working between her legs.

Anger, mixed with a deep crying need of him, made Victoria push hard at his hands, trying to free herself from him. His mouth was following hers, trying to quiet her protests.

"You're arrogant—a real arrogant bastard!" she managed.

His hands gripped her arms like steel. His face drew back. In the dim light from the single light pole, she could see his fury. "Don't ever say that to me again," he said between his teeth."

"You are *hurting* me, Carlo."

"You are hurting yourself," he said, holding her as roughly as before. "Take back what you said. Take it back and—"

A free hand pounded at him, tried to slap him. "I *hate* you!" I—"

"You *love* me and you know you love me." He had pinned her down. "Now we are going to stay just this way until you calm down." His face was just above hers, his body against hers, one knee pushing between her legs. He stayed perfectly still, insisting that she do the same. The warmth of his body on hers, its very heaviness, seemed to press the life from her. She felt a gentle swaying motion from his hips —the slightest move. And then his full lips open, touching hers with a feathery touch, another, and then his whispers beckoning, his hands no longer harsh, but gentle, and he was saying, "I love you, Victoria Donati. I will never love another woman. You are all I want—ever want. Love me. . . . *Show* me. . . . Love me. . . . Now. . . . Tell me that there's no one else . . . never anyone else . . . just me. You . . . me . . . That's right—here . . . closer to the edge of the seat . . ."

When it was over, he propped himself up, pushed her damp hair off her face. "Why are you crying?" he asked softly.

"*Us.* What are we going to do about us, Carlo? How could it ever work?"

He took out his handkerchief, dried her face, pulled her into his arms quietly, let her cry until she was through. "I don't know. I really don't know." He took a long breath. "I'm not good enough for you. Let's face it—you were right, I have my own kind. I'm not on your side of the mountain. I'm a good enough viticulturist. I've even had an offer from one of the big new conglomerates coming into the valley buying up acreage, developing new vineyards. A new thing is happening in Napa Valley. Starting slowly, but happening. I can make money, more money than I ever dreamed of when you first brought me up here on your horse and hid me in the bunkhouse." He laughed a hollow laugh. "But I'm still the *foreman*, and you're—how do they say it?— 'old Napa.' You'll be inheriting your grandmother's big house and this place up here."

Her voice was thick with tears. "That's plenty for both of us, isn't it?"

"It's more than what's *enough*—moneywise. I've got to hold my head up. I've got a different kind of pride than you. You see, I'm not ashamed at all of being half Mexican. I'm learning to be proud of it. That side of my heritage has been a damn sight nicer to me than the other side." He leaned his head back against the back seat, closed his eyes a moment, one arm loosely around her. She had her head against his shoulder, one hand on his chest where she could feel the heavy, steady pounding of his heart. "I went up to Jamison Wiley James's house one time," he said, a bitter irony in his voice. "I was about ten—eleven maybe. I marched right up to the front door. A big black man answered, told me to go to to the back. I went to the back. A black woman asked me what did I want. I told her I wanted to see Mr. James. I wanted to see my father." He bit his bottom lip. "She started laughing. She spread her hands out as if she'd heard the funniest joke ever told. The more she laughed, the louder I yelled. I just remember yelling and yelling that I wanted to see my father."

"*Did* you see him?"

"No. I got a fast shove off the back steps by the same big black man who opened the front door. He told me to run while the running was good or I might not live to talk about it. He said he wouldn't lay a hand on me but there were people in the house who would. So I took his advice. I never went back. But I saw inside for one quick minute. I saw the fine big house. Maybe—maybe I'm trying to get inside that house through you, Victoria. I've asked myself that. I asked myself if I'm loving you, dreaming about you, wanting you every day of my life just so I think I can be inside that big house of my father's."

"That wouldn't make your love so real, then. Is that what you're telling me, Carlo?" The tears were burning her eyes again, but she was blinking them back in the darkness there against his shoulder.

He pulled her tightly against him. "I don't know what any of it is. I just know I've been sick at heart. I can't take it. I'm no good for Blanca either. I'm making her life miserable. I'm not nice to her. I'm nice one minute, say, and do the wrong thing the next. She's going back to Candido's."

Victoria stiffened, sat up. "So Blanca walked out on you and you suddenly just had to see me again—is that it!"

He drew over into the opposite corner, one leg up on the seat. "No, that is *not* it. I told you the truth. Every word is the truth."

"Blanca—why did you have to bring *her* into it, when we had—when I told you I loved you!"

"Because Blanca has been part of my life." He took out a package of cigarettes, lit one, handed it to her automatically; lit another. The smell of the smoke broke the tension between them, became, that

561

moment, like something alive, a needed presence. After a long inhalation, Victoria herself leaned back. They were sitting there in the darkness now, side by side, not touching, as though staring ahead at some distant vanishing point in a car that wasn't moving, that was driverless.

She spoke first. "What will you do?"

The cigarette made a red glow as he drew in smoke. "Take the best job, I think. Your father—I'll have to figure the best way to tell him."

"He'll think it's because you aren't loyal. He thought that when Henry Ried left for better wages. He'll probably offer you more money. Then what?"

"I'll tell him I can't stay because I'm in love with you."

"No—don't do that!"

"Why? Are you ashamed for your father to know? He's treated me like his own son. I think he might understand. He's a kind, gentle man. A very gentle man . . ." He let smoke drift around him. "I love your father as if he were really my father."

"I'm not ashamed—I just don't want you to tell him." She ran her hand over her eyes. "Then you are going—this is the end?"

"Victoria . . . I don't—I can't see a way that it would work. I hate saying things are the end. Maybe I'll just take a vacation. I'll tell David I need some time off. A sabbatical. I'll make up some excuse about going down to study with the Wentes, some damn thing. Maybe that's the best way. I don't really want to stay in Napa Valley. Knowing you're here. Knowing I could come up here like this—or, if I *didn't*, what we were missing. When we're so right for each other . . . when everything fits. When we could have such beautiful children together. When I could be a loving man."

He opened his door, got out, stood with his chin lifted, letting the mountain wind whip across his face. He ground out the cigarette butt, waited for her to get out and come around. She was straightening her skirt, trying to smooth her hair down. He took her by the shoulders, kissed her ever so lightly on the lips. "I think I will go south. Take a few months off. See if I can get my head straight."

"I think that sounds better than just saying everything is over—ended." She got in under the wheel. Started the motor.

Carlo closed her door, checked to be sure it was shut tightly; hit the metal roof of her car with the flat palms of his hands. "Take it easy driving down the mountain—okay?"

"Sure. You do the same," she said, barely able to speak for the pain knotting her throat. As she backed up, turned around and headed out down the narrow driveway, his Studebaker came slowly behind her. Through the rearview mirror she saw the two round headlights like monster eyes waving, tracking her down.

"I'll never be free of you, Carlo Carducci!" she cried out in some deep echoing valley in the back of her mind.

Victoria didn't see Carlo again until the next year—in August, 1955, when David decided it was time to pick the first white grapes and to have the priest come up for the blessing. They had not expected Carlo, since no one knew that he was back in Napa Valley.

Victoria had asked Janet Cutler to arrange a picnic, set up on tables on the stone veranda, where by one o'clock the sun would have swung around so that the wisteria vines would give them a cooling shade—the whole valley having been caught in a stifling heat wave.

Before the priest arrived, Victoria talked a little with the new Davis graduate David had hired, young good-looking Tate Williams from Fresno, who would do some work in the vineyards as needed; his major training, however, had been in marketing and production. He was blond, built like a football player, and had a wonderful, ready laugh which made Victoria happy to have him around. Too, she felt that their weakest area on Spring Mountain was marketing. For with stepped-up production, as David was now planning, they could not, as she saw it, rely on mailing lists exclusively. Too, she wanted the Donati name known in wider circles. Even David, who had been at first dismayed to learn Carlo was leaving, was seeing the advantage of having hired Tate Williams, more or less to fill Carlo's place.

Victoria was leaning against the redwood post, looking out at the workers pulling the gondola into place for the ritual of the blessing, and was laughing at something Tate had just said, when she looked up to see Carlo coming up the pathway, a white jacket slung over one shoulder, blue-and-white striped shirt open at the collar, his navy-blue trousers crisply tailored. She felt as if someone had drawn a quick tight rope around her chest. She saw him smiling, shaking hands with David, with Dick Cutler, giving a friendly wave to some of the pickers, as though he knew them in another way but was on his own equal terms with them. When he saw Victoria and Tate Williams standing side by side, his smile disappeared; but he came forward, put one foot on the edge of the stone veranda, so very near her own. "Hello. Surprised to see me? I got in yesterday—heard from one of your pickers last night you were starting the crush today. Thought I'd come up, make sure you aren't shorthanded. Be around for the blessing."

She introduced him to Tate. Before they could say much, Chip Brosius was leading a frail Sarah up the walk. Though of late she had announced she wouldn't travel beyond a three-mile radius, Chip had talked her into coming up for the blessing. She hadn't made any explanation to anyone as to why she was limiting her travels to three miles, except to say, "Three's as good a number as any. Better than four, which is unlucky."

She stepped up on the stone veranda, patted Carlo on the arm. "Where have *you* been, young man? You've forgotten me! Everybody forgets these days." She looked at Victoria, at Janet Cutler, at Tate Williams. "Good gracious, there're so many new faces up here on Spring Mountain. I feel like a stranger in my own house." She sat down in the nearest wrought-iron chair. "I regard this as still being my house. I was married in it. I helped raise three boys in it. You were born here, Victoria. And now they tell me that it's filled up with boxes of wine—that I'll hate what I find." She looked out at the vineyards. "I see that the view hasn't changed any. Howell Mountain looks the same. The vines—they never look much different, I guess."

"Do you mean you can *see* Howell Mountain?" Victoria asked.

"I certainly can! Without glasses. I told you vitamins help. But on this hot day I'm not getting out there in the blistering sun to hear the priest do all that mumble-jumble. I'll watch the ceremony from here. I'll drink a little toast—that's what we used to do to celebrate the harvest. Made it fun—like a party."

"We're having a picnic—the toasts after the blessing, Grandmother."

"Well, go on out there and get it over with. I'm hungry. I don't want to wait around to eat!"

At the gondola of the first-picked grapes, Carlo came over and stood by Victoria. They were standing across from David, who Victoria thought looked pale, as if he didn't feel well. But he had been up since dawn seeing that every man knew his job.

The priest had just finished and headed back, walking slowly and talking aimlessly with Dick and Janet Cutler and Tate Williams; David and Chip Brosius were ambling toward Carlo and Victoria. As in a daze, Victoria realized something was wrong. But her father had slid toward the ground so silently, so quickly, having only in that one brief instant clutched at his shirt and tried to hold himself up on one knee before crumpling on the ground.

Carlo shot past her, was the first to reach him. Feverishly, he was tearing at his shirt, trying to pump life back into him. "Get a doctor!

Somebody get a doctor!" he cried out. Then in a low voice to David's stilled ear, in rhythm with the artificial respiration he was giving, he was saying, "Come on . . . try . . . please . . . breathe for me . . . please."

"Can't we put something under his head—something?" Victoria said numbly, as if by their getting his head out of the dirt it would be all right again.

Then Father O'Brien was there over him, saying the incantations for the dead. Wide-eyed Mexican pickers stood in a silent ring of their own, some crossing themselves. Janet Cutler flung her arms around her husband, Dick, sobbed openly.

"Grandmother . . . we'd better go to Grandmother," Victoria said, wondering where the sound came from when she was numb all over.

The priest and Carlo were guiding Victoria toward the veranda, where Sarah's reedlike voice called out irritably, "What's all that commotion out there? Did somebody have a sunstroke? I knew it was too hot a day to be out in the sun!"

Delia and Anne arrived barely in time for the funeral. On Sunday, the day before both girls wanted to leave to get back to their respective worlds in New York City, Chip Brosius came to read David's will and go over his assets.

"David wanted a share-and-share-alike distribution of his assets, but he wanted Victoria to inherit the deed to the Donati property on Spring Mountain. Which means that when we divide these twelve hundred shares, the value of Spring Mountain must be amortized out in ratio to the market value of the shares in the Fuller-Brunner Winery —negotiations being in process now for the final liquidation and sale of it to the Minnehaha Brewery Company. Because of that delay, it may be a while yet before we can get this will in probate."

Anne, who had draped herself across the settee out on the brick terrace, where they had gone in search of a cooler place, looked restless, as though she hadn't really been listening to anything Chip said. She sat up abruptly. "*I've* got to have money right away. I simply have to have some money. Someone has got to help me get it!"

Victoria, sitting by Delia (whose hair had been cut off short all over her head; who was wearing a dress made from burlap; sandals strapped around her legs up to her knees; enormous Indian bracelets riding one arm; a pendant around her neck), asked in a whispering voice, "What's wrong with Anne? She acts crazy."

"She's stoned out of her mind. Or she needs a fix, is my guess," Delia said under her breath.

Sarah, who had been spending most of her time in her room since David's death, as though something vital had snapped inside her, suddenly came out on the terrace, helped by a sad-eyed Li Po. He waited until she was safely seated, then went slowly back into the house.

Anne was reaching for a glass of wine, her hand shaking. "Grandmother, did you hear what I *said*? They're telling me the money won't be available for months. I've got to have money. Will you tell this man —will you tell someone to get some money for me?"

Sarah clasped her hands tightly together, her lap making a cradle for them. Her pale, age-faded eyes narrowed, as if applying some invisible magnifying glass of her own to this strange, pale-looking, clammy-skinned girl. "*Money?* You look to me like you need a good hot dish of oatmeal! Something to put some flesh on your bones. Some of Li Po's herbs to get the color back to your skin."

"I don't need *herbs!*" Anne said, her eyes wide.

Delia got up, hurried to Anne, spoke in her ear, was pulling her up, guiding her toward the door. More for the sake of Sarah, Delia said, "She's upset over Father's death. I think I'll call a doctor. What local doctor do you suggest?"

"I don't *like* doctors," Sarah snorted.

Chip Brosius seemed to guess at the problem. "I have someone for you to call. Try Francoli—the only one listed. Tell him I asked you to call. Explain your problem and ask him to come right out here if he will. Tell him the old Reynolds place—that's how he knows this house."

When they had quieted down, Chip continued, "There is one other person, to whom David bequeathed eighty acres of vineyards. Sarah, I believe these acres are from those you deeded over to David some time ago."

"I deeded over *six hundred* and eighty acres to him—not eighty."

"I know that. He has left the eighty in Cabernet to Carlo Carducci. He names the plot number, the accessor's parcel number. I guess I overlooked that. I would have had Carlo come by."

"Is he around?" Victoria asked quietly.

"A good question. I'll find out. Someone told me he was working with the Farm Workers Union organizers down around Stockton someplace. That he and his cousin—some young lawyer, one of those Mexican smart alecks—are ringleaders now."

Victoria got up, stood near her grandmother. "Do you know that for a fact, Mr. Brosius?"

He looked at her, startled, not accustomed to being called anything by the family except Chip. "I'm saying what I heard. That's the word that's out. There's some agitation going on among the pickers. Maybe you don't get much of it up on Spring Mountain—maybe Carlo has been part of the reason. But there are other growers who could tell you a different story. There are some who're predicting loyal Mexicans here in Napa Valley will take sides against their own people if they ever do something stupid and march into Napa Valley the way they're stirring up such a fuss down south."

"I don't think you should spread rumors," she snapped. "You aren't here to speak against Carlo Carducci, whom my father loved as his own son!" She let the door slam behind her.

It was Delia who got up, lifted her eyebrows. "If you're through, I think I'm going to try to get out of Napa Valley tonight. New York seems tame to me in comparison."

But Sarah was not going to let Delia get by her so easily. "That's right! Pack up, hurry back. Don't think I haven't taken note of how you and Anne come to see us only when you both need money. Don't think my will doesn't take note of it! When *I* die you might as well *stay* in New York City. It will hardly pay you to come after the pittance you're getting from me."

Soon after Chip Brosius had gone—having mumbled to himself that he wasn't sure if the Donatis weren't all a little crazy after a day like today—the doctor arrived, examined Anne. Delia and Victoria called him into the kitchen, being sure that Sarah was out on the brick terrace out of earshot.

"What should we do?" Victoria asked. "She's addicted, isn't she?"

"Yes—badly. You've got to get her someplace now for treatment. We have a few places. There's the federal drug center in Lexington, Kentucky. That might be your best bet. I'll be glad to help."

"Then we'll do it," Delia said. "Tell us what we have to do. We can't let our sister go on this way. We're all Donatis, and Donatis stick together."

Later, when she and Victoria were up in Victoria's bedroom, when Sarah had allowed Li Po to take her to her room and bring supper to her on a tray, Delia stretched out across the ancient Hubbard bed, looked up at the high ceiling of the old mansion. "Anne will hate us for a while—but that man she's living with is killing her. He does all her camera work—what little there is to do these days. In modeling they're always searching for a new look. Anne's face is old hat now. Plus, look at her." She sat up, looked at Victoria sitting at her dresser absently brushing her thick red hair, lost in her own troubled thoughts.

"You're the beauty of the family—but why do you look so *sad?* I mean, other than losing Pop? Something's eating away at you." They were silent. A small bedside clock ticked. Outside the window a bluejay was chasing a squirrel down the rough bark of a huge oak tree, squawking noisily. "Come on, tell big sister. I'm used to looking into people's eyes, looking deeper than your red hair and your fabulous skin, my dear. As an artist, that's my forte. Come on—I'm a good listener."

Victoria put the brush down. "What do you do when you love the wrong man in life?"

Delia put her hands on her forehead, then raked her sensitive fingers through her short-cropped hair. "You *would* ask me that one! Honey, finding the right man has been my nemesis." She let out a sigh. "Who is it? Anyone I know? You had plenty of men in Greenwich Village mad about you when you were there. Look, if you ever want a man, come to New York! With *your* looks, my God! You're certainly going to be able to afford it. Looks as if Grandmother is leaving you everything—which, really, she should. I don't blame her. You two have always been close. Loved each other."

Victoria was staring out the window, watching the raucous bluejay perched there with something shiny in its mouth. "I've been thinking about that—the inheritance. That this isn't fair to you or Anne. I'm having Chip divide those shares between the two of you, evenly. Now they're thinking they'll be worth around fifteen hundred dollars each. Six hundred times fifteen hundred—not a bad sum. You'll have taxes to pay, but it will be immediate money. Mine—most of my inheritance will be tied up in the land. In vines. In the winery."

Delia came over, hugged Victoria. She was shorter, rounder-armed. She looked up at Victoria's haunted blue eyes, at her exquisitely chiseled features. "I love you, baby sister. If you ever want to get the hell out of Napa Valley you can be my guest in New York, any time."

Victoria kept her arms about Delia for a moment, felt tears stinging her eyes. "Thank you. I'll remember that. But I guess this place is part of me. Spring Mountain especially—it's in my blood. I've got my work cut out for me with Dad gone. We were quite a good team. He had that old-school way. The experience. A remarkable nose. A patience for making wine. But he was willing to change certain things. He was giving me such free rein to experiment. I wish—it never occurred to me that he would just . . . *die.* He had so much I wanted to learn from him! I'm scared now. He built the name of Donati into something in the real wine world. What if I tear down what he did? What if I'm not good enough!"

"You will be. Look, he wasn't always perfect. Was he ever really satisfied with his wines? I don't remember him ever seeming all that pleased about what he had done."

"He wasn't. What winemaker ever is? But I'm not what he was. I can never be."

Delia stood back, lifted one eyebrow. "But try—not to be David Donati, winemaker, but Victoria Donati! I had to learn that. That I couldn't be Cézanne or Picasso or Matisse. I had to be myself. I had to believe in my own unique vision. And don't we all have to do that, whatever we're after in life?"

After a moment, she went over, starting stuffing things into a suitcase. "That doctor is nice. He says I should go with her to Lexington. That he'll send someone else along."

"If you need money, I have plenty," Victoria said. "I'd go along, but I—we're in the middle of the crush and we'll be shorthanded as it is. There aren't that many good oenologists around. We're still short of skilled help. I couldn't possibly leave right now."

"Maybe you could advance a loan to me. Victoria, it's damn nice of you to split the shares. You don't have to."

"I want to. It's my gift."

"It might help to get Anne well." Delia folded a blouse. "It might give Anne a whole new start in life."

"That's worth more than owning some shares I didn't help earn with my own hands."

It was spring of 1956 before the distribution of the money from the sale of the Fuller-Brunner Winery took place. Because the Minnehaha Brewery Company wanted to keep an old Napa Valley family name associated with its wine, the name was changed from Fuller-Brunner to the Jacob Brunner Winery, with an imprint on the label, "Since 1872." Anton tried to slap a lawsuit on the new owners, protesting the use of his great-grandfather's name and stating that Jacob Brunner had been a famous grower but never had made wine, and that therefore the label was misleading. The judge ruled that the name Jacob Brunner could be used, but the wording should be changed to say: "Vineyards established since 1872."

Phyllis's children, who had legally dropped the name Brunner long ago, made a brief visit to Napa Valley to see about putting the Cugnot house—as it was still called by Napa Valley natives—on the market. The vineyards had been sold as part and parcel of the winery itself. Bernard was twenty-seven years old; Frances had just had her thirty-first birthday—and her third divorce, awarded a month before she arrived. Victoria invited them over to Sarah's for tea. The visit was strained, with a nervous Bernard—who looked eerily like Anton—constantly looking at his watch.

"How is Aunt Phyllis?" Victoria asked, when they had not asked to see any of the valley's tourist spots or taken her up on her offer to drive them up to Spring Mountain.

Frances stretched out long legs, let smoke drift about her face, which was long and angular but more attractive than her mother's had been. "*Mother*, darling, is hopeless. She lives in that horrible old beach house—won't let let us spend a dime on repairs. She's totally eccentric. But still shrewd with money! She gets richer by the hour, as our lawyers tell us. It is truly disgusting the amount of money she has and won't let go. She lives nearly like a pauper. But we do have our trusts. We aren't exactly impoverished. We can *wait*. She can't live much longer, with her cirrhosis." She twisted enormous diamond rings into an upright position on her right hand. "Isn't it ghastly, seeing people get old? Your grandmother—how old is she these days? I hear she didn't want to come down. Is she well?"

"Yes. She's eighty-two now. She more or less rations out her energies. Is very selective about what she does with her time, whom she sees. She complains that most people have really very little to say worth listening to."

Bernard stood up. "We've got to dash. Sorry to break this up. We mustn't miss our plane, Sis. I couldn't bear to miss our plane!" He lifted his eyebrows, gave Frances an exasperated, knowing look.

"We're going to Bermuda for the winter. We do have plans, and though Napa Valley is marvelously quaint and charming, we have to get back to Boston, tidy up certain affairs."

That same year, in June, Carlo stopped by to tell Victoria that he was turning over his eighty acres of Cabernets to the management of a Mexican cousin. "He's from Colima. His name is Miguel Díaz. He's the son of my second cousin. Pepe, I call him. We went to school in Stockton together. He's ready now to take his bar exams. His full name, a name Napa Valley may come to know in time, is Daniel Ramírez Díaz." He spoke the name slowly, with an emphasis intended to make her curious.

They were standing out on the stone veranda on Spring Mountain. Sarah had not been well lately, and Victoria was in a hurry to get back to look in on her. She was not actually all that needed by Sarah; but she was trying to convince herself that it was urgent that she hurry—

anything to get away from Carlo, from that arrogant look he was giving her, as if he were some special genie born out of Bacchus's own private pitcher.

"I'll walk to your car with you," he said, breaking into an easy long-legged stride alongside her as she hurried down the stone pathway.

"What are you up to these days? Still unionizing?"

He didn't answer. When she reached her car, took out her key, unlocked it—her father had trained her to keep it locked, a practice carried over from Prohibition days, to keep thirsty searchers from looking in a winemaker's car—Carlo put one hand flat on top of the blue Buick sedan. "You need a good polish job," he said. He leaned over, looked in the back seat, lifted one eyebrow. "Looks like a junkyard back there. Don't you ever clean out your car?"

"I think I asked *you* a question!" she said, getting in behind the wheel. "I heard you were a big-time organizer."

"You heard wrong. There's some organizing going on. *I'm* not part of it. Pepe is. Pepe's in the thick of it."

"Daniel Ramírez Díaz?" Victoria started the car.

Carlo folded his arms across the open window, put his face inside next to hers. "Aren't you going to kiss me goodbye? I won't be back for a long time. I'm enrolled in school—full time. Going after that big degree. All the way to the top."

She looked around, kept her mouth rigid as his lips brushed across hers. He drew back, still smiling that mocking smile that made her want to slap his face.

"Are *you* going to be a lawyer, too?" Her voice was laced with bitterness.

"No. Viticulturist. Sticking strictly with the land. I want to learn all I can about modern science." He pushed back, both hands on the open windowsill. "Have you still got Golden Boy working for you? The Williams guy?"

"Yes. Plus a few others. I'm getting qualified people now. Why?"

"I thought there might be something more—you seemed intrigued with him."

"He's nice. I like him."

"Do you love him?"

"No, Carlo, I don't love him." She pressed her foot down on the clutch, reached for the gearshift. "Does that make you happy? Is that what you wanted to hear?"

"Maybe. Maybe if you had said you loved him it would be a little easier." With that, Carlo gave one last slap with the palm of his hand to the metal top of the car and went over to where his own highly polished maroon-red Studebaker was parked carefully in the shade, looking hardly a day older than when he had bought it. He did not look back when he slammed the door behind him. This time, he let his foot jam to the floor as he spun the car around and tore off down the driveway.

26

Knowing that Carlo Carducci was gone now from the Napa Valley, Victoria tried to get him out of her mind. She was beginning to accept dates with Tate Williams. She enjoyed his spontaneous way of suddenly suggesting after a long day at the winery that they drive to San Francisco for a Japanese dinner at his favorite little restaurant on Post Street, or go to North Beach Restaurant. She went to Fresno with him one weekend to meet his parents, ranchers who owned land adjacent to the Kings River, who were warmhearted, generous, in a simple, direct way that comes with people who work the land.

At times, he would insist she go with him in the four-wheel-drive Jeep he had bought from war surplus; when he would take her up Oat Hill Mine Road, or to the top of Glass Mountain, where he would drive through thick chalky-white volcanic dust and say, "Wonder what kinds of vines would do well here—what kind of Cabernet or Chardonnay we could get in these high places?"

But regardless of what they had in common, as hard as she tried, she could not make herself fall in love with Tate. When he brought up any suggestion of romance, quickly she changed the subject to something related to winemaking, to fractional blending, malo-lactic fermentation, variety evaluation, new antiseptics and clarification agents, when or when not to use the centrifuge, to add bentonite, how long to leave the juice on the lees, to punch the cap down or pump over—anything but the subject of love, of any serious relationship whatsoever.

Besides the winery, she had her hands full with Sarah, whose mind was beginning to slip. There would be moments when she would seem amazingly astute; other times she would ask, "When is David coming home? Has he decided to stay up on Spring Mountain?"

Li Po was not much better. Though he kept pretty much to himself in his room off the kitchen, Victoria was afraid he was going to burn the house down some night forgetting to turn off the gas burner.

She wished now she had stayed with electricity and never had butane brought in. She could smell his incense; she was afraid he might have candles burning and let one of those catch something on fire. Because she was having to spend more and more time on Spring Mountain at the winery, she decided to hire a permanent housekeeper to look after both her grandmother and Li Po.

Through her grandmother's friend Martha Cantrell—who herself was confined to a wheelchair with a broken hip—she found a practical nurse, a big-shouldered, warmhearted widow who lived in a trailer court, who was willing to move in full time if she could bring along her two miniature poodles. Her name was Maude Bly. Though Victoria did not like the yapping from Cain and Abel, the poodles, Maude's hefty presence gave her more freedom to concentrate on the winery.

Sarah herself seemed contented with Maude. Sometimes she did not recognize Victoria. One morning when Victoria had been out on the brick terrace quickly drying her hair in the warm sunshine before going to Spring Mountain, Sarah asked, "Are you one of the Mulligan girls? They're the only redheads I know in Napa Valley."

But there would be the other times with her grandmother when Victoria would sit beside her—usually in Sarah's favorite spot facing southwest—and Sarah would reminisce, vividly recounting to Victoria the day she and Adam Donati had met or the day they were married. "I'll never forget coming down those stairs up there in the big stone house on Spring Mountain—those Alfieri girls playing the wedding march and all you children singing in those wobbling voices and squirming around waiting to throw the rice bags." Victoria never corrected her, to tell her that it had been her mother, Lilliana, who had been one of the children. She would simply nod her head, encourage Sarah to go on.

"I used to love the dinners, the harvest celebrations. Sitting out on the stone veranda looking out at the view. This is a nice view here—I look *up* at the mountain ridges instead of *down* on the world. Sometimes—don't laugh—sometimes I think I see Adam up there, riding across those hills on his black stallion . . . riding back and forth waiting for me. Sometimes I see him, sometimes I don't. It's worth it, sitting here until my feet go to sleep sometimes—waiting for those times when he's there."

The harvest of 1960 was not one of the grape industry's best. Again a surplus was on the market, and the government was taking steps to establish a set-aside program—mostly in the San Joaquin Valley, where the main surplus was felt. Carlo Carducci had just graduated from California State University in Fresno, where he had been enrolled the past four years in the Department of Agricultrual Industry and Education. The week following his graduation he had turned thirty. Though he had been offered several positions around Fresno— had been strongly tempted with one from the Penny Newman Grain Company—he decided that before he made up his mind he would go back to Napa Valley, telling himself that he wanted to see if his eighty acres were being managed properly.

He had planned to arrive around the fifteenth of June. On the night when he had gone out to celebrate his graduation with his cousin Pepe and some of Pepe's friends, he had found out some disturbing news about an offshot group of activists who had left Pepe's more conservative approach to union organization and were planning a campaign in the Napa Valley, where Pepe feared there might even be some violence.

"Why Napa?" Carlo had asked, feeling a surge of loyalty, a strong rise of protectiveness shooting through him.

"Because Napa Valley, as they say, is the most biased, the most prejudiced of all. In their language, it's the shits."

"What do they know about it?"

"They *know*—okay, they know! They're trying to get the NAACP, CORE—black groups—to join in with the grape workers."

"Exactly what do they expect to accomplish, these midnight-raider types?"

"From what I gather, more propaganda than anything else. A few scare tactics. Get the press's attention. Call attention all over the country to the workers' plight by using the most bourgeois area to show contrast."

"What are you doing to stop it?" Carlo asked angrily.

"Staying out of it—staying from here to there out of it so we won't be associated with that bunch of hotheads. We're working toward *goals*—long-range goals. This kind of business from Gutiérrez's men will put us back another fifty goddam years!"

"I think you should do something. You should stop them. You should make a statement."

Pepe had waved him back to his seat. "Have another beer. Look, I'll make a statement through the union when the time comes. Official channels. We're going straight, all the way—peacefully. One of these days we'll whittle away at it until we accomplish what we're after."

"Okay. I'm going to Napa. I'll be staying with your father. Will you let me know if you hear anything that I ought to know?"

Pepe laughed. "Like what? Like if they're going after your girl friend, huh? Is that what's bothering you? You haven't been much interested in the cause until now—why are you so hot under the collar all of a sudden over tactics?"

"I just want to be kept informed—as a landowner."

Pepe, who was short, stocky, round-raced, looked up at the towering, good-looking Carlo standing over him. "Sure—sure, Carlo. If I find anything out I think you ought to know I'll let Pop know about it. But that will be strictly personal—between family. Not as an official statement from the union. Have you got that?"

By the time the crush got under way, that year of 1960, Victoria had made several changes on Spring Mountain. It had cost much more than she had planned on spending; but she was pleased with the converted stable, the added space for concentrating on making white wines, for storing the new stainless-steel tanks, for the installation of the dejuicer system, a new stemmer-crusher—even some space for small oak barrels for the Chardonnay, with the two-foot-thick stone walls of the old stable giving their own kind of built-in temperature control.

Where she was in charge of the white wines, she had put Tate Williams in charge of the reds. He did his crushing and open fermenting up at the regular old winery, where again she had spent enormous sums putting on a new roof, refurbishing it generally, even reinforcing the tunnels with concrete. She had intended to have a concrete floor poured at the stables, but that added expense would have to wait. She had had the workmen use a cheap wooden floor. With the stainless steel it wasn't the same messy process, anyway.

Though she had heard some of the talk about the straggly group of union agitators marching into the valley waving banners and telling some they were going to take over in ten years, no one seemed much alarmed about their presence. They were mostly after the new corporate structure, the Jacob Brunner Winery, it seemed. There had been a barn-burning in Yountville that was thought to be arson by their hands, but no proof was uncovered. A few minor mishaps had been attributed to them—such as gondolas being found turned upside down.

At one point, Victoria had asked Tate Williams about it. "Sounds more like some heavy Halloween pranks to me. How do they think they can change a big outfit like those powers behind Brunner's? I saw a few of them marching, I guess toward Krug's or Beringers'. A sorry-looking bunch—looked kind of pitiful to me with those ratty banners. There were a few television cameras around. Some reporters trying to get some kind of news to put on the air and liven things up. Nothing to worry about."

"Do you think they have valid beefs?"

He shrugged his shoulders. "The growers around here have a good program. Give them the benefits they're claiming they don't have. That's *my* opinion. I hear there are some Mexicans getting together to chase them out of Napa County. Some pickers are carrying weapons— ready to fight if they have to." He had gone over a polyculture yeast he wanted to try out with her that was new from the Pasteur Institute, and to ask what fining she wanted with the Pinot Noir. "I'm going to Fresno this weekend. My folks' thirty-fifth wedding anniversary. I've got Dick Cutler geared to look after my end of things. I'll be back Monday. Do you think you can manage? You wouldn't come along with me, would you? They'd love to have you. You know that."

"No. Thank you. Please take along a case of wine as my gift. I have to look in on my grandmother. I have my work cut out up here. I've got to get in here and get this bentonite added to some wine."

Victoria had not intended to work that Saturday. She was exhausted. She could use a day sleeping in late. But with the crew finishing picking, with the regular staff off for the weekend, it would give her a chance to catch up on some paperwork; to work in some relative quiet for a change.

It was sundown when she finally decided to lock up and head down Spring Mountain. Maude Bly had asked for the next day off, so Victoria would be at home with Sarah all day—maybe rest while Sarah napped.

She had just stepped out on the stone veranda when Carlo's voice caught her like a knife stab itself. "Good, you're still here. I was afraid I'd miss you." He propped one hand on the redwood post, grinned at her.

"Carlo—I guess you startled me! When did you get back? How are you?" Her heart was pounding as he always made it do; after four years, nothing, she thought dismally, had changed.

"I've been here, but I've been pretty busy. Seems that Brunner's, who contracted my Cabernets, have been cheating Miguel. Paid him about half what they were supposed to. I've been busy with lawyers. Other things."

"Yes, I'd imagine that you have been." She looked at him, shrugged her shoulders. "Well, good to see you. Did you graduate? What—where are you these days, generally?"

"Trying to make up my mind what to do, now that I have my degree and a few job offers. If I'll stay around here or go back to the Fresno area. I've got some nice friends down that way."

"Anyone special?"

"No—not the way I think you meant that question. How about you? Not married yet?"

"No. I'm a bona-fide old maid. Twenty-eight years old and still single. No hope in sight." She lifted one eyebrow, pushed her shoulder-length red hair off her face. "I guess I'd better be getting on down the mountain. It's been a long day around here."

He stopped her, put his hands on her upper arms. "Victoria—I feel exactly the same. You know that, don't you? That hasn't changed at all for me. How about you? or do you—"

"I don't think about it! I've got my hands full with positive things. With the reality of running this place and trying to make some decent wines. Get them marketed properly. Keep the Donati name up there where it belongs."

They walked in strained silence down the pathway, past the vineyards, toward the stable with her new equipment, her expensive dejuicer, the stainless-steel tanks, the new wood floor.

"How about dinner?" he asked, waiting while she opened the car door.

She looked at him quietly, studying his handsome face, his deep-blue eyes, a part of her crying out to say yes, to fling herself at him. Instead, her voice came remarkably evenly: "Carlo, let's not do this to ourselves. We decided back then it wouldn't work. So has anything changed? Are we any different now than we were then?"

"Older. You're more beautiful. You are, you know."

"Don't flatter me. I'm exhausted tonight. I'm going home and take a long hot bath. Then I'm going to bed and sleep at least twelve hours. If you're going to be around for a while, maybe you can give me a rain check on dinner."

He shrugged his shoulders. "Maybe you're right. Nothing's different." He was looking around as she started the motor. "Have you had any trouble from the—agitators, I guess you call them? Any pickets? Any threats?"

"No. Why?" She detected a seriousness, a concern in his voice.

"I'd keep an eye out for a while, just in case. I—well, being who I am, I hear things you wouldn't. Speaking Spanish, I pick up on certain things."

"Like what?" Her hands were gripped tightly around the steering wheel. She wasn't sure if Carlo was using this as some new tactic of his own to entice her, make her vulnerable again, or if he was trying to warn her about something.

"I don't want to frighten you. I came up here today not to ask you out for dinner. I know how you feel. I know what we *don't* have—okay? But I did hear some talk that because you're the only woman winemaker around, and rich, you'd make good news coverage. They're out for publicity more than anything. But I wouldn't want you to get hurt. Not over that bunch." He dug his hands into his pockets. "I also want you to know that if anything should happen, *I* have nothing to do with them—nor does my cousin Pepe. He's with the real union, the big movement. They don't go in for these underhanded methods. Burning barns—that kind of thing."

"Well, I guess I say thanks for telling me. Goodbye, Carlo. Oh, lock the gate after you, will you, please?"

It was about nine o'clock that night, after Victoria had bathed, rested, was feeling better again, when Maude's poodles started an endless yapping that got on her nerves. She didn't want to do anything to upset Maude, since the poodles would be gone for the day tomorrow, so she decided that she would take a drive, just to get out.

She told Maude she was going to a movie, since Maude liked simple explanations. Instinctively, she headed out for St. Helena. Carlo had upset her. She wished now that she had been the last one to drive out. Could she depend on him to have closed and locked the gate? Four years had gone by—he wasn't the same Carlo Carducci, maybe.

When she got near the top of Spring Mountain, she found the gate locked. Now that she was here, she told herself, she might as well go on into the laboratory a few minutes. She had some papers, charts, some new file cabinets and bookshelves she could get straightened out. It would be a good feeling on Monday morning to come in and have all those little details taken care of. A place for everything for a change, now that the new expansion was finished.

A strong wind was blowing. She drove through the gate, went back and placed the lock so that it appeared to be locked but would be easy to get open when she came back out. She wouldn't stay much more than an hour, she told herself.

Because it was dark, with only a sliver of a moon, she decided to drive the car to the back door. She wasn't afraid on Spring Mountain —she had never been afraid—but she *was* alone. And Carlo had made her a little nervous with his talk about agitators.

Victoria unlocked the back door of the old stone house, went into the kitchen-laboratory. Her past few years of intense work had formed habits that began taking over automatically as soon as she took off her corduroy jacket and looked about at what should be the first job to tackle. In a jumbly box in one corner were old records, journals. She went to those, heaved the heavy box up on a work counter, drew up a tall stool and began going through them.

Time began to drop away. She had found old ledgers going back to 1888—invoices, peculiar brandy forms for the government. It started her mind racing. She should build glass cases for these things—start a Donati Winery museum right here on the premises. After all, the stone buildings had become a well-known Napa Valley landmark. She should protect and pass on down the Donati history of winemaking!

The hall clock struck eleven-thirty. She was tired. She should get back down valley. She slid her arms back inside the beige corduroy jacket that matched her skirt. Went into the main front hallway to turn out a light she had left on. For a moment she stared up the steps, trying to envision her grandmother a young woman coming down to the sounds of the wedding march and children singing—to feel the living history inside these thick stone walls. What a wonderful house it would be, she thought, if it were converted back to family use, filled up with lots of children. She tugged at her sleeves, then snapped out the hallway light. If she ever did meet the right man, and, if she did, one who would ask her to marry him . . . *we would have such beautiful children,* Carlo had said to her once.

Well, she *wasn't* married and she saw little chance of children! It was going to be midnight, and all dreams turned into pumpkins and mice then, didn't they?"

She walked briskly to the back door, was turning to put the key in the latch, when she whirled around, saw the fire shooting out from the bunkhouse windows, from the roof of the stable.

Her first reaction during the seizure of panic was to run toward it—as if it would put the fire out somehow. Then she was flinging open the back door, running to the telephone. After she had shouted her message to what she hoped had been the right fire department in St. Helena, she went out the door, running toward what represented most of the actual money she had inherited. The dejuicing equipment, the stainless steel tanks—how damaged would they be? The oak barrels with the Chardonnay from last vintage, the records . . .

At the end of the pathway, she saw the red taillights bobbing out of sight down the driveway; heard the muffler—a broken muffler—roaring off. And over to her right, under a single light bulb on the telephone pole, she saw the familiar maroon-red of Carlo's Studebaker.

She stood, frozen with panic, with fear, with the closest thing to hatred she had ever known. So Carlo was the one who was the ringleader of the agitators! He had tricked her! She half ran toward the door of the stable, wondering blindly if she could find a hose, something, maybe even catch Carlo in the act of pouring on more gasoline or whatever it was they had used.

It was then that she saw the foot sticking out of the front door—the huge double front door where freight wagons had once rolled.

From inside the stable, she heard the crashing sound of timber falling. She grabbed the heel of the shoe, pulled, then the other, crying out to no one, to everyone, "*Help.* Won't somebody please *help* me!"

And then as she got the heavy body out away from the fire, was pulling it as though dragging a rolled-up rug, then she saw the blood—saw that it was Carlo! And as she bent down, she saw the knife jutting out of his back. Her scream was as though the knife had been plunged into her own lungs.

Later, she did not remember having got him inside the Studebaker, or the scrambling for the right key, or how she had got him into the seat at all. She had been sure that he was dead. Yet she had felt his heart. She had heard a gurgling gasp—a hideous sound. He was *alive*—she must get him to the hospital!

She careened wildly down Spring Mountain, Carlo's head slumped over on her—yet she couldn't move to stop. At Main Street she bore down, hoping a policeman would give chase and then lead her, help her. Policemen were always after speedsters, weren't they? Their sirens and red lights would surely come bearing down on her any moment.

Get him out of this valley! It was like a drumbeat going through her head. She could have headed up Deer Park Road toward the St. Helena Sanitarium, but something primitive was pressing her foot harder and harder on the gas pedal. Once Carlo had said to her, *The outlines of those mountains look like a witch's profile to me sometimes. . . .*

The hospital was—she thought she remembered right—on Trancas. She was driving down the very middle of the highway, the speedometer going past ninety now. *Policeman, where are you?* she was silently screaming to herself.

And then, somehow, she was under bright lights at the emergency entrance. She was running, shouting at people in white uniforms bent over charts at a desk. Then a stretcher was being pushed out and men in white jackets were opening the Studebaker, lifting out Carlo's limp form.

A nurse took her by the arm, took her into a room with blinding white lights that smelled of medicines. Ammonium was being waved under her nose. Bitter, acrid smelling salts. "There—take a deep breath. . . . Relax . . . . Lower your head between your knees a moment . . . . Feeling a little faint there, eh? You'll be okay now."

"Carlo—is he dead?"

"The doctors are working with him now. We can't tell yet." The nurse had a kindly, square face. Her hair was short, dyed a stiff blond. She led Victoria out. "As soon as you're up to it, the policemen want to talk with you—ask you some questions."

Victoria had no idea what time it was. She went over and over the answers; listened to the same questions endlessly repeated, it seemed to her.

"Yes, I've known Carlo Carducci for years. He worked for my father. . . . No, I don't know anything about his relatives. . . . About Díaz or Candido's. . . . . He was a loyal employee. He did come and warn me there were agitators. . . . . No, I don't know who those agitators were. I have no idea whom he meant. I don't know if he knew them or not. . . . I don't know *when* he got back to Napa Valley. . . . I don't think he had anything to do with setting the fire. I think he was trying to stop them and someone stabbed him. He was trying to help me—to save my winery, my investment on Spring Mountain. . . ." And then she began to cry.

"Maybe you'd better get home and get some rest," a burly red-faced policeman suggested.

"No—I'm staying here. But someone—if he has these relatives, someone should notify them. I know Miguel Díaz is in charge of his eighty acres."

"You said you didn't know his relatives."

"I know that Miguel Díaz is his cousin. Yes, he did tell me that, when my father left him that property in his will."

"Do you know the name Daniel Ramírez Díaz?"

"No. I do not know that man. Maybe I have heard the name. I don't know that man. Why?"

"Where does Miguel Díaz live?"

"St. Helena—I believe on Dowdell. I'm not sure."

When the policemen had quit asking questions, she went back to where she knew the doctors were working over Carlo. "How is he?" she asked the nurse at the desk.

"He's conscious. He's cooperating."

"What do you mean—cooperating?"

"They are having to drain his lungs. He is responding. He feels the needles." The nurse smiled. "That is good, you see—that he *feels*. Are you a relative? His wife? Could you fill out these admission forms for him?"

"He was . . . My father more or less raised him, I guess. No, I'm not a relative. But—he's very close to me. Dear to me." She started crying.

"We need to know if he has insurance."

"I'll pay—you can charge it to me." She took the forms. "What are they doing to him now?" she asked anxiously.

"Many things at once. They're getting blood plasma to him as fast as they can. He's lost a lot of blood."

At four o'clock, a startled, round-faced Miguel, followed by two younger Mexican men, hurried in, looked about as though lost. Victoria got up wearily, went over, introduced herself. Miguel spoke broken English. She tried as best she could to explain the situation as she knew it. The men spoke rapid, low-voiced Spanish with each other; went over and sat down on a leather couch in the emergency waiting room. Victoria felt their stares. Was relieved when the one named Fernando picked up a magazine, leafed through it, looking at the pictures.

"I drove him down—in his Studebaker," Victoria said lamely at one point when Miguel got up, paced the floor, looked at the nurse, who kept charting.

It was about five o'clock, Victoria guessed. Outside, the sky would be lifting its night shade, the birds would be starting in with their singing, she thought wearily, as she heard the droning voice of a page: "Dr. Ginsberg, please report to Emergency . . . . Dr. Ginsberg . . ."

Her eyes were dry, burning, when the doctor in charge of the emergency room came up to them. "Are you folks all with Mr. Carducci? Are you family?"

"They are." Victoria had jumped up. "I'm Victoria Donati—it happened at my place. I brought him down here. How is he?"

She thought the doctor looked at her curiously. "We think he has about a fifty-fifty chance right now of pulling through this. We've got the blood stopped. He's getting plasma still. We have to get him into X ray and see the extent of his head wound. If we can locate the broken-off tip of the knife. A neurosurgeon, Dr. Ginsberg, is here, I believe. I hear his page. We sent for him to take charge." He looked at Victoria. "I'd suggest you go on home. I'll ask his relatives to stay."

"I'd be *glad* to. I—"

"No, we're letting only family. Until he's off critical."

• •

It was seven-thirty on Sunday morning when Victoria drove up, in Carlo's Studebaker, at Sarah's. Her beige jacket was bloodstained. Every muscle ached with fatigue.

Maude Bly met her at the back door. "This house has been like a three-ring circus! Are *you* all right? You know about the fire at the winery? Police, firemen, everybody in Napa County calling up here since midnight!" She saw Victoria's face. "I'm staying. Go on to bed. I'll be here."

At six o'clock that evening, Maude Bly came with a pot of coffee to awaken Victoria. "The police want you to call—no later than in the morning. They're making a report on the fire."

"Tell them it will be in the morning," Victoria said, scrambling out of bed, getting dressed. "I've got to get to the hospital, see how Carlo is," she said frantically, not having intended sleeping that long.

But when she hurried up to the room number in the hospital that the admissions-desk clerk had given her, she was stopped by a strong-jawed policeman. "Sorry—nobody but immediate family admitted. And them one at a time. Doctors' orders."

She stood there exasperated. "But my father raised him. He worked for us for years. I'm his—*friend*."

"Ask the nurse. Me, I just follow orders. Nobody goes in here without permission from the desk. That's my job."

"He's not a criminal!" she cried out. "He's a *victim*—why are you treating him like a criminal?"

"Lady, I'm just doing what I'm told to do. A Mexican got stabbed. They don't know why, who, or how just yet. Until he gives a statement I stay here. As much for his sake as anybody's."

A narrow-faced older nurse looked up at her over horn-rimmed glasses. "Sorry, dear. Dr. Ginsberg says absolutely no visitors except family. No exceptions."

"Could you at least tell me how he is? Is *that* allowed?"

"Here comes the doctor—ask him."

Victoria turned to a small, nervous-looking man poring over a chart as he hurried down the hall. "Dr. Ginsberg—could you tell me how Carlo Carducci is? It was my place where he was hurt."

He squinted at her. "These Mexicans are tough. We think he's over the crisis. Unless some unforeseen complication comes up—yes, I think he'll pull through."

"Dr. Ginsberg—Carlo Carducci is not Mexican altogether. He is part—Texan."

He was already turning to the nurse, having written out more orders, reaching for the chart with the blood-pressure readings. "Order a CBC, stat. He's O-negative. Have we got plenty of blood on hand? We've got to get him ready for surgery—get that broken-off tip of the blade out of there if we can. I'm setting up surgery for tomorrow, if nothing else goes wrong." He turned back to Victoria. "Give him about a week, then come back for a visit. At regular visiting hours, of course'"

Victoria went back down the hallway, her pulses racing with indignation. She went back to the policeman. "Is it possible for you to ask whatever member of his family is in there with him now to come out in the hallway? Is *that* permissible?"

He shrugged indifferently, opened the door a crack, motioned to Miguel, who came out, smiled at Victoria wearily.

"How is he? You look exhausted! Could I get something for *you*?"

"My boy, Fernando, and Pepe are coming. Then I go home." His eyes filled with tears. "The pain—he hurts so bad. They don't give him nothing. Here, maybe the brain, they are afraid . . . I can't look—he hurts. . . ."

She found herself putting her arm around him, trying to console the older man. She insisted on going to the cafeteria, brought back a sandwich and a carton of milk for him; waited to be sure the policeman handed it to him. She was just begrudgingly leaving when she saw the two men; one she guessed to be Pepe, and the other she recognized as Fernando.

"Pepe?"

He stopped, whirled around, his eyes in an instant making their alert appraisal. He nodded to Fernando to go on and relieve Miguel. He stood in front of Victoria, looking up at her, since he was three or four inches shorter than she, even in his polished high-heeled boots. He put his hands inside the slit pockets of a leather coat. "You're the girl that Jerrod—you're the Donati girl?"

"Yes. I'm sorry—I'm so sorry this happened! I found him—I did the best I could, getting him in the car. I drove a hundred miles an hour. This hospital—I thought it was the best." Her eyes were fighting back a rush of hot tears. She didn't know why she felt she had to apologize, to explain herself to this strange little man rocking back on his heels, narrowing his eyes in that measuring way he had.

"You know that he must have loved you very much to go through this for you? You know that, don't you?"

"I—it's . . ."

"Yeah, I know how it is. Look, you want me to give him a message? Tell him you were here?"

"Oh, *yes*. If he needs *any*thing—I'd pay for special nurses, I'd do anything that might help. They won't let me in—please tell him that." She held her lip between her teeth to keep it from trembling. "I'll be here as soon as they'll let me."

"His car—Miguel will send somebody to your place to pick up the Studebaker. He'll want to know his car is safe. He loves that Studebaker."

"Sure. It might have some blood on the front seat. I didn't—there wasn't any time—"

"Sure. We understand. We'll get it cleaned up for him before he gets out of here."

All that week, Victoria tried to keep her mind on what was needed from her on Spring Mountain. Intermittently, she called the hospital, was told the same: "No, ma'am, he is not allowed visitors as yet. Sorry, ma'am, his condition is listed as satisfactory. I cannot tell you more than that. . . . Yes, we will see that your message is delivered."

She sent flowers. She tried calling Dr. Ginsberg; got his answering service: "May I have your name and number, please? Your message? You want to know how Carlo Carducci in Room 328 is doing? I will give your message to Dr. Ginsberg."

Tate Williams had greeted her at the winery Monday morning, tried to put his arms around her consolingly. But she had pulled away from him. She was still in a state of shock. She went with the insurance adjuster through the charred ruins of the stable. "It's a loss—a total loss," she mumbled, looking about at the roofless old stone building, the timbers, everything wooden burned out, at the stainless-steel tanks—some toppled, some standing like glistening cold fingers.

"At least they didn't touch your main winery. You have your red wines and some good Chardonnay stored," Tate said reassuringly. "Your insurance covers most of your loss, doesn't it?"

"How do you measure loss?" she asked numbly, thinking of Carlo, of what he was going through. She ached to see him. To sit by him. How she envied Miguel—soft-eyed, round-faced Miguel, who was *family*. Who could sit there in the darkened corner and answer if Carlo called. Or Fernando, or Pepe. All of them taking relays, all of them needed. Wanted. *Family*. "Are you his *wife?*" the nurse in the emergency room had asked. Why hadn't she lied? Would they have demanded her marriage certificate? She could have said, "Yes, of course I'm his wife!"

On Friday, when she had been so sure they would tell her it would be all right to come by, when she was told she was still forbidden to visit Carlo Carducci, Victoria looked about at Janet Cutler, at Tate

Williams. "I'm going home. I'm exhausted. I'll see everyone Monday. Do you mind?"

"Get some rest," Tate said briskly. "We'll be here. You can depend on us."

She drove into the driveway around four-thirty. A disheveled Maude Bly met her at the back door, a poodle tucked under each arm.

"These poor little dogs. If this hasn't been a day around here! They're out of their minds." Maude sat down, patted each on its pom-pom head, where she had just tied fresh blue ribbons.

Victoria tossed her car keys on the kitchen table, went over to the refrigerator and took out a bottle of cold Chenin Blanc, poured out a glass half full, sat down opposite Maude. "I've had a bad day, too. What went on here?"

Maude gave the poodles a little shove down to the kitchen floor, plopped her huge elbows across the table. "First of all, your grandmother has been talking off the wall all day—that is, until just a little while ago. Now you'd think she's clear as a bell. I tell you, it beats the daylights out of me how that sweet little thing can be nutty as a fruit-cake one hour and then before you turn around twice she's sitting up there sharp as a whip! Keeping anybody on his toes with some of the things she comes out with." She tossed a tiny rubber ball at the poodle named Cain, the gray one; laughed when the solid black one, Abel, yapped angrily. Then she shook her head. "It was that bunch of China-men that got Cain and Abel so upset."

"What Chinamen?"

"Li Po's cousins. They came to get him today. Said it was time to take him to their place."

"You mean Li Po's gone? Like that? They simply came and took him?"

"They most certainly did. Said it was their custom, their faith, to look after their old with proper respect—if you can say *heathens* have a faith."

Victoria put the wineglass down, got up, looked at Maude with disbelief. "What did Li Po say? How did Grandmother take it? They've been together so long. He's been a part of our family as long as I can remember—as long as we've had a Donati family!"

"Honey, your grandmother, like I said, was jabbering a mile a minute most of the day about things you or anybody else never heard about! And when that poor little thing went waddling in there to tell her goodbye, well, she went off on this talking jag about watercress down at the springhouse and telling him to to do this and that—not to forget the sugar and cream for Adam's tea, and to put starch in the curtains. Well, it was pitiful! He left this house carrying that little sack full of stuff, bawling like a baby."

"Did they say where they were taking him?" Victoria was furious. "I didn't give him severance pay, get to tell him goodbye—anything!"

"So don't get so worked up, honey. It's not that they took him to China! They just took him down to Napa City, where they run that restaurant over on Third Street and that laundry over there back of the courthouse. Probably got him stuck off in the back someplace." She picked up the black poodle. "You just stop biting your brother's ears, young man!" Then she looked up as Victoria started up the back stairs. "Why don't you go in and see your grandmother while she's not so fuzzyheaded? I shampooed her hair this morning, too. I was washing my dogs and thought there wasn't a reason in this world I shouldn't shampoo her hair too. She's the cutest little thing—I scrubbed her all up. Put a nice pink bed jacket on her. Like I said, she's all of a sudden clearheaded as she can be. In her day she must have been a real crackerjack. Smart as a whip."

"She was quite a lady."

Victoria found Sarah propped up against a pile of fluffy pillows in the fourposter bed that had come down through the Hubbard family —one that had belonged to the woman for whom she herself had been named: Victoria Hubbard.

At first Sarah appeared to be asleep. Maude had combed the wispy, thinned-out white hair back off her scrubbed wizened face. Where, with her poodles, she had tied blue ribbons on their pompoms, with Sarah she had tied a pink ribbon to match the bed jacket. For a moment, Victoria stood at the foot of the bed, looking at the gentle face, at the hands folded across the quilted satin comforter, at the brown age spots and the blue veins like cords interlaced where thin fingers had seemed to grasp for one another. Then she pulled a chair next to the bed, reached out, took her grandmother's left hand, and placed it between both of hers.

Sarah opened her age-faded, watery blue eyes, looked at Victoria, recognized her and smiled. "I was wondering where you were. When you were coming to see me," she said in a crackly voice.

"Did I ever tell you—do you know how much, how very much, I love you, Grandmother?" Victoria said softly, patting Sarah's hand. "Do you know what you've meant to me in my life?"

Sarah tilted her head to one side, her eyes glistening, alive with

588

humor. "Surely, I know. I knew the first time I ever saw you—when your proud daddy pointed out your crop of red hair. When you came out squalling—fighting the world the very minute you were born. I knew you had gumption. That you'd be a special granddaughter. And you *have* been. You're the only one I give a hoot about—who gives a hoot about me. Your Grandfather Adam Donati would have been awfully proud of you, too, young lady! But he'd have to get used to the idea that you're a *woman* winemaker. That a woman's running the show up there on Spring Mountain!" She chuckled. "He was proud of me because I went to Wellesley and knew more than the average run of the mill around Napa Valley. But he always insisted on being the boss. He was Old World that way. European. He made sure I stayed in my place." She seemed to clutch Victoria's fingers, holding on to them as though it might keep her firmly fixed to her thoughts, her fast-fading, slippery memory. "I loved him, though. When you love a man, you understand his weak points. You learn to live with them. You're just glad you have all the rest."

Victoria smoothed Sarah's hair down on her forehead. Then Sarah reached over, patted Victoria's hand this time.

"But Adam would be in a stew about you right now if he knew you hadn't got married yet. He'd be wondering why you don't have that big stone house up there filled up with Donati boys by now. He always took it for granted there would be lots of heirs so that what he stood for—everything up there on Spring Mountain—would be passed on down, one generation to the next."

She was getting tired. Victoria's hand lingered a moment on her forehead, which felt unusually cold to her. "Are you warm enough with that coverlet? Do you need more covers, dear?"

"I don't need a thing. But maybe you can tell me something that nobody else seems to know. Whatever in this wide world happened to Luigi Pascarella, who built Spring Mountain? And to Joseph? To Adam's own boy, Joseph? That woman who gives me my bath said she would ask and find out."

At that moment Maude Bly hurried in, carrying a tray with a glass of orange juice and a medicine glass filled with mineral oil. "What did I hear you just say! Don't you remember what I just told you about two days ago?" Maude lifted her eyebrows at Victoria knowingly. "Didn't I tell you that my sister Eva told me that Luigi Pascarella died three years ago from diabetes? That his brother Cesare is rich as King Midas? Now, don't you remember that? And didn't I tell you that Joseph Donati lives in Vallejo—runs a flea-bitten grocery store, when he isn't down-and-out drunk?" She put a strong, sure arm under the pillows, lifted Sarah's head to more of a sitting position. "It's time for your orange juice and your medicine. Here, which one you want to take first—a sip of orange juice and then the oil, or the oil and the orange juice all at once?"

Sarah's hand came out like a bird claw. "I *told* you—orange juice has sugar in it and it's bad for me! I told you I like my glass of red wine right now."

Maude stood up, put her hands on her hips. "If I'm going to take care of you, you have to take your medicine and do what's right, what's good for you!"

"Give her the wine," Victoria said quietly. "Give her what she wants, for God's sake!"

Maude's big square face flushed. "Well, tomorrow, when I go to Eva's for a rest—and believe you me I could use a few days off—let's just see how *you* get along with her, with her changing one minute to the next!"

It was sometime during the middle of the night when Victoria awakened, vaguely aware that someone was knocking on her door, calling her name out in a strange way. She sat up, her heart racing, reaching through the darkness for the lamp. Was it Carlo? Was she on Spring Mountain? Who was it out there? The hospital—maybe something had happened, complications . . .

She scrambled over the edge of the high fourposter bed, pulled a robe around her, made her way, as in a fog, toward the door.

Maude Bly stood there, her coarse gray hair standing out, her eyes wide, her plaid flannel men's-style bathrobe buttoned unevenly. "I thought I heard her yelling out—I was sleeping like a log. I could swear I heard her yelling something about Adam and a horse." She put both hands up around her chin, as if trying to pull what she had to say into clearer words. "I got up like I always do—being sure she didn't do anything funny like trying to get out of bed by herself and break a hip while she was at it. So I got in there as fast as I usually do. But there she was—just propped up on her pillows the way I left her." Maude looked as if she wasn't seeing for a moment. "She just plain *died*."

Victoria first called Dede, who said, "Sweetheart, I'd love to come be with you, but I've got to finish a painting for this exhibit—my first truly important one. I have twenty-two canvases. I'm assured of critics. It's so exciting. Wish me *luck*. Do you think you could get through with the funeral and all in time to be here for my opening?"

She located Anne at Juilliard, had her called out from a piano class. "She finally *died*? . . . She lived to be so old, didn't she? Victoria, I couldn't possibly come right now. You see, I'm just now getting my perspective. I go to my analyst twice a week—he's superb. He's doing wonderful things for my head. I'm so sorry you're having to do all this by yourself. You *do* understand?"

Actually, she did understand, Victoria told herself. Besides, what could they do if they came? She didn't think she could handle any added demands on her energies right now, either. Each day she managed to call the hospital, regardless of her own inner turmoil and everyone seeming to need her at once, either regarding the estate or about the recent fire at the winery. And each day she was told that, no, Mr. Carducci could not receive visitors other than his immediate family just yet. Again, she sent flowers; she asked the nurse to relay her messages that she had called, was there, should he need her for anything.

It was Wednesday, the second week of November, two and a half weeks since Carlo had been stabbed on Spring Mountain. Chip Brosius had outlined the terms of Sarah's last will and testament. "You are her sole heir, essentially, except for small insignificant bequests. She stipulates that you may keep the land, separate and apart from the mansion and the immediate twenty acres surrounding the house. You may sell all or one or keep them. She requests that should it be a choice, she preferred that you would keep the house on Spring Mountain and sell this one here on the valley floor. Actually, she left you as much free rein as possible. If you want to pull out, you can. You could sell everything. David didn't have that opportunity. There were times I was sure he would have gone a thousand miles to turn his back on Napa Valley."

She smiled. "He might have, but I doubt it. He loved Spring Mountain. He was tied to the land—and I guess I am, too. I couldn't leave it if I wanted to, paper or no paper."

"I'd suggest you sell this big place, then. What would you do with it? Such a big house. No family. A single girl."

"You're right, Chip. I'd like to put it up for sale—my grandmother's house. Not Spring Mountain. I never want to sell *it*, I've decided. Would you see to it that this house goes on the market? Not the vineyards—just the house and the surrounding twenty acres? Ask around, find out what a fair market price is."

Chip was finished with their business by three o'clock. Victoria hurried across the black-and-white marble-tiled foyer and half ran up the curved stairs to her room, where quickly she took down the blue dress that once Carlo had said he liked to see her wear. She looked in the mirror, ran the brush over her shoulder-length red hair, dabbed on a touch of powder where her nose was shiny, a smear of lipstick, perfume behind her ears, on her wrists. She slipped out of her regular comfortable loafers, worked her feet into a pair of pumps, dumped the contents of her old brown leather bag into a purse to match the navy-blue leather pumps, and hurried back downstairs. Regular visiting hours at the hospital were from two to four. Even if they told her that Carlo Carducci was not allowed visitors outside of the family yet, she would pretend she was there calling on someone who could have visitors.

After two and a half weeks, even with the surgery to remove the knife-blade tip, he should be feeling a lot better. Maybe they were even letting him up. Surely the policeman wouldn't be stationed outside his door. They had had plenty of time to clear that up, get a statement.

She drove faster than usual down Highway 29, her hands gripped nervously around the wheel. She wasn't sure how she would say it, how she would tell him that she *knew*, that she had made up her mind once and for all that nothing else mattered.

She passed through Yountville, saw to her left the old Groezsinger Winery. The old depot. To her right, the Veterans' Hospital. There were the long stretches of vineyards coming up. She thought suddenly of vines, of the roots down in the ground, those native Mission roots with a sturdy resistance to disease, onto which fine varietals were grafted. Maybe she should put it to Carlo in those terms: that she had seen now that it wasn't what the root was, it was what one gathered off the vine itself.

She had reached Trancas Avenue; waited for the light; turned left. Maybe he would laugh at that. Maybe she should come right out and say it: "Carlo, I love you. Nothing else matters. I want to be your wife and have your babies and live on Spring Mountain with you for the rest of our lives. You take care of the vineyards and I'll take care of the winemaking; together we'll take care of our children. Of Spring Mountain's heirs."

She pulled into the visitors' parking lot; drove around looking for a place; finally found one. She hurried into the side entrance, her neck and her face feeling flushed, her heart pounding. The elevator took forever, she thought, impatient for the creaking noises to rumble, shudder to a halt, the doors to open and fly with her up to the third floor.

If Miguel, Fernando, Pepe, any of them, were there, she'd simply ask them to step outside. It was her turn! She had waited long enough, *family* or not. . .

There was no one in the elevator. She pressed the button for the third floor, her hand trembling. *What if they stopped her?* She must remember to walk down the corridor as nonchalantly as though she were expected; had every right to be marching into Room 328. From habit, as though hearing Sarah's admonishing voice, she pulled her stomach in, straightened her back, lifted her chin. When she came to the corner where the nurses' station jutted out like a watchtower, she did not look right or left. As she thought she remembered correctly, 328 was down to the right, the next to the last door, near the end of the hall.

Above, a loudspeaker droned a page: "Drs. Bowers, Fittipoldi, and Morrison, please call the operator. . . . Drs. Bowers . . . "

The highly polished linoleum floors in twelve-inch squares seemed to tilt, lurch higher than the floor. Then she was there. She looked up, quickly rechecking the number, a little surprised to find the door open wide.

At first she thought she had made a mistake. Number 328—that *was* his room number. She had called it every day. Though he had not been allowed a telephone in his room, she had asked the nurse on the floor, "Mr. Carlo Carducci in Room 328, bed B . . ."

She stared numbly at the empty, crisply clean room that showed no signs of occupancy. Perhaps they had transferred him to another room, she thought, hurrying out into the hallway, walking briskly toward the nurses' station, not letting her high heels click by keeping her step gingerly light.

A plump, jolly-faced brown-haired nurse was laughing at something an intern had just said. The intern was thumbing through a chart.

"Excuse me. In Room 328, bed B—could you please tell me to what room Mr. Carducci has been transferred?"

The nurse looked up, stretched. "Let me see—I've been on vacation . . . . Room 328—isn't that the only empty room we have on this floor? . . . *Carducci?*"

"Yes, Carlo Carducci. He was—he was stabbed. Dr. Ginsberg operated on him a couple of weeks ago. I was told yesterday that he couldn't have visitors—except family . . . I've been waiting to come see him—"

"The Mexican—Carducci?" The intern looked up, stubbed out a cigarette. "I wrote out his dismissal order last night. He insisted on going home. We called Dr. Ginsberg—he told me to write the order. Sure, he left last night."

"I don't understand!" Victoria cried out, feeling that her blood was draining from her. "How could he just be dismissed when they weren't even letting him have visitors?"

The intern looked annoyed. "He signed his own release. He had to sign a paper that the hospital isn't responsible."

"But *why?* Where did he go?"

The intern shrugged. "Who knows? He said something—I believe I recall that he mentioned Fresno. But I wouldn't say that's positive. Ask down at the information desk in the lobby. Maybe they know."

For a moment Victoria stared blindly about, looking back down the hallway toward 328, back toward the elevator. She saw the nurse putting a Chiclet into her mouth, taking a chart out of the rack. She half ran down the hallway, saw the stairway exit and flung open the heavy door, plunged down the hollow-sounding metal stairway, trying not to trip in her high heels.

At the desk in the main lobby, a thin-faced middle-aged woman whose hair was tightly waved and stiff with hair spray, her face powdered heavily with a pinkish flaky coat, looked up, kept the telephone receiver to her ear. "Yes, may I help you?"

"Carlo Carducci—he went home last night, a late dismissal. Do you know—could you please tell me *where* he went? I must—I have to find out! It's urgent."

The woman cradled the phone under her chin. "Hold on, please," she said into it; reached across to a card index, ran down it. "We have a Carlyle. Here's a Carlson . . . . Carslund. How do you spell that?"

"C-a-r-d-u-c-c-i, Carducci. Carlo."

"We don't have anyone by that name. Sorry."

Victoria stood for a moment, feeling as if the desk, the floor, the revolving door were all going around and around. She hurried to where she saw people streaming in, pushed out past them. The fresh air made her feel better. She hurried toward the parking lot, got in and drove her car back out Trancas, heading toward Highway 29. When she saw a telephone booth at a gas station, she pulled in; looked up Dr. Ginsberg's office number.

A nasal-sounding receptionist answered. "Carlo Carducci—with a C as in *cat?* . . . Has he been a patient recently in Dr. Ginsberg's office? . . . I'm sorry, if he hasn't been a patient in the office we won't have a record of him. Doctor frequently operates on emergency—if he happens to be on call . . . A *stabbing* case, you say? . . . My dear, we have our share of those. Mexicans—always fighting with knives. I'm sorry, I can't help you. Why don't you check with the hospital? Try Medical Records . . . It's past four—they may be closed for today. In the morning—yes, try Medical Records."

Victoria slammed the phone down, got back into the car, bore down on the gas pedal and headed back up valley, racing now toward

St. Helena. Dowdell . . . She would find Miguel if she had to ask at every house.

She was only vaguely aware of the blur of vineyards whizzing past. When she passed Sarah's mansion—her own now, the one listed for sale—she barely glanced that way. She saw the new Jacob Brunner Winery—the new enormous storage facilities that had caused such an outcry throughout the valley from natives who did not want anything built to disturb the quiet character and the Victorian quaintness of the valley, anything that would jar the eye.

To her left, Inglenook made an oblique distorted picture of faded yellow with rust-red roofs. Beaulieu, the Oakville Country Store to her right, all seemed to weave like vines across her panic—the gray numb area behind her actual seeing eye that was keeping the car on her side of the road. Dowdell—it was on the right. There were big houses and little houses on Dowdell. There was a huge estate at the end of it. Victorian houses, some tiny houses closer to the highway.

It was not a paved road, and there were holes from past winter rains. She bumped across them, saw two children out chasing an old car tire, pushing it around like a wheel of fortune, their legs flying out like spokes as they ran, staggering this way and that, trying to keep the tire from falling.

She pulled up, leaned out. "Please—Miguel Díaz? Do you know where he lives?"

The boy, who was about eight years old, his eyes like huge chestnuts, pointed. "Over there—that blue house."

"It's not blue—it's gray," the girl, who was younger, said.

"Thank you!" Victoria felt foolish that a spurt of triumph had shot through her. She pulled into the dirt driveway, got out, hurried up the steps to a narrow door with a curtained glass window in it. She knocked furiously. She was not sure if those were sounds inside or her hopes that they were sounds. She looked about, saw the pots of geraniums lined in a neat row against the wall. A swing, dangling from chains, swung gently with a surge of breeze. A lop-eared, short-haired skinny dog came out from under the porch, did not bark, but looked at her through fuzzy eyes, then slunk back where he had been.

She saw the fingertips ease the curtain back just enough for brown eyes to peer out. Then the door opened and Miguel stood there, solemn-faced.

"Carlo—please, where is he, Miguel?" Victoria asked, hearing her own plaintive sound. "I must—I have to see him. Talk with him. They wouldn't let me come to the hospital."

"He asked the doctor. He didn't want anybody to come."

"Not even me! *Why?* Why wouldn't he see me, Miguel?"

"He's a proud man."

"Please, Miguel—listen to me," Victoria begged. "I knew—I knew today, for the first time, that I love him. Really love him. I made up my mind—I want to marry him." Tears of desperation hung in her eyes. "Is he here?"

He shook his head. "No. He went with Pepe. Last night. Pepe drove the Studebaker. They went back to Fresno."

"Where in Fresno? Tell me. I'm going there. I have to find him!"

Again Miguel shook his head. "He did not tell me. My son, Pepe, he said he did not want anybody to know, not even me."

She was crying now. "But if he'd just let me *tell* him . . . I must let him know how I feel, Miguel!"

"I am sorry. I cannot—no, I don't know."

She swiped at her face. Embarrassed, she turned her back, went to the edge of the tiny porch, looked out across the way at a newly planted vineyard, the young scions only inches tall, the grape sticks, thin lonely markers, marching like stick soldiers. He was still standing at the door, not coming out, not moving.

When she was calmer, when she could see clearly without any blurring of the even rows of the grape sticks, she turned back and faced the short round-faced man. "Miguel, if you hear from Carlo, if Pepe or Carlo contacts you in any way, at any time, will you promise me that you will tell him what I just told you? That I love him. That —that he must come back and talk with me. Let me tell him in my own words!"

"I don't think he will come back. He told me he was through with Napa Valley. It was like a witch, a bad witch, for him."

"But he owns land here! Won't he come back to his land?"

Miguel shrugged his shoulders. "I know only what he said. Pepe— he is going to work with Pepe."

"As an organizer?"

"I just know he said he was going to work with Pepe—for something that was right."

Victoria drove slowly back down Dowdell Lane. The children with the tire were gone now. She waited for a truck, a line of cars to go by, then turned right; headed on through St. Helena; turned left on Madrona; right, toward Spring Mountain.

She was not in a hurry now. The curves seemed to bend, wrap around in slow motion. The car and the road, her hands and her foot on the gas pedal were all one and the same. It was sundown. It was going to be dark pretty soon. She didn't like driving the mountain road after dark, regardless of how many times she had driven up and down it, how well she knew every twist, every grade, every sharp descent.

The gate was locked, which meant that everybody had left for the day. She felt a sinking feeling, as though she had been abandoned.

As she got out of the car, unlocked the gate, pulled through, went back to be sure it was locked securely behind her, she told herself, They have *their* homes, their families, to go to.

The long narrow driveway seemed to draw her forward as if caught in some tree-lined tunnel. To her right she felt the great hollow emptiness of the dense woods. She remembered herself that they were alive with deer, birds, squirrels, any number of living things.

Under the light pole, she parked the car, got out, looked about at the fading sun, at the oranges and muted lavenders that would soon be gone.

As she headed up the stone pathway, her ankles felt as if they had turned very thick—as if her legs had been stuffed with sawdust.

She stopped on the stone veranda, leaned against the redwood post, absently letting the wind whip her hair across her face. Across the vineyards, she heard the dry rustling sound that came just before the leaves fell. Beyond them, she saw Howell Mountain glowing in a soft rosy cast reflected from the western sunset. A long lumpy roll of clouds seemed caught, suspended across the valley.

As if driven by some silent force, she stepped off the veranda, headed out through the vineyards, past that place where her father had fallen—hurrying now, picking out steps, again, faster. All about her she heard the crisp, crumply sound of grape leaves hanging like ancient parchment from vines ready for the winter's rest. As she pushed on, her high heels dug into the dirt. Then she was standing on the edge of the knoll, where she could look south, far down the valley, or north, to the commanding slopes of Mount St. Helena.

She stood there, looking south, looking north. The wind whipped her blue dress about her knees, sent strands of her hair out like earth-red streamers about her face.

The lumpy clouds were thinning out, weightless, in slow, rolling motion . . . changing shapes . . . like strong darker arms reaching out in embrace . . . melting now into thin, trailing white wisps, like her grandmother's hair. . . .

And then her grandmother's face seemed to wash before her, wrapping about her.

When she could see again, she turned quickly, heading back toward the stone house that stood in looming silhouette against the last traces of the dark, purplish-black sunset.

Suddenly she stopped, in the middle of the vineyard, reached out, touching one of the thick, scaly, gnarled trunks of a very old vine.

She locked both hands around its trunk, grasping it as though its pulse of flowing sap, that strength gathering down deeply in its ancient root, would pour into her own numb fingers.

Carlo used to help care for these very vines. . . .

And hadn't her father always said that Carlo showed all the signs of having been truly born to the land—of being a *steward* of the land?

Wouldn't that be the reason why her father had willed those eighty acres of choice Cabernets, those special Rutherford-dust Cabernets, to him in the first place?

And if that was so, how could he just walk out on his land—forsake the very thing he had been born to do?

A fluttering, like fledglings afraid to fly just yet, seemed to be taking place inside her chest, encircling her heart, making her pulse beat faster.

Carlo had left Napa Valley before. But hadn't he always come back at harvest? Last time he had just walked up the stone pathway, that white jacket slung across his shoulder, that smile stretched out across his face, that bearing-down grin, that look that went right through her . . .

She was walking faster now toward the stone veranda, breaking into a half-run—as if by getting there soon enough she might find him hurrying to meet her.

On the stone veranda, she looked down toward where she had left her car parked. There was no sign of a maroon Studebaker. Only the blue dusty hood of her Buick.

With the sun down, the wind had turned cold. She should have brought her jacket, she thought, fishing in her jumbly purse for the key to the front door of the old stone house.

As she turned it in the ancient lock, a voice in the back of her mind said, *Next harvest* . . . That really wasn't so far away, when she thought about it. And pretend—*no, say that he would come back!* If they should decide to get married right away and start their babies— oh, there would be so much to do, to have ready, before then!

There would be the entire house to restore—ceilings to mend, wallpaper to be steamed off, new wiring, a new roof . . .

She pushed the huge front door open eagerly, stepped into the hallway just as the enormous old grandfather's clock began a resounding striking out of the hour of six o'clock.

For a moment, Victoria stood there, as if caught in the center of those clanging, bonging rings of sound, rings circling wider and wider, lifting, now spreading out until they were flattened against the high-beamed ceiling, where even their echoes became lost whispers.

Still she stood there, looking up now at the stairway where her grandmother had made her descent to the wedding march. Then to her right, into the cavernous empty dining room, where, yes, she would bring back up to Spring Mountain that huge mahogany table, some of those wonderful old Hubbard pieces, maybe that Oriental screen stored in the attic at her grandmother's . . .

Granted, there was a lot to do. But she would be ready for him by next harvest. She'd really just have to be!